THE WAR OF SOULS
VOLUME THREE

DRAG⊙NS
of a
VANISHED MOON

Margaret Weis and Tracy Hickman

DRAGONS OF A VANISHED MOON

Cover art by Matt Stawicki
Cartography by Dennis Kauth
First Printing: June 2002
Library of Congress Catalog Card Number: 2001092207

9 8 7 6 5 4 3 2 1

US ISBN: 0-7869-2740-2
UK ISBN: 0-7869-2741-0
620-88602-001-EN

U.S., CANADA,
ASIA, PACIFIC, & LATIN AMERICA
Wizards of the Coast, Inc.
P.O. Box 707
Renton, WA 98057-0707
+1-800-324-6496

EUROPEAN HEADQUARTERS
Wizards of the Coast, Belgium
P.B. 2031
2600 Berchem
Belgium
+32-70-23-32-77

Visit our web site at **www.wizards.com/dragonlance**

by Margaret Weis and Tracy Hickman

CHRONICLES
Dragons of Autumn Twilight
Dragons of Winter Night
Dragons of Spring Dawning

LEGENDS
Time of the Twins
War of the Twins
Test of the Twins

The Second Generation
Dragons of Summer Flame

THE WAR OF SOULS
Dragons of a Fallen Sun
Dragons of a Lost Star
Dragons of a Vanished Moon

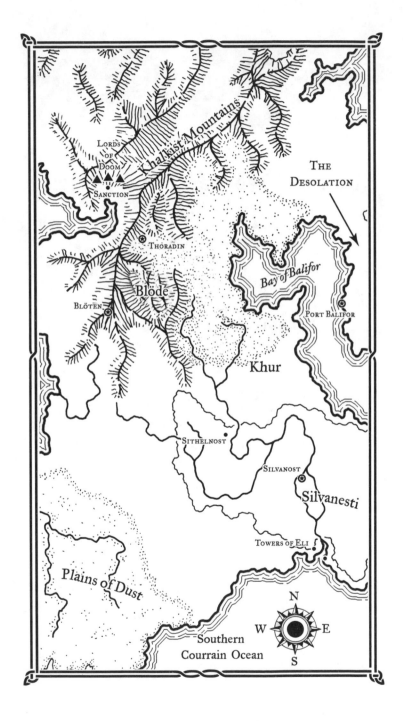

Dedication

To those who fight the never ending battle against the darkness, this book is respectfully dedicated.

Book I

I

Lost Souls

In the dungeon of the Tower of High Sorcery, that had once been in Palanthas but now resided in Nightlund, the great archmagus Raistlin Majere had conjured a magical Pool of Seeing. By gazing into this pool, he was able to follow and sometimes shape events transpiring in the world. Although Raistlin Majere had been dead many long years, his magical Pool of Seeing remained in use. The wizard Dalamar, who had inherited the Tower from his *Shalafi*, maintained the magic of the pool. A veritable prisoner in the Tower that was an island in the river of the dead, Dalamar had often made use of the pool to visit in his mind those places he could not travel in his body.

Palin Majere stood now at the pool's edge, staring into the unwavering blue flame that burned in the center of the still water and was the chamber's only light. Dalamar was close beside him, his gaze fixed on the same unwavering fire. Although the mages could have seen events transpiring anywhere in the world, they watched intently an event that was happening quite close to them, an event taking place at the top of the very Tower in which they stood.

Goldmoon of the Citadel of Light, and Mina, Lord of the Night, leader of the Dark Knights of Neraka, were to meet in the laboratory that had once belonged to Raistlin Majere. Goldmoon had already arrived at the strange meeting place. The laboratory was cold and dark and shadowed. Dalamar had left her a lantern, but its light was feeble and served only to emphasize the darkness that could never truly be illuminated, not if every lantern and every candle on Krynn should burst into flame. The darkness that was the soul of this dread Tower had its heart here in this chamber, which in the past had been a scene of death and pain and suffering.

In this chamber, Raistlin Majere had sought to emulate the gods and create life, only to fail utterly, bringing into the world misbegotten, shambling, pathetic beings known as the Live Ones, who had lived out their wretched existence in the room where the two wizards now stood. In the chamber, the Blue Dragonlady Kitiara had died, her death as brutal and bloody as her life. Here stood the Portal to the Abyss, a link between the realm of the mortal and realm of the dead, a link that had long ago been severed and was nothing now but a home to mice and spiders.

Goldmoon knew the dark history of this room. She must be considering that now, Palin thought, watching her image that shimmered on the surface of the pool. She stood in the laboratory, her arms clasped about her. She shivered not with the cold, but with fear. Palin was concerned. He could not remember—in all the years that he had known her—seeing Goldmoon afraid.

Perhaps it was the strange body that Goldmoon's spirit inhabited. She was over ninety. Her true body was that of an elderly woman—still vigorous, still strong for her years, but with skin marked and marred with time, a back that was starting to stoop, fingers that were gnarled, but whose touch was gentle. She had been comfortable with that body. She had never feared or regretted the passage of the years that had brought the joy of love and birth, the sorrow of love and death. That body had been taken from her the night of the great storm, and she had been given another body, a stranger's body, one that was young and beautiful, healthful and vibrant. Only the eyes were the eyes of the woman Palin had known throughout his life.

She is right, he thought, this body doesn't belong to her. It's borrowed finery. Clothing that doesn't fit.

"I should be with her," Palin muttered. He stirred, shifted, began to pace restlessly along the water's edge. The chamber was made of stone and was dark and chill, the only light the unwavering flame that burned in the heart of the dark pool, and it illuminated little and gave no warmth. "Goldmoon looks strong, but she's not. Her body may be that of someone in her twenties, but her heart is the heart of a woman whose life has spanned nine decades. The shock of seeing Mina again—especially as she is—may kill her."

"In that case, the shock of seeing you beheaded by the Dark Knights would probably do very little for her either," returned Dalamar caustically. "Which is what she would see if you were to march up there now. The Tower is surrounded by soldiers. There must be at least thirty of them out there."

"I don't think they'd kill me," said Palin.

"No? And what would they do? Tell you to go stand in a corner with your face to the wall and think what a bad boy you've been?" Dalamar scoffed.

"Speaking of corners," he added suddenly, his voice altering, "did you see that?"

"What?" Palin jerked his head, looked around in alarm.

"Not here! There!" Dalamar pointed into the pool. "A flash in the eyes of dragons that guard the Portal."

"All I see is dust," Palin said after a moment's intense gaze, "and cobwebs and mouse dung. You're imagining things."

"Am I?" Dalamar asked. His sardonic tone had softened, was unusually somber. "I wonder."

"You wonder what?"

"A great many things," said Dalamar.

Palin eyed the dark elf closely but could not read on that gaunt and drawn face a single thought stirring behind the dark eyes. In his black robes, Dalamar was indistinguishable from the darkness of the chamber. Only his hands with their delicate fingers could be seen, and they appeared to be hands that lacked a body. The long-lived elf was presumably in the prime of life, but his wasted form, consumed by the fever of frustrated ambition, might have belonged to an elder of his race.

I shouldn't be casting aspersions. What does he see when he looks at me? Palin asked himself. A shabby, middle-aged man. My face wan and wasted. My hair graying, thin. My eyes the embittered eyes of one who has not found what he was promised.

I stand on the edge of wondrous magic created by my uncle, and what have I done, except fail everyone who ever expected anything of me. Including myself. Goldmoon is just the most recent. I should be with her. A hero like my father would be with her, no matter that it meant sacrificing his freedom, perhaps his life. Yet here I am, skulking in the basement of this Tower.

"Stop fidgeting, will you?" Dalamar said irritably. "You'll slip and fall in the pool. Look there." He pointed excitedly to the water. "Mina has arrived." Dalamar rubbed his thin hands. "Now we will see and hear something to our advantage."

Palin halted on the edge of the pool, wavering in his decision. If he left immediately, walked the corridors of magic, he might yet reach Goldmoon in time to protect her. Yet, he could not pull himself away. He stared down at the pool in dread fascination.

"I can see nothing in this wizard's murk," Mina was saying loudly. "We need more light."

The light in the chamber grew brighter, so bright that it dazzled eyes accustomed to the darkness.

"I didn't know Mina was a mage," said Palin, shading his eyes with his hand.

"She's not," said Dalamar shortly. He cast Palin a strange glance. "Doesn't that tell you something?"

Palin ignored the question, concentrated on the conversation.

"You . . . you are so beautiful, Mother," Mina said softly, awed. "You look just as I imagined."

Sinking to her knees, the girl extended her hands. "Come, kiss me, Mother," she cried, tears falling. "Kiss me as you used to. I am Mina. Your Mina."

"And so she was, for many years," murmured Palin, watching in sorrowful concern as Goldmoon advanced unsteadily to clasp her adopted child in her arms. "Goldmoon found Mina washed up on the shore, presumably the survivor of some terrible ship wreck, though no wreckage or bodies or any other survivors were ever discovered. They brought her to the Citadel's orphanage. Intelligent, bold, fearless, Mina charmed all, including Goldmoon, who took the child to her heart. And then, one day, at the age of fourteen, Mina ran away. We searched, but we could find no trace of her, nor could anyone say why she had gone, for she had seemed so happy. Goldmoon's heart broke, then."

"Of course, Goldmoon found her," Dalamar said. "She was meant to find her."

"What do you mean?" Palin glanced at Dalamar, but the elf's expression was enigmatic.

Dalamar shrugged, said nothing, gestured back to the dark pool.

"Mina!" Goldmoon whispered, rocking her adopted daughter. "Mina! Child . . . why did you leave us when we all loved you so much?"

"I left for love of you, Mother. I left to seek what you wanted so desperately. And I found it, Mother! I found it for you.

"Dearest Mother." Mina took hold of Goldmoon's hands and pressed them to her lips. "All that I am and all that I have done, I have done for you."

"I . . . don't understand, child," Goldmoon faltered. "You wear the symbol of evil, of darkness. . . . Where did you go?

Where have you been? What has happened to you?"

Mina laughed. "Where I went and where I have been is not important. What happened to me along the way—that is what you must hear.

"Do you remember, Mother, the stories you used to tell me? The story about how you traveled into darkness to search for the gods? And how you found the gods and brought faith in the gods back to the people of the world?"

"Yes," said Goldmoon. She had gone so very pale that Palin determined to be with her, cost him what it might.

He began to chant the words of magic. The words that came out of his mouth, however, were not the words that had formed in his brain. Those words were rounded, smooth, flowed easily. The words he spoke were thick and square-sided, tumbled out like blocks dropped on the floor.

He halted, angry at himself, forced himself to calm down and try again. He knew the spell, could have said it backward. He might well have said it backward, for all the sense it made.

"You're doing this to me!" Palin said accusingly.

Dalamar was amused. "Me?" He waved his hand. "Go to Goldmoon, if you want. Die with her, if you want. I'm not stopping you."

"Then who is? This One God?"

Dalamar regarded him in silence a moment, then turned back to gaze down into the pool. He folded his hands in the sleeves of his robes. "There was no past, Majere. You went back in time. There was no past."

"You told me the gods were gone, Mother," Mina said. "You told me that because the gods were gone we had to rely on ourselves to find our way in the world. But I didn't believe that story, Mother.

"Oh"—Mina placed her hand over Goldmoon's mouth, silencing her—"I don't think you lied to me. You were mistaken, that was all. You see, I knew better. I knew there was a god for I heard the voice of the god when I was little and our boat sank and I was cast alone into the sea. You found me on the shore, do you remember, Mother? But you never knew how I came to be there, because I promised I would never tell. The others drowned, but I was saved. The god held me and supported me and sang to me when I was afraid of the loneliness and dark.

"You said there were no gods, Mother, but I knew you were wrong. So I did what you did. I went to find god and bring god back to you. And I've done that, Mother. The miracle of the storm. That is the One God. The miracle of your youth and beauty. That is the One God, Mother."

"Now do you understand, Majere?" Dalamar said softly.

"I think I am beginning to," said Palin. His broken hands clasped tightly together. The room was cold, his fingers ached with the chill. "I would add, 'the gods help us,' but that might be out of place."

"Hush!" Dalamar snapped. "I can't hear. What did she say?"

"You asked for this," Goldmoon demanded, indicating her altered body with a gesture. "This is not me. It is your vision of me. . . ."

"Aren't you pleased?" Mina continued, not hearing her or not wanting to hear. "I have so much to tell you that will please you. I've brought the miracle of healing back into the world with the power of the One God. With the blessing of the One, I felled the shield the elves had raised over Silvanesti and I killed the treacherous dragon Cyan Bloodbane. A truly monstrous green dragon, Beryl, is dead by the power of the One God. The elven nations that were corrupt and faithless have both been destroyed, their people dead."

"The elven nations destroyed!" Dalamar gasped, his eyes burning. "She lies! She cannot mean that!"

"Strange to say this, but I do not think Mina knows how to lie," Palin said.

"But in death, they will find redemption," Mina preached. "Death will lead them to the One God."

"I see blood on these hands," Goldmoon said, her voice

tremulous. "The blood of thousands! This god you have found is terrible god. A god of darkness and evil!"

"The One God told me you would feel this way, Mother," Mina responded. "When the other gods departed and you thought you were left alone, you were angry and afraid. You felt betrayed, and that was only natural. For you *had* been betrayed. The gods in which you had so misguidedly placed your faith fled in fear. . . ."

"No!" Goldmoon cried out. She rose unsteadily to her feet and fell away from Mina, holding out her hand in warding. "No, Child, I don't believe it. I won't listen to you."

Mina seized Goldmoon's hand.

"You *will* listen, Mother. You must, so that you will understand. The gods fled in fear of Chaos, Mother. All except one. One god remained loyal to the people she had helped to create. One only had the courage to face the terror of the Father of All and of Nothing. The battle left her weak. Too weak to make manifest her presence in the world. Too weak to fight the strange dragons that came to take her place. But although she could not be with her people, she gave gifts to her people to help them fight the dragons. The magic that they called the wild magic, the power of healing that you know as the power of the heart . . . those were her gifts. Her gifts to you."

"If those were her gifts, then why did the dead need to steal them for her . . ." said Dalamar softly. "Look! Look there!" He pointed to the still water.

"I see." Palin breathed.

The heads of the five dragons that guarded what had once been the Portal to the Abyss began to glow with an eerie radiance, one red, one blue, one green, one white, one black.

"What fools we have been," Palin murmured.

"Kneel down," Mina commanded Goldmoon, "and offer your prayers of faith and thanksgiving to the One True God. The One God who remained faithful to her creation—"

"No, I don't believe what you are telling me!" Goldmoon said, standing fast. "You have been deceived, Child. I know this One God. I know her of old. I know her tricks and her lies and deceits."

Goldmoon looked at the five-headed dragon.

"I do not believe your lies, Takhisis!" Goldmoon said defiantly. "I will never believe that the blessed Paladine and Mishakal left us to your mercy!"

"They didn't leave, did they?" Palin said.

"No," Dalamar said. "They did not."

"You are what you have always been," Goldmoon cried. "A god of Evil who does not want worshipers, you want slaves! I will never bow down to you! I will never serve you!"

White fire flared from the eyes of the five dragons. Palin watched in horror to see Goldmoon begin to wither in the terrible heat.

"Too late," said Dalamar with terrible calm. "Too late. For her. And for us. They'll be coming for us soon. You know that."

"This chamber is hidden—" Palin began.

"From Takhisis?" Dalamar gave a mirthless laugh. "She knew of this chamber's existence long before your uncle showed it to me. How could anything be hidden from the 'One God'? The One God who stole away Krynn!"

"As I said, what fools we have been," said Palin.

"You yourself discovered the truth, Majere. You used the device to journey back to Krynn's past, yet you could go back only to the moment Chaos was defeated. Prior to that, there was no past. Why? Because in that moment, Takhisis stole the past, the present, and the future. She stole the world. The clues were there, if we'd had sense enough to read them."

"So the future Tasslehoff saw—"

"—will never come to pass. He leaped forward to the future that was supposed to have happened. He landed in the future that is now happening. Consider the facts: a strange-looking sun in the sky; one moon where there were once three; the patterns of the stars are vastly different; a red star burns in the heavens where one had never before been seen; strange dragons appear from out of nowhere. Takhisis brought the world here, to this part

---

of the universe, wherever that may be. Thus the strange sun, the single moon, the alien dragons, and the One God, all-powerful, with no one to stop her."

"Except Tasslehoff," said Palin, thinking of the kender secreted in an upstairs chamber.

"Bah!" Dalamar snorted. "They've probably found him by now. Him and the gnome. When they do, Takhisis will do with him what we planned to do—she will send him back to die."

Palin glanced toward the door. From somewhere above came shouted orders and the sound of feet running to obey. "The fact Tasslehoff is here at all proves to me that the Dark Queen is not infallible. She could not have foreseen his coming."

"Cling to that if it makes you happy," said Dalamar. "I see no hope in any of this. Witness the evidence of the Dark Queen's power."

They continued to watch the reflections of time shimmering in the dark pool. In the laboratory, an elderly woman lay on the floor, her white hair loose and unbound around her shoulders. Youth, beauty, strength, life had all been snatched away by the vengeful goddess, angry that her generous gifts had been spurned.

Mina knelt beside the dying woman. Taking hold of Gold-moon's hands, Mina pressed them again to her lips. "Please, Mother. I can restore your youth. I can bring back your beauty. You can begin life all over again. You will walk with me, and together we will rule the world in the name of the One God. All you have to do is to come to the One God in humility and ask this favor of her, and it will be done."

Goldmoon closed her eyes. Her lips did not move.

Mina bent close. "Mother," she begged. "Mother, do this for me if not for yourself. Do this for love of me!"

"I pray," said Goldmoon in a voice so soft that Palin held his breath to hear, "I pray to Paladine and Mishakal that they forgive me for my lack of faith. I should have known the truth," she said softly, her voice weakening as she spoke the words with her dying breath, "I pray that Paladine will hear my prayer and he will come . . . for love of Mina . . . For love of all . . ."

Goldmoon sank, lifeless, to the floor.

"Mother," said Mina, bewildered as a lost child, "I did this for you. . . ."

Palin's eyes burned with tears, but he was not sure for whom it was he wept—for Goldmoon, who had brought light into the world, or for the orphan girl, whose loving heart had been snared, tricked, deceived by the darkness.

"May Paladine hear her dying prayer," Palin said quietly.

"May I be given bat wings to flap around this chamber," Dalamar retorted. "Her soul has gone to join the river of the dead, and I fancy that our souls will not be far behind."

Footsteps clattered down the stairs, steel swords banged against the sides of the stone walls. The footsteps halted outside their door.

"I don't suppose anyone found a key?" asked a deep, rumbling voice.

"I don't like this, Galdar," said another. "This place stinks of death and magic. Let's get out of here."

"We can't get in if there's no key, sir," said a third. "We tried. It wasn't our fault we failed."

A moment's pause, then the first voice spoke, his voice firm. "Mina gave us our orders. We will break down the door."

Blows began to rain on the wooden door. The Knights started to beat on it with their fists and the hilts of their swords, but none sounded very enthusiastic.

"How long will the spell of warding hold?" Palin asked.

"Indefinitely, against this lot," said Dalamar disparagingly. "Not long at all against Her Dark Majesty."

"You are very cool about this," said Palin. "Perhaps you are not overly sorry to hear that Takhisis has returned."

"Say, rather, that she never left," Dalamar corrected with fine irony.

Palin made an impatient gesture. "You wore the black robes. You worshiped her—"

"No, I did not," said Dalamar so quietly that Palin could barely hear him over the banging and the shouting and the thundering on the door. "I worshiped Nuitari, the son, not the mother. She could never forgive me for that."

"Yet, if we believe what Mina said, Takhisis gave us both the magic—me the wild magic and you the magic of the dead. Why would she do that?"

"To make fools of us," said Dalamar. "To laugh at us, as she is undoubtedly laughing now."

The sounds of fists beating at the door suddenly ceased. Quiet descended on those outside. For a hope-filled moment, Palin thought that perhaps they had given up and departed. Then came a shuffling sound, as of feet moving hastily to clear a path. More footsteps could be heard—lighter than those before.

A single voice called out. The voice was ragged, as if it were choked by tears.

"I speak to the wizard Dalamar," called Mina. "I know you are within. Remove the magical spell you have cast on the door that we may meet together and talk of matters of mutual interest."

Dalamar's lip curled slightly. He made no response, but stood silent, impassive.

"The One God has given you many gifts, Dalamar, made you powerful, more powerful than ever," Mina resumed, after a pause to hear an answer that did not come. "The One God does not ask for thanks, only that you serve her with all your heart and all your soul. The magic of the dead will be yours. A million million souls will come to you each day to do your bidding. You will be free of this Tower, free to roam the world. You may return to your homeland, to the forests that you love and for which you long. The elven people are lost, seeking. They will embrace you as their leader, bow down before you, and worship you in my name."

Dalamar's eyes closed, as if in pain.

He has been offered the dearest wish of his heart, Palin realized. Who could turn that down?

Still, Dalamar said nothing.

"I speak now to you, Palin Majere," Mina said, and it seemed to Palin that he could see her amber eyes shining through the closed and spell-bound door. "Your uncle Raistlin Majere had the power and the courage to challenge the One God to battle. Look at you, his nephew. Hiding from the One God like a child who fears punishment. What a disappointment you have been. To your uncle, to your family, to yourself. The One God sees into your heart. The One God sees the hunger there. Serve the One God, Majere, and you will be greater than your uncle, more honored, more revered. Do you accept, Majere?"

"Had you come to me earlier, I might have believed you, Mina," Palin answered. "You have a way of speaking to the dark part of the soul. But the moment is passed. My uncle, wherever his spirit roams, is not ashamed of me. My family loves me, though I have done little to deserve it. I do thank this One God of yours for opening my eyes, for making me see that if I have done nothing else of value in this life, I have loved and been loved. And that is all that truly matters."

"A very pretty sentiment, Majere," Mina responded. "I will write that on your tomb. What of you, Dark Elf? Have you made your decision? I trust you will not be as foolish as your friend."

Dalamar spoke finally, but not to Mina. He spoke to the blue flame, burning in the center of the still pool of dark water.

"I have looked into the night sky and seen the dark moon, and I have thrilled to know that my eyes were among the few eyes that could see it. I have heard the voice of the god Nuitari and reveled in his blessed touch as I cast my spells. Long ago, the magic breathed and danced and sparkled in my blood. Now it crawls out of my fingers like maggots swarming from a carrion carcass. I would rather be that corpse than be a slave to one who so fears the living that she can trust only servants who are dead."

A single hand smote the door. The door and the spell that guarded it shattered.

Mina entered the chamber. She entered alone. The jet of flame that burned in the pool shone in her black armor, burned in her heart and in her amber eyes. Her shorn red hair glistened. She was might and power and majesty, but Palin saw that the amber eyes were red and swollen, tears stained her cheeks, grief for Goldmoon. Palin understood then the depth of the Dark Queen's perfidy, and he had never hated Takhisis so much as he hated her now. Not for what she had done or was about to do to him, but for what she had done to Mina and all the innocents like her.

Mina's Knights, fearful of the powerful wizards, hung back upon the shadowy stairs. Dalamar's voice raised in a chant, but the words were mumbled and inarticulate, and his voice faded slowly away. Palin tried desperately to summon the magic to him. The spell dissolved in his hands, ran through his fingers like grains of sand from a broken hourglass.

Mina regarded them both with a disdainful smile. "You are nothing without the magic. Look at you—two broken-down, impotent old men. Fall on your knees before the One God. Beg her to give you back the magic! She will grant your pleas."

Neither Palin nor Dalamar moved. Neither spoke.

"So be it," said Mina.

She raised her hand. Flames burned from the tips of her five fingers. Green fire, blue and red, white, and the red-black of embers lit the Chamber of Seeing. The flames merged together to form two spears forged of magic. The first spear she hurled at Dalamar.

The spear struck the elf in the breast, pinned him against the wall of the Chamber of Seeing. For a moment, he hung impaled upon the burning spear, his body writhing. Then his head sagged, his body went limp.

Mina paused. Holding the spear, she gazed at Palin.

"Beg," she said to him. "Beg the One God for your life."

Palin's lips tightened. He knew a moment's panicked fear, then pain sheared through his body. The pain was so horrific, so agonizing that it brought its own blessing. The pain made his last living thought a longing for death.

2

The Significance of the Gnome

Dalamar had said to Palin, "You do understand the significance of the gnome?"

Palin had not understood the significance at that moment, nor had Tasslehoff. The kender understood now. He sat in the small and boring room in the Tower of High Sorcery, a room that was pretty much devoid of anything interesting: sad-looking tables and some stern-backed chairs and a few knick-nacks that were too big to fit in a pouch. He had nothing to do except look out a window to see nothing more interesting than an immense number of cypress trees—more trees than were absolutely necessary, or so Tas thought—and the souls of the dead wandering around among them. It was either that or watch Conundrum sort through the various pieces of the shattered Device of Time Journeying. For now Tas understood all too well the significance of the gnome.

Long ago—just how long ago Tasslehoff couldn't remember, since time had become extremely muddled for him, what with leaping forward to one future that turned out wasn't the proper future and ending up in this future, where all anyone wanted to do was send him back to the past to die—anyhow, long ago, Tasslehoff Burrfoot had, through no fault of his own (well, maybe a little) ended up quite by accident in the Abyss.

Having assumed that the Abyss would be a hideous place where all manner of perfectly horrible things went on—demons eternally torturing people, for example—Tas had been most frightfully disappointed to discover that the Abyss was, in fact, boring. Boring in the extreme. Nothing of interest happened. Nothing of disinterest happened. Nothing at all happened to anyone, ever. There was nothing to see, nothing to handle, nothing to do, nowhere to go. For a kender, it was pure hell.

Tas's one thought had been to get out. He had with him the Device of Time Journeying—this same Device of Time Journeying that he had with him now. The device had been broken—just as it was broken now. He had met a gnome—similar to the gnome now seated at the table across from him. The gnome had fixed the device—just as the gnome was busy fixing it now. The one big difference was that then Tasslehoff had *wanted* the gnome to fix the device, and now he didn't.

Because when the Device of Time Journeying was fixed, Palin and Dalamar would use it to send him—Tasslehoff Burrfoot— back in time to the point where the Father of All and of Nothing would squash him flat and turn him into the sad ghost of himself he'd seen wandering about Nightlund.

"What did you do with this device?" Conundrum muttered irritably. "Run it through a meat grinder?"

Tasslehoff closed his eyes so he wouldn't have to see the gnome, but he saw him anyway—his nut-brown face and his wispy hair that floated about his head as though he were perpetually poking his finger into one of his own inventions, perhaps the steam-powered preambulating hubble-bubble or the locomotive, self-winding rutabaga slicer. Worse, Tas could see the light of cleverness shining in the gnome's beady eyes. He'd seen that light before, and he was starting to feel dizzy. *What did you do with this device? Run it through a meat grinder?* were exactly the same words—or very close to them—that the previous gnome had said in the previous time.

To alleviate the dizzy feeling, Tasslehoff rested his head with its topknot of hair (going only a little gray here and there) on his hands on the table. Instead of going away, the uncomfortable dizzy feeling spiraled down from his head into his stomach, and spread from his stomach to the rest of his body.

A voice spoke. The same voice that he'd heard in a previous time, in a previous place, long ago. The voice was painful. The voice shriveled his insides and caused his brain to swell, so that it pressed on his skull, and made his head hurt horribly. He had heard the voice only once before, but he had never, ever wanted to hear it again. He tried to stop his ears with his hands, but the voice was inside him, so that didn't help.

You are not dead, said the voice, and the words were exactly the same words the voice had spoken so long ago, *nor were you sent here. You are not supposed to be here at all.*

"I know," said Tasslehoff, launching into his explanation. "I came from the past, and I'm supposed to be in a different future—"

A past that never was. A future that will never be.

"Is that . . . is that my fault?" Tas asked, faltering.

The voice laughed, and the laughter was horrible, for the sound was like a steel blade breaking, and the feel was of the slivers of the broken blade piercing his flesh.

Don't be a fool, kender. You are an insect. Less than an insect. A mote of dust, a speck of dirt to be flicked away with a brush of my hand. The future you are in is the future of Krynn as it was meant to be but for the meddlings of those who had neither the wit nor the vision to see how the world might be theirs. All that happened once will happen again, but this time to suit my purposes. Long ago, one died on a Tower, and his death rallied a Knighthood. Now, another dies on a Tower and her death plunges a nation into despair. Long ago, one was raised up by the miracle of the blue crystal staff. Now the one who wielded that staff will be raised up—to receive me.

"You mean Goldmoon!" Tasslehoff cried bleakly. "She used the blue crystal staff. Is Goldmoon dead?"

Laughter sliced through his flesh.

"Am I dead?" he cried. "I know you said I wasn't, but I saw my own spirit."

You are dead and you are not dead, replied the voice, *but that will soon be remedied.*

"Stop jabbering!" Conundrum demanded. "You're annoying me, and I can't work when I'm annoyed."

Tasslehoff's head came up from the table with a jerk. He stared at the gnome, who had turned from his work to glare at the kender.

"Can't you see I'm busy here? First you moan, then you groan, then you start to mumble to yourself. I find it most distracting."

"I'm sorry," said Tasslehoff.

Conundrum rolled his eyes, shook his head in disgust, and went back to his perusal of the Device of Time Journeying. "I think that goes here, not there," the gnome muttered. "Yes. See? And then the chain hooks on here and wraps around like so. No, that's not quite the way. It must go . . . Wait, I see. This has to fit in there first."

Conundrum picked up one of the jewels from the Device of Time Journeying and fixed it in place. "Now I need another of these red gizmos." He began sorting through the jewels. Sorting through them now, as the other gnome, Gnimsh, had sorted through them in the past, Tasslehoff noted sadly.

The past that never was. The future that was hers.

"Maybe it was all a dream," Tas said to himself. "That stuff about Goldmoon. I think I'd know if she was dead. I think I'd feel sort of smothery around the heart if she was dead, and I don't feel that. Although it is sort of hard to breathe in here."

Tasslehoff stood up. "Don't you think it's stuffy, Conundrum? I think it's stuffy," he answered, since Conundrum wasn't paying any attention to him.

"These Towers of High Sorcery are always stuffy," Tas added, continuing to talk. Even if he was only talking to himself, hearing his own voice was far, far better than hearing that other, terrible voice. "It's all those bat wings and rat's eyeballs and moldy, old books. You'd think that with the cracks in these walls, you'd get a nice breeze, but that doesn't seem to be the case. I wonder if Dalamar would mind very much if I broke one of his windows?"

Tasslehoff glanced about for something to chuck through the windowpane. A small bronze statue of an elf maiden, who didn't seem to be doing much with her time except holding a wreath of flowers in her hands, stood on a small table. Judging by the dust, she hadn't moved from the spot for half a century or so and therefore, Tas thought, she might like a change of scenery. He picked up the statue and was just about to send the elf maiden on her journey out the window, when he heard voices outside the Tower.

Feeling thankful that the voices were coming from outside the Tower and not inside him, Tas lowered the elf maiden and peered curiously out the window.

A troop of Dark Knights had arrived on horseback, bringing with them a horse-drawn wagon with an open bed filled with straw. The Knights did not dismount but remained on their horses, glancing uneasily at the circle of dark trees that surrounded them. The horses shifted restlessly. The souls of the dead crept around the boles of the trees like a pitiful fog. Tas wondered if the riders could see the souls. He was sorry he could, and he did not look at the souls too closely, afraid he'd see himself again.

Dead but not dead.

He looked over his shoulder at Conundrum, bent almost double over his work and still mumbling to himself.

"Whoo-boy, there are a lot of Dark Knights about," Tas said loudly. "I wonder what these Dark Knights are doing here? Don't you wonder about that, Conundrum?"

The gnome muttered, but did not look up from his work. The device was certainly going back together in a hurry.

"I'm sure your work could wait. Wouldn't you like to rest a bit and come see all these Dark Knights?" Tas asked.

"No," said Conundrum, establishing the record for the shortest gnome response in history.

Tas sighed. The kender and the gnome had arrived at the Tower of High Sorcery in company with Tas's former companion and longtime friend Goldmoon—a Goldmoon who was ninety years old if she was a day but had the body and face of a woman of twenty. Goldmoon told Dalamar that she was meeting someone at the Tower. Dalamar took Goldmoon away and told Palin to take Tasslehoff and the gnome away and put them in a room to wait—making this a waiting room. It was then Dalamar had said, *You do understand the significance of the gnome?*

Palin had left them here, after wizard-locking the door. Tas knew the door was wizard-locked, because he'd already used up his very best lockpicks in an effort to open it without success. The day lockpicks fail is a day wizards are involved, as his father had been wont to say.

Standing at the window, staring down at the Knights, who appeared to be waiting for something and not much enjoying the wait, Tasslehoff was struck by an idea. The idea struck so hard that he reached up with the hand that wasn't holding onto the bronze statue of the elf maiden to feel if he had a lump on his head. Not finding one, he glanced surreptitiously (he thought that was the word) back at the gnome. The device was almost back together. Only a few pieces remained, and those were fairly small and probably not terribly important.

Feeling much better now that he had a Plan, Tas went back to observing what was happening out the window, thinking that now he could properly enjoy it. He was rewarded by the sight of an immense minotaur emerging from the Tower of High Sorcery. Tas was about four stories up in the Tower, and he could look right down on the top of the minotaur's head. If he chucked the statue out the window now, he could bean the minotaur.

Clunking a minotaur over the head was a delightful thought, and Tas was tempted. At that moment, however, several Dark Knights trooped out of the Tower. They bore something between them—a body covered with a black cloth.

Tas stared down, pressing his nose so hard against the glass pane that he heard cartilage crunch. As the troop carrying the body moved out of the Tower, the wind sighed among the cypress trees, lifted the black cloth to reveal the face of the corpse.

Tasslehoff recognized Dalamar.

Tas's hands went numb. The statue fell to the floor with a crash.

Conundrum's head shot up. "What in the name of dual carburetors did you do that for?" he demanded. "You made me drop a screw!"

More Dark Knights appeared, carrying another body. The wind blew harder, and the black cloth that had been thrown carelessly over the corpse slid to the ground. Palin's dead face looked up at the kender. His eyes were wide open, fixed and staring. His robes were soaked in blood.

"This is my fault!" Tas cried, riven by guilt. "If I had gone back to die, like I was supposed to, Palin and Dalamar wouldn't be dead now."

"I smell smoke," said Conundrum suddenly. He sniffed the air. "Reminds me of home," he stated and went back to his work.

Tas stared bleakly out the window. The Dark Knights had started a bonfire at the base of the Tower, stoking it with dry branches and logs from the cypress forest. The wood crackled. The smoke curled up the stone side of the Tower like some noxious vine. The Knights were building a funeral pyre.

"Conundrum," said Tasslehoff in a quiet voice, "how are you coming with the Device of Time Journeying? Have you fixed it yet?"

"Devices? No time for devices now," Conundrum said importantly. "I have this contraption about fixed."

"Good," said Tasslehoff.

Another Dark Knight came out of the Tower. She had red hair, cropped close to her head, and Tasslehoff recognized her. He'd seen her before, although he couldn't recall where.

The woman carried a body in her arms, and she moved very slowly and solemnly. At a shouted command from the minotaur, the other Knights halted their work and stood with their heads bowed.

The woman walked slowly to the wagon. Tas tried to see who it was the woman carried, but his view was blocked by the minotaur. The woman lowered the person gently into the wagon. She backed away and Tasslehoff had a clear view.

He'd assumed that the person was another Dark Knight, maybe one who'd been wounded. He was astonished to see that the person in the wagon was an old, old woman, and Tas knew immediately that the old woman was dead. He felt very sorry and wondered who she was. Some relation of the Dark Knight with the red hair, for she arranged the folds of the woman's white gown around her and then brushed out with her fingers the woman's long, flowing, silver-white hair.

"So Goldmoon used to brush out my hair, Galdar," said the woman.

Her words carried clearly in the still air. Much too clearly, as far as Tas concerned.

"Goldmoon." Tas felt a lump of sadness rise up in his throat. "She *is* dead. Caramon, Palin . . . Everyone I love is dead. And it's my fault. I'm the one who *should* be dead."

The horses drawing the wagon shifted restlessly, as if anxious to leave. Tas glanced back at Conundrum. Only two tiny jewels remained to be stuck on somewhere.

"Why did we come here, Mina?" The minotaur's booming voice could be heard clearly. "You have captured Solanthus, given the Solamnics a sound spanking and sent them running home to mama. The entire Solamnic nation is yours now. You have done what no one else has been able to do in the entire history of the world—"

"Not quite, Galdar," Mina corrected him. "We must still take Sanction, and we must take it by the time of the Festival of the Eye."

"The . . . festival?" The minotaur's forehead wrinkled. "The Festival of the Eye. By my horns, I had almost forgotten that old celebration." He grinned. "You are such a youngling, Mina, I'm surprised you know of it at all. It hasn't been celebrated since the three moons vanished."

"Goldmoon told me about the festival," said Mina, gently stroking the dead woman's wrinkled cheek. "That it was held on the night when all three moons—the red, the white, and the black—converged, forming the image of a great staring eye in the heavens. I should like to have seen that sight."

"Among humans, it was a night for riot and revelry, or so I have heard. Among my people, the night was honored and reverenced," Galdar stated, "for we believed the Eye to be the eye of Sargas, our god—*former* god," he added hastily, with a sidelong glance at Mina. "Still, what has some old festival to do with capturing Sanction? The three moons are gone, and so is the eye of the gods."

"There will be a festival, Galdar," said Mina. "The Festival of the New Eye, the One Eye. We will celebrate the festival in the Temple of Huerzyd."

"But the Temple of Huerzyd is in Sanction," Galdar protested. "We are on the other side of the continent from Sanction, not to mention the fact that Sanction is firmly in control of the Solamnic Knights. When will the festival occur?"

"At the appointed time," said Mina. "When the totem is assembled. When the red dragon falls from the skies."

"Ugh," Galdar grunted. "Then we should be marching to Sanction now and bringing with us an army. Yet we waste our time at this fell place." He cast a glance of enmity at the Tower. "Our march will be further slowed if we must cart along the body of this old woman."

The bonfire roared and crackled. The flames leaped up the stone walls of the Tower, charring them. Smoke swirled about Galdar, who batted irritably at it, and drifted in through the window. Tas coughed, covered his mouth with his hand.

"I am commanded to bring the body of Goldmoon, princess of the Qué-shu, bearer of the blue crystal staff, to Sanction, to the Temple of Huerzyd on the night of the Festival of the New Eye. There a great miracle will be performed, Galdar. Our journey will not be slowed. All will move as has been ordered. The One God will see to that."

Mina raised her hands over the body of Goldmoon and lifted up her voice in prayer. Orangish-yellow light radiated from her hands. Tas tried to look into the light to see what was happening, but the light was like tiny pieces of glass in his eyes, made them burn and hurt so that he was forced to shut them tight. Even then he could see the glare right through them.

Mina's praying ceased. The bright light slowly faded. Tasslehoff opened his eyes.

The body of Goldmoon lay enshrined in a sarcophagus of golden amber. Encased in the amber, Goldmoon's body was once again youthful, beautiful. She wore the white robes she had worn in life. Feathers adorned her hair, that was gold threaded with silver—yet all now held fast in amber.

Tas felt the sick feeling in his stomach rise up into his throat. He choked and clutched the window ledge for support.

"This coffin you've created is very grand, Mina," said Galdar, and the minotaur sounded exasperated, "but what do you plan to do with her? Cart her about as a monument to this One God? Exhibit her to the populace? We are not clerics. We are soldiers. We have a war too fight."

Mina stared at Galdar in silence, a silence so large and terrible that it absorbed into itself all sound, all light, snatched away the air they breathed. The awful silence of her fury withered Galdar, who shrank visibly before it.

"I'm sorry, Mina," he mumbled. "I didn't mean—"

"Be thankful that I know you, Galdar," said Mina. "I know that you speak from your heart, without thinking. But someday, you will go too far, and on that day I will no longer be able to protect you. This woman was more than mother to me. All I have done in the name of the One God, I have done for her."

Mina turned to the sarcophagus, placed her hands upon the amber, and bent near to look at Goldmoon's calm, still face. "You told me of the gods who had been but were no more. I went in search of them—for you!"

Mina's voice trembled. "I brought the One God to you, Mother. The One God gave you back your youth and your beauty. I thought you would be pleased. What did I do wrong? I don't understand." Mina's hands stroked the amber coffin, as if smoothing out a blanket. She sounded bewildered. "You will change your mind, dear Mother. You will come to understand. . . ."

"Mina . . ." Galdar said uneasily, "I'm sorry. I didn't know. Forgive me."

Mina nodded. She did not turn her head.

Galdar cleared his throat. "What are your orders concerning the kender?"

"Kender?" Mina repeated, only half-hearing him.

"The kender and the magical artifact. You said they were in the Tower."

Mina lifted her head. Tears glistened on her cheeks. Her face was pale, the amber eyes wide. "The kender." Her lips formed the words, but she did not speak them aloud. She frowned. "Yes, of course, go fetch him. Quickly! Make haste!"

"Do you know where he is, Mina?" Galdar asked hesitantly. "The Tower is immense, and there are many rooms."

Mina raised her head, looked directly at Tas's window, looked directly at Tas, and pointed.

"Conundrum," said Tasslehoff in a voice that didn't sound to him like his own voice but belonged to some altogether different person, a person who was well and truly scared. "We have to get out of here. Now!"

He backed precipitously away from the window.

"There, it's finished," said Conundrum, proudly displaying the device.

"Are you sure it will work?" Tas asked anxiously. He could hear footsteps on the stairs, or at least he thought he could.

"Or course," Conundrum stated, scowling. "Good as new. By the way, what did it do when it *was* new?"

Tas's heart, which had leaped quite hopefully at the first part of the gnome's statement, now sank.

"How do you know it works if you don't know what it does?"

Tas demanded. He could quite definitely hear footsteps. "Never mind. Just give it to me. Quickly!"

Palin had wizard-locked the door, but Palin was . . . wasn't here anymore. Tas guessed that the wizard-lock wasn't here either. He could hear footsteps and harsh breathing. He pictured the large and heavy minotaur, tromping up all those stairs.

"I thought at first it might be a potato peeler," Conundrum was saying. He gave the device a shake that made the chain rattle. "But it's a bit small, and there's no hydraulic lift. Then I thought—"

"It's a device that sends you traveling through time. That's what I'm going to do with it, Conundrum," Tasslehoff said. "Journey back through time. I'd take you with me, but I don't think you'd much like where I'm going, which is back to the Chaos War to be stepped on by a giant. You see, it's my fault that everyone I love is dead, and if I go back, they won't be dead. I'll be dead, but that doesn't matter because I'm already dead—"

"Cheese grater," said Conundrum, regarding the device thoughtfully. "Or it could be, with a few modifications, a meat grinder, maybe, and a—"

"Never mind," said Tasslehoff, and he drew in a deep breath to give himself courage. "Just hand me the device. Thank you for fixing it. I hate to leave you here in the Tower of High Sorcery with an angry minotaur and the Dark Knights, but once I'm stepped on, they might not be here anymore. Would you please hand me the device?"

The footsteps had stopped, but not the harsh breathing. The stairs were steep and treacherous. The minotaur had been forced to halt his climb to catch his breath.

"Combination fishing rod and shoe tree?" guessed the gnome.

The minotaur's footsteps started again.

Tas gave up. One could be polite for only so long. Especially to a gnome. Tas made a grab for the device. "Give it to me!"

"You're not going to break it again?" Conundrum asked, holding it just out of the kender's reach.

"I'm not going to break it!" Tasslehoff said firmly. With a another lunge, he succeeded in nabbing the device and wrenched it out of the gnome's hand. "If you'll watch closely, I'll show you how it works. I hope," he muttered to himself.

Holding the device, Tas said a little prayer in his heart. "I know you can't hear me, Fizban . . . Or maybe you can but you're so disappointed in me that you don't want to hear me. I'm truly sorry. Truly, truly sorry." Tears crept into his eyes. "I never meant to cause all this trouble. I only wanted to speak at Caramon's funeral, to tell everyone what a good friend he was to me. I never meant for this to happen. Never! So, if you'll help me just once to go back to die, I'll stay dead. I promise."

"It's not doing anything," Conundrum grumbled. "Are you sure it's plugged in?"

Hearing the footsteps growing louder and louder, Tas held the device over his head.

"Words to the spell. I have to say the words to the spell. I know the words," the kender said, gulping. "It goes . . . It goes . . . Thy time is thine . . . Around it you journey . . . No, that can't be right. Travel. Around it you travel . . . and something, something expanses . . ."

The footsteps were so close now that he could feel the floor shake.

Sweat beaded on the kender's forehead. He gulped again and looked at the device, as if it might help him. When it didn't, he shook it.

"Now I see how it got broken in the first place," said Conundrum severely. "Is this going to take long? I think hear someone coming."

"Grasp firmly the beginning and you'll end up at the end. No, that's wrong," Tas said miserably. "All of it's wrong. I can't remember the words! What's the matter with me? I used to know it by heart. I could recite it standing on my head. I know because Fizban made me do it. . . ."

There came a thundering crash on the door, as of a heavy minotaur shoulder bashing into it.

Tas shut his eyes, so that he wouldn't hear what was going on outside the door. "Fizban made me say the spell standing on my head backwards. It was a bright, sunny day. We were in a green meadow, and the sky was blue with these little puffy white clouds, and the birds were singing, and so was Fizban until I asked him politely not to. . . ."

Another resounding crash and a sound of wood splintering.

Thy time is thy own.
Though across it you travel.
Its expanses you see.
Whirling across forever.
Obstruct not its flow.
Grasp firmly the end and the beginning.
Turn them forward upon themselves.
All that is loose shall be secure
Destiny be over your own head.

The words flooded Tasslehoff's being, as warm and bright as the sunshine on that spring day. He didn't know where they came from, and he didn't stick around to ask.

The device began to glow brightly, jewels gleaming.

The last sensation Tas felt was that of a hand clutching his. The last sound Tas heard was Conundrum's voice, crying out in panic, "Wait! There's a screw loose—"

And then all sound and sensation was lost in the wonderful and exciting rushing-wind noise of the magic.

3

The Punishment for Failure

T he kender is gone, Mina," Galdar reported, emerging
from the Tower.

"Gone?" Mina turned away from the amber coffin that
held the body of Goldmoon to stare at the minotaur. "What do
you mean? That's impossible? How could he escape—"

Mina gave a cry of anguish. Doubling over in wrenching pain,
she sank to her knees, her arms clasped around her, her nails digging into her bare flesh in transports of agony.

"Mina!" Galdar cried in alarm. He hovered over her, helpless,
baffled. "What has happened? Are you wounded? Tell me!"

Mina moaned and writhed upon the ground, unable to
answer.

Galdar glared around at her Knights. "You were supposed to
be guarding her! What enemy has done this?"

"I swear, Galdar!" cried one. "No one came near her—"

"Mina," said Galdar, bending over her, "tell me where you are
hurt!"

Shuddering, in answer, she placed her hand on the black hauberk she wore, placed her hand over her heart.

"My fault!" she gasped through lips that bled. She had bitten down on them in her torment. "My fault. This . . . my punishment."

Mina remained on her knees, her head bowed, her hands clenched. Rivulets of sweat ran down her face. She shivered with fevered chills. "Forgive me!" she gasped, the words were flecked with blood. "I failed you. I forgot my duty. It will not happen again, I swear on my soul!"

The spasms of wracking pain ceased. Mina sighed, shuddering. Her body relaxed. She drew in deep breaths and rose, unsteadily, to her feet.

Her Knights gathered around her, wondering and ill at ease.

"Alarm's over," Galdar told them. "Go back to your duties."

They went, but not without many backward looks. Galdar supported Mina's unsteady steps.

"What happened to you?" he asked, eyeing her anxiously. "You spoke of punishment. Who punished you and for what?"

"The One God," said Mina. Her face was streaked with sweat and drawn with remembered agony, the amber eyes gray. "I failed in my duty. The kender was of paramount importance. I should have retrieved him first. I . . ." She licked her bloodied lips, swallowed. "I was so eager to see my mother, I forgot about him. Now he is gone, and it is my fault."

"The One God did this to you?" Galdar repeated, appalled, his voice shaking with anger. "The One God hurt you like this?"

"I deserved it, Galdar," Mina replied. "I welcome it. The pain inflicted on me is nothing compared to the pain the One God bears because of my failure."

Galdar frowned, shook his head.

"Come, Galdar," she said, her tone chiding, "didn't your father whip you as a child? Didn't your battle master beat you when you made a mistake in training? Your father did not strike you out of malice. The battle master did not hit you out of spite. Such punishment was meant for your own good."

"It isn't the same," Galdar growled. He would never forget the sight of her, who had led armies to glorious conquest, on her knees in the dirt, writhing in pain.

"Of course, it is the same," Mina said gently. "We are all children of the One God. How else are we to learn our duty?"

Galdar had no reply. Mina took his silence for agreement.

"Take some of the men and search every room in the Tower. Make certain the kender is not hiding in any of them. While you are gone, we will burn these bodies."

"Must I go back in there, Mina?" said Galdar, his voice heavy with reluctance.

"Why? What do you fear?" she asked.

"Nothing living," he replied, with a dark scowl at the Tower.

"Don't be afraid, Galdar," said Mina. She cast a careless glance at the bodies of the wizards, being dragged to the funeral pyre. "Their spirits cannot harm you. They go to serve the One God."

A bright light shone in the heavens. Distant, ethereal, the light was more radiant than the sun, made that orb seem dim and tarnished by comparison. Dalamar's mortal eyes could not look long at the sun, lest he be blinded, but he could stare at this beautiful, pure light forever, or so he imagined. Stare at it with an aching longing that rendered all that he was, all that he had been, paltry and insignificant.

As a very small child, he had once looked up in the night sky above his homeland to see the silver moon. Thinking it a bauble, just out of his reach, he wanted it to play with. He demanded his parents fetch it for him, and when they did not, he wept in anger and frustration. He felt that way now. He could have wept, but he had no eyes to weep with, no tears to fall. The bright and beautiful light was out of reach. His way to it was blocked. A barrier as thin as gossamer and strong as adamant stretched in front of him. Try as he might, he could not move past that barrier, a prison wall that surrounded a world.

He was not alone. He was one prisoner among many. The souls of the dead roamed restlessly about the prison yard of their bleak existence, all of them looking with longing at the radiant light. None of them able to attain it.

"The light is very beautiful," said a voice that was soft and beguiling. "What you see is the light of a realm beyond, the next stage of your soul's long journey. I will release you, let you travel there, but first you must bring me what I need."

He would obey. He would bring the voice whatever it wanted, so long as he could escape this prison. He had only to bring the magic. He looked at the Tower of High Sorcery and recognized it as having something to do with what he was, what he had been, but all that was gone now, behind him. The Tower was a veritable storehouse for the magic. He could see the magic glistening like streams of gold dust among the barren sand that had been his life.

The other, restless souls streamed into the Tower, now bereft of the one who had been its master. Dalamar looked at the radiant light, and his heart ached with longing. He joined the river of souls that was flowing into the Tower.

He had almost reached the entrance when a hand reached out and seized hold of him, held him fast. The voice, angry and frustrated itself, hissed at him, "Stop."

"Stop!" Mina commanded. "Halt! Do not burn the bodies. I have changed my mind."

Startled, the Knights let loose their hold. The corpses flopped limply to the ground. The Knights exchanged glances. They had never seen Mina like this, irresolute and vacillating. They didn't like it, and they didn't like to see her punished, even by this One God. The One God was far away, had little to do with them. Mina was near, and they worshiped her, idolized her.

"A good idea, Mina," said Galdar, emerging from the Tower. He glared balefully at the dead wizards. "Leave the vultures to be eaten by vultures. The kender is not in the Tower. We've searched high, and we've searched low. Let's get out of this accursed place."

Fire crackled. Smoke curled about the Tower, as the mournful dead curled about the boles of the cypress trees. The living waited in hopeful expectation, longing to leave. The dead waited patiently, they had nowhere to go. All of them wondered what Mina meant to do.

She knelt beside Dalamar's body. Clasping one hand over the medallion she wore around her neck, she placed her other hand on the mage's mortal wounds. The staring eyes looked up vacantly.

Softly, Mina began to sing.

Wake, love, for this time wake.
Your soul, my hand does take.
Leave the darkness deep.
Leave your endless sleep.

Dalamar's flesh warmed beneath Mina's hand. Blood tinged the gray cheeks, warmed the chill limbs. His lips parted, drew in breath in a shivering gasp. He quivered and stirred at her touch. Life returned to the corpse, to all but the eyes. The eyes remained vacant, empty.

Galdar watched in scowling disapproval. The Knights stared in awe. Always before, Mina had prayed over the dead, but she had never brought them back to life. The dead serve the One God, she had told them.

"Stand up," Mina ordered.

The living body with the lifeless eyes obeyed, rose to its feet.

"Go to the wagon," Mina ordered. "There await my command."

The elf's eyelids shivered. His body jerked.

"Go to the wagon," Mina repeated.

Slowly, the mage's empty eyes shifted, looked at Mina.

"You will obey me in this," said Mina, "as you will obey me in all things, else I will destroy you. Not your body. The loss of this lump of flesh would be of little consequence to you now. I will destroy your soul."

The corpse shuddered and, after a moment's hesitation, shuffled off toward the wagon. The Knights fell back before it, gave it wide berth, although a few started to grin. The shambling thing looked grotesque. One of the Knights actually laughed aloud.

Horrified and repelled, Galdar saw nothing funny in this. He had spoken glibly of leaving the corpses to the vultures, and he could have done that without a qualm—they were wizards, after all—but he didn't like this. There was something wrong with this, although he couldn't quite say what or why it should so disturb him.

"Mina, is this wise?" he asked.

Mina ignored him. Singing the same song over the second wizard, she placed her hand upon his chest. The corpse sat up.

"Go join your fellow in the wagon," she commanded.

Palin's eyes blinked. A spasm contorted his features. Slowly, the hands with their broken fingers started to raise up, reach out, as if to grab and seize hold of something only he could see.

"I will destroy you," Mina said sternly. "You will obey me."

The hands clenched. The face contorted in agony, a pain that seemed far worse than the pain of death.

"Go," said Mina, pointing.

The corpse gave up the fight. Bowing its head, it walked to the wagon. This time, none of the Knights laughed.

Mina sat back, pale, wan, exhausted. This day had been a sad one for her. The death of the woman she loved as a mother, the anger of her god. She drooped, her shoulders sagged. She seemed scarcely able to stand under her own power. Galdar was moved to pity. He longed to comfort and support her, but his duty came first.

"Mina, is this wise?" he repeated in a low voice, for her ears alone. "Bad enough we must haul a coffin about Ansalon, but now we are further burdened by these two . . . things." He didn't know what name to call them. "Why have you done this? What purpose does it serve?" He frowned. "It unsettles the men."

The amber eyes regarded him. Her face was drawn with fatigue and grief, but the eyes shone clear, undimmed, and, as always, they saw right through him.

"It unsettles you, Galdar," she said.

He grunted. His mouth twisted.

Mina turned her gaze to the corpses, sitting on the end of the wagon, staring out at nothing.

"These two wizards are tied to the kender, Galdar."

"They are hostages, then?" said Galdar, cheering up. This was something he could understand.

"Yes, Galdar, if you want to think of it that way. They are hostages. When we recover the kender and the artifact, they will explain to me to how it works."

"I'll put an extra guard on them."

"That will not be necessary," Mina said, shrugging. "Think of them not so much as prisoners, but as animated slabs of meat."

She gazed at them, her expression thoughtful. "What would you say to an army of such as these, Galdar? An army of soldiers who obey commands without question, soldiers who fight without fear, who have inordinate strength, who fall, only to rise again. Isn't that the dream of every commander? We hold their souls in thrall," she continued, musing, "and send forth their bodies to do battle. What would you say to that, Galdar?"

Galdar could think of nothing to say. Rather, he could think of too much to say. He could imagine nothing more heinous, nothing more obscene.

"Fetch my horse, Galdar," Mina ordered. "It is time we left this place of sorrow."

Galdar did as he was told, obeyed that order eagerly.

Mounting her horse, Mina took her place at the head of the mournful caravan. The Knights fell in around the wagon, forming an honor guard for the dead. The wagon's driver cracked his whip, and the heavy draft horses heaved against the harness. The wagon and its strange burden lurched forward.

The souls of the dead parted for Mina, as did the trees. A trail opened up through the thick and tangled wood that surrounded the Tower of High Sorcery. The trail was smooth, for Mina would not have the coffin jostled. She turned often in her saddle to look back to the wagon, to the amber sarcophagus.

Galdar took his customary place at Mina's side.

The bodies of the two wizards sat on the back of the wagon, feet dangling, arms flaccid, hands resting in their laps. Their eyes stared straight ahead behind them. Once, Galdar glanced back at them. He saw two wispy entities trailing after the living corpses, like silken scarves caught in the wagon wheels.

Their souls.

He looked quickly away and did not look back again.

4

The Death of Skie

The silver dragon had no idea how much time had passed since he had first entered the caverns of Skie, the mighty blue dragon. The blind silver, Mirror, had no way of judging time, for he could not see the sun. He had not seen it since the day of that strange and terrible storm, the day he'd heard the voice in the storm and recognized it, the day the voice had commanded that he bow down and worship, the day he'd been punished for his refusal, struck by the bolt that left him sightless and disfigured. That day was months past. He had wandered the world since, stumbling about in human form, because a blind human can walk, whereas a blind dragon, who cannot fly, is almost helpless.

Hidden away in this cave, Mirror knew nothing but night, felt nothing but night's cool shadows.

Mirror had no notion how long he had been here in the lair with the suffering blue dragon. It might have been a day or a year since Skie had sought to make demands of the One God. Mirror had been an unwitting witness to their encounter.

Having heard the voice in the storm and recognized it, Mirror had come seeking an answer to this strange riddle. If the voice was that of Takhisis, what was she doing in this world when all the other gods had departed? Thinking it over, Mirror had decided that Skie might be the one to provide him with information.

Mirror had always had questions about Skie. Supposedly a Krynn dragon like himself, Skie had grown larger and stronger and more powerful than any other blue dragon in the history of the world. Skie had purportedly turned on his own kind, slaying and devouring them as did the dragon overlords. Mirror had often wondered: Had Skie had truly turned upon his own kind? Or had Skie joined his own kind?

With great difficulty, Mirror had managed to find Skie's lair and enter it. He had arrived in time to witness Skie's punishment by Mina for his presumption, for his perceived disloyalty. Skie had sought to kill Mina, but the lightning bolt meant to slay her reflected off her armor, struck him. The immense blue dragon was mortally wounded.

Desperate to know the truth, Mirror had done what he could to heal Skie. He had been only partially successful. He was keeping the Blue alive, but the barbs of the gods are powerful weapons, and Mirror, though a dragon, was mortal.

Mirror left his charge only to fetch water for them both.

Skie drifted in and out of consciousness. During the times he was awake and lucid, Mirror was able to question the blue dragon about the One God, a god to whom Mirror was now able to give a name. These conversations took place over long periods of time, for Skie was rarely able to remain conscious long.

"She stole the world," Skie said at one point, shortly after he first regained his senses. "Stole it away and transported it to this part of the universe. She had long planned out her actions. All was in readiness. She awaited only the right moment."

"A moment that came during the Chaos War," Mirror said. He paused, asked quietly, "How are you feeling?"

"I am dying," Skie returned bluntly. "That's how I am feeling."

Had Mirror been human, he would have told some comforting falsehood intended to sooth the dying dragon's final moments. Mirror was not human, although he now walked in human form. Dragons are not given to telling falsehoods, not even those meant to comfort. Mirror was wise enough to know that such lies bring comfort only to the living.

Skie was a warrior dragon. A blue dragon, he had flown into battle countless times, had sent many of his foes plummeting to their deaths. He and his former rider, the infamous Kitiara uth Matar, had cut a swath of terror and destruction across half of Ansalon during the War of the Lance. After the Chaos War, Skie had been one of the few dragons in Ansalon to hold his own against the alien dragon overlords, Malys and Beryl, finally rising in power to take his place among them. He had slaughtered and gorged on other dragons, gaining in strength and power by devouring his own kind. He had built a hideous totem of the skulls of his victims.

Mirror could not see the totem, but he could sense it nearby. He heard the voices of the dead, accusing, angry, crying out for revenge. Mirror had no love for Skie. Had they met in battle, Mirror would have fought to defeat his foe and rejoiced in his destruction.

And Skie would have rejoiced in such a death. To die as a warrior, to fall from the skies with the blood of your foe wet on your talons, the taste of lightning on your tongue. That was the way Skie would have wanted to die. Not this way, not lying helpless, trapped in his lair, his life passing from him in labored, gasping breaths; his mighty wings stilled; his bloodied talons twitching and scrabbling on the rock floor.

No dragon should die this death, Mirror thought to himself. Not even my worst enemy. He regretted having used his magic to bring Skie back to life, but Mirror had to know more about this One God, he had to find out the truth. He inured himself against pity for his foe and continued asking questions. Skie did not have much time left to answer.

"You say Takhisis planned this removal," Mirror said, during another conversation. "You were part of her plan."

Skie grunted. Mirror could hear the massive body shift itself in an effort to ease the pain.

"I was the most important part, curse the eon I met the conniving bitch. I was the one who discovered the Portals. Our world, the world where I and others of my kind were born, is not like this world. We do not share our world with the short-lived, the soft-bodies. Ours is a world of dragons."

Skie was not able to say this without many pauses for breath and grunts of pain. He was determined to continue his tale. His voice was weak, but Mirror could still hear the anger, like a rumble of distant thunder.

"We roamed our world at will and fought ferocious battles for survival. These dragons you see here, this Beryl and this Malys, they seem to you enormous and powerful, but in comparison to those who ruled our world, they are small and pitiful creatures. That was one reason they came to this world. But I jump ahead of myself.

"I could see, as could others of our kind, that our world was growing stagnant. We had no future, our children had no future but to eat or be eaten. We were not advancing, we were regressing. I was not the only one to seek a way off the world, but I was the first to be successful. Using my magic, I discovered the roads that led through the ethers to worlds far beyond our own. I grew skilled at traveling these roads. Often the roads saved my life, for if I was threatened by one of the Elders, I had only to jump into the ethers to escape.

"It was while I was inside the ethers that I came upon Her Dark Majesty." Skie ground his teeth as he spoke, as if he would be glad to grind her between them. "I had never seen a god before. I had never before beheld anything so magnificent, never been in the presence of such power. I bowed before her and offered myself to her as her servant. She was fascinated by the roads through the ethers. I was not so enamored of her that I foolishly revealed their secrets to her, but I gave her enough information so that she could see how they might be of use to her.

"Takhisis brought me to her world that she called Krynn. She told me that on Krynn she was but one of many gods. She was the most powerful, she said, and because of that, the others feared her and were constantly conspiring against her. She would one day be triumphant over them, and on that day she would give me rich reward. I would rule Krynn and the soft-bodies who lived on it. This was to be my world in exchange for my services. Needless to say, she lied."

Anger stirred in Mirror, anger at the overweening ambition that gave no thought or care to any of those living on the world that was apparently little more than a bauble to Queen Takhisis. Mirror took care to keep his own anger hidden. He had to hear all that Skie had to tell. Mirror had to know what had happened. He could not change the past, but he might be able to affect the future.

"I was young then," Skie continued, "and the young of our species are the size of the blue dragons on Krynn. Queen Takhisis paired me with Kitiara—a favorite of the Dark Queen. Kitiara . . ."

Skie was silent, remembering. He gave a deep sigh, an aching sigh of longing. "Our battles together were glorious. For the first time, I learned that one could fight for more than survival—one could fight for honor, for the joy of the battle, for the glory in victory. At first, I despised the weaklings who inhabit this world: humans and the rest. I could not see why the gods permitted them to exist. Soon, I came to find them fascinating—Kitiara, especially. Courageous, bold, never doubting herself, knowing exactly what she wanted and reaching out to seize it. Ah, what a goddess *she* would have made."

Skie paused. His breath came with a painful catch. "I will see her again. I know I will. Together, we will fight . . . and ride once more to glory. . . ."

"And all this time," Mirror said, leading Skie back to the main topic, "you worked for Takhisis. You established the road that would take her here, to this part of the universe."

"I did. I made all ready for her. She had only to wait for the right time."

"But, surely, she could not have foreseen the Chaos War?" A terrible thought came to Mirror. "Or did that come about through her machinations?"

Skie snorted in disgust. "Clever Takhisis may be, but she is not that clever. Perhaps she had some inkling that Chaos was trapped inside the Graygem. If so, she had only to wait—for what is time to her, she is a god—for some fool to let him loose. If it had not been that, she would have found some other means. She was constantly watching for her chance. As it was, the Chaos War played right into her hands. All was in readiness. She made a show of fleeing the world, withdrawing her support and her power, leaving those who relied on her helpless. She had to do that, for she would need all her power for the enormous task that awaited her.

"The moment came. In the instant that Chaos was defeated, the energy released was immense. Takhisis harnessed that energy, combined it with her own power, and wrenched the world free of its moorings, brought it along the roads I had created with my magic, and set it here, in this part of the universe. All of this happened so fast that no one on the world was aware of the shift. The gods themselves, caught up in the desperate battle for survival, had no inkling of her plan, and once they realized what was happening, they were so depleted of their own power that they were helpless to stop her.

"Takhisis snatched the world away from them and hid it from their sight. All proceeded as she had planned. Bereft of the gods' blessing, stripped of their magic, the people of the world were thrown into turmoil and despair. She herself was exhausted, so weak that she was reduced to almost nothing. She needed time to heal herself, time to rest. But she wasn't worried. The longer the people were without a god, the greater their need. When she returned, they would be so thankful and relieved that they would be her abject slaves. She made one minor miscalculation."

"Malys," said Mirror. "Beryl and the rest."

"Yes. They were intrigued by this new toy that had suddenly dropped down among them. Weary of struggling to survive in their world, they were only too happy to take over this one. Takhisis was too weak to stop them. She could do nothing but watch in helpless frustration as they seized rulership of the world. Still, she lied to me and continued to promise me that someday, when she was again powerful, she would destroy the usurpers and give the world to me. I believed her for a while, but the years passed, and Malystryx and Beryl and the rest grew more powerful still. They killed the dragons of Krynn and feasted on them and built their totems, and I heard nothing from Takhisis.

"As for me, I could see this world degenerating into a world like the one I had left. I looked back with joy to my days of battle with Kitiara. I wanted nothing more to do with my kind, nothing more to do with the pathetic wretches who populated this place. I went to Takhisis and demanded payment.

"'Keep the world,' I said to her. 'I have no need of it. I do not want it. Restore Kitiara to me. We will travel the roads together. Together we will find a world where glory awaits us.' "

"She promised me she would. In a place called the Gray, I would find Kitiara's soul. I saw the Gray. I went there. Or thought I did." Skie rumbled deep in his chest. "You heard the rest. You heard Mina, the Dark Queen's new toady. You heard her tell me how I had been betrayed."

"Yet, others saw you depart. . . ."

"Others saw what she meant them to see, just as all saw what she meant them to see at the end of the Chaos War."

Skie fell silent, brooding over his wrongs. Mirror listened to the blue dragon's labored breathing. Skie might live for hours or days. Mirror had no way of knowing. He could not find out where Skie was wounded, and Skie himself would not tell him. Mirror wondered if the wound was not so much heart-deep as soul-deep.

Mirror changed the subject to turn Skie's thoughts. "Takhisis faced a new threat—the dragon overlords."

"The overlords." Skie grunted. "Yes, they were a problem. Takhisis had hoped that they would continue to fight and eventually slay each other, but the overlords agreed to a truce. Peace was declared. People began to grow complacent. Takhisis feared that soon people would start to worship the overlords, as some were already doing, and have no need of her. The Dark Queen was not yet strong enough to battle them. She had to find a way to increase her power. She had long recognized and lamented the waste of energy that passed out of the world with the souls of the dead. She conceived a way to imprison the dead within the world, and thus she was able to use them to steal away the wild magic and feed it to her. When she deemed she was strong enough to return, she came back, the night of the storm."

"Yes," said Mirror. "I heard her voice. She called to me to join her legions, to worship her as my god. I might have, but something stopped me. My heart knew that voice, if my head did not. And so I was punished. I—"

He halted. Skie had begun to stir, trying to lift his great bulk from the floor of the lair.

"What is it? What are you doing?"

"You had best hide yourself," said Skie, struggling desperately to regain his feet. "Malys is coming."

"Malys!" Mirror repeated, alarmed.

"She has heard I am dying. Those cowardly minions who used to serve me must have raced to her with the glad tidings. The great vulture comes to steal my totem. I should let her! Takhisis has usurped the totems for her own use. Malys takes her worst enemy to bed with her every night. Let the red monster come. I will fight her with my last breath—"

Skie might be raving, as Mirror truly thought he was, but the Blue's advice to hide was sound. Even had he not been blind, Mirror would have avoided a fight with the immense red dragon, much as he hated and loathed her. Mirror had seen too many of his kind caught and crushed in the mighty jaws, set ablaze by her horrific fire. Brute strength alone could not overcome this alien creature. The largest, strongest dragon ever to walk Krynn would be no match for Malystryx.

Not even a god had dared face her.

Mirror shifted back to human form. He felt very fragile and vulnerable in the soft skin, the thin and delicate bones, the paltry musculature. Yet, a blind human could manage in this world. Mirror began to grope his way around Skie's massive body. Mirror planned to retreat, move deeper into the twisting maze of corridors in the Blue's labyrinthine lair. Mirror was feeling his way about, when his hand touched something smooth and cold.

A shiver passed through his arm. Mirror could not see, but he knew immediately what he had touched—Skie's totem, made of skulls of his victims. Shuddering, Mirror snatched his hand away and almost lost his balance in his haste. He stumbled into the wall, steadied himself, used the wall to guide his steps.

"Wait," Skie's voice hissed through the dark corridors. "You did me a favor, Silver. You kept me from death by her foul hands. Because of you, I can die on my own terms, with what dignity I have left. I will do you a favor in return. The others of your kind—the Golds and Silvers—you've searched for them, and you cannot find them. True enough?"

Mirror was reluctant to admit this, even to a dying blue dragon. He made no reply but continued groping his way along the passage.

"They did not flee in fear," Skie continued. "They heard Takhisis's voice the night of the storm. Some of them recognized it, understood what it meant. They left the world to try to find the gods."

Mirror paused, turned his sightless face to the sound of Skie's voice. Outside, he could now hear what Skie had heard long before him—the beating of enormous wings.

"It was a trap," Skie said. "They left, and now they cannot return. Takhisis holds them prisoner, as she holds the souls of the dead prisoner."

"What can be done to free them?" Mirror asked.

"I have told you all I know," Skie replied. "My debt to you is paid, Silver. You had best make haste."

Moving as fast as possible, Mirror slipped and slid down the passage. He had no notion of where he was going, but guessed that he was traveling deeper into the lair. He kept his right hand on the wall, moved with the wall, never let go. Thus, he reasoned, he would be able to find his way out. When he heard Malys's voice, strident and high-pitched—an odd sound to come from such a massive creature—Mirror halted. Keeping his hand firmly against the wall, he hunkered down onto the smooth floor, shrouded in the lair's cool darkness. He quieted even his breathing, fearful that she might hear him and come seeking him.

Mirror crouched in the blue dragon's lair and awaited the outcome with dread.

Skie knew he was dying. His heart lurched and shivered in his rib cage. He fought for every breath. He longed to lie down and rest, to close his eyes, to lose himself in the past. To once more spread his wings that were the color of heaven and fly up among the clouds. To hear Kitiara's voice again, her firm commands, her mocking laughter. To feel her hands, sure and capable, on the reins, guiding him unerringly to the fiercest, hottest part of the battle. To revel again in the clash of arms and smell the blood, to feel the flesh rend beneath his talons and hear Kitiara's exultant battle cry, challenging all comers. To return to the stables, have his wounds dressed, and wait for her to come, as she always did, to sit down beside him and relive the battle. She would come to him, leaving behind those puny humans who sought to love her. Dragon and rider, they were a team—a deadly team.

"So, Skie," said a voice, a hated voice. Malys's head thrust inside the entrance to the lair, blotted out the sunlight. "I was misinformed. You're not dead yet, I see."

Skie roused himself. His dreams, his memories had been very real. This was unreality.

"No, I am not dead," he growled. His talons dug deep into the rock, fighting against the pain, forcing himself to remain standing.

Malys insinuated more of her great bulk inside his lair—her head and shoulders, front talons and neck. Her wings remained folded at her side, her hind feet and tail dangled down the cliff face. Her small, cruel eyes swept over him disdainfully. Discounting him, she searched for the reason she had come—his totem. She found it, elevated in the center of the lair, and her eyes glistened.

"Don't mind me," she said coolly. "You were dying, I believe. Please continue. I don't mean to interrupt. I just came to collect a few mementos of our time together."

Reaching out her talon, Malys began to weave a magical web around the skulls of his totem. Skie saw eyes in the skulls of the totem. He could sense his Queen's presence. Takhisis had no care for him. Not anymore. He was of no use to her now. She had eyes only for Malys. Fine. Skie wished them joy together. They deserved each other.

His legs trembled. They could not support his weight any longer, and he slumped to the floor of his lair. He was angry with himself, furious. He had to fight, to take a stand, to at least leave his mark upon Malys. He was so weak, shivering. His heart pounded as if it would burst in his chest.

"Skie, my lovely Blue!" Kitiara's voice came to him, mocking, laughing. "What, you sluggard, still asleep? Wake up! We have battles to fight this day. Death to deal. Our enemies do not slumber, you may be certain of that."

Skie opened his eyes. There she stood before him, her blue dragon armor shining in the sun. Kitiara smiled her crooked smile and, lifting her arm, she pointed.

"There stands your foe, Skie. You have one fight left in you. One more battle to go. Then you may rest."

Skie raised his head. He could not see Malys. His sight was going rapidly, draining away with his life. He could see Kitiara, though, could see where she pointed. He drew in a breath, his last breath. He had better make it a good one.

The breath mingled with the sulfur in his belly. He exhaled.

Lightning cracked and sizzled, split the air. Thunder boomed, shook the mountain. The sound was horrendous, but he could still hear Malys's shriek of rage and pain. He could not see what damage he had done to her, but he guessed it had been considerable.

Enraged, Malys attacked him. Her razor-sharp talons dug through his scales, ripped apart his flesh, tore a gaping hole in his flank.

Skie felt nothing, no more pain, no more fear.

Pleased, he let his head sink to the floor of his lair.

"Well done, my lovely Blue," came Kitiara's voice, and he was proud to feel the touch of her hand on the side of his neck. "Well done. . . ."

Skie's weak thunderbolt had caused Malys no real harm, beyond a jarring, tingling sensation that danced through her body and knocked a large chunk of scaly flesh off the joint of her upper left foreleg. She felt the pain more to her pride than to her great, bloated body, and she lashed out at the dying Skie, ripping and rending his flesh until the lair was awash with blood. Eventually, she realized she was doing nothing but maltreating an unfeeling corpse.

Her fury spent, Malys resumed her dismantling of his totem, prepared it for transport back to her lair in the new Goodlund Range, the Peak of Malys.

Gloating over her prize, eyeing with satisfaction the large number of skulls, Malys could feel her own power swell just handling them.

She had never had much use for Krynn dragons. In a world where they were the dominant species, Krynn dragons were feared and revered by the rest of the world's puny inhabitants and had thus become spoiled. Sometimes, it was true, Krynn's soft-skins had taken up arms against the dragons. Malys had heard accounts of these contests from Skie, heard him go on and on about some event known as the War of the Lance, about the thrill of battle and the bonds formed between dragonrider and dragon.

Clearly Skie had been away from his native world for too long, if he considered such childlike flailings to be true battles. Malys had gone up against a few of these dragonriders, and she'd never seen anything so amusing in her life. She thought back to her old world, where not a day went by but that some bloody fight erupted to establish hierarchy among the clan.

Survival had been a daily battle, then, one reason Malys and the others had been glad to find this fat and lazy world. She did not miss those cruel times, but she tended to look back upon them with nostalgia, like an old war veteran reliving his past. She and her kind had taught these weakling Krynn dragons a valuable lesson—those who survived. The Krynn dragons had bowed down before her, had promised to serve and worship her. And then came the night of that strange storm.

The Krynn dragons changed. Malys could not say exactly what was different. The Reds and Blacks and Blues continued to serve her, to come when summoned and answer her every beck and call, but she had the feeling they were up to something. She would often catch them in whispered conversations that broke off whenever she appeared. And, of late, several had gone missing. She'd received reports of Krynn dragons bearing dragonriders—Dark Knights of Neraka—into battle against the Solamnics at Solanthus.

Malys had no objections to the dragons killing Solamnics, but she should have been consulted first. Lord Targonne would have done so, but he had been slain, and it was in the reports of his death that Malys had first heard the most disturbing news of all— the appearance on Krynn of a god.

Malys had heard rumors of this god—the very god who had brought the world to this part of the universe. Malys had seen no signs of this god, however, and could only conclude that the god had been daunted by her arrival and had abandoned the field. The idea that the god might be lying low, building up her strength, never occurred to Malys—not surprising, for she came from a world devoid of guile, a world ruled by strength and might.

Malys began to hear reports of this One God and of the One God's champion—a human girl-child named Mina. Malys did not pay much attention to these, mainly because this Mina did nothing to annoy Malys. Mina's actions actually pleased Malys. Mina removed the shield from over Silvanesti and destroyed the sniveling, self-serving green dragon, Cyan Bloodbane. The Silvanesti elves were properly cowed, crushed beneath the boots of the Dark Knights.

Malys had not been pleased to hear that her cousin Beryl was about to attack the land of the Qualinesti elves. Not that Malys cared anything for the elves, but such actions broke the pact. Malys didn't trust Beryl, didn't trust her ambition and her greed. Malys might have been tempted to intervene and put a stop to this, but she had been assured by Lord Targonne, late leader of the Dark Knights, that he had the situation under control. Too late Malys found out that Targonne didn't even have his own situation under control.

Beryl flew off to attack and destroy Qualinesti, and she was successful. The Qualinesti elves were now fleeing the wreckage of their homeland like the vermin they were. True, Beryl managed to get herself killed in the process, but she had always been an impulsive, over-emotional, irrational nincompoop.

The green dragon's death was reported to Malys by two of Beryl's minions—red dragons, who cringed and groveled properly but who, Malys suspected, were chortling out of the sides of their mouths.

Malys did not like the way these reds gloated over her cousin's death. They didn't show the proper respect. Nor did Malys like what she heard of the reports of Beryl's death. It had the whiff of the god about it. Beryl might have been a braying donkey of a dragon, but she was an immense and powerful beast, and Malys could not envision any circumstances under which a band of elves could have taken her down without divine assistance.

One of the Krynn dragons gave Malys the idea of seizing Beryl's totem. He had happened to mention the totem, wondered what they were going to do with it. Power radiated from the totem still, even after Beryl's death. There was some talk among her surviving human generals that they might make use of it themselves, if they could figure out how to harness the magic.

Appalled by the idea of humans laying their filthy hands on something so powerful and sacred as the totem, Malys flew immediately to claim it for herself. She used her magic to transport it to her lair, added the skulls of Beryl's victims to the skulls of her own. She drew upon the magic and felt it well up inside her, making her stronger, more powerful than ever. Then came the report from Mina that she had slain the mighty Skie.

Malys wasted no time. So much for this god. She had best creep back into whatever hole she had crawled out of. Malys wrapped Skie's totem in magic and prepared to carry it off. Pausing, she glanced at the mangled remains of the great blue dragon, and wondered if she should add his head to the totem.

"He does not deserve such distinction," Malys said, shoving aside a bit of Skie's bone and flesh with a disdainful toe. "Mad, that's what he was. Insane. His skull would likely be a curse."

She glowered at the wound on her shoulder. The bleeding had stopped, but the burned flesh stung and ached, the damage to the muscle was causing her front foreleg to stiffen. The wound would not impede her flying, however, and that was all that mattered.

Gathering up the skulls in her magical web, Malys prepared to depart. Before leaving, she sniffed the air, took one last look around. She had noticed something strange on her arrival—an odd smell. At first she'd been unable to determine the nature of the smell, but now she recognized it. Dragon. One of those Krynn dragons and, unless Malys was much mistaken, a Krynn metallic dragon.

Malys searched the chamber of Skie's lair in which his body lay, but found no trace of a metallic dragon: no golden scales lying about, no silver scrapings on the walls. At length, Malys gave up. Her wound pained her. She wanted to return to the dark and restful sanctuary of her lair and build up her totem.

Holding fast to the web-encased skulls of the totem and favoring her wounded leg, Malys wormed her massive body out of the lair of the dead Blue and flapped off eastward.

5

The Silver Dragon and the Blue

Mirror remained in hiding until he was certain beyond doubt that Malys was gone and that she would not return. He had heard the battle, and he'd even felt pride in Skie for standing up to the heinous red dragon, experienced a twinge of pity at Skie's death. Mirror heard Malys's furious roar of pain, heard her rip apart Skie's body. When he felt a trickle of warm liquid flow past his hand, Mirror guessed that it was Skie's blood.

Yet now that Malys was gone, Mirror wondered what he would do. He put his hand to his maimed eyes, cursed his handicap. He was in possession of important information about the true nature of the One God. He knew what had become of the metallic dragons, and he could do nothing about any of it.

Mirror realized he was going to have to do something—go in search of food and water. The odor of dragon blood was strong, but through it he could just barely detect the scent of water. He used his magic to shift back to his dragon form, for his sense of smell was better in that form than this puny human body. He invariably looked forward to the shifting, for he felt cramped and vulnerable in the frail, wingless human form, with its soft skin and fragile bones.

He flowed into the dragon's body, enjoying the sensation as a human enjoys in a long, luxurious stretch. He felt more secure with his armored scales, felt better balanced on four legs than on two. He could see far more clearly, could spot a deer running through a field miles below him.

Or, rather, I could have once seen more clearly, he amended.

His sense of smell now much more acute, he was soon able to find a stream that flowed through the cavernous lair.

Mirror drank his fill and then, his thirst slaked, he next considered easing his hunger pangs. He smelled goat. Skie had brought down a mountain goat and not yet had a chance to eat it. Once he quieted the rumblings of his belly, Mirror would be able to think more clearly.

He hoped to avoid returning to the main chamber where the remnants of Skie's body lay, but his senses told him that the goat meat he sought was in that chamber. Hunger drove Mirror back.

The floor was wet and slippery with blood. The stench of blood and death hung heavy in the air. Perhaps it was this that dulled Mirror's senses or perhaps the hunger made him careless. Whatever the reason, he was startled beyond measure to hear a voice, dire and cold, echo in the chamber.

"I thought at first you must be responsible for this," said the dragon, speaking in the language of dragons. "But now I realize that I was wrong. You could not have brought down the mighty Skie. You can barely move about this cavern without bumping into things."

Calling defensive magical spells to mind, Mirror turned his sightless head to face the unknown speaker—a blue dragon, by the sound of his voice and the faint scent of brimstone that hung about him. The blue must have flown in the main entrance to Skie's lair. Mirror had been so preoccupied with his hunger that he had not heard him.

"I did not slay Skie," said Mirror.

"Who did, then? Takhisis?"

Mirror was surprised to hear her name, then realized that he shouldn't be. He was not the only one to have recognized that voice in the storm.

"You might say that. The girl called Mina wielded the magical bolt that brought about his death. She acted in self-defense. Skie attacked her first, claiming that she had betrayed him."

"Of course she betrayed him," said the Blue. "When did she ever do anything else?"

"I am confused," said Mirror. "Are we speaking of Mina or Takhisis?"

"They are one and the same, to all intents and purposes. So what are you doing here, Silver, and why is the stench of Malys heavy about the place?"

"Malys took away Skie's totem. Skie was mortally wounded, yet he still managed to defy her. He wounded her, I think, though probably not severely. He was too weak. She did this to him in retaliation."

"Good for him," growled the Blue. "I hope gangrene sets in and she rots. But you didn't answer my first question, Silver. Why are you here?"

"I had questions," said Mirror.

"Did you receive answers?"

"I did," said Mirror.

"Were you surprised to hear these answers?"

"No, not really," Mirror admitted. "What is your name? I am called Mirror."

"Ah, the Guardian of the Citadel of Light. I am called Razor. I am"—the Blue paused and when he next spoke, his voice was heavy and tinged with grief—"I was the partner of Marshal Medan of Qualinesti. He is dead, and I am on my own now. You, being a Silver, might be interested to hear that Qualinesti has been destroyed," Razor added. "The Lake of Death, the elves call it. That is all that is left of the once-beautiful city."

Mirror was suspicious, wary. "I can't believe this!"

"Believe it," said Razor grimly. "I saw the destruction with my own eyes. I was too late to save the Marshal, but I did see the great, green dragon Beryl meet her death." His tone held grim satisfaction.

"I would be interested to hear the account," said Mirror.

The Blue chuckled. "I imagine you would. The elves of Qualinesti were warned of her coming, and they were ready for her. They stood on their rooftops and fired thousands of arrows at her. Attached to each arrow was cord that someone had strengthened with magic. The elves thought it was their magic, naturally. It wasn't. It was her magic."

"Takhisis?"

"Simply ridding herself of another rival and the elves at the same time. The thousands of strands of magical cord formed a net over Beryl, dragged her down from the skies. The elves planned to kill her as she lay helpless on the ground, but their plans went awry. The elves had worked with the dwarves, you see, to dig tunnels beneath the ground of Qualinesti. Many elves managed to escape through these tunnels, but, in the end, they proved to be Qualinesti's undoing. When Beryl landed on the ground, her great weight caused the tunnels to collapse, forming a huge chasm. She sank deep into the ground. The waters of the White-Rage River left their banks and flowed into the chasm, flooding Qualinesti and turning it into a gigantic lake. A Lake of Death."

"Beryl dead," Mirror murmured. "Skie dead. The Qualineseti lands destroyed. One by one, Takhisis rids herself of her enemies."

"Your enemies, too, Silver," said Razor. "And mine. These overlords, as they call themselves, have slain many of our kind. You should rejoice in our Queen's victory over them. Whatever you may think of her, she is the goddess of our world, and she fights for us."

"She fights for no one but herself," Mirror retorted. "As she has always done. This is all her fault. If Takhisis had not stolen away the world, these overlords would have never found us. Those who have died would be alive today: dragons, elves, humans, kender. The great dragons murdered them, but Takhisis herself is ultimately responsible for their deaths, for she brought us here."

"Stole the world . . ." Razor repeated. His claws scratched against the rock. He shifted his tail slowly back and forth, his wings stirred restlessly. "So that is what she did."

"According to Skie, yes. So he told me."

"And why would he tell you, Silver?" Razor asked, sneering.

"Because I tried to save his life."

"He a blue dragon, your most hated enemy! And you tried to save his life!" Razor scoffed. "I am not some hatchling to swallow this kender tale."

Mirror couldn't see the Blue, but he could guess what he looked like. A veteran warrior, his blue scales would be shining clean, perhaps with a few scars of his prowess on his chest and head.

"My reasons for saving him were cold-blooded enough to satisfy even you," Mirror returned. "I came to Skie seeking answers to my questions. I could not let him die and take those answers to the grave with him. I used him. I admit it. I am not proud of myself, but at least, because of my aid, he managed to live long enough to strike a blow against Malys. For that, he thanked me."

The Blue was silent. Mirror could not tell what Razor was thinking. His claws scraped the rock, his wings brushed the blood-tainted air of the lair, his tail swished back and forth. Mirror had spells ready, should Razor decide to fight. The contest would not be equal—a seasoned, veteran Blue against a blind Silver. But at least, like Skie, Mirror would leave his mark upon his enemy.

"Takhisis stole the world." Razor spoke in thoughtful tones. "She brought us here. She is, as you say, responsible. Yet, she is our goddess as of old, and she fights to avenge us against our enemies."

"Her enemies," said Mirror coldly. "Else she would not bother."

"Tell me, Silver," Razor challenged, "what did you feel when you first heard her voice. Did you feel a stirring in your heart, in your soul? Did you feel nothing of this?"

"I felt it," Mirror admitted. "When I first heard the voice in the storm, I knew it to be the voice of a god, and I thrilled to hear it. The child whose father beats him will yet cling to that parent, not because he is a good or wise parent, but because he is the only parent the child knows. But then I began to ask questions, and my questions led me here."

"Questions," Razor said dismissively. "A good soldier never questions. He obeys."

"Then why haven't you joined her armies?" Mirror demanded. "Why are you here in Skie's lair, if not to ask questions of him?"

Razor had no response. Was he brooding, thinking things over or was he angry, planning to attack? Mirror couldn't tell, and he was suddenly tired of this conversation, tired and hungry. At the thought of food, his stomach rumbled.

"If we are going to battle," Mirror said, "I ask that we do it after I have eaten. I am famished, and unless I am mistaken, I smell fresh goat meat in the lair."

"I am not going to fight you," said Razor impatiently. "What honor is there in fighting a blind foe? The goat you seek is over to your left, about two talon-lengths away. My mate's skull is in one of those totems. Perhaps, if we had not been brought to this place, she would be alive today. Still," the Blue added moodily, slashing his tail, "Takhisis *is* my goddess."

Mirror had no help to offer the Blue. Mirror had solved his own crisis of faith. His had been relatively easy, for none of his kind had ever worshiped Takhisis. Their love and their loyalty belonged to Paladine, God of Light.

Was Paladine out there somewhere searching for his lost children? After the storm, the metallic dragons left to find the gods, or so Skie had said. They must have failed, for Takhisis remained unrivaled. Yet, Mirror believed, Paladine still exists. Somewhere the God of Light is looking for us. Takhisis shrouds us in darkness, hides us from his sight. Like castaways lost at sea, we must find a way to signal those who search the vast ocean that is the universe.

Mirror settled down to devour the goat. He did not offer to share. The Blue would be well fed, for he could see his prey. When Mirror walked the land in human form, he carried a begging bowl, lived off scraps. This was the first fresh meat he'd eaten in a long time and he meant to enjoy it. He had some notion now of what he could do, if he could only find the means to do it. First, though, he had to rid himself of this Blue, who appeared to think he had found a friend.

Blues are social dragons, and Razor was in no hurry to leave. He settled down to chat. He had seemed initially a dragon of few words, but now they poured out of him, as though he was relieved to be able to tell someone what was in his heart. He described the death of his mate, he spoke with sorrow and pride of Marshal Medan, he talked about a Dark Knight dragonrider named Gerard. Mirror listened with half his brain, the other half toying with an idea.

Fortunately, eating saved him from the necessity of replying beyond a grunt or two. By the time Mirror's hunger was assuaged, Razor had once more fallen silent. Mirror heard the dragon stir and hoped that finally the Blue was ready to leave.

Mirror was mistaken. Razor was merely shifting his bulk to obtain a more comfortable position.

If I can't get rid of him, Mirror decided dourly, I'll make use of him.

"What do you know of the dragon-skull totems?" Mirror asked cautiously.

"Enough." Razor growled. "As I said, my mate's skull adorns one of them. Why do you ask?"

"Skie said something about the totems. He said"—Mirror had to do some fancy mental shuffling to keep from revealing all Skie had said about the totems and the missing metallic dragons—"something about Takhisis having taken them over, subverted them to her own use."

"What does that mean? It's all very vague," Razor stated.

"Sorry, but he didn't say anything more. He sounded half crazy when he said it. He may have been raving."

"From what I have heard, one person alone knows the mind of Takhisis, and that is the girl Mina, the leader of the One God's armies. I have spoken to many dragons who have joined her. They say that this Mina is beloved of Takhisis and that she carries with her the goddess's blessing. If anyone knows the mystery of the totems, it would be Mina. Not that this means much to you, Silver."

"On the contrary," Mirror said thoughtfully, "it might mean more than you imagine. I knew Mina as a child."

Razor snorted, skeptical.

"I am Guardian of the Citadel, remember?" Mirror said. "She was a foundling of the Citadel. I knew her."

"Perhaps you did, but she would consider you her enemy now."

"So one would think," Mirror agreed. "But she came upon me only a few months ago. I was in human shape, blind, weak, and alone. She knew me then and spared my life. Perhaps she remembered our experiences together when she was a child. She was always asking questions—"

"She spared you out of sentimental weakness." Razor snorted. "Humans, even the best of them, all have this failing."

Mirror said nothing, carefully hid his smile. Here was a blue dragon who could grieve for his dead rider and still chide a human for being sentimentally attached to people from her youth.

"Still, in this instance, the failing could prove useful to us," Razor continued. He gave a refreshing shake, from his head to the tip of his tail, and flexed his wings. "Very well. We will confront this Mina, find out what is going on."

"Did you say 'we'?" Mirror asked, astounded. He truly thought he hadn't heard correctly, although the words "we" and "I" in the language of dragons are very distinct and easily distinguished.

"I said"—Razor lifted his voice, as though Mirror were deaf, as well as blind—"that we will go together to confront this Mina and demand to know our Queen's plans—"

"Impossible," said Mirror shortly. Whatever he himself planned, it did not involve partnering with a Blue. "You see my handicap."

"I see it," said Razor. "A grievous injury, yet it does not seem to have stopped you from doing what you needed to do. You came here, didn't you?"

Mirror couldn't very well deny that. "I travel on foot, slowly. I am forced to beg for food and shelter—"

"We don't have time for such nonsense. Begging! Of humans!" Razor shook his head so that his scales rattled. "I would think you would have much rather died of starvation. You must ride with me. Time is short. Momentous events are happening in the world. We don't have time to waste trudging along at a human's pace."

Mirror didn't know what to say. The idea of a blind silver dragon riding on the back of a Blue was so utterly ludicrous as to make him sorely tempted to laugh out loud.

"If you do not come with me," Razor added, seeing that Mirror was apparently having trouble making up his mind, "I will be forced to slay you. You speak very glibly about certain information Skie gave you, yet you are vague and evasive when it comes to the rest. I think Skie told you more than you are willing to admit to me. Therefore you will either come with me where I can keep an eye on you, or I will see to it that the information dies with you."

Mirror had never more bitterly regretted his blindness than at this moment. He supposed that the noble thing to do would be to defy the Blue and die in a brief and brutal battle. Such a death would be honorable, but not very sensible. Mirror was, so far as he knew, one of two beings on Krynn who were aware of the departure of his fellow gold and silver dragons, who had flown off on the wings of magic to find the gods, only to be trapped and imprisoned by the One God. Mina was the other being who knew this, and although Mirror did not think that she would tell him anything, he would never know for certain until he had spoken to her.

"You leave me little choice," said Mirror.

"Such was my intent," Razor replied, not smug, merely matter-of-fact.

Mirror altered his form, abandoning his strong, powerful dragon body for the weak, fragile body of a human. He took on the aspect of a young man with silver hair, wearing the white robes of a mystic of the Citadel. He wore a black cloth around his hideously injured eyes.

Moving slowly on his human feet, he groped about with his human hands. His shuffling footsteps stumbled over every rock in the lair. He slipped in Skie's blood and fell to his knees, cutting the weak flesh. Mirror was thankful for one blessing—he did not have to see the look of pity on Razor's face.

The Blue was a soldier, and he made no gibes at Mirror's expense. Razor even guided Mirror's steps with a steadying talon, assisted him to crawl upon the Blue's broad back.

The stench of death was strong in the lair where lay Skie's maltreated corpse. Both Blue and Silver were glad to leave. Perched on the ledge of the cavern, Razor drew in a breath of fresh air, spread his wings and took to the clouds. Mirror held on tightly to the Blue's mane, pressed his legs into Razor's flanks.

"Hold on," Razor warned. He soared high into the air, wheeled about in a huge arc. Mirror guessed what Razor planned and held on tightly, as he'd been ordered.

Mirror felt Razor's lungs expand, felt the expulsion of breath. He smelt the brimstone and heard the sizzle and crackle of lightning. A blast and the sound of rock splitting and shattering, then the sound of tons of rock sliding down the cliff face, rumbling and roaring amidst the thunder of the lightning bolt. Razor unleashed another blast, and this time it sounded to Mirror as if the entire mountain was falling into rubble.

"Thus passes Khellendros, known as Skie," said Razor. "He was a courageous warrior and loyal to his rider, as his rider was loyal to him. Let this might be said of all of us when it comes our time to depart this world."

His duty done to the dead, Razor dipped his wings in a final salute, then wheeled and headed off in a different direction.

Mirror judged by the warmth of the sun on the back of his neck that they were flying east. He held fast to Razor's mane, feeling the rush of wind strong against his face. He envisioned the trees, red and gold with the coming of autumn, like jewels set against the green velvet cloth of the grasslands. He saw in his mind the purple-gray mountains, capped by the first snows of the seasons. Far below, the blue lakes and snaking rivers with the golden blot of a village, bringing in the autumn wheat, or the gray dot of a manor house with all its fields around it.

"Why do you weep, Silver?" Razor asked.

Mirror had no answer, and Razor, after a moment's thought, did not repeat the question.

6

The Stone Fortress of the Mind

he Wilder elf known as the Lioness watched her husband with growing concern. Two weeks had passed since they had heard the terrible news of the Queen Mother's death and the destruction of the elven capital of Qualinost. Since that time, Gilthas, the Qualinesti's young king, had barely spoken a word to anyone—not to her, not to Planchet, not to the members of their escort. He slept by himself, covering himself in his blanket and rolling away from her when she tried to offer him the comfort of her presence. He ate by himself, what small amount he ate. His flesh seemed to melt from his bones, and he'd not had that much to spare. He rode by himself, silent, brooding.

His face was pale, set in grim, tight lines. He did not mourn. He had not wept since the night they'd first heard the dreadful tidings. When he spoke, it was only to ask a single question: how much farther until they reached the meeting place?

The Lioness feared that Gilthas might be slipping back into the old sickness that had plagued him during those early years of his enforced rulership of the Qualinesti people. King by title and prisoner by circumstance, he had fallen into a deep depression that left him lethargic and uncaring. He had often spent days sleeping in his bed, preferring the terrors of the dream world to those of reality. He had come out of it, fighting his way back from the dark waters in which he'd nearly drowned. He'd been a good king, using his power to aid the rebels, led by his wife, who fought the tyranny of the Dark Knights. All that he had gained seemed to have been lost, however. Lost with the news of his beloved mother's death and the destruction of the elven capital.

Planchet feared the same. His Majesty's bodyguard and valet-de-chamber, Planchet had been responsible, along with the Lioness, in luring Gilthas away from his nightmare world back to those who loved and needed him.

"He blames himself," said the Lioness, riding alongside Planchet, both gazing with concern on the lonely figure, who rode alone amidst his bodyguards, his eyes fixed unseeing on the road ahead. "He blames himself for leaving his mother there to die. He blames himself for the plan that ended up destroying the city and costing so many hundreds of lives. He cannot see that because of his plan Beryl is dead."

"But at a terrible cost," said Planchet. "He knows that his people can never return to Qualinost. Beryl may be dead, but her armies are not destroyed. True, many were lost, but according to the reports, those who remain continue to burn and ravage our beautiful land."

"What is burned can be restored. What is destroyed can be rebuilt. The Silvanesti went back to their homes to fight the dream," said the Lioness. "They took back their homeland. We can do the same."

"I'm not so sure," Planchet returned, his eyes fixed on his king. "The Silvanesti fought the dream, but look where it led them—to even greater fear of the outside world and an attempt to isolate themselves inside the shield. That proved disastrous."

"The Qualinesti have more sense," insisted the Lioness.

Planchet shook his head. Not wanting to argue with her, he let the subject drop. They rode several miles in silence, then Planchet said quietly, "You know what is truly wrong with Gilthas, don't you?"

The Lioness said nothing for long moments, then replied softly, "I think I do, yes."

"He blames himself for not being among the dead," said Planchet.

Her eyes filling with tears, the Lioness nodded.

Much as he now loathed this life, Gilthas was forced to live it. Not for his sake, for the sake of his people. Lately he began to wonder if that was reason enough to go on enduring this pain. He saw no hope for anyone, anywhere in this world. Only one thin strand tethered him to this life: the promise he had made to his mother. He had promised Laurana that he would lead the refugees, those who had managed to escape Qualinesti and who were waiting for him on the edges of the Plains of Dust. A promise made to the dead is a promise that must be fulfilled.

Still, they never rode past a river but he looked into it and imagined the peace he would find as the waters closed over his head.

Gilthas knew his wife grieved for him and worried about him. He knew or suspected that she was hurt that he had withdrawn from her, retreated to the stone-walled fortress in which he hid from the world. He would have liked to open the gates and let her come inside, but that required effort. He would have to leave the sheltered corner in which he'd taken refuge, advance into the sunlight, cross the courtyard of memory, unlock the gate to admit her sympathy, a sympathy he did not deserve. He couldn't bear it. Not yet. Maybe not ever.

Gilthas blamed himself. His plan had proven disastrous. His plan had brought destruction to Qualinesti and its defenders. His plan had caused his mother's death. He shrank from facing the refugees. They would think him a murderer—and rightly so. They would think him a coward—and rightly so. He had run away and left his people to die. Perhaps they would accuse him of having deliberately plotted the Qualinesti's downfall. He was part human, after all. In his depression, nothing was too outrageous or fantastic for him to believe.

He toyed with the idea of sending an intermediary, of avoiding facing the refugees directly.

"How very like the coward you are," Gilthas said to himself with a sneer. "Shirk that responsibility, as you've shirked others."

He would face them. He would suffer their anger and pain in silence as his due. He would relinquish the throne, would hand over everything to the Senate. They could choose another ruler. He would return to the Lake of Death, where lay the bodies of his mother and his people, and the pain would end.

Thus were the dark thoughts of the young elven king as he rode, day after day, by himself. He looked straight ahead toward a single destination—the gathering place for the refugees of Qualinost, those who had, through the gallant efforts of the dwarves of Thorbardin, escaped through tunnels that the dwarves had dug deep beneath the elven lands. There to do what he had to do. He would fulfill his promise, then he would be free to leave . . . forever.

Sunk in these musings, he heard his wife's voice speak his name.

The Lioness had two voices—one her wifely voice, as Gilthas termed it, and the other her military commander voice. She made the shift unconsciously, not aware of the difference until Gilthas had pointed it out to her long ago. The wife's voice was gentle and loving. The commander's voice could have cut down small trees, or so he teasingly claimed.

He closed his ears to the gentle and loving wife's voice, for he did not feel he deserved love, anyone's love. But he was king, and he could not shut out the voice of the military commander. He knew by the sound she brought bad news.

"Yes, what is it?" he said, turning to face her, steeling himself.

"I have received a report . . . several reports." The Lioness paused, drew in a deep breath. She dreaded telling him this, but she had no choice. He was king. "The armies of Beryl that we thought were scattered and destroyed have regrouped and reformed. We did not think this was possible, but it seems they have a new leader, a man named Samuval. He is a Dark Knight, and he follows a new Lord of the Night, a human girl called Mina."

Gilthas gazed at his wife in silence. Some part of him heard and understood and absorbed the information. Another part crawled farther into the dark corner of his prison cell.

"This Samuval claims he serves a god known as the One God. The message he brings his soldiers is this: The One God has wrenched Qualinesti from the elves and means to give it back to the humans, to whom this land rightly belongs. Now, all who want free land have only to sign on to serve with this Captain Samuval. His army is immense, as you can imagine. Every derelict and ne'er-do-well in the human race is eager to claim his share of our beautiful land. They are on the march, Gilthas," the Lioness said in conclusion. "They are well armed and well supplied and moving swiftly to seize and secure Qualinesti. We don't have much time. We have to warn our people."

"And then do what?" he asked.

The Lioness didn't recognize his voice. It sounded muffled, as if he were speaking from behind a closed door.

"We follow our original plan," she said. "We march through the Plains of Dust to Silvanesti. Only, we must move faster than we had anticipated. I will send riders on ahead to alert the refugees—"

"No," said Gilthas. "I must be the one to tell them. I will ride day and night if need be."

"My husband . . ." The Lioness shifted to the wife voice, gentle, loving. "Your health—"

He cast her a look that silenced the words on her lips, then turned and spurred his horse. His sudden departure took his bodyguard by surprise. They were forced to race their horses to catch up with him.

Sighing deeply, the Lioness followed.

The place Gilthas had chosen for the gathering of the elven refugees was located on the coast of New Sea, close enough to Thorbardin so that the dwarves could assist in the defense of the refugees, if they were attacked, but not near enough to make the dwarves nervous. The dwarves knew in their heads that the forest-loving elves would never think of living in the mighty underground fortress of Thorbardin, but in their hearts the dwarves were certain that everyone on Ansalon must secretly envy them their stronghold and would claim Thorbardin for themselves, if they could.

The elves had also to be careful not to draw the ire of the great dragon Onysablet, who had taken over what had once been New Coast. The land was now known as New Swamp, for she had used her foul magicks to alter the landscape into a treacherous bog. To avoid traveling through her territory, Gilthas was going to attempt to cross the Plains of Dust. A vast no-man's land, the plains were inhabited by tribes of barbarians, who lived in the desert and kept to themselves, taking no interest in the world outside their borders, a world that took very little interest in them.

Slowly, over several weeks, the refugees straggled into the meeting place. Some traveled in groups, streaming through the tunnels built by the dwarves and their giant dirt-devouring worms. Others came singly or by twos, escaping through the forests with the help of the Lioness's rebel forces. They left behind their homes, their possessions, their farmland, their crops, their lush forests and fragrant gardens, their beautiful city of Qualinost with its gleaming Tower of the Sun.

The elves were confident they would be able to return to their beloved homeland. The Qualinesti had always owned this land, or so it seemed to them. Looking back throughout history, they could not find a time when they had not claimed this land. Even after the elven kingdoms had split in twain following the bitter Kinslayer Wars, creating the two great elven nations, Qualinesti and Silvanesti, the Qualinesti continued to rule and inhabit land that had already been theirs.

This uprooting was temporary. Many among them still remembered how they had been forced to flee their homeland during the War of the Lance. They had survived that and returned to make their homes stronger than before. Human armies might come and go. Dragons might come and go, but the Qualinesti nation would remain. The choking smoke of burning would soon be blown away. The green shoots would shove up from underneath the black ash. They would rebuild, replant. They had done it before, they would do it again.

So confident were the elves of this, so confident were they in the defenders of their beautiful city of Qualinost, that the mood in the refugee camps, which had been dark at first, became almost merry.

True, there were losses to mourn, for Beryl had taken delight in slaughtering any elves she caught out in the open. Some of the refugees had been killed by the dragon. Others had run afoul of rampaging humans or been caught by the Dark Knights of Neraka and beaten and tortured. But the numbers of dead were surprisingly few, considering that the elves had been facing destruction and annihilation. Through the planning of their young king and the help of the dwarven nation, the Qualinesti had survived. They began to look toward the future and that future was in Qualinesti. They could not picture anything else.

The wise among the elves remained worried and troubled, for they could see certain signs that all was not well. Why had they not heard any news from the defenders of Qualinesti? Wildrunners had been stationed in the city, ready to speed swiftly to the refugee camps. They should have been here by now with either good news or bad. The fact that they had not come at all was deeply disturbing to some, shrugged off by others.

"No news is good news," was how the humans put it, or "No explosion is a step in the right direction," as the gnomes would say.

The elves pitched their tents on the sandy beaches of New Sea. Their children played in the gently lapping waters and made castles in the sand. At night they built fires of driftwood, watching the ever-changing colors of the flames and telling stories of other times the elves had been forced to flee their homeland—stories that always had a happy ending.

The weather had been beautiful, with unusually warm days for this late in the year. The seawater was the deep, blue-black color that is seen only in the autumn months and presages the coming of the winter storms. The trees were heavily laden with their harvest gifts, and food was plentiful. The elves found streams of fresh water for drinking and bathing. Elven soldiers stood guard over the people by day and by night, dwarven soldiers watched from the forests, keeping one eye alert for invading armies and one eye on the elves. The refugees waited for Gilthas, waited for him to come tell them that the dragon was defeated, that they could all go home.

"Sire," said one of the elven body guards, riding up to Gilthas, "you asked me to tell you when we were within a few hours' ride of the refugee camp. The campsite is up ahead." The elf pointed. "Beyond those foothills."

"Then we will stop here," said Gilthas, reigning in his horse. He glanced up at the sky, where the pale sun shone almost directly overhead. "We will ride again when dusk falls."

"Why do we halt, my husband?" the Lioness asked, cantering up in time to hear Gilthas give his instructions. "We have nearly broken our necks to reach our people, and, now that we are near, we stop?"

"The news I have to tell should be told only in darkness," he said, dismounting, not looking at her. "The light of neither sun nor moon will shine on our grief. I resent even the cold light of the stars. I would pry them from the skies, if I could."

"Gilthas—" she began, but he turned his face from her and walked away, vanishing into the woods.

At a sign from the Lioness, his guard accompanied him, maintaining a discreet distance, yet close enough to protect him.

"I am losing him, Planchet," she said, her voice aching with pain and sorrow, "and I don't know what to do, how to reclaim him."

"Keep loving him," Planchet advised. "That is all you can do. The rest he must do himself."

Gilthas and his retinue entered the elven refugee encampment in the early hours of darkness. Fires burned on the beach. Elven children were sprightly shadows dancing amidst the flames. To them, this was a holiday, a grand adventure. The nights spent in the dark tunnels with the gruff-voiced and fearsome looking dwarves were now distant memories. School lessons were suspended, their daily chores remitted. Gilthas watched them dance and thought of what he must tell them. The holiday would end this night. In the morning, they would begin a bitter struggle, a struggle for their very lives.

How many of these children who danced so gaily around the fire would be lost to the desert, succumbing to the heat and the lack of water, or falling prey to the evil creatures reputed to roam the Plains of Dust? How many more of his people would die? Would they survive as a race at all, or would this be forever known as the last march of the Qualinesti?

He entered the camp on foot without fanfare. Those who saw him as he passed were startled to see their king—those who recognized him as their king. Gilthas was so altered that many did not know him.

Thin and gaunt, pale and wan, Gilthas had lost almost any trace of his human heritage. His delicate elven bone-structure was more visible, more pronounced. He was, some whispered in awe, the very image of the great elven kings of antiquity, of Silvanos and Kith-Kanan.

He walked through the camp, heading for the center, where blazed a large bonfire. His retinue stayed behind, at a command from the Lioness. What Gilthas had to say, he had to say alone.

At the sight of his face, the elves silenced their laughter, ceased their storytelling, halted the dancing, and hushed their children. As word spread that the king had come among them, silent and alone, the elves gathered around him. The leaders of the Senate came hastily to greet him, clucking to themselves in irritation that he had robbed them of a chance to welcome him with proper ceremony. When they saw his face—deathlike in the firelight—they ceased their cluckings, forgot their welcoming speeches, and waited with dire foreboding to hear his words.

Against the music of the waves, rolling in one after the other, chasing each other to shore and falling back, Gilthas told the story of the downfall of Qualinesti. He told it clearly, calmly, dispassionately. He spoke of the death of his mother. He spoke of the heroism of the city's defenders. He lauded the heroism of the dwarves and humans who had died defending a land and a people not their own. He spoke of the death of the dragon.

The elves wept for their Queen Mother and for loved ones now surely dead. Their tears slid silently down their faces. They did not sob aloud lest they miss hearing what came next.

What came next was dreadful.

Gilthas spoke of the armies under this new leader. He spoke of a new god, who claimed credit for ousting the elves from their homeland and who was handing that land over to humans, already pouring into Qualinesti from the north. Hearing of the refugees, the army was moving rapidly to try to catch them and destroy them.

He told them that their only hope was to try to reach Silvanesti. The shield had fallen. Their cousins would welcome them to their land. To reach Silvanesti, however, the elves would have to march through the Plains of Dust.

"For now," Gilthas was forced to tell them, "there will be no homecoming. Perhaps, with the help of our cousins, we can form an army that will be powerful enough to sweep into our beloved land and drive the enemy from it, take back what they have stolen. But although that must be our hope, that hope is far in the future. Our first thought must be the survival of our race. The road we walk will be a hard one. We must walk that road together with one goal and one purpose in our hearts. If one of us falls out, all will perish.

"I was made your king by trickery and treachery. You know the truth of that by now. The story has been whispered among you for years. The Puppet King, you called me."

He cast a glance at Prefect Palthainon as he spoke. The prefect's face was set in a sorrowful mask, but his eyes darted this way and that, trying to see how the people were reacting.

"It would have been best if I had remained in that role," Gilthas continued, looking away from the senator and back to his people. "I tried to be your ruler, and I failed. It was my plan that destroyed Qualinesti, my plan that left our land open to invasion."

He raised his hand for silence, for the elves had begun to murmur among themselves.

"You need a strong king," Gilthas said, raising his voice that was growing hoarse from shouting. "A ruler who has the courage and the wisdom to lead you into peril and see you safely through it. I am not that person. As of now, I abdicate the throne and renounce all my rights and claims to it. I leave the succession in the hands of the Senate. I thank you for all the kindness and love that you have shown me over the years. I wish I had done better by you. I wish I was more deserving."

He wanted to leave, but the people had pressed close about him and, much as he needed to escape, he did not want to force a path through the crowd. He was forced to wait to hear what the Senate had to say. He kept his head lowered, did not look into the faces of his people, not wanting to see their hostility, their anger, their blame. He stood waiting until he was dismissed.

The elves had been shocked into silence. Too much had happened too suddenly to absorb. A lake of death where once stood their city. An enemy army behind them, a perilous journey to an uncertain future ahead of them. The king abdicating. The senators thrown into confusion. Dismayed and appalled, they stared at each other, waited for someone to speak the first word.

That word belonged to Palthainon. Cunning and conniving, he saw this disaster as a means to further his own ambition. Ordering some elves to drag up a large log, he mounted it and, clapping his hands, called the elves loudly to silence, a command that was completely unnecessary, for not even a baby's cry broke the hushed stillness.

"I know what you are feeling, my brethren," the prefect stated in sonorous tones. "I, too, am shocked and grieved to hear of the tragedy that has befallen our people. Do not be fearful. You are in good hands. I will take over the reins of leadership until such time as a new king is named."

Palthainon pointed his bony finger at Gilthas. "It is right that this young man has stepped down, for he brought this tragedy upon us—he and those who pulled his strings. Puppet King. Yes, that best describes him. Once Gilthas allowed himself to be guided by my wisdom and experience. He came to me for advice, and I was proud and happy to provide it. But there were those of his own family who worked against me. I do not name them, for it is wrong to speak ill of the dead, even though they sought continuously to reduce my influence."

Palthainon warmed to his topic. "Among those who pulled the puppet's strings was the hated and detested Marshal Medan—the true engineer of our destruction, for he seduced the son as he seduced the mother—"

Rage—white-hot—struck the fortress prison in which Gilthas had locked himself, struck it like the fiery bolt of a blue dragon. Leaping upon the log on which Palthainon stood, Gilthas hit the elf a blow on the jaw that sent him reeling. The prefect landed on his backside in the sand, his fine speech knocked clean out of his head.

Gilthas said nothing. He did not look around. He jumped off the log and started to shove his way through the crowd.

Palthainon sat up. Shaking his muzzy head, he spat out a tooth and started to sputter and point. "There! There! Did you see what he did! Arrest him! Arrest—"

"Gilthas," spoke a voice out of the crowd.

"Gilthas," spoke another voice and another and another.

They did not chant. They did not thunder his name. Each elf spoke his name calmly, quietly, as if being asked a question and giving an answer. But the name was repeated over and over throughout the crowd, so that it carried with it the quiet force of the waves breaking on the shore. The elderly spoke his name, the young spoke his name. Two senators spoke it as they assisted Palthainon to his feet.

Astonished and bewildered, Gilthas raised his head, looked around.

"You don't understand—" he began.

"We do understand," said one of the elves. His face was drawn, marked with traces of recent grief. "So do you, Your Majesty. You understand our pain and our heartache. That is why you are our king."

"That is why you have always been our king," said another, a woman, holding a baby in her arms. "Our true king. We know of the work you have done in secret for us."

"If not for you, Beryl would be wallowing in our beautiful city," said a third. "We would be dead, those of us who stand here before you."

"Our enemies have triumphed for the moment," said yet another, "but so long as we keep fast the memory of our loved nation, that nation will never perish. Some day, we will return to claim it. On that day, you will lead us, Your Majesty."

Gilthas could not speak. He looked at his people who shared his loss, and he was ashamed and chastened and humbled. He did not feel he had earned their regard—not yet. But he would try. He would spend the rest of his life trying.

Prefect Palthainon spluttered and huffed and tried to make himself heard, but no one paid any attention to him. The other senators crowded around Gilthas.

Palthainon glared at them grimly, then, seizing hold of the arm of an elf, he whispered softly, "The plan to defeat Beryl was my plan all along. Of course, I allowed His Majesty to take credit for it. As for this little dust-up between us, it was all just a misunderstanding, such as often happens between father and son. For he is like a son to me, dear to my heart."

The Lioness remained on the outskirts of the camp, her own heart too full to see or speak to him. She knew he would seek her out. Lying on the pallet she spread for both of them, on the edge of the water, near the sea, she heard his footsteps in the sand, felt his hand brush her cheek.

She put her arm around him, drew him beside her.

"Can you forgive me, beloved?" he asked, lying down with a sigh.

"Isn't that the definition of being a wife?" she asked him, smiling.

Gilthas made no answer. His eyes were closed. He was already fast asleep.

The Lioness drew the blanket over him, rested her head on his chest, listened to his beating heart until she, too, slept.

The sun would rise early, and it would rise blood red.

7

AN UNEXPECTED JOURNEY

Following the activation of the Device of Time Journeying, Tasslehoff Burrfoot was aware of two things: impenetrable darkness and Conundrum shrieking in his left ear, all the while clutching his (Tasslehoff's) left hand so tightly that he completely lost all sense of feeling in his fingers and his thumb. The rest of Tas could feel nothing either, nothing under him, nothing over him, nothing next to him—except Conundrum. Tas couldn't tell if he was on his head or his heels or an interesting combination of both.

This entertaining state of affairs lasted an extremely long time, so long that Tas began to get a bit bored by it all. A person can stare into impenetrable darkness only so long before he thinks he might like a change. Even tumbling about in time and space (if that's what they were doing, Tas wasn't at all sure at this point) grows old after you've been doing it a long while. Eventually you decide that being stepped on by a giant is preferable to having a gnome shrieking continuously in your ear (remarkable lung capacity, gnomes) and nearly pinching your hand off at the wrist.

This state of affairs continued for a good long while until Tasslehoff and Conundrum slammed down, bump, into something that was soft and squishy and smelled strongly of mud and pine needles. The fall was not a gentle one and knocked the boredom out of the kender and the shrieks out of the gnome.

Tasslehoff lay on his back, making gasping attempts to catch what would probably be the last few breaths he would ever take. He looked up, expecting to see Chaos's enormous foot poised above him. Tas had just a few seconds in which to explain matters to Conundrum, who was about to be inadvertently squished.

"We're going to die a hero's death," said Tasslehoff with his first mouthful of air.

"What?" Conundrum shrieked with his first mouthful of air.

"We're going to die a hero's death," Tasslehoff repeated.

Then he suddenly realized that they weren't.

Absorbed in preparing both himself and the gnome for an imminent demise, Tasslehoff had not taken a close look at their surroundings. He assumed that all he would be seeing was the ugly underside of Chaos's foot. Now that he had time to notice, he saw above him not a foot, but the dripping needles of a pine tree in a rain storm.

Tasslehoff felt his head to see if he had received a severe bump, for he knew from past experience that severe bumps to the head can cause you to see the most remarkable things, although those were generally starbursts, not dripping pine needles. He could find no signs of a bump, however.

Hearing Conundrum drawing in another large breath, undoubtedly preparatory to letting loose another ear-piercing shriek, Tasslehoff raised his hand in a commanding gesture.

"Hush," he whispered tensely, "I thought I heard something."

Now, if truth be told, Tasslehoff had not heard something. Well, he had. He'd heard the rain falling off the pine needles, but he hadn't heard anything dire, which is what his tone implied. He'd only pretended that in order to shut off the gnome's shrieks. Unfortunately, as is often the way with transgressors, he was immediately punished for his sin, for the moment he pretended to hear something dire, he *did* hear something dire—the clash of steel on steel, followed by a crackling blast.

In Tas's experience as a hero, only two things made sounds like that: swords beating against swords and fireballs exploding against just about anything.

The next thing he heard was more shrieking, only this time it was not, blessedly, Conundrum. The shrieking was some distance away and had the distinct sound of dying goblin to it, a notion that was reinforced by the sickening smell of burnt goblin hair. The shrieking ended summarily, then came a crashing, as of large bodies running through a forest of dripping wet pine needles. Thinking these might be more goblins and realizing that this was an inopportune time to be running into goblins, especially those who have just been fireball-blasted, Tasslehoff squirmed his way on his belly underneath a sheltering, low-hanging pine bough and dragged Conundrum in after him.

"Where are we?" Conundrum demanded, lifting up his head out of the mud in which they were lying. "How did we get here? When are we going back?"

All perfectly sound, logical questions. Trust a gnome, thought Tas, to go right to the heart of the matter.

"I'm sorry," said Tas, peering out through the wet pine needles, trying to see what was going on. The crashing sounds were growing louder, which meant they were coming closer. "But I don't know. Any of it."

Conundrum gaped. His chin fell so far it came back up with mud on it. "What do you mean you don't know?" he gasped, swelling with indignation. "You brought us here."

"No," said Tas with dignity, "I didn't. *This* brought us here." He indicated the Device of Time Journeying that he was holding in his hand. "When it wasn't supposed to."

Seeing Conundrum sucking in another huge breath, Tas fixed the gnome with a withering stare. "So I guess you didn't fix it, after all."

The breath wheezed out of Conundrum. He stared at the device, muttered something about missing schematics and lack of internal directives, and held out his mud-covered hand. "Give it to me. I'll take a look at it."

"No, thank you," said Tasslehoff, shoving the device into a pouch and closing the flap. "I think I should hold onto it. Now hush!" Turning back to stare out from under the pine bough, Tas put his fingers to his lips. "Don't let on we're here."

Contrary to most gnomes, who never see anything outside of the inside of Mount Nevermind, Conundrum was a well-traveled gnome who'd had his share of adventures, most of which he hadn't enjoyed in the slightest. Nasty, bothersome things, adventures. Interrupted a fellow's work. But he had learned an important lesson—the best way to survive adventures was to lie hidden in some dark and uncomfortable place and keep your mouth shut. This he was good at doing.

Conundrum was so good at hiding that when Tasslehoff, who was not at all good at this sort of thing, started to get up with a glad and joyful cry to go to meet two humans who had just run out of the forest, the gnome grabbed hold of the kender with a strength borne of terror and dragged him back down.

"What in the name of all that's combustible do you think you're doing?" Conundrum gasped.

"They're not burnt goblins, like I first thought," Tas argued, pointing. "That man is a Solamnic Knight. I can tell by his armor. And the other man is a mage. I can tell by his robes. I'm just going to go say hello and introduce myself."

"If there is one thing that I have learned in my travels," said Conundrum in a smothered whisper, "it is that you never introduce yourself to anyone carrying a sword or wearing wizard's robes. Let them go their way, and you go your way."

"Did you say something?" said the strange mage, turning to his companion.

"No," said the Knight, raising his sword and looking keenly about.

"Well, somebody did," said the mage grimly. "I distinctly heard voices."

"I can't hear anything for the sound of my own heart beating." The Knight paused, listening, then shook his head. "No, I can't hear a thing. What did it sound like? Goblins?"

"No," the mage said, peering into the shadows.

The man was a Solamnic by his looks, for he had long, blond hair that he wore braided to keep out of his way. His eyes were blue, keen, and intense. He wore robes that might have started out red but were now so stained with mud, charred with smoke, and smeared with blood that their color was indistinguishable in the gray light of the rainy day. A glint of golden trim could be seen at the cuffs and on the hem.

"Look at that!" gasped Tasslehoff, agog with amazement, "He's carrying Raistlin's staff!"

"Oddly enough," the mage was saying, "it sounded like a kender."

Tasslehoff clapped his hand over his mouth. Conundrum shook his head bleakly.

"What would a kender be doing here in the middle of a battle field?" asked the Knight with a smile.

"What does a kender do anywhere?" the mage returned archly, "except cause trouble for those who have the misfortune to encounter him."

"How true," sighed Conundrum gloomily.

"How rude," muttered Tasslehoff. "Maybe I won't go introduce myself to them, after all."

"So long as it was not goblins you heard," the Knight said. He cast a glance over his shoulder. "Do you think we've stopped them?"

The Knight wore the armor of a Knight of the Crown. Tas had first taken him to be an older man, for the Knight's hair had gone quite gray, but after watching him awhile, Tas realized that the Knight was far younger than he appeared at first glance. It was his eyes that made him look older—they had a sadness about them and a weariness that should not have been seen in one so young.

"We've stopped them for the time being," the mage said. Sinking down at the foot of the tree, he cradled the staff protectively in his arms.

The staff was Raistlin's, all right. Tasslehoff knew that staff well, with its crystal ball clutched in the golden dragon's claw. He remembered the many times he'd reached out to touch it, only to have his hand smacked.

"And many times I've seen Raistlin hold the staff just like that," Tas said softly to himself. "Yet that mage is most certainly *not* Raistlin. Maybe he's stolen Raistlin's staff. If so, Raistlin will want to know who the thief is."

Tas listened with all his ears, as the old kender saying went.

"Our enemy now has a healthy fear of your sword and my magic," the mage was saying. "Unfortunately, goblins have an even healthier fear of their own commanders. The whip will soon convince them to come after us."

"It will take them time to regroup." The Knight squatted down beneath the tree. Picking up a handful of wet pine needles, he began to clean the blood off his sword. "Time enough for us to rest, then try to find our way back to our company. Or time for them to find us. They are undoubtedly out searching for us even now."

"Searching for *you*, Huma," said the mage with a wry smile. He leaned back against the tree and wearily closed his eyes. "They will not be looking very hard for me."

The Knight appeared disturbed by this. His expression grave, he concentrated on his cleaning, rubbing hard at a stubborn speck. "You have to understand them, Magius—" he began.

"Huma . . ." Tas repeated. "Magius . . ." He stared at the two, blinked in wonder. Then he stared down at the Device of Time Journeying. "Do you suppose . . . ?"

"I understand them quite well, Huma," Magius returned. "The average Solamnic Knight is an ignorant, superstitious dolt, who believes all the dark tales about wizards told to him by his nursery maid in order to frighten him into keeping quiet at night, in consequence of which he expects me to start leaping through camp naked, gibbering and ranting and transforming him into a newt with a wave of my staff. Not that I couldn't do it, mind you," Magius continued with a quirk of his brow and the twist of an infectious smile. "And don't think I haven't considered it. Spending five minutes as a newt would be an interesting change for most of them. Expand their minds, if nothing else."

"I don't think I'd much care for life as a newt," said Huma.

"You, alone, are different, my friend," Magius said, his tone softening. Reaching out his hand, he rested it on the Knight's wrist. "You are not afraid of new ideas. You are not afraid of that which you do not understand. Even as a child, you did not fear to be my friend."

"You will teach them to think better of wizards, Magius," said Huma, resting his hand over his friend's. "You will teach them to view magic and those who wield it with respect."

"*I* will not," said Magius coolly, "for I really have no care what they think of me. If anyone can change their obsolete, outdated and outmoded views, you are the one to do it. And you had best do it quickly, Huma," he added, his mocking tone now serious. "The Dark Queen's power grows daily. She is raising vast armies. Countless thousands of evil creatures flock to her standard. These goblins would never before have dared to attack a company of Knights, but you saw with what ferocity they struck us this morning. I begin to think that it is not the whip they fear, but the wrath of the Dark Queen should they fail."

"Yet she will fail. She must fail, Magius," said Huma. "She and her evil dragons must be driven from the world, sent back to the Abyss. For if she is not defeated, we will live as do these wretched goblins, live our lives in fear." Huma sighed, shook his head. "Although, I admit to you, dear friend, I do not see how that is possible. The numbers of her minions are countless, their power immense—"

"But you do defeat her!" Tasslehoff cried, unable to restrain himself any longer. Freeing himself from Conundrum's frantic grasp, Tas scrambled to his feet and burst out from underneath the pine trees.

Huma jumped up, drawing his sword in one, swift movement. Magius extended the staff with the crystal held fast in the dragon's claw, aimed the staff at the kender, and began to speak words that Tas recognized by their spidery sound as being words of magic.

Knowing that perhaps he didn't have much time before *he* was turned into a newt, Tasslehoff accelerated his conversation.

"You raise an army of heroes, and you fight the Queen of Darkness herself, and while you die, Huma, and you die, too, Magius—I'm really very sorry about that, by the way—you do send all the evil dragons back to— ulp"

Several things happened simultaneously with that "ulp." Two large, hairy, and foul-smelling goblin hands grabbed hold Conundrum, while another yellow-skinned, slavering-jawed goblin seized hold of Tasslehoff.

Before the kender had time to draw his blade, before Conundrum had time to draw his breath, a blazing arc of lightning flared from the staff and struck the goblin who had hold of Conundrum. Huma ran his sword through the goblin trying to drag off Tas.

"There are more goblins coming," said Huma grimly. "You had best take to your heels, Kender."

Flapping goblin feet could be heard crashing through the trees, their guttural voices raised in hideous howls, promising death. Huma and Magius stood back to back, Huma with his sword drawn, Magius wielding his staff.

"Don't worry!" Tasslehoff cried. "I have my knife. It's called Rabbit-slayer." Opening a pouch, he began searching among his things. "Caramon named it. You don't know him—"

"Are you mad?" Conundrum screamed, sounding like the noon whistle at Mount Nevermind, a whistle that never, on any account, goes off at noon.

A hand touched Tasslehoff on the shoulder. A voice in his ear whispered, "Not now. It is not yet time."

"I beg your pardon?" Tasslehoff turned to see who was talking. And kept turning. And turning.

Then he was still, and the world was turning, and it was all a mass of swirling color, and he didn't know if he was on his head or his heels, and Conundrum was at his side, shrieking, and then it was all very, very dark.

In the midst of the darkness and the turning and the shrieking, Tasslehoff had one thought, one important thought, a thought so important that he made sure to hang onto it with all his brain.

"I found the past. . . ."

8

The Coming of the God

Rain fell on the Solamnic plains. The rain had been falling without letup since the Knights' crushing defeat by Mina's force at the city of Solanthus. Following the loss of the city, Mina had warned the surviving Knights that she meant next to take the city of Sanction. She had also told them to think on the power of the One God, who was responsible for the Solamnic's defeat. This done, she had bidden them ride off in safety, to spread the word of the One God.

The Knights didn't have much choice but to glumly obey the command of their conqueror. They rode for days through the rain, heading for Lord Ulrich's manor house, located about fifty miles east of Solanthus. The rain was chill and soaked everything. The Knights and what remained of their meager force were wet through, coated with mud, and shivering from the cold. The wounded they brought with them soon grew feverish, and many of them died.

Lord Nigel, Knight of the Crown, was one of the dead. He was buried beneath a rock cairn, in the hopes that at some future date his relatives would be able to remove the body and give him proper burial in his family's vault. As Gerard helped place the heavy stones over the corpse, he couldn't help but wonder if Lord Nigel's soul had gone to join the army that had defeated the Solamnic Knights—the army of the dead. In life, Lord Nigel would have shed his last drop of blood before he betrayed the Knighthood. In death, he might become their enemy.

Gerard had seen the souls of other Solamnic Knights drifting on the fearful tide of the river of souls. He guessed that the dead had no choice, they were conscripts, constrained to serve. But who or what did they serve? The girl, Mina? Or someone or something more powerful?

Lord Ulrich's manor house was constructed along simple lines. Built of stone quarried from the land on which the house stood, it was solid, massive, with square towers and thick walls. Lord Ulrich had sent his squire ahead to warn his lady wife of their coming, and there were roaring fires, fresh rushes on the floors, hot bread and mulled wine waiting for them on their arrival. The Knights ate and drank, warmed themselves and dried out their clothes. Then they met in council to try to determine what to do next.

Their first move was obvious—they sent messengers riding in haste to Sanction to warn the city that the Knights of Neraka had taken Solanthus and that they were threatening to march next on Sanction. Before the loss of Solanthus, the Knights would have scoffed at this notion. The Dark Knights of Neraka had been laying siege to Sanction for months without any success. Solamnic Knights insured that the port remained open and that supplies flowed into the city, so that while the besieged citizens didn't live well, they didn't starve either. The Solamnics had once almost broken the siege, but had been driven back by strange mischance. The siege continued, the balance held, neither side making any headway against the other.

But that had been before Solanthus had fallen to an army of dead souls, living dragons, a girl called Mina, and the One God.

These all figured large in the discussions and arguments that rang throughout the great hall of the manor house. A large, rectangular room, the hall had walls of gray stone covered with a few splendid tapestries depicting scenes illustrative of texts from the Measure. Thick, beeswax candles filled the hall with light. There were not enough chairs, so the Knights stood gathered around their leaders, who sat behind a large, ornately carved wooden table.

Every Knight was permitted his say. Lord Tasgall, Lord of the Rose and head of the Knights' Council, listened to them all in patient silence—including Odila, whose say was extremely uncomfortable to hear.

"We were defeated by a god," she told them, as they shifted and muttered and glanced askance at each other. "What other power on Krynn could hurl the souls of the dead against us?"

"Necromancers," suggested Lord Ulrich.

"Necromancers raise the bodies of the dead," Odila stated. "They drag skeletons from the ground to fight against the living. They have never had power over the souls of the dead."

The other Knights were glum, bedraggled, dour. They looked and felt defeated. By contrast, Odila was invigorated, exalted. Her wet, black hair gleamed in the firelight, her eyes sparked as she spoke of the god.

"What of death knights such as Lord Soth?" Lord Ulrich argued. The pudgy Lord Ulrich had lost considerable weight during the long, dispirited journey. Loose skin sagged around his mouth. His usually cheerful face was solemn, his bright eyes shadowed.

"You prove my point, my lord," Odila replied coolly. "Soth was cursed by the gods. Only a god has such power. And this god is powerful."

She raised her voice to be heard among the angry cries and denunciations. "You have seen that for yourself! What other force could create legions of souls and claim the loyalty of the dragons. You saw them! You saw them on the walls of Solanthus—red and white, black and green and blue. They were not there in the service of Beryl. They were not there in the service of Malys or any other of the dragon overlords. They were there in the service of Mina. And Mina is there in the service of the One God."

Odila's words were drowned out by jeers and boos, but that meant only that she'd struck a weak point in their armor. None could deny a word she said.

Lord Tasgall, the elder Knight, graying, upright, stern of bearing and countenance, shouted repeatedly for order and banged his sword hilt upon the table. Eventually order was restored. He looked at Odila, who remained standing, her head with its two thick, black braids thrown back in defiance, her face flushed.

"What is your proposal—" he began, and when one of the Knights hissed, the Lord Knight silenced him with a withering glance.

"We are a people of faith," said Odila. "We have always been people of faith. I believe that this god is trying to speak to us and that we should listen—"

The Knights thundered in anger, many shaking their fists.

"A god who brings death!" cried one, who had lost his brother in the battle.

"What of the old gods?" Odila shouted back. "*They* dropped a fiery mountain on Krynn!"

Some of the Knights were silenced by this, had no argument. Others continued to rant and rage.

"Many Solamnics lost their faith after the Cataclysm," Odila continued. "They claimed that the gods had abandoned us. Then we came to find out during the War of the Lance that we were the ones who had abandoned the gods. And after the Chaos War, when we woke to find the gods missing, we cried out again that they had left us. Perhaps again that is not the case. Perhaps this Mina is a second Goldmoon, coming to bring us the truth. How do we know until we investigate? Ask questions?"

How, indeed? Gerard asked himself, the seeds of a plan starting to take root in his mind. He couldn't help but admire Odila, even as he wanted to grab her by the shoulders and shake her until her teeth rattled. She alone had the courage to say aloud what needed to be said. Too bad she lacked the tact to say it in such a way that didn't start fistfights.

The hall erupted into chaos with people arguing for and against and Lord Tasgall banging his sword hilt with such force that chips flew from the wooden table. The wrangling continued far into the night, and eventually two resolutions were presented for consideration. A small but vocal group wanted to ride to Ergoth, where the Knights still held firm, there to lick their wounds and build up their strength. This plan was favored by many until someone sourly pointed out that if Sanction fell they might build up their strength from now until the end of forever and they wouldn't be strong enough to retake all that they had lost.

The other resolution urged the Knights to march to Sanction, there to reinforce the Knights already defending that disputed city. But, argued the minority, how do we even know they mean to go to Sanction? Why would this girl give away her plans? It is a trick, a trap. Thus they argued, back and forth. No one mentioned anything about the One God.

The council itself was divided. Lord Ulrich was in favor of riding to Sanction. Lord Siegfried, who replaced the late Lord Nigel on the council, was from Ergoth and argued that the Knights would do better to retreat.

Gerard glanced at Odila, who stood near him. She was thoughtful and very quiet, her eyes dark and shadowed. She apparently had no more arguments to present, nothing more to say. Gerard should have realized silence was a bad sign for the glib-tongued young woman. As it was, he was too absorbed in his own thoughts and plans to pay much attention to her beyond wondering what she'd expected to accomplish in the first place. When next he looked around at her, to ask her if she wanted to go get something to eat, he found that she had gone.

Lord Tasgall rose to his feet. He announced that the council would take both matters under advisement. The three retired to discuss the matter in private.

Thinking that his own proposed plan of action might aid their decision making, Gerard left his fellows, who were still arguing, and went in search of the Lord Knights. He found them closeted in what had once been an old chapel dedicated to the worship of Kiri-Jolith, one of the old gods and one favored by the Solamnic Knights.

Retainers in the service of Lord Ulrich stood guard at the door. Gerard told them he had a matter of urgency to bring before the council and then, having been standing for hours, he sank thankfully onto a bench outside the chapel to await the Lord Knights' pleasure. While he waited, he went over his plans once more, searching for any flaw. He could find none. Confident and excited, he waited impatiently for the Knights to summon him.

At length, the guard came to him and said that they would see him now. As Gerard entered the old chapel, he realized that the council had already reached a decision. He guessed, by the way Lord Ulrich was smiling, that the decision was to march to Sanction.

Gerard was kept waiting a moment longer while Lord Siegfried conferred in a low voice with Lord Tasgall. Gerard glanced with interest around the old chapel. The walls were made of rough-hewn stone, the floor lined with wooden benches, worn smooth by years of use. The chapel was small, for it was a private chapel, intended for the family and servants. An altar stood at the front. Gerard could just barely make out the symbol of Kiri-Jolith—the head of a buffalo—carved in relief.

Gerard tried to picture in his mind what the chapel had been like all those many years ago, when the Lord Knight and his lady wife and their children, their retinue and their servants, had come to this place to worship their god. The ceiling would have been hung with bright banners. The priest—probably a stern, warrior-type—would have taken his place at the front as he prepared to read from the Measure or relate some tale of Vinas Solamnus, the founder of the Knighthood. The presence of the god would have been felt in this chapel. His people would have been comforted by that presence and would have left to go about their daily lives strengthened and renewed.

His presence was lacking now, when it was sorely needed.

"We will hear you now, Sir Gerard," said Lord Tasgall with a touch of impatience, and Gerard realized with a start that this was the second time he'd been addressed.

"I beg your pardon, my lords," said Gerard, bowing.

Receiving an invitation to advance and speak, he did so, outlining his plan. The three Knights listened in silence, giving no hint of their feelings. In conclusion, Gerard stated, "I could provide you with the answer to one question, at least, my lords—whether in truth this Mina does intend to march to Sanction or if that was a ruse to divert us from her true goal. If so, I might be able to discover the nature of that goal."

"The risk you run is very great," observed Lord Siegfried, frowning.

"'The greater the risk, the greater the glory,'" quoted Lord Ulrich, with a smile.

"I would it were so, my lord," said Gerard with a shrug, "but, in truth, I will not be in all that much danger. I am known to the Dark Knights, you see. They would have little reason to question my story."

"I do not approve of the use of spies," stated Lord Siegfried, "much less one of our own Knights acting in such a demeaning capacity. The Measure forbids it."

"The Measure forbids a lot of things," said Lord Tasgall dryly. "I, for one, tend to choose common sense over rules that have been handed down in the distant past. I do not command you to do this, Sir Gerard, but if you volunteer—"

"I do, my lord," said Gerard eagerly.

"—then I believe that you can be of inestimable help to us. The council has determined that the Knights will ride to the support of Sanction. I am convinced that this Mina does mean to attack and therefore we cannot delay. However, I would be glad to receive confirmation of this and to learn of any plans she has for the capture of the city. Even with dragons, she will find her way difficult, for there are many underground structures where armies can be safely concealed from attack."

"Then, too, her own armies may be susceptible to the dragon-fear," stated Lord Ulrich. "She may use dragons against us, only to watch helplessly as her own troops flee the field in terror."

The dead won't flee in terror, thought Gerard, but he kept that thought to himself. He knew by their grim expressions and grimmer faces that the Knights understood that as well as he did.

"Good luck to you, Sir Gerard," said Lord Tasgall, rising to his feet to shake hands.

Lord Ulrich also shook hands heartily. Lord Siegfried was stiff and solemn and clearly disapproving, but he made no further argument and actually wished Gerard luck, although he did not shake hands.

"We'll say nothing of this plan to anyone, gentlemen," said Lord Tasgall, glancing around at the others.

This agreed to, Gerard was about to take his departure when the retainer entered to say that a messenger had arrived with urgent news.

Since this might have some impact on Gerard's plan, Lord Tasgall gave a sign that he was to remain. The messenger entered. Gerard was alarmed to recognize a young squire from the household of Lord Warren, commander of the outpost of Solamnic Knights that protected Solace, location of Gerard's last posting. Gerard tensed, sensing dire news. The young man was mud-spattered, his clothes travel-worn. He strode forward, came to stand in front of Lord Tasgall. Bowing, he held out a sealed scrollcase.

Lord Tasgall opened the scrollcase, drew out the scroll, and began to read. His countenance changed markedly, his eyebrows raised. He looked up, amazed.

"Do you know what this contains?" Lord Tasgall asked.

"Yes, my lord," answered the squire. "In case the message was lost, I committed it to memory to relate to you."

"Then do so," said Lord Tasgall, leaning on the table. "I want these gentlemen to hear. I want to hear myself," he added in a low voice, "for I can scarce believe what I have read."

"My lords," said the squire, facing them, "three weeks ago, the dragon Beryl launched an attack against the elven nation of Qualinesti."

The Knights nodded. None were surprised. Such an attack had been long foreseen. The messenger paused to draw breath and consider what he would say next. Gerard, in a fever of impatience to hear news of his friends in Qualinesti, was forced to clench his fists to keep from dragging the information out of the man's throat.

"My lord Warren regrets to report that the city of Qualinost was completely destroyed in the attack. If the reports we have received are to be believed, Qualinost has disappeared off the face of Ansalon. A great body of water covers the city."

The Knights stared, astounded.

"The elves did manage to take their enemy down with them. The dragon overlord, Beryl, is dead."

"Excellent news!" said Lord Ulrich.

"Perhaps there is a god, after all," said Lord Siegfried, making a weak joke at which no one laughed.

Gerard bounded across the room. Grasping the startled messenger by the collar, Gerard nearly lifted the young man off the floor. "What of the elves, damn you? The Queen Mother, the young king? What of them? What has happened to them?"

"Please, sir—" the messenger exclaimed, rattled.

Gerard dropped the gasping young man. "I beg your pardon, sir, my lords," he said, lowering his strident tones, "but I have recently been in Qualinesti, as you know, and I came to care deeply for these people."

"Certainly, we understand, Sir Gerard," said Lord Tasgall. "What news do you have of the king and the royal family?"

"According to the survivors who managed to reach Solace, the Queen Mother was killed in the battle with the dragon," said the messenger, eyeing Gerard distrustfully and keeping out of his reach. "She is being proclaimed a hero. The king is reported to have escaped safely and is said to be joining the rest of his people, who fled the dragon's wrath."

"At least with the dragon dead, the elves can now go back to Qualinesti," said Gerard, his heart heavy.

"I am afraid that is not the case, my lord," the messenger replied grimly. "For although the dragon is dead and her armies dispersed, a new commander arrived very shortly afterward to take control. He is a Knight of Neraka and claims he was present during the attack on Solanthus. He has rallied what was left of Beryl's armies and overrun Qualinesti. Thousands flock to his standard for he has promised wealth and free land to all who join him."

"What of Solace?" asked Lord Tasgall anxiously.

"For the moment, we are safe. Haven is free. Beryl's forces who held control of that city abandoned their posts and traveled south to be in on the looting of the elven nation. But my lord believes that once this Lord Samuval, as he calls himself, has a firm grip on Qualinesti, he will next turn his gaze upon Abanasinia. Thus does my lord request reinforcements. . . ."

The messenger paused, looked from one lord knight to another. None met the man's pleading gaze. They looked at each other and then looked away. There were no reinforcements to send.

Gerard was so shaken that he did not immediately recognize the name Samuval and call to mind the man who had escorted him through Mina's camp. He would remember that only when he was on the road to Solanthus. For now, all he could think about was Laurana, dying in battle against the great dragon, and his friend and enemy, the Dark Knight commander, Marshal Medan. True, the Solamnics would never mention him or name Medan a hero, but Gerard guessed that if Laurana had died, the gallant Marshal had preceded her in death.

Gerard's heart went out to the young king, who must now lead his people in exile. Gilthas was so young to have such terrible responsibility thrust upon him, young and untried. Would he be up to the task? Could anyone, no matter how old and experienced, be up to that task?

"Sir Gerard . . ."

"Yes, my lord."

"You have leave to go. I suggest that you depart tonight. In all the turmoil, no one will think to question your disappearance. Do you have everything you need?"

"I need to make arrangements with the one who is to carry my messages, my lord." Gerard had no more luxury for sorrow. Someday, he hoped to have the chance to avenge the dead. But, for now, he had to make certain that he did not join them. "Once that is accomplished, I am ready to depart on the instant."

"My squire, Richard Kent, is young, but sensible, and an expert horseman," said Lord Tasgall. "I will appoint him to be your messenger. Would that be satisfactory?"

"Yes, my lord," said Gerard.

Richard was summoned. Gerard had seen the young man before and been impressed with him. The two soon settled where Richard was to wait to hear from Gerard and how they were going to communicate. Gerard saluted the Knights of the council, then departed.

Leaving the chapel of Kiri-Jolith, Gerard entered the sodden wet courtyard, ducked his head to keep the rain out of his eyes. His first thought was to find Odila, to see how she was faring. His second and better thought convinced him to leave her alone. She would ask questions about where he was going and what he was planning, and he'd been ordered to tell no one. Rather than lie to her, he decided it would be easier to not speak to her at all.

Taking a circuitous route to avoid the possibility of bumping into her or anyone else, he went to gather up what he needed. He did not take his armor, nor even his sword. Going to the kitchen, he packed some food in a saddlebag, snagged some water, and a thick cape that had been hung in front of the fire to dry. The cape was still damp in places and smelled strongly of wet sheep that had been baked in an oven, but it was ideal for his purpose. Clad only in his shirt and breeches, he wrapped himself in the cape and headed for the stables.

He had a long ride ahead of him—long, wet, and lonely.

9

The Plains of Dust

The rain that drenched the northlands of Ansalon and was such a misery to the Solamnic Knights would have been welcome to the elves in the south, who were just starting their journey through the Plains of Dust. The Qualinesti elves had always gloried in the sun. Their Tower was the Tower of the Sun; their king, the Speaker of the Sun. The sun's light banished the darkness and terrors of the night, brought life to the roses and warmth to their houses. The elves had loved even the new sun, that had appeared after the Chaos War, for though its light seemed feeble, pale, and sickly at times, it continued to bring life to their land.

In the Plains of Dust, the sun did not bring life. The sun brought death.

Never before had any elf cursed the sun. Now, after only a few days' travel through the empty, harsh land under the strange, glaring eye of this sun—an eye that was no longer pale and sickly but fierce and unforgiving as the eye of a vengeful goddess—the elves grew to hate the sun and cursed it bleakly as it rose with malevolent vindictiveness every morning.

The elves had done what they could to prepare for their journey, but none, except the runners, had ever traveled so far from their homeland, and they had no idea what to expect. Not even the runners, who maintained contact with Alhana Starbreeze of the Silvanesti, had ever crossed the Plains of Dust. Their routes took them north through the swamp land of the dragon overlord Onysablet. Gilthas had actually considered trying to travel these routes, but rejected the idea almost immediately. While one or two could creep through the swamps undetected by the dragon or the evil creatures who served her, an entire populace could not escape her notice. The runners reported that the swamp grew darker and more dangerous, as the dragon extended her control over the land, so that few who ventured into it these days came out alive.

The rebel elves—most of them Wilder elves, who were accustomed to living out-of-doors—had a better idea of what the people would face. Although none of them had ever ventured out into the desert, they knew that their lives might well depend on being able to flee at a moment's notice, and they knew better than to burden themselves with objects that are precious in life, but have no value to the dead.

The majority of the refugees had yet to learn this hard lesson. The Qualinesti elves had fled their homes, made a dangerous journey through dwarven tunnels or traveled by night under the shelter of the trees. Even so, many had managed to bring along bags and boxes filled with silken gowns, thick woolen robes, jewels and jewel boxes, books containing family histories, toys and dolls for the children, heirlooms of all types and varieties. Such objects held sweet remembrances of their past, represented their hope for the future.

Acting on the advice of his wife, Gilthas tried to convince the people that they should leave their heirlooms and jewels and family histories behind. He insisted that every person carry as much water as he or she could possibly manage, along with food enough for a week's journey. If that meant an elf maiden could no longer carry her dancing shoes, so be it. Most thought this stricture harsh in the extreme and grumbled incessantly. Someone came up with the idea of building a litter that could be dragged along behind and soon many of the elves began lashing together tree limbs to haul their goods. Gilthas watched and shook his head.

"You will never force them to abandon their treasures, my love," said the Lioness. "Do not try, lest they come to hate you."

"But they will never make it alive through the desert!" Gilthas gestured to an elven lord who had brought along most of his household possessions, including a small striking clock. "Don't they understand that?"

"No," the Lioness said bluntly, "but they will. Each person must make the decision to leave his past behind or die with it hanging about his neck. Not even his king can make that decision for him." Reaching out, she rested her hand over his. "Remember this, Gilthas, there are some who would *rather* die. You must steel yourself to face that."

Gilthas thought of her words as he trudged over the wind-swept rock that flowed like a harsh, hard, and barren red-orange sea to the blue horizon. Looking back across the land that shimmered in the hot sun, he saw his people straggling along behind. Distorted by the waves of heat rising from the rock, they appeared to waver in his vision, to lengthen and recede as he watched. He had placed the strongest at the rear of the group to assist those who were having difficulty, and he set the Wilder elves to keep watch along the flanks.

The first few days of their march, he had feared being attacked by the human armies rampaging through Qualinesti, but after traveling in the desert, he soon realized that here they were safe—safe because no one in his right mind would ever waste his energy chasing after them. Let the desert kill them, his enemies would say. Indeed, that seemed likely.

"We're not going to make it," Gilthas realized.

The elves did not know how to dress for the desert. They discarded their clothes in the heat and many were terribly burned by the sun. The litters now served a useful purpose—carrying those too burned or sick to walk. The heat sapped strength and energy, so that feet stumbled and heads bowed. As the Lioness had predicted, the elves began to divest themselves of their past. Although they left no mark on the rock, the tale of their passage could be read in the abandoned sacks and broken chests dumped off the litters or thrown down by weary arms.

Their pace was slow—heartbreakingly slow. According to the maps, they would have to cross two hundred and fifty miles of desert before they reached the remnants of the old King's Highway that led into Silvanesti. Managing only a few miles a day, they would run out of both food and water long before they reached the midpoint. Gilthas had heard that there were places in the desert where one could find water, but these were not marked on the maps, and he didn't know how to locate them.

He had one hope—the hope that had led him to dare to make this treacherous journey. He must try to find the Plainspeople who made their homes in this forbidding, desolate land. Without their help, the Qualinesti nation would perish.

Gilthas had naively supposed that traveling the Plains of Dust was similar to traveling in other parts of Ansalon, where one could find villages or towns within a day's journey along the route. He had been told that there was a village of Plainspeople at a place called Duntol. The map showed Duntol to be due east from Thorbardin. The elves traveled east, walking straight into the morning sun, but they saw no signs of a village. Gazing across the empty expanse of glistening red rock, Gilthas could see for miles in all directions and in all directions he saw no sign of anything except more rock.

The people were drinking too much water. He ordered that waterskins be collected by the Wilder elves and rationed. The same with the food.

At the loss of their precious water, the elves became angry and afraid. Some fought, others pleaded with tears in their eyes. Gilthas had to be harsh and stern, and some of the elves turned from cursing the sun to cursing their king. Fortunately for Gilthas—his one single stroke of luck—Prefect Palthainon was so badly sunburned that he was too sick to cause trouble.

"When the water runs out, we can bleed the horses and live off their blood for a few days," said the Lioness.

"What happens when the horses die?" he asked.

She shrugged.

The next day, two of the sunburn victims died. The elves could not bury them, for no tool they owned would break through the solid rock. They could find no stones on the windswept plains to cover the bodies. They finally wrapped them in woolen capes and lowered the bodies with ropes into deep crevices in the rock.

Light-headed from walking in the blazing sun, Gilthas listened to the keening of those who mourned the dead. He stared down into the crevice and thought dazedly how blissfully cool it must be at the bottom. He felt a touch on his arm.

"We have company," said the Lioness, pointing north.

Gilthas shaded his eyes, tried to see against the harsh glare. In the distance, wavering in the heat, he could make out three riders on horseback. He could not discern any details—they were shapeless lumps of darkness. He stared until his eyes watered, hoping to see the riders approaching, but they did not move. He waved his arms and shouted until his parched throat was hoarse, but the riders simply stood there.

Unwilling to lose any more time, Gilthas gave the order for the people to start walking.

"Now the watchers are on the move," said the Lioness.

"But not toward us," said Gilthas, sick with disappointment.

The riders traveled parallel to the elves, sometimes vanishing from sight among the rocks, but always reappearing. They made their presence known, made the elves aware that they were being watched. The strange riders did not appear threatening, but they had no need to threaten. If they viewed the elves as an enemy, the blazing sun was the only weapon they required.

Hearing the wailing of children in his ears and the moans of the ill and dying, Gilthas could bear it no longer.

"You're going to talk to them," the Lioness said, her voice cracking from lack of water.

He nodded. His mouth was too parched to waste words.

"If they are Plainspeople, they have no love for strangers trespassing in their territory," she warned. "They might kill you."

He nodded again and took hold of her hand, raised it to his lips, kissed it. Turning his horse's head, he rode off toward the north, toward the strange riders. The Lioness called a halt to the march. The elves sank down on the burning rock. Some watched their young king ride off, but most were too tired and dispirited to care what happened to him or them.

The strange riders did not gallop forth to meet Gilthas, nor did they gallop off. They waited for him to come to them. He could still make out very few details, and as he drew closer, he could see why. The strangers were enveloped in white garments that covered them from head to toe, protecting them from the sun and the heat. He could also see that they carried swords at their sides.

Dark eyes, narrowed against the sun, stared at him from the shadows cast by the folds of cloth swathed around their heads. The eyes were cold, dispassionate, gave no indication of the thoughts behind them.

One rider urged his horse forward, putting himself forth as the leader. Gilthas took note of him, but he kept glancing at a rider who kept slightly apart from the rest. This rider was extremely tall, towered over the heads of the others, and, although Gilthas could not say why, instinct led him to believe that the tall man was the person in charge.

The lead rider drew his sword, held it out before him and shouted out a command.

Gilthas did not understand the words. The gesture spoke for itself, and he halted. He raised his own sunburned hands to show that he carried no weapons.

"*Bin'on du'auth*," he said, as best he could talk for his cracked lips. "I give you greeting."

The stranger answered with a swarm of unfamiliar words that

buzzed about the king's ears, all of them sounding alike, none making any sense.

"I am sorry," Gilthas said, flushing and shifting to Common, "but that is all I know of your language." Speaking was painful. His throat was raw.

Waving the sword, the stranger spurred his horse and rode straight at Gilthas. The king did not move, did not flinch. The sword whistled harmlessly past his head. The stranger wheeled, galloped back, bringing his horse to a halt in a flurry of sand and a fine display of riding skill.

He was about to speak, but the tall man raised his hand in a gesture of command. Riding forward, he eyed Gilthas approvingly.

"You have courage," he said, speaking Common.

"No," Gilthas returned. "I am simply too tired to move."

The tall man laughed aloud at this, but his laughter was short and abrupt. He motioned for his comrade to sheathe his sword, then turned back to Gilthas.

"Why do the elves, who should be living on their fat land, leave their fat land to invade ours?"

Gilthas found himself staring at the waterskin the man carried, a waterskin that was swollen and beaded with drops of cool water. He tore his gaze away and looked back at the stranger.

"We do not invade your land," he said, licking his dry lips. "We are trying to cross it. We are bound for the land of our cousins, the Silvanesti."

"You do not plan to take up residence in the Plains of Dust?" the tall man asked. He was not wasteful of his words, spoke only what was needful, no more, no less. Gilthas guessed that he was not one to waste anything on anyone, including sympathy.

"Trust me, no, we do not," said Gilthas fervently. "We are a people of green trees and cold, rushing water." As he spoke these words, a homesickness welled up inside him so that he could have wept. He had no tears. They had been burned away by the sun. "We must return to our forests, or else we will die."

"Why do you flee your green land and cold water?" the tall man asked.

Gilthas swayed in the saddle. He had to pause to try to gather enough moisture in his throat to continue speaking. He failed. His words came out a harsh whisper.

"The dragon, Beryl, attacked our land. The dragon is dead, but the capital city, Qualinost, was destroyed in the battle. The lives of many elves, humans, and dwarves were lost defending it. The Dark Knights now overrun our land. They seek our total annihilation. We are not strong enough to fight them, so we must—"

The next thing Gilthas knew, he was flat on his back on the ground, staring up at the unwinking eye of the vengeful sun. The tall man, wrapped in his robes, squatted comfortably at his side, while one of his comrades dribbled water into Gilthas's lips.

The tall man shook his head. "I do not know which is greater— the courage of the elves or their ignorance. Traveling in the heat of the day, without the proper clothing . . ." He shook his head again.

Gilthas struggled to sit up. The man giving him water shoved him back down.

"Unless I am much mistaken," the tall man continued, "you are Gilthas, son of Lauralanthalasa and Tanis Half-elven."

Gilthas stared, amazed. "How did you know?"

"I am Wanderer," said the tall man, "son of Riverwind and Goldmoon. These are my comrades." He did not name them, apparently leaving it up to them to introduce themselves, something they did not seem disposed to do. Obviously a people of few words. "We will help you," he added, "if only to speed you through our land."

The offer was not very gracious, but Gilthas took what he could get and was grateful for it.

"If you must know," Wanderer continued, "you have my mother to thank for your salvation. She sent me to search for you."

Gilthas could not understand this in the slightest, could only suppose that Goldmoon had received a vision of their plight.

"How is . . . your mother?" he asked, savoring the cool drops of tepid water that tasted of goat, yet were better to him than the finest wine.

"Dead," said Wanderer, gazing far off over the plains.

Gilthas was taken aback by his matter-of-fact tone. He was about to mumble something consoling, but the tall man interrupted him.

"My mother's spirit came to me the night before last, and told me to travel south. I did not know why, and she did not say. I thought perhaps I might find her body on this journey, for she told me that she lies unburied, but her spirit disappeared before she could tell me where."

Gilthas again began to stammer his regrets, but Wanderer paid no heed to his words.

"Instead," Wanderer said quietly, "I find you and your people. Perhaps you know how to find my mother?"

Before Gilthas could answer, Wanderer continued on. "I was told she fled the Citadel before it was attacked by the dragon, but no one knows where she went. They said that she was in the grip of some sort of madness, perhaps the scattered wits that come to the very old. She did not seem mad to me when I saw her spirit. She seemed a prisoner."

Gilthas thought privately that if Goldmoon was not mad, her son certainly was—all this talk of spirits and unburied bodies. Still, Wanderer's vision had saved their lives, and Gilthas could not very well argue against it. He answered only that he had no idea where Goldmoon was, or if she was dead or alive. His heart ached, for he thought of his own mother, lying unburied at the bottom of a new-formed lake. A great weariness and lethargy came over him. He wished he could lie here for days, with the taste of cool water on his lips. He had his people to think of, however. Resisting all admonitions to remain prone, Gilthas staggered to his feet.

"We are trying to reach Duntol," he said.

Wanderer rose with him. "You are too far south. You will find an oasis near here. There your people may rest for a few days and build up their strength before you continue your journey. I will send my comrades to Duntol for food and supplies."

"We have money to pay for it," Gilthas began. He swallowed the words when he saw Wanderer's face darken in anger. "We will find some way to repay you," he amended lamely.

"Leave our land," Wanderer reiterated sternly. "With the dragon seizing ever more land to the north, our resources are stretched as it is."

"We intend to," said Gilthas, wearily. "As I have said, we travel to Silvanesti."

Wanderer gazed long at him, seemed about to say more, but then apparently thought better of it. He turned to his companions and spoke to them in the language of the Plainspeople. Gilthas wondered what Wanderer had been about to say, but his curiosity evaporated as he concentrated on just remaining upright. He was glad to find that they had given his horse water.

Wanderer's two companions galloped off. Wanderer offered to ride with Gilthas.

"I will show you how to dress yourselves to protect your fair skin from the sun and to keep out the heat," Wanderer said. "You must travel in the cool of the night and the early morning, sleep during the heat of the day. My people will treat your sick and show you how to build shelters from the sun. I will guide you as far as the old King's Highway, which you will be able to follow to Silvanesti. You will take that road and leave our land and not return."

"Why do you keep harping on this?" Gilthas demanded. "I mean no offense, Wanderer, but I cannot imagine anyone in his right mind wanting to live in a place like this. Not even the Abyss could be more empty and desolate."

Gilthas feared his outburst might have angered the Plainsman and was about to apologize, when he heard what sounded like a smothered chuckle come from behind the cloth that covered Wanderer's face. Gilthas remembered Riverwind only dimly, when he and Goldmoon had visited his parents long ago, but he was suddenly reminded of the tall, stern-faced hunter.

"The desert has its own beauty," said Wanderer. "After a rain, flowers burst into life, scenting the air with their sweetness. The red of the rock against the blue of the sky, the flow of the cloud shadows over the rippling sand, the swirling dustdevils and the rolling tumbleweed, the sharp scent of sage. I miss these when I am gone from them, as you miss the thick canopy of incessantly dripping leaves, the continuous rain, the vines that tangle the feet, and the smell of mildew that clogs the lungs."

"One man's Abyss is another man's Paradise, it seems," said Gilthas, smiling. "You may keep your Paradise, Wanderer, and you are welcome to it. I will keep my trees and cool water."

"I hope you will," said Wanderer, "but I would not count upon it."

"Why?" Gilthas asked, alarmed. "What do you know?"

"Nothing for certain," said Wanderer. Checking his horse, he turned to face Gilthas. "I was of two minds whether to tell you this or not. These days, rumors drift upon the wind like the cottonwood seeds."

"Yet, obviously, you give this rumor credence," Gilthas said.

When Wanderer still did not speak, Gilthas added, "We intend to go to Silvanesti no matter what has happened. I assure you, we have no plans to remain any longer in the desert than is necessary for us to cross it."

Wanderer gazed out across the sand to the mass of elves, bright spots of color that had blossomed among the rocks without benefit of life-giving rain.

"The rumors say that Silvanesti has fallen to the Dark Knights." Wanderer turned his dark eyes to Gilthas. "You've heard nothing of this?"

"No," replied Gilthas. "I have not."

"I wish I could give you more details, but, needless to say, your people do not confide in us. Do you believe it?"

Even as Gilthas shook his head firmly in the negative, his heart sank. He might speak confidently before this stranger and before his people, but the truth was that he had heard nothing from the exiled Silvanesti queen, Alhana Starbreeze, in many weeks, not since before the fall of Qualinost. Alhana Starbreeze had been waging a concerted fight to reenter Silvanesti, to destroy the shield that surrounded it. The last Gilthas had heard, the shield had fallen and she and her forces were poised on the border, ready to enter her former homeland. One might argue that Alhana's messengers would have a difficult time finding him, since he'd been on the move, but the Silvanesti Wildrunners were friends with the eagles and the hawks and all whose sight was keen. If they had wanted to find him, they could have. Alhana had sent no runners, and perhaps this explained why.

Here was yet another burden to bear. If this was true, they were not fleeing danger, they were running headlong toward it. Yet, they could not stay in the desert.

At least if I have to die, let it be under a shade tree, Gilthas thought.

He straightened in the saddle. "I thank you for this information, Wanderer. Forewarned is forearmed. Now I should no longer delay telling my people that help is coming. How many days will take us to reach the King's Highway?"

"That depends on your courage," said Wanderer. Gilthas could not see the man's lips, due to the folds of cloth that swathed his face, but he saw the dark eyes warm with a smile. "If all your people are like you, I should not think the journey will take long at all."

Gilthas was grateful for the compliment. He wished he had earned it. What is taken for courage might only be exhaustion, after all.

10

Breaking Into Prison

Gerard planned to enter Solanthus on foot. He stabled the animal at a roadhouse about two miles from the city—a roadhouse recommended by young Richard. Taking the opportunity to eat a hot meal (about the best that could be said for it), Gerard caught up on the local gossip. He put out that he was a sell-sword, wondered if there might be work in the great city.

He was immediately told all he needed and more than he wanted to know about the disastrous rout of the Solamnic Knights and the takeover of the city by the Dark Knights of Neraka. There had not been many travelers after the fall of Solanthus several weeks ago, but the inn's mistress was hopeful that business would soon improve. Reports coming from Solanthus indicated that the citizens were not being tortured and slaughtered in droves as many had feared, but that they were well treated and encouraged to go about their daily lives as though nothing had happened.

Oh, certainly, a few people had been hauled off to prison, but they had probably deserved it. The person in charge of the Knights, who was said to be a slip of a girl, was not lopping off heads, but was preaching to the people of a new god, who had come to take care of them. She had gone so far as to order an old temple of Paladine cleaned out and restored, to be dedicated to this new god. She went about the city healing the sick and performing other miracles. The people of Solanthus were becoming enamored of her.

Trade routes between Solanthus and Palanthas, long closed, had now been reopened, which made the merchants happy. All in all, the innkeeper stated, things could be worse.

"I heard there were evil dragons about," Gerard said, dunking his stale bread in the congealing gravy, the only way to make either palatable. "And worse than that." He lowered his voice. "I heard that the dead walked in Solanthus!"

The woman sniffed. She'd heard something along these lines, but she'd seen nothing of any dragons herself, and no ghost had come to the roadhouse asking for food. Chuckling at her own humor, she went bustling off to provide indigestion to some other unsuspecting guest, leaving Gerard to feed the rest of his meal to the roadhouse dog and ponder what he'd heard.

He knew the truth of the matter. He'd seen the red and blue dragons flying above the city, and he'd seen the souls of the dead surrounding the city's walls. The hair still rose on the back of his neck whenever he thought about that army of empty eyes and gaping mouths, wispy hands with ragged fingers that stretched out to him over the gulf of death. No, that had been very real. Inexplicable, but real.

He was startled to hear that the people of Solanthus were being so well treated, but not much surprised to hear that they had apparently taken Mina to their hearts. He'd had only a brief talk with the charismatic leader of the Dark Knights, and yet he retained a vivid picture of her: he could see the fell, amber eyes, hear the timbre of her voice, recall every word she'd spoken. Did the fact that she was treating the Solanthians well make his job easier or more difficult? He argued one way and the other and at length came to the conclusion that the only way to find out was to go there and see for himself.

Paying for his meal and for the stabling of the horse for a week, Gerard set out for Solanthus on foot.

Coming within sight of the city walls, he did not immediately enter. He sat down in a grove of trees, where he could see but not be seen. He needed more information on the city, and he needed that information from a certain type of person. He had been sitting there for about thirty minutes when a wicket at the main gate opened up and several small bodies shot out, as though forcibly propelled from behind.

The small bodies picked themselves up, dusted themselves off as though this were nothing out of the ordinary, and, after shaking hands all round, set off upon their separate ways.

One of the small bodies happened to pass quite close to Gerard. He called out, accompanying his call with a friendly gesture, and the small body, which belonged to a kender, immediately came over to chat.

Reminding himself that this was for a worthy cause, Gerard braced himself, smiled in a friendly manner at the kender, and invited him to be seated.

"Goatweed Tangleknot," said the kender, by way of introduction. "My goodness, but you're ugly," he added cheerfully, peering up into Gerard's pockmarked face, admiring his corn-yellow and recalcitrant hair. "You're probably one of the ugliest humans I've ever met."

The Measure promised that all who made the supreme sacrifice for the sake of their country would be rewarded in the afterlife. Gerard figured that this particular experience should gain him a suite of rooms in some celestial palace. Gritting his teeth, he said he knew he wouldn't win any prizes as queen of the May dance.

"And you have *very* blue eyes," said Goatweed. "Uncomfortably blue, if you don't mind my saying so. Would you like to see what I have in my pouches?"

Before Gerard could answer, the kender dumped out the contents of several pouches and began happily to sort through them.

"You just left Solanthus," Gerard said, interrupting Goatweed
in the middle of a story about how he'd come by a hammer that
had once belonged to some unfortunate tinker. "What's it like
inside there? I heard that it had been taken over by Dark Knights?"

Goatweed nodded vigorously. "It's about the same as usual.
The guards round us up and throw us out. Except that now they
take us first to this place that used to belong to the Mystics, and
before that it was a temple of some old god or other. They
brought in a group of Mystics from the Citadel of Light and
talked to them. That was fun to watch, I tell you! A girl stood up
in front of them, dressed up like a knight. She had very strange
eyes. Very strange. Stranger than your eyes. She stood in front of
the Mystics and told them all about the One God, and she
showed them a pretty lady stored up in an amber box and told
them that the One God had already performed one miracle and
given the pretty lady her youth and beauty and the One God was
going to perform another miracle and bring the pretty lady back
to life.

"The Mystics stared at the pretty lady, and some of them
began to cry. The girl asked the Mystics if they wanted to know
more about this One God, and those who said they did were
marched off one way, and those who said that they didn't were
marched off another, including some old man called the Star-
master or something like that. And then the girl came to us and
asked us lots of questions, and then she told *us* all about this new
god who has come to Krynn. And then she asked us if we'd like
to worship this new god and serve the new god."

"And what did you say?" Gerard was curious.

"Why, I said 'yes,' of course," said Goatweed, astonished that
he could suppose otherwise. "It would be rude *not* to, don't you
think? Since this new god has taken all this trouble to come here
and everything, shouldn't we do what we can to be encouraging?"

"Don't you think it might be dangerous to worship a god you
don't know anything about?"

"Oh, I know a lot about this god," Goatweed assured him. "At least, as much as seems important. This god has a great liking for kender, the girl told us. A very great liking. So great that this god is searching for one very special kender in particular. If any of us find this kender, we're supposed to bring him to the girl and she'll give us a huge reward. We all promised we would, and that's the very thing I'm off to do. Find this kender. You haven't seen him, by any chance?"

"You're the first kender I've seen in days," said Gerard. And hopefully the last, he added mentally. "How do you manage to get into the city without—"

"His name," said Goatweed, fixated on his quest, "is The Tasslehoff Burrfoot, and he—"

"Eh?" Gerard exclaimed, astonished. "What did you say?"

"Which time? There was what I said about Solanthus and what I said about the girl and what I said about the new god—"

"The kender. The special kender. You said his name was Burrfoot? Tasslehoff Burrfoot?"

"*The* Tasslehoff Burrfoot," Goatweed corrected. "The 'The' is very important because he can't be just any Tasslehoff Burrfoot."

"No, I guess he couldn't be," said Gerard, thinking back to the kender who had started this entire adventure by managing to get himself locked inside the Tomb of Heroes in Solace.

"Although, to make sure," Goatweed continued, "we're supposed to bring any Tasslehoff Burrfoot we find to Sanction for the girl to have a look at."

"You mean Solanthus," said Gerard.

Goatweed was absorbed in examining with interest a bit of broken blue glass. Holding it up, he asked eagerly, "Do you think that's a sapphire?"

"No," said Gerard. "It's a piece of broken blue glass. You said you were supposed to take this Burrfoot to Sanction. You mean Solanthus. The girl and her army are in Solanthus, not Sanction."

"Did I say Sanction?" Goatweed scratched his head. After some thought, he nodded. "Yes, I said Sanction, and I meant Sanction. The girl told us that she wasn't going to be in Solanthus long. She and her army were all heading off to Sanction, where the new god was going to establish a huge temple, and it was in Sanction where she wanted to see Burrfoot."

That answers one of my questions, Gerard thought to himself.

"*I* think it's a sapphire," Goatweed added, and slid the broken glass back into his pouch.

"I once knew a Tasslehoff Burrfoot—" Gerard began hesitantly.

"Did you?" Goatweed leaped to his feet and began to skip around Gerard in excitement. "Where is he? How do I find him?"

"I haven't seen him for a long time," Gerard said, motioning the kender to calm down. "It's just that I was wondering what makes this Burrfoot so special."

"I don't think the girl said, but I may be mistaken. I'm afraid I dozed off for a bit at about that point. The girl kept us sitting there a very long time, and when one of us tried to get up to leave, a soldier stuck us with a sword, which isn't as exciting as it sounds like it might be. What was the question?"

Patiently, Gerard repeated it.

Goatweed frowned, a practice that is commonly known to aid the mental process, then said, "All I can remember is that he is very special to the One God. If you see this Tasslehoff friend of yours, will you be sure to tell him the One God is looking for him? And please mention my name."

"I promise," said Gerard. "And now, you can do me a favor. Say that a fellow had a very good reason for *not* entering Solanthus through the front gate, what's another way a fellow could get inside?"

Goatweed eyed Gerard shrewdly. "A fellow about your size?"

"About," said Gerard, shrugging.

"What would this information be worth to a fellow about your size?" Goatweed asked.

Gerard had foreseen this, and he brought forth a pouch containing an assortment of interesting and curious objects he'd appropriated from the manor house of Lord Ulrich.

"Take your pick," he said.

Gerard regretted this immediately, for Goatweed was thrown

into an agony of indecision, dithering over the lot, finally ending up torn between a rusty caltrop and an old boot missing its heel.

"Take them both," Gerard said.

Struck by such generosity, Goatweed described a great many places whereby one could sneak unnoticed into Solanthus. Unfortunately, the kender's descriptions were more confusing than helpful, for he often jumped forward to add details about one he hadn't described yet or fell backward to correct information about one he'd described fifteen minutes earlier.

Eventually, Gerard pinned Goatweed down and made him go over each in detail—a time-consuming and frustrating process, during which Gerard came perilously close to strangling Goatweed. At length, Gerard had three locations in mind: one he deemed most suitable to his needs and the other two as back-up. Goatweed required Gerard to swear on his yellow hair that he would never, never divulge the location of the sites to anyone. Gerard did so, wondering if Goatweed himself had taken that very same vow and considering it highly likely.

After this came the hard part. Gerard had to rid himself of the kender, who had by now decided that they were best friends, if not brothers or maybe cousins. The loyal Goatweed was quite prepared to travel with Gerard for the rest of his days. Gerard said that was fine with him, he was going to lounge about here for a good long while. Maybe take a nap. Goatweed was free to wait.

Fifteen minutes passed, during which the kender developed the fidgets and Gerard snoozed with one eye open to see that he didn't lose anything of value. Finally Goatweed could stand the strain no longer. He packed up his treasure and departed, coming back several times to remind Gerard that if he saw The Tasslehoff Burrfoot, he was to send him straight to the One God and mention that his friend Goatweed was to receive the reward. Gerard promised and finally managed to rid himself of the kender. He had several hours to wait until darkness, and he whiled away his time trying to figure out what Mina wanted with Tasslehoff Burrfoot.

Gerard couldn't imagine that Mina had any great love for kender. The magical Device of Time Journeying the kender carried was probably the prize the girl was after.

"Which means," said Gerard to himself, "that if the kender can be found, we should be the ones to find him."

He made a mental note to tell the Solamnic Knights to be on the lookout for any kender calling himself Tasslehoff Burrfoot and to seize and hold said kender for safekeeping and, above all, not let him fall into the hands of the Dark Knights. This settled, Gerard waited for nightfall.

II

The Prison House of Death

erard had no difficulty slipping unobserved into the city. Although his first choice had been blocked up—showing that the Dark Knights were working to stop up all the "rat holes"—they had not yet found the second. True to his vow, Gerard never revealed the location of the entrance site.

The streets of Solanthus were dark and empty. According to the innkeeper, a curfew had been imposed on the city. Patrols marched through the streets, forcing Gerard to duck and dodge to avoid them, sliding into a shadowed doorway, ducking behind piles of rubbish in an alleyway.

What with hiding from the patrols and an imperfect knowledge of the streets, Gerard spent a good two hours roaming about the city before he finally saw what he'd been looking for—the walls of the prison house.

He huddled inside a doorway, keeping watch and wondering how he was going to manage to sneak inside. This had always been the weak point of his plan. Breaking into a prison was proving just as difficult as breaking out.

A patrol marched into the courtyard, escorting several curfew violators. Listening as the guard made his report, Gerard found out that all the taverns had been shut down by order of the Dark Knights. A tavern owner, trying to cut his losses, had secretly opened his doors to a few regular customers. The private party had turned rowdy, drawing the attention of the patrols, and now the customers and the proprietor were all being incarcerated.

One of the prisoners was singing at the top of his lungs. The proprietor wrung his hands and demanded to know how he was supposed to feed his family if they took away his livelihood. Another prisoner was sick on the pavement. The patrol wanted to rid themselves of their onerous burden as quickly as possible, and they beat on the door, yelling for the gaoler.

He arrived, but he didn't look pleased. He protested that the jail cells were filled to overflowing, and he didn't have room for any more. While he and the patrol leader argued, Gerard slid out of his doorway, darted across the street, and took his place at the back of the group of prisoners.

He pulled the hood of his cloak over his head, hunched his shoulders, and crowded as close to the others as possible. One of the prisoners glanced at him, and his eyes blinked. Gerard held his breath, but after staring at him a moment, the man broke into a drunken grin, leaned his head on Gerard's shoulder, and burst into tears.

The patrol leader threatened to march away and leave the prisoners in the street, adding that he would most certainly report this obstruction of his duty to his superiors. Cowed, the gaoler flung open the door of the prison and shouted for the prison guards. The prisoners were handed over, and the patrol marched off.

The guards herded Gerard and the others into the cell block.

The moment the gaoler came in sight, the prisoners began shouting. The gaoler paid no attention to them. Shoving his prisoners into any cell that could accommodate them, the gaoler and his guards left with all haste.

The cell in which they stuffed Gerard was already so packed that he didn't dare sit down for fear of being trampled. Adjoining cells were just as bad, some filled with men, others with women, all of them clamoring to be set free. The stench of unwashed bodies, vomit, and waste was intolerable. Gerard retched and clamped his hand over his nose and mouth, trying desperately and unsuccessfully to filter the smell through his fingers.

Gerard shoved his way through the mass of bodies toward the back of the cell, as far from the overflowing slop bucket as he could manage. He had feared he and his clothes might look too clean for what he planned, but he no longer had to worry about that. A few hours in here and the stench would cling to him so that he doubted if he could ever be free of it. After a brief time spent convincing himself that he was not going to throw up, he noticed that a neighboring cell—one that was large and spacious— appeared to be empty.

Nudging one of his cellmates in the ribs, Gerard jerked a thumb in that direction.

"Why don't they put some of us in there?" he asked.

"You can go in there if you want to," said the prisoner, with a dark glance. "Me, I'll stay here."

"But it's empty," Gerard protested.

"No, it ain't. You just can't see 'em. Good thing, too." The man grimaced. "Bad enough lookin' at 'em by daylight."

"What are they?" asked Gerard, curious.

"Wizards," the man grunted. "At least, that's what they was. I ain't sure what they are now."

"Why? What's wrong with them?"

"You'll see," the man predicted dourly. "Now let me get some sleep, will you?"

Squatting down on the floor, the man closed his eyes. Gerard figured he should try to rest, too, although he guessed gloomily it would be impossible.

He was pleasantly amazed to wake up some hours later to find daylight struggling to make its way inside the slit windows. Rubbing the sleep from his eyes, he looked with interest at the occupants of the neighboring cell, wondering what made the wizards so very formidable.

Startled, Gerard pressed his face against the bars that separated the two cells.

"Palin?" Gerard called out in a low voice. "Is that you?"

He honestly wasn't certain. The mage looked like Palin. But if this was Palin, the usually conscientious mage had not bathed or shaved or combed his hair or taken any care of his appearance for weeks. He sat on a cot, staring at nothing, eyes empty, his face expressionless.

Another mage sat on another cot. This mage was an elf, so emaciated that he might have been a corpse. He had dark hair, unusual in the elves, who tended to be fair, and his skin was the color of bleached bone. He wore robes that might have started out black in color, but grime and dust had turned them gray. The elf sat still and lifeless as Palin, the same expression that was no expression on his face.

Gerard called Palin's name again, this time slightly louder so that it could be heard over the coughing, hacking, wheezing, shouting, and complaining of his fellow prisoners. He was about to call again when he was distracted by a tickling sensation on his neck.

"Damn fleas," he muttered, slapping at it.

The mage lifted his head, looked up.

"Palin! What are you doing here? What's happened to you? Are you hurt? Drat these fleas!" Gerard scrubbed viciously at his neck, wriggled about in his clothes.

Palin stared vacantly at Gerard for long moments, as if waiting for him to do something or say something more. When Gerard only repeated his earlier questions, Palin shifted his eyes away and once more stared at nothing.

Gerard tried several more times but finally gave up and concentrated on ridding himself of the itching vermin. He managed to do so at last, or so he assumed, for the tickling sensation ceased.

"What happened to those two?" Gerard asked his cellmate.

"Dunno," was the answer. "They were like that when I was brought here, and that was three days ago. Every day, someone comes in and gives 'em food and water and sees that they eat it. All day, they just sit like that. Gives a fellow the horrors, don't it."

Yes, Gerard thought, indeed it did. He wondered what had happened to Palin. Seeing splotches of what appeared to be dried blood on his robes, Gerard concluded that the mage had been beaten or tortured so much that his wits had left him. His heart heavy with pity, Gerard scratched absently at his neck, then turned away. He couldn't do anything to help Palin now, but, if all went as he planned, he might be able to do something in the future.

He squatted down in the cell, keeping his distance from a loathsome-looking straw mattress. He had no doubt that's where he'd picked up the fleas.

"Well, that was a waste of time," remarked Dalamar.

The elf's spirit lingered near the prison's single window. Even in this twilight world that he was forced to inhabit—neither dead nor alive—he felt as if he were suffocating inside the stone walls. He found it comforting at least to imagine he was breathing fresh air.

"What were you trying to accomplish?" he asked. "I take it you weren't indulging in a practical joke."

"No, no joke," said Palin's spirit quietly. "If you must know, I was hoping to be able to contact the man, to speak to him."

"Bah!" Dalamar snorted. "I would have thought you had more sense. He cares nothing for us. None of them do. Who is he, anyhow?"

"His name is Gerard. He's a Solamnic Knight. I knew him in Qualinesti. We were friends . . . well, maybe not friends. I don't think he liked me. You know how Solamnics feel about mages, and I wasn't very pleasant company, I have to admit. Still"—Palin remembered what it was to sigh—"I thought perhaps I might be able to communicate with him, just as my father was able to communicate with me."

"Your father loved you, and he had something of importance to relate to you," said Dalamar. "Besides, Caramon was quite thoroughly dead. We are not, at least I must suppose we are not. Perhaps that has something to do with it. What were you hoping he could do for you, anyhow?"

Palin was silent.

"Come now," said Dalamar. "We are hardly in a position to keep secrets from one another."

If that is true, Palin thought, than what do you do on those solitary rambles of yours? And don't tell me you are lingering beneath the pine trees to enjoy nature. Where do *you* go and why?

For a long time after their return from death, the mages' spirits remained tethered to the bodies they had once inhabited, as a prisoner is chained to a wall. Dalamar, restless, searching for a way back to life, was the first to discover that their bonds were self-created. Perhaps because they were not wholly dead, their spirits were not enslaved to Takhisis, as were the souls caught up in the river of the dead. Dalamar was able to sever the link that bound body and soul together. His spirit left its jail, left Solanthus, or so he told Palin, although he didn't say where he had gone. Yet, even though he could leave, the mage was always forced to return.

Their spirits tended to be as jealous of their bodies as any miser of the chest that holds his wealth. Palin had tried venturing out into the sad world of the other imprisoned souls only to be consumed by fear that something might happen to his body in his absence. He flitted back to find it still sitting there, staring at nothing. He knew he should feel glad, and part of him was, but another part was bitterly disappointed. After that, he did not leave his body. He could not join with the dead souls, who neither saw nor heard him. He did not like to be around the living for the same reason.

Dalamar was often away from his body, though never for long. Palin was convinced that Dalamar was meeting with Mina, trying to bargain with her for the return of his life. He could not prove it, but he was certain it was so.

"If you must know," said Palin, "I was hoping to persuade Gerard to kill me."

"It would never work," said Dalamar. "Don't you think I've already considered it?"

"It might," Palin insisted. "The body lives. The wounds we suffered are healed. Killing the body again might sever the cord that binds us."

"And once again, Takhisis would bring us back to this charade of life. Haven't you figured out why? Why does our Queen feed us and watch over us as the *Shalafi* once fed and cared for those poor wretches he termed the Live Ones? We are her experiment, as they were his. The time will come when she will determine if her experiment has succeeded or failed. *She* will determine it. We will not. Don't you think I've tried?"

He spoke the last bitterly, confirming Palin's suspicions.

"First," Palin said, "Takhisis is not my queen, so don't include me in your thinking. Second, what do you mean— experiment? She's obviously keeping us around to make use of the magical Device of Time Journeying, should she ever get hold of it."

"In the beginning that was true. But now that we've done so well—thrived, so to speak—she's starting to have other ideas. Why waste good flesh and bone by letting it rot in the ground when it could be animated and put to use? She already has an army of souls. She plans to augment her forces by creating an army of corpses to go along with it."

"You sound very certain."

"I am," said Dalamar. "One might say I've heard it from the horse's mouth."

"All the more reason for us to end this," said Palin firmly. "I—"

Dalamar's spirit made a sudden move, darted quickly back to be near the body.

"We are about to have visitors," he warned.

Guards entered the cells, dragging along several kender, tied together with ropes around their waists. The guards marched the kender through the cells to the clamorous amusement of the other prisoners. Then jeering and insults ceased abruptly. The prison grew hushed, quiet.

Mina walked along the rows of cells. She glanced neither to the right nor the left, took no interest in those behind the bars. Some of the prisoners looked at her with fear, some shrank from her. Others reached out their hands in wordless pleading. She ignored them all.

Halting in front of the cell in which the bodies of the two mages were incarcerated, Mina took hold the rope and dragged the assorted kender forward.

"Every one of them claims to be Tasslehoff Burrfoot," she said, speaking to the corpses. "Is one of these the kender I seek? Do either of you recognize him?"

Dalamar's corpse responded with a shake of the head.

"Palin Majere?" she asked. "Do you recognize any of these kender?"

Palin could tell at a glance that none of them were Tasslehoff, but he refused to answer. If Mina imagined she had the kender, let her waste her time finding out otherwise. He sat there, did nothing.

Mina was not been pleased at his show of defiance.

"Answer me," she commanded. "You see the shining light, the realms beyond?"

Palin saw them. They were his constant hope, his constant torment.

"If you have any thought of freedom, of obtaining your soul's wish to leave this world, you will answer me."

When he did not, she clasped her hand around the medallion she wore at her throat.

"Just tell her!" Dalamar hissed at him. "What does it matter? A simple search of the kender will reveal that they don't have the device. Save your defiance for something truly important."

Palin's corpse shook its head.

Mina released her hold on the medallion. The kender, most of them protesting that they were too The Tasslehoff Burrfoot, were marched away.

Watching them go, Palin wondered how Tasslehoff—the real one—had managed to evade capture for so long. Mina and her God were both growing increasingly frustrated.

Tasslehoff and his device were the bedbugs keeping the Queen from having a really good night's sleep. The knowledge of her vulnerability must nip at her constantly, for no matter how powerful she grew, the kender was out there when and where he should not be.

If anything happened to him—and what kender ever lived to a ripe old age?—Her Dark Majesty's grand schemes and plans would come to naught. That might be a comforting thought, but for the fact that Krynn and its people would come to naught, as well.

"All the more reason to remain alive," Dalamar stated with vehemence, speaking to Palin's thoughts. "Once you join that river of death, you will drown and be forever at the mercy of the tide, as are those poor souls who are out there now. We still have a modicum of free will, as you just discovered. That is the flaw in the experiment, the flaw that Takhisis has yet to correct. She has never liked the concept of freedom, you know. Our ability to think and act for ourselves has always been her greatest enemy. Unless she somehow finds a way to deprive us of that, we must cling to our one strength, keep fast hold of it. Our chance will come, and we must be ready to seize it."

Our chance or yours? Palin wondered. He was half-amused by Dalamar, half-angry at him, and on reflection, wholly ashamed of himself.

As usual, he thought, I've been sitting around feeling sorry for myself while my self-serving, ambitious colleague has been out and doing. No more. I will be just as selfish, just as ambitious as any two Dalamars. I may be lost in a foreign country, hobbled hand and foot, where no one speaks my language and they are all deaf, dumb, and blind to boot. Yet, some way, some how, I will find someone who sees me, who hears me, who understands me.

Your experiment will fail, Takhisis, Palin vowed. The experiment itself will see to that.

12

In the Presence of the God

The day Gerard spent in the cell was the worst day of his life. He hoped he would grow used to the smell, but that proved impossible, and he caught himself seriously wondering if breathing was actually worth it. The guards tossed food inside and brought buckets of water for drinking, but the water tasted like the smell, and he gagged as he swallowed. He was gloomily pleased to note that the day gaoler, who appeared none too intelligent, was, if possible, more harassed and confused than the night man.

Late in the afternoon, Gerard began to think that he'd miscalculated, that his plan wasn't as good as he'd thought and that there was every possibility he would spend the rest of his life in this cell. He'd been caught by surprise when Mina had entered the cells, accompanying the kender. She was the last person he wanted to see. He kept his face hidden, remained crouched on the floor until she had gone.

After a few more hours, when it appeared that no one else was likely to come, Gerard was beginning to have second thoughts about this mission. Suppose no one came? He was reflecting that he wasn't nearly as smart as he'd thought he was, when he heard a sound that improved his spirits immensely—the rattle of steel, the clank of a sword.

Prison guards carried clubs, not swords. Gerard leaped to his feet. Two members of the Dark Knights of Neraka entered the prison cells. They wore their helmets with the visors lowered (probably to keep out the smell), cuirasses over woolen shirts, leather breeches, and boots. They kept their swords sheathed but their hands on the hilts.

Immediately the prisoners set up a clamor, some demanding to be freed, others pleading to be able to talk to someone about the terrible mistake that had been made. The Dark Knights ignored them. They headed for the cell where the two mages sat staring at the walls, oblivious to the uproar.

Lunging forward, Gerard managed to thrust his arm between the bars and seize hold of the sleeve of one of the Dark Knights. The man whipped around. His companion drew his sword, and Gerard might have lost his hand had he not snatched it away.

"Captain Samuval!" Gerard shouted. "I must see Captain Samuval."

The Knight's eyes were glints of light in the shadow of his helm. He lifted his visor to get a better view of Gerard.

"How do you know Captain Samuval?" he demanded.

"I'm one of you!" Gerard said desperately. "The Solamnics captured me and locked me up in here. I've been trying to convince the great oaf who runs this place to set me free, but he won't listen. Just bring Captain Samuval here, will you? He'll recognize me."

The Knight stared at Gerard a moment longer, then snapped his visor shut and walked over to the cell that held the mages. Gerard could do nothing more but hope that the man would tell someone, would not leave him here to die of the stink.

The Dark Knights escorted Palin and his fellow mage out of the cellblock. The prisoners fell back as the mages shuffled past, not wanting anything to do with them. The mages were gone for more than an hour. Gerard spent the time wondering if the Knight would tell someone. Hopefully, the name of Captain Samuval would spur the Knight to action.

The clanking of swords announced the Knights' return. They deposited their catatonic charges back on their cots. Gerard hastened forward to try to talk to the Dark Knight again. The prisoners were banging on the cell bars and shrieking for the guards when the commotion suddenly ceased, some swallowing their cries so fast that they choked.

A minotaur entered the cells. The beast-man, who had the face of a bull made even more ferocious by the intelligent eyes that looked out of the mass of shaggy brown fur, was so tall that he was forced to walk with his head bowed to avoid raking his sharp horns against the low ceiling. He wore a leather harness that left bare his muscular torso. He was armed with numerous weapons, among them a heavy sword that Gerard doubted if he could have lifted with two hands. Gerard guessed rightly that the minotaur was coming to see him, and he didn't know whether to be worried or thankful.

As the minotaur approached his cell, the other prisoners scrambled to see who could reach the back fastest. Gerard had the front of the cell all to himself. He tried desperately to remember the minotaur's name, but it eluded him.

"Thank goodness, sir," he said, making do. "I was beginning to think I'd rot in here. Where's Captain Samuval?"

"He is where he is," the minotaur rumbled. His small, bovine eyes fixed on Gerard. "What do you want with him?"

"I want him to vouch for me," said Gerard. "He'll remember me, I'm sure. You might remember me, too, sir. I was in your camp just prior to the attack on Solanthus. I had a prisoner—a female Solamnic Knight."

"I remember," said the minotaur. The eyes narrowed. "The Solamnic escaped. She had help. Yours."

"No, sir, no!" Gerard protested indignantly. "You've got it all wrong! Whoever helped her, it wasn't me. When I found out she was gone, I chased after her. I caught her, too, but we were close to the Solamnic lines. She shouted, and before I could shut her up"—he drew his hand across his throat—"the Solamnics came to her rescue. They took me prisoner, and I've been locked here ever since."

"Our people checked to see if there were any Knights being held prisoner after the battle," said the minotaur.

"I tried to tell them then," said Gerard, aggrieved. "I've been telling them ever since! No one believes me!"

The minotaur said nothing in reply, just stood staring. Gerard had no way of knowing what the beast-man was thinking beneath those horns.

"Look, sir," said Gerard, exasperated, "would I be in this stinking hole if my story wasn't true?"

The minotaur stared at Gerard a moment longer. Turning on his heel, he stalked off to the end of the corridor to confer with the gaoler. Gerard saw the jailer peer at him and then shake his head and fling up his hands helplessly.

"Let him out," ordered the minotaur.

The gaoler hurried to obey. Fitting the key in the lock, he opened the cell door. Gerard walked out to the tune of muttered curses and threats from his fellow prisoners. He didn't care. At that moment, he could have hugged the minotaur, but he thought his reaction should be one of indignation, not relief. He flung a few curses himself and glowered at the gaoler.

The minotaur laid a heavy hand on Gerard's shoulder. The hand was not there in the spirit of friendship. The minotaur's nails dug painfully into Gerard's shoulder.

"I will take you to Mina," said the minotaur.

"I plan to pay my respects to Lord of the Night Mina," said Gerard, "but I can't appear before her like this. Give me some time to wash up and find some decent clothes—"

"She will see you as you are," said the minotaur, adding, as an afterthought, "She sees all of us as we are."

This being precisely what he feared, Gerard was not in the least eager to be interviewed by Mina. He had hoped to be able to retrieve his knightly accoutrements (he knew the storehouse where the Solamnics had stashed them) and blend in with the crowd, hang about the barracks with the other Knights and soldiers, pick up the latest gossip, discover who'd been given orders to do what, then leave to make his report.

There was no help for it, however. The minotaur (whose name was Galdar, Gerard finally remembered), marched Gerard out of the prison. Gerard cast a last glance at Palin as he left. The mage had not moved.

Shaking his head, feeling a shiver run through him, Gerard accompanied the minotaur through the streets of Solanthus.

If anyone would know Mina's plans, it was Galdar. The minotaur was not the talkative type, however. Gerard mentioned Sanction a couple of times, but the minotaur answered only with a cold, dark glower. Gerard gave up and concentrated on seeing what he could of life in Solanthus. People were out in the streets, going about their daily routine, but they did so in a fearful and hurried manner, keeping their heads down, not wanting to meet the eyes of the numerous patrols.

All the taverns were closed, their doors ceremoniously sealed by a band of black cloth that had been stretched across them. Gerard had always heard the saying about courage being found at the bottom of a jug of dwarf spirits, and he supposed that was why the taverns had been shut down. The black cloth was stretched across other shops, as well—most notably mageware shops and shops that sold weapons.

They came within sight of the Great Hall, where Gerard had been brought to trial. Memories came back to him forcibly, particularly memories of Odila. She was his closest friend, his only friend, really, for he was not the type to make friends easily. He was sorry now that he hadn't said good-bye to her and at least given her some hint of what he planned.

Galdar steered Gerard past the Great Hall. The building teemed with soldiers and Knights, for it had apparently been taken over as a barracks. Gerard thought they might stop here, but Galdar led him to the old temples that stood near the hall.

These temples had been formerly dedicated to the gods most favored by the Knights—Paladine and Kiri-Jolith. The temple of Kiri-Jolith was the older of the two and slightly larger, for Kiri-Jolith was considered the Solamnics' special patron. Paladine's temple, constructed of white marble, drew the eye with its simple but elegant design. Four white columns adorned the front. Marble steps, rounded so that they resembled waves, flowed down from the portico.

The two temples were attached by a courtyard and a rose garden. Here grew the white roses, the symbol of the Knighthood. Even after the departure of the gods and, subsequently, the priests, the Solamnics had kept up the temples and tended the rose gardens. The Knights had used the temples for study or for meditation. The citizens of Solanthus found them havens of peace and tranquility and could often be seen walking here with their families.

"Not surprising this One God looks on them with covetous eyes," Gerard said to himself. "I'd move here in a minute if I were out wandering the universe, searching for a home."

A large number of the citizens stood gathered around the outer doors of the temple of Paladine. The doors were closed, and the crowd appeared to be awaiting admittance.

"What's going on, sir?" Gerard asked. "What are all these people doing here? They aren't threatening to attack, are they?"

A tiny smile creased the minotaur's muzzle. He almost chuckled. "These people have come to hear about the One God. Mina speaks to crowds like this every day. She heals the sick and performs other miracles. You will find many residents of Solanthus worshiping in the temple."

Gerard had no idea what to say to this. Anything that came to mind would only land him in trouble and so he kept his mouth shut. They were walking past the rose garden when a brilliant flash of sunlight reflecting off amber caught his eye. He blinked, stared, then stopped so suddenly that Galdar, irritated, almost yanked off his arm.

"Wait!" Gerard cried, appalled. "Wait a minute." He pointed. "What is that?"

"The sarcophagus of Goldmoon," said Galdar. "She was once the head of the Mystics of the Citadel of Light. She was also the mother of Mina—her adopted mother," he felt compelled to add. "She was an old, old woman. Over ninety, so they say. Look at her. She is young and beautiful again. Thus does the One God grant favor to the faithful."

"A lot of good that does her if she's dead," Gerard muttered, his heart aching, as he looked at the body encased in amber. He remembered Goldmoon vividly, remembered her beautiful, golden hair that seemed spun with silver moonbeams, remembered her face, strong and compassionate and lost, searching. He couldn't find the Goldmoon he had known, though. Her face, seen beneath the amber, was the face of no one, anyone. Her gold and silver hair was amber-colored. Her white robes amber. She'd been caught in the resin, like all the rest of the insects.

"She will be granted life again," said Galdar. "The One God has promised to perform a great miracle."

Gerard heard an odd tone in Galdar's voice and he glanced, startled, at the minotaur. Disapproving? That was hard to be believe. Still, as Gerard thought back over what he knew of the minotaur race, he had always heard them described as devout followers of their former god, Sargonnas, who was himself a minotaur. Perhaps Galdar was having second thoughts about this One God. Gerard marked that down as a hunch he might be able to make use of later.

The minotaur gave Gerard a shove, and he had to continue walking. He looked back at the sarcophagus. Many of the citizenry were standing around the amber coffin, gaping at the body inside and sighing and ooohing and aahing. Some were on their knees in prayer. Gerard kept twisting his head to look around, forgot to watch where he was going, and tripped over the temple stairs. Galdar growled at him, and Gerard realized he had better keep his mind on his own business or he'd end up in a coffin himself. And the One God wasn't likely to perform any miracle on him.

The temple doors opened for Galdar, then shut behind him, to the great disappointment of those waiting outside.

"Mina!" they called out, chanting her name. "Mina! Mina!"

Inside, the temple was shadowed and cool. The pale light of the sun, that seemed to have to work hard to shine through the stained glass windows, formed weak and watery patterns of blue, white, green, and red on the floor, criss-crossed with black bars. The altar had been covered with a cloth of white velvet. A single person knelt there. At the sound of their footfalls in the still temple, the girl raised her head and glanced over her shoulder.

"I am sorry to disturb you in your prayers, Mina," said Galdar in a subdued voice that echoed eerily in the still temple, "but this is a matter of importance. I found this man in the prison cells. You may remember him. He—"

"Sir Gerard," said Mina. Rising, she moved away from the altar, walked down the central aisle. "Gerard uth Mondar. You brought that young Solamnic Knight to us. Odila was her name. She escaped."

Gerard had his story all ready, but his tongue stuck firmly to the roof of his mouth. He had not thought he could ever forget those amber eyes, but he had forgotten the powerful spell they could cast over any person caught in their depths. He had the feeling that she knew all about him, knew everything he had done since they last parted, knew exactly why he was here. He could lie to her, but he would be wasting his time.

Still, he had to try, futile as it might be. He stumbled through his tale, thinking all the while that he sounded exactly like a guilty child lying to avoid the strap and the woodshed.

Mina listened to him with grave attention. He ended by saying that he hoped that he would be permitted to serve her, since he understood that his former commander, Marshal Medan, had died in the battle of Qualinesti.

"You grieve for the Marshal and for the Queen Mother, Laurana," said Mina.

Gerard stared at her, dumbfounded.

She smiled, the amber eyes shone. "Do not grieve for them. They serve the One God in death as they both unwittingly served the One God in life. So do we all serve the One God, whether we will or no. The rewards are greater for those who serve the One God knowingly, however. Do you serve the One God, Gerard?"

Mina came nearer to him. He saw himself small and insignificant in her amber eyes, and he suddenly wanted very much to do something to make her proud of him, to win her favor.

He could do so by swearing to serve the One God, yet in this, if in nothing else, he must speak the truth. He looked at the altar, and he listened to the stillness, and it was then he knew for a certainty that he was in the presence of a god and that this god saw through to his very heart.

"I . . . I know so little of this One God," he stammered evasively. "I cannot give you the answer you want, Lady. I am sorry."

"Would you be willing to learn?" she asked him.

"Yes" was all he needed to say to remain in her service, yet the truth was that he didn't want to know anything at all about this One God. Gerard had always done very well without the gods. He didn't feel comfortable in the presence of this one.

He mumbled something unintelligible, even to himself. Mina seemed to hear what she wanted to hear from him, however. She smiled.

"Very well. I take you into my service, Gerard uth Mondar. The One God takes you into service, as well."

At this, the minotaur made a disgruntled rumbling sound.

"Galdar thinks you are a spy," said Mina. "He wants to kill you. If you are a spy, I have nothing to hide. I will tell you my plans freely. In two days time, an army of soldiers and Knights from Palanthas will join us, adding another five thousand to our number. With that army and the army of souls, we will march on Sanction. And we will take it. Then we will rule all of the northern part of Ansalon, well on our way to ruling all of this continent. Do you have any questions?"

Gerard ventured a feeble protest. "Lady, I am not—"

Mina turned from him. "Open the doors, Galdar," she ordered. "I will speak to the people now." Glancing back at Gerard, she added, "You should stay to hear the sermon, Sir Gerard. You might find my words instructive."

Gerard could do nothing but acquiesce. He glanced sidelong at Galdar, caught the minotaur glowering back at him. Clearly, Galdar knew him for what he was. Gerard must take care to keep out of the minotaur's way. He supposed he should be thankful, for he'd accomplished his mission. He knew Mina's plans—always provided she was telling the truth—and he had only to hang about for a couple of days to see if the army from Palanthas showed up to confirm it. His heart was no longer in his mission, however. Mina had killed his spirit, as effectively as she might have killed his body.

We fight against a god. What does it matter what we do?

Galdar flung wide the temple doors. The people streamed inside. Kneeling before Mina, they pleaded with her to touch them, to heal them, to heal their children, to take away their pain. Gerard kept an eye on Galdar. The minotaur watched a moment, then walked out.

Gerard was about to sidle out the door when he saw a troop of Knights marching up the stairs. They had with them a prisoner, a Solamnic, to judge by the armor. The prisoner's arms were bound with bowstrings, but she walked with her head held high, her face set in grim determination.

Gerard knew that face, knew the expression on that face. He groaned softly, swore vehemently, and hastily drew back into the deepest shadows, covering his face with his hands as though overcome by reverence.

"We captured this Solamnic trying to enter the city, Mina," said one of the Knights.

"She's a bold one," said another. "Walked right in the front gate wearing her armor and carrying her sword."

"Surrendered her sword without a fight," added the first. "A fool and a coward, like all of them."

"I am no coward," said Odila with dignity. "I chose not to fight. I came here of my own accord."

"Free her," said Mina, and her voice was cold and stern. "She may be our enemy, but she is a Knight and deserves to be treated with dignity, not like a common thief!"

Chastened, the Knights swiftly removed the bindings from Odila's arms. Gerard had stepped into the shadows, afraid that if she looked around and saw him, she might give him away. He soon realized he could spare himself the worry. Odila had no eyes for anyone except Mina.

"Why have you come all this way and risked so much to see me, Odila?" Mina asked gently.

Odila sank to her knees, clasped her hands.

"I want to serve the One God," she said.

Mina bent down, kissed Odila on the forehead.

"The One God is pleased with you."

Mina removed the medallion she wore on her breast, fastened the medallion around Odila's neck.

"You are my cleric, Odila," said Mina. "Rise and know the blessings of the One God."

Odila rose, her eyes shining with exaltation. Walking to the altar, she joined the other worshipers, knelt in prayer to the One God. Gerard, a bitter taste in his mouth, walked out.

"Now what in the Abyss do I do?" he wondered.

13

The Convert

Absorbed into the main body of the Dark Knights of Neraka, Gerard was assigned to patrol duty. Every day, he and his small band of soldiers marched through their assigned portion of Solanthus, keeping the populace in check. His task was not difficult. The Dark Knights under Mina's command had acted swiftly to round up any members of the community who might have given them trouble. Gerard had seen most of them inside the prison.

As for the rest, the people of Solanthus appeared to be in a state of shock, stunned by the recent, disastrous turn of events. One day they were living in the only free city in Solamnia, and the next day their city was occupied by their most hated enemy. Too much had happened too quickly for them to comprehend. Given time, they might organize and become dangerous.

Or they might not.

Always a devout people, the Solamnics had grieved over the absence of their gods. Feeling an absence and a lacking in their lives, they were interested in hearing about this One God, even if they didn't plan on believing what they heard. The adage goes that while elves strive to be worthy of their gods, humans require that their gods be worthy of them. The citizens of Solanthus were naturally skeptical.

Every day, the sick and the wounded came or were carried to the former temple of Paladine, now the temple of the One God. The lines for miracles were long and the lines waiting to view the miracle maker were longer still. The elves of far-off Silvanesti, so Mina had told them, had bowed down to the One God and proclaimed their devotion. By contrast, the humans of Solanthus started fistfights, as those who believed in the miracles took umbrage with those who claimed they were tricks. After two days of patrol duty, Gerard was ordered to cease walking the streets (where nothing happened) and to start breaking up fights in the temple.

Gerard didn't know if he was glad for this change in assignment or not. He'd spent the last two days trying to decide if he should confront Odila and try to talk some sense into her or if he should continue to avoid her. He didn't think she'd give him away, but he wasn't certain. He couldn't understand her sudden religious fervor and therefore no longer trusted her.

Gerard had never really been given the choice of worshiping the gods, so he hadn't wasted much thought on the matter. The presence or absence of the gods had never made much difference to his parents. The only change that had occurred in their lives when the gods left was that one day they said prayers at the table and the next day they didn't. Now Gerard was being forced to think about it, and in his heart he could sympathize with those who started the fights. He wanted to punch someone, too.

Gerard sent off his report to Richard, who was waiting for it at the roadhouse. He gave the Knights' Council all the information he'd gleaned, confirming that Mina planned to march to Sanction.

Counting the reinforcements expected to arrive from Palanthas, Mina had over five thousand soldiers and Knights under her command. A small force, yet with this force she planned to take the walled city that had held out against double that number of troops for over a year. Gerard might have laughed at the notion, except that she'd taken Solanthus—a city considered impregnable—with far fewer troops than that. She'd taken Solanthus using dragons and the army of souls, and she spoke of using dragons and the army of souls to take Sanction. Recalling the terror of that night he'd fought the dead, Gerard was convinced that nothing could withstand them. He said as much to the Knights' Council, although they hadn't asked for his opinion.

His assignment now completed, he could have left Solanthus, returned to the bosom of the Solamnic Knighthood. He stayed on, however, at risk of his life, he supposed, for Galdar considered him a spy. If that was true, no one paid much attention to him. No one watched him. He was not restricted in his movements. He could go anywhere, talk to anyone. He was not admitted to Mina's inner circle, but he didn't lose by that, for apparently Mina had no secrets. She freely told everyone who asked what she and the One God meant to do. Gerard was forced to concede that such supreme confidence was impressive.

He stayed in Solanthus, telling himself that he would remain to see if Mina and her troops actually marched out, headed east. In truth, he was staying because of Odila, and the day he took up his duties at the temple was the day he finally admitted as much to himself.

Gerard stationed himself at the foot of the temple steps, where he could keep a watchful eye on the crowd, who had gathered to hear Mina speak. He posted his men at intervals around the courtyard, trusting that the sight of armed soldiers would intimidate most of the troublemakers. He wore his helmet, for there were those in Solanthus who might recognize him.

Mina's own Knights, under the command of the minotaur, surrounded her, kept watch over her, guarding her not so much from those who would do her harm, but from those who would have adored her to death. Her speech concluded, Mina walked among the crowd, lifting up children in her arms, curing the sick, telling them all of the One God. The skeptical watched and jeered, the faithful wept and tried to fling themselves at Mina's feet. Gerard's men broke up a few fights, hauled the combatants off to the already crowded prisons.

When Mina's steps began to falter, the minotaur stepped in and called a halt. The people still waiting for their share of the miracles groaned and wailed, but he told them to come back tomorrow.

"Wait a moment, Galdar," said Mina, her voice carrying clearly over the tumult. "I have good news to tell the people of Solanthus."

"Silence!" Galdar shouted, but the effort was needless. The crowd immediately hushed, leaned forward eagerly to hear her words.

"People of Solanthus," Mina cried. "I have just received word that the dragon overlord, Khellendros, also known as Skie, is dead. Only a few days earlier, I told you that the dragon overlord, Beryl, was dead, as well as the wicked dragon known as Cyan Bloodbane."

Mina raised her arms and her eyes to the heavens. "Behold, in their defeat, the power of the One God!"

"Khellendros dead?" The whisper went through the crowd, as each person turned to his neighbors to see what their reaction was to such astonishing news.

Khellendros had long ruled over much of the old nation of Solamnia, exacting tribute from the citizens of Palanthas, using the Dark Knights to keep the people in line and the steel flowing into the dragon's coffers. Now Khellendros was dead.

"So when does this One God go after Malys?" someone yelled.

Gerard was appalled to find that the someone was himself.

He'd had no idea he was going to shout those words. They'd burst out before he could stop them. He cursed himself for a fool, for the last thing he wanted to do was draw attention to himself. Snapping shut the visor of his helm, he glared around, as if searching for the person who had spoken. He did not fool Mina, however. Her amber gaze pierced the eyeslits of his helmet with unerring accuracy.

"After I have taken Sanction," Mina said coolly, "then I will deal with Malys."

She acknowledged the cheers of the crowd with a gesture toward heaven, indicating that their praise belonged to the One God, not to her. Turning, she disappeared inside the temple.

Gerard's skin burned so hot it was a wonder that his steel helm didn't melt around his ears. He expected to feel the heavy hand of the minotaur close around his neck any moment, and when someone touched his shoulder, he nearly crawled out of his armor.

"Gerard?" came a puzzled voice. "Is that you in there?"

"Odila!" he gasped in relief, uncertain whether to hug her or hit her.

"So now you're back to being a Dark Knight," she said. "I must concede that drawing your pay from two coffers is a good way to make a living, but don't you find yourself getting confused? Do you flip a coin? 'Which armor do I put on this morning? Heads Dark Knight, tails Solamnic—'"

"Just shut up, will you," Gerard growled. Grabbing her by the arm, he glanced around to see if anyone had been listening, then hauled her off to a secluded part of the rose garden. "Apparently finding religion hasn't caused you to lose your twisted sense of humor."

He yanked off his helm, glared at her. "You know perfectly well why I'm here."

She eyed him, frowning. "You didn't come after me, did you?"

"No," he answered, which was truth enough.

"Good," she said, her face clearing.

"But now that you mention it—" Gerard began.

Her frown returned.

"Listen to me, Odila," he said earnestly, "I came at the behest of the Knights' Council. They sent me to find out if Mina's threat to attack Sanction is real—"

"It is," said Odila coolly.

"I know that now," said Gerard. "I'm on an intelligence-gathering mission—"

"So am I," she said, interrupting, "and my mission is far more important than yours. You are here to gain information about the enemy. You are here to listen at keyholes and count the numbers of troops and how many siege engines they have."

She paused. Her gaze shifted to the temple. "I am here to find out about this god."

Gerard made a sound.

She looked back at him. "We Solamnics can't ignore this, Gerard, just because it makes us uncomfortable. We can't deny this god because the god came to an orphan girl and not to the Lord of the Rose. We have to ask questions. It is only in the asking that we find answers."

"And what have you found out?" Gerard asked unwillingly.

"Mina was raised by Goldmoon at the Citadel of Light. Yes, I was surprised to hear that myself. Goldmoon told Mina stories of the old gods, how she—Goldmoon—brought knowledge of the gods back to the people of Ansalon when everyone thought the gods had left the world in anger. Goldmoon showed them that it was not the gods who had left mankind but mankind who had left the gods. Mina asked if that might be what was happening now, but Goldmoon told her no, that this time the gods had gone, for there were those who spoke to Paladine and the other gods before they left and who were told that the gods departed the world to spare the world the wrath of Chaos.

"Mina didn't believe this. She knew in her heart that Goldmoon was wrong, that there was a god on this world. It was up to Mina to find the god, as Goldmoon had once found the gods. Mina ran away. She searched for the gods, always keeping her heart open to hear the voice of the gods. And, one day, she heard it.

"Three years, Mina spent in the presence of the One God, learning the One God's plans for the world, plans for us, learning how to put those plans in motion. When the time was right and

Mina was strong enough to bear the burden of the task given to her, she was sent to lead us and tell us of the One God."

"That answers some of the questions about Mina," said Gerard, "but what about this One God? So far all I've seen is that this god is a sort of press-gang for the dead."

"I asked Mina about that," Odila said, her face growing solemn at the memory of that terrible night she and Gerard had fought the dead souls. "Mina says that the souls of the dead serve the One God willingly, joyfully. They are glad to remain among the living in the world they love."

Gerard snorted. "They didn't look glad to me."

"The dead do no harm to the living," Odila said sharply. "If they seem threatening, it is only because they are so eager to bring the knowledge of the One God to us."

"So that was proselytizing?" Gerard said. "While the souls preach to us of the One God, Mina and her soldiers fly red dragons into Solanthus. They kill a few hundred people in the process, but I suppose that's just more evangelical work. More souls for the One God."

"You saw the miracles of healing Mina performed," said Odila, her gaze clear and level. "You heard her tell of the deaths of two of the dragon overlords who have long terrorized this world. There *is* a god in this world, and all your gibes and snide comments won't change that."

She thrust a finger accusingly into his chest. "You're afraid. You're afraid to find out that maybe you're *not* in control of your own destiny. That maybe the One God has a plan for you and for all of us."

"If you're saying I'm afraid to find out I'm a slave to this One God, then you're right!" Gerard returned. "I make my own decisions. I don't want any god making them for me."

"You've done so well so far," Odila said caustically.

"Do you know what *I* think?" Gerard returned, jabbing his finger in her chest with a force that shoved her backward a step. "I think you made a mess of your life, and now you're hoping this god will come along and fix everything."

Odila stared at him, then she rounded on her heel, started to walk away. Gerard leaped after her, caught hold of her by the arm.

"I'm sorry, Odila. I had no right to say that. I was just angry because I don't understand this. Any of it. And, well, you're right. It does frighten me."

Odila kept her head turned away, her face averted, but she didn't try to break loose of his grip.

"We're both in a tough situation here," Gerard said, lowering his voice. "We're both in danger. We can't afford to quarrel. Friends?"

He let go her arm, held out his hand.

"Friends," Odila said grudgingly, turning around to shake hands. "But I don't think we're in any danger. I honestly believe that the entire Solamnic army could walk in here and Mina would welcome them with open arms."

"And a sword in each hand," Gerard muttered beneath his breath.

"What did you say?"

"Nothing important. Listen, there's something you can do for me. A favor—"

"I won't spy on Mina," Odila stated firmly.

"No, no, nothing like that," Gerard said. "I saw a friend of mine in the dungeon. His name is Palin Majere. He's a wizard. He doesn't look well, and I was wondering if maybe Mina could . . . er . . . heal him. Don't tell her I said anything," he added hurriedly. "Just say that you saw him and you were thinking . . . I mean, it should sound like your idea. . . ."

"I understand," Odila said, smiling. "You really do believe that Mina has god-given powers. This proves it."

"Yes, well, maybe," said Gerard, not wanting to start another argument. "Oh, and one thing more. I hear that Mina is searching for Tasslehoff Burrfoot, the kender who was with me. You remember him?"

"Of course." Odila's eyes were suddenly alert and focused, intent on Gerard's face. "Why? Have you seen him?"

"Look, I have to ask—what does this One God want with Tasslehoff Burrfoot. Is this some sort of joke?"

"Far from it," said Odila. "This kender is not supposed to be here."

"Since when is a kender supposed to be anywhere?"

"I'm serious. This is very important, Gerard. Have you seen him?"

"No," said Gerard, thankful he didn't have to lie to her. "Remember about Palin, will you? Palin Majere? In the prison?"

"I'll remember. And you keep watch for the kender."

"I will. Where can we meet?"

"I am always here," Odila said, gesturing toward the Temple.

"Yeah, I guess you are. Do you . . . um . . . pray to this One God?" Gerard asked uncomfortably.

"Yes," said Odila.

"Have your prayers been answered?"

"You're here, aren't you?" Odila said. She wasn't being glib. She was serious. With a smile and a wave, she walked back toward the temple.

Gerard gaped at her, speechless. Finally, he found his tongue. "I'm not . . ." he shouted after her. "I didn't . . . You didn't . . . Your god didn't . . . Oh, what's the use!"

Figuring that he was confused enough for one day, Gerard turned on his heel and stalked off.

The minotaur, Galdar, saw the two Solamnics deep in discussion. Convinced that both of them were spies, he sauntered their direction in hopes of hearing something of their conversation. One drawback to being a minotaur in a city of humans was that he could never blend in with his surroundings. The two stood near the amber sarcophagus of Goldmoon, and using that as cover, he edged near. All he could hear was a low murmur, until at one point they forgot themselves and their voices rose.

"You're afraid," he heard the the female Solamnic say in accusing tones. "You're afraid to find out that maybe you're *not* in control of your own destiny. That maybe the One God has a plan for you and for all of us."

"If you're saying I'm afraid to find out I'm a slave to this One God, then you're right!" the Knight returned angrily. "I make my own decisions. I don't want any god making them for me."

At that point their voices dropped again. Even though they were talking theology, not sedition, Galdar was still troubled. He remained standing in the shadow of the sarcophagus until long after they had both gone, one returning to the temple and the other heading back to his quarters. The Knight's face was red with anger and frustration. He muttered to himself as he walked and was so absorbed in his thoughts that he passed within a foot of the enormous minotaur and never noticed him.

Solamnics and minotaurs have always had much in common—more in common than not, although, throughout history, it was the "not" that divided them. Both the Solamnics and the minotaurs place high emphasis on personal honor. Both value duty and loyalty. Both admire courage. Both reverenced their gods when they had gods to worship. Both gods were gods of honor, loyalty and courage, albeit one god fought for the side of light and the other for the side of darkness.

Or was it truly that? Might not it be said that one god, Kiri-Jolith, fought for the side of the humans and that Sargas fought for the minotaurs? Was it race that divided them, not daylight and night shadow? Humans and minotaurs both told tales of the famous Kaz, a minotaur who had been a friend of the great Solamnic Knight, Huma.

But because one had horns and a snout and was covered with fur and the other had soft skin and a puny lump of a nose, the friendship between Kaz and Huma was considered an anomaly. The two races had been taught to hate and distrust each other for centuries. Now the gulf between them was so deep and wide and ugly that neither could cross.

In the absence of the gods, both races were deteriorating. Galdar had heard rumors of strange doings in the minotaur homeland—rumors of murder, treachery, deceit. As for the

Solamnics, few young men and women in this modern age wanted to endure the rigors and constraints and responsibilities of the Knighthood. Their numbers were dwindling, their backs were to the wall. And they had a new enemy—a new god.

Galdar had seen in Mina the end of his quest. He had seen in Mina a sense of duty, honor, loyalty, and courage—the ways of old. Yet, certain things Mina had said and done had begun to trouble Galdar. The foremost of these was the horrible rebirth of the two wizards.

Galdar had no use for wizards. He could have watched these two being tortured without a qualm, could have slain them with his own hand and never given the matter another thought. But the sight of their lifeless bodies being used as mindless slaves gave him a sick feeling in the pit of his stomach. He could not look at the two shambling corpses without feeling his gorge rise.

Worst was the One God's punishment of Mina for losing the kender. Recalling the sacrifices Mina had made, the physical pain she had endured, the torment, the exhaustion, thirst, and starvation, all in the name of the One God, then to see her suffering like that, Galdar was outraged.

Galdar honored Mina. He was loyal to Mina. His duty lay with Mina. But he was beginning to have doubts about this One God.

The Solamnic's words echoed in Galdar's mind. *If you're saying I'm afraid to find out I'm a slave to this One God, then you're right! I make my own decisions. I don't want any god making them for me.*

Galdar did not like thinking of himself as a slave to the will of this One God or any god. More important, he didn't like seeing Mina as a slave to this One God, a slave to be whipped if she failed to do the god's bidding.

Galdar decided to do what he should have done long ago. He needed to find out more about this One God. He could not speak of this to Mina, but he could speak of it to this Solamnic female.

And perhaps kill two with one blow, as the saying went among minotaurs, in reference to the well-known tale of the thieving kender and the minotaur blacksmith.

14

Faith in the One God

Over a thousand Knights and soldiers from Palanthas entered the city of Solanthus. Their entry was triumphant. Flags bearing the emblems of the Dark Knights as well as flags belonging to individual Knights whipped in the wind. The Dark Knights who served in Palanthas had grown wealthy, for although much of the tribute had gone to the late dragon Khellendros and still more had been sent to the late Lord of the Night Targonne, the high-ranking Knights of Palanthas had done all right for themselves. They were in a good mood, albeit a bit concerned over rumors that had reached them concerning the new, self-proclaimed Lord of the Night—a teen-age girl.

These officers could not imagine how any right-thinking veteran soldier could take orders from a chit who should be dreaming of dancing around the Maypole, not leading men into battle. They had discussed this on the march to Solanthus and had privately agreed among themselves that there must be some shadowy figure working behind the scenes—this minotaur, who was said never to stir far from Mina's side. He must be the true leader. The girl was a front, for humans would never follow a minotaur. There were some who pointed out that few men would follow a slip of a girl into battle, either, but others replied knowingly that she performed tricks and illusions to entertain the ignorant, dupe them into fighting for her.

No one could argue with her success, and so long as it worked, they had no intention of destroying those illusions. Of course, as intelligent men, they would not be fooled.

As had others before them, the officers of the Palanthas Knighthood met Mina with boisterous bravado, preparing to hear her with outward composure, inward chuckles. They came away pale and shaken, quiet and subdued, every one them trapped in the resin of the amber eyes.

Gerard faithfully recorded their numbers in a coded message to the Knighthood. This was his most important missive yet, for this confirmed that Mina meant to attack Sanction and she meant to march soon. Every blacksmith and weaponsmith in the city was pressed into duty, working day and night, making repairs on old weapons and armor and turning out new ones.

Her army would move slowly. It would take weeks, maybe months, to march through the woods and trek across the grasslands and into the mountains that surrounded Sanction. Watching the preparations and thinking of this prolonged march, Gerard developed a plan of attack that he included along with his report. He had little hope that the plan would be adopted, for it involved fighting by stealth, hitting the flanks of the army as it crawled across the ground, striking their supply trains, attacking swiftly, then disappearing, only to strike again when least expected.

Thus, he wrote, *did the Wilder elves of Qualinesti succeed in doing great damage to the Dark Knights who occupied that land. I realize that this is not an accepted means of fighting for the knighthood, for it is certainly not chivalric nor honorable nor even particularly fair. However, it is effective, not only in reducing the numbers of the enemy but in destroying the morale of the troops.*

Lord Tasgall was a sensible man, and Gerard actually thought that he might toss aside the Measure and act upon it. Unfortunately, Gerard couldn't find any way of delivering the message to Richard, who'd been instructed to return to the roadhouse on a weekly basis to see if Gerard had more information.

Gerard was now being watched day and night, and he had a good idea who was to blame. Not Mina. The minotaur, Galdar.

Too late Gerard had noticed the minotaur eavesdropping on his conversation with Odila. That night, Gerard discovered Galdar was having him watched.

No matter where Gerard went, he was certain to see the horns of the minotaur looming over the crowd. When he left his lodging, he found one of Mina's Knights loitering about in the street outside. The next day, one of his patrol members fell mysteriously ill and was replaced. Gerard had no doubt that the replacement was one of Galdar's spies.

He had no one to blame but himself. He should have left Solanthus days ago instead of hanging about. Now he had not only placed himself in danger, he'd imperiled the very mission he'd been sent to accomplish.

During the next two days, Gerard continued to perform his duties. He went to the temple as usual. He had not seen Odila since the day they'd spoken and was startled to see her standing alongside Mina today. Odila searched the crowd until she found Gerard. She made a small gesture, a slight beckoning motion. When Mina left, and the supplicants and idlers had departed. Gerard hung around outside, waiting.

Odila emerged from the temple. She shook her head slightly, indicating he was not to speak to her, and walked past him without a glance.

As she passed, she whispered, "Come to the temple tonight an hour before midnight."

Gerard sat gloomily on his bed, waiting for the hour Odila had set. He whiled away the time, by staring in frustration at the scrollcase containing the message that should have been in the hands of his superiors by now. Gerard's quarters were in the same hall once used to house the Solamnic Knights. He had at first been assigned a room already occupied by two other Knights, but he'd used some of the money he'd earned from the Dark Knights to buy his way into a private chamber. The chamber was, in reality, little more than a windowless storage room located on the first level. By the lingering smell, it had once been used to store onions.

Restless, he was glad to leave it. He walked openly into the streets, pausing only long enough to lace up his boot and to catch a glimpse of a shadow detaching itself from a nearby doorway. Resuming his pace, he heard light footfalls behind him.

Gerard had a momentary impulse to whirl around and confront his shadow. He resisted the impulse, kept walking. Going straight to the temple, he entered and found a seat on a stone bench in a corner of the building.

The temple's interior was dark, lit by five candles that stood on the altar. Outside, the sky was clouded over. Gerard could smell rain in the air, and within a few moments, the first drops began to fall. He hoped his shadow got soaked to the skin.

The flames of the candles wavered in a sudden gust stirred up by the storm. A robed figure entered the temple from a door in the rear. Pausing at the altar, she fussed with the candles for a moment, then, turning, walked down the aisle. Gerard could see her silhouetted against the candlelight, and although he could not see her face, he knew Odila by her upright bearing and the tilt of her head.

She sat down beside him, slid closer to him. He shifted on the stone bench, moved nearer to her. They were the only two in the temple, but they kept their voices low.

"Just so you know, I'm being followed," he whispered.

Alarmed, Odila turned to stare at him. Her face was pale against the candle-lit darkness. Her eyes were smudges of shadow. Reaching out her hand, she fumbled for Gerard's, found it, and clasped hold tightly. He was astonished, both at the fact that she was seeking comfort and by the fact that her hand was cold and trembling.

"Odila, what is it? What's wrong?" he asked.

"I found out about your wizard friend, Palin," she said in a smothered voice, as if she found it hard to draw breath. "Galdar told me."

Odila's shoulders straightened. She turned to him, looked him in the eyes. "Gerard, I've been a fool! Such a fool!"

"We're a pair of them, then," he said, patting her hand clumsily.

He felt her stiff and shivering, not comforted by his touch. She didn't seem to hear his words. When she spoke, her voice was muffled.

"I came here hoping to find a god who could guide me, care for me, comfort me. Instead I've found—" She broke off, said abruptly. "Gerard, Palin's dead."

"I'm not surprised," Gerard said, with a sigh. "He didn't look well—"

"No, Gerard!" Odila shook her head. "He was dead when you saw him."

"He wasn't dead," Gerard protested. "He was sitting on his cot. After that, I saw him get up and walk out."

"And I'm telling you that he was dead," she said, turning to face him. "I don't blame you for not believing me. I didn't believe it myself. But I . . . Galdar took me to see him. . . ."

He eyed her suspiciously.

"Are you drunk?"

"I wish I were!" Odila returned, but with sudden, savage vehemence. "I don't think there's enough dwarf spirits in the world to make me forget what I've seen. I'm cold sober, Gerard. I swear it."

He looked at her closely. Her eyes were focused, her voice shaking but clear, her words coherent.

"I believe you," he said slowly, "but I don't understand. How could Palin be dead when I saw him sitting and standing and walking?"

"He and the other wizard were both killed in the Tower of High Sorcery. Galdar was there. He told me the whole story. They died, and then Mina and Galdar found out that this kender they were searching for was in the Tower. They went to find him, only they lost him. The One God punished Mina for losing the kender. Mina said that she needed the wizards' help to find him, and . . . and she . . . she gave them back their lives."

"If she did, they didn't look any too pleased by it," Gerard said, thinking of Palin's empty eyes, his vacant stare.

"There's a reason for that," Odila returned, her voice hollow. "She gave them their lives, but she didn't give them their souls. The One God holds their souls in thrall. They have no will to think or act on their own. They are nothing more than puppets, and the One God holds the strings. Galdar says that when the kender is captured, the wizards will know how to deal with him and the device he carries."

"And you think he's telling the truth?"

"I *know* he is. I went to see your friend, Palin. His body lives, but there is no life in his eyes. They're both corpses, Gerard. Walking corpses. They have no will of their own. They do whatever Mina tells them to do. Didn't you think it was strange the way they both just sit there, staring at nothing?"

"They're wizards," Gerard said lamely, by way of excuse.

Now that he looked back, he wondered he hadn't guessed something was wrong. He felt sickened at the thought.

Odila moistened her lips. "There's something else," she said, dropping her voice so that it was little more than a breath. Gerard had to strain to hear her. "Galdar told me that the One God is so pleased by this that she has ordered Mina to use the dead in battle. Not just the souls, Gerard. She is supposed to give life back to the bodies."

Gerard stared at her, aghast.

"It doesn't matter that Mina plans to attack Sanction with a ridiculously small army," Odila continued relentlessly. "None of her soldiers will ever die. If they do, Mina will just raise them up and send them right back into battle—"

"Odila," said Gerard, his voice urgent, "we have to leave here. Both of us. You don't want to stay, do you?" he asked suddenly, uncertain.

"No," she answered emphatically. "No, not after this. I am sorry I ever sought out this One God."

"Why did you?" Gerard asked.

She shook her head. "You wouldn't understand."

"I might. Why do you think I wouldn't?"

"You're so . . . self-reliant. You don't need anyone or anything. You know your own mind. You know who you are."

"Cornbread," he said, recalling her disparaging nickname for him. He had hoped to make her smile, but she didn't even seem to have heard him. Speaking of his feelings like this wasn't easy for him. "I'm looking for answers," he said awkwardly, "just like you. Just like everyone. Like you said, in order to find the answers, you have to ask questions." He gestured outside the temple, to the steps where the worshipers congregated every day. "That's what's the matter with half these people around here. They're like starving dogs. They are so hungry to believe in something that they take the first handout that's offered and gulp it down, never dreaming that the meat might be poisoned."

"I gulped," said Odila, sighing. "I wanted what everyone claimed they had in the old days. You were right when you said I hoped that the One God would fix my life. Make everything better. Take away the loneliness and the fear—" She halted, embarrassed to have revealed so much.

"I don't think even the old gods did that, at least from what I've been told," Gerard said. "Paladine certainly didn't solve all Huma's problems. If anything, he heaped more on him."

"Unless you believe that Huma chose to do what he did," said Odila softly, "and that Paladine gave him strength to do it." She paused, then added, in bleak despair, "We can't do anything to this god, Gerard. I've seen the mind of this god! I've seen the immense power this god wields. How can such a powerful god be stopped?"

Odila covered her face with her hands.

"I've made such a mess of things. I've dragged you into danger. I know the reason you've stayed around Solanthus, so don't try to deny it. You could have left days ago. You *should* have. You stayed around because you were worried about me."

"Nothing matters now because both of us are going to leave," Gerard said firmly. "Tomorrow, when the troops march out, Mina and Galdar will be preoccupied with their own duties. There will be such confusion that no one will miss us."

"I want to get out of here," Odila said emphatically. She jumped to her feet. "Let's leave now. I don't want to spend another minute in this terrible place. Everyone's asleep. No one will miss me. We'll go back to your quarters—"

"We'll have to leave separately. I'm being followed. You go first. I'll keep watch."

Reaching out impulsively, Odila took hold of his hand, clasped it tightly. "I appreciate all you've done for me, Gerard. You are a true and loyal friend."

"Go on," he said. "Quickly. I'll keep watch."

Releasing his hand with a parting squeeze, she started walking toward the temple doors, which were never locked, for worshipers of the One God were encouraged to come to the temple at any time, day or night. Odila gave the doors an impatient push and they opened silently on well-oiled hinges. Gerard was about to follow when he heard a noise by the altar. He glanced swiftly in that direction, saw nothing. The candle flames burned steadily. No one had entered. Yet he was positive he'd heard something. He was still staring at the altar, when he heard Odila give a strangled gasp.

Gerard whipped around, his hand on his sword. Expecting to find that she had been accosted by some guard, he was surprised to see her standing in the open doorway, alone.

"Now what's the matter?" He didn't dare go to her. The person following him would be watching for him. "Just walk out the damn door, will you?"

Odila turned to stare at him. Her face glimmered so white in the darkness, that he was reminded uncomfortably of the souls of the dead.

She spoke in a harsh whisper that carried clearly in the still night. "I can't leave!"

Gerard swore beneath his breath. Keeping a tight grip on his sword, he sidled over to the wall, hoping to remain unseen. Reaching a point near the door, he glared at Odila.

"What do you mean you won't leave?" he demanded in low and angry tones. "I risked my neck coming here, and I'll be damned if I'm going to leave without you. If I have to carry you—"

"I didn't say I won't leave!" Odila said, her breath coming in gasps. "I said I *can't*!"

She took a step toward the door, her hands outstretched. As she came nearer the door, her movements grew sluggish, as if she were wading into a river, trying to move against a swift-flowing current. Finally, she came to a halt and shook her head.

"I . . . can't!" she said, her voice choked.

Gerard stared in perplexity. Odila was trying her best, that much was clear. Something was obviously preventing her from leaving.

His gaze went from her terrified face to the medallion she wore around her neck.

He pointed at it. "The medallion! Take it off!"

Odila raised her hand to the medallion. She snatched back her fingers with a pain-filled cry.

Gerard grabbed the medallion, intending to rip it off her.

A jolting shock sent him staggering back against the doors. His hand burned and throbbed. He stared helplessly at Odila. She stared just as helplessly back.

"I don't understand—" she began.

"And yet," said a gentle voice, "the answer is simplicity itself."

Hand on his sword hilt, Gerard turned to find Mina standing in the doorway.

"I want to leave," Odila said, managing with a great effort to keep her voice firm and steady. "You have to let me go. You can't keep me here against my will."

"I am not keeping you here, Odila," said Mina.

Odila tried again to walk through the door. Her jaw clenched, and she strained every muscle. "You are lying!" she cried. "You have cast some sort of evil spell on me!"

"I am no wizard," said Mina, spreading her hands. "You know that. You know, too, what binds you to this place."

Odila shook her head in violent negation.

"Your faith," said Mina.

Odila stared, baffled. "I don't—"

"But you do. You believe in the One God. You said so yourself. 'I've seen the mind of this god! I've seen the immense power this god wields.' You have placed your faith in the One God, Odila, and in return, the One God claims your service."

"Faith shouldn't make anyone a prisoner," Gerard said angrily.

Mina turned her eyes on him, and he saw with dismay the images of thousands of people frozen in their amber depths. He had the terrible feeling that if he looked long enough, he would see himself there.

"Describe to me a faithful servant," said Mina, "or, better yet, a faithful knight. One who is faithful to his Order. What must he do to be termed 'faithful'?"

Gerard stubbornly kept silent, but that didn't matter, because Mina answered her own question.

Her tone was fervent, her eyes glowed with an inner light. "A faithful servant performs loyally and without question all the duties his master asks of him. In return, the master clothes him and feeds him and protects him from harm. If the servant is disloyal, if he rebels against his master, he is punished. Just so the faithful knight who is duty-bound to obey his superior. If he fails in his duty or rebels against authority, what happens to him? He is punished for his oath breaking. Even the Solamnics would punish such a knight, wouldn't they, Sir Gerard?"

She is the faithful servant, Gerard realized. She is the faithful knight. And this makes her dangerous, perhaps the most dangerous person to have ever lived on Krynn.

Her argument was flawed. He knew that, in some deep part of him, but he couldn't think why. Not while staring into those amber eyes.

Mina smiled gently at him. Because he had no answer, she assumed she had won. She turned the amber eyes back to Odila.

"Deny your belief in the One God, Odila," Mina said to her, "and you will be free to go."

"You know I cannot," Odila said.

"Then the One God's faithful servant will remain here to perform her duties. Return to your quarters, Odila. The hour is late. You will need your rest, for we have much to do tomorrow to prepare for the battle that will see the fall of Sanction."

Odila bowed her head, started to obey.

"Odila!" Gerard risked calling.

She kept walking. She did not look back at him.

Mina watched her depart, then turned to Gerard. "Will we see you among the ranks of our Knights as we march in triumph to Sanction, Sir Gerard? Or do you have other duties that call you away? If you do, you may go. You have my blessing and that of the One God."

She knows! Gerard realized. She knows I'm a spy, yet she does nothing. She even offers me the chance to leave! Why doesn't she have me arrested? Tortured? Killed? He wished suddenly that she would. Even death would be better than the notion in the back of his mind that she was using him, allowing him to think he was acting of his own free will, when all the time, whatever he did, he was carrying out the will of the One God.

"I'll ride with you," Gerard said grimly and stalked past her through the door.

On the steps of the temple he halted, stared in the darkness, and announced in a loud voice, "I'm going back to my quarters! Try to keep up, will you?"

Entering his room, Gerard lit a candle, then went to his desk and stood staring for long moments at the scrollcase. He opened it, removed the paper that detailed his plans to defeat Mina's army. Deliberately, grimly, he ripped the paper into small pieces. That done, he fed the pieces, one by one, to the candle's flame.

15

The Lame and the Blind

ina's army left Solanthus the next day. Not all the army marched, for she was forced to leave behind troops enough to occupy what was presumably a hostile city. Its hostility was largely a myth, judging by the number of Solanthians who turned out to cheer her and wish her well and press gifts upon her—so many that they would have filled the wagon that contained the amber sarcophagus, had Mina permitted it. She told them instead to give the gifts to the poor in the name of the One God. Weeping, the people of Solanthus blessed her name.

Gerard could have wept, too, but for different reasons. He'd spent the night wondering what to do, whether to go or stay. He decided finally to remain with the army, ride with them to Sanction. He told himself it was because of Odila.

She rode with the army. She sat in the wagon with the corpse of Goldmoon, imprisoned in amber, and the corpses of the two wizards, imprisoned in their own flesh. Viewing the wretched, ambulating corpses, Gerard wondered that he had not known the truth the moment he saw Palin, with his staring, vacant eyes. Odila did not glance at Gerard as the wagon rumbled past.

Galdar looked at him, dark eyes baleful. Gerard stared back. The minotaur's displeasure gave Gerard one consolation. The fact that he was accompanying Mina's army so obviously angered the minotaur that Gerard felt he must be doing something right.

As he cantered out the gates, taking up a position in the rear, as far from Mina as he could get and still be part of her army, his horse nearly ran down two beggars, who scrambled hastily to get out of his way.

"I'm sorry, gentlemen" said Gerard, reigning in his horse. "Are you hurt, either of you?"

One beggar was an older man, human, with gray hair and a gray, grizzled beard. His face was seamed with wrinkles and browned from the sun. His eyes were a keen, glittering blue, the color of new-made steel. Although he limped and leaned upon a crutch, he had the air and bearing of a military man. This was borne out by the fact that he wore what appeared to be the faded, tattered remnants of some sort of military uniform.

The other beggar was blind, his wounded eyes wrapped in a black bandage. He walked with one hand resting on the shoulder of his comrade, who guided him along his way. This man had white hair that shone silver in the sun. He was young, much younger than the other beggar, and he lifted his sightless head at the sound of Gerard's voice.

"No, sir," said the first beggar gruffly. "You did but startle us, that is all."

"Where is this army bound?" the second beggar asked.

"Sanction," said Gerard. "Take my advice, sirs, keep clear of the temple of the One God. Even though they could heal you, I doubt it's worth the price."

Tossing each beggar a few coins, he turned his horse's head, galloped off down the road, and was soon enveloped in a cloud of dust raised by the army.

The citizens of Solanthus watched until Mina was long out of sight, then they turned back to their city, which seemed bleak and empty now that she was gone.

"Mina marches on Sanction," said the blind beggar.

"This confirms the information we received last night," said the lame beggar. "Everywhere we go, we hear the same thing. Mina marches on Sanction. Are you satisfied now, at last?"

"Yes, Razor, I am satisfied," the blind man replied.

"About time," Razor muttered. He hurled the coins Gerard had given him at the blind man's feet. "No more begging! I have never been so humiliated."

"Yet, as you have seen, this disguise permits us to go where we will and talk to whom we want, from thief to knight to nobleman," Mirror said mildly. "No one has any clue that we are more than we seem. The question now is, what do we do? Do we confront Mina now?"

"And what would you say to her, Silver?" Razor raised his voice to a mocking lilt. "'Where, oh where, are the pretty gold dragons? Where, oh where, can they be?'"

Mirror kept silent, not liking how close Razor had come to the mark.

"I say we wait," Razor continued. "Confront her in Sanction."

"Wait until Sanction has fallen to your Queen, you mean," Mirror stated coldly.

"And I suppose you're going to stop her, Silver? Alone, blind?" Razor snorted.

"You would have me walk into Sanction, alone and blind," said Mirror.

"Don't worry, I won't let anything happen to you. Skie told you more than you've let on. I intend to be there when you have your conversation with Mina."

"Then I suggest you pick up that money, for we will need it," said Mirror. "These disguises that have worked well thus far will aid us all the more in Sanction. What better excuse to speak to Mina than to come before her as two seeking miracles?"

Mirror could not see the expression on Razor's face, but he

could imagine it—defiant at first, then glum, as he realized that what Mirror said made sense.

He heard the scrape of the coins being snatched irritably from the ground.

"I believe you are enjoying this, Silver," Razor said.

"You're right," Mirror returned. "I can't think when I've had this much fun."

16

An Unexpected Meeting

Like leaves flung from out the center of the cyclone, the gnome and the kender fluttered to the ground. That is, the kender—with his gaily colored clothes—fluttered. The gnome landed heavily, resulting in a subsequent cessation of breathing for a few heart-stopping minutes. Lack of breath also resulted in a cessation of the gnome's shrieking, which, considering where they found themselves, was undeniably a good thing.

Not that they knew right away where they were. All Tasslehoff knew, as he looked about, was where he wasn't, which was anywhere he'd been up to this point in his life. He was standing—and Conundrum was lying—in a corridor made of enormous blocks of black marble that had been polished to a high gloss. The corridor was lit sporadically with torches, whose orange light gave a soft and eerie glow to the corridor. The torches burned clean, for no whisper of air stirred. The light did nothing to remove the gloom from the corridor. The light only made the shadows all that much darker by contrast.

No whisper, no sound at all came from anywhere, though Tas listened with all his might. Tas made no sound either, and he hushed Conundrum as he helped the gnome to his feet. Tas had been adventuring most of his life, and he knew his corridors, and without doubt, this corridor had the smothery feeling of a place where you want to be quiet, very quiet.

"Goblins!" was the first word Conundrum gasped.

"No, not goblins," said Tasslehoff in a quiet tone that was meant to be reassuring. He rather spoiled by it by adding cheerfully, "Probably worse things than goblins down here."

"What do you mean?" Conundrum wheezed and clutched at his hair distractedly. "Worse than goblins! What could be worse than goblins? Where are we anyway?"

"Well, there's lots worse than goblins," whispered Tas upon reflection. "Draconians, for instance. And dragons. And owlbears. Did I ever tell you the story about the Uncle Trapspringer and the owlbear? It all began—"

It all ended when Conundrum doubled up his fist and punched Tasslehoff in the stomach.

"Owlbears! Who cares about owlbears or your blasted relations? I could tell you stories about my cousin Strontiumninety that would make your hair fall out. Your teeth, too. Why did you bring us here, and where is here, anyway?"

"*I* didn't bring us anywhere," returned Tasslehoff in irritable tones when he could speak again. Being struck soundly and unexpectedly in the stomach tended to make a fellow irritable. "The device brought us here. And I don't know where 'here' is anymore than you do. I— Hush! Someone's coming."

When in a dark and smothery feeling corridor, it is always a good idea to see who is coming before giving them a chance to see you. That's the maxim Uncle Trapspringer had always taught his nephew, and Tas had found that, in general, it was a good plan. For one thing, it allowed you to leap out of the darkness and give the person a grand surprise. Tasslehoff took hold of the collar of Conundrum's shirt and dragged the gnome behind a black, marble pillar.

A single figure walked the corridor. The figure was robed in black and was not easily distinguishable from either the darkness of the corridor or the black, marble walls. Tasslehoff had his first good view of the figure as it passed beneath one of the torches. Even in the darkness, able to see only the dimmest, shadowiest outline of the figure, Tasslehoff had the strange and squirmy feeling in his stomach (probably left over from being struck) that he knew this person. There was something about the walk that was slow and halting, something about the way the person leaned upon the staff he was carrying, something about the staff that gave off a very soft, white light.

"Raistlin!" Tasslehoff breathed, awed.

He was about to repeat the name in a much louder voice, accompanied by a whoop and a shout and a rushing forward to give his friend, whom he hadn't seen in a long time and presumed to be dead, an enormous hug.

A hand grasped his shoulder, and a voice said softly, "No. Leave him be."

"But he's my friend," Tas said to Conundrum. "Not counting the time he murdered another friend of mine, who was a gnome, by the way."

Conundrum's eyes opened wide. He clutched at Tas nervously. "This friend of yours. He doesn't make it a practice of . . . of m-m-murdering gnomes, does he?"

Tas missed this because he was staring at Conundrum, noting that the gnome had hold of Tasslehoff's sleeve with one hand and his shirt front with the other. This accounted for two hands and, so far as Tas knew, gnomes came with only two hands. Which meant there was a hand left over, and that hand was holding Tasslehoff firmly by the shoulder. Tasslehoff twisted and squirmed to see who had hold of him, but the pillar behind which they were standing cast a dark shadow, and all he could see behind him was more darkness.

Tas looked round at the other hand—the hand that was on his shoulder—but the hand wasn't there. Or at least, it was there because he could feel it, but it wasn't there because he couldn't see it.

Finding this all very strange, Tasslehoff looked back at Raistlin. Knowing Raistlin as he did, Tas was forced to admit that there were times when the mage had not been at all friendly to the kender. And there was the fact that Raistlin *did* murder gnomes. Or at least, he had murdered one gnome for fixing the Device of Time Journeying. This very device, although not this very gnome. Raistlin wore the black robes now, and he had been wearing black robes then, and while Tasslehoff found Conundrum extremely annoying at times, he didn't want to see the gnome murdered. Tasslehoff decided that for Conundrum's sake he would keep silent and not jump out at Raistlin, and he would forgo the big hug.

Raistlin passed very near the kender and the gnome. Conundrum was, thank goodness, speechless with terror. Through a heroic effort on his part, Tasslehoff kept silent, though the absent gods alone knew what this cost him. He was rewarded with an approving squeeze by the hand on his shoulder that wasn't there, which, all in all, didn't make him feel as good as it might have under the circumstances.

Raistlin was apparently deep in thought, for his head was bowed, his walk slow and abstracted. He stopped once to cough, a racking cough that so weakened him he was forced to lean against the wall. He choked and gagged, his face grew deathly pale. Blood flecked his lips. Tas was alarmed, for he'd seen Raistlin have these attacks before but never one this bad.

"Caramon had a tea he used to fix for him," Tas said, starting forward.

The hand pressed him back.

Raistlin raised his head. His golden eyes shone in the torchlight. He looked about, up and down the corridor.

"Who spoke?" he said in his whispering voice. "Who spoke that name? Caramon? Who spoke, I say?"

The hand dug into Tasslehoff's shoulder. He had no need of its caution, however. Raistlin looked so very strange and his expression was so very terrible that the kender would have kept silent, regardless.

"No one," said Raistlin, at last able to draw a ragged breath. "I am imagining things." He mopped his brow with the hem of his black velvet sleeve, then smiled sardonically. "Perhaps it was my own guilty conscience. Caramon is dead. They are all dead, drowned in the Blood Sea. And they were all so shocked when I used the dragon orb and departed, leaving them to their fate. Amazed that I would not meekly share in their doom."

Recovering his strength, Raistlin drew away from the wall. He steadied himself with the staff, but did not immediately resume his walk. Perhaps he was still too weak.

"I can see the look on Caramon's face now. I can hear his blubbering." Raistlin pitched his voice high, spoke through his nose. "'But . . . Raist—'" He ground his teeth, then smiled again, a most unpleasant smile. "And Tanis, that self-righteous hypocrite! His illicit love for my dear sister led him to betray his friends, and yet he has the temerity to accuse *me* of being faithless! I can see them all—Goldmoon, Riverwind, Tanis, my brother—all staring at me with great cow eyes."

Again, his voice rose to mimic. "'At least save your brother . . .'" The voice resumed its bitter monologue. "Save him for what? A lawn ornament? His ambition takes him no further than the bed of his latest conquest. All my life, he has been the manacles that bound my hands and shackled my feet. You might as well ask me to leave my prison but take along my chains. . . ."

He resumed his walk, moving slowly down the corridor.

"You know, Conundrum," whispered Tasslehoff, "I said he was my friend, but it takes a lot of work to like Raistlin. Sometimes I'm not sure it's worth the effort. He's talking about Caramon and the rest drowning in the Blood Sea, but they didn't drown. They were rescued by sea elves. I know because Caramon told me the whole story. And Raistlin knows they weren't drowned because he saw them again. But if he thinks that they're drowned, then obviously he doesn't yet know that they weren't, which means that he must be somewhere between the time he thought they drowned and the time he finds that they didn't.

Which means," Tas continued, awed and excited, "that I've found another part of the past."

Hearing this, Conundrum eyed the kender suspiciously and backed up a few steps. "You haven't *met* my cousin, Stroniumninety, have you?"

Tas was about to say that he hadn't had the pleasure when the sound of footsteps rang through the corridor. The footsteps were not those of the mage, who barely made any noise at all beyond the occasional rasping cough and the rustle of his robes. These footsteps were large and imposing, thunderous, filling the corridor with noise.

The hand that wasn't on Tasslehoff's shoulder pulled him back deeper into the shadows, cautioning him with renewed pressure to keep quiet. The gnome, with finely honed instincts for survival so long as steam-powered pistons weren't in the offing, had already pressed himself so far into the wall that he might have been taken for the artistic renderings of some primitive tribe.

A man as large as his footfalls filled the corridor with sound and motion and life. He was tall and brawny, wore heavy, ornately designed armor that seemed a part of his anatomy for all that it slowed him down. He carried under his arm the horned helm of a Dragon Highlord. An enormous sword clanked at his side. He was obviously on his way somewhere with a purpose in mind, for he walked rapidly and with intent, looking neither to the right nor the left. Thus he very nearly ran down Raistlin, who was forced to fall back against the wall at the man's coming or be crushed.

The Dragon Highlord saw the mage, acknowledged his presence with no more than a sharp glance. Raistlin bowed. The Dragon Highlord continued on his way. Raistlin started to go his, when suddenly the Highlord halted, spun round on his heel.

"Majere," boomed the voice.

Raistlin halted, turned. "My Lord Ariakas."

"How do you find things here in Neraka? Your quarters comfortable?"

"Yes, my lord. Quite adequate for my simple needs," Raistlin replied. The light of the crystal ball atop his staff glimmered ever so slightly. "Thank you for asking."

Ariakas frowned. Raistlin's response was polite, servile, as the Dragon Highlord had a right to respect. Ariakas was not a man to note subtleties, but apparently even he had heard the sardonic tone in the mage's raspy voice. The Highlord could not very well rebuke a man for a tone, however, so he continued.

"Your sister Kitiara says that I am to treat you well," said Ariakas gruffly. "You have her to thank for your post here."

"I owe my sister a great deal," Raistlin replied.

"You owe me more," said Ariakas grimly.

"Indeed," said Raistlin with another bow.

Ariakas was plainly not pleased. "You are a cool one. Most men cringe and cower when I speak to them. Does nothing impress you?"

"*Should* anything impress me, my lord?" Raistlin returned.

"By our Queen," Ariakas cried, laying his hand on the hilt of his sword, "I could strike off your head for that remark!"

"You could try, my lord," said Raistlin. He bowed again, this time more deeply than before. "Forgive me, sir, I did not mean the words the way they sounded. Of course, I find you impressive. I find the magnificence of this city impressive. But just because I am impressed does not mean I am fearful. You do not admire fearful men, do you, my lord?"

"No," said Ariakas. He stared at Raistlin intently. "You are right. I do not."

"I would have you admire me, my lord," said Raistlin.

Ariakas continued to stare at the mage. Then, suddenly, the Highlord burst out laughing. His laughter was enormous. It rolled and crashed through the corridor, smashed the gnome up against the wall. Tasslehoff felt dazed by it, as though he'd been struck in the head by a large rock. Raistlin winced slightly, but held his ground.

"I don't admire you yet, mage," said Ariakas, when he had regained control of himself. "But someday, Majere, when you have proven yourself, maybe I will."

Turning on his heel, still chuckling, he continued on his way down the corridor.

When his footfalls had died away and all was once again silent, Raistlin said softly, "Someday, when I have proven myself, my lord, you will do more than admire me. You will fear me."

Raistlin turned and walked away, and Tasslehoff turned to try to see who it was who didn't have hold of his shoulder, and he turned and turned and kept on turning. . . .

Book 2

I

Meeting of the Gods

The gods of Krynn met in council, as they had done many times since the world had been stolen away from them. The gods of light stood opposite the gods of darkness, as day stands opposite night, with the gods of neutrality divided evenly in between. The children of the gods stood together, as they always did.

These council sessions had accomplished little in the past except to sometimes soothe raging tempers and cheer crushed spirits. One by one, each of the gods came forth to tell of searching that had been done in vain. Many were the journeys taken by each god and goddess to try to find what was lost. Long and dangerous were some of these treks through the planes of existence, but one and all ended in failure. Not even Zivilyn, the all-seeing, who existed in all times and in all lands, had been able to find the world. He could see the path Krynn and its people would have taken into the future, but that path was populated now by the ghosts of might-havebeens. The gods were close to concluding sorrowfully that the world was lost to them forever.

When each had spoken, Paladine appeared to them in his radiance.

"I bring glad tidings," he said. "I have heard a voice cry out to me, the voice of one of the children of the world. Her prayer rang through the heavens, and its music was sweet to hear. Our people need us, for as we had suspected, Queen Takhisis now rules the world unchallenged."

"Where is the world?" Sargonnas demanded. Of all the gods of darkness, he was the most enraged, the most embittered, for Queen Takhisis had been his consort, and he felt doubly betrayed. "Tell us and we will go there immediately and give her the punishment she so richly deserves."

"I do not know," Paladine replied. "Goldmoon's voice was cut off. Death took her and Takhisis holds her soul in thrall. Yet, we now know the world exists. We must continue to search for it."

Nuitari stepped forth. The god of the magic of darkness, he was clad all in black. His face, that of a gibbous moon, was white as wax.

"I have a soul who begs an audience," he said.

"Do you sponsor this?" Paladine asked.

"I do," Nuitari answered.

"And so do I." Lunitari came forward in her red robes.

"And so do I." Solinari came forth in his silver robes.

"Very well, we will hear this soul," Paladine agreed. "Let this soul come forward."

The soul entered and took his place among them. Paladine frowned at the sight, as did most of the other gods, light and darkness alike, for none trusted this soul, who had once tried to become a god himself.

"Raistlin Majere has nothing to say that I want to hear," Sargonnas stated with a snarl and turned to depart.

The others grumbled their agreement—all but one.

"I think we should listen to him," Mishakal said.

The other gods turned to look at her in surprise, for she was the consort of Paladine, a loving goddess of healing and compassion. She knew better than most the harm and suffering and sorrow that this man had brought upon those who loved and trusted him.

"He made reparation for his crimes," Mishakal continued, "and he was forgiven."

"Then why has his soul not departed with the rest?" Sargonnas demanded. "Why does he linger here, except to take advantage of our weakness?"

"Why does your soul remain, Raistlin Majere," Paladine asked sternly, "when you were free to move on?"

"Because half of me is missing," returned Raistlin, facing the god, meeting his eyes. "Together, my brother and I came into this world. Together, we will leave it. We walked apart for much of our lives. The fault was mine. If I can help it, we will not be separated in death."

"Your loyalty is commendable," said Paladine dryly, "if a bit belated. But I do not understand what business you have with us."

"I have found the world," said Raistlin.

Sargonnas snorted. The other gods stared at Raistlin in troubled silence.

"Did you hear Goldmoon's prayer as well?" Paladine asked.

"No," Raistlin responded. "I could hardly be expected to, could I? I did hear something else, though—a voice chanting words of magic. Words I recognized, as perhaps none other could. I recognized, as well, the voice that spoke them. It belonged to a kender, Tasslehoff Burrfoot."

"That is impossible," said Paladine. "Tasslehoff Burrfoot is dead."

"He is and he isn't, but I will come to that later," Raistlin said. "His soul remains unaccounted for." He turned to Zivilyn. "In the future that was, where did the kender's soul go after his death?"

"He joined his friend Flint Fireforge," said Zivilyn readily.

"Is his soul there now? Or does the grumbling dwarf wait for him still?"

Zivilyn hesitated, then said, "Flint is alone."

"A pity you did not notice this earlier," Sargonnas growled at Zivilyn. The minotaur god turned his glare at Raistlin. "Suppose this blasted kender *is* alive. What was he doing speaking words of magic? I never had much use for you mages, but at least you had sense enough to keep kender from using magic. This story of yours smells of yesterday's fish to me."

"As for the magic words he spoke," Raistlin replied, unperturbed by the minotaur god's gibe, "they were taught to him by an old friend of his, Fizban, when he gave into his hands the Device of Time Journeying."

The gods of darkness raised a clamor. The gods of magic looked grave.

"It has long been decreed that none of the Gray Gemstone races should ever be given the opportunity to travel through time," said Lunitari accusingly. "We should have been consulted in this matter."

"In truth, I gave him the device," said Paladine with a fond smile. "He wanted to attend the funeral of his friend Caramon Majere to do him honor. Quite logically assuming that he would die long before Caramon, Tasslehoff asked for the device so that he could go forward into the future to speak at the funeral. I thought this a noble and generous impulse, and thus I permitted it."

"Whether that was wise or not, you know best, Great One," Raistlin said. "I can affirm that Tasslehoff did travel forward in time once, but he missed, arriving at the funeral too late. He came back, thinking he would go again. As for what happened after that, the following is surmise, but since we know kender, I believe we can all agree that the premise I put forth is logical.

"One thing came up, then another, and Tasslehoff forgot all about traveling to Caramon's funeral until he was just about to be crushed by Chaos. At that moment, with only a few seconds of life left, Tas happened to recall this piece of unfinished business. He activated the device, which carried him forward in time. He arrived in the future, as he intended, except that it was a different future. Quite by mischance, the kender found the world. And I have found the kender."

For long moments, no one spoke. The gods of magic glanced at one another, their thoughts in perfect accord.

"Then take us there," said Gilean, the keeper of the book of knowledge.

"I would not advise it," Raistlin returned. "Queen Takhisis is extraordinarily powerful now. She is watchful. She would be aware of your coming far in advance, and she has made preparations to receive you. Should you return now, weak and unprepared to face her, she might well destroy you."

Sargonnas rumbled deep in his chest. The thunder of his ire echoed through the heavens. The other gods were scornful, suspicious, or solemn, depending on the nature of each.

"You have another problem," Raistlin continued. "The people of the world believe that you abandoned them in their hour of greatest need. If you enter the world now, you will not find many who will welcome you."

"My people know I did not abandon them!" Sargonnas cried, clenching his fist.

Raistlin bowed, made no reply. He kept his gaze upon Paladine, who looked troubled.

"There is something in what you say," said Paladine at last. "We know how the people turned against us after the Cataclysm. Two hundred years passed before they were ready to accept us back. Takhisis knows this, and she would gladly use the distrust and anger of the people against us. We must proceed slowly and cautiously, as we did then."

"If I might suggest a plan," Raistlin said.

He detailed his idea. The gods listened, most of them. When he concluded, Paladine glanced around the circle.

"What say you all?"

"We approve," said the gods of magic, speaking together with one voice.

"I do not," said Sargonnas in anger.

The other gods remained silent, some doubtful, others disapproving.

Raistlin looked at each of them in turn, then said quietly, "You do not have an eternity to mull this over and debate among yourselves. You may not even have one second. Is it possible that you do not see the danger?"

"From a kender?" Sargonnas laughed.

"From a kender," said Nuitari. "Because Burrfoot did not die when he was supposed to have died, the moment of his death hangs suspended in time."

Solinari caught up his cousin's words, so that they seemed to come from the same throat. "If the kender dies in a time and place that is not his own, Tasslehoff will not defeat Chaos. The Father of All and Nothing will be victorious, and he will carry out his threat to destroy us *and* the world."

"The kender must be discovered and returned to the time and place of his death," Lunitari added, her voice stern. "Tasslehoff Burrfoot must die when and where he was supposed to die or we all face annhilation."

The three voices that were distinct and separate and yet seemed one voice fell silent.

Raistlin glanced around again. "I take it I have leave to go?"

Sargonnas muttered and grumbled, but in the end he fell silent.

The other gods looked to Paladine.

At length, he nodded.

"Then I bid you farewell," said Raistlin.

When the mage had departed, Sargonnas confronted Paladine. "You heap folly upon folly," the minotaur stated accusingly. "First you give a powerful magical artifact into the hands of a kender, then you send this twisted mage to fight Takhisis. If we are doomed, you have doomed us."

"Nothing done out of love is ever folly," Paladine returned. "If we face great peril, we now do so with hope." He turned to Zivilyn. "What do you see?"

Zivilyn looked into eternity.

"Nothing," he replied. "Nothing but darkness."

2

The Song of the Desert

Mina's army moved east, heading for Sanction. The army traveled rapidly, for the skies were clear, the air cool and crisp, and they met no opposition. Blue dragons flew above them, guarding their march and scouting out the lands ahead. Rumor of their coming spread. Those along their route of march quaked in fear when they heard that they lay in the path of this conquering army. Many fled into the hills. Those who could not flee or had nowhere to go waited fearfully for destruction.

Their fears proved groundless. The army marched through villages and past farms, camped outside of towns. Mina kept her soldiers under strict control. Supplies they could have taken by force, they paid for. In some cases, when they came to an impoverished house or village, the army gave of what they had. Manor houses and castles they could have razed, they let stand. Everywhere along their route, Mina spoke to the people of the One God. All they did, they did in the name of the One God.

Mina spoke to the high born and the low, to the peasant and the farmer, the blacksmith and the innkeeper, the bard and the tinker, the noble lord and lady. She brought healing to the sick, food to the hungry, comfort to the unhappy. She told them how the old gods had abandoned them, left them to the scourge of these alien dragons. But this new god, the One God, was here to take care of them.

Odila was often at Mina's side. She took no part in the proceedings, but she watched and listened and fingered the amulet around her neck. The touch no longer seemed to cause her pain.

Gerard rode in the rear, as far as possible from the minotaur, who was always in the front ranks with Mina. Gerard guessed that Galdar had been ordered to leave him alone. Still, there was always the possibility of an "accident." Galdar could not be faulted if a poisonous snake happened to crawl into Gerard's bedroll or a broken tree branch came crashing down on his head. Those few times when the two were forced by circumstance to meet, Gerard saw by the look in the minotaur's eyes that Gerard was alive only because Mina willed it.

Unfortunately, riding in the rear meant that Gerard was back among those who guarded the wagon carrying the sarcophagus of Goldmoon and the two wizards. The phrase, "More dead than alive" came to Gerard's mind as he looked at them, and he looked at them often. He didn't like to. He couldn't stand the sight of them, sitting on the end of the wagon, bodies swaying to and fro with the motion of the bumpy ride, feet and arms dangling, heads drooping. Every time he watched them, he rode away sickened, vowing that was the last time he would have anything to do with them. The next day he was drawn to stare at them, fascinated, repulsed.

Mina's army marched toward Sanction, leaving behind not fire and smoke and blood, but cheering crowds, who tossed garlands at Mina's feet and sang praises of the One God.

Another group marched east, traveling almost parallel to Mina's army, separated by only a few hundred miles. Their march was slower because it was not as organized and the land through which they traveled was not as hospitable. The same sun that shone brightly on Mina seared the elves of Qualinesti as they struggled across the Plains of Dust, heading for what they hoped would be safe sanctuary in the land of their kin, the Silvanesti. Every day, Gilthas blessed Wanderer and the people of the plains, for without their help, not a single elf would have crossed the desert alive.

The Plainspeople gave the elves enveloping, protective clothing that kept out the heat of the day and held body warmth for the cold nights. The Plainspeople gave the elves food, which Gilthas suspected they could ill afford to share. Whenever he questioned them about this, the proud Plainspeople would either ignore him or cast him such cold glances that he knew that to continue to ask questions would offend them. They taught the elves that they should march during the cool parts of the morning and night and seek shelter against the sweltering heat of the afternoon. Finally, Wanderer and his comrades offered to accompany the elves and serve as guides. Gilthas knew, if the rest of the elves did not, that Wanderer had a twofold purpose. One was beneficent—to make certain the elves survived the crossing of the desert. The other was self-serving—to make certain the elves crossed.

The elves had come to look very much like the Plainspeople, dressing in baggy trousers and long tunics and wrapping themselves in many layers of soft wool that protected them from the desert sun by day and the desert chill by night. They kept their faces muffled against the stinging sand, kept delicate skin shielded from exposure. Having lived close to nature, with a respect for nature, the elves soon adapted to the desert and lost no more of their people. They could never love the desert, but they came to understand it and to honor its ways.

Gilthas could tell that Wanderer was uneasy at how swiftly the elves were adapting to this hard life. Gilthas tried his best to convince the Plainsman that the elves were a people of forests and gardens, a people who could look on the red and orange striated rock formations that broke the miles of endless sand dunes and see no beauty, as did the Plainspeople, but only death.

One night, when they were nearing the end of their long journey, the elves arrived at an oasis in the dark hours before the dawn. Wanderer had decreed that here the elves could rest this night and throughout the day tomorrow, drinking their fill and renewing their strength before they once more took up their weary journey. The elves made camp, set the watch, then gave themselves to sleep.

Gilthas tried to sleep. He was weary from the long walk, but sleep would not come. He had fought his way out of the depression that had plagued him. The need to be active and responsible for his people had been beneficial. He had a great many cares and worries still, not the least of which was the reception they might receive in Silvanesti. He was thinking of these matters, and restless, he left his bedroll, taking care not to wake his slumbering wife. He walked into the night to stare up at the myriad stars. He had not known there were so many. He was awed and even dismayed by their number. He was staring thus, when Wanderer found him.

"You should be sleeping," said Wanderer.

His voice was stern, he was giving a command, not making idle conversation. He had not changed from the day Gilthas had first met him. Taciturn, quiet, he never spoke when a gesture would serve him instead. His face was like the desert rock, formed of sharp angles marred by dark creases. He smiled, never laughed, and his smile was only in his dark eyes.

Gilthas shook his head. "My body yearns for sleep, but my mind prevents it."

"Perhaps the voices keep you awake," said Wanderer.

"I've heard you speak of them before," Gilthas replied, intrigued. "The voices of the desert. I have listened, but I cannot hear them."

"I hear them now," said Wanderer. "The sighing of the wind among the rocks, the whispering of the sand floes. Even in the silence of the night, there is a voice that we know to be the voice of the stars. You cannot see the stars in your land or, if you can, they are caught and held prisoner by the tree branches. Here"— Wanderer waved his hand to the vast vault of star-studded sky that stretched from horizon to horizon—"the stars are free, and their song is loud."

"I hear the wind among the rocks," said Gilthas, "but to me it is the sound of a dying breath whistling through gaping teeth. Yet," he added, pausing to look around him, "now that I have traveled through this land, I must admit that there is a beauty to your night. The stars are so close and so numerous that some-times I *do* think I might hear them sing." He shrugged. "If I did not feel so small and insignificant among them, that is."

"That is what truly bothers you, Gilthas," said Wanderer, reaching out his hand and touching Gilthas on his breast, above his heart. "You elves rule the land in which you live. The trees form the walls of your houses and provide you shelter. The orchids and the roses grow at your behest. The desert will not be ruled. The desert will not be subjugated. The desert cares nothing about you, will do nothing for you except one thing. The desert will always be here. Your land changes. Trees die and forests burn, but the desert is eternal. Our home has always been, and it will always be. That is the gift it gives us, the gift of surety."

"We thought our world would never change," said Gilthas quietly. "We were wrong. I wish you a better fate."

Returning to his tent, Gilthas felt exhaustion overcome him. His wife did not waken, but she was sleepily aware of his return, for she reached out her arms and drew him close. He listened to the voice of her heart beating steadily against his. Comforted, he slept.

Wanderer did not sleep. He looked up at the stars and thought over the words of the young elf. And it seemed to Wanderer that the song of the stars was, for the first time since he'd heard it, mournful and off-key.

The elves continued their trek, their progress slow but steady. Then came the morning the Lioness shook her husband awake.

"What?" Gilthas asked, fear jolting him from sleep. "What is it? What is wrong?"

"For a change, nothing," she said, smiling at him through her rampant, golden curls. She sniffed the air. "What do you smell?"

"Sand," said Gilthas, rubbing his nose, that always seemed clogged with grit. "Why? What do you smell?"

"Water," said the Lioness. "Not the muddy water of some oasis but water that runs swift and fast and cold. There is a river nearby. . . ." Her eyes filled with tears, her voice failed her. "We have done it, my husband. We have crossed the Plains of Dust!"

A river it was, yet no river such as the Qualinesti had ever before seen. The elves gathered on its banks and stared in some dismay at the water, that flowed red as blood. The Plainspeople assured them that the water was fresh and untainted, the red color came from the rocks through which the river ran. The elves might have still hesitated, but the children broke free of their parents' grasp and rushed forward to splash in the water that bubbled around the roots of giant cottonwood and willow trees. Soon what remained of the Qualinesti nation was laughing and splashing and rollicking in the River Torath.

"Here we leave you," said Wanderer. "You can ford the river at this point. Beyond, only a few miles distant, you will come upon the remains of the King's Highway that will take you to Silvanesti. The river runs along the highway for many miles, so you will have water in abundance. The foraging is good, for the trees that grow along the river give of their fruits at this time of year."

Wanderer held out his hand to Gilthas. "I wish you good fortune and success at your journey's end. And I wish for you that someday you will hear the song of the stars."

"May their song never fall silent for you, my friend," said Gilthas, pressing the man's hand warmly. "I can never thank you enough for what you and your people have done—"

He stopped speaking, for he was talking to Wanderer's back. Having said all that was needed, the Plainsman motioned to his comrades, led them back into the desert.

"A strange people," said the Lioness. "They are rude and uncouth and in love with rocks, which is something I will never understand, but I find that I admire them."

"I admire them, too," said Gilthas. "They saved our lives, saved the Qualinesti nation. I hope that they never have reason to regret what they have done for us."

"Why should they?" the Lioness asked, startled.

"I don't know, my love," Gilthas replied. "I can't say. Just a feeling I have."

He walked away, heading for the river, leaving his wife to gaze after him with a look of concern and consternation.

3

The Lie

A lhana Starbreeze sat alone in the shelter that had been shaped for her by those elves who still had some magical power remaining to them, at least enough to command the trees to provide a safe haven for the exiled elven queen. As it turned out, the elves did not need their magic, for the trees, which have always loved the elves, seeing their queen sorrowful and weary to the point of collapse, bent their branches of their own accord. Their limbs hung protectively over her, their leaves twined together to keep out the rain and the wind. The grass formed a thick, soft carpet for her bed. The birds sang softly to ease her pain.

The time was evening, one of the few quiet times in Alhana's unquiet life. These were busy times, for she and her forces were living in the wilderness, fighting a hit-and-run war against the Dark Knights: raiding prison camps, attacking supply ships, making daring forays into the city itself to rescue elves in peril. For the moment, though, all was peaceful. The evening meal had been served. The Silvanesti elves under her command were settling down for the night. For the moment, no one needed her, no one demanded that she make decisions that would cost more elven lives, shed more elven blood. Alhana sometimes dreamed of swimming in a river of blood, a dream from which she could never escape, except by drowning.

Some might say—and some elves did—that the Dark Knights of Neraka had done Alhana Starbreeze a favor. She had once been deemed a dark elf, exiled from her homeland for daring to try to bring about peace between the Silvanesti and their Qualinesti cousins, for daring to marry a Qualinesti in order to unite their two squabbling realms.

Now, in their time of greatest trouble, Alhana Starbreeze had been accepted back by her people. The sentence of exile had been lifted from her formally by the Heads of House who remained alive after the Dark Knights had completed their occupation of the capital, Silvanost. Alhana's people now embraced her. Kneeling at her feet, they were loud in their lamentations for the "misunderstanding." Never mind that they had tried to have her assassinated. In the very next breath, they cried to her, "Save us! Queen Alhana, save us!"

Samar was furious with her, with her people. The Silvanesti had invited the Dark Knights into their city and turned away Alhana Starbreeze. Not so many weeks before, they had fallen on their knees before the leader of the Dark Knights, a human girl called Mina. The Silvanesti had been warned of Mina's treachery, but they had been blinded by the miracles she performed in the name of the One God. Samar had been among those who had warned them that they were fools to put their trust in humans—miracles or not. The elves had been all astonishment and shock and horror when the Dark Knights had turned on them, set up their slave camps and prisons, killed any who opposed them.

Samar was grimly pleased that the Silvanesti had at last come to revere Alhana Starbreeze, the one person who had remained loyal to them and fought for them when they had reviled her. He was less pleased with his queen's response, which was forgiving, magnanimous, patient. He would have seen them cringe and grovel to obtain her favor.

"I cannot punish them, Samar," Alhana said to him on the evening on which the sentence of exile had been lifted. She was now free to return to her homeland—a homeland ruled over by the Dark Knights of Neraka, a homeland she was going to have to fight to reclaim. "You know why."

He knew why: All she did was for her son, Silvanoshei, who was the king of Silvanesti. An unworthy son, as far as Samar was concerned. Silvanoshei had been the person responsible for admitting the Knights of Neraka into the city of Silvanost. Enamored of the human girl, Mina, Silvanoshei was the cause of the downfall of the Silvanesti people.

Yet the people adored him and still claimed him as their king. Because of him, they followed his mother. Because of Silvanoshei, Samar was on a perilous journey, forced to leave his queen at the most desperate time in the ancient history of Silvanesti, forced to go chasing over Ansalon after this very son. Although few knew it, Silvanoshei, the king of the Silvanesti, had run away the very night Samar and other elves had risked their lives to rescue him from the Dark Knights.

Few knew he was gone, because Alhana refused to admit it, either to her people or to herself. Those elves who had been with them the night of his departure knew, but she had sworn them to secrecy. Long loyal to her, loving her, they had readily agreed. Now Alhana kept up the pretense that Silvanoshei was ill and that he was forced to remain in seclusion until he had healed.

Meantime, Alhana was confident he would return. "He is off sulking somewhere," she told Samar. "He will get over this infatuation and come to his senses. He will come back to me, to his people."

Samar did not believe it. He tried to point out to Alhana the evidence of the tracks of horse's hooves. The elves had brought no horses with them. This animal was magical, had been sent for Silvanoshei. He wasn't coming back. Not then, not ever. At first

Alhana had refused even to listen to him. She had forbidden him to speak of it. But as the days passed and Silvanoshei did not return, she was forced to admit, with a breaking heart, that Samar might be right.

Samar had been gone long weeks now. During this time, Alhana had kept up the pretense that Silvanoshei was with them, sick and confined to his tent. She even went so far as to maintain his tent, pretend to go visit him. She would sit on his empty bed and talk to him, as if he were there. He would come back, and when he did, he would find her waiting for him, with all in readiness as if he had never left.

Alone in her bower, Alhana read and reread her latest message from Samar, a message carried by a hawk, for these birds had long served as messengers between the two. The message was brief—Samar not being one to waste words—and it brought both joy and sorrow to the anxious mother, dismay and despair to the queen.

I have picked up his trail at last. He took a ship from Abanasinia, sailed north to Solamnia. There he traveled to Solanthus in search of this female, but she had already marched eastward with her army. Silvanoshei followed her.

Other news I have heard. The city of Qualinost has been utterly destroyed. A lake of death now covers what remains of Qualinost. The Dark Knights now ravage the countryside, seizing land and making it their own. It is rumored that many Qualinesti escaped, including Laurana's son, Gilthas, but where they are or what has happened to them is unknown. I spoke to a survivor, who said that it is certain that Lauranalanthalsa was slain in the battle, along with many hundreds of Qualinesti, as well as dwarves of Thorbardin and some humans who fought alongside them. They died heroes. The evil dragon Beryl was killed.

I am on the trail of your son. I will report when I can.
Your faithful servant,
Samar

Alhana whispered a prayer for the soul of Laurana and the souls of all those who had perished in the battle. The prayer was to the old gods, the departed gods, who were no longer there to heed it. The beautiful words eased her grief, even if she knew in her heart that they held no meaning. She prayed, too, for the Qualinesti exiles, hoping that the rumor of their escape was true. Then, concern for her son banished all other thoughts from her mind.

"What witchery has this girl worked on you, my son?" she said softly, absently smoothing the vellum on which Samar had written his note. "What foul witchery . . ."

A voice spoke from outside her shelter, calling her name. The voice belonged to one of her elite guard, a woman who had served her long, through many difficult and dangerous times. She was known to Alhana to be stoic, reserved, never showing any emotion, and the queen was startled and alarmed now to hear a tremor in the woman's voice.

Fears of all kinds and sorts crowded around Alhana. She had to steel herself to react calmly. Crumpling the vellum in her hand, she thrust it into the bosom of her chemise, then ducked out of the sheltering vines and branches to face the woman. She saw with her a strange elf, someone unknown to her.

Or was he unknown? Or simply forgotten? Alhana stared at him closely. She knew this young man, she realized. Knew the lines of his face, knew the eyes that held in them a sadness and care and crushing responsibility to mirror her own. She could not place him, probably due to the foreign garb he wore— the long and enveloping robes of the barbarians who roamed the desert.

She looked to her guard for answers.

"The scouts came across him, my queen," said the woman. "He will not give his name, but he claims to be related to you through your honored husband, Porthios. He is Qualinesti, beneath all these layers of wool. He does not come armed into our lands. Since he may be what he claimed, we brought him to you."

"I know you, sir," Alhana said. "Forgive me, I cannot give you a name."

"That is understandable," he replied with a smile. "Many years and many trials separate us. Yet"—his voice softened, his eyes were warm with admiration—"I remember you, the great lady so wrongfully imprisoned by her people—"

Alhana gave a glad cry, flung herself into his arms. Even as she embraced him, she remembered the mother he had lost, who would never more put her arms around her son. Alhana kissed him tenderly, for her sake and that of Laurana's, then she stepped back to look at him.

"Those trials of which you speak have aged you more than the corresponding years. Gilthas of the House of Solostaran, I am pleased beyond measure to see you safe and well, for I just heard the sad news concerning your people. I hoped that what I heard was rumor and gossip and that it would prove false, but, alas, I see the truth in your eyes."

"If you have heard that my mother is dead and that Qualinost is destroyed, then you have heard the truth," Gilthas said.

"I am sorry beyond measure," Alhana said, taking his hand in her own and holding it fast. "Please, come inside, where you may be comfortable, for I see the weariness of many weeks of travel lie on you. I will have food and water brought to you."

Gilthas accompanied Alhana into the shelter. He ate the food that was offered, though Alhana could see he did so out of politeness rather than hunger. He drank the water with a relish he could not disguise, drank long and deep, as if he could never get enough.

"You have no idea how good this water tastes to me," he said, smiling. He glanced around. "But when am I going to have a chance to greet my cousin, Silvanoshei? We have never met, he and I. We heard the sad rumor that he had been slain by ogres and were glad to receive news that this was not true. I am eager to embrace him."

"I regret to say that Silvanoshei is not well, Gilthas," said Alhana. "He was brutally beaten by the Dark Knights when they seized Silvanost and barely escaped with his life. He keeps to his tent on the order of the healers and is not permitted to have any company."

She had told this lie so often that she was able to tell it now without a break in her voice. She could meet the young man's eyes and never falter. He believed her, for his face took on a look of concern.

"I am sorry to hear this. Please accept my wishes for his swift recovery."

Alhana smiled and changed the subject. "You have traveled far and on dangerous roads. Your journey must have been a hard and perilous one. What can I do for you, Nephew? May I call you that, although I am only your aunt by marriage?"

"I would be honored," said Gilthas, his voice warm. "You are all the family I have left now. You and Silvanoshei."

Alhana's eyes filled with sudden tears. He was all the family she had, at this moment, with Silvanoshei lost to her. She clasped his hand, and he held fast to hers. She was reminded of his father, Tanis Half-Elven. The memory was heartening, for the times in which they had known each other had been fraught with peril, yet they had overcome their foes and gone on to find peace, even if only for a short while.

"I come to ask a great boon of you, Aunt Alhana," he said. He gazed at her steadfastly. "I ask that you receive my people."

Alhana stared at him, bewildered, not understanding.

Gilthas gestured to the west. "Three days' ride from here, on the border of Silvanesti, a thousand exiles from Qualinesti wait to receive your permission to enter the land of our cousins. Our home is destroyed. The enemy occupies it. We lack the numbers to fight them. Someday," he said, his chin lifting and pride lighting his eyes, "we will return and drive the Dark Knights from our land and reclaim what is ours.

"But that day is not today," he continued, the light fading, darkened by shadow. "Nor is it tomorrow. We have traveled across the Plains of Dust. We would have died there but for the help of the people who call that terrible land home. We are weary and desperate. Our children look to us for comfort, and we have none to give them. We are exiles. We have nowhere to go. Humbly we come to you, who left so long ago, and humbly we ask that you take us in."

Alhana looked long at him. The tears that had burned in her eyes now slid unchecked down her cheeks.

"You weep for us," he said brokenly. "I am sorry to have brought this trouble to you."

"I weep for us all, Gilthas," Alhana said. "For the Qualinesti people, who have lost their homeland, and for the Silvanesti, who are fighting for ours. You will not find peace and sanctuary here in these forests, my poor nephew. You find us at war, battling for our very survival. You did not know this when you set out, did you?"

Gilthas shook his head.

"You know this now?" she asked.

"I know," he said. "I heard the news from the Plainspeople. I had hoped they exaggerated—"

"I doubt it. They are a people who see far and speak bluntly. I will tell you what is happening, and then you can decide if you want to join us."

Gilthas would have spoken, but Alhana raised her hand, silenced him. "Hear me out, Nephew." She hesitated a moment, underwent some inward struggle, then said, "You will hear from some of our people that my son was bewitched by this human girl, Mina, the leader of the Dark Knights. He was not the only Silvanesti to fall under her fatal spell. Our people sang songs of praise to her as she walked through the streets. She performed miracles of healing, but there was a price—not in coin but in souls. The One God wanted the souls of the elves to torment and enslave and devour. This One God is not a loving god, as some of our people mistakenly thought, but a god of deceit and vengeance and pain. Those elves who served the One God were taken away. We have no idea where. Those elves who refuse to serve the One God were killed outright or enslaved by the Dark Knights.

"The city of Silvanost is completely under the control of the Dark Knights. Their forces are not yet large enough to extend that control, and so we are able to maintain our existence here in the forests. We do what we can to fight against this dread foe, and we have saved many hundreds of our people from torture and death. We raid the prison camps and free the slaves. We harass the patrols. They fear our archers so much that no Dark Knight now dares set foot outside the city walls. All this we do, but it is not enough. We lack the forces needed to retake the city, and every day the Dark Knights add to its fortifications."

"Then our warriors will be a welcome addition," said Gilthas quietly.

Alhana lowered her eyes, shook her head. "No," she said, ashamed. "How could we ask that of you? The Silvanesti have treated you and your people with contempt and disdain all these years? How could we ask you to give your lives for our country?"

"You forget," said Gilthas, "that our people have no country. Our city lies in ruins. The same foe that rules your land rules ours." His fist clenched, his eyes flashed. "We are eager to take retribution. We will take back your land, then combine our forces to take back our own."

He leaned forward, his face alight. "Don't you see, Alhana? This may be the impetus we need to heal the old wounds, to once more unite our two nations."

"You are so young," Alhana said. "Too young to know that old wounds can fester so that the infection strikes to the very heart, turning it sick and putrid. You do not know that there are some who would see all of us fall rather than one of us rise. I tried to unite our people. I failed and this is what has come of my failure. I think it is too late. I think that nothing can save our people."

He gazed at her in consternation, clearly disturbed by her words.

Alhana rested her hand on his. "Maybe I am wrong. Perhaps your young eyes see more clearly. Bring your people into the safety of the forest. Then you must go before the Silvanesti and tell them of your plight and ask them to admit you into their lands."

"Ask them? Or do you mean beg them?" Gilthas rose, his expression cool. "We do not come before the Silvanesti as beggars."

"There, you see," Alhana said sadly. "You have been infected. Already, you jump to conclusions. You should ask the Silvanesti because it is politic to ask. That is all I meant." She sighed. "We corrupt our young, and thus perishes hope for anything better."

"You are sorrowful and weary and worried for your son. When he is well, he and I— Alhana," Gilthas said, alarmed, for she had sunk down upon a cushion and begun weeping bitterly. "What is wrong? Should I call someone? One of your ladies?"

"Kiryn," Alhana said in a choked voice. "Send for Kiryn."

Gilthas had no notion who this Kiryn was, but he ducked outside the shelter and informed one of the guards, who dispatched a runner. Gilthas went back inside the shelter, stood ill at ease, not knowing what to do or say to ease such wrenching grief.

A young elf entered the dwelling. He looked first at Alhana, who was struggling to regain her composure, then at Gilthas. Kiryn's face flushed with anger.

"Who are you? What have you said—"

"No, Kiryn!" Alhana raised her tearstained face. "He has done nothing. This is my nephew, Gilthas, Speaker of the Sun of the Qualinesti."

"I beg your pardon, Your Majesty," said Kiryn, bowing low. "I had no way of knowing. When I saw my queen—"

"I understand," said Gilthas. "Aunt Alhana, if I inadvertently said or did anything to cause you such pain—"

"Tell him, Kiryn," Alhana ordered in a tone that was low and terrible to hear. "Tell him the truth. He has a right . . . a need to know."

"My queen," said Kiryn, glancing at Gilthas uncertainly, "are you certain?"

Alhana closed her eyes, as if she would thankfully close them upon this world. "He has brought his people across the desert. They came to us for succor, for their capital city is destroyed, their land ravaged by the Dark Knights."

"Blessed *E'li!*" exclaimed Kiryn, calling, in his astonishment, upon the absent god Paladine or E'li, as the elves know him.

"Tell him," said Alhana, sitting with her face averted from them, hidden behind her hand.

Kiryn motioned Gilthas to draw near. "I tell you, Your Majesty, what only a few others know, and they have taken vows of secrecy. My cousin, Silvanoshei, is not wounded. He does not lie in his tent. He is gone."

"Gone?" Gilthas was puzzled. "Where has he gone? Has he been captured? Taken prisoner?"

"Yes," said Kiryn gravely, "but not the way you mean. He has become obsessed with a human girl, a leader of the Dark Knights called Mina. We believe that he has run off to join her."

"You *believe?*" Gilthas repeated. "You do not know for sure?"

Kiryn shrugged, helpless. "We know nothing for certain. We rescued him from the Dark Knights, who were going to put him to death. We were escaping into the wilderness when a magical sleep came over us. When we awoke, Silvanoshei was gone. We found the tracks of a horse's hooves. We tried to follow the hoofprints, but they entered the Than-Thalas River, and although we searched upstream and down, we could not find any more tracks. It was as if the horse had wings."

Alhana spoke, her voice muffled. "I have sent my most trusted friend and advisor after my son, to bring him back. I have told the Silvanesti people nothing about this. I ask you to say nothing of this to anyone."

Gilthas was troubled. "I don't understand. Why do you keep his disappearance secret?"

Alhana lifted her head. Her eyes were swollen with her grief, red-rimmed. "Because the Silvanesti people have taken him to their hearts. He is their king, and they follow him, when they would not willingly follow me. All I do, I do in his name."

"You mean you make the hard decisions and face the danger, while your son, who should be sharing your burden, chases after a petticoat," Gilthas began sternly.

"Do not criticize him!" Alhana flared. "What do you know of

what he has endured? This female is a witch. She has ensorcelled him. He does not know what he is doing."

"Silvanoshei was a good king until he had the misfortune to meet Mina," said Kiryn defensively. "The people came to love and respect him. He will be a good king when this spell is broken."

"I thought you should know the truth, Gilthas," Alhana said stiffly, "since you have responsibilities of your own you must bear, decisions you must make. I ask only that you do as Kiryn does, respect my wishes and say nothing of this to anyone. Pretend, as we pretend, that Silvanoshei is here with us."

Her tone was cold, her eyes beseeching. Gilthas would have given much to have been able to ease her pain, to lift her burdens. But, as she said, he bore burdens himself. He had responsibilities, and they were to his people.

"I have never yet lied to the Qualinesti, Aunt Alhana," he said, as gently as he could. "I will not start now. They left their homeland on my word, they followed me into the desert. They have given their lives and the lives of their children into my hands. They trust me, and I will not betray that trust. Not even for you, whom I love and honor."

Alhana rose to her feet, her fists clenched at her sides. "If you do this, you will destroy all that I have worked for. We might as well surrender to the Dark Knights now." Her fists unclenched, and he saw that her hands trembled. "Give me some time, Nephew. That is all I ask. My son will return soon. I know it!"

Gilthas shifted his gaze from her to Kiryn, looked long and intently at the young elf. Kiryn said nothing, but his eyes flickered. He was clearly uncomfortable.

Alhana saw Gilthas's dilemma.

"He is too kind, too polite, too mindful of my pain to speak the words that must be burning on his tongue," she said herself. "If he could, he would say to me, *This is not my doing. I am not at fault. This is your son's doing. Silvanoshei has failed his people. I will not follow in those same footsteps.*"

Alhana was angry with Gilthas, jealous of him and proud of him, all in the same scalding moment. She envied Laurana suddenly, envied her death that brought blessed silence to the turmoil, an end to pain, an end to despair. Laurana had died a hero's death, fighting to save her people and her country. She had left behind a legacy of which she could be proud, a son she could honor.

"I tried to do what was right," Alhana said to herself in misery, "but it all has ended up so terribly wrong."

Her loved husband Porthios had vanished and was presumed to be dead. Her son, her hope for the future, had run away to leave her to face that future alone. She might tell herself he had been ensorcelled, but deep in her heart, she knew better. He was spoiled, selfish, too easily swayed by passions she had never had the heart to check. She had failed her husband, she had failed her son. Her pride refused to let her admit it.

Pride would be her downfall. Her pride had been wounded when her people turned against her. Her pride had caused her to attack the shield, to try to reenter a land that didn't want her. Now her pride forced her to lie to her people.

Samar and Kiryn had both counseled against it. Both had urged her to tell the truth, but her pride could not stomach it. Not her pride as a queen, but her pride as a mother. She had failed as a mother and now all would see that failure. She could not bear for people to regard her with pity. That, more than anything else, was the true reason she had lied.

She had hoped that Silvanoshei would come back, admit that he had been wrong, ask to be forgiven. If that had happened, she could have overlooked his downfall. She knew now after reading Samar's letter that Silvanoshei would never come back to her, not of his own free will. Samar would have to drag him back like an errant schoolboy.

She looked up to find Gilthas looking at her, his expression sympathetic, grave. In that moment, he was his father. Tanis Half-Elven had often looked at her with that same expression as she underwent some inward battle, fought against her pride.

"I will keep your secret, Aunt Alhana," Gilthas said. His voice was cool, he was clearly unhappy with what he was doing. "As long as I can."

"Thank you, Gilthas," she said, grateful and ashamed for having to be grateful. Her pride! Her damnable pride. "Silvanoshei will return. He will hear of our plight and come back. Perhaps he is already on his way."

She pressed her hand over her bosom, over Samar's letter that said entirely the opposite. Lying had become so easy, so very easy.

"I hope so," said Gilthas somberly.

He took her hand in his own, kissed it respectfully. "I am sorry for your trouble, Aunt Alhana. I am sorry to have added to your trouble. But if this brings about the reunification of our two nations, then someday we will look back upon the heartbreak and turmoil and say that it was worth it."

She tried to smile, but the stiffness of her lips made her mouth twitch. She said nothing, and so in silence they parted.

"Go with him," she told Kiryn, who remained behind. "See to it that he and his people are made welcome."

"Your Majesty—" Kiryn began uneasily.

"I know what you are going to say, Kiryn. Do not say it. All will be well. You will see."

After both had left, she stood in the doorway of the shelter, thinking of Gilthas.

"Such pretty dreams," she said softly. "The dreams of youth. Once I had pretty dreams. Now, like my pretty gowns, they hang about me in rags and in tatters. May yours fit better, Gilthas, and last longer."

4

Waiting and Waiting

eneral Dogah, leader of the Dark Knights in Silvanost, was having his own problems. The Dark Knights used blue dragons as scouts, patrolling the skies above the thick and tangled forests. If the dragons caught sight of movement on the ground, they swooped down and, with their lightning breath, laid waste to entire tracts of forest land.

These dragon scouts saw the large gathering of people in the desert but had no idea they were Qualinesti. The scouts thought them the barbarians, the Plainspeople, fleeing the onslaught of the dragon overlord Sable. General Dogah wondered what to do about this migration. He had no orders concerning the Plainspeople. His forces were limited, his hold on Silvanost tenuous at best. He did not want to start war on another front. He dispatched a courier on dragonback with an urgent message for Mina, telling her about the situation and asking for orders.

The courier had some difficulty locating Mina, for he flew first to Solanthus, only to find that her army had left there and was on the march for Sanction.

After another day's flying, the courier located her. He sped back with this reply, short and terse.

General Dogah
  These are not Plainspeople. They are Qualinesti exiles. Destroy them.

  In the name of the One God,
                              Mina

Dogah sent off his dragonriders to do just that, only to find, in the interim, that the Qualinesti had disappeared. No trace of them could be found anywhere. He received this report with a bitter curse, for he knew what it meant. The Qualinesti had managed to escape into the forests of Silvanesti and were now beyond his reach.

Here were yet more elves to attack his patrols and fire flaming arrows at his supply ships. To add to his woes, the dragons began bringing reports that the ogres, long enraged at the Knights for stealing their land, were massing on the northern Silvanesti border that adjoined Blöde, undoubtedly hoping to seize some elven land in return.

And to make matters worse, Dogah was having morale trouble. So long as Mina had been around to enchant them and entrance them, the soldiers were committed to her cause, dedicated and enthusiastic followers. But Mina had been gone many long weeks now. The soldiers and the Knights who commanded them were isolated in the middle of a strange and unfriendly realm, where enemies lurked in every shadow—and Silvanesti was a land of shadows. Arrows came out of the skies to slay them. Even the vegetation seemed intent on trying to kill them. Tree roots tripped them, dead limbs dropped on their heads, forests lured them into tangles from which few ever returned.

Not a single supply ship had sailed down the river in the past week. The elves set fire to those that made the attempt. The soldiers had no food other than what the elves ate, and no human could subsist on leaves and grass for long. The meat-hungry humans dared not enter the woods to hunt, for, as they soon discovered, every creature in the forest was a spy for the elves.

The elves of the city of Silvanost, seemingly cowed by the might of the Dark Knights, were growing bolder. None of Dogah's men dared venture into the city alone lest they risk being found dead in an alley. The men began to grouse and grumble.

Dogah issued orders to torture more elves, but such entertainment could keep his troops occupied for only so long. He was fortunate in that there were no desertions. This was not due to loyalty, as he well knew, but to the fact that the men were too terrified of the elves and the forest that sheltered them to flee.

Now, with the knowledge that a thousand more elves had joined those already in the forest, the mutinous rumblings grew loud as thunder, so that Dogah could not remain deaf to them. He himself began to doubt. When he could not see himself reassuringly reflected in her amber eyes, his trust in Mina started to wane.

He dispatched another urgent message to Mina, telling her that the Qualinesti had escaped his best efforts to destroy them, that morale was in the privies, and that unless something happened to change the situation, he would have no choice but to pull out of Silvanesti or face mutiny.

Dark-bearded and, these days, dark-faced and gloomy, the short, stocky Dogah sat alone (he had very little trust even in his own bodyguards these days) in his quarters, drank elven wine that he wished mightily was a liquor far stronger, and waited for Mina's reply.

The Qualinesti entered the forest to be coolly welcomed by their long-estranged cousins, the Silvanesti. A polite cousinly kiss of greeting was exchanged, and then spears and arrows were thrust into Qualinesti hands. If they were going to relocate to Silvanesti, they had better be prepared to fight for it.

The Qualinesti were only too happy to oblige. They saw this

as a chance to avenge themselves on those who had seized their own realm and were now laying waste to it.

"When do we attack?" they demanded eagerly.

"Any day now," was the response from the Silvanesti. "We are waiting for the right time."

"Waiting for the right time?" the Lioness asked her husband. "For what 'right time' do we wait? I have talked to the scouts and spies. We outnumber the Dark Knights who are bottled up in Silvanost. Their morale sinks faster than a shipwrecked dwarf in full battle armor. Now is the opportune time to attack them!"

The two spoke in the shelter that had been provided for them—a hutch made of woven willow branches on the side of a bubbling stream. The space was small and cramped, but they were luckier than most of the elves, for they had a place of their own (due to Gilthas's royal rank) and some privacy. Most of the elves slept in the boughs of living trees or the hollowed-out boles of dead ones, inside caves or simply lying in the grass under the stars. The Qualinesti had no complaints. After their trek through the desert, they asked for nothing more than to sleep on crisp-smelling pine needles, lulled by the gentle murmur of the falling rain.

"You tell me nothing that I don't already know," said Gilthas morosely. He had taken to wearing clothing more typical of his people—the long, belted tunic, woollen shirt, and stockings in woodland colors. But he had folded neatly and put away safely the coverings of the desert.

"There are problems, however. The Silvanesti are spread out all over the land. Some are stationed along the river to disrupt the Dark Knights' supply lines. Others hide near the city of Silvanost, to make certain that any patrol that has nerve enough to leave the city does not return intact. Still others are scattered along the borders . . ."

"The wind, the hawk, the squirrel carry messages," returned the Lioness. "If the orders were sent now, most of the Silvanesti could be gathered outside Silvanost in a week's time. Days go by, and the orders are not given. We must skulk about in the forest and wait. Wait for what?"

Gilthas knew, but he could not answer. He kept silent, was forced let his wife fume.

"We know what will happen if the opportunity is missed! Thus did the Dark Knights take over our homeland during the Chaos War. The same will be true of the Silvanesti, if we don't act now. Is it your cousin, Silvanoshei, who holds back? He is young. Probably he doesn't understand. You must speak to him, Gilthas, explain to him—"

She knew her husband well. At the look on her face, the words clotted on her tongue.

The Lioness eyed him narrowly. "What is it, Gilthas? What's wrong? Something about Silvanoshei, isn't it?"

Gilthas looked at her ruefully. "Am I so transparent? Kings should be cloaked in inscrutability and mystery."

"My husband," said the Lioness, unable to keep from laughing, "you are inscrutable and mysterious as a crystal goblet. The truth inside you is plain for all the world to see."

"The truth . . ." Gilthas made a wry face. "The truth is, my dear, that Silvanoshei could not lead his people in a three-legged race, much less lead them to war. He is nowhere near here, nowhere near Silvanesti. I promised Alhana I would say nothing, but now a fortnight has passed and it seems to me that the time for lying has come to an end. Although"—Gilthas shook his head—"I fear that the truth will do more harm than good. The Silvanesti follow Alhana now only because she speaks in the name of her son. Some still view her with suspicion, see her as a 'dark elf.' If they find out the truth, that she has been lying to them, I fear they will never believe her again, never listen to her."

The Lioness looked into her husband's eyes. "That leaves you, Gilthas."

Now it was his turn to laugh. "I am everything that they despise, my dear. A Qualinesti with human blood thrown in. They will not follow me."

"Then you must persuade Alhana to tell her people the truth."

"I don't believe she can. She has told the lie so long that, for her, the lie has become the truth."

"So what do we do?" the Lioness demanded. "Live here in the forest until we take root along with the trees? We Qualinesti could attack the Dark Knights—"

"No, my dear," said Gilthas firmly. "The Silvanesti have permitted us to enter their homeland, that much is true, but they view us with suspicion, nonetheless. There are those who think we are here to usurp their homeland. For the Qualinesti to attack Silvanost—"

"The Qualinesti are *not* attacking Silvanost. The Qualinesti are attacking the Dark Knights *in* Silvanost," argued the Lioness.

"That is not how the Silvanesti will view it. You know that as well as I do."

"So we sit and do nothing."

"I do not know what else we can do," said Gilthas somberly. "The one person who could have united and rallied his people has been lured away. Now the only people left to lead the elves are a dark elf queen and a half-human king."

"Yet sooner or later someone must take the lead," the Lioness said. "We must follow someone."

"And where would that someone lead them?" Gilthas asked somberly, "except to our own destruction."

General Dogah drank his way through several barrels of wine. His problems increased daily. Six soldiers ordered to stand guard on the battlements refused to obey. Their officer threatened them with the lash. They attacked him, beat him severely, and ran off, hoping to lose themselves in the streets of Silvanost. Dogah sent his troops after the deserters, intending to string them up to serve as examples to the rest.

The elves saved him the cost of rope. The bodies of the six were delivered to the castle. Each had died in some gruesome, grotesque manner. A note found on one, scrawled in Common, read, *A gift for the One God.*

That night, Dogah sent another messenger to Mina, pleading for either reinforcements or permission to withdraw. Although, he thought glumly, he had no idea where he would withdraw to. Everywhere he looked, he saw enemies.

Two days later, the messenger finally returned.

General Dogah
    Hold your ground. Help is on the way.

    In the name of the One God.
                              Mina

That wasn't much comfort.

Every day, Dogah cautiously mounted the walls of Silvanost, peered out to the north, the south, the east, and the west. The elves were out there. They had him surrounded. Every day, he expected the elves to attack.

Days passed, and the elves did nothing.

5

The Hedge Maze

asslehoff Burrfoot was, at that moment in time feeling extremely put-out, put-upon, dizzy, and sick to his stomach. Of the three feelings, the dizzy feeling predominated, so that he was finding it hard to think clearly. Plain, wooden floors and good, hard ground had once seemed mundane objects as far as he was concerned, but now Tasslehoff thought fondly, wistfully, longingly of ground or floor or any solid surface beneath his feet.

He also thought longingly of his feet returning to their proper place as feet and not thinking themselves his head, which they were continually doing, for he always looked for them below and found them above. The only good thing to happen to Tasslehoff was that Conundrum had screamed himself hoarse and could now make only feeble croaking sounds.

Tas blamed everything on the Device of Time Journeying. He wondered sadly if this whirling and turning and dropping in on various points of time was going to go on eternally, and he was a bit daunted at the prospect. Then it occurred to him that sooner or later, the device was bound to land him back in the time where he'd be stepped on by Chaos. All in all, not a bright prospect.

Such thoughts ran through his head, which was constantly whirling and twirling through time. He thought them through as best he could, given the dizzy feeling, and suddenly a fresh thought popped in. Perhaps the owner of the voice that he heard in his ear and the hand that he felt on his shoulder could do something about this endless whirling. He made up his mind that the moment they landed again, he would do everything in his power to see the hand's owner.

Which he did. The very minute he felt firm ground (blessed ground!) beneath his feet, he stumbled around (rather wobbly) to look behind him.

He saw Conundrum and Conundrum's hand, but that was the wrong hand. No one else was about, and Tas immediately knew why. He and the gnome were standing in what appeared to be a field blackened by fire. Some distance away, crystal buildings caught the last glow of evening, glimmered orange or purple or gold as the dying rays of the sun painted them. The air was still tainted with the smell of burning, although the fire that had consumed the vegetation had been put out some time ago. He could hear voices, but they were far distant. From somewhere came the sweet and piercing music of a flute.

Tasslehoff had the vague notion that he'd been here before. Or maybe he'd been here after before. What with all the time jumping, he wasn't certain about anything anymore. The place looked familiar, and he was about to set off in search of someone who could tell him where he was, when Conundrum gave a wheezing gasp.

"The Hedge Maze!"

Tas looked down and looked sideways, and he realized that Conundrum was right. They were standing in what remained of the Hedge Maze after the red dragons had destroyed it with their fiery breath. The walls of leaves were burnt down to the ground.

The paths that wound and twisted between them—leading those who walked the paths deeper into the maze—were laid bare. The maze was a maze no longer. Tas could see the pattern clearly, the white paths standing out starkly against the black. He could see every twist, every turning, every whorl, every jog, every dead end. He saw the way to the heart of the Hedge Maze and he saw the way out. The silver stair stood naked, exposed. He could see plainly now that it led up and up to nowhere, and with a queasy flutter of the stomach, he remembered his leap off the top and his dive into the smoke and the flame.

"Oh, my!" whispered Conundrum, and Tas remembered that mapping the Hedge Maze had been the gnome's Life Quest.

"Conundrum," said Tas somberly. "I—"

"You can see everything," said the gnome.

"I know," said Tas, patting the gnome's hand. "And I—"

"I could walk from one end to the other," said Conundrum, "and never get lost."

"Maybe you could find some other line of work," Tas suggested, wanting to be helpful. "Although I'd stay away from the repair of magical devices—"

"It's perfect!" Conundrum breathed. His eyes filled with happy tears.

"What?" Tas asked, startled. "What's perfect?"

"Where's my parchment?" Conundrum demanded. "Where's my ink bottle and my brush?"

"I don't have an ink bottle—"

Conundrum glared at him. "Then what good are you? Never mind," he added huffily. "Ah, ha! Charcoal! That'll do."

He plopped down on the burnt ground. Spreading out the hem of his brown robes, he picked up a charred stick and began slowly and laboriously tracing the route of the burnt Hedge Maze on the fabric.

"This is so much easier," he muttered to himself. "I don't know why I didn't think of it sooner."

Tasslehoff felt the familiar touch of the hand on his shoulder. The jewels of the Device of Time Journeying began to sparkle and glitter with golden and purple light, a reflection of the setting sun.

"Goodbye, Conundrum," Tas called, as the paths of the Hedge Maze began to swirl in his vision.

The gnome didn't look up. He was concentrating on his map.

6

The Strange Passenger

A t a small port in southern Estwilde, the strange passenger disembarked from the ship on which he had sailed across New Sea. The captain was relieved to be rid of his mysterious passenger and more relieved to be rid of the passenger's fiery-tempered horse. Neither the captain nor any of the crew knew anything about the passenger. No one ever saw his face, which he kept hidden beneath the hood of his cloak.

Such seclusion had raised much speculation among the crew about the nature of their passenger, most of it wild and all of it wrong. Some guessed the passenger was a woman, disguised as a man, for the cabin boy had once caught a glimpse of a hand that, according to him, was slender and delicate in appearance. Others suspected him to be a wizard of some sort for no other reason than that wizards were known to wear hooded cloaks and that they were always mysterious and never to be trusted. Only one sailor stated that he believed the passenger to be an elf, hiding his face because he knew that the humans aboard ship would not take kindly to one of his race.

The other sailors scoffed at this notion and, since the conversation was being held at dinner, they threw weevily biscuits at the head of the man who made it. He offered his hunch as a wager, and everyone took him up on it. He became a wealthy man, relatively speaking, at the end of the voyage, when a gust of wind blew back the passenger's hood as he was leading his horse down the gangplank to reveal that he was, indeed, an elf.

No one bothered to ask the elf what brought him to this part of Ansalon. The sailors didn't care where the elf had been or where he was going. They were only too happy to have him off their ship, it being well known among seafarers that the sea elves—those who purportedly make their homes in the watery deeps—will try to scuttle any ship carrying one of their land-bound brethren in order to persuade them to live the remainder of their lives below the sea.

As for Silvanoshei, he never looked back, once he had set foot on land. He had no care for the ship or the sailors, although both had sped him across New Sea at a truly remarkable rate of speed. The wind had blown fair from the day they set forth, never ceasing. There had been no storms—a miracle this late in the season. Yet no matter how fast the ship sailed, it had not sailed fast enough for Silvanoshei.

He was overjoyed when he first set foot on land, for this was the land on which Mina walked. Every step brought him closer to that loved face, that adored voice. He had no idea where she was, but the horse knew. Her horse, which she had sent for him. The moment he set foot on shore, Silvanoshei mounted Foxfire, and they galloped off so fast that he never knew the name of the small port in which they'd landed.

They traveled northwest. Silvanoshei would have ridden day and night, if he could, but the horse (miraculous animal though it was) was a mortal horse and required food and rest, as did Silvanoshei himself. At first he bitterly grudged the time they must spend resting, but he was rewarded for his sacrifice.

The very first night away from the ship, Silvanoshei fell in with a merchant caravan bound for the very same port town he'd recently left.

Many humans would have shunned a lone elf met by chance on the road, but merchants view every person as a potential customer and thus they tend not to be prejudiced against any race (except kender). Elven coin being just as good (or oftentimes better) than human, they cordially invited the young elf, whose clothing, though travel-stained, was of fine quality, to share their repast. Silvanoshei was on the verge of loftily refusing—he wanted to do nothing but sit by himself and dream of amber eyes—when he heard one of them speak the name, "Mina."

"I thank you gentlemen and ladies for your hospitality," said Silvanoshei, hurrying over to sit by their roaring fire. He even accepted the tin plate of dubious stew they offered him, although he didn't eat it, but surreptitiously dumped it in the bushes behind him.

He still wore the cloak he had worn on board ship, for the weather this time of year was cool. He removed the hood, however, and the humans were lost in admiration for this handsome youth, with his wine-colored eyes, charming smile and a voice that was sweet and melodious. Seeing that he'd eaten his stew quickly, one of the women offered him more.

"You're as thin as last year's mattress," she said, filling a plate, which he politely declined.

"You mentioned the name 'Mina,' " Silvanoshei said, trying to sound casual, though his heart beat wildly. "I know someone of that name. She wouldn't be an elf maid, by chance?"

At this they all laughed heartily. "Not unless elf maids wear armor these days," said one.

"I heard tell of an elf maid who wore armor," protested another, who seemed of an argumentative nature. "I recall my grandfather singing a song about her. Back in the days of the War of the Lance, it was."

"Bah! Your grandfather was an old souse," said a third. "He never went anywhere, but lived and died in the bars of Flotsam."

"Still, he's right," said one of the merchant's wives. "There was an elf maid who fought in the great war. Her name was Loony-tarry."

"Lunitari was the old goddess of magic, my dear," said her friend, another one of the wives, with a nudge of her elbow. "The ones who went away and left us to the mercy of these huge, monstrous dragons."

"No, I'm sure it wasn't," said the first wife, offended. "It was Loony-tarry, and she slew one of the foul beasts with a gnomish device called a dragonlunch. So called because she rammed it down the beast's gullet. And I wish another such would come and do the same to these new dragons."

"Well, from what we hear, this Mina plans to do just that," said the first merchant, trying to make peace between the two women, who were muttering huffily at each other.

"Have you seen her?" Silvanoshei asked, his heart on his lips. "Have you seen this Mina?"

"No, but she's all anyone's talking about in the towns we've passed through."

"Where is she?" Silvanoshei asked. "Is she close by?"

"She's marching along the road to Sanction. You can't miss her. She rides with an army of Dark Knights," answered the argumentative man dourly.

"Don't you take that amiss, young sir," said one of the wives. "Mina may wear black armor, but from what we hear, she has a heart of pure gold."

"Everywhere we go, we see some child she's healed or some cripple she's made to walk," said her friend.

"She's going to break the siege of Sanction," added the merchant, "and give us our port back. Then we can quit trekking halfway across the continent to sell our wares."

"And none of you think this is wrong?" said the argumentative man angrily. "Our own Solamnic Knights are in Sanction, trying to hang onto it, and you're cheering on this leader of our enemies."

This precipitated a lively discussion, which led at last to the majority of the group being in favor of whichever side would at last open up the ports to shipping once again. The Solamnics had tried to break out of Sanction and failed. Let this Mina and her Dark Knights see what they could do.

Shocked and horrified to think of Mina placing herself in such danger, Silvanoshei slipped away to lie awake half the night sick with fear for her. She must not attack Sanction! She must be dissuaded from such a dangerous course of action.

He was up and away with the first light of dawn. He had no need to urge the horse. Foxfire was as anxious to return to his mistress as was his rider. The two pushed themselves to the limit, the name "Mina" sounding with every hoofbeat, every beat of Silvanoshei's heart.

Several days after their encounter with Silvanoshei, the merchant caravan arrived in a port town. Leaving their husbands to set up camp, the two women went to visit the marketplace, where they were stopped by another elf, who was loitering about the stalls, accosting all new-comers.

This elf was an "uppity" elf, as one of the wives stated. He spoke to them, as one said, "like we were a bit of something that dropped in the dog's dish."

Still, they took the elf's money readily enough and told him what he wanted to know in exchange for it.

Yes, they had run into a young elf dressed like a fine gentleman on the road. A polite, well-spoken young man. Not like *some*, said the merchant's wife with a telling look. She could not recall where he said he'd been going, but she did remember that they had talked about Sanction. Yes, she supposed it was possible that he might be going to Sanction, but she thought it just as possible he might be going to the moon, for all she knew of the matter.

The older elf, whose face was grim and manner chill, paid them off and left them, traveling the same road as Silvanoshei.

The two wives knew immediately what to make of it.

"That young man was his son and has run away from home," said the first, nodding sagely.

"I don't blame him," said the second, looking after the elf irately. "Such a sour-faced old puss as that."

"I wish now I'd thrown him off the trail," said the first. "It would have served him right."

"You did what you thought was best, my dear," said her friend, craning her neck to see how many silver coins had been taken in. "It's not up to us to get involved in the affairs of the likes of such outlandish folk."

Linking arms, the two headed for the nearest tavern to spend the elf's money.

7

Faith's Convicts

ina's forces moved relentlessly, inexorably toward Sanction. They continued to march unopposed, met no resistance on the way. Mina did not ride with her legions but traveled on ahead of them, entering cities, villages, and towns to work her miracles, spread the word of the One God, and round up all the kender. Many wondered at this last. Most assumed she meant to slay the kender (and few would have been sorry), but she only questioned them, each and every one, asking about a particular kender who called himself Tasslehoff Burrfoot.

Many Tasslehoffs presented themselves to her, but none was ever The Tasslehoff Burrfoot. Once they had all been questioned, Mina would then release the kender and send them on their way, with promise of rich reward should they find this Burrfoot.

Every day, kender arrived at the camp in droves, bringing with them Tasslehoff Burrfoots of every shape and description in hopes of receiving the reward. These Tasslehoffs included not only kender but dogs, pigs, a donkey, a goat, and once an extremely irate and hung-over dwarf. Trussed and bound, he was dragged into camp by ten kender, who proclaimed he was The Tasslehoff Burrfoot trying to disguise himself in a false beard.

The humans and the kender of Solamnia and Throt and East-wilde were as enchanted with Mina as the elves of Silvanesti had been. They viewed her with deep suspicion when she rode in and followed after her with prayers and songs when she left. Castle after castle, town after town fell to Mina's charm, not her might.

Gerard had long ago given up hoping that the Solamnic Knights would attack. He guessed that Lord Tasgall intended to concentrate his efforts in Sanction rather than try to halt Mina along the way. Gerard could have told them they were wasting their time. Every day, Mina's army grew larger, as more and more men and women flocked to her standard and the worship of the One God. Although the pace her officers set was fast and the troops were forced to be up with the dawn and march until nightfall, morale was high. The march had more the feeling of a wedding procession, hastening forward to joyous celebration, rather than marching toward battle, carnage, and death.

Gerard still did not see much of Odila. She traveled in Mina's retinue and was often away from the main body of the force. Either she went by consent or she was forced to go, Gerard could not be sure, for she carefully avoided any contact with him. He knew that she did this for his own safety, but he had no one else to talk to, and he felt he would have risked the danger just for the chance to share his thoughts—dark and pessimistic as they were—with someone who would understand.

One day Gerard's contemplations were interrupted by the minotaur, Galdar. Discovering Gerard riding in the rear, the minotaur tersely ordered him to take his place at the front with the rest of the Knights. Gerard had no choice but to obey, and he spent the rest of the march traveling under the minotaur's watchful eye.

Why Galdar didn't kill him was a mystery to Gerard, but then Galdar himself was a mystery. Gerard felt Galdar's beady eyes on him often, but the look in them was not so much sinister as it was speculative.

Gerard kept to himself, rebuffing the attempts by his "comrades" to make friends. He could not very well share the cheerful mood of the Dark Knights nor participate in discussions of how many Solamnics they were going to gut or how many Solamnic heads they were going to mount on pikes.

Because of his morose silence and perverse nature, Gerard soon acquired the reputation as a dour, unsociable man, who was little liked by his "fellow" Knights. He didn't care. He was glad to be left alone.

Or perhaps not so alone. Whenever he roamed off by himself, he would often look up to find Galdar shadowing him.

The days stretched into weeks. The army traveled through Estwilde, wound north through Throt, entered the Khalkist Mountains through the Throtyl Gap, then headed due south for Sanction. As they left the more populated lands behind, Mina returned to the army, riding in the vanguard with Galdar, who now paid far more attention to Mina than he did to Gerard, for which Gerard was grateful.

Odila also returned, but she rode in the rear, in the wagon carrying the amber sarcophagus. Gerard would have liked to have found a way to talk to her, but the one time he lagged behind, hoping he wouldn't be missed, Galdar sought him out and ordered him to maintain his position in the ranks.

Then the day came that a mountain range appeared on the horizon. They saw it first as a dark blue smudge, which Gerard mistook for a bank of dark blue storm clouds. As the army drew closer, he could see plumes of smoke drifting from the summits. He looked upon the active volcanoes known as the Lords of Doom—the guardians of Sanction.

"Not long now," he thought, and his heart ached for the defenders of Sanction, watching and waiting. They would be confident, certain their defenses would hold. They had held for over a year now; why should they expect anything different?

He wondered if they'd heard rumors about the horrific army of the dead that had attacked Solanthus. Even if they had, would they believe what they heard? Gerard doubted it. He would not have believed such tales himself. He wasn't certain, thinking back on it, that he believed it even now. The entire battle had the unreal disconnection of a fever dream. Did the army of the dead march with Mina? Gerard sometimes tried to catch a glimpse of them, but, if the dead were with them, this fell ally traveled silently and unseen.

Mina's army entered the foothills of the Khalkists and began the climb that would lead them to the pass through the Lords of Doom. In a valley, Mina halted their march, telling them they would remain here for several days. She had a journey to make, she said, and, in her absence, the army would prepare for the push through the mountains. Everyone was ordered to have armor and weapons in good condition, ready for battle. The blacksmith set up his forge, and he and his assistants spent the days mending and making. Hunting parties were sent out to bring in fresh meat.

They had only just set up camp on the first day when the elf prisoner was captured.

He was dragged into camp by several of the outriders who patrolled the army's flanks, scouring the area for any sign of the enemy.

Gerard was at the smith's, having his sword mended and finding it strange to think that the very enemy who might soon be spitted on that sword was now working hard to fix it. He had determined that he would take the opportunity of Mina's absence to try to convince Odila to escape with him. If she refused, he would ride off for Sanction alone, to take the news to them of the approaching enemy. He had no idea how he was going to manage this, how he was going to elude Galdar or, once he reached Sanction, how he was going to pass through the hordes of the enemy who had the city surrounded, but he figured he would deal with all that later.

Bored with waiting, tired of his own gloomy thoughts, he heard a commotion and walked over to see what was going on.

The elf was mounted on a red horse of fiery temper and disposition, for no one was able to get near the beast. The elf himself seemed uneasy on his mount, for when he reached down a hand to try to sooth the animal, the horse flung his head about and bit at him. The elf snatched his hand back and made no further move to touch the horse.

A crowd had gathered around the elf. Some knew him, apparently, for they began to jeer, bowing before him mockingly, saluting the "king of Silvanesti" with raucous laughter. Gerard eyed the elf curiously. He was dressed in finery that might have suited a king, though his cloak of fine wool was travel-stained and his silken hose were torn, his gold-embroided doublet worn and frayed. He paid no attention to his detractors. He searched the camp for someone, as did the horse.

The crowd parted, as it always did whenever Mina walked among them. At the sight of her, the eyes of both horse and rider fixed on her with rapt attention.

The horse whinnied and shook his head. Mina came to Foxfire, laid her head against his, ran her hand over his muzzle. He draped his head over her shoulder and closed his eyes. His journey ended, his duty done, he was home, and he was content. Mina patted the horse and looked up at the elf.

"Mina," said the young man, and her name, as he spoke it, was red with his heart's blood. He slid down off the horse's back, stood before her. "Mina, you sent for me. I am here."

Such aching pain and love was in the elf's voice that Gerard was embarrassed for the young man. That his love was not reciprocated was obvious. Mina paid no attention to the elf, continued to lavished her attention on the horse. Her disregard for the young man did not go unnoticed. Mina's Knights grinned at one another. Bawdy jests were whispered about. One man laughed out loud, but his laughter ceased abruptly when Mina shifted her amber eyes to him. Ducking his head, his face red, he slunk away.

Mina finally acknowledged the elf's presence. "You are welcome, Your Majesty. All is in readiness for your arrival. A tent for you has been prepared next to mine. You have come in good time. Soon we march on Sanction to lay claim to that sacred city in the name of the One God. You will be witness to our triumph."

"You can't go to Sanction, Mina!" said the elf. "It's too dangerous . . ." His words faltered. Glancing around the crowd of black-armored humans, he seemed to have only just now realized that he had ridden into a camp of his enemies.

Mina saw and understood his unease. She cast a stern look around the crowd, quelled the jokes and silenced the laughter.

"Let it be known throughout the army that the king of the elves of the land of Silvanesti is my guest. He is to be treated with the same respect you treat me. I make each and every one of you responsible for his safety and well being."

Mina's gaze went searchingly about the camp and, to Gerard's great discomfiture, halted when it reached him.

"Sir Gerard, come forward," Mina ordered.

Aware that every man and woman in camp was staring at him, Gerard felt the hot blood suffuse his face, even as a cold qualm gripped his gut. He had no idea why he was being singled out. He had no choice but to obey.

Saluting, he kept quiet, waited.

"Sir Gerard," said Mina gravely, "I appoint you as special bodyguard for the elven king. His care and comfort are your responsibility. I choose you because you have had considerable experience dealing with elves. As I recall, you served in Qualinesti before coming to us."

Gerard could not speak, he was so astonished, primarily at Mina's cursed cleverness. He was her avowed enemy, a Solamnic Knight come to spy on her. She knew that. And because he was a Solamnic Knight, he was the only person in her army to whom she could entrust the life of the young elven king. Set a prisoner to guard a prisoner. A unique concept, yet one that must work in Gerard's case.

"I am sorry, but I fear that this duty will keep you out of the battle for Sanction, Sir Gerard," Mina continued. "It would never do for His Majesty to be exposed to that danger, and so you will remain with him in the rear, with the baggage train. But there will be other battles for you, Sir Gerard. Of that, I am certain."

Gerard could do nothing but salute again. Mina turned her back, walked away. The elf stood staring after her, his face bleak and pale. Many in the army remained to stare and, now that Mina had departed, resume their gibes at the elf's expense. Some started to grow downright nasty.

"Come on," said Gerard and, seeing that the elf was not going to move unless prompted, he grabbed hold of the elf's arm and hauled him off bodily. Gerard marched the elf through the camp toward the area where Mina had raised her tent. Sure enough, another tent had been set up a short distance from hers. The tent was empty, awaiting the arrival of this strange guest.

"What is your name?" Gerard asked grumpily, not feeling kindly disposed toward this elf, who had further complicated his life.

The elf didn't hear at first. He kept looking about, trying to find Mina.

Gerard asked again, this time raising his voice.

"My name is Silvanoshei," the elf replied. He spoke Common fluently, though his accent was so thick it was hard to understand him. The elf looked directly at Gerard, the first time he'd done so since Gerard had been put in charge of him.

"I don't recognize you. You weren't with her in Silvanesti, were you?"

No need to specify which "her" he was talking about. Gerard could see plainly that for this young man, there was only one "her" in the world.

"No," said Gerard shortly. "I wasn't."

"Where has she gone now? What is she doing?" Silvanoshei asked, looking about again. "When will she come back?"

Mina's tent and those of her bodyguards stood apart from the main camp, off to themselves. The noise of the camp faded behind them. The show was over. The Knights and soldiers went back to the business of making ready for war.

"Are you really king of the Silvanesti elves?" Gerard asked.

"Yes," said Silvanoshei absently, preoccupied by his search, "I am."

"Then what in the Abyss are you doing here?" Gerard demanded bluntly.

At that moment, Silvanoshei saw Mina. She was far distant, galloping on Foxfire across the valley. The two were alone, happy together, racing the wind with wild abandon. Seeing the pain in the young man's eyes, Gerard answered his own question.

"What did you say?" Silvanoshei asked, sighing and turning around. Mina had ranged out of sight. "I didn't hear you."

"Who's ruling your people in your absence, Your Majesty?" Gerard asked accusingly. He was thinking of another elven king—Gilthas—who had sacrificed so much to save his people. Not run away from them.

"My mother," said Silvanoshei. He shrugged. "It's what she's always wanted."

"Your mother rules," said Gerard skeptically. "Or the Dark Knights of Neraka? I hear they've taken over Silvanesti."

"Mother will fight them," said Silvanoshei. "She enjoys fighting. She has always enjoyed it, you know. The battle and the danger. It's what she lives for. I hate it. Our people, dying and suffering. Dying for her. Always dying for her. She drinks their blood, and it keeps her beautiful. But it poisoned me."

Gerard stared at him in perplexity. Even though the elf had been speaking Common, Gerard had no idea what he was talking about. He might have asked, but at that moment, Odila emerged from a tent that was set up next to Mina's. She stopped at the sight of Gerard, flushed self-consciously, then turned swiftly and walked off.

"I will fetch you some hot water, Your Majesty," Gerard offered, keeping an eye on her. "You'll want to freshen up and clean away the dust of the road. And I'll bring food and drink. You look as if you could use it."

That much was true. Elves were always thin, but this young elf was emaciated. Apparently he was trying to live on love. Gerard's anger started to fade. He was beginning to feel sorry for this young man, who was as much a prisoner as any of them.

"As you wish," said Silvanoshei, not caring. "When do you think Mina will return?"

"Soon, Your Majesty," said Gerard, almost shoving the young man into the tent. "Soon. You should be rested."

Having rid himself of his responsibility, at least for the moment, he hurried after Odila, who was walking through the camp.

"You've been avoiding me," he said in an undertone, catching up to her.

"For your own good," she replied, still walking. "You should leave, take word to the Knights in Sanction."

"I was planning to." He jerked his thumb back over his shoulder. "Now I have this besotted young elf king on my hands. I've been assigned duty as his bodyguard."

Odila halted, stared at him. "Truly?"

"Truly."

"Mina's idea?"

"Who else?"

"How clever," Odila remarked, continuing on.

"My thoughts exactly," said Gerard. "You don't happen to know what she plans to do with him, do you? I can't think she's romantically inclined."

"Of course not," said Odila. "She told me all about him. He may not look it at the moment, but he has the potential to be a strong and charismatic leader of the elven nation. Mina saw the threat and acted to remove it. I don't know much about elven politics, but I gather that the Silvanesti will not willingly follow anyone but him."

"Why doesn't she just kill him?" Gerard asked. "Death would be more merciful that what she's doing to him now."

"His death makes him a martyr, gives his people a cause for which they would fight. Now, they do nothing but sit and twiddle their thumbs, waiting for him to come back. There's Galdar watching us," she said suddenly. "I should go on alone. Don't come with me."

"But where are you going?"

She did not look at him. "It is my task to take food to the two wizards. Force them to eat."

"Odila," said Gerard, holding her back, "you still believe in the power of this One God, don't you?"

"Yes," she said, casting him a swift and defiant glance.

"Even though you know it's an evil power?"

"An evil power that heals the sick and brings peace and comfort to hundreds," Odila returned.

"And restores hideous life to the dead!"

"Something only a god could do." Odila faced him squarely. "I believe in this god, Gerard, and, what's more, so do you. That's the real reason you're here."

Gerard tried to come up with a glib rejoinder, but found he couldn't. Was this what the voice in his heart was trying to tell him? Was he here of his own free will, or was he just one more prisoner?

Seeing he had no response, Odila turned and left him.

Gerard stood in troubled silence, watched her make her way through the bustling camp.

8

Knight of the Black Rose

he journey this time was brief. Tas had barely started to grow annoyed with the tumbling about when he was suddenly right side up and standing solidly on his own two feet. Time, once again, stopped.

He exhaled in relief and looked around.

The Hedge Maze was gone. Conundrum was gone. Tas stood alone in what must have once been a beautiful rose garden. The garden was beautiful no longer, for everything in it had died. Dried rose blossoms, that had once been red, were now dark as sorrow. Their heads hung drooping on the stems that were brown and withered. Dead leaves from years that knew nothing but winter lay in piles beneath a crumbling stone wall. A path made of broken flagstones led from the dead garden into a manor house, its walls charred and blackened by long-dead flames. Tall cypress trees surrounded the manor house, their enormous limbs cutting off any vestige of sunlight, so that if night fell, it came only as a deepening of day's shadows.

Tasslehoff thought that he had never in his life seen any place that made him feel so unutterably sad.

"What are you doing here?"

A shadow fell over the kender. A voice spoke, a voice that was fell and cold. A knight, clad in ancient armor, stood over him. The knight was dead. He had been dead for many centuries. The body inside the armor had long ago rotted away. The armor was the body now, flesh and bone, muscle and sinew, tarnished and blackened with age, charred by the fires of war, stained with the blood of his victims. Red eyes, the only light in an eternal darkness, were visible through the slit visor of the helm. The red eyes flicked like flame over Tasslehoff. Their gaze was painful, and the kender flinched.

Tasslehoff stared at the apparition before him, and a most unpleasant feeling stole over him, a feeling he had forgotten because it was such a horrible feeling that he didn't like to remember it. His mouth filled with a bitter taste that stung his tongue. His heart lurched about in his chest as though it were trying to run away, but couldn't. His stomach curled up in a ball and searched for some place to hide.

He tried to answer the question, but the words wouldn't come out. He knew this knight. A death knight, Lord Soth had taught the kender fear, a sensation that Tasslehoff had not liked in the least. The thought came that perhaps Lord Soth might not remember him, and it occurred to Tas that it might be a good thing if Lord Soth didn't, for their last meeting hadn't been all that friendly. That notion was quickly dispelled by the words that bit at the kender like winter's bitter wind.

"I don't like to repeat myself. What are you doing here?"

Tas had been asked that question a lot in his long life, although never quite with this shade of meaning. Most of the time the question was: "What are you doing *here?*" said in tones that implied the questioner would be glad if whatever he was doing *here* he would do it someplace else. Other times, the question was: "What are you *doing* here?" which really meant stop *doing* that immediately. Lord Soth had placed the emphasis on the "you" making it "What are *you* doing here?" which meant that he was referring to Tasslehoff Burrfoot directly. Which meant that he recognized him.

Tasslehoff made several attempts to answer, none of which were successful, for all that came out of his mouth was a gargle, not words.

"Twice I asked you a question," said the death knight. "And while my time in this world is eternal, my patience is not."

"I'm trying to answer, sir," returned Tas meekly, "but you cause the words to get all squeezed up inside of me. I know that this is impolite, but I'm going to have to ask you a question before I can answer yours. When you say "here," what exactly do you mean by that?" He mopped sweat from his forehead with the sleeve of his hand and tried to look anywhere except into those red eyes. "I've been to lots of 'heres,' and I'm a bit muddled as to where your 'here' is."

Soth's red eyes shifted from Tasslehoff to the Device of Time Journeying, clutched in the kender's stiff fingers. Tas followed the death knight's gaze.

"Oh, uh, this," Tas said, gulping. "Pretty, isn't it? I came across it on my . . . er . . . last trip. Someone dropped it. I plan on returning it. Isn't it lucky I found it? If you don't mind, I'll just put it away—" He tried to open one of his pouches, but his hands wouldn't quit shaking.

"Don't worry," said Soth. "I won't take it from you. I have no desire for a device that would carry me backward in time. Unless"—he paused, the red eyes grew shadowed—"unless it would take me back to undo what I did. Perhaps then I might make use of it."

Tas knew full well that he could never stop Lord Soth from taking the device if he wanted it, but he meant to give it a good try. The courage that is true courage and not merely the absence of fear rose up in Tasslehoff, and he fumbled for the knife, Rabbit Slayer, that he wore on his belt. He didn't know what good his little knife could do against a death knight, but Tas was a Hero of the Lance. He had to try.

Fortunately, his courage was not tested.

"But what would be the use?" said Lord Soth. "If I had it to do over again, the outcome would be the same. I would make the same decisions, commit the same heinous acts. For that was the man I was."

The red eyes flickered. "If I could go back, knowing what I know, maybe then my actions would be different. But our souls can never go back. They can only go forward. And some of us are not even permitted to do that. Not until we have learned the hard lessons life—and death—teach us."

His voice, already cold, grew colder still, so that Tas stopped sweating and began to shiver.

"And now we are no longer given the chance to do that."

The red eyes flared again. "To answer your question, kender, you are in the Fifth Age, the so-called 'Age of Mortals'." The helmed head shifted. He lifted his hand. The tattered cape he wore stirred with his motion. "You stand in the garden of what was once my dwelling place and is now my prison."

"Are you going to kill me?" Tas asked, more because it was a question he might be expected to ask than because he felt threatened. A person has to take notice of you in order to threaten you, and Tas had the distinct impression that he was of less interest to this undead lord than the withered stems or the dried-up rose petals.

"Why should I kill you, kender?" Soth asked. "Why should I bother?"

Tas gave the matter considerable thought. In truth, he could find no real reason why Soth should kill him, other than one.

"You're a death knight, my lord," Tas said. "Isn't killing people your job?"

"Death was not my job," Soth replied tonelessly. "Death was my joy. And death was my torment. My body has died, but my soul remains alive. As the torture victim suffers in agony when he feels the red-hot brand sear his flesh, so I suffer daily, my soul seared with my rage, my shame, my guilt. I have sought to end it, sought to drown the pain in blood, ease the pain with ambition. I was promised that the pain would end. I was promised that if I helped my goddess achieve her reward, I would be given my reward. My pain would end, and my soul would be freed. These promises were not kept."

The red eyes flicked over Tasslehoff, then roved restlessly to the withered and blackened roses.

"Once I killed out of ambition, for pleasure and for spite. No more. None of that has any meaning to me now. None of that drowned the pain.

"Besides," Soth added off-handedly, "in your case, why should I bother to kill you? You are already dead. You died in the Fourth Age, in the last second of the Fourth Age. That is why I ask, why are you here? How did you find this place, when even the gods cannot see where it is hidden?"

"So I *am* dead," Tas said to himself with a little sigh. "I guess that settles it."

He was thinking it strange that he and Lord Soth should have something in common, when a voice, a living voice, called out, "My lord! Lord Soth! I seek an audience with you!"

A hand closed over the kender's mouth. Another strong hand wrapped around him, and he was suddenly enveloped in the folds of soft black robes, as if night had taken on shape and form and dropped over his head. He could see nothing. He could not speak, could barely breathe, for the hand was positioned right over his nose and mouth. All he could smell—oddly enough— was rose-petals.

Tas might have strongly protested this rude behavior, but he recognized the living voice that had called out to Lord Soth, and he was suddenly quite glad that he had the strange hand to help him keep quiet, for even though sometimes he meant to be very quiet, words had a tendency to leap out of his throat before he could stop them.

Tas wriggled a bit to try to free up his nose for breathing, which—dead or not—his body required him to do. This accomplished, he held perfectly still.

Lord Soth did not immediately answer the call. He, too, recognized the person who had called out, although he had never before met her or seen her. He knew her because the two of them were bound together by the same chain, served the same master. He knew why she had come to him, knew what she meant to ask of him. He did not know what his answer would be, however. He knew what he wanted it to be, yet doubted if he had the courage.

Courage. He smiled bitterly. Once he'd imagined himself afraid of nothing. Over time, he'd come to realize he'd been afraid of everything. He had lived his life in fear: fear of failure, fear of weakness, fear that people would despise him if they truly knew him. Most of all, he had feared she would despise him, once she found out that the man she adored was just an ordinary man, not the paragon of virtue and courage she believed him.

He had been given knowledge by the gods that might have prevented the Cataclysm. He had been riding to Istar when he had been confronted by a group of elven women, misguided followers of the Kingpriest. They told him lies about his wife, told him she had been unfaithful to him and that the child she carried was not his. His fear caused him to believe their stories, and he had turned back from the path that might have been his salvation. Fear had stopped his ears to his wife's protestations of innocence. Fear had made him murder that which he truly loved.

He stood thinking of this, remembering it all yet again, as he had been doomed to remember so many, many times.

Once more he stood in the blooming garden where she tended the roses with her own hands, not trusting the gardener he had hired to do the work for her. He looked with concern at her hands, her fair skin torn and scratched, marred with drops of blood.

"Is it worth it?" he asked her. "The roses cause you so much pain."

"The pain lasts for but a moment," she told him. "The joy of their beauty lasts for days."

"Yet with winter's chill breath, they wither and die."

"But I have the memory of them, my love, and that brings me joy."

Not joy, he thought. Not joy, but torment. Memory of her smile, her laughter. Memory of the sorrow in her eyes as the life faded from them, taken by my hand. Memory of her curse.

Or was it a curse? I thought so then, but now I wonder. Perhaps it was, in truth, her blessing on me.

Leaving the garden of dead roses, he entered the manor house that had stood for centuries, a monument to death and fear. He took his seat in the chair that was covered with the dust of ages, dust that his incorporeal body never disturbed. He sat in that chair and stared, as he had stared for hour after hour after hour, at the bloodstain upon the floor.

There she fell.

There she died.

For eons he had been doomed to hear the recital of his wrongs sung to him by the spirits of those elven women who had been his undoing and who were cursed to live a life that was no life, an existence of torment and regret. He had not heard their voices since the Fifth Age began. How many years that was he did not know, for time had no meaning to him. The voices were part of the Fourth Age, and they had remained with the Fourth Age.

Forgiven, at last. Granted permission to leave.

He sought forgiveness, but it was denied him. He was angry at the denial, as his queen had known he would be. His anger snared him. Thus Takhisis caught him in her trap and bound him fast and carried him here to continue on his wretched existence, waiting for her call.

The call had come. Finally.

Footsteps of the living brought him out of his dark reverie. He looked up to see this representative of Her Dark Majesty and saw a child clad in armor, or so he first thought. Then he saw that what he had mistaken for a child was a girl on the edge of womanhood. He was reminded of Kitiara, the only being who had, for a brief time, been able to ease his torment. Kitiara, who never knew fear except once, at the very end of her life, when she looked up to see him coming for her. It was then, when he gazed into her terror-stricken eyes, that he understood himself. She had given him that much, at least.

Kitiara was gone now, too, her soul moving on to wherever it needed to go. Was this to be another? Another Kitiara, sent to seduce him?

No, he realized, looking into the amber eyes of the girl who stood before him. This was not Kitiara, who had done what she did for her own reasons, who had served no one but herself. This girl did all for glory—the glory of the god. Kitiara had never willingly sacrificed anything in order to achieve her goals. This girl had sacrificed everything, emptied herself, left herself a vessel to be filled by the god.

Soth saw the tiny figures of thousands of beings held fast in the amber eyes. He felt the warm amber slide over him, try to capture and hold him, just another insect.

He shook his helmed head. "Don't bother, Mina," he told the girl. "I know too much. I know the truth."

"And what is that truth?" Mina asked. The amber eyes tried again to seize hold of him. She was not one to give up, this woman-child.

"That your mistress will use you and then abandon you," Soth said. "She will betray you, as she has betrayed everyone who ever served her. I know her of old, you see."

He felt the stirrings of his queen's anger, but he chose to ignore it. Not now, he told her. You cannot use that against me now.

Mina was not angry. She seemed saddened by his response. "How can you say that of her when she went to such trouble to bring you with her? You are the only one so honored. All the rest . . ." She waved her hand to indicate the chamber, empty of its ghosts, or so it must seem to her. To him, the chamber was crowded. "All the rest were banished to oblivion. You alone were granted the privilege of remaining with this world."

"Oblivion is it? Once I believed that. Once I feared the darkness, and thus she kept her hold on me. Now I know differently. Death is not oblivion. Death frees the soul to travel onward."

Mina smiled, pitying his ignorance. "You are the one who has been deceived. The souls of the dead went nowhere. They vanished into the mist, wasted, forgotten. The One God now takes the souls of the dead unto her and gives them the opportunity to remain in this world and continue to act for the good of the world."

"For the good of the god, you mean," said Soth. He stirred in his chair, which gave him no comfort. "Let us say I find myself grateful to this god for the privilege of remaining in the world. Knowing this god as I do of old, I know that she expects my gratitude to take on a tangible form. What is it she requires of me?"

"Within a few days time, armies of both the living and the dead will sweep down on Sanction. The city will fall to my might." Mina did not speak with bravado. She stated a fact, nothing more. "At that time, the One God will perform a great miracle. She will enter the world as she was long meant to do, join the realms of the mortal and the immortal. When she exists in both realms, she will conquer the world, rid it of such vermin as the elves, and establish herself as the ruler of Krynn. I am to be made captain of the army of the living. The One God offers you the captaincy of the army of the dead."

"She 'offers' me this?" Soth asked.

"Offers it. Yes, of course," said Mina.

"Then she will not be offended if I turn down her offer," said Soth.

"She would not be offended," Mina replied, "but she would be deeply grieved at your ingratitude, after all that she has done for you."

"All she has done for me." Soth smiled. "So this is why she brought me here. I am to be a slave leading an army of slaves. My answer to this generous offer is 'no.'

"You made a mistake, my queen," called Soth, speaking to the shadows, where he knew she lay coiled, waiting. "You used my anger to keep your talons in me, and you dragged me here so that you could make use of me still. But you left me alone too long. You left me to the silence in which I could once more hear my wife's beloved voice. You left me to the darkness that became my light, for I could once more see my wife's beloved face. I could see myself, and I saw a man consumed by his fear. And it was then I saw you for what you are.

"I fought for you, Queen Takhisis. I believed your cause was mine. The silence taught me that it was you who fed my fear, raising around me a ring of fire from which I could never escape. The fire has gone out now, my queen. All around me is nothing but ashes."

"Beware, my lord," said Mina, and her tone was dire. "If you refuse this, you risk the god's anger."

Lord Soth rose to his feet. He pointed to a stain upon the stone floor.

"Do you see that?"

"I see nothing," said Mina, with an indifferent glance, "nothing except the cold, gray rock."

"I see a pool of blood," said Lord Soth. "I see my beloved wife lying in her blood. I see the blood of all those who perished because my fear kept me from accepting the blessing the gods offered to me. Long have I been forced to stare at that stain, and long have I loathed the very sight of it. Now, I kneel on it," he said, bending his knees on the stone, "I kneel in her blood and the blood of all who died because I was afraid. I beg her to forgive me for the wrong I did to her. I beg them all to forgive me."

"There can be no forgiveness," said Mina sternly. "You are cursed. The One God will cast your soul into the darkness of unending pain and torment. Is this what you choose?"

"Death is what I choose," said Lord Soth. Reaching beneath the breast plate of his armor, he drew forth a rose. The rose was long dead, but its vibrant color had not faded. The rose was red as her lips, red as her blood. "If death brings unending torment, then I accept that as my fitting punishment."

Lord Soth saw Mina reflected in the red fire of his soul. "Your god has lost her hold on me. I am no longer afraid."

Mina's amber eyes hardened in anger. Turning on her heel, she left him kneeling on the cold stone, his head bowed, his hands clasped over the thorns and dried leaves and crumpled petals of the red rose. Mina's footfalls reverberated through the manor house, shook the floor on which he knelt, shook the charred and broken walls, shook the blackened beams.

He felt pain, physical pain, and he looked in wonder at his hand. The accursed armor was gone. The thorns of the dead rose pierced his flesh. A tiny drop of blood gleamed on his skin, more red than the petals.

A beam above him gave way and crashed down beside him. Shards of splintered wood flew from the shattered beam, punctured his flesh. He gritted his teeth against the pain of his wounds. This was the Dark Queen's last, desperate attempt to keep her hold on him. He had been given back his mortal body.

She would never know, but she had, in her ignorance, granted him a final blessing.

She lay coiled in the shadows, certain of her triumph, waiting for his fear to once more bind him to her, waiting for him to cry out that he had been wrong, waiting for him to plead and grovel for her to spare him.

Lord Soth lifted the rose to his lips. He kissed the petals, then scattered them over the blood that stained the gray stone red. He cast off the helm that had been his flesh and bone for so many empty years. He tore off the breastplate and hurled it far from him, so that it struck the wall with a clank and a clatter.

Another beam fell, hurled by a vengeful hand. The beam struck him, crushed his body, drove him to the floor. His blood flowed freely, mingled with his dear wife's blood. He did not cry out. The pain of dying was agony, but it was an agony that would soon end. He could bear the pain for her sake, for the pain her soul had born for him.

She would not be waiting for him. She had long ago made her own journey, carrying in her arms their son. He would make his solitary way after them, lost, alone, seeking.

He might never find them, the two he had so wronged, but he would dedicate eternity to the search.

In that search, he would be redeemed.

Mina stalked through the rose garden. Her face was livid and cold as a face carved of marble. She did not look back to see the final destruction of Dargaard Keep.

Tasslehoff, peeping out from behind a fold of blackness, saw her leave. He did not see where she went, for at that moment the massive structure collapsed, falling in upon itself with a thunderous crash that sent clouds of dust and debris roiling up into the air.

A gigantic block of stone smashed down into the rose garden. He was extremely surprised to find that he wasn't underneath it, for it fell right where he'd been standing, but, like thistledown, he floated on the winds of ruin and death and was lifted above them into the pure, chill blue of a cloudless, sunlit sky.

9

The Attack on Sanction

The city of Sanction had been besieged for months. The Dark Knights threw everything they had against it. Countless numbers died in the shadows of Sanction's walls, on both sides of Sanction's walls, died for no reason, for the siege could not be broken. When Mina's army marched into view, Sanction's defenders laughed to see it, for how could such pitifully small numbers of men make any difference?

They did not laugh long. The city of Sanction fell to the army of souls in a single day.

Nothing could halt the advance of the dead. The moats of sluggish, hot lava flowing from the Lords of Doom that kept the living at bay, were no barrier to the souls. The newly built and strengthened earthwork fortifications against which the army of the Dark Knights had thrown themselves time and again without success now stood as monuments to futility. The thick, gray mist of hapless souls flowed down the sides of the mountains, filled the valleys like a rising tide, and boiled up and over the fortifications. Besieger and besieged alike fled before the terrifying dead.

Mina's sappers had no need to batter down the gates that led into the city or breach the walls. Her troops had only to wait until the gates were flung open from within by the panic-stricken defenders. Fleeing the army of the dead, they soon joined their ranks. Mina's Knights, hidden among the ghastly mist, cut down the living without mercy. Led by Galdar, the army stormed through the gates to do battle in the city.

Mina fought her battles in the foothills around Sanction, doing what she could to quell the panic of the army of besiegers, who were just as terrified as their enemy. She rode among them, halting their flight, urging them back to battle.

She seemed to be everywhere upon the battlefield, galloping swiftly on her red horse to wherever she was needed. She rode without care for her own safety, often leaving her bodyguards far behind, spurring their steeds frantically to keep up.

Gerard did not take part in the battle. True to her word, Mina posted him and his prisoner, the elf king, atop a ridgeline overlooking the city.

Along with the elf, Gerard and four other Dark Knights guarded the wagon carrying the amber sarcophagus of Goldmoon and the two dead wizards. Odila rode with the wagon. Like Gerard, her gaze was fixed on the battle in which she could take no part. Frustrated, helpless to do anything to aid his fellow Knights, Gerard followed the battle from his detested safe vantage point. Mina shone with a pale, fey light that made her a rallying point anywhere on the field.

"What is that strange fog that fills the valley?" Silvanoshei asked, staring down from his horse in wonder.

"That strange fog is not fog, Your Majesty. That is an army of dead souls," Gerard answered grimly.

"Even the dead adore her," Silvanoshei said. "They come to fight for her."

Gerard glanced at the wagon, carrying the bodies of the two dead mages. He wondered if Palin's soul was on that battlefield,

Tell us what you think about *Dragons of a Vanished Moon*, the third book in the War of Souls trilogy. Please answer the following questions and mail the card to us. You'll be entered in a random drawing for a **Dragonlance**® Legends Gift Set. Five winners will be chosen!

1. Overall, how would you rate *Dragons of a Vanished Moon*?

Excellent				Poor
☐ 5	☐ 4	☐ 3	☐ 2	☐ 1

2. How would you rate *Dragons of a Vanished Moon* on each of the following features?

FEATURE	Excellent				Poor
Cover art	☐ 5	☐ 4	☐ 3	☐ 2	☐ 1
Cover copy	☐ 5	☐ 4	☐ 3	☐ 2	☐ 1
Title	☐ 5	☐ 4	☐ 3	☐ 2	☐ 1
Story	☐ 5	☐ 4	☐ 3	☐ 2	☐ 1
Value for price	☐ 5	☐ 4	☐ 3	☐ 2	☐ 1

3. Please rank each of the following five items according to how important each one is to you in deciding whether to purchase a particular fantasy novel.

(1 indicates that the factor is the most important in making this decision, 2 indicates it is the next most important, and so on. Please use the numbers 1 through 5 only once each.)

FACTOR	Rank
Author	
Cover	
Series	
Reviews/Bestseller list	
Recommendations from friends/relatives	

4. Which of the following elements do you look for in a fantasy novel? (Please check all that apply.)

☐ Humor ☐ Romance
☐ Action ☐ Dark setting
☐ Suspense ☐ Well-developed characters
☐ Intricate plots ☐ Other, please specify:

5. How would you rate your interest in novels with the following types of settings?

SETTING	Very Interested				Not At All Interested
Heroic fantasy (*Dragonlance* and *Forgotten Realms*®, for example)	☐ 5	☐ 4	☐ 3	☐ 2	☐ 1
Space fantasy (*Star Wars*™, for example)	☐ 5	☐ 4	☐ 3	☐ 2	☐ 1
Postapocalyptic (*Mad Max*, for example)	☐ 5	☐ 4	☐ 3	☐ 2	☐ 1
Horror (Stephen King and Dean Koontz, for example)	☐ 5	☐ 4	☐ 3	☐ 2	☐ 1
Alternate history (Harry Turtledove, for example)	☐ 5	☐ 4	☐ 3	☐ 2	☐ 1
Intrigue/Spy (Robert Ludlum, for example)	☐ 5	☐ 4	☐ 3	☐ 2	☐ 1
War/Action (W. E. B. Griffin and Mack Bolen, for example)	☐ 5	☐ 4	☐ 3	☐ 2	☐ 1

6. If you were to purchase ten novels over the next year, how many of each of the following types of novels would you purchase?

TYPE	Number of this type you would purchase (Total = 10)
Heroic fantasy	
Space fantasy	
Postapocalyptic	
Horror	
Intrigue/Spy	
Alternate history	
War/Action	
Other, please specify:	

7. Which of the following Wizards of the Coast® novel series do you read regularly? (Please check all that apply.)

☐ Dragonlance ☐ Forgotten Realms
☐ Magic: The Gathering® ☐ Legend of the Five Rings™
☐ Other, please specify:

8. What types of fiction do you read regularly? (Please check all that apply.)

☐ Fantasy ☐ Horror
☐ Mystery ☐ Historical
☐ Science fiction ☐ Action/Adventure
☐ Romance ☐ Classical literature
☐ Other, please specify:

9. What is your gender?
☐ Male ☐ Female

10. What is your birth date?

Month	Day	Year

Full Name:

Address:

City/Town: **State/Province:**

ZIP/Postal Code:

Country:

Phone:

Email:

☐ Please check here if you DO wish to be contacted or receive promotional offers.

BUSINESS REPLY MAIL

FIRST-CLASS MAIL   PERMIT NO. 609   RENTON, WA

POSTAGE WILL BE PAID BY ADDRESSEE

ATTN.: CONSUMER RESPONSE
WIZARDS OF THE COAST
PO BOX 980
RENTON WA   98057-9960

fighting for Mina. He guessed how much Palin "adored" her. He could have pointed this out to the besotted young elf, but he kept quiet. The young man wouldn't listen, anyway. Gerard sat his horse in grim silence.

The din of battle, the cries of the dying, rose up from the mist of souls that grew thicker by the moment. Gerard suddenly saw it all in a blood-drenched haze, and he determined to ride down to join that desperate battle, though he knew from the outset that he could do no good and would only die in the attempt.

"Gerard!" Odila called out.

"You can't stop me!" he cried angrily, and then, when the red haze cleared a bit, he saw she wasn't trying to stop him. She was trying to warn him.

Four of Mina's Knights, who were supposed to be guarding the elf, spurred their horses, surrounded him.

He had no idea how they had divined his intention, but he drew his sword, fiercely glad to have this chance to do battle. Their first words astonished him.

"Ride off, Gerard," said one, a man named Clorant. "This is not your fight. We mean you no harm."

"It is my fight, you bloody bastards—" Gerard began. His words of defiance sputtered out.

They were not staring at him. Their hate-filled eyes stared behind him, at the elf. Gerard remembered the jeers and catcalls he'd heard when the elven king rode into camp. He glanced over his shoulder. Silvanoshei was not armed. He would be defenseless against these four.

"What happens to the pointy-ear is none of your concern, Gerard," Clorant said. His tone was dire. He was in deadly earnest. "Ride on, and don't look back."

Gerard had to grapple with himself, squelch his rage, force himself to think calmly and rationally. All the while, he cursed Mina for seeing into his heart.

"You boys have got yourselves all turned around," Gerard said. Trying his best to sound casual, he edged his horse so that it was between Clorant and the young elf. Gerard pointed. "The fight's in that direction. Behind you."

"You won't get into trouble with Mina, Gerard," Clorant promised. "We have our story all thought out. We're going to tell her we were attacked by an enemy patrol that had been lurking up in the mountains. We drove them off, but in the confusion the elf was killed."

"We'll drag a couple of bodies up here," added another. "Bloody ourselves up some. Make it look real."

"I'll be happy to bloody any one of you," said Gerard, "but it's not going to come to that. This elf's not worth it. He's no threat to anybody."

"He's a threat to Mina," said Clorant. "He tried to kill her when we were in Silvanesti. The One God brought her back to us, but the next time the bastard might succeed."

"If he did try to kill her, let Mina deal with him," said Gerard.

"She can't see through his tricks and deceits," said Clorant. "We have to protect her from herself."

He's a jealous lover, Gerard realized. Clorant is in love with Mina himself. Every one of them is in love with her. That's the real reason they want to kill this elf.

"Give me a sword. I can fight my own battles," declared Silvanoshei, riding up alongside Gerard. The elf cast him a proud and scornful glance. "I don't need you to fight them for me."

"You young fool," Gerard growled out of the side of his mouth. "Shut up, and let me handle this!"

Aloud he said, "Mina ordered me to guard him, and I'm bound to obey. I took an oath to obey, the same as you. There's a concept floating around called honor. Maybe you boys have heard of it?"

"Honor!" Clorant spat on the ground. "You talk like a cursed Solamnic. You have a choice, Gerard. You can either ride off and let us deal with the elf, in which case we'll see to it that you don't get into trouble, or you can be one of the corpses we leave on the field to prove our story. Don't worry," he sneered. "We'll tell Mina that you died 'with honor.' "

Gerard didn't wait for them to come at him. He didn't even wait for Clorant to finish his speech but spurred his horse toward him. Their swords clanged together on the word, "honor."

"I'll deal with this bastard," shouted Clorant. "The rest of you kill the elf!"

Leaving Clorant to take care of Gerard, the other three galloped toward the elf. Gerard heard Silvanoshei shout in Elvish, heard one of the Knights curse, and then a thud and a clatter of metal. Risking a glance, Gerard saw to his amazement that Silvanoshei, with no weapon but his own hands, had thrown himself bodily on one of the armored Knights, carried him off his horse and onto the ground. The two floundered, grappling for the knight's loose sword. The Knight's comrades circled around the combatants, waiting a chance to strike the elf, not wanting to risk hitting their friend.

Gerard had his own problems. Fighting an armed foe on horseback is not so much a matter of skilled thrust and parry between two swordsmen as a bludgeoning, slashing battle to try to unseat your foe.

Their horses snorted and churned up the ground with their hooves. Clorant and Gerard circled each other, swords swinging wildly, striking any part of the body that came into view., neither making much headway. Gerard's fist smashed into Clorant's jaw, his sword sliced through the chain mail of the man's upper arm. Gerard himself was not wounded, but he was the one at a disadvantage. Clorant had only to defend himself, keep Gerard occupied so that he could not save the elf.

Another glance showed Gerard that Silvanoshei had managed to grab the fallen Knight's sword. Taking up a defensive position, Silvanoshei grimly eyed his foes, two of whom were still mounted and still armed. The fallen Knight was staggering to his feet.

Raising his sword, one Knight sent his horse at a gallop straight at Silvanoshei, intending to behead him with a slashing downward stroke. Desperate, Gerard turned his back on Clorant. Gerard was leaving himself wide open, but he had no other recourse if he wanted to save the elf's life. Gerard spurred his horse, so that the startled animal leaped ahead, his intent being to gallop between the two combatants, putting himself between the elf and his attacker.

Clorant struck Gerard from behind. His sword thunked against Gerard's helm, setting his ears to ringing and scattering his wits. Then Clorant was at Gerard side. A sword flashed in the sunlight.

"Stop this!" a woman shouted, her voice shaking with fury. "In the name of the One God, stop this madness!"

The Knight galloping down on the elf pulled so hard on the reins that his horse reared and practically upended both of them. Gerard had to rein in his steed swiftly or crash into the floundering animal. He heard Clorant suck in his breath, heard him try to check his horse.

Gerard lowered his sword, looked about to see who had spoken. He could tell by Clorant's wild-eyed stare and guilty expression that he thought the voice was Mina's. Gerard knew it wasn't. He recognized the voice. He could only hope that Odila had the nerve to pull this off.

Her face livid, her robes whipping about her ankles, Odila marched into the midst of the sweating, bleeding, deadly fray. She thrust aside a sword with her bare hand.

Glaring around at them, her eyes burning, she looked directly at Clorant. "What is the meaning of this? Did you not hear Mina's command that this elf was to be treated with the same respect you show her?" Odila sent a flashing glance at each one of them in turn, not excluding Gerard. "Put away your weapons! All of you!"

She was taking a great risk. Did these men view her as a true cleric, a representative of the One God, someone as sacred as Mina herself? Or did they see her as nothing more than a follower, no different from themselves?

The men hesitated, glanced uncertainly at each other. Gerard kept quiet, tried to look as guilty and dismayed at the rest. He cast one warning glance at the elf, but Silvanoshei had the sense to keep his mouth shut. He panted, gasping for breath, kept wary watch on his enemies.

Odila's gaze hardened, her eyes narrowed. "In the name of the One God put down your weapons," she ordered again, and this time she pointed at Clorant, "lest your sword hand wither with my displeasure and fall from your arm!"

"Will you tell Mina about this?" Clorant asked sullenly.

"I know that you did what you did out of misguided care for Mina," said Odila, her voice softening. "You have no need to protect her. The One God holds Mina in the palm of her hand. The One God knows what is best for Mina and for us all. This elf lives only because the One God wills it." Odila pointed in the direction of Sanction. "Return to the battle. Your true foe lies down there."

"Will you tell Mina?" Clorant persisted, and there was fear in his voice.

"I won't," said Odila, "but you will. You will confess to her what you have done and seek her forgiveness."

Clorant lowered his sword and, after a moment's hesitation, thrust it into his sheath. He made a motion for his comrades to do the same. Then, casting a final, loathing glance at the elf, he turned his horse's head and galloped down the hill, heading for Sanction. His friends rode after him.

Exhaling a great sigh of relief, Gerard slid down from his horse.

"Are you all right?" he asked Silvanoshei, looking him over. He saw a few splashes of blood on his clothes but nothing serious.

Silvanoshei drew away from him, stared at him suspiciously. "You—a Dark Knight—risked your life to save mine. You fought your own comrades. Why?"

Gerard could not very well tell him the truth. "I didn't do it for you," he said gruffly. "I did it for Mina. She ordered me to guard you, remember?"

Silvanoshei's face smoothed. "That makes sense. Thank you."

"Thank Mina," muttered Gerard ungraciously.

His movements stiff and painful, he limped over to Odila. "Well acted," he said in low tone. "That was quite a performance.

Though, I'm curious—what would have happened if Clorant had called your bluff? I thought he was going to for a minute there. What would you have done then?"

"It's strange," Odila said. Her gaze was abstracted, her voice soft and introspective. "At the moment I made the threat, I knew I had the power to carry it out. I could have withered his hand. I could have."

"Odila—" he began to remonstrate with her.

"It doesn't matter if you believe me or not," Odila said bleakly. "Nothing can stop the One God."

Clasping the medallion she wore around her neck, she walked back to the wagon.

"Nothing can stop the One," Odila repeated. "Nothing."

10

City of Ghosts

R iding in the vanguard of the triumphant army as they entered, unopposed, Sanction's West Gate and marched victorious along the famous Shipmaker's Road, Gerard looked at the city and saw nothing but ghosts: ghosts of the past, ghosts of the present, ghosts of prosperity, ghosts of war.

He remembered what he'd heard of Sanction, remembered— as if it had happened to someone else and not to him—talking to Caramon Majere about hoping to be sent to Sanction. *Someplace where there is real fighting going on,* he had said or, if he had not said it, he had thought it. He looked back on that ghost of himself and saw a callow youth who didn't have sense enough to know when he was well off.

What must Caramon have thought of me? Gerard flushed as he remembered some of his foolish spoutings. Caramon Majere had fought in many wars. He knew the truth about glory—that it was nothing more than a bloodstained and rusted old sword hanging on the wall of an old man's memory. Riding past the bodies of those who had defended Sanction, Gerard saw the true glory of war: the carrion birds flapping down to pluck out eyeballs, the flies that filled the air with their horrid buzzing, the burial crews laughing and joking as they filled wheelbarrows with bodies and dumped them into mass graves.

War was a thief who dared accost Death, robbing that majestic noble of his dignity, stripping him bare, tossing him in a pit, and covering him with lime to stop the stench.

Gerard was grateful for one blessing: The dead were laid to rest. At the end of the battle, Mina—her armor covered with blood, herself unscathed—knelt beside the first of the hastily dug trenches meant to receive the dead and prayed over them. Gerard watched in stomach-clenching horror, more than half expecting the bloodied corpses to rise up, seize their weapons, and fall into ranks at Mina's command.

Fortunately, that did not happen. Mina commended the spirits to the One God, urged them all to serve the One God well. Gerard glanced at Odila, who stood not far from him. Her head was bowed, her hands clasped.

Gerard was angry at her and angry at himself for being angry. Odila had done nothing more than speak the truth. This One God was all-seeing, all-knowing, all-powerful. There was nothing they could do to stop the One. He was loathe to face the truth. That was all. Loathe to admit defeat.

After the ceremony for the dead ended, Mina mounted her horse and rode into the city, which was, for the most part, deserted.

During the War of the Lance, Sanction had been an armed camp dedicated to the Queen of Darkness, headquarters for her armies. The draconians had been born in the temple of Luerkhisis. Lord Ariakas had his headquarters in Sanction, trained his troops here, kept his slaves here, tortured his prisoners here.

The Chaos War and the departure of the gods that brought devastation to many parts of Ansalon delivered prosperity to Sanction. At first, it seemed that Sanction must be destroyed and that no one would rule it, for the lava flows spilling from the Lords of Doom threatened to bury the city. A man called Hogan

Bight arrived to save Sanction from the mountains' wrath. Using powerful magicks that he never explained, he diverted the flow of lava, drove out the evil people who had long ruled the city. Merchants and others seeking to better their lives were invited in and, almost overnight, Sanction grew prosperous, as goods flowed into its wharves and docks.

Seeing its wealth, needing access to its ports, the Dark Knights had wanted Sanction back under their control, and now they had it.

With Qualinost destroyed, Silvanesti occupied, and Solamnia under her rulership, it might be truly said that those parts of Ansalon that were not under Mina's control were not worth controlling. She had come full circle, back to Sanction where her legend had begun.

Having been warned of Mina's march on their city, the citizens of Sanction, who had weathered the siege without any great hardship, heard the rumors of the advancing army of Dark Knights, and fearing that they would be enslaved, their homes looted, their daughters raped, their sons slain by their cruel conquerers, they took to their boats or their horse carts, putting out to sea or heading for the mountains.

Only a few remained behind: the poor who did not have the means to leave; the infirm, the elderly, the sick who could not leave; kender (a fact of nature); and those entrepreneurs who had no care for any god, who owed no allegiance to any government or cause except their own. These people lined the streets to watch the entry of the army, their expressions ranging from dull apathy to eager anticipation.

In the case of the poor, their lives were already so miserable that they had nothing to fear. In the case of the entrepreneurs, their eyes fixed greedily on two enormous, wooden, iron-bound chests that had been transported under heavy guard from Palanthas. Here was much of the wealth of the Dark Knights, wealth that the late Lord Targonne had so covetously amassed. The wealth was now to be shared with all those who had fought for Mina, or so the rumor ran.

Reinforce religious fervor with bags of steel coins—a wise move, Gerard thought, and one guaranteed to win her the hearts, as well as the souls, of her soldiers.

The army advanced along Shipbuilder's Road into a large marketplace. One of Gerard's fellow Knights, who had once visited Sanction, stated that this was known as the Souk Bazaar, and that it was usually so crowded with people that one scarcely had room enough to draw a breath, let alone walk. That was not true now. The only people around were a few enterprising hoodlums taking advantage of the commotion to raid the abandoned stalls.

Calling a halt at this central location, Mina proceeded to take control of the city. She dispatched guards under trustworthy officers to seize the warehouses, the taverns, the mageware shops, and the shops of the money-lenders. She sent another group of guards, led by the minotaur Galdar, to the impressive palace where lived the city's governor, the mysterious Hogan Bight. The guards had orders to arrest him, take him alive if he cooperated, kill him if he didn't. Hogan Bight continued to be a mystery, however, for Galdar returned to report that the man was nowhere to be found and no one could tell when they'd last seen him.

"The palace is empty and would make an ideal dwelling place for you, Mina," said Galdar. "Shall I order the troops to make it ready for your arrival?"

"The palace will be military headquarters," said Mina, "but not my dwelling place. The One God does not reside in grand palaces, and neither will I."

She glanced at the wagon carrying the body of Goldmoon in the amber coffin. Goldmoon's body had not withered, had not decayed. Frozen in the amber, she seemed forever young, forever beautiful. The wagon had been given an honored place in the procession, following directly after Mina, surrounded by an honor guard of her Knights.

"I will dwell in what was once called the Temple of Huerzyd but is now known as the Temple of the Heart. Detain any of the Mystics who remain in the temple. Put them somewhere secure, for their own safety. Treat them with respect and tell them that I look forward to meeting with them. You will escort the body of Goldmoon to the temple and carry the sarcophagus inside to be placed before the altar. You will feel at home, Mother," said Mina, speaking softly to the still, cold face of the woman imprisoned in amber.

Galdar did not appear particularly pleased at his assignment. He did not question Mina, however. The wagon and its guard of honor rolled out of the bazaar, heading for the temple, which was located in the northern part of the city.

Seated astride her irritable horse, Mina proceeded to issue commands. Her Knights crowded around her, eager to serve, hoping for a look, a word, a smile. Gerard held back, not wanting to get caught in the crush of men and horses. He needed to know what he was to do with the elf, but he wasn't in any hurry. He was glad to have this time to think, determine what his next move was going to be. He didn't like at all what was happening to Odila. Her talk of withering hands frightened him. Medallion or no medallion, he was going to find a way to get her out of here, if he had to bash her over the head and haul her out bodily.

Gerard suddenly felt a fierce determination to do something— anything—to fight this One God, even if he caused the One God less harm than a bee sting. One bee might not do much damage, but if there were hundreds of bees, thousands . . . He'd heard stories of dragons fleeing such swarms. There had to be—

"Hey, Gerard," called someone. "You've lost your prisoner."

Gerard came to himself with a jolt. The elf was no longer at his side. Gerard had no fear—or hope—that Silvanoshei would try to escape. He knew right where to look for him. Silvanoshei was urging his horse forward, trying to force his way through the armed circle of Knights surrounding Mina.

Cursing them both beneath his breath, Gerard spurred his horse. The Knights around Mina were aware of the elf and were deliberately blocking his passage. Silvanoshei set his jaw and continued to determinedly and stubbornly pursue his course. One of the Knights, whose horse was jostled by Silvanoshei's horse, turned to stare at him. The Knight was Clorant, his face bruised and swollen, his lip bloodied. The split lip pulled back in a grimace. Silvanoshei hesitated, then pushed ahead. Clorant tugged sharply on the reins, jerking his horse's head. The animal, annoyed, took a nip at Silvanoshei's horse, which bared its teeth. In the confusion, Clorant gave Silvanoshei a shove, trying to unseat him. Silvanoshei managed to cling to the saddle. He shoved back.

Gerard guided his steed through the melee and caught up with the elf, jostling Clorant's arm in passing.

"This is not a good time to interrupt Mina, Your Majesty," Gerard said in an undertone to the elf. "Maybe later." He reached for the reins of Silvanoshei's horse.

"Sir Gerard," called Mina. "Attend me. Bring His Majesty with you. The rest of you, make way."

At Mina's command, Clorant was forced to edge his horse backward, so that Gerard and Silvanoshei could ride past. Clorant's dark, grim gaze followed them. Gerard could feel it tickle the back of his neck as he rode to receive his orders.

Removing his helm, Gerard saluted Mina. Due to his fight with Clorant, Gerard's face was bruised, dried blood matted his hair. Most of the other Knights looked the same or worse, though, after the battle. Gerard was hoping Mina wouldn't notice.

She might not have noticed him, but she gazed intently at Silvanoshei, whose shirt was sliced open and stained with blood, his traveling cloak covered with dirt.

"Sir Gerard," Mina said gravely, "I entrusted His Majesty to you, to keep him safely out of the affray. I see you both bruised and bloodied. Did either of you take serious harm?"

"No, Madam," replied Gerard.

He refused to call her Mina, as did her other Knights. Like a medicine made of alum and honey, her name, sweet at first, left a bitter taste on his tongue. He said nothing more about the fight with Clorant and his fellow Knights. Neither did Silvanoshei. After assuring her that he was not injured, the elf fell silent. No one in the crowd of waiting Knights spoke. Here and there, a horse shifted beneath a restless rider. By now all Mina's Knights knew about the affray. Perhaps they had even been in on the conspiracy.

"What are your orders, Madam?" Gerard asked, hoping to let the matter drop.

"That can wait. What happened?" Mina persisted.

"A Solamnic patrol came out of nowhere, Madam," said Gerard evenly. He looked straight into the amber eyes. "I think they hoped to seize our supply wagon. We drove them away."

"His Majesty fought them, too?" asked Mina, with a half smile.

"When they saw he was an elf, they sought to rescue him, Madam."

"I didn't want to be rescued," Silvanoshei added.

Gerard's lips tightened. That statement was true enough.

Mina cast the young elf a cool glance, then turned her attention back to Gerard.

"I saw no bodies."

"You know Solamnics, Madam," he replied evenly. "You know what cowards they are. We rattled our swords at them, and they ran away."

"I *do* know Solamnics," Mina replied, "and contrary to what you believe, Sir Gerard, I have a great respect for them."

Mina's amber gaze swept over the line of Knights, unerringly picked out the four who had been involved. Her gaze fixed longest on Clorant, who tried to defy it, but ended up squirming and cringing. Finally, she turned her amber eyes back to Silvanoshei, another insect caught in the warm resin.

"Sir Gerard," said Mina, "do you know where to find the City Guard Headquarters?"

"No, Madam," said Gerard. "I have never been in Sanction. But I have no doubt I can locate it."

"There you will find secure prison cells. You will escort His Majesty to these cells and make certain that he is locked in one of them. See to his comfort. This is for your own protection, Your Majesty," Mina added. "Someone might try to 'rescue' you again, and the next time you might not have such a valiant defender."

Gerard glanced at Silvanoshei, then looked away. The sight was too painful. Her words might have been a dagger thrust in the elf's gut. His face drained of life. Even the lips lost their color. In the young man's livid face, the burning eyes were the only life.

"Mina," he said quietly, desperately. "I have to know one thing. Did you ever love me? Or have you just been using me?"

"Sir Gerard," said Mina, turning away. "You have your orders."

"Yes, Madam," he said. Taking the reins from the elf's hand, he started to lead his horse away.

"Mina," pleaded Silvanoshei. "I deserve at least that much. To know the truth."

Mina glanced back at him, over her shoulder.

"My love, my life is the One God."

Gerard led the elf's horse away.

The City Guard Headquarters turned out to be south of the West Gate by a few blocks. The two rode in silence through the streets that had been deserted when the army marched in, but were now filling rapidly with the soldiers of the army of the One God. Gerard had to watch where they were going to avoid riding down anyone, and their progress was slow. He glanced back in concern for Silvanoshei, saw his face set, his jaw clenched, his eyes staring down at the hands that gripped the pommel so tightly the knuckles were chalk white.

"Women." Gerard grunted. "It happens to all of us."

Silvanoshei smiled bitterly and shook his head.

Well, he's right, Gerard admitted. None of the rest of us had a god involved in our love-making.

They rode past the West Gate. Gerard had been harboring a vague notion that he and the elf might be able to escape during the confusion, but he discarded that idea immediately. The road was clogged with Mina's troops, and more remained on the field outside the city. Every man they passed cast Silvanoshei a dark, frowning glance. More than one muttered threats.

Mina is right, Gerard decided. Prison is probably the safest place for the young man. If any place is safe for Silvanoshei in Sanction.

The city guards had either fled the guardhouse or been killed. Mina had placed one of her Knights in charge. The Knight glanced without interest at Silvanoshei, listened with impatience to Gerard's insistence that the young man be placed under special guard. The Knight jerked a thumb in the direction of the cell block. A brief search turned up the keys.

Gerard escorted his prisoner to a cell in darkest corner of the block, hoping he would escape notice.

"I'm sorry about this, Your Majesty," said Gerard.

Silvanoshei shrugged, sat down on the stone block that passed for a bed. Gerard shut the cell door, locked it.

At the sound of key turning, Silvanoshei raised his head. "I should thank you for saving my life."

"I'll bet now you wished I'd let them kill you," said Gerard, sympathetic.

"*Their* swords would have been less painful," Silvanoshei agreed with a pale flicker of a smile.

Gerard glanced around. They were the only two in the cell-blocks. "Your Majesty," he said quietly. "I can help you escape. Not now—there's something else I have to do first. But soon."

"Thank you, sir. But you'd be putting yourself in danger for nothing. I can't escape."

"Your Majesty," said Gerard, his voice hardening, "you saw her, you heard her. You have no chance with her! She doesn't love you. She's all wrapped up in this . . . this god of hers."

"Not only hers. My god, too," he said, speaking with an eerie calm. "The One God promised me that Mina and I would be together."

"Do you still believe that?"

"No," Silvanoshei said, after a moment. The word seemed wrenched from him. "No, I don't."

"Then be ready. I'll come back for you."

Silvansoshei shook his head.

"Your Majesty," said Gerard, exasperated, "do you know the reason Mina lured you here away from your kingdom? Because she knows that your people will not follow anyone but you. The

Silvanesti are sitting around waiting for you to return to them. Go back and be their king, the king she fears!"

"Go back to be their king." Silvanoshei's mouth twisted. "Go back to my mother, you mean. Go back to ignominy and shame, tears and rebukes. I would sit in this prison cell the rest of my life—and we elves live a long, long time—rather than face that."

"Look, damn it, if it was just you, I'd let you rot here," Gerard said grimly. "But you're their king, like it or not. You have to think about your people."

"I am," said Silvanoshei. "I will."

Rising to his feet, he walked over to Gerard, tugging on a ring as he came. "You're a Solamnic Knight, as Mina said, aren't you? Why are you here? To spy on Mina?"

Gerard glowered, shrugged, didn't answer.

"You don't have to admit it," said Silvanoshei. "Mina saw into your heart. That's why she set you to guard me. If you're serious about wanting to help me—"

"I am, Your Majesty," said Gerard.

"Then take this." Silvanoshei handed through the cell bars a blue, glittering ring. "Somewhere out there—close by, I'm certain—you will find an elven warrior. His name is Samar. He has been sent by my mother to bring me back home. Give him this ring. He will recognize it. I've worn it since I was a child. When he asks you how you came by it, tell him you took it from my corpse."

"Your Majesty—"

Silvanoshei thrust the ring at him. "Take it. Tell him I am dead."

"Why would I lie? And why would he believe me?" Gerard asked, hesitating.

"Because he will want to believe you," said Silvanoshei. "And by this action, you will free me."

Gerard took the ring, that was a circlet of sapphires, small enough to fit a child's hand.

"How will I find this Samar?"

"I will teach you a song," said Silvanoshei. "An old elven children's song. My mother used it as a signal if ever she needed to warn me of danger. Sing the song as you ride. Samar will hear it, and he will be intensely curious as to how you—a human— would know this song. He will find you."

"And then slit my throat—"

"He'll want to interrogate you first," said Silvanoshei. "Samar is a man of honor. If you tell him the truth, he'll know you for a man of honor, as well."

"I wish you'd reconsider, Your Majesty," Gerard said. He was starting to like this young man, even as he deeply pitied him.

Silvanoshei shook his head.

"Very well," said Gerard, sighing. "How does this song go?"

Silvanoshei taught the song to Gerard. The words were simple, the melody melancholy. It was a song meant to teach a child to count. "'*Five for the fingers on each hand. Four for the legs upon a horse.*'"

The last line he knew he would never forget.

"'*One is one and all alone and evermore shall be so.*'"

Silvanoshei went to the stone bed, lay down upon it, turned away his face.

"Tell Samar I am dead," he reiterated softly. "If it's any comfort to you, Sir Knight, you won't be telling a lie. You'll be telling him the truth."

II

To Free the Snared Bird

Gerard emerged from the prison to find that night had fallen. He looked up the street and down, even took a casual saunter behind the prison, and saw no one lurking in a doorway or hiding in the shadows.

"This is my chance," he muttered. "I can ride out of the gate, lose myself in the confusion of the troops setting up camp, find this Samar, and start over from there. That's what I'll do. Leaving now is logical. It makes sense. Yes, that's definitely what I'm going to do."

But even as he said this to himself, even as he told himself repeatedly that this was his best course of action, he knew very well that he wouldn't. He would go find Samar, he had to go—he had promised Silvanoshei he would, and that was a promise he planned to keep, even if he didn't plan to keep any of the rest of the promises he'd made to the young man.

First, he had to talk to Odila. The reason was, of course, that he hoped to persuade her to come with him. He had thought up some very fine arguments against this One God and he planned to use them.

The Temple of the Heart was an ancient building that pre-dated the Cataclysm. Dedicated to the worship of the old gods of Light, the temple had been built at the foot of Mount Grishnor and was reputed to be the oldest structure in Sanction, probably built when Sanction was little more than a fishing village. Various rumors and legends surrounded the temple, including one that the foundation stone had been laid by one of the Kingpriests, who'd had the misfortune to be shipwrecked. Washing up on this shore, the Kingpriest had given thanks to Paladine for his survival. To show his gratitude, he built a temple to the gods.

After the Cataclysm, the temple might have suffered the same fate as many other temples during that time, when people took out their anger on the gods by attacking and destroying their temples. This temple remained standing, unscathed, mostly due to the rumor that the spirit of that same Kingpriest lingered here, refusing to allow anyone to harm his tribute to the gods. The temple suffered from neglect, but that was all.

Following the Chaos War, the vengeful spirit must have departed, for the Mystics of the Citadel of Light moved into the temple without encountering any ghosts.

A small, square, unimposing structure of white marble, the temple had a steeply pitched roof that soared up among the trees. Beneath the roof was a central altar chamber—the largest and most important room in the temple. Other rooms surrounded the altar and were there to support it: sleeping quarters for the priests, a library, and so forth. Two sets of double doors led into the temple from the front.

Deciding that he would make faster time in the crowded streets on foot, Gerard stabled his horse in a hostelry near the West Gate and walked north to where the temple stood on a hill, somewhat isolated from the city, overlooking it.

He found a few people gathered in front of the temple, listening to Mina telling them of the miracles of the One God. An elderly man frowned exceedingly, but most of the others appeared interested.

The temple flared with lights, both inside and out. Huge double doors were propped open. Under Galdar's command, the Knights were carrying Goldmoon's amber sarcophagus into the altar room. The head of the minotaur was easily seen, his horns and snout silhouetted against the flames of torches that had been placed in sconces on the walls. Mina kept close watch on the procedure, glancing often in the direction of the procession to make certain that the sarcophagus was being handled carefully, that her Knights were behaving with dignity and respect.

Pausing in the deep shadows of a night-shrouded tree to reconnoiter, and, hopefully, try to catch a glimpse of Odila, Gerard watched the amber sarcophagus move slowly and with stately formality into the temple. He heard Galdar issue a sharp rebuke at one point, saw Mina turn her head swiftly to look. She was so concerned that she lost the thread of her exhortation and was forced to think a moment to remember where she'd left off.

Gerard could never ask for a better time to talk to Odila than this, while Galdar was supervising the funeral detail and Mina was proselytizing. When a group of Knights walked toward the temple, carrying Mina's baggage, Gerard fell in behind them.

The Knights were in a good mood, talking and laughing over what a fine joke it was on the do-gooder Mystics that Mina had taken over their temple. Gerard couldn't see the humor himself, and he doubted very much if Mina would have been pleased had she overheard them.

The Knights entered through another set of double doors, heading for Mina's living quarters. Looking through an open door on his left into a blaze of candle light, Gerard saw Odila standing beside the altar, directing the placement of the amber sarcophagus on several wooden trestles.

Gerard hung back in the shadows, hoping for a chance to catch Odila alone. The Knights lumbered in with their burden, deposited it with much grunting and groaning and a yelp and a curse, as one of the men dropped his end of the coffin prematurely, causing it to pinch the fingers of another man's hand. Odila issued a sharp rebuke. Galdar growled a threat. The men pushed and shoved, and soon the crystal sarcophagus was in place.

Hundreds of white candles burned on the altar, probably placed there by Odila's hands. The reflection of the candles burned in the amber, so that it seemed Goldmoon lay in the midst of a myriad tiny flames. The light illuminated her waxen face. She looked more peaceful than Gerard remembered, if such a thing were possible. Perhaps, as Mina had said, Goldmoon was pleased to be home.

Gerard wiped his sleeve across his forehead. The candles gave off a surprising amount of heat. Gerard found a seat on a bench in the back of the altar room. He moved as quietly as he could, holding his sword to keep it from knocking against the wall. He couldn't see very well, having stared into the candle flames, and he bumped into someone. Gerard was about to make his excuses when he saw, with a shudder, that his companion was Palin. The mage sat unmoving on the bench, stared unblinking into the candle flames.

Touching the mage's flaccid arm was like touching a warm corpse. Feeling his gorge rise, Gerard moved hastily to another bench. He sat down, waited impatiently for the minotaur to leave.

"I will post a guard around the sarcophagus," Galdar stated.

Gerard muttered a curse. He hadn't counted on that.

"No need," Odila said. "Mina is coming to worship at the altar, and she has given orders that she is to be left alone."

Gerard breathed more freely, then his breathing stopped altogether. The minotaur was half-way out the door when he paused, sent a searching gaze throughout the altar room. Gerard froze in place, trying desperately to remember whether or not minotaur have good night vision. It seemed to him that Galdar saw him, for the beady, bovine eyes stared straight at him. He waited tensely for Galdar to call to him, but, after a moment's scrutiny, the minotaur walked out.

Gerard wiped away the sweat that was now running down his face and dripping off his chin. Slowly and cautiously, he edged out from the rows of benches and walked toward the front of the altar. He tried to be quiet, but leather creaked, metal rattled.

Odila was swathed in candlelight. Her face was partially turned toward him, and he was alarmed to see how thin and wasted she had grown. Riding for weeks in the wagon, doing nothing but listening to Mina's harangues and force-feeding the mages had caused her fine muscle tone to diminish. She could probably still wield her sword, but she wouldn't last two rounds with a healthy, battle-hardened opponent.

She no longer laughed or spoke much, but went about her duties in silence. Gerard hadn't liked this god before. Now he was starting to actively hate the One God. What sort of god stamped out joy and was offended by laughter? No sort of god he wanted to have anything to do with. He was glad he'd come to talk to her, hoped to be able to convince her to abandon this and come away with him.

But even as the hope was born, it died within him. One look at her face as she bent over the candles and he knew he was wasting his time.

He was suddenly reminded of an old poacher's trick for snaring a bird. You attach berries at intervals to a long, thin cord tied to a stake. The bird eats the berries, one by one, ingesting the cord at the same time. When the bird reaches the end of the cord, it tries to fly away, but by now the cord is wound up inside its vitals, and it cannot escape.

One by one, Odila had consumed the berries attached to the lethal cord. The last was the power to work miracles. She was tied to the One God, and only a miracle—a reverse miracle—would cut her free.

Well, perhaps friendship was that sort of miracle.

"Odila—" he began.

"What do you want, Gerard?" she asked, without turning around.

"I have to talk to you," he said. "Please, just a moment. It won't take long."

Odila sat down on a bench near the amber sarcophagus. Gerard would have been happier sitting farther back, out of the light and the heat, but Odila wouldn't move. Tense and preoccupied, she cast frequent glances at the door, glances that were half-nervous, half-expectant.

"Odila, listen to me," said Gerard. "I'm leaving Sanction. Tonight. I came to tell you that and to try to convince you to leave with me."

"No," she said, glancing at the door. "I can't leave now. I have too much to do here before Mina comes."

"I'm not asking you to go on a picnic!" he said, exasperated. "I'm asking you to escape this place with me, tonight! The city is in confusion, what with soldiers marching in and out. No one knows what's going on. It'll be hours before some sort of order is established. Now's the perfect time to leave."

"Then go," she said, shrugging. "I don't want you around anyway."

She started to rise. He grabbed her arm, gripped her wrist tightly, and saw her wince with pain.

"You don't want me around because I remind you of what you used to be. You don't like this One God. You don't like the change that's come over you anymore than I do. Why are you doing this to yourself?"

"Because, Gerard," Odila said wearily, as if she'd gone over the same argument again and again, "the One God is a god. A god who came to this world to care for us and guide us."

"Where? Off the edge of a precipice?" Gerard demanded. "After the Chaos War, Goldmoon found her guide in her own heart. Love and caring, compassion, truth, and honor did not leave with gods of light. They are inside each of us. Those are our guides or they should be."

"At her death, Goldmoon turned to the One God," said Odila, glancing at the still, calm face entombed in amber.

"Did she?" Gerard demanded harshly. "I wonder about that. If she really did embrace the One God, why didn't the One God keep her alive to go around shouting her miracle to the world? Why did the One God feel it necessary to stop her mouth in death and lock her up in an amber prison?"

"She will be freed, Mina says," said Odila defensively. "On the Night of the New Eye, the One God will raise Goldmoon from the dead, and she will come forth to rule the world."

Gerard released her hand, let go of her. "So you won't come with me?"

Odila shook her head. "No, Gerard, I won't. I know you don't understand. I'm not as strong as you are. I'm all by myself in the dark forest, and I'm afraid. I'm glad to have a guide, and if the guide is not perfect, neither am I. Goodbye, Gerard. Thank you for your friendship and your caring. Go on your journey safely in the name of the—"

"One God?" he said grimly. "No, thanks."

Turning, he walked out of the altar room.

The first place Gerard went was to the army's central command post, located in the former Souk Bazaar, whose stalls and shops had been replaced by a small city of tents. Here, the contents of the strongboxes were being distributed.

Taking his place in line, Gerard felt a certain satisfaction in taking the Dark Knights' steel. He'd earned it, no question about that, and he would need money for his journey back to Lord Ulrich's manor or wherever the Knights were consolidating their forces.

After receiving his pay, he headed for the West Gate and freedom. He put Odila out of his mind, refused to let himself think about her. He removed most of his armor—the braces and greaves and his chain mail, but continued to wear the cuirass and helm. Both were uncomfortable, but he had to consider the possibility that sooner or later Galdar might grow tired of shadowing Gerard and just stab him in the back.

The bulk of the two towers of the West Gate loomed black against the red light that shone from the lava moat surrounding the city. The gates had been shut. The gate guards weren't about to open them until they'd had a good look at Gerard and heard his story—that he was a messenger dispatched to Jelek with word of their victory. The guards wished him a good journey and opened a wicket gate to let him ride through.

Glancing back to see the walls of Sanction lined with men, Gerard was once more profoundly and grudgingly impressed with Mina's leadership and her ability to impose discipline and order on her troops.

"She will grow in strength and in power every day she remains here," he remarked gloomily to himself as his horse cantered through the gate. Ahead of him was the harbor and beyond that the black expanse of New Sea. A whiff of salt air was a welcome relief from the continuous smell of sulfur and brimstone that lingered in the air of Sanction. "And how are we to fight her?"

"You can't."

A hulking figure blocked his path. Gerard recognized the voice, as his horse recognized the stench of minotaur. The horse snorted and reared, and Gerard had his hands full trying to remain on the animal's back, during which frantic few moments he lost any opportunity he might have had to either run the minotaur down or gallop away and leave him standing in the dust.

The minotaur drew closer, his bestial face faintly illuminated by the red glow of the lava that made Sanction's night perpetual twilight. Galdar grabbed hold of the horse's bridle.

Gerard drew his sword. He had no doubt that this was going to be their final confrontation, and he was not in much doubt about how it would end. He'd heard tales of how Galdar had once cut a man in two with a single stroke of his massive sword. One glance at the knotty muscles of the arms and the smooth, sleek muscles of the minotaur's hairy chest attested to the veracity of the storyteller.

"Look, Galdar," Gerard said, interrupting the minotaur as he was about to speak, "I've had a bellyful of sermons, and I'm fed up with being watched day and night. You know that I'm a Solamnic Knight sent here to spy on Mina. I know you know, so let's just end this right now—"

"I would like to fight you, Solamnic," said Galdar, and his voice was cold. "I would like to kill you, but I am forbidden."

"I figured as much," said Gerard, lowering his sword. "May I ask why?"

"You serve her. You do her bidding."

"Now, see here, Galdar, you and I both know that I'm not riding to do Mina's bidding—" Gerard began, then stopped, growing confused. Here he was, arguing for his own death.

"By *her*, I do not mean Mina," said Galdar. "I mean the One God. Have you never thought to find out the name?"

"Of the One God?" Gerard was becoming increasingly annoyed by this conversation. "No. To be honest, I never really gave a rat's—"

"Takhisis," said Galdar.

"—ass," said Gerard, and then fell silent.

He sat on his horse in the road in the darkness, thinking, it all makes sense. It all makes bloody, horrible, awful sense. No need to ask him if he believed the minotaur. Deep inside, Gerard had suspected this truth all along.

"Why are you telling me this?" he demanded.

"I am not allowed to kill you," Galdar said dourly, "but I can kill your spirit. I know your plans. You carry a message from that wretched elf king to his people, begging them to come save him. Why do you think Mina chose you to take the elf to prison, if not to be his 'messenger'? She *wants* you to bring his people here. Bring the entire elven nation. Bring the Knights of Solamnia—what is left of them. Bring them all here to witness the glory of Queen Takhisis on the Night of the New Eye."

The minotaur released the horse's bridle. "Ride off, Solamnic. Ride to whatever dreams of victory and glory you have in your heart and know, as you ride, that they are nothing but ash.

Takhisis controls your destiny. All you do, you do in her name. As do I."

Giving Gerard an ironic salute, the minotaur turned and walked back to the walls of Sanction.

Gerard looked up at the sky. Clouds of smoke rolling from the Lords of Doom obliterated the stars and the moon. The night was dark above, fire-tinged below. Was it true that somewhere out there, Takhisis watched him? Knew all he thought and planned?

"I have to go back," Gerard thought, chilled. "Warn Odila." He started to turn his horse's head, then halted. "Maybe that's what Takhisis *wants* me to do. If I go back, perhaps she'll see to it that I lose my chance to talk with Samar. I can't do anything to help Odila. I'll ride on."

He turned his horse's head the other way, then stopped. "Takhisis wants me to talk to the elf. Galdar said as much. So maybe I shouldn't! How can I know what to do? Or does it even make any difference?"

Gerard stopped dead in his tracks.

"Galdar was right," he said bitterly. "He would have done me a favor by sticking a plain, ordinary, everyday sword in my gut. The blade he's left there now is poisoned, and I can never rid myself of it. What do I do? What *can* I do?"

He had only one answer, and it was the one he'd given Odila.

He had to follow what was in his heart.

12

The New Eye

As he stalked back toward the West Gate, Galdar was disappointed to find that he didn't feel as pleased with himself as he should have. He had hoped to infect the confident and self-assured Solamnic with the same sickness that infected him. He'd done what he'd set out to accomplish— the angry, frustrated expression on the Solamnic's face had proven that. But Galdar found he couldn't take any satisfaction from his victory.

What had he hoped? That the Solamnic would prove him wrong?

"Bah!" Galdar snorted. "He's caught in the same coil as the rest of us, and there's no way out. Not now. Not ever. Not even in death."

He rubbed his right arm, which had begun to ache persistently, and found himself wishing he could lose it again, so much did it pain him. Once he'd been proud of that arm, the arm that Mina had restored to him, the first miracle she'd ever performed in the name of the One God. Now he caught himself fingering his sword with some vague notion of hacking off the arm himself. He wouldn't, of course. Mina would be angry with him and, worse, she would be hurt and saddened. He could endure her anger, he'd felt its lash before. He could never do anything to hurt her. Most of the pent-up fury and resentment he felt toward Takhisis was based not on her treatment of him but the way she treated Mina, who had sacrificed everything, even her life, for her goddess.

Mina had been rewarded. She'd been given victory over her enemies, given the power to perform miracles. But Galdar knew Takhisis of old. The minotaur race had never thought very highly of the goddess, who was the consort of the minotaur god, Sargas, or Sargonnas, as the other races called him. Sargas had remained with his people to fight Chaos until the bitter end, when—so legend had it—he had sacrificed himself to save the minotaur race. Takhisis would never dream of sacrificing herself for anything. She expected sacrifices to be made to her, demanded them in return for her dubious blessings.

Perhaps that is what she has in mind for Mina. Galdar grew uneasy listening to Mina's constant talk of this "great miracle" Takhisis was going to perform on the Night of the New Eye. Takhisis never gave something for nothing. Galdar had only to feel the throbbing pain of the goddess's displeasure with him to know that. Mina was so trusting, so guileless. She could never understand Takhisis's deceitfulness, her treacherous and vindictive nature.

That, of course, was why Mina had been chosen. That and because she was beloved of Goldmoon. Takhisis would not pass up a chance to inflict pain on anyone, most especially on Goldmoon, who had thwarted her in the past.

I could tell all this to Mina, Galdar thought as he entered the temple. I could tell her, but she wouldn't hear me. She hears only one voice these days.

The Temple of the Heart, now the Temple of the One God. How Takhisis must revel in that appellation! After an eternity of being one of many, now she was one and all powerful.

He shook his horned head gloomily.

The temple grounds were empty. Galdar went first to Mina's quarters. He did not truly expect to find her there, although she must be exhausted after the day's battle. He knew where she would be. He wanted to check to make certain that everything was prepared for her when she finally chose to go to bed.

He glanced into the room that had once been the room for the head of the Order, probably that old fool who'd scowled all through Mina's sermon. Galdar found all in readiness. Everything had been arranged for her comfort. Her weapons were here, as was her armor, carefully arranged on a stand. Her morning star had been polished, the blood cleaned from it and from her armor. Her boots were free of dirt and blood. A tray of food stood on a desk near the bed. A candle burned to light her way in the darkness. Someone had even thought of placing some late-blooming wildflowers in a pewter cup. Everything in the room attested to the love and devotion her troops felt for her.

For her. Galdar wondered if she realized that. The men fought for her, for Mina. They shouted her name when she led them forth to battle. They shouted her name in victory.

Mina . . . Mina . . .

They did not shout, "For the One God." They did not shout, "For Takhisis".

"And I'll wager you don't like that," Galdar said to the darkness.

Could a god be jealous of a mortal?

This god could, Galdar thought, and he was suddenly filled with fear.

Galdar entered the altar room, stood blinking painfully while his eyes became accustomed to the light of the candles blazing on the altar. Mina was alone, kneeling before the altar in prayer. He could hear her voice, murmuring, halting, then murmuring again, as if she were receiving instructions.

The other Solamnic, the female Knight turned priestess, lay stretched out on a bench, asleep. She slept soundly on her hard bed. Mina's own cloak covered the female. Galdar could never remember her name.

Goldmoon, in her amber coffin, slept as well. The two mages sat in the back of the chamber, where'd they'd been planted. He could see their forms, shadowy in the candlelight. His gaze flicked over them quickly, went back to Mina. The sight of the wretched mages gave him the horrors, made the hair rise on his spine, ripple down his back.

Someday perhaps his own corpse would sit there quietly, staring at nothing, doing nothing, waiting for Takhisis's orders.

Galdar walked toward the altar. He tried to move quietly, out of respect for Mina, but minotaurs are not made for stealthy movement. His knee bumped a bench, his sword clanked and clattered at his side, his footfalls boomed, or so it seemed to him.

The female Solamnic stirred uneasily, but she was too deeply drowned in sleep to waken.

Mina did not hear him.

Walking up to stand behind her, he spoke to her quietly, "Mina."

She did not lift her head.

Galdar waited a moment, then said, "Mina" again and placed his hand gently on her shoulder.

Now she turned, now she looked around. Her face was pale and drawn with fatigue. Smudged circles of weariness surrounded her amber eyes, whose bright gleam was dimmed.

"You should go to bed," he told her.

"Not yet," she said.

"You were all over the battlefield," he persisted. "I couldn't keep up with you. Everywhere I looked, there you were. Fighting, praying. You need your rest. We have much to do tomorrow and in the days following to fortify the city. The Solamnics will attack us. Their spy rides to alert them even now. I let him go," Galdar growled, "as you commanded. I think it was a mistake. He's in league with the elf king. The Solamnics will make some deal with the elves, bring the might of both nations down on us."

"Most likely," said Mina.

She held out her hand to Galdar. He was privileged to help

her rise to her feet. She retained his hand—his right hand—in her own, looked up into his eyes.

"All is well, Galdar. I know what I am doing. Have faith."

"I have faith in you, Mina," Galdar said.

Mina cast him a disappointed glance. Releasing his hand, she turned away from him to face the altar. Her look and her silence were her rebuke, that and the sudden gut-twisting pain in his arm. He clamped his lips shut, massaged his arm, and stubbornly waited.

"I have no more need of you, Galdar," Mina said. "Go to your bed."

"I do not sleep until you sleep, Mina. You know that. Or you should, after all this time together."

Her head bowed. He was astonished to see two tears glitter in the candlelight, slide down her cheeks. She whisked them both swiftly away.

"I know, Galdar," she said in muffled voice that tried to be gruff but failed, "and I do appreciate your loyalty. If only . . ." She paused, then, glancing back at him, she said, almost shyly, "Will you wait here with me?"

"Wait for what, Mina?"

"For a miracle."

Mina lifted her hands in a commanding gesture. The flames leaped and swelled, burning brighter and hotter. A wave of searing heat smote Galdar in the face, causing him to gasp for breath and lift his hand to shield himself.

A breath filled the chamber, blew on the flames, caused them to grow stronger, burn higher. Banners and tapestries graced with emblems sacred to the Mystics hung behind the altar. The flames licked the fringe of the tapestries. The fabric caught fire.

The heat grew in intensity. Smoke coiled around the altar and around Goldmoon's amber sarcophagus. The Solamnic female began to cough and choke and woke herself up. She stared in fearful amazement, jumped to her feet.

"Mina!" she cried. "We must get out of here!"

The flames spread rapidly from the banners to the wooden beams that supported the steep ceiling. Galdar had never seen fire move so fast, as if the wood and the walls had been soaked with oil.

"If your miracle is to burn down this temple, then the Solamnic is right," Galdar bellowed over the roar of the fire. "We must get out of here now, before the ceiling collapses."

"We are in no danger," Mina said calmly. "The hand of the One God protects us. Watch and wonder and glory in her power."

The gigantic wooden ceiling beams were now ablaze. At any moment, they would start to crumble and break apart, come crashing down on top of them. Galdar was just about to grab hold of Mina and carry her out bodily, when he saw, to his utter confusion, that the flames consumed the beams entirely. Nothing was left of them. No cinders fell, no fiery timbers came thundering down in a rush of sparks. The holy fire devoured the wood, devoured the ceiling, devoured whatever materials had been used to build the roof. The flames consumed and then went out.

Nothing was left of the temple roof, not even ashes. Galdar stared into the night sky that glittered with stars.

The corpses of the two mages sat on their bench, unseeing, uncaring. They could have perished in the flames and never made a sound, spoken no word of protest, done nothing to save themselves. At a sharply spoken command from Mina, the bodies of the mages rose to their feet and moved toward the altar. Walking without seeing where they were going, they came to a halt when Mina ordered them to stop—near Goldmoon's amber sarcophagus—and stood once more staring at nothing.

"Watch!" said Mina softly. "The miracle begins."

Galdar had seen many wondrous and terrible sights in his long life, particularly that part of it that revolved around Mina. He had never seen anything like this, and he stared, thunderstruck.

A hundred thousand souls filled the night sky. The ghostly mist of their hands, their faces, their diaphanous limbs blotted out the stars. Galdar stared, aghast, amazed, to see that in their ephemeral hands, the dead carried the skulls of dragons.

Reverently, gently, the souls of the dead lowered the first skull through the charred opening where the roof had been and placed the skull on the floor, before the altar.

The skull was enormous, that of a gold dragon—Galdar could tell by the few golden scales that clung to the bone and gleamed pathetically in the flickering candlelight. Though the altar room was large, the skull filled it.

The dead brought down another skull, that of a red dragon. The dead placed the skull of the red dragon down beside that of the gold.

Shouts and cries rose up from outside. Seeing the flames, people came running to the Temple. The shouts ceased as they gazed in shock at the wondrous and fearful sight of dragon skulls, hundreds of them, spiraling down out of the dark night, cradled in the arms of the dead.

Methodically, the dead piled the skulls one on top of the other, the largest skulls on the bottom to form a secure base, the skulls of smaller dragons piled on top of that. The mound of skulls rose higher and higher, stacking up well above what would have been the height of the steep-pitched roof.

Galdar's mouth went dry. His eyes burned, his throat constricted so that he had difficulty speaking.

"This is a skull totem from one of the dragon overlords!" he cried.

"*Three* of the dragon overlords to be precise," Mina corrected.

The totem increased in height, now taller than the tallest trees, and still the dead continued to bring more skulls to add to it.

"This is the totem of Beryllinthranox the Green and of Khellendros the Blue and of Malystryx the Red. As Malystryx stole the totems of the other two, so the dead steal hers."

Galdar's stomach shriveled. His knees weakened. He was forced to grab hold of the altar to remain standing. He was terrified, and he was not ashamed to admit to his terror.

"You have stolen Malys's totem? The dragon will be furious,

Mina. She will find out who has taken the totem, and she will come here after you!"

"I know," said Mina calmly. "That is the plan."

"She will kill you, Mina!" Galdar gasped. "She will kill us all. I know this foul dragon. No one can stand up to her. Even her own kind are terrified of her."

"Look, Galdar," said Mina softly.

Galdar turned his reluctant gaze back to the pile of skulls that was now almost complete. One last skull, that of a small white dragon, was laid upon the top. The dead lingered for a moment, as if admiring their handiwork. A chill wind blew down from the mountainside, shredded the souls into wisps of fog, and dispersed them with a puff.

The eyes of dead dragons began to shine from their hollow eye sockets. It seemed to Galdar that he could hear voices, hundreds of voices, raised in a triumphant paean. A shadowy form took shape above the totem, coiled around it covetously. The shadowy form became clearer, more distinct. Scales of many colors gleamed in the candlelight. An enormous tail curled around the totem's base, the body of a giant dragon circled it. Five heads rose over the totem. Five heads attached to one body and that body attached to the totem.

The body lacked substance, however. The five heads were daunting, but they were not real heads, not as real as the skulls of the dead over which they hovered. The eyes of the dead dragons gleamed bright. Their light was almost blinding, and suddenly it lanced straight into the heavens.

The light of the totem blazed through the sky, and there, looking down upon them, was a single eye. The eye of the goddess.

White, staring, the eye gazed down at them, unblinking.

The body of the five-headed dragon grew more distinct, gained in substance and in strength.

"The power of the totem feeds the One God as the totem once fed Malys," Mina said. "With each passing moment, the One God comes closer to entering the world, joining the mortal and immortal. On the Night of the Festival of the New Eye, the

One God will become the paradox, she will take a mortal form and imbue it with immortality. In that moment, she will rule over all that is in the heavens and all that is below. She will rule over the living and the dead. Her victory will be assured, her triumph complete."

She will take a mortal form. Galdar knew then why they'd been forced to cart the body of Goldmoon across Ansalon, haul it up mountains, and hoist it out of valleys.

Takhisis's final revenge. She would enter the body of the one person who had fought life-long against her, and she would use that body to seduce and enthrall and entrap the trusting, the innocent, the guileless.

He could hear outside the temple a hubbub of voices, raised in excitement, babbling and clamoring at the sight of this new moon in the heavens. The cry raised, "Mina! Mina!"

She would go out to them, bask in the light and warmth of their affection, far different from that chill, cold light. She would tell them that this was the work of the One God, but no one would pay any attention.

"Mina . . . Mina . . ."

She walked out the door of the ruined temple. Galdar heard the swelling cheer raised when she appeared, heard it reverberate off the sides of the mountains, echo to the heavens.

To the heavens.

Galdar looked up at the five heads of the ethereal dragon, swaying over the totem, consuming its power. The single eye burned, and he realized in that moment that he was closer to this goddess than Mina was or ever could be.

The trusting, the innocent, the guileless.

Galdar wanted his bed, wanted to sleep and forget all this in dark oblivion. He would break his own rule this night. Mina was with those who adored her. She had no need of him. He was about to depart, when he heard a moan.

The Solamnic female crouched on the floor, huddled within herself, staring up, appalled, at the monster that writhed and coiled above her.

She, too, had seen the truth.

"Too late," he said to her as he passed by on his way to his bed. "Too late. For all of us."

13

Restless Spirits

T he bodies of the two mages stood where they had been told to stand, near the amber sarcophagus in the Temple of the Heart, now the Temple of the One God. The spirit of only one of the mages was there to watch the building of the totem. Dalamar's spirit had departed with the arrival of the skull-bearing dead. Palin continued to watch the totem grow, a monument to the strengthening power of Queen Takhisis. He had no idea where Dalamar had gone. The spirit of the dark elf was often absent, gone more than he was around.

Palin still found it disconcerting to be away from his body for any period of time, but had been venturing farther these past few days. He was growing increasingly alarmed, for he realized—as did all the dead—that Takhisis was very close to the time when she would make her triumphant entry into the world.

Palin watched the totem grow and, with it, Takhisis's power. Takhisis could take many forms, but when dealing with dragons, she preferred her dragon form. Five heads, each of a different color and species of dragon, emerged from a body of massive power and strength. The head of the red dragon was brutal, vicious. Flames flickered in the nostrils. The head of the blue was sleek, elegant, and deadly. Lightning crackled from between the razor-sharp fangs. The head of the black was cunning, sly, and dripped poison acid. The head of the white was cruel, calculating, and radiated a bone-numbing chill. The head of the green was devious and clever. Noxious fumes spewed from the gaping jaws.

This was Takhisis on the immortal plane, the Takhisis the dead served in dread terror, the Takhisis whom Palin hated and loathed and, despite himself, felt moved to worship. For in the eyes of the five dragons was the mind of the god, a mind that could span the vastness of eternity and see and understand the limitless possibilities and, at the same time, number all the drops in the swelling seas and count the grains of sand in the barren desert.

The sight of the Dark Queen hovering around the skulls of the dead dragons, receiving the accolades of the dead dragons, was too much for him to bear. Palin tore his spirit from his body and flitted restlessly out into the darkness.

He found it difficult to give up the habits of the living, and so he roamed the streets of Sanction in his spirit form as he might have done in his living form. He walked around buildings, when he might have passed through them. Physical objects were no barrier to a spirit, yet they blocked him. To walk through walls—to do something that was so completely against the laws of nature—would be to admit that he had lost any connection to life, to the physical part of life. He could not do that, not yet.

His spirit form did allow him easy passage through the streets that were clogged with people, everyone running to the newly proclaimed Temple of the One God to see the miracle. If he had been alive and breathing, Palin would have been swept up in the mob or run down, just as were two beggars floundering in the street. One, a lame man, had his crutch knocked out from under him. The other, a blind man, had lost his cane and was groping about helplessly with his hands, trying to find it.

Instinctively, Palin started to offer them help, only to remember what he was, remember there was no help he could give. Drifting nearer, Palin noted that the blind man looked familiar—the silver hair, the white robes. . . . The silver hair especially. He couldn't see the man's face, which was covered by bandages to hide the hideous wound that had robbed him of his sight. Palin knew the blind man, but he couldn't place him. The man was out of context, not where he was supposed to be. The Citadel of Light came to Palin's mind, and he suddenly recalled where he had seen this man before. This man, who was no man.

Using the eyes of the spirit world, Palin saw the true forms of the two beggars, forms that existed on the immortal plane and thus could not be banished, although they had taken other shapes in the mortal world. A silver dragon—Mirror—former guardian of the Citadel of Light stood side by side, wing-tip to wing-tip with a blue dragon.

Palin remembered then what it was to hope.

Dalamar's spirit was also abroad this night. The dark elf ventured much farther afield than Palin. Unlike Palin, Dalamar let no physical barrier impede him. Mountains were for him as insubstantial as clouds. He passed through the solid rock walls of Malys's lair, penetrated its labyrinthine chambers with the ease of blinking an eye or drawing a breath.

He found the great, red dragon sleeping, as he had been accustomed to finding her on previous occasions. Yet, this time, there was a difference. On his earlier visits, she'd slept deeply and peacefully, secure in the knowledge that she was supreme ruler of this world and there were none strong enough to challenge her. Now, her sleep was troubled. Her huge feet twitched, her eyes roved behind closed lids, her nostrils inflated. Saliva drooled from her jaw, and a growl rumbled deep in her chest. She dreamed—an unpleasant dream, seemingly.

That would be nothing, compared to her waking.

"Most Great and Gracious Majesty," Dalamar said.

Malys opened one eye, another sign that her slumber was not restful. Usually Dalamar had to speak to her several times or even summon one of her minions to come wake her.

"What do you want?" she growled.

"To make you aware of what is transpiring in the world while you sleep."

"Yes, go on," Malys said, opening the other eye.

"Where is your totem, Majesty?" Dalamar asked coolly.

Malys turned her massive head to look reassuringly upon her collection of skulls, trophies of her many victories, including those over Beryl and Khellendros.

Her eyes widened. Her breath escaped in a sizzling hiss. Rearing up with such force that she caused the mountain to quiver, she turned her head this way and that.

"Where is it?" she bellowed, lashing out with her tail. Granite walls cracked at the blows, stalactites crashed down from the ceiling, shattered on her red scales. She paid them no attention. "Where is the thief? Who has stolen it? Tell me!"

"I will tell you," Dalamar said, ignoring her fury, for she could do him no harm. "But I want something in exchange."

"Always the shrewd bargainer!" she hissed with a flicker of flame from out her teeth.

"You are aware of my present lamentable condition," said Dalamar, extending his hands to exhibit his ghostly form. "If you recover the totem and defeat the person who has unlawfully taken it, I ask that you use your magic to restore my soul to my living body."

"Granted," said Malys with a twitch of her clawed foot. Her head leaned forward. "Who has it?"

"Mina."

"Mina?" Malys repeated, baffled. "Who is this Mina and why has she taken my totem? *How* has she taken it? I smell no thief! No one has been in my lair! No thief could transport it!"

"Not even an army of thieves," Dalamar agreed. "An army of the dead could. And did."

"Mina . . ." Malys breathed the name with loathing. "Now I remember. I heard it said that she commanded an army of souls. What rubbish!"

"The 'rubbish' stole away the totem while you slept, Majesty, and they have rebuilt it in Sanction, in what was once known as the Temple of the Heart, but is now known as the Temple of the One God."

"This so-called One God again," snarled Malys. "This One God is starting to annoy me."

"The One God could do far more than annoy you, Majesty," said Dalamar coolly. "This One God was responsible for the destruction of Cyan Bloodbane, your cousin Beryl, and Khellendros the Blue—next to yourself, the three mightiest dragons in Krynn. This One God has encompassed the fall of Silvanesti, the destruction of Qualinost, the defeat of the Solamnic Knights in Solanthus, and now she has been victorious in Sanction. You alone stand in the way of her absolute triumph."

Malys glowered, silent, brooding. He had spoken harshly, and although she didn't like to hear it, she couldn't deny the truth.

"She steals my totem. Why?" Malys asked sullenly.

"It has not been your totem for a long time," Dalamar replied. "The One God has been subverting the souls of the dead dragons who once worshiped her. She has been using the power of their souls to fuel her own power. By stealing the totems of your cousin and Khellendros, you played into the One God's hands. You made the souls of the dead dragons more powerful still. Do not underestimate this goddess. Although she was weakened and near destruction when first she came to this world, she has recovered her strength, and she is now poised to lay claim to a prize she has long coveted."

"You speak as if you know this goddess," said Malys, eyeing Dalamar with contempt.

"I do know her," said Dalamar, "and so do you—by reputation. Her name is Takhisis."

"Yes, I've heard of her," said Malys, with a dismissive flick of a claw. "I heard she abandoned this world during the war with Father Chaos."

"She did not abandon it," said Dalamar. "She stole it and brought it here, as she had long planned to do with the aid of Khellendros. Did you never stop to think how this world suddenly came into being in this part of the universe? Did you never wonder?"

"No, why should I?" Malys returned angrily. "If food falls into the hands of a starving man, he does not question, he eats!"

"You dined exceedingly well, Majesty," Dalamar agreed. "It is a shame that afterward you did not take out the garbage. The souls of the dead dragons have recognized their queen, and they will do anything she requires. You are sadly outnumbered, Your Majesty."

"Dead dragons have no fangs." Malys sneered. "I face a puny god who has a child for a champion and who must rely on expired souls for her might. I will recover my totem and deal a death blow to this god."

"When does Your Majesty plan to attack Sanction?" Dalamar asked.

"When I am ready," Malys growled. "Leave me now."

Dalamar bowed low. "Your Majesty will not forget her promise—to restore my soul to my body. I could be of so much more use to you as one whole person."

Malys waved a claw. "I do not forget my promises. Now go."

Closing her eyes, she let her massive head sink to the floor.

Dalamar was not fooled. For all her appearance of nonchalance, Malys had been shaken to the core of her being. She might sham sleep, but inside the fires of her rage burned bright and hot.

Satisfied that he had done all he could—here, at least—Dalamar departed.

The totem grew inside the fire-ravaged Temple. Mina's Knights and soldiers cheered her and called her name. Takhisis's shadow hovered over the totem, but few could see her. They did not look for her. They saw Mina, and that was all they cared about.

In Sanction's streets, now almost completely emptied, the silver dragon Mirror groped about for his beggar's staff, that had been knocked out of his hands.

"What is happening?" he asked his companion, who silently handed him his staff. "What is going on? I hear a tumult and a great cry."

"It is Takhisis," said Razor. "I can see her. She has revealed herself. Many of my brethren circle in the heavens, shouting her name. The dead dragons cry out to her. I hear the voice of my mate among them. Red, blue, white, black, green, living, dead—all swear their loyalty to her. She grows in power as I speak."

"Will you join them?" Mirror asked.

"I have been thinking long on what you said back in the cave of the mighty Skie," said Razor slowly. "How none of the calamities that have befallen this world would have happened if it had not been for Takhisis. I hated and detested Paladine and the other so-called gods of light. I cursed his name, and if I had a chance to kill one of his champions, I took that chance and gloried in it. I longed for the day when our queen might rule uncontested.

"Now that day has come, and I am sorry for it. She has no care for us." Razor paused, then said, "I see you smiling, Silver. You think 'care' is the wrong word. I agree. Those of us who followed the Dark Queen are not noted for being caring individuals. Respect. That is the word I want. Takhisis has no respect for those her serve her. She uses them until they are no longer of value to her, then she casts them aside. No, I will not serve Takhisis."

"But will he work actively against her?" a familiar voice whispered in Mirror's ear. "If you will vouch for him, I can use his help, as well as yours."

"Palin?" Mirror turned gladly in the direction of the voice. He reached out his hand toward the source of the voice, but felt no warm hand clasp his in return.

"I cannot see you or touch you, but I hear you, Palin," Mirror said. "And even your voice seems far away and distant, as though you speak from across a wide vale."

"So I do," said Palin. "Yet, together, perhaps we can cross it. I want you to help me destroy this totem."

Dalamar's spirit joined the river of souls flowing toward the Temple of the One, as other rivers flow toward the sea. His spirit paid no heed to the rest, but concentrated on his next objective. The other souls ignored him. They would not have heard him if he had spoken. They did not see him. They heard only one voice, saw only one face.

On arriving, Dalamar broke free of the torrent that spiraled around and around the totem of dragon skulls. The immense monument towered high in the air, visible for miles, or so said some of the thousands who stood staring at it in awe and admiration, exulting in Mina's victory over the hated red dragon, Malys.

Dalamar flicked the totem a glance. It was impressive, he had to admit. He then shifted his mind to more urgent matters. Guards stood posted at the temple doors. None with substantial bodies were being admitted inside the temple. His spirit flowed past the guards and into the altar room. He made certain that his body was safe, noted with some suprise that Palin's spirit was abroad this night.

Palin's departure was such an unusual occurrence that, despite the urgency of his errand, Dalamar paused to ponder where he might be, what the mage's soul could be up to. Dalamar wasn't concerned. He considered Palin as devious as a bowl of porridge.

"Still," Dalamar reminded himself, "he is Raistlin's nephew. And while porridge may be pale and lumpy, it is also thick and viscous. Much can be concealed beneath that bland surface."

The souls whirled in frenetic ecstasy around the totem, as thick as smoke rising from water-soaked wood. Millions of faces streamed past Dalamar any instant he chose to look. He continued on his way, moved ahead with the next stage of his plan.

Mina stood alone at the candle-lit altar. Her back to the totem, she stared, rapt, into the flames. The big minotaur was nearby. Where Mina was, the minotaur was.

"Mina, you are exhausted," Galdar pleaded. "You can barely stand. You must come to your bed. Tomorrow . . . who knows what tomorrow will bring? You should be rested."

"I thought you went to bed, Galdar," said Mina.

"I did," the minotaur growled. "I could not sleep. I knew I would find you here."

"I like to be here," said Mina in a dreamy voice. "Close to the One God. I can feel her holy presence. She folds me in her arms and lifts me up with her."

Mina raised her gaze upward into the night sky, now visible since the roof of the temple had been destroyed. "I am warm when I am with her, Galdar. I am warm and loved and fed and clothed and safe in her arms. When I come back to this world, I am cold and starving and thirsty. It is a punishment to be here, Galdar, when I would so much rather be up there."

Galdar made a rumbling sound in his throat. If he had doubts, he knew better than to speak them. He said only, "Yet, while you are down here, Mina, you have a job to do for the One God. You will not be able to do that job if you are sick with fatigue."

Mina reached out her hand, placed it on the minotaur's arm. "You are right, Galdar. I am being selfish. I will come to bed, and I will even sleep late in the morning."

Mina turned to look at the totem. Her amber eyes shone as if she still stared into the flames. "Isn't it magnificent?"

She might have said more, but Dalamar took care to enter her line of sight. He bowed low.

"I seek but a moment of your time, Mina," said Dalamar, bowing again.

"Go on ahead and make certain that my chamber is prepared, Galdar," Mina ordered. "Don't worry. I will come shortly."

Galdar's bestial eyes passed over the place where Dalamar's spirit hovered. Dalamar could never decide if the minotaur saw him or not. He didn't think so, but he had the feeling that Galdar knew his spirit was there. The minotaur's nose wrinkled, as though he smelled something rotten. Then with a grunting snort, Galdar turned away and left the altar room.

"What do you want?" Mina asked Dalamar. Her tone was calm, composed. "Have you word of the magical device carried by the kender?"

"Alas, no, Mina," said Dalamar, "but I do have other information. I have dire news. Malys is aware that you are the one who has stolen her totem."

"Indeed," said Mina, smiling slightly.

"Malys will come to take it back, Mina. The dragon is furious. She sees you now as a threat to her power."

"Why are you telling me all this, wizard?" Mina asked. "Surely, you are not fearful for my safety."

"No, Mina, I am not," said Dalamar coolly. "But I am fearful for my own if something should happen to you. I will help you defeat Malys. You will need a wizard's help to fight against this dragon."

"How will you, in your sorry state, help me?" Mina asked, amused.

"Restore my soul to my body. I am one of the most powerful wizards in the history of Krynn. My help to you could be invaluable. You have no leader for the dead. You tried to recruit Lord Soth and failed."

The amber eyes flickered. She was displeased.

"Yes, I heard about that," Dalamar said. "My spirit travels the world. I know a great deal about what is transpiring. I could be of use to you. I could be the one to lead the dead. I could seek out the kender and bring him and the device to you. Burrfoot knows me, he trusts me. I have made a study of the Device of Time Journeying. I could teach you to use it. I could use my magic to help you fight the dragon's magic. All this I could do for you—but only as living man."

Dalamar saw himself reflected in the amber eyes—a wisp, more insubstantial than spider's silk.

"All this you will do for me and more, if I require it," Mina said, "not as living man but as living corpse." She lifted her head proudly. "As for your help against Malys, I have no need of your aid. The One God supports me and fights at my side. I need no other."

"Listen to me, Mina, before you go," insisted Dalamar, as she was turning away. "In my youth, I came to your One God as a lover comes to his mistress. She embraced me and caressed me and promised me that one day we would rule the world, she and I. I believed her, I trusted in her. My trust was betrayed. When I was no longer of use to her, she cast me to my enemies. She will do the same to you, Mina. When that day comes, you will need an ally of my strength and power. A living ally, not a corpse."

Mina paused, glanced back at him. She wore a thoughtful look. "Perhaps there is something in what you say, wizard."

Dalamar watched her warily, not trusting this sudden about-face. "There is, I assure you."

"Your faith in the One God was betrayed. She might say the same of you, Dalamar the Dark. Lovers often quarrel, a silly quarrel, soon forgotten, neither of them remembering."

"I remember," said Dalamar. "Because of her betrayal, I lost everything I ever loved and valued. Do you think I would so readily forget?"

"She might say that you put all that you loved and valued above her," Mina said, "that she was the one forsaken. Still, after all this time, it doesn't matter who was at fault. She values your affection. She would like to prove she still loves you by restoring to you everything you lost and more."

"In return for what?" Dalamar asked warily.

"A pledge of your affection."

"And? . . ."

"A small favor."

"And what is this 'small' favor?"

"Your friend, Palin Majere—"

"He is not my friend."

"That makes this easier, then," Mina said. "Your fellow wizard conspires against the One God. She is aware of his plots and schemings, of course. She would have no trouble thwarting them, but she has much on her mind these days, and she would appreciate your help."

"What must I do?" Dalamar asked.

Mina shrugged. "Nothing much. Simply alert her when he is about to act. That is all. She will take care of the matter from there."

"And in return?"

"You will be restored to life. You will be given all you ask for, including the leadership of the army of souls, if that is what you want. In addition . . ." Mina smiled at him. The amber eyes smiled.

"Yes? In addition?"

"Your magic will be restored to you."

"*My* magic," Dalamar emphasized. "I do not want the magic she borrowed from the dead and then loaned to me. I want the magic that once lived inside me!"

"You want the god's magic. She promises."

Dalamar thought back to all the promises Takhisis had made him, all the promises she had broken. He wanted this so much. He wanted to believe.

"I will," he said softly.

14

The Ring and the Cloak

Days, weeks, had passed since the Qualinesti elves had arrived in Silvanesti. How long they had been here, Gilthas could not say, for one day blended into another in the timeless woods. And though his people were content to allow one day to slide off time's silken strand and fall into the soft green grass, Gilthas was not. He grew increasingly frustrated. Alhana kept up the pretense that Silvanoshei was recovering inside his tent. She spoke of him to her people, giving details of what he said and what he ate and how he was slowly mending. Gilthas listened in shock to these lies, but, after a time, he came to the conclusion that Alhana actually believed them. She had woven the threads of falsehood into a warm blanket and was using that blanket to shield herself from the cold truth.

The Silvanesti listened to her and asked no questions— something else that was incomprehensible to Gilthas.

"We Silvanesti do not like change," explained Kiryn in response to Gilthas's frustration. "Our mages halted the changing of the seasons, for we could not bear to see the green of spring wither and die. I know you cannot understand this, Gilthas. Your human blood runs hot, will not let you sit still. You count the seconds because they are so short and slip away so fast. The human side of you revels in change."

"Yet change comes!" said Gilthas, pacing back and forth, "whether the Silvanesti will it or not."

"Yes, change has come to us," said Kiryn with a sad smile. "Its raging torrent has washed away much of what we loved. Now the waters are calmer, we are content to float on the surface. Perhaps we will wash up on some quiet shore, where no one will find us or touch us or harm us ever again."

"The Dark Knights are desperate," said Gilthas. "They are outnumbered, they have no food. Their morale is low. We should attack now!"

"What would be the outcome?" asked Kiryn, shrugging. "The Dark Knights are desperate, as you say. They will not go down without a fight. Many of our people would die."

"And many of the enemy would die," said Gilthas impatiently.

"The death of one human is as the crushing of an ant—there are so many left and so many more to come. The death of a single elf is like the falling of a mighty oak. None will grow up to take his place for hundreds of years, if then. So many of us have died already. We have so little left to us, and it is all precious. How can we waste it?"

"What if the Silvanesti knew the truth about Silvanoshei?" Gilthas asked grimly. "What would happen then?"

Kiryn looked out into the green leaves of the never changing forest. "They know, Gilthas," he said quietly. "They know. As I said, they do not like change. It easier to pretend that it is always springtime."

Eventually, Gilthas had to quit worrying about the Silvanesti and start worrying about his own people. The Qualinesti were beginning to splinter into factions. One was led, unfortunately, by his wife. The Lioness sought revenge, no matter what the cost.

She and those like her wanted to fight the humans in Silvanost, drive them out, whether the Silvanesti would join them or not. It fell to Gilthas to argue time and again that under no circumstances could the Qualinesti launch an attack against the lord city of their cousins. No good could come of this, he argued. It would lead to more years of bitter division between the two nations. He could see this so clearly that he wondered how others could be so blind.

"You are the one who is blind," said the Lioness angrily. "No wonder. You stare constantly into the darkness of your own mind!"

She left him, moved out of their tent, going to live among her Wilder elf troops. Gilthas grieved at this quarrel—the first since their marriage—but he was king first, not loving husband. Much as he longed to give in, he could not, in good conscience, permit her to have her way.

Another faction of Qualinesti was being seduced by the Silvanesti way of life. Their hearts bruised and aching, they were content to live in the dreamlike state in the beautiful forest that reminded them of the forests of their homeland. Senator Palthainon, the leader of this faction, slavishly flattered the Silvanesti, dropping hints into their ears that Gilthas, because he was part human, was not the right ruler of the Qualinesti and could never be. Gilthas was erratic and wayward, as are all humans, and not to be trusted. If it had not been for the staunch and steadfast courage of Senator Palthainon, the Qualinesti would have never made it across the desert alive, and so on and so forth.

Some of the Qualinesti knew this to be untrue, and many argued in favor of their king, but the rest, while they applauded Gilthas's courage, would not have been sorry to see him go. He was the past, the pain, the gaping wound. They wanted to start to heal. As for the Silvanesti, they did not trust Gilthas to begin with, and Palthainon's whispers did not help.

Gilthas felt as though he had walked into a quagmire. Relentlessly, inch by agonizing inch, he was being sucked down into some nameless doom. His struggles caused him to sink further, his cries went unheeded. The end was approaching so slowly that no one else seemed to be aware of it. Only he could see it.

The stalemate continued. The Dark Knights hid in Silvanost, afraid to come out. The elves hid in the forest, unwilling to move.

Gilthas had taken to walking the forests alone these days. He wanted no company for his gloom-ridden thoughts, had even banished Planchet. Hearing a bestial cry from the air, he looked up, and his blood thrilled. A griffin, bearing a rider, circled above the trees, searching for a safe place to land. Change, for good or ill, was coming.

Gilthas hastened through the forest to where Alhana had established her camp, about thirty miles south of the border between Silvanesti and Blöde. The majority of the Silvanesti force was in this location, along with the refugees who had fled or been rescued from the capital city of Silvanost, and the Qualinesti refugees. Other elven forces were located along the Thon-Thalas River, with more lurking in the Bleeding Woods that surrounded Silvanost. Although scattered, the elven forces were in constant contact, using the wind, the creatures of woods and air, and runners to speed messages from one group to another.

Gilthas had wandered far from the campsite, and he was some time retracing his steps. When he arrived, he found Alhana in company with an elf who was a stranger to him. The elf was dressed as a warrior, and by the looks of his weathered face and travel-stained clothing, he had been on the road for many long months. Gilthas could tell by the warmth in Alhana's voice and the agitation in her manner that this elf was someone special to her. Alhana and the strange elf disappeared inside her shelter before Gilthas had a chance to make himself known.

Seeing Gilthas, Kiryn waved him over.

"Samar has returned."

"Samar . . . the warrior who went in search of Silvanoshei?"

Kiryn nodded.

"And what of Silvanoshei?" Gilthas looked in the direction of Alhana's tent.

"Samar came back alone," said Kiryn.

An agonized cry came from Alhana's shelter. The cry was quickly smothered and was not repeated. Those waiting tensely outside glanced at each other and shook their heads. A sizeable crowd had formed in the small clearing. The elves waited in respectful silence, but they waited, determined to hear the news for themselves.

Alhana came out to speak to them, accompanied by Samar, who stood protectively at her side. Samar reminded Gilthas of Marshal Medan, a resemblance that would not have been appreciated by either one. Samar was an older elf, probably near the same age as Alhana's husband, Porthios. Years of exile and warfare had etched the delicate bone structure of the elven face into granite, sharp and hard. He had learned to bank the fire of his emotions so that he gave away nothing of what he was thinking or feeling. Only when he looked at Alhana did warmth flicker in his dark eyes.

Alhana's face, surrounded by the mass of black hair, was normally pale, the pure white of the lily. Now her skin was completely without color, seemed translucent. She started to speak, but could not. She shuddered, pain wracked her as if it might rend her bone by bone. Samar reached out a supportive arm. Alhana thrust him aside. Her face hardened into firm resolve. Mastering herself, she looked out upon the silent watchers.

"I give my words to the wind and to the rushing water," said Alhana. "Let them carry the words to my people. I give my words to the beasts of the forests and the birds of the air. Let them carry my words to my people. All of you here, go forth and carry my words to my people and to our cousins, the Qualinesti." Her gaze touched on Gilthas but only for an instant.

"You know this man—Samar, my most trusted commander and loyal friend. Many long weeks ago, I sent him on a mission. He has returned from that mission with news of importance." Alhana paused, moistened her lips. "In telling you what Samar has told me, I must make an admission to you. When I claimed that Silvanoshei, your king, was ill inside his tent, I lied. If you want to know why I told this lie, you have only to look about you. I told the lie in order keep our people together, to keep us unified and to keep our cousins united beside us. Because of the lie, we are strong, when we might have been terribly weakened. We will need to be strong for what lies ahead."

Alhana paused, drew in a shivering breath.

"What I tell you now is the truth. Shortly after the battle of Silvanost, Silvanoshei was captured by the Dark Knights. We tried to rescue him, but he was taken away from us in the night. I sent Samar to try to find out what had become of him. Samar has found him. Silvanoshei, our king, is being held prisoner in Sanction."

The elves made soft sounds, as of a breath of wind blowing through the branches of the willow, but said nothing.

"I will let Samar tell you his tale."

Even as Samar spoke to the people, he had a care for Alhana. He stood near her, ready to assist her if her strength failed.

"I met a Knight of Solamnia, a brave and honorable man." Samar's dark eyes swept the crowd. "For those who know me, this is high praise. This Knight saw Silvanoshei in prison and spoke to him, at peril of his own life. The Knight bore Silvanoshei's cloak and this ring."

Alhana held up the ring for all to see. "The ring is my son's. I know it. His father gave it to him when he was a child. Samar also recognized it."

The elves looked from the ring to Alhana, their expressions troubled. Several officers, standing near Kiryn, nudged him and urged him forward.

Kiryn advanced. "May I have permission to speak, gracious Queen?"

"You may, Cousin," said Alhana, regarding him with an air of defiance as if to say, "You may speak, but I do not promise to listen."

"Forgive me, Alhana Starbreeze," Kiryn said respectfully, "for doubting the word of such a great and renowned warrior as

Samar, but how do we know we can trust this human Knight? Perhaps it is a trap."

Alhana relaxed. Apparently this wasn't the question she had been anticipating.

"Let Gilthas, ruler of the Qualinesti, son of the House of Solostaran, come forward."

Wondering what this had to do with him, Gilthas walked out of the crowd to make his bow to Alhana. Samar's stern gaze flicked over Gilthas, who had the impression of being weighed in the balance. Whether he came out the winner or the loser in Samar's estimation, the young king had no way of judging.

"Your Majesty," said Samar, "when you were in Qualinesti, did you know a Solamnic by the name of Gerard uth Mondar?"

"Yes, I did," said Gilthas, startled.

"You consider him a man of courage, of honor?"

"I do," said Gilthas. "He is all that and more. Is this the Knight of whom you spoke?"

"Sir Gerard said he heard that the king of the Qualinesti and survivors of that land were going to try to reach safe haven in our land. He expressed deep sorrow for your loss but rejoiced that you are safe. He asked to be remembered to you."

"I know this Knight. I know of his courage, and I can attest to his honor. You are right to trust his word. Gerard uth Mondar came to Qualinesti under strange circumstances, but he left that land a true friend carrying with him the blessing of our beloved Queen Mother Lauranalanthalasa. His was one of the last blessings my mother ever bestowed."

"If both Samar and Gilthas attest to the honor of this Knight, then I have no more to say against him," said Kiryn. Bowing, he returned to his place within the circle.

Over a hundred elves had gathered. They were quiet, said nothing, but exchanged glances. Their silence was eloquent. Alhana could proceed, and she did so.

"Samar has brought other information. We can now give a name to this One God. The One God came to us in the name of peace and love, but that turned out to be part of her despicable plan to ensnare and destroy us. And now we know why. The name of the One God is an ancient one. The One God is Takhisis."

Like a pebble dropped into still water, the ripples of this astounding news spread among the elves.

"I cannot explain to you how this terrible miracle came about," Alhana continued, her voice growing stronger and more majestic with every word. The elves were with her now. She had their full support. All questions about the human Knight were forgotten, overshadowed by the dark wings of an ancient foe. "But we do not need to know. At last, we can put a name to our enemy and it is an enemy that we can defeat, for we have defeated her in the past.

"The Solamnic Knight, Gerard, carries word of this to the Knights' Council," Samar added. "The Solamnics are forming an army to attack Sanction. He urges the elves to be part of this force, to rescue our king. What say you?"

The elves gave a cheer that caused the branches of the trees to shake. Hearing the commotion, more and more elves came running to the site, and they raised their voices. The Lioness arrived, her Wilder elves behind her. Her face was aglow, her eyes alight.

"What is this I hear?" she cried, sliding from her horse and racing to Gilthas. "Is it true? Are we going to war at last?"

He did not answer her, but she was too excited to notice. Turning from him, she sought out those soldiers among the Silvanesti. Before this, they would have never deigned to speak to a Wilder elf, but now they answered her eager questions with joy.

Alhana's officers clustered around her and around Samar, offering suggestions, making plans, discussing what routes that they would take and how fast they could possibly reach Sanction and who would be permitted to go and who would be left behind.

Gilthas alone stood silent, listening to the tumult. When he finally spoke, he heard his own voice, heard the human sound to it, deeper and harsher than the voices of the elves.

"We must attack," he said, "but our target should not be Sanction. Our target is Silvanost. When that city is secure, then we turn our eyes to the north. Not before."

The elves stared at him in shocked disapproval, as if he were a guest at a wedding who had gone berserk and smashed all the gifts. The only elf who paid any heed to him was Samar.

"Let us hear the Qualinesti king," he orderd, raising his voice over the angry rumblings.

"It is true that we have defeated Takhisis in the past," Gilthas told his glowering audience, "but we had the help of Paladine and Mishakal and the other gods of light. Now Takhisis is the One God, alone and supreme. Her defeat will not be easy.

"We will have to march hundreds of miles from our homeland, leaving our own land in the hands of the enemy. We will join a fight with humans to attack and try to win a human city. We will make sacrifices for which we will never be rewarded. I do not say that we should *not* join this battle against Takhisis," Gilthas added. "My mother, as all of you know, fought among humans. She fought to save human cities and human lives. She made sacrifices for which no one ever thanked her. This battle against Takhisis and her forces is a battle that I believe is worth fighting. I counsel only that we make certain we have a homeland to which to return. We have lost Qualinesti. Let us not lose Silvanesti."

Hearing his impassioned words, the Lioness's expression softened. She came to stand at his side.

"My husband is right," she said. "We should attack Silvanost and hold it secure before we send a force to rescue the young king."

The Silvanesti looked at them with hostile eyes. A half-human and a Wilder elf. Outsiders, aliens. Who were they to tell the Silvanesti and even the Qualinesti what to do? Prefect Palthainon stood beside Alhana, whispering in her ear, undoutedly urging her to pay no attention to the "puppet king." Gilthas found one ally among them—Samar.

"The king of our cousins speaks wisely, Your Majesty," said Samar. "I think we should heed his words. If we march to Sanction, we leave behind us an enemy who may well attack and slay us when our backs are turned."

"The Dark Knights are trapped in Silvanost like bees caught in a jar," replied Alhana. "They bumble about, unable to escape. Mina has no intention of sending reinforcements to the Dark Knights in Silvanost. If she was going to, she would have done so by now. I will leave a small force behind to keep up the illusion that a larger force has them surrounded. When we return, triumphant, we will deal with these Dark Knights, my son and I," she added proudly.

"Alhana," Samar began.

She cast him a glance, her violet eyes wine-dark and chill.

Samar said nothing more. Bowing, he took up his stance behind his queen. He did not look at Gilthas, nor did Alhana. The decision had been made, the matter closed.

Silvanesti and Qualinesti gathered eagerly around her, awaiting her commands. The two nations were united at last, united in their determination to march to Sanction. After a moment's worried look at her husband, the Lioness squeezed his hand for comfort, then she, too, hastened over to confer with Alhana Starbreeze.

Why couldn't they see? What blinded them?

Takhisis. This is her doing, Gilthas said to himself. Now free to rule the world unchallenged, she has seized hold of love's sweet elixir, stirred it with poison, and fed it to both the mother and her son. Silvanoshei's love for Mina turns to obsession. Alhana's love for her son muddles her thoughts. And how can we fight this? How can we fight a god when even love—our best weapon against her—is tainted?

15

The Rescue of a King

Elves could be dreamy and lethargic, spend all their daylight hours watching the unfolding of the petals of a rose or sit hushed and rapt beneath the stars for nights on end. But when they are stirred to action, the elves astonish their humans observers with their quickness of thought and of movement, their ability to make swift decisions and carry them through, their resolve and determination to overcome any and all obstacles.

If either Alhana or Samar slept in the next few days, Gilthas had no idea when. Day and night, the stream of people coming and going from her tree shelter never ceased. He himself was one of them, for as ruler of his people, he was included in all important decisions. He said very little, however, although Alhana graciously took pains to invite him to share his opinion. He knew quite well that his opinion was not valued. In addition, he had such small knowledge of the lands through which they must pass that he was not much help anyway.

He was surprised to see how readily the Silvanesti and Qualinesti looked to Alhana, once an outcast, a dark elf, for leadership. His surprise ended when he heard her detail the outlines of her plan. She knew the mountainous lands through which they must march, for she had hidden her forces there for many years. She knew every road, every deer path, every cave. She knew war, and she knew the hardships and terrors of war.

No Silvanesti commander had such extensive knowledge of the lands they would traverse, the forces they might have to fight, and soon the most obdurate of them deferred to Alhana's superior knowledge and swore loyalty to her. Even the Lioness, who would lead her Wilder elves, was impressed.

Alhana's plan for the march was brilliant. The elves would travel north into into Blöde, land of their enemies, the ogres. This might appear to be suicidal, but many years ago, Porthios had discovered that the Khalkist mountain range split in two, hiding with its tall peaks a series of valleys and gorges nestled in the center. By marching in the valleys, the elves could use the mountains to guard their flanks. The route would be long and arduous, but the elven army would travel light and swift. They hoped to be safely through Blöde before the ogres knew they were there.

Unlike human armies, who must cart about blacksmith forges and heavily laden supply wagons, the elves wore no plate or chain armor, carried no heavy swords or shields. The elves relied on the bow and arrow, making good use of the skill for which elven archers are renowned. Thus the elven army could cover far greater distances than their human counterparts. The elves would have to travel swiftly, for within only a few short weeks the winter snows would start to fall in the mountains, sealing off the passes.

Much as he admired Alhana's plan of battle, every fiber in Gilthas's body cried out that it was wrong. As Samar had said, they should not march ahead, leaving the enemy in control behind. Gilthas grew so despondent and frustrated that he knew he must stop going to the meetings. Yet, the Qualinesti needed to be represented. He turned to the man who had been his friend for many years, a man who had, along with his wife, helped to lift Gilthas from the debilitating depression that had once sought to claim him.

"Planchet," said Gilthas, early one morning, "I am dismissing you from my service."

"Your Majesty!" Planchet stared, aghast and dismayed. "Have I done anything or said anything to displease you? If so, I am truly sorry—"

"No, my friend," said Gilthas, smiling a smile that came from the heart, not from diplomacy. He rested his arm on the shoulder of the man who had stood by his side for so long. "Do not protest the use of that word. I say 'friend,' and I mean it. I say adviser and mentor, and I mean that, too. I say father and councilor, and I mean those, as well. All these you have been to me, Planchet. I do not exaggerate when I say that I would not be standing here today if it were not for your strength and your wise guidance."

"Your Majesty," Planchet protested, his voice husky. "I do not deserve such praise. I have been but the gardener. Yours is the tree that has grown strong and tall—"

"—from your careful nurturing."

"And this is the reason I must leave His Majesty?" Planchet asked quietly.

"Yes, because now it is your time to nurture and watch over others. The Qualinesti need a military leader. Our people clamor to march to Sanction. You must be their general. The Lioness leads the Kagonesti. You will lead the Qualinesti. Will you do this for me?"

Planchet hesitated, troubled.

"Planchet," said Gilthas, "Prefect Palthainon is already trying to squirm his way into this position. If I appoint you, he will grumble and gripe, but he will not be able to stop me. He knows nothing of military matters, and you are a veteran with years of experience. You are liked and trusted by the Silvanesti. Please, for the sake of our people, do this for me."

"Yes, Your Majesty," Planchet replied at once. "Of course. I thank you for your faith in me, and I will try to be worthy of it. I know that Your Majesty is not in favor of this course of action, but I believe that it is the right one. Once we defeat Takhisis and drive her from the world, the shadow of dark wings will be lifted, the light will shine on us, and we will remove the enemy from both our lands."

"Do you truly think so, Planchet?" Gilthas asked in somber tones. "I have my doubts. We may defeat Takhisis, but we will not defeat that on which she thrives—the darkness in men's hearts. Thus I think we would be wise to drive out the enemy that holds our homes, secure our homeland and make it strong, then march out into the world."

Planchet said nothing, appeared embarrassed.

"Speak your thoughts, my friend," said Gilthas, smiling. "You are now my general. You have an obligation to tell me if I am wrong."

"I would say only this, Your Majesty. It is these very isolationist policies that have brought great harm to the elves in the past, causing us to be mistrusted and misunderstood by even those who might have been our allies. If we fight alongside the humans in this battle, it will prove to them that we are part of the larger world. We will gain their respect and perhaps even their friendship."

"In other words," said Gilthas, smiling wryly, "I have always been one to languish in my bed and write poetry—"

"No, Your Majesty," said Planchet, shocked. "I never meant—"

"I know what you meant, dear friend, and I hope you are right. Now, you'll be wanted in the next military conference that is convening shortly. I have told Alhana Starbreeze of my decision to name you general, and she approves of it. Whatever decisions you make, you make them in my name."

"I thank you for your trust, Your Majesty," said Planchet. "But what will you do? Will you march with us or remain behind?"

"I am no warrior, as you well know, dear friend. What small skill I have with the sword I have you to thank for it. Some of our people cannot travel, those with children to care for, the infirm and the elderly. I am considering remaining behind with them."

"Yet, think, Your Majesty, Prefect Palthainon marches with us. Consider that he will attempt to insinuate himself into Alhana's trust. He will demand a part in any negotiations with humans, a race he detests and despises."

"Yes," said Gilthas wearily. "I know. You had best go now, Planchet. The meeting will convene shortly, and Alhana requires that everyone be prompt in their attendance."

"Yes, Your Majesty," said Planchet, and with one final, troubled glance at his young king, he departed.

Within a far shorter time than anyone could have imagined, the elves were prepared to march. They left behind a force as the home guard to watch over those who could not make the long trek north, but the force was small, for the land itself was their best defender—the trees that loved the elves would shelter them, the animals would warn them and carry messages for them, the caverns would hide them.

They left behind another small force to maintain the illusion that an elven army had the city of Silvanost surrounded. So well did this small force play its part that General Dogah, shut up in the walls of a city he'd come to loathe, had no idea that his enemy had marched away. The Dark Knights remained imprisoned inside their victory and cursed Mina, who had left them to this fate.

The kirath remained to guard the borders. Long had they walked within the gray desolation left behind by the shield. Now they rejoiced to see small green shoots thrusting up defiantly through the gray dust and decay. The kirath took this as a hopeful sign for their homeland and their people, who had themselves almost withered and died, first beneath the shield, then beneath the crushing boot of the Dark Knights.

Gilthas had made up his mind to stay behind. Two days before the march, Kiryn sought him out.

Seeing the elf's troubled face, Gilthas sighed inwardly.

"I hear you plan to remain in Silvanesti," Kiryn said. "I think you should change your mind and come with us."

"Why?" asked Gilthas.

"To guard the interests of your people."

Gilthas said nothing, interrogated him with a look.

Kiryn flushed. "I was given this information in confidence."

"I do not want you to break a vow," said Gilthas. "I have no use for spies."

"I took no vow. I think Samar wanted me to tell you," said Kiryn. "You know that we march through the Khalkist Mountains, but do you know how we plan to make our way into Sanction?"

"I know so little of the territory—" Gilthas began.

"We will ally ourselves with the dark dwarves. March our army through their underground tunnels. They are to be well-paid."

"With what?" Gilthas asked.

Kiryn stared down at the leaf-strewn forest floor. "With the money you have brought with you from Qualinesti."

"That wealth is not mine," Gilthas said sharply. "It is the wealth of the Qualinesti people. All that we have left."

"Prefect Palthainon offered it to Alhana, and she accepted."

"If I protest, there will be trouble. My attendance on this ill-fated venture will not change that."

"No, but now Palthainon, as highest-ranking official, has charge of the wealth. If you come, you take your people's trust into your keeping. You may be forced to use it. There may not be another way. But the decision would be yours to make."

"So now it comes to this," Gilthas muttered when Kiryn had gone. "We pay off the darkness to save us. How far do we sink into darkness before we become the darkness?"

On the day the march began, the Silvanesti left their beloved woods with dry eyes that looked to the north. They marched in silence, with no songs, no blaring horns, no crashing cymbals, for the Dark Knights must never know that they were leaving, the ogres must not be warned of their coming. The elves marched in the shadows of the trees to avoid the eyes of watchful blue dragons, circling above.

When they crossed the border of Silvanesti, Gilthas paused to look behind him at the rippling leaves that flashed silver in the sunlight, a brilliant contrast to the gray line of decay that was the forest's boundary, the shield's legacy. He gazed long, with the oppressive feeling in his heart that once he crossed, he could never go back.

A week after the Silvanesti army had departed, Rolan of the kirath walked his regular patrol along the border. He kept his gaze fixed on the ground, noting with joy in his heart a small sign that nature was fighting a battle against the evil caused by the shield.

Although the shield's deadly magic was gone, the destruction wrought by its evil magic remained. Whatever plant or tree the shield had touched had died, so the borders of Silvanesti were marked by a gray, grim line of death.

Yet now, beneath the gray shroud of desiccated leaves and withered sticks, Rolan found tiny stalks of green emerging triumphantly from the soil. He could not tell yet what they were: blades of grass or delicate wildflowers or perhaps the first brave shoot of what would become a towering oak or a flame-colored maple. Maybe, he thought with a smile, this was some common, humble plant he tended—dandelion or catnip or spiderwort. Rolan loved this, whatever it might turn out to be. The green of life sprouting amidst death was an omen of hope for him and for his people.

Carefully, gently he replaced the shroud, which he now thought of as a blanket, to protect the frail young shoots from the harsh sunlight. He was about to move on when he caught whiff of a strange scent.

Rolan rose to his feet, alarmed. He sniffed the air, trying hard to place the peculiar odor. He had never smelled anything like it: acrid, animal. He heard distant sounds that he recognized as the crackling of breaking tree limbs, the trampling of vegetation. The sounds grew louder and more distinct, and above them came sounds more ominous: the warning cry of the hawk, the scream of the timid rabbit, the panicked bleat of fleeing deer.

The foul animal scent grew strong, overwhelming, sickening. The smell of meat-eaters. Drawing his sword, Rolan put his fingers to his lips to give the shrill, penetrating whistle that would alert his fellow kirath to danger.

Three enormous minotaurs emerged from the forest. Their horns tore the leaves, their axes left gashes in the tree limbs as they impatiently hacked at the underbrush that blocked their way. The minotaurs halted when they saw Rolan, stood staring him, their bestial eyes dark, without expression.

He lifted his sword, made ready to attack.

A bovine smell engulfed him. Strong arms grabbed him. He felt the prick of the knife just below his ear; swift, bitter pain as the knife slashed across his throat . . .

The minotaur who slew the elf dumped the body onto the ground, wiped the blood from his dagger. The minotaur's companions nodded. Another job well done. They proceeded through the forest, clearing a path for those who came behind.

For the hundreds who came behind. For the thousands.

Minotaur forces tramped across the border. Minotaur ships with their painted sails and galleys manned by slaves sailed the waters of the Thon-Thalas, traveling south to the capital of Silvanost, bringing General Dogah the reinforcements he had been promised.

Many kirath died that day, died as did Rolan. Some had the chance to fight their attackers, most did not. Most were taken completely by surprise.

The body of Rolan of the kirath lay in the forest he had loved. His blood seeped below the gray mantle of death, drowned the tiny green shoots.

16

Odila's Prayer, Mina's Gift

n the night, the eyes of the dead dragons within the skulls that made up the totem gleamed bright. The phantom of the five-headed dragon floated above the totem, causing those who saw it to marvel. In the night, in the darkness that she ruled, Queen Takhisis was powerful and reigned supreme. But, with the light of the sun, her image faded away. The eyes of the dead dragons flickered and went out, as did the candles on the altar, so that only wisps of smoke, blackened wicks, and melted wax remained.

The totem that appeared so magnificent and invulnerable in the darkness was by daylight a pile of skulls—a loathsome sight, for bits of scales or rotted flesh still clung to the bones. By day, the totem was a stark reminder to all who saw it of the immense power of Malys, the dragon overlord who had built it.

The question on everyone's lips was not *if* Malys would attack, but when. Fear of her coming spread through the city. Fearing massive desertions, Galdar ordered the West Gate closed. Although publicly Mina's Knights maintained a show of nonchalance, they were afraid.

When Mina walked the streets every day, she lifted fear from the hearts of all who saw her. When she spoke every night of the power of the One God, the people listened and cheered, certain that the One God would save them from the dragon. But when Mina departed, when the sound of her voice could no longer be heard, the shadow of red wings spread a chill over Sanction. People looked to the skies with dread.

Mina was not afraid. Galdar marveled at her courage, even as it worried him. Her courage stemmed from her faith in Takhisis, and he knew the goddess was not worthy of such faith. His one hope was that Takhisis needed Mina and would thus be loath to sacrifice her. One moment he had convinced himself she would be safe, the next he was convinced that Takhisis might use this means to rid herself of a rival who had outlasted her usefulness.

Compounding Galdar's fears was the fact that Mina refused to tell him her strategy for defeating Malys. He tried to talk to her about it. He reminded her of Qualinost. The dragon had been destroyed, but so had a city.

Mina rested her hand reassuringly on the minotaur's arm. "What happened to Qualinost will not happen to Sanction, Galdar. The One God hated the elves and their nation. She wanted to see them destroyed. The One God is pleased with Sanction. Here she plans to enter the world, to inhabit both the physical plane and the spiritual. Sanction and its people will be safe, the One God will see to that."

"But then what is your strategy, Mina?" Galdar persisted. "What is your plan?"

"To have faith in the One God, Galdar," said Mina, and with that, he had to be content, for she would say no more.

Odila was also worried about the future, worried and confused and distraught. Ever since the souls had built the totem and she had recognized the One God as Queen Takhisis, Odila had felt very much like one of the living dead mages. Her body ate and drank and walked and performed its duties, but she was absent from that body. She seemed to stand apart, staring at it uncaring, while mentally she groped in the storm-ridden darkness of her soul for answers, for understanding.

She could not bring herself to pray to the One God. Not any longer. Not since she knew who and what the One God was. Yet, she missed her prayers. She missed the sweet solace of giving her life into the hands of Another, some Wise Being who would guide Odila's steps and lead her away from pain to blissful peace. The One God had guided Odila's steps but not to peace. The One God had led her to turmoil and fear and dismay.

More than once Odila clasped the medallion at her throat and was prepared to rip it off. Every time her fingers closed around the medallion, she felt the metal's warmth. She remembered the power of the One God that had flowed through her veins, the power to halt those who had wanted to slay the elven king. Her hand fell away, fell limp at her side. One morning, watching the sun's red rays give a sullen glow to the clouds that hung perpetually over the Lords of Doom, Odila decided to put her faith to the test.

Odila knelt before the altar that was near the totem of dragon skulls. The room smelled of death and decay and warm, melting wax. The heat of the candles was a contrast to the cold draught that blew in from the gaping hole in the roof, whistled eerily through the teeth of the skulls. Sweat from the heat chilled on Odila's body. She wanted very much to flee this terrible place, but the medallion was warm against her cold skin.

"Queen Takhisis, help me," she prayed, and she could not repress a shudder at speaking that name. "I have been taught all my life that you are a cruel god who has no care for any living being, who sees us all as slaves meant to obey your commands. I have been taught that you are ambitious and self-serving, that you mock and denigrate those principles that I hold dear: honor, compassion, mercy, love. Because of what you are, I should not believe in you, I should not serve you. And yet . . ."

Odila lifted her eyes, gazed up into the heavens. "You are a god. I have witnessed your power. I have felt it thrill inside me. How can I choose *not* to believe in you? Perhaps . . ." Odila hesitated, uncertain. "Perhaps you have been maligned. Misjudged. Perhaps you *do* care for us. I ask this not for myself, but for someone who has served you faithfully and loyally. Mina faces terrible danger. I am certain that she intends to try to fight Malys alone. She has faith that you will fight at her side. She has put her trust in you. I fear for her, Queen Takhisis. Show me that my fears are unfounded and that you care for her, if you care for no one else."

She waited tensely, but no voice spoke. No vision came. The candle flames wavered in the chill wind that flowed through the altar room. The bodies of the mages sat upon their benches, staring unblinking into the flames. Yet, Odila's heart lightened, her burden of doubt eased. She did not know why and was pondering this when she became aware of someone standing near the altar.

Her eyes dazzled by the bright light of hundreds of candles, she couldn't see who was there.

"Galdar?" she said, at last making out the minotaur's hulking form. "I didn't hear you or see you enter. I was preoccupied with my prayers."

She wondered uneasily if he had overheard her, if he was going to berate her for her lack of faith.

He said nothing, just stood there.

"Is there something you want from me, Galdar?" Odila asked. He'd never wanted anything of her before, had always seemed to distrust and resent her.

"I want you to see this," he said.

In his hands, he carried an object bound in strips of linen, tied up with rope. The linen had once been white, but was now so stained by water and mud, grass and dirt that the color was a dull and dingy brown. The ropes had been cut, the cloth removed, but both appeared to have been clumsily replaced.

Galdar placed the object on the altar. It was long and did not seem particularly heavy. The cloth concealed whatever was inside.

"This came for Mina," he continued. "Captain Samuval sent it. Unwrap it. Look inside."

Odila did not touch it. "If it is a gift for Mina, it is not for me to—"

"Open it!" ordered Galdar, his voice harsh. "I want to know if it is suitable."

Odila might have continued to refuse, but she was certain now that Galdar had heard her prayer, and she feared that unless she agreed to this, he might tell Mina. Gingerly, her fingers trembling from her nervousness, Odila tugged at the knots, removed the strips of cloth. She was unpleasantly reminded of the winding cloths used to bind the bodies of the dead.

Her wonder grew as she saw what lay beneath, her wonder and her awe.

"Is it what Samuval claims it to be?" Galdar demanded. "Is it a dragonlance?"

Odila nodded wordlessly, unable to speak.

"Are you certain? Have you ever seen one before?" Galdar asked.

"No, I haven't," she admitted, finding her voice. "But I have heard stories of the fabled lances from the time I was a little girl. I always loved those stories. They led me to become a Knight."

Odila reached out her hand, ran her fingers along the cold, smooth metal. The lance gleamed with a silver radiance that seemed apart and separate from the yellow flames of the candles.

If all the lights in the universe were snuffed out, Odila thought, even the light of sun and moon and stars, the light of this lance would still shine bright.

"Where did Captain Samuval find such a treasure?" she asked.

"In some old tomb somewhere," said Galdar. "Solace, I think."

"Not the Tomb of the Heroes?" Odila gasped.

Snatching her hand back from the lance, she stared at Galdar in horror.

"I don't know," said Galdar, shrugging. "He didn't say what the tomb was called. He said the tomb brought him bad luck, for when the locals caught him and his men inside, they attacked in such numbers that he barely escaped with his life. He was even set upon by a mob of kender. This was one of the treasures he managed to bring along with him. He sent it to Mina with his regards and respect."

Odila sighed and looked back at the lance.

"He stole it from the dead," said Galdar, frowning. "He said himself it was bad luck. I do not think we should give it to Mina."

Before Odila could answer, another voice spoke from out of the darkness.

"Do the dead have need of this lance anymore, Galdar?"

"No, Mina," he said, turning to face her. "They do not."

The light of the lance shone bright in Mina's amber eyes. She took hold of it, her hand closing over it. Odila flinched when she saw Mina touch it, for there were some who claimed that the fabled dragonlances could be used only by those who fought on the side of light and that any others who touched them would be punished by the gods.

Mina's hand grasped the lance firmly. She lifted the lance from the altar, hefted it, regarded it with admiration.

"A lovely weapon," she said. "It seems almost to have been made for me." Her gaze turned to Odila. The amber eyes were warm as the medallion around Odila's throat. "An answer to a prayer."

Placing the lance upon the altar, Mina reverently knelt before it.

"We will thank the One God for this great blessing."

Galdar remained standing, looking stern. Odila sank down before the altar. Tears flowed down Odila's cheeks. She was grateful for Mina's sake that her prayer had been answered. Her tears were not for something found, however, but for something lost. Mina had been able to grip the lance, to lift it from the altar, to hold it in her hand.

Odila looked down at her own hands through her tears. The tips of the fingers that had touched the dragonlance were blistered and burned, and they hurt so that she wondered if she would ever again be free of the pain.

17

The Volunteer

Night had come again to Sanction. Night was always a relief to the inhabitants, for it meant that they'd survived another day. Night brought Mina out to speak them of the One God, speeches in which she lent them some of her courage, for when in her presence they were emboldened and ready for battle against the dragon overlord.

Having lived for centuries within the shadows of the Lords of Doom, the city of Sanction was essentially fireproof. Buildings were made of stone, including the roofs, for any other material, such as thatch, would have long ago burned away. True, it was said that the breath of dragons had the power to melt granite, but there was no defense against that, except to hope desperately that whoever spread the rumor was exaggerating.

Every soldier was being hastily trained in archery, for with a target this large, even the rankest amateur could hardly miss. They hauled catapults up onto the wall, hoping to fling boulders at Malys, and they trained their ballistae to shoot into the sky. These tasks accomplished, they felt they were ready, and some of the boldest called upon Malys to come and have done with it. Still, all were relieved when night fell and they'd lived through another day, never mind that dread came again with morning.

The blue dragon Razor, still forced to rove about Sanction in human guise, watched the preparations with the keen interest of a veteran soldier and told Mirror about them in detail, adding his own disapproval or approval, whichever seemed warranted. Mirror was more interested in the totem, in what it looked like, where it was positioned in the city. Razor had been supposed to reconnoiter, but he'd been wasting time among the soldiers.

"I know what you're thinking," Razor said suddenly, stopping himself in the midst of describing the precise workings of a catapult. "You're thinking that none of this will make any difference. None will have any effect on that great, red bitch. Well, you're right. And," he added, "you're wrong."

"How am I wrong?" Mirror asked. "Cities have used catapults before to defend against Malys. They've used archers and arrows, heroes and fools, and none have survived."

"But they have never had a god on their side," stated Razor.

Mirror tensed. A silver dragon, loyal to Paladine, he had long feared that Razor would revert to his old loyalties, to Queen Takhisis. Mirror had to proceed carefully. "So you are saying we should abandon our plan to help Palin destroy the totem?"

"Not necessarily," said Razor evasively. "Perhaps, reconsider, that is all. Where are you going?"

"To the temple," said Mirror. Shrugging off Razor's guiding hand, the blind silver dragon in human guise started off on his own, tapping his way with his staff. "To view the totem for myself, since you will not be my eyes."

"This is madness!" Razor protested, following after him with his fake limp. Mirror could hear the pounding of the crutch on the bricks. "You said before that Mina saw you in your beggar form on the road and immediately recognized you as the guardian of the Citadel of Light. She knows you by sight, both as a human and in your true form."

Mirror began to rearrange the bandages he wore wrapped about his damaged eyes, tugging them down so that they covered his face.

"It is a risk I must take. Especially if you are wavering in your decision."

Razor said nothing. Mirror could no longer hear the crutch thumping along beside him and assumed that he was going alone. He had only the vaguest idea where the temple was located. He knew only that it was on a hill overlooking the city.

So, he calculated, if I walk uphill, I am bound to find it.

He was startled to hear Razor's rasping breath in his ear. "Wait, stop. You've blundered into a cul-de-sac. I'll guide you, if you insist on going."

"Will you help me destroy the totem?" Mirror demanded.

"That I must think about," said Razor. "If we are going, we should go now, for the temple is most likely to be empty."

The two wended their way through the mazelike streets. Mirror was thankful for Razor's guidance, for the blind silver could have never found his way on his own.

What will Palin and I do if Razor decides to shift his allegiance? Mirror wondered. A blind dragon and a dead wizard out to defeat a goddess. Well, if nothing else, maybe Takhisis will get a bellyache from laughing.

The noise made by the crowds told Mirror they were close to the temple. And there was Mina, telling them of the wonders and magnificence of the One God. She was persuasive, Mirror had to admit. He had always liked Mina's voice. Even as a child, her tone had been mellow and low and sweet to hear.

As he listened, he was taken back to those days in the Citadel, watching Mina and Goldmoon together—the elderly woman in the sunset of her life, the child bright with the dawn. Now Mirror could not see Mina for the darkness, and not the darkness of his own blind eyes.

Razor led him past the crowd. The two proceeded quietly, not to draw attention to themselves, and entered the ruined temple that now stood as a monument to the dragon skull totem.

"Are we alone?" Mirror asked.

"The bodies of the two wizards sit in a corner."

"Tell me about them," said Mirror, his heart aching. "What are they like?"

"Like corpses propped up at their own funerals," said Razor dourly. "That is all I will say. Be thankful you cannot see them."

"What of their spirits?"

"I see no signs of them. All to the good. I have no use for wizards, living or dead. We don't need their meddling. Here, now. You stand before the totem. You can reach out and touch the skulls, if you want."

Mirror had no intention of touching anything. He had no need to be told he stood before the totem. Its magic was powerful, potent—the magic of a god. Mirror was both drawn to it and repelled by it.

"What does the totem look like?" he asked softly.

"The skulls of our brethren, stacked one on top of the other in a grotesque pyramid," Razor answered. "The skulls of the larger support the smaller. The eyes of the dead burn in the sockets. Somewhere in that pile is the skull of my mate. I can feel the fire of her life blaze in the darkness."

"And I feel the god's power residing within the totem," said Mirror. "Palin was right. This is the doorway. This is the Portal through which Takhisis will walk into the world at last."

"I say, let her," said Razor. "Now that I see this, I say let Takhisis come, if her help is needed to slay Malystryx."

Mirror could smell the flickering candles, if he could not see them. He could feel their heat. He could feel, as Razor felt, the heat of his own anger and his longing for revenge. Mirror had his own reasons for hating Malys. She had destroyed Kendermore, killed Goldmoon's dearly loved husband Riverwind and their daughter. Malys had murdered hundreds of people and displaced thousands more, driving them from their homes, terrorizing them as they fled for her own cruel amusement. Standing before the totem that Malys had built of the bones of those she had devoured, Mirror began to wonder if Razor might not be right.

Razor leaned near, whispered in his ear. "Takhisis has her faults, I admit that freely. But she is a god, and she is our god, of our world, and she's all we've got. You have to concede that."

Mirror conceded nothing.

"You can't see them," Razor continued relentlessly, "but there are the skulls of silver dragons in that totem. A good many of them. Don't you want to avenge their deaths?"

"I don't need to see them," said Mirror. "I hear their voices. I hear their death cries, every one of them. I hear the cries of their mates who loved them and the cries of the children who will never be born to them. My hatred for Malys is as strong as yours. To rid the world of this terrible scourge, you say I must choke down the bitter medicine of Takhisis's triumph."

Razor shrugged. "She is our god," he repeated. "Of our world."

A terrible choice. Mirror sat on the hard bench, trying to decide what to do. Lost in his thoughts, he forgot where he was, forgot he was in the camp of his enemies. Razor's elbow dug into his side.

"We have company," the blue warned softly.

"Who is it? Mina?" Mirror asked.

"No, the minotaur who is never far from her side. I told you this was a bad idea. No, don't move. It's too late now. We're in the shadows. Perhaps they won't take notice of us. Besides," the Blue added coolly, "we might learn something."

Indeed, Galdar did not notice the two beggars as he entered the altar room. At least, not immediately. He was preoccupied with his own worries. Galdar knew Mina's plan, or he thought he did. He hoped he was wrong, but his hope wasn't very strong, probably because he knew Mina so well.

Knew Mina and loved her.

All his life, Galdar had heard legends of a famous minotaur hero known as Kaz, who had been a friend of the famous Solamnic hero, Huma. Kaz had ridden with Huma in his battle against Queen Takhisis. The minotaur had risked his life for Huma many times, and Kaz's grief at Huma's death had been lifelong. Although Kaz had been on the wrong side of the war, as far as the minotaur were concerned, he was honored among his people to this day for his courage and valor in warfare. A minotaur admires a valiant warrior no matter which side he fights on.

As for his friendship with a human, few minotaurs could understand that. True, Huma had been a valiant warrior—for a human. Always that qualification was added. In minotaur legends, Kaz was the hero, saving Huma's life time and again, at the end of which, Huma is always humbly grateful to the gallant minotaur, who accepts the human's thanks with patronizing dignity.

Galdar had always believed these legends, but now he was starting to think differently. Perhaps, in truth, Kaz had fought with Huma because he loved Huma, just as Galdar loved Mina. There was something about these humans. They wormed their way into your heart.

Their puny bodies were so frail and fragile, and yet they could be tough and enduring as the last hero standing in the blood-stained arena of the minotaur circus.

They never knew when they were defeated, these humans, but fought on when they should have laid down and died. They led such pitifully short lives, but they were always ready to throw away these lives for a cause or a belief, or doing something as foolish and noble as rushing into a burning tower to save the life of a total stranger.

Minotaurs have their share of courage, but they are more cautious, always counting the cost before spending their coin. Galdar knew what Mina planned, and he loved her for it, even as his heart ached to think of it. Kneeling beside the altar, he vowed that she would not go into battle alone if there was any way he could stop her. He did not pray to the One God. Galdar no longer prayed to the One God, ever since he'd found out who she was. He never said a word to Mina about this—he would take his secret to the grave with him—but he would not pray to Queen Takhisis, a goddess whom he considered treacherous and completely without honor. The vow he made, he made within himself.

His prayer concluded, he rose stiffly from the altar. Outside, he could hear Mina telling the admiring crowds that they had no need to fear Malys. The One God would surely save them. Galdar had heard it all before. He no longer heard it now. He heard Mina's voice, her loved voice, but that was all. He guessed that was all most of those listening heard.

Galdar fidgeted near the altar, waiting for Mina, and it was then he saw the beggars. The altar room was crowded during the day, for the inhabitants of Sanction, mostly soldiers, came to make offerings to the One God or to gape at the totem or to try to catch a glimpse of Mina and touch her or beg her blessing. At night, they went to hear her, to hide themselves beneath the blanket of her courage. After that, they went to their posts or to their beds. Few worshipers came to the altar room at night, one reason Galdar was here.

This night, a blind man and a lame beggar sat on a bench near the altar. Galdar had no use for mendicants. No minotaur does. A minotaur would starve to death before he would dream of begging for even a crust. Galdar could not imagine what these two were doing in Sanction and wondered why they hadn't fled, as had many of their kind.

He eyed them more closely. There was something about them that made them different from other beggars. He couldn't quite think what it was—a quiet confidence, capability. He had the feeling that these were no ordinary beggars and he was about to ask them a few questions when Mina returned.

She was exalted, god-touched. Her amber eyes shone. Approaching the altar, she sank down, almost too tired to stand, for during these public meetings, she poured forth her whole soul, giving everything to those who listened, leaving nothing for herself. Galdar forgot the strange beggars, went immediately to Mina.

"Let me bring you some wine, something to eat," he offered.

"No, Galdar, I need nothing, thank you," Mina replied. She sighed deeply. She looked exhausted.

Clasping her hands, she said a prayer to the One God, giving thanks. Then, appearing refreshed and renewed, she rose to her feet. "I am only a little tired, that is all. There was a great crowd tonight. The One God is gaining many followers."

They follow you, Mina, not the One God, Galdar might have said to her, but he kept silent. He had said such things to her in the past, and she had been extremely angry. He did not want to risk her ire, not now.

"You have something to say to me, Galdar?" Mina asked. She reached out to remove a candle whose wick had been drowned in molten wax.

Galdar arranged his thoughts. He had to say this carefully, for he did not want to offend her.

"Speak what is in your heart," she urged. "You have been troubled for a long time. Ease your burden by allowing me to share it."

"You are my burden, Mina," said Galdar, deciding to do as she said and open his heart. "I know how you plan to fight Malys on dragonback. You have the dragonlance, and I assume that the One God will provide you with a dragon. You plan to go up alone to face her. I cannot allow you to do that, Mina. I know what you are about to say." He raised his hand, to forestall her protest. "You will not be alone. You will have the One God to fight at your side. But let there be another at your side, Mina. Let me be at your side."

"I have been practicing with the lance," Mina said. Opening her hand, she exhibited her palm, that was red and blistered. "I can hit the bull's-eye nine times out of ten."

"Hitting a target that stands still is much different from hitting a moving dragon," Galdar growled. "Two dragonriders are most effective in fighting aerial battles, one to the keep the dragon occupied from the front while the other attacks from the rear. You must see the wisdom in this?"

"I do, Galdar," said Mina. "True, I have been studying the combat in my mind, and I know that two riders would be good." She smiled, an impish smile that reminded him of how young she was. "A thousand riders would be even better, Galdar, don't you think?"

He said nothing, scowled at the flames. He knew where she was leading him, and he could not stop her from going there.

"A thousand would be better, but where would we find these thousand? Men or dragons?" Mina gestured to the totem. "Do you remember all the dragons who celebrated when the One God consecrated this totem? Do you remember them circling the totem and singing anthems to the One God? Do you remember, Galdar?"

"I remember."

"Where are they now? Where are the Reds and the Greens, the Blues and the Blacks? Gone. Fled. Hiding. They fear I will ask them to fly against Malys. And I can't blame them."

"Bah! They are all cowards," said Galdar.

He heard a sound behind him and glanced around. He'd forgotten the beggars. He eyed them closely, but if either of them had spoken neither seemed inclined to do so now. The lame beggar stared down at the floor. As for the blind beggar, his face was so swathed in bandages that it was difficult to tell if he had a mouth, much less whether he had used it. The only other two beings in the room were the wizards, and Galdar had no need to look at them. They never moved unless someone prodded them.

"I'll make you a bargain, Galdar," Mina said. "If you can find a dragon who will voluntarily carry you into battle, you can fly at my side."

Galdar grunted. "You know that is impossible, Mina."

"Nothing is impossible for the One God, Galdar," Mina told him, gently rebuking. She knelt down again before the altar, clasped her hands. Glancing up at Galdar, she added, "Join me in my prayers."

"I have already made my prayer, Mina," said Galdar heavily. "I have duties to attend to. Try to get some rest, will you?"

"I will," she said. "Tomorrow will be a momentous day."

Galdar looked at her, startled. "Will Malys come tomorrow, Mina?"

"She will come tomorrow."

Galdar sighed and walked out into the night. The night may bring comfort to others but not to him. The night brought only morning.

Mirror felt Razor's human body shift restlessly on the bench beside him. Mirror sat with his head lowered, taking care that Mina did not see him, although he suspected he could have leaped up and done a dance with bells and tambour and she would have been oblivious to him. She was with her One God. For now, she had no care or concern for what transpired on this mortal plane. Still, Mirror kept his head down.

He was troubled and at the same time relieved. Perhaps this was the answer.

"You would like to be the dragon that Galdar seeks, is that right?" Mirror asked in a quiet undertone.

"I would," Razor said.

"You know the risk you take," said Mirror. "Malys's weapons are formidable. Fear of her alone drove a nation of kender mad, so it is claimed by the wise. Her flaming breath is said to be hotter than the fires of the Lords of the Doom."

"I know all this," Razor returned, "and more. The minotaur will find no other dragon. Craven cowards, all of them. No discipline. No training. Not like the old days."

Mirror smiled, thankful that his smile was hidden beneath the bandages.

"Go, then," he said. "Go after the minotaur and tell him that you will fight by his side."

Razor was silent. Mirror could feel his astonishment.

"I cannot leave you," Razor said, after a pause. "What would you do without me?"

"I will manage. Your impulse is brave, noble, and generous. Such weapons are our strongest weapons against her." By *her*, Mirror did not mean Malys, but he saw no reason to clarify his pronoun.

"Are you certain?" Razor asked, clearly tempted. "You will have no one to guard you, protect you."

"I am not a hatchling," Mirror retorted. "I may not be able to see, but lack of sight does not hamper my magic. You have done your part and more. I am glad to have known you, Razor, and I honor you for your decision. You had best go after the minotaur. You two will need to make plans, and you will not have much time to make them."

Razor rose to his feet. Mirror could hear him, feel him moving at his side. The Blue's hand rested on Mirror's shoulder, perhaps for the last time.

"I have always hated your kind, Silver. I am sorry for that, for I have discovered that we have more in common than I realized."

"We are dragons," said Mirror simply. "Dragons of Krynn."

"Yes," said Razor. "If only we had remembered that sooner."

The hand lifted. Its warm pressure gone, Mirror felt the lack. He heard footsteps walking swiftly away, and he smiled and shook his head. Reaching out his hand, groping about, he found Razor's crutch, tossed aside.

"Another miracle for the One God," said Mirror wryly. Taking the crutch, he secreted it beneath the bench.

As he did so, Mina's voice rose.

"Be with me, my god," she prayed fervently, "and lead me and all who fight with me to glorious victory against this evil foe."

"How can I refuse to echo that prayer?" Mirror asked himself silently. "We are dragons of Krynn, and though we fought against her, Takhisis was our goddess. How can I do what Palin asks of me? Especially now that I am alone."

Galdar made the rounds, checking on the city's defenses and the state of Sanction's defenders. He found all as he expected. The defenses were as good as they were going to get, and the defenders were nervous and gloomy. Galdar said what he could to raise their spirits, but he wasn't Mina. He couldn't lift their hearts, especially when his own was crawling in the dust.

Brave words he'd spoken to Mina about fighting at her side against Malys. Brave words, when he knew perfectly well that when Malys came he'd be among those watching helplessly from the ground. Tilting his head, he scanned the skies. The night air was clear, except for the perpetual cloud that roiled out of the Lords of Doom.

"How I would love to astonish her," he said to the stars. "How I long to be there with her."

But he was asking the impossible. Asking a miracle of a goddess he didn't like, didn't trust, couldn't pray to.

So preoccupied was Galdar that it took him some time— longer than it should have—for him to realize he was being followed. This was such a strange occurrence that he was momentarily taken aback. Who could be following him and why? He would have suspected Gerard, but the Solamnic Knight had left Sanction long ago, was probably even now urging the Knights to rise up against them. Everyone else in Sanction, including the Solamnic female, was loyal to Mina. He wondered, suddenly, if Mina was having him followed, if she no longer trusted him. The thought made him sick to his stomach. He determined to know the truth.

Muttering aloud something about needing fresh air, Galdar headed for the temple gardens that would be dark and quiet and secluded this time of night.

Whoever was following him either wasn't very good at it or wanted Galdar to notice him. The footfalls were not stealthy, not padded, as would be those of a thief or assassin. They had a martial ring to them—bold, measured, firm.

Reaching a wooded area, Galdar stepped swiftly to one side, concealed himself behind the bole of a large tree. The footsteps came to a halt. Galdar was certain that the person must have lost him, was astonished beyond measure to see the man walk right up to him.

The man raised his hand, saluted.

Galdar started instinctively to return the salute. He halted, glowering, and rested his hand on his sword's hilt.

"What do you want? Why do you sneak after me like a thief?" Peering more closely at the person, Galdar recognized him and was disgusted. "You filthy beggar! Get away from me, scum. I have no money—"

The minotaur paused. His gaze narrowed. His hand tightened its grasp on the hilt, half-drew the sword from its sheath. "Weren't you lame before? Where is your crutch?"

"I left it behind," said the beggar, "because I no longer need it. I want nothing of you, sir," he added, his tone respectful. "I have something to give you."

"Whatever it is, I don't want it. I have no use for your kind. Begone and trouble me no more or I'll have you thrown in prison." Galdar reached out his hand, intending to shove the man aside.

The night shadows began to shimmer and distort. Tree branches cracked. Leaves and twigs and small limbs rained down around him. Galdar's hand touched a surface hard and solid as armor, but this armor wasn't cold steel. It was warm, living.

Gasping, Galdar staggered backward, lifted his astounded gaze. His eyes met the eyes of a blue dragon.

Galdar stammered something, he wasn't sure what.

The blue dragon drew in a huge breath and expelled it in satisfaction and immense relief. Fanning his wings, he luxuriated in a stretch and sighed again. "How I hate that cramped human form."

"Where . . . ? What . . . ?" Galdar continued to stammer.

"Irrelevant," said the dragon. "My name is Razor. I happened to overhear your conversation with your commander in the temple. She said that if you could find a dragon that would carry you into battle against Malys, you could fight at her side. If you truly meant what you said, warrior; if you have the courage of your convictions, then I will be your mount."

"I meant what I said," Galdar growled, still trying to recover from the shock. "But why would you do this? All your brethren have fled, and they are the sensible ones."

"I am"—the dragon paused, corrected himself with grave dignity—"I *was* the dragon attached to Marshal Medan. Did you know him?"

"I did," said Galdar. "I met him when he came to visit Lord Targonne in Jelek. I was impressed. He was a man of sense, a man of courage and of honor. A valiant Knight of the old school."

"Then you know why I do this," said Razor, with a proud toss of his head. "I fight in his name, in his memory. Let's be clear about that from the outset."

"I accept your offer, Razor," said Galdar, joy filling his soul. "I fight for the glory of my commander. You fight for the memory of yours. We will make this battle one of which they will sing for centuries!"

"I was never much for singing," said Razor dourly. "Neither was the Marshal. So long as we kill that red monstrosity, that is all I care about. When do you think she will attack us?"

"Mina says tomorrow," said Galdar.

"Then tomorrow I will be ready," said Razor.

18

Day's Dawning

A tremor shook the city of Sanction in the early hours before the dawn. The rippling ground dumped sleepers from their beds, sent the crockery spilling to floor, and set all the dogs in the city to barking. The quake jarred nerves that were already taut.

Almost before the ground had ceased to tremble, crowds began to gather outside the temple. Although no official word had been given or orders gone out, rumors had spread, and by now every soldier and Knight in Sanction knew that this was the day Malys would attack. Those not on duty (and even some who were) left their billets and their posts and flocked to the temple. They came out of a hunger to see Mina and hear her voice, hear her reassurance that all would be well, that victory would be theirs this day.

As the sun lifted over the mountains, Mina emerged from the temple. Customarily at her appearance a resounding cheer went up from the crowd. Not this day. Everyone stared, hushed and awed.

Mina was clad in glistening armor black as the frozen seas. The helm she wore was horned, the visor black, rimed with gold. On the breastplate was etched the image of a five-headed dragon. As the first rays of the sun struck the armor, the dragon began to shimmer eerily, shifting colors, so that some who saw it thought it was red, while others thought it was blue, and still others swore it was green.

Some in the audience whispered in excited voices that this was armor once worn by the Dragon Highlords, who had fought for Takhisis during the fabled War of the Lance.

In her gloved hand, Mina held a weapon whose metal burned like flame as it caught the rays of the rising sun. She lifted the weapon high above her head in a gesture of triumph.

At this, the crowd raised a cheer. They cheered long and loud, crying, "Mina, Mina!" The cheers rebounded off the mountains and thundered over the plains, shaking the ground like another tremor.

Mina knelt upon one knee, the lance in her hand. The cheering ceased as people joined her in prayer, some calling upon the One God, many more calling upon Mina.

Rising to her feet, Mina turned to face the totem. She handed the lance to a priestess of the One God, who stood beside her. The priestess was clad in white robes, and whispers went about that she was a former Solamnic Knight who had prayed to the One God and been given the dragonlance, which she had in turn given to Mina. The Solamnic held the lance steady, but her face was contorted by pain, and she often bit her lip as if to keep from crying out.

Mina placed her hands upon two of the enormous dragon skulls that formed the totem's base. She cried out words that no one could understand, then stepped back and raised her arms to the heavens.

A being rose from the totem. The being had the shape and form of an enormous dragon, and those standing near the totem tumbled back in terror.

The dragon's brown-colored scaly skin stretched taut over its skull, neck, and body. The skeleton could be seen clearly through the parchmentlike skin: the round disks of the neck and spine, the large bones of the massive rib cage, the thick and heavy bones of the gigantic legs, the more delicate bones of the wings and tail and feet. Sinews were visible and tendons that held the bones together. Missing were the heart and blood vessels, for magic was the blood of this dragon, vengeance and hatred formed the beating heart. The dragon was a mummified dragon, a corpse.

The wing membranes were dried and tough as leather, their span massive. The shadow of the wings spread over Sanction, doused the rays of the sun, turned dawning day to sudden night.

So horrible and loathsome was the sight of the putrid corpse hanging over their heads that the cheers for Mina died, strangled, in the throats of those who had raised them. The stench of death flowed from the creature, and with the stench came despair that was worse than the dragonfear, for fear can act as a spur to courage, while despair drains the heart of hope. Most could not bear to look at it, but lowered their heads, envisioning their own deaths, all of which were pain-filled and terrifying.

Hearing their cries, Mina took pity on them and gave to them from her own strength.

She began to sing, the same song they'd heard many times, but now with new meaning.

> The gathering darkness takes our souls,
>   Embracing us in chilling folds,
> Deep in a Mistress's void that holds
>   Our fate within her hands.
>
> Dream, warriors, of the dark above
>   And feel the sweet redemption of
> The Night's Consort, and of her love
>   For those within her bands.

Her song helped quell their fears, eased their despair. The soldiers called her name again, vowed that they would make her proud of them. Dismissing them, she sent them to do their duties with courage and with faith in the One God. The crowd left, Mina's name on their lips.

Mina turned to the priestess, who had been holding the lance all this time. Mina took the lance from her.

Odila snatched her hand away, hid her hand behind her back.

Mina raised the visor of her helm. "Let me see," she said.

"No, Mina," Odila mumbled, blinking back tears. "I would not burden you—"

Mina grabbed hold of Odila's hand, brought it forth to the light. The palm was bloodied and blackened, as if it had been thrust into a pit of fire.

Holding Odila's hand, Mina pressed her lips to it. The flesh healed, though the wound left terrible scars. Odila kissed Mina and bade her good fortune in a soundless voice.

Holding the lance, Mina looked up to the death dragon. "I am ready," she said.

The image of an immortal hand reached out of the totem. Mina stepped upon the palm and the hand lifted her gently from the ground, carried her safely through the air. The hand of the goddess raised her higher than the treetops, higher than the skulls of the dragons stacked one atop the other. The hand halted at the side of the death dragon. Mina stepped off the hand, mounted the dragon's back. The corpse had no saddle, no reins that anyone could see.

Another dragon appeared on the eastern horizon, speeding toward Sanction. People cried out in fear, thinking that this must be Malys. Mina sat astride the death dragon, watched and waited.

As the dragon came in sight, cries of fear changed to wild cheering. The name, "Galdar" flew from mouth to mouth. His horned head, silhouetted against the rising sun, was unmistakable.

Galdar held in his hand an enormous pike of the kind usually thrust into the ground to protect against cavalry charges. The pike's heavy weight was nothing to him. He wielded it with as much ease as Mina wielded the slender dragonlance.

In his other hand, he held the reins of his mount, the blue dragon, Razor.

Galdar lifted the pike and shook it in defiance, then raised his voice and gave a mighty roar, a minotaur battle cry. An ancient cry, the words called upon the god Sargas to fight at the warrior's side, to take his body if he fell in the fray, and to smite him if he faltered. Galdar had no idea where the words came from as he shouted them. He supposed he must have heard this cry when he was a child. He was astonished to hear the words come from his mouth, but they were appropriate, and he was pleased with them.

Mina raised her visor to greet him. Her skin, in stark contrast to the black of the helm, was bone white. Her eyes shone with her own excitement. He saw himself in the amber mirror, and for the first time he was not a bug trapped in their molten gold. He was himself, her friend, her loyal comrade. He could have wept. Perhaps he did weep. If so, his battle lust burned away the tears before they could shame him.

"You will not go alone into battle this day, Mina!" Galdar roared.

"The sight of you gladdens my heart, Galdar," Mina shouted. "This is a miracle of the One God. It is among the first we will see this day, but not the last."

The blue dragon bared his teeth, a sparkle of lightning flickered from his clenched jaws.

Perhaps Mina was right. Truly, this did feel miraculous to Galdar, as wonderful a miracle as the tales of heroes of old.

Mina lowered her visor. A touch of her hand upon the corpse dragon caused it to lift its head, spread its wings, and soar into the sky, carrying her high above the clouds. The Blue glanced back at Galdar to ascertain his orders. Galdar indicated they were to follow.

The city of Sanction dwindled in size. The people were tiny black dots, then they disappeared. Higher the Blue climbed into the cold, clear air, and the world itself grew small beneath him. All was quiet, profoundly quiet and peaceful. Galdar could hear only the creak of the dragon's wings, then even that stopped as the beast took advantage of a thermal to soar effortlessly among the clouds.

All sounds of the world ceased, so that it seemed to Galdar that he and Mina were the only two left in it.

On the ground below, the people watched until they could no longer catch sight of Mina. Many still continued to watch, staring into the sky until their necks ached and their eyes burned. Officers began shouting orders, and the crowd started to disperse. Those on duty went to their posts, to take up positions on the walls. A vast number of people continued to crowd around the temple, talking excitedly of what they had seen, speaking of Malys's easy defeat and how from this day forth Mina and the Knights of the One God would be the rulers of Ansalon.

Mirror lingered near the totem, waiting for Palin's spirit to join him. The Silver did not wait long.

"Where is the blue dragon?" Palin asked immediately, alarmed by his absence.

Palin's words came to the Silver clearly, so clearly that Mirror could almost believe they were spoken by the living, except that they had a strange feel to them, a spidery feel that brushed across his skin.

"You have only to look in the sky above you to see where Razor has gone," said Mirror. "He fights his own battle in his own way. He leaves us to fight ours—whatever that may be."

"What do you mean? Are you having second thoughts?"

"That is the nature of dragons," said Mirror. "We do not rush into things headlong like you humans. Yes, I have been having second thoughts and third and fourth thoughts as well."

"This is nothing to joke about," said Palin.

"Too true," said Mirror. "Have you considered the consequences of your proposed actions? Do you know what destroying the totem will do? Especially destroying it as Malys attacks?"

"I know that this is the only opportunity we will have to destroy the totem," said Palin. "Takhisis has all her attention focused on Malys, as does everyone else in Sanction. If we miss this chance, we will not have another."

"What if, in destroying the totem, we give the victory to Malys?"

"Malys is mortal. She will not live forever. Takhisis will. I admit," Palin continued, "that I do not know what will be the consequences of the destruction of the totem. But I do know this. Every day, every hour, every second I am surrounded by the souls of the dead of Krynn. Their numbers are countless. Their torment is unspeakable, for they are driven by a hunger that can never be assuaged. She makes them promises she has no intention of keeping, and they know this, and yet they do her bidding in the pitiful hope that one day she will free them. That day will never come, Mirror. You know that, and I know it. If there is a chance that the totem's destruction will stop her from entering the world, then that is a chance we must take."

"Even if it means that we are all burned alive by Malys?" Mirror asked.

"Even if it means that," said Palin.

"Leave me a while," said Mirror. "I need to think this over."

"Do not think too long," Palin cautioned. "For while dragons think, the world moves under them."

Mirror stood alone, wrestling with his problem. Palin's words were meant to remind Mirror of the old days when the dragons of light lay complacent and sleepy in their lairs, ignoring the wars raging in the world. The dragons of light spoke smugly and learnedly of evil: evil destroys its own, good redeems its own, they said. Thus they spoke and thus they had slept and thus the Dark Queen stole their eggs and destroyed their children.

The wind shifted, blowing from the west. Mirror sniffed, caught the scent of blood and brimstone, faint, but distinct.

Malys.

She was far distant still, but she was coming.

Locked in his prison house of darkness, he heard the people around him talking glibly of the approaching battle. He could find it in his heart to pity them. They had no idea of the horror that was winging toward them. No idea at all.

Mirror groped his way past the totem, heading for the temple. He moved slowly, forced to tap out a clear path with his staff, bumping it into people's shins, knocking against trees, stumbling off the path and bumbling into flower gardens. The soldiers swore at him. Someone kicked him. He kept the rising sun on his left cheek and knew he was heading in the direction of the temple, but he should have reached it by now. He feared that he had veered off course. For all he knew, he could be headed up the mountain—or off it.

He cursed his own helplessness and came to a standstill, listening for voices and the clues they might give. Then a hand touched his outstretched hand.

"Sir, you appear to be lost and confused. Can I be of aid?"

The voice was a woman's, and it had a muffled, choked sound to it, as though she had been weeping. Her touch on his hand was firm and strong, he was startled to feel calluses on her palm, the same that could be felt on the hands of those who wielded a sword. Some female Dark Knight. Odd that she should trouble herself with him. He detected a Solamnic accent, though. Perhaps that was the reason. Old virtues are comfortable, like old clothes, and hard to part with.

"I thank you, Daughter," he said humbly, playing his role of beggar. "If you could lead me into the temple, I seek counsel."

"There we are alike, sir," said the woman. Linking her arm in his, she slowly guided his steps. "For I, too, am troubled."

Mirror could hear the anguish in her voice, feel it in the trembling of her hand.

"A burden shared is a burden halved," he said gently. "I can listen, if I cannot see."

Even as he spoke, he could hear, with his dragon soul, the beating of immense wings. The stench of Malys grew stronger. He had to make his decision.

He should break off this conversation and go about his own urgent business, but he chose not to. The silver dragon had lived long in the world. He did not believe in accidents. This chance meeting was no chance. The woman had been drawn to him out of compassion. He was touched by her sadness and pain.

They entered the Temple. He groped about with his hand, until he found what he sought.

"Stop here," he said.

"We have not reached the altar," said the woman. "What you touch is a sarcophagus. Only a little farther."

"I know," Mirror said, "but I would rather remain here. She was an old friend of mine, you see."

"Goldmoon?" The woman was startled, wary. "A friend of yours?"

"I came a long way to see her," he said.

Palin's voice whispered to him, soft and urgent. "Mirror, what are you doing? You cannot trust this woman. Her name is Odila. She was once a Solamnic Knight, but she has been consumed by darkness."

"A few moments with her. That's all I ask," Mirror replied softly.

"You may take all the time you want with her, sir," said Odila, mistaking his words. "Although the time we have is short before Malys arrives."

"Do you believe in the One God?" Mirror asked.

"Yes," said Odila, defiantly. "Don't you?"

"I believe in Takhisis," said Mirror. "I revere her, but I do not serve her."

"How is that possible?" Odila demanded. "If you believe in Takhisis and revere her, it follows that you must serve her."

"My reply takes the form of a story. Were you with Goldmoon when she died?"

"No," Odila said. Her voice softened. "No one but Mina was with her."

"Yet there were witnesses. A wizard named Palin Majere saw and heard their conversation, during which Takhisis revealed her true nature to Goldmoon. That was a moment of triumph for Takhisis. Goldmoon had long been her bitter enemy. How sweet it must have been for Takhisis to tell Goldmoon that it was she who gave Goldmoon the power of the heart, the power to heal and to build and to create. Takhisis told Goldmoon that this power of the heart stemmed not from the light but from the darkness. Takhisis hoped to convince Goldmoon to follow her. The goddess promised Goldmoon life, youth, beauty. All in return for her service, her worship.

"Goldmoon refused to accept. She refused to worship the goddess who had brought such pain and sorrow to the world. Takhisis was angry. She inflicted on Goldmoon the burden of her years, made her old and feeble and near death. The goddess hoped Goldmoon would die in despair, knowing that Takhisis had won the battle, that she would be the 'one god' for now and forever. Goldmoon's dying words were a prayer."

"To Takhisis?" Odila faltered.

"To Paladine," said Mirror. "A prayer asking for his forgiveness for having lost her faith, a prayer reaffirming her belief."

"But why did she pray to Paladine when she knew he could not answer?" Odila asked.

"Goldmoon did not pray for answers. She knew the answers. She had long carried the truth of his wisdom and his teachings in her soul. Thus, even though she might never again see Paladine or hear his voice or receive his blessings, he was with her, as he had always been. Goldmoon understood that Takhisis had lied. The good that Goldmoon had done came from her heart, and that good could never be claimed by darkness. The miracles would always come from Paladine, because he had never left her. He was always with her, always a part of her."

"It is too late for me," said Odila, despairing. "I am beyond redemption. See? Feel this." Grasping his hand, she placed his fingers on her palm. "Scars. Fresh scars. Made by the blessed dragonlance. I am being punished."

"Who punishes you, Daughter?" Mirror asked gently. "Queen Takhisis? Or the truth that is in your heart?"

Odila had no answer.

Mirror sighed deeply, his own mind at ease. He had his answer. He knew now what he must do.

"I am ready," he said to Palin.

19

Malys

Galdar and Mina flew together, though not side by side. The blue dragon, Razor, kept his distance from the death dragon. He would not come near the foul corpse, did nothing to hide his disgust. Galdar feared that Mina might be offended by the Blue's reaction, but she did not seem to notice, and he came at last to realize that she saw nothing except the battle that lay ahead. All else, she had shut out of her mind.

As for Galdar, even though he was certain that his own death lay ahead of him, he had never been so happy, never been so much at peace. He thought back to the days when he'd been a one-armed cripple, forced to lick the boots of such scum as his former talon leader, the late and unlamented Ernst Magit. Galdar looked back along the path of time that had brought him to this proud moment, fighting alongside her, the one who had saved him from that bitter fate, the one who had restored his arm and, in so doing, restored his life. If he could give that life for her, to save her, that was all he cared about.

They flew high into the air, higher than Galdar had ever flown on dragonback before. Fortunately, he was not one of those who are cursed with vertigo. He did not enjoy flying on dragonback—the minotaur has not been born who enjoys it— but he did not fear it. The two dragons soared above the peaks of the Lords of Doom. Galdar looked down, fascinated, to see the fiery red innards of the mountains boiling and bubbling inside deep cavities of rock. The dragons flew in and out of the clouds of steam spewing from the mountains, keeping watch for Malys, hoping to see her first, hoping for the advantage of surprise.

The surprise came, but it was on them. Galdar and Mina and the dragons were keeping watch on the horizon when Mina gave a sudden shout and pointed downward. Malys had used the clouds herself to evade their watchfulness. She was almost directly below them and flying fast for Sanction.

Galdar had seen red dragons before and been awed by their size and their might. The red dragons of Krynn were dwarf dragons, compared to Malystrx. Her massive head could have swallowed him and his Blue in one snap of the jaws. Her talons were large enough to uproot mountains, and sharp as the mountain peaks. Her tail could flatten those peaks, obliterate them, make of them piles of dust. He stared at the dragon in dry-mouthed wonder, his hand clutching the pike so that his fingers ached.

Galdar had a sudden vision of the fire belching from Malys's belly, the dragonfire that could melt stone, consume flesh and bone in an instant, set the seas to boiling. He was about to order Razor to chase after her, but the dragon was an old campaigner and knew his business, probably better than Galdar. Swift and silent, Razor folded his wings to his sides and dived down upon his foe.

The death dragon matched Razor's speed, then outdid him. Mina lowered her visor. Galdar could not see her face, but he knew her so well that he had no need to. He could envision her: pale, fey. She and the death dragon were far ahead of him now. Galdar cursed and kicked at the Blue as if he were a horse, urging him to keep up. Razor did not feel the minotaur's kicks, nor did he need any urging. He was not going to be left behind.

The dragon flew so fast that the stinging wind brought tears to Galdar's eyes, forced his eyelids shut. Try as he might, he could not keep them open except for quick peeks now and then. Malys was a red blur through the tears that never had a chance to fall, for the wind whipped them away.

Razor did not slacken his speed. Despite the wind in Galdar's eyes, this maddened flight was exhilarating, just as the first wild charge in battle was exhilarating. Galdar gripped his pike, leveled it. The notion came to him that Razor meant to crash headlong into Malys, ram her as one ship rams another, and though that would mean Galdar's death, he had no care about that, no care for himself at all. A strange calm came over him. He had no fear. He wanted to deal death, to kill this beast. Nothing else mattered.

He wondered if Mina, gripping the dragonlance, had the same idea. He envisioned the two of them, dying together in blood and in fire, and he was exalted.

Malystryx's target was Sanction. She had the city in sight. She could see its buglike inhabitants, who were just now starting to feel the terror of her might. Malys did not fear attack from the air, for she never imagined that anyone—not even this Mina—would be so crazed as to fight her from dragonback. Happening to glance up for no other reason than to enjoy the prospect of the bright blue sky, Malys was shocked to the depth of her soul to see two dragonriders plummeting down on her.

She was so startled that for a moment she doubted her senses. That moment almost proved to be her last, for her foes were on her with a suddenness that took away her breath. An instinctive, banking move saved her, carried her out of their path. The attacking dragons were flying too fast to be able to halt. They sailed past her and began to pull up, both of them circling around for another attack.

Malys kept her eye on them, but she did not immediately fly to annihilate them. She held back, wary, watchful, waiting to see what they would do next. No need to exert herself. She had only to wait until the dragonfear, which she knew how to wield better than any other dragon who had ever existed on Krynn, caused these pitiful, lesser dragons to blanch and break, turn tail and flee. Once they had their backs to her, then she would slay them.

Malys waited, watched in glee to see the blue dragon falter in his flight, while his minotaur rider cowered on his back. Certain those two were not a threat, Malys turned her attention to the other dragon and its rider. She was annoyed to note that the other dragon had not halted in its banking turn, but was coming straight for her. Malys suddenly understood why her fear did not work on this one. She had seen enough dragon corpses to recognize one more.

So this One God could raise the dead. Malys was more irritated than impressed, for now she would have to rethink her battle strategy. This creaking, worm-eaten, grotesque monstrosity could not be defeated by terror and would not succumb to pain. It was already dead, so how could she kill it? This was going to be more work than she'd anticipated.

"First you use the souls of the dead to rob me," Malys roared. "Now you bring a moldering, mummified relic to fight me. What do you and this small and desperate god of yours expect me to do? Scream? Faint? I have no fear of the living or the dead. I have fed upon both. And I will soon feed upon you!"

Malys watched her enemies carefully, trying to guess what they would do, even as she plotted her next attack. She discounted the blue dragon. The creature was in a sad state. She could smell the reek of his dread and his rider was not much better. The rider of the dead dragon was different. Malys hovered before Mina, letting the human get a good look at the power of her foe. She could not possibly win. No god could save her.

Malys knew the impression she must make upon the human. The largest living being on all of Krynn, the red dragon was enormous, dwarfing all native dragons. A snap of Malys's massive jaws could sever the spine of the mummy dragon. A single claw was as large as this human who dared to challenge her. Beyond that, Malys wielded a magical power that had raised up mountains.

She opened her jaws, let the molten fire drool from her mouth, pool around her sharp fangs. She flexed the claws that were stained brown with blood, claws that had once pierced the scales of a gold dragon and ripped out the still-beating heart. She twitched the huge tail that could crack a red dragon's skull or break its neck, sending it plummeting to the ground while its hapless rider could do nothing but scream to see obliteration rushing up at him.

Few mortals had ever been able to withstand the horror of Malys's coming, and it seemed that Mina could not. She froze on the back of the mummified beast. She tried to keep her head up, but the terror of what she saw seemed to crush her, for she drooped and shrank, then lowered her head as if she knew death was coming and could not bear to look at it.

Malys was pleased and relieved. Opening her mouth, she drew in a breath of air that would mix with the brimstone in her belly and be unleashed in a gout of flame, cremating what was left of the corpse dragon and turn this minion of the so-called One God into a living torch.

Mina did not lower her head in fear. She lowered her head in prayer, and her god did not abandon her. Mina raised her head, looked directly at Malys. In her hand she held the dragonlance.

Silver light shone from the lance, light as sharp as the lance itself. The stabbing light struck Malys full in the eyes, for she'd been staring straight at it. Momentarily blinded, she choked upon the flaming breath, swallowed most of it. Thwarted in her attack she blinked her eyes, tried to rid them of the dazzling light.

"For the One God!" Mina cried.

Galdar knew they were finished. He hoped that they were finished. He longed for easeful death to end the fear that dissolved his organs so that he was literally drowning in his own terror. Beneath him, he could feel Razor shivering, hear the clicking of his teeth and feel tremor after tremor shake the Blue's body.

Then Mina called upon Takhisis, and the goddess answered. The dragonlance flared like a bursting star. Silver light shot through Galdar's darkness, channeled the fear into his muscles and his sinews and his brain. Razor let out a roar of defiance, and Galdar lifted his voice to match.

Mina gestured with the lance, and Galdar understood. They were not going to charge again, but would try another dive, attacking Malys from above. The red dragon, in her arrogance, had slowed her flight. They would wheel and attack her before she could recover.

The two dragons banked and began their dive. Malys gave one flap of her mighty wings, then another, and suddenly she was speeding straight at them with deadly intent. Her jaws gaped wide.

Razor anticipated the Red's attack. The Blue veered off, flipping over backward to avoid the blast of flame that came so close it singed the scales on his belly.

The world reeled beneath Galdar's horns. The minotaur's stomach rolled. Dangling upside down in the harness that held him to the saddle, he clung frantically to the pommel with one hand, his weapon with the other. The harness had been built for human dragonriders, not for a minotaur. Galdar could only hope that the straps held his weight.

Razor rolled out of his turn. Galdar was upright again, the world was back where it was supposed to be. He looked hastily about to see what had become of Mina. For a moment, he could not find her, and his heart nearly burst with fear.

"Mina!" he shouted.

"Below us!" Razor called out.

She was very far below them, flying close to the ground,

flying underneath Malys, who was now caught between the two of them.

Malys's attention fixed on the Blue. A lazy flap of her wings and suddenly she was driving straight for them. Razor turned tail, beat his wings frantically.

"Fly, damn you!" Galdar snarled, although he could see that Razor was using every ounce of strength to try to outdistance the large red dragon.

Galdar looked back over his shoulder to see that the race was hopeless, lost before it could be won. Razor gasped for breath. His wings pumped. The muscles of the dragon's body flexed and heaved. Malys was barely even puffing. She seemed to fly effortlessly. Her jaws parted, fangs gleamed. She meant to snap the Blue's spine, dislodge his rider, send Galdar falling thousands of feet to his death on the rocks below.

Galdar gripped his pike.

"We're not going to make it!" he shouted at Razor. "Turn and close with her!"

The blue dragon wheeled. Galdar looked into Malys's eyes. He gripped the pike, prepared to launch it down her throat.

Malys opened her jaws, but instead of snapping at the Blue, she gave a gasp.

Mina had flown up underneath Malys. Wielding the dragonlance, Mina struck the Red in the belly. The lance sliced through the outer layer of red scales, ripped open a gash in the dragon's gut.

Malys's gasp was more astonishment than pain, for the lance had not done her serious damage. The shock and, worse than that, the insult angered her. She flipped in mid-air, tail over head, claws reaching and teeth gnashing.

The death dragon proved itself adept at maneuvering. Flying rapidly, ducking and dodging, it scrambled to keep clear of the red dragon's wild flailings. The death dragon dived. Galdar and his Blue rose and then banked for another attack.

Malys was growing weary of this battle, which was no longer fun for her. She could exert herself to some purpose when she tried, and now she stretched her wings and sought speed. She would catch this corpse and rend it bone from rotting bone, peel off its flesh and crush it into dust. And she would do the same to its rider.

Galdar had never seen anything move so fast. He and Razor flew after Malys, but they could not hope to catch up with her, not before she had slain Mina.

Malys breathed out a blast of flame.

Galdar screamed in defiance and kicked the flanks of the Blue. He might not be able to save Mina but he would avenge her.

Hearing the flame belch forth, the dead dragon lowered its head, nose down, and spread its leather wings. The ball of fire burst on its belly, spread along the wings. Galdar roared in rage, a roar that changed to a howl of glee.

The dragonlance gleamed in the flames. Mina lifted the lance, waved it to show Galdar she was safe. The death dragon's leathery wings and body shielded her from the fire. The maneuver was not without cost. The corpse's leather wings were ablaze. Tendrils of smoke snaked into the air. No matter that the corpse could neither feel pain nor die. Without the membrane of its wings, it could not remain airborne.

The death dragon began to lose altitude, flame dancing along the skeletal remains of its wings.

"Mina!" Galdar shouted in wrenching agony. He was helpless to save her.

Its wings consumed by the fire, the death dragon spiraled downward.

Certain that one foe was doomed, Malys turned her attention back to Galdar. The minotaur cared nothing about himself. Not anymore.

"Takhisis," he prayed. "I do not matter. Save Mina. Save her. She has given her all for you. Spare her life!"

In answer to his prayer, a third dragon appeared. This dragon was neither dead nor living. Shadowy, without substance, the five heads of this dragon flowed into the body of the dead dragon. The goddess herself had come to join in the battle.

The dead dragon's leathery wings began to shimmer with an eerie light. Even as flames continued to burn, the corpse pulled out of its death spiral only a short distance above the ground.

Galdar raised a mighty cheer and brandished his pike, hoping to draw Malys's attention from Mina.

"Attack!" he roared.

Razor needed no urging. He was already in a steep dive. The blue dragon bared his teeth. Galdar felt a rumbling in the dragon's belly. A bolt of lightning shot forth from the Blue's jaws. Crackling and sizzling, the lightning bolt struck Malys on the head. The concussive blast that followed nearly knocked Galdar from the saddle.

Malys jerked spasmodically as the electricity surged through her body. Galdar thought for a moment that the jolt had finished her, and his heart leaped in his chest. The lightning dissipated. Malys shook her head groggily, like a fighter who has received a blow to the nose, then she reared back, opened her jaws and came at them.

"Take me close!" Galdar cried.

Razor did as commanded. He swept in low over Malys's head. Galdar flung the pike with all his strength into the dragon's eye. He saw the pike pierce the eyeball, saw the eye redden and the dragon blink frantically.

Nothing more. And that blow had cost him dearly.

Razor's move had carried them too close to the dragon to be able to escape her reach. Galdar's strike had not taken Malys out of the battle, as he hoped. The huge pike looked puny, sticking out of Malys's eye. She felt it no more than he might feel an eyelash.

Her head reared up. She lunged at them, jaws snapping.

Galdar had one chance to save himself. He flung himself from the saddle, grabbed hold of Razor around the neck and held on. Malys drove her teeth into the blue dragon's body. The saddle disappeared in her maw.

Blood poured down Razor's flanks. The blue dragon cried out in pain and in fury as he struggled desperately to fight his attacker, lashing out with his forelegs and his hind legs, slapping at her with his tail. Galdar could do nothing but hang on. Splashed with the Blue's warm blood, Galdar clung to Razor's neck.

Malys shook the blue dragon like a dog shakes a rat to break its spine. Galdar heard a sickening crunch of bone, and Razor gave a horrifying scream.

Mina looked up to see the blue dragon clasped in Malys's jaws. She could not see Galdar and assumed that he was dead. Her heart ached. Among all those who served her, he was most dear to her. Mina could see clearly the wound on the dragon's belly. A trail of glistening, dark red marred the fire-orange red of the scales. Yet, the wound was not mortal.

The dead dragon's wings were sheets of flame, and the flames were spreading to the body. Soon Mina would be sitting on a dragon made of fire. She felt the heat, but it was an annoyance, nothing more. She saw only her enemy. She saw what she must do to defeat the enemy.

"Takhisis, fight with me!" she cried and, raising her lance, she pointed upward.

Mina heard a voice, the same voice she had heard call to her at the age of fourteen. She had run away from home to seek out that voice.

"I am with you," said Takhisis.

The goddess spread her arms, and they became dragon wings. The burning wings of the death dragon lifted into the air, propelled by the wings of the goddess. Faster and faster they flew, the air fanning the flames on the dragon, whipping them so that the fire swirled about Mina. Her armor protected her from the flames but not from the heat. Imbued with the spirit of the god, she did not feel the burning, hot metal start to sear her skin. She saw clearly that victory must be theirs. The wounded underbelly of the red dragon came closer and closer. Malys's blood dripped down on Mina's upturned face.

And then, suddenly, Takhisis was gone.

Mina felt the absence of the goddess as a rush of chill air that snatched away her breath, left her suffocating, gasping. She was alone now, alone on a dragon that was disintegrating in fire. Her goddess had left her, and Mina did not know why.

Perhaps, Mina thought frantically, this is a test.

Takhisis had administered such tests before when Mina had first found the One God and offered to be her servant. Those tests had been hard, demanding that she prove her loyalty in blood, word, and deed. She had not failed one of them. None had been as hard as this one, though. She would not survive this one, but that made no difference, because, in death, she would be with her goddess.

Mina willed the death dragon that was now a dragon of fire to keep going, and either her will or the dragon's own momentum carried it up those last few feet.

The blazing dragon crashed into Malys's body with tremendous force. The blood dripping from the wound began to bubble and boil, so hot were the flames.

Lifting the dragonlance, Mina drove it with all her strength into the dragon's belly. The lance pierced through the weakened scales, opened a gaping wound in the flesh.

Engulfed in blood and in fire, Mina held fast to the lance and prayed to the goddess that she might now be found worthy.

Malys felt pain, a pain such as she'd never before experienced. The pain was so dreadful that she released her hold on the blue dragon. Her bellowings were horrible to hear. Galdar wished he could cover his ears so that he could blot out the sound. He had to endure it, though, for he dared not move or he would lose his hold and fall to his death. He and Razor were spiralling downward. The Lords of Doom that had been small beneath Galdar now towered over him. The jagged rocks of the mountainous terrain would make for a bone-crunching landing.

Razor had taken a mortal wound, but the dragon was still alive and with unbelievable courage was struggling desperately to remain in control. Although Razor knew he was doomed, he was fighting to save his rider. Galdar did what he could to help, hanging on and trying not move. Every flap of the dragon's wings must be agony, for Razor gasped and shuddered with the pain, but he was slowly descending. He searched with his dimming vision for a clear spot on which to land.

Clinging to the neck of the dying dragon, Galdar looked up to see Mina sitting astride wings of fire. The dragon's entire body was in flames. Flames raced up the dragonlance. The fiery dragon rammed Malys, struck her in the belly. Mina jabbed the dragonlance straight into the wound she'd already made. Malys's belly split wide open. A great, gushing rush of black blood poured out of the dragon.

"Mina!" Galdar cried out in anguish and despair, as a terrifying roar from Malys obliterated his words.

Malys screamed her death scream. She knew that death scream. She'd heard it often. She'd heard it from the Blue as she shattered his spine. Now it was her turn. The death scream rose, bubbling with agony and fury, from her throat.

Blinded by the dragon's blood, abandoned by her god, Mina yet held fast to the dragonlance. She thrust the lance up into the dreadful wound, guided the lance to pierce Malys's heart.

The red dragon died in that moment, died in midair. Her body plunged from the sky, smashed onto the rocks of the Lords of Doom below. She carried her slayer down with her.

20

BliNoiNG LiGht

So pent up and excited were the defenders of Sanction that they gave a cheer when Malys's huge, red body emerged from shredded clouds.

The cheers sank, as did their courage, when the dragonfear washed over Sanction in a tidal wave that crushed hope and severed dreams and brought every person in the city face to face with the dread image of his own doom. The archers who were supposed to fire arrows at the gleaming red scales threw down their bows and fell to their bellies and lay there shivering and whimpering. The men at the catapults turned and fled their posts.

The stairs leading up to the battlements were clogged with the terrified troops so that none could go up and none could go down. Fights broke out as desperate men sought to save themselves at the expense of their fellows. Some were so maddened by the fear that they flung themselves off the walls. Those who managed to control their fear tried to calm the rest, but they were so few in number that they made little difference. One officer who tried to halt the flight of his panic-stricken men was struck down with his own sword, his body trampled in the rush.

Stone walls and iron bars were no barrier. A prisoner in the guard house near the West Gate, Silvanoshei felt the fear twist inside him as he lay on his hard bed in his dark cell, dreaming of Mina. He knew he was forgotten, but he could never forget her and he spent entire nights in hopeless dreams that she would walk through that cell door, walk with him again the dark and tangled path of his life.

The jailer had come to the cells to give Silvanoshei his daily food ration, when Malys's dragonfear washed over the city. The jailer's duty was onerous and boring, and he liked to brighten it by tormenting the prisoners. The elf was an easy target, and, although the jailer was forbidden to harm Silvanoshei physically, he could and did torment him verbally. The fact that Silvanoshei never reacted or responded did not faze the jailer, who imagined that he was having a devastating effect on the elf. In reality, Silvanoshei rarely even heard what the man said. His voice was one of many: his mother's, Samar's, his lost father's, and the voice that had made him so many promises and kept none. Real voices, such as the jailers, were not as loud as these voices of his soul, were no more than the chattering of the rodents that infested his cell.

The dragonfear twisted inside Silvanoshei, caught in his throat, strangling and suffocating. Terror jolted him out of the nether world in which he existed, flung him onto the hard floor of reality. He crouched there, afraid to move.

"Mina save us!" moaned the jailer, shivering in the doorway. He made a lunge at Silvanoshei, caught hold of his arm with a grip that nearly paralyzed the elf.

The jailer broke into slobbering tears and clung to Silvanoshei as if he'd found an elder brother.

"What is it?" Silvanoshei cried.

"The dragon! Malys," the jailer managed to blurt out. His teeth clicked together so he could barely talk. "She's come. We're all going to die! Mina save us!"

"Mina!" Silvanoshei whispered. The word broke the shackling fear. "What has Mina to do with this?"

"She's going to fight the dragon," the jailer burbled, wringing his hands.

The prison erupted into chaos as the guards fled and the prisoners screamed and shouted and flung themselves against the bars in frantic efforts to escape the horror.

Silvanoshei pushed away the quivering, blubbering mound that had once been the jailer. The cell door stood open. He ran down the corridor. Men pleaded with him to free them, but he paid no heed to them.

Emerging outside, he drew in a deep breath of air that was not tainted with the stink of unwashed bodies and rat dung. Looking into the blue sky, he glimpsed the red dragon—a huge, bloated monster hanging in the heavens. His eager, searching gaze flicked past Malys without interest. Silvanoshei scanned the heavens and at last found Mina. His sharp elven eyesight could see better than most. He could see the tiny speck that gleamed silver in the sunlight.

Silvanoshei stood in the middle of the street, staring upward. People ran past him, dashed into him, shoved him and jostled him in their mindless panic. He paid no attention, fended off hands, fought to keep his feet, and fought to keep his gaze fixed upon that small sparkle of light.

When Malys appeared, Palin discovered that there was one advantage to being dead. The dragonfear that plunged Sanction's populace into chaos had no effect upon him. He could look upon the great red dragon and feel nothing.

His spirit hovered near the totem. He saw the fire blaze in the eyes of the dead dragons. He heard their cries for revenge rise up to the heavens, rise up to Takhisis. Palin never doubted himself. His duty was clear before him. Takhisis must be stopped or at least slowed, her power diminished. She had invested much of that power into the totem, planning to use it as a doorway into the world, to merge the physical realm and the spiritual. If she succeeded she would reign supreme. No one—spirit or mortal—would be strong enough to fight her.

"You were right," said Mirror, who stood by Palin's side. "The city has gone mad with terror."

"It will wear off soon—" Palin began. He broke off abruptly.

Dalamar's spirit emerged from among the dragon skulls.

"The view of the battle is better from the box seats," Dalamar said. "You do not have feet, you know, Majere. You are not bound to the ground. Together you and I can sit at our ease among the clouds, watch every thrust and parry, see the blood fall like rain. Why don't you join me?"

"I have very little interest in the outcome," said Palin. "Whoever wins, we are bound to lose."

"Speak for yourself," Dalamar said.

To Palin's discomfiture, Dalamar's spirit was taking an unusual interest in Mirror.

Could Dalamar see both the man and the silver dragon? Could Dalamar have guessed their plan? If he knew, would he attempt to thwart them, or was he preoccupied with his own schemes? That Dalamar had schemes of his own, Palin did not doubt. Palin had never fully trusted Dalamar, and he had grown more wary of him these past few days.

"The battle goes well," Dalamar continued, his soul's gaze fixed on Mirror. "Malys is fully occupied, that much is certain. People are calming down. The dragonfear is starting to abate. Speaking of which, your blind beggar friend appears to be remarkably immune to dragonfear. Why is that, I wonder?"

What Dalamar said was true. The dragonfear was fading away. Soldiers who had been hugging the ground and screaming that they were all going to die were sitting up, looking sheepish and embarrassed.

If we are going to do this, we have to act now, realized Palin. What danger can Dalamar be to us? He can do nothing to stop them. Like me, he has no magic.

A roaring bellow boomed among the mountains. People in the street stared upward, began to shout and point to the sky.

"A dragon has drawn blood," said Mirror, peering upward. "Hard to say which, though."

Dalamar's spirit hung in the air. The eyes of his soul stared at them as if he would delve the depths of theirs. Then, suddenly, he vanished.

"The outcome of this fight means something to him, that is certain," said Palin. "I wonder which horse he is backing."

"Both, if he can find a way," said Mirror.

"Could he see your true form, do you think?" Palin asked.

"I believe that I was able to hide from him," said Mirror. "But when I begin to cast my magic, I can no longer do so. He will see me for what I am."

"Then let us hope the battle proves interesting enough to keep him occupied," said Palin. "Do you have fur and amber . . . ? Ah, sorry, I forgot," he added, seeing Mirror smile. "Dragons have no need of such tools for their spell casting."

Now that the battle had begun, the totem's magic intensified. Eyes in the skulls burned and glittered with a fury so potent it shone from ground to heaven. The single eye, the New Eye, gleamed white, even in the daylight. The magic of the totem was strong, drew the dead to it. The souls of the dead circled the totem in a pitiful vortex, their yearning a torment fed by the goddess.

Palin felt the pain of longing, a longing for what is lost beyond redemption.

"When you cast your spell," he said to Mirror, the longing for the magic an aching inside him, "the dead will swarm around you, for yours is a magic they can steal. The sight of them is a terrible one, unnerving—"

"So there is at least one advantage to being blind," Mirror remarked, and he began to cast the spell.

Dragons, of all the mortal beings on Krynn, are born with the ability to use magic. Magic is inherent to them, a part of them like their blood and their shining scales. The magic comes from within.

Mirror spoke the words of magic in the ancient language of dragons. Coming from a human throat, the words lacked the rich resonance and rolling majesty that the silver dragon was accustomed to hearing, sounded thin and weak. Small or large, the words would accomplish the goal. The first prickles of magic began to sparkle in his blood.

Wispy hands plucked at his scales, tore at his wings, brushed across his face. The souls of the dead now saw him for what he was—a silver dragon—and they surged around him, frantic for the magic that they could feel pulsing inside his body. The souls reached out to him with their wispy hands and pleaded with him. The souls clung to him and hung from him like tattered scarves. The dead could do him no harm. They were an annoyance, like scale mites. But scale mites did nothing more than raise an irritating itch. Scale mites did not have voices that cried out in desperation, begging, beseeching. Hearing the despair in the voices, Mirror realized he had spoken truly. There was an advantage to being blind. He did not have to see their faces.

Even though the magic was inherent to him, he still had to concentrate to cast the spell, and he found this difficult. The fingers of the souls raked his scales, their voices buzzed in his ears.

Mirror tried to concentrate on one voice—his voice. He concentrated on the words of his own language, and their music was comforting and reassuring. The magic burned within him, bubbled in his blood. He sang the words and opened his hands and cast the magic forth.

Although Dalamar guessed that his fellow mage was up to something, he had discounted Palin as a threat. How could he be? Palin was as impotent as Dalamar when it came to magic. True, Dalamar would not let that stop him. He had schemed and connived so that whichever way the bread landed, he'd still have the butter side up.

Yet, there was something strange about that blind beggar. Probably the fellow was or fancied himself a wizard. Probably Palin had concocted some idea that they could work together, although what sort of magical rabbit they would be able to pull out of their joint hats was open to debate. If they were able to come up with a rabbit at all, the souls of the dead would grab it and rip it apart.

Satisfied, Dalamar felt it safe to leave Palin and his blind beggar to bumble about in the darkness while he went to witness first hand the gladiatorial contest between Malys and Mina. Dalamar was not overly interested in which one won. He viewed the battle with the cold, dispassionate interest of the gambler who has all his bets covered.

Malys breathed blazing fire on the corpse dragon, the leather wings erupted into flames. Malys chortled, thinking she was the victor.

"Don't count your winnings yet," Dalamar advised the red dragon, and he was proven right.

Takhisis advanced onto the field of battle. Reaching out her hand, she touched the death dragon. Her spirit flowed into the body of the burning corpse, saving Mina, her champion.

At that moment, Dalamar's soul heard the sound of a voice chanting. He could not understand the words, but he recognized the language of dragons, and he was alarmed to realize by the cadence and the rhythm that the words were magic. His spirit fled the battle, soared back to the temple. He saw a spark of bright light and realized immediately that he had made a mistake—perhaps a fatal mistake.

As Dalamar the Dark had misjudged the uncle, so had he misjudged the nephew. Dalamar saw in an instant what Palin planned.

Dalamar recognized the blind beggar as Mirror, guardian of the Citadel of Light, one of the few silver dragons who had dared remain in the world after all the others had so mysteriously fled. He saw the dead surrounding Mirror, trying to feed off the magic he was casting, but the dragon would be poor pickings. The dead might leech some of the magic, but they would not seriously impede Mirror's spellcasting. Dalamar knew immediately what the two were doing, knew it as well as if he had plotted it with them.

Dalamar looked back to the battle. This was Takhisis's moment of victory, the moment she would avenge herself on this dragon who had dared moved in to take over her world. The Dark Queen had been forced to endure Malys's taunts and gibes in seething silence. She had been forced to watch Malys slay her minions and use their power—that should have been her power.

At last, Takhisis had grown strong enough to challenge Malys, to wrench away the souls of the dead dragons, who now worshiped their queen and gave their power to their queen. Dragons of Krynn, their souls were hers to command.

Long had Takhisis watched and worked and waited for this moment when she would remove the last obstacle to stand in her way of taking full and absolute control of her world. Concentrating on the foe in front, Takhisis was oblivious to the danger creeping up on her from behind.

Dalamar could warn Takhisis. He had but to say one word and she would run to protect her totem. She could not afford to do otherwise. She had worked hard to create the door for her entry and she was not about to have it slammed shut in her face. There would be other days to fight Malys, other champions to fight Malys if she lost Mina.

Dalamar hesitated.

True, Takhisis had offered him rich reward—a return to his body and the gifting of the magic to go with it.

Dalamar reached out with his soul and touched the past, touched the memory that was all that was left to him: the memory of the magic. He would do anything, say anything, betray, destroy anyone for the sake of the magic.

The thought that he must abase himself before Takhisis was galling to him. Once years ago, when the magic had been his to command, he had been open in his defiance of the Dark Queen. Nuitari, her son, had no love for his mother and could always be counted upon to defend his worshipers against her. Nuitari was gone now. The power the dark god of magic had lavished on his servant was gone.

Dalamar must now abase himself before the Dark Queen, and he knew that Takhisis would not be generous in her victory over him. Yet, for the magic, he could do even this.

Takhisis straddled the world, watching the battle in which she took such a keen interest. Her champion was winning. Mina flew straight up at Malys, the gleaming dragonlance in her hand.

Dalamar knelt in the dust and bowed his head low and said humbly, "Your Majesty . . ."

Mirror could not see the magic, but he could feel it and hear it. The spell flowed from his fingers as bolts of jagged, blue lightning that crackled and sizzled. The air smelled of brimstone. He could see the blazing bolts in his mind's eye, see them striking a skull, dancing from that skull to another, from the skull of a gold to the skull of a red, from that skull to the skull touching it, and round and round, jumping from one to the next, in a blazing, fiery chain.

"Is the spell cast?" Mirror cried.

"It is cast," said Palin, watching in awe.

He wished Mirror could see this sight. The lightning sizzled and danced. Blue-white, the bolts jumped from one skull to the next, so fast that the eye could not follow them. As the lightning struck each skull, that skull began to glow blue-white, as though dipped in phosphorus. Thunder boomed and blasted, shaking the ground, shaking the totem.

Power built in the totem, the magic shuddered in the air. The voices of the dead fell silent as the voices of the living raised in a terrible clamor, screaming and crying out. Feet pounded, some running toward the totem, others running away.

Watching Mirror cast the spell, Palin recited to himself the words of magic that for him held no meaning, but which were imprinted on his soul. His body sat unmoved, uncaring, on a bench in the temple. Exultant, his soul watched lightning leap from skull to skull, setting each afire.

The magic reverberated, hummed, grew stronger and stronger. The white-hot fire burned bright. The intense heat drove back those gathered around the totem. The skulls of the dragons now had eyes of white flame.

In the heavens, thunder rolled. The New Eye glared down on them.

Dark clouds, thick and black, shot through with bolts of orange and red, bubbled and boiled and frothed. Tendrils of destruction twisted down from the storm, raising dust clouds and uprooting trees. Hail pelted, smashed into the ground.

"Do your damndest, Takhisis," cried Palin to the thundering, angry voice of the storm. "You are too late."

The black clouds blanketed Sanction with darkness and rain and hail. A gust of wind blew on the totem. Torrential rains deluged the city, trying desperately to douse the magic.

The rain was like oil on the fire. The wind fanned the flames. Mirror could not see the fire, but he could feel the searing heat. He staggered backward, stumbling over benches, backed into the altar. His groping hands found purchase, cool and smooth. He recognized by touch the sarcophagus of Goldmoon, and it seemed to him that he could hear her voice calm and reassuring. Mirror crouched beside the sarcophagus, though the heat grew ever more intense. He kept his hand upon it protectively.

A ball of fire formed in the center of the totem, shining bright as a lost star fallen to the ground. Light, bright and white as starlight, began to shine within the eyes of the dragons. The light grew brighter and brighter until none of the living could look at it, but were forced to cover their eyes.

The fire grew in strength and intensity, burning purely and radiantly, its luminous brilliance so dazzling that Mirror could see it through his blindness, saw bursting, blue-white flame and the petals of flame drifting up into the heavens. The rain had no effect on the magical fire. The wind of the goddess's fury could not diminish it.

The light shone pure white at its heart. The skulls of the dragons shattered, burst apart. The totem teetered and swayed, then fell in upon itself, dissolving, disintegrating.

The New Eye stared into the white heart of the blaze. Blood-red, the Eye fought to maintain its gaze, but the pain proved too much.

The Eye blinked.

The Eye vanished.

Darkness closed over Mirror, but he no longer cursed it, for the darkness was blessed, safe and comforting as the darkness from which he'd been born. His trembling hand ran over the smooth, cool surface of the sarcophagus. There came a ringing sound as of shattering glass, and he felt cracks in the surface, felt them spread through the amber like winter ice melting in the spring sun.

The sarcophagus broke apart, the bits and pieces falling around him. He felt a soft touch on his hand that was like ashes drifting on the wind.

"Goodbye, dear friend," he said.

"The blind beggar!" a voice like thunder rumbled. "Slay the blind beggar. He has destroyed the totem! Malys will kill us! Malys will kill us all."

Voices cried out in anger. Footsteps pounded. Fists began to pummel him.

A rock struck Mirror and another.

Palin watched, exultant, as the totem fell. He saw the sarcophagus destroyed and, though he could not find Goldmoon's spirit, he rejoiced that her body would no longer be held in thrall, that she would not longer be a slave of Takhisis.

He would be called to account. He would be made to pay. He could not avoid it, could not hide, for though her eye might have been blinded, Takhisis was still master. Her presence in the world had not been banished, merely diminished. He remained a slave, and there was nowhere he could hide that her dogs would not sniff him out, hunt him down.

He waited to accept his fate, waited near the crumbling ruins of the totem, waited beside the pitiful shell of flesh that was his body. The dogs were not long in coming.

Dalamar appeared, materializing out of the smoking ruins of the burning skulls.

"You should not have done this, Palin. You should not have interfered. Your soul faces oblivion. Darkness eternal."

"What is to be your reward for your service to her?" Palin asked. "Your life? No"—he answered his own question—"you cared little for your life. She gave you back the magic."

"The magic is life," said Dalamar. "The magic is love. The magic is family. The magic is wife. The magic is child."

Inside the temple, Palin's body sat on the hard bench, stared unseeing at the candle flames that wavered, fearful and helpless, in the storm winds that swept through the room.

"How sad," he said, as his spirit started to ebb, water receding from the shoreline, "that only at the end do I know what I should have known from the start."

"Darkness eternal," Dalamar echoed.

"No," said Palin softly, "for beyond the clouds, the sun shines."

Rough hands seized hold of Mirror. Angry, panicked voices clamored in his ear, so many at once that he could not possibly understand them. They mauled him, pulled him this way and that, as they screeched and argued between themselves about what to do with him. Some wanted to hang him. Others wanted to rend him apart where he stood.

The silver dragon could always slough off this puny human guise and transform into his true shape. Even blind, he could defend himself against a mob. He spread his arms that would become his silver wings and lifted his head. Joy filled him even as danger closed in on him. In a moment, he would be himself, shining silver in the darkness, riding the winds of the storm.

Shackles clamped over his wrists. He almost laughed, for no iron forged of man could hold him. He tried to shake them off, but the shackles would not fall, and he realized that they were not forged of iron, but of fear. Takhisis made them and she clamped them on him. Strive as he might, he could not transform himself. He was chained to his human body, shackled to this two-legged form, and in that form, blind and alone, he would die.

Mirror fought to escape his captors, but his thrashings only goaded them to further torment. Rocks and fists struck him. Pain shot through him. Blow after blow rained down on him. He slumped to the ground.

He heard, as in a dream of pain, a strong, commanding voice speak out. The voice was powerful, and it quelled the clamor.

"Back away!" Odila ordered. Her voice was cold and stern and accustomed to being obeyed. "Leave him alone or know the wrath of the One God!"

"He used some sort of magic to destroy the totem!" a man cried. "I saw him!"

"He's done away with the moon!" cried another. "Done something foul and unnatural that will curse us all!"

Other voices joined in the accusing clamor, demanded his death.

"The magic he used is the magic of the One God," Odila told them. "You should be down on your knees, praying for the One God to save us from the dragon, not maltreating a poor beggar!"

Her strong, scarred hands took firm hold of him, lifted him up.

"Can you walk?" she whispered to him, low and urgent. "If so, you must try."

"I can walk," he told her.

A trickle of warm blood seeped down into the bandages he wore around his eyes. The pain in his head eased, but he felt cold and clammy and nauseous. He staggered to his feet. Her arms wrapped around him, supported his faltering steps.

"Good," Odila whispered in his ear. "We're going to walk backward." Taking a firm grip on him, she suited her action to her words. He stumbled with her, leaning on her.

"What is happening?" he asked.

"The mob is holding back for the moment. They feel my power, and they fear it. I speak for the One God, after all." Odila sounded amused, reckless, joyful. "I want to thank you," she said, her voice softening. "I was the one who was blind. You opened my eyes."

"Let's go after him," someone shouted. "What's stopping us? She's not Mina! She's just some traitor Solamnic."

Odila let go of Mirror, moved to stand defensively in front of him. He heard a roar as the mob surged forward.

"A traitor Solamnic with a club, not a sword," Odila said to him. He heard the splintering of wood, guessed that she had smashed up one of the benches. "I'll hold them off as long as I can. Make your way behind the altar. You'll find a trapdoor—"

"I have no need for trapdoors," Mirror said. "You will be my eyes, Odila. I will be your wings."

"What the—" she began, then she gasped. He heard her drop the club.

Mirror spread his arms. Fear was gone. The Dark Queen had no power over him. He could see, once again, the radiant light. As it had destroyed the totem, so it burned away the shackles that bound him. His human body, so frail and fragile, small and cramped, was transformed. His heart grew and expanded, blood pulsed through massive veins, fed his strong taloned legs and an enormous silver-scaled body. His tail struck the altar, smashed it, sent the candles tumbling to the floor in a river of melted wax.

The mob that had surged forward to kill a blind beggar fell all over itself trying to escape a blind dragon.

"No saddle, Sir Knight," he told Odila. "You'll have to hang on tight. Grasp my mane. You'll need to lean close to my head to be able to tell me where we are going. What of Palin?" he asked, as she caught hold of his mane and pulled herself up on his back. "Can we take him with us?"

"His body is not there," Odila reported.

"I feared as much," said Mirror quietly. "And the other one? Dalamar."

"He is there," said Odila. "He sits alone. His hands are stained with blood."

Mirror spread his wings.

"Hold on!" he shouted.

"I'm holding," said Odila. "Holding fast."

In her hand was the medallion that bore on it the image of the five-headed dragon. The medallion burned her scarred fingers. The pain was minor compared to the pain that seared her when she touched the dragonlance. Clasping the medallion, Odila tore it off.

The silver dragon gave a great leap. His wings caught the winds of the storm, used them to carry him aloft.

Odila brought the medallion to her lips. She kissed it, then, opening her fingers, she let the medallion fall. The medallion spiraled down into the pile of dust that was now all that remained of Malys's monument to death.

Mina's followers witnessed the breathtaking battle. They cheered to see Malys fall, gasped in horror as Mina fell in flames along with her foe.

Desperately they waited to see her rise again from the fire, as she had done once before. Smoke drifted up from the mountain, but it brought no Mina with it.

Silvanoshei had watched with the rest. He started walking. He would go to the temple. Someone there would have news. As he walked, as the blood flowed and his stiff muscles warmed, he came gradually to realize that not only was he still alive, he was free.

People milled about in the streets, shocked and confused. Some wept openly. Some simply wandered aimlessly, not knowing what to do next, waiting for someone to come and tell them. Some spoke of the battle, reliving it, relating over and over what they had seen, trying to make it real. People jabbered about the moon and that it was gone and so was the One God, if the One God had ever been, and that now Mina was gone too. No one paid any attention to Silvanoshei. Everyone was too caught up in his own despair to care about an elf.

I could walk out of Sanction, Silvanoshei said to himself, and no one would lift a finger to stop me.

He had no thought of leaving Sanction, however. He could not leave, not until he knew for certain what had become of Mina. Arriving at the temple, he found a huge throng of people gathered around the totem and he joined them, staring in dismay at the pile of ashes that had once been the glory of Queen Takhisis.

Silvanoshei stared into the ashes and he saw what he had been, saw what he might have been.

He saw the events that had led him to this point, saw them with his soul that never sleeps, always watches. He saw the terrible night the ogres attacked. He saw himself— consumed with hatred for his mother and for the life she had forced him to lead, consumed with fear and guilt when it seemed that she might die at the hands of the ogres. He saw himself running through the darkness to save her, and he saw himself proud to think that he would be the one to save his people. He saw the lightning bolt that sent him tumbling into unconsciousness. He saw himself falling down the hill to land at the base of the shield and then he saw what he had not been able to see with mortal eyes. He saw the dark hand of the goddess lift the shield so that he could enter.

Staring into the darkness, he saw the darkness staring back at him, and he realized that he had looked into the Dark Queen's eyes many times before, looked into them without blinking or turning away.

He heard again words that Mina had said to him on that first night they had come together. Words that he had tossed aside as nonsense, meaningless, without importance.

You do not love me. You love the god you see in me.

Everything his mother yearned for, he had been given. She had wanted to rule Silvanesti. He was the king of Silvanesti. She had longed to be loved by the people. They loved him. That was his revenge, and it had been sweet. But that was only part of the revenge. The best part was that he had thrown it all away. Nothing he could have done had the power to hurt his mother more.

If the goddess had used him, it was because Takhisis had gazed deeply into the eyes of his soul and had seen one eye wink.

21

The Dead and Dying

Razor's strength gave out while they were still airborne. He could no longer move his wings, and he began to twist downward in an uncontrolled dive. Galdar had the terrifying image of sheer-sided, jagged rocks stabbing upward. Razor crashed headlong into a small grove of pine trees.

For a heart-stopping moment, all Galdar could see was a blur of orange rocks and green trees, blue dragon scales and red blood. He squinched his eyes tight shut, gripped the dragon with all the strength of his massive body, buried his head in the dragon's neck. Buffeted and jolted, he heard the rending and snapping of limbs and bones, smelled and tasted the sharp odor of pine needles and the iron-tinged smell of fresh blood. A branch struck him on the head, nearly ripping off his horn. Another smote him on the back of his shoulder. Shattered branches tore at his legs and arms.

Suddenly, abruptly, they slammed to a halt.

Galdar spent a long moment doing nothing except gasping for breath and marveling that he was still alive. Every part of him hurt. He had no idea if he was seriously wounded or not. He moved, gingerly. Feeling no sharp, searing pain, he concluded that no bones were broken. Blood dribbled down his nose. His ears rang, and his head throbbed. He felt Razor give a shuddering sigh.

The dragon's head and upper portion of his shattered body rested in the pine trees that had broken beneath his weight. Disentangling himself from a nest of twisted, snapped branches, Galdar slid down off the dragon's back. He had the woozy impression that the blue dragon was resting in a cradle of pine boughs. The lower half of the dragon's body—the broken wings and tail—trailed behind him onto the rocks, leaving a smear of blood.

Galdar looked swiftly about for Malys's carcass. He saw it, off in the distance. Her corpse was easy to located. In death, she made her final mountain—a glistening, red mound of bloody flesh. Smoke and flame drew his eye. Fire consumed the death dragon, the flames spreading to the scrub pine. Farther down in the valley lay Sanction, but he couldn't see the city. Dark thunderclouds swirled beneath him. Where he stood, the sun shone brightly, so brightly that it had apparently eclipsed that New Eye, for he could not see it.

He did not take time to search for it. His main concern was Mina. He was frantic with worry about her and wanted nothing more than to go off immediately to search for her. But the minotaur owed his life to the heroics of the blue dragon. The least Galdar could do was to stay with him. No one, minotaur or dragon, should die alone.

Razor was still alive, still breathing, but his breaths were pain-filled and shallow. Blood flowed from his mouth. His eyes were starting to grow dim, but they brightened at the sight of Galdar.

"Is she . . ." The blue dragon choked on his own blood, could not continue.

"Malys is dead," Galdar said, deep and rumbling. "Thank you for the battle. A glorious victory that will be long remembered.

You die a hero. I will honor your memory, as will my children and my children's children and their children after."

Galdar had no children, nor was there any likelihood he would ever have any. His words were the ancient tribute given to a warrior who has fought valiantly and died with honor. Yet Galdar spoke them from the depth of his soul, for he could only imagine what terrible agony these last few moments were for the dying dragon.

The blue dragon gave another shudder. His body went limp.

"I did my duty," he breathed, and died.

Galdar lifted his head and gave a howl of grief that echoed among the mountains—a final, fitting tribute. This done, he was free at last to follow his aching heart, to find out what had happened to Mina.

I should not be worried, he told himself. I have seen Mina survive poisoning, emerge whole and unscarred from her own flaming funeral pyre. The One God loves Mina, loves her as perhaps she has never before loved a mortal. Takhisis will protect her darling, watch over her.

Galdar told himself that, told himself repeatedly, but still he worried.

He scanned the rugged rocks around the carcass of the dragon. Chunks of flesh and gore were splattered about a wide area, the rocks were slippery with the mess. He hoped to see Mina come striding toward him, that exalted glow in her eyes. But nothing moved on the rocky outcropping where the dragon had fallen. The birds of the air had fled at her coming, the animals gone to ground. All was silent, except for a fierce and angry wind that hissed among the rocks with an eerie, whistling sound.

The rocks were difficult enough to navigate without the blood and blubber. Climbing was slow going, especially when every movement brought the pain of some newly discovered injury. Galdar found his pike. The weapon was covered with blood, and the blade was broken. Galdar was pleased to retrieve it. He would give it to Mina as a memento.

Search as he might, he could not find her. Time and again, he roared out, "Mina!" The name came back a hundredfold, careening off the sides of the mountains, but there was no answering call. The echoes faded away into silence. Climbing up and over a jumble of boulders, Galdar came at last to Malys's carcass.

Looking at the wreckage of the gigantic red dragon, Galdar felt nothing, not elation, not triumph, nothing except weariness and grief and a wonder that any of them had come out of this confrontation alive.

"Perhaps Mina didn't," said a voice inside him, a voice that sent shudders through him.

"Mina!" He called again, and he heard, in answer, a groan.

Malys's red-scaled and blood-smeared flank moved.

Alarmed, Galdar lifted the broken pike. He looked hard at the dragon's head, that lay sideways on the rocks, so that only one eye was visible. That eye stared, unseeing, at the sky. The neck was twisted and broken. Malys could not be alive.

The groan was repeated and a weak voice called out, "Galdar!"

With a cry of joy, Galdar flung down the pike and bounded forward. Beneath the belly of the dragon he saw a hand, covered with blood and moving feebly. The dragon had fallen on top of Mina, pinning her beneath.

Galdar put his shoulder to the fast cooling mass of blubber and heaved. The dragon's carcass was heavy, weighing several hundred tons. He might as well have tried to shift the mountain.

He was frantic with worry now, for Mina's voice sounded weak. He put his hands on the belly that had been slit wide open. Entrails spewed out; the stench was horrible. He gagged, tried to stop breathing.

"I can barely lift this, Mina," he called to her. "You must crawl out. Make haste. I can't hold it for long."

He heard something in reply but could not understand, for her voice was muffled. He gritted his teeth and bent his knees and, sucking in a great breath of air, he gave a grunt and heaved upward with all his might. He heard a scrabbling sound, a pain-filled gasping for breath, and a muffled cry. His muscles ached and burned, his arms grew wobbly. He could hold on no longer. With a loud shout of warning, he dropped the mass of flesh and stood gasping for breath amid the putrid remains. He looked down to find Mina lying at his feet.

Galdar was reminded of a time when Mina had been invited to bless a birthing. Galdar hadn't wanted to be there, but Mina had insisted and, of course, he'd obeyed. Looking down at Mina, Galdar remembered vividly the tiny child, so frail and fragile, covered in blood. He knelt by Mina's side.

"Mina," he said, helpless, afraid to touch her, "where are you hurt? I cannot tell if this is your blood or the dragon's."

Her eyes opened. The amber was bloodshot, rimmed with red. She reached out her hand, grasped Galdar's arm. The move caused her pain. She gasped and shivered but still managed to cling to him.

"Pray to the One God, Galdar," she said, her voice no more than a whisper. "I have done something . . . to displease her . . . Ask her . . . to forgive . . ."

Her eyes closed. Her head lolled to one side. Her hand slipped from his arm. His own heart stopping in fear, Galdar put his hand on her neck to feel for her pulse. Finding it, he gave a great sigh of relief.

He lifted Mina in his arms. She was light as he remembered that newborn babe to have been.

"You great bitch!" Galdar snarled. He was not referring to the dead dragon.

Galdar found a small cave, snug and dry. The cave was so small that the minotaur could not stand to his full height, but was forced to crouch low to enter. Carrying Mina inside, he laid her down gently. She had not regained consciousness, and although this scared him, he told himself this was good, for otherwise she would die of the pain.

Once in the cave, he had time to examine her. He stripped away her armor, tossed it outside to lie in the dust. The wounds she had sustained were terrible. The end of her leg bone protruded from the flesh, that was bloody, purple, and grotesquely swollen. One arm no longer looked like an arm, but like something hanging in a butcher's stall. Her breathing was ragged and caught in her throat. Every breath was a struggle, and more than once he feared she lacked the strength to take another. Her skin was burning hot to the touch. She shivered with the cold that brings death.

He no longer felt the pain of his own wounds. Whenever he made a sudden move and a sharp jab reminded him, he was surprised, wondered vaguely where it came from. He lived only for Mina, thought only of her. Finding a stream a short distance from the cave, he rinsed out his helm, filled it with water, carried it back to her.

He laved her face and touched her lips with the cool liquid, but she could not drink. The water trickled down her blood-covered chin. Up here in these rocks he would find no herbs to treat her pain or bring down her fever. He had no bandages. He had a rough sort of battlefield training in healing, but that was all, and it was not much help. He should amputate that shattered leg, but he could not bring himself to do it. He knew what it was for a warrior to live as a cripple.

Better she should die. Die in the glorious moment with the defeat of the dragon. Die as a warrior victorious over her foe. She was going to die. Galdar could do nothing to save her. He could do nothing but watch her life bleed away. He could do nothing but be by her side so that she would not die alone.

Darkness crept into the cave. Galdar built a fire inside the cavern's entrance to keep her warm. He did not leave the cavern again. Mina was delirious, fevered, murmuring incoherent words, crying out, moaning. Galdar could not bear to see her suffer, and more than once, his hand stole to his dagger to end this swiftly, but he held back. She might yet regain consciousness, and he wanted her to know, before she died, that she died a hero and that he would always love and honor her.

Mina's breathing grew erratic, yet she struggled on. She fought very hard to live. Sometimes her eyes opened and he saw the agony in them and his heart wrenched. Her eyes closed again without showing any signs of recognition, and she battled on.

He reached out his hand, wiped the chill sweat from her forehead.

"Let go, Mina," he said to her, tears glimmering on his eyelids. "You brought down your enemy—the largest, most powerful dragon ever to inhabit Krynn. All nations and people will honor you. They will sing songs of your victory down through the ages. Your tomb will be the finest ever built in Ansalon. People will travel from all over the world to pay homage. I will lay the dragonlance at your side and the put the monstrous skull of the dragon at your feet."

He could see it all so clearly. The tale of her courage would touch the hearts of all who heard it. Young men and women would come to her tomb to pledge themselves to lives of service to mankind, be it as warrior or healer. That she had walked in darkness would be forgotten. In death, she was redeemed.

Still, Mina fought on. Her body twitched and jerked. Her throat was ragged and raw from her screams.

Galdar could not bear it. "Release her," he prayed, not thinking what he was doing or saying, his only thought of her. "You've done with her! Release her!"

"So this is where you have her hidden," said a voice.

Galdar drew his dagger, twisted to his feet, and emerged from the cave all in one motion. The fire stole away his night vision. Beyond the crackling flames, all was darkness. He was a perfect target, standing there in the firelight, and he moved swiftly. Not too far away. He would never leave Mina, let them do what they might to him.

He blinked his eyes, tried to pierce the shadows. He had not heard the sound of footfalls or the chink of armor or the ring of steel. Whoever it was had come upon him by stealth, and that boded no good. He made certain to hold his dagger so it did not reflect the firelight.

"She is dying," he said to whoever was out there. "She has not long to live. Honor her dying and allow me to remain with her to the end. Whatever is between us, we can settle that afterward. I pledge my word."

"You are right, Galdar," said the voice. "Whatever is between us, we will settle at a later date. I gave you a great gift, and you returned my favor with treachery."

Galdar's throat constricted. The dagger slid from the suddenly nerveless right hand, landed on the rocks at his feet with a clash and a clatter. A woman stood at the mouth of the cave. Her figure blotted out the light of the fire, obliterated the light of the stars. He could not see her face with his eyes, for she had yet to enter the world in her physical form, but he saw her with the eyes of his soul. She was beautiful, the most beautiful thing he had ever seen in his life. Yet her beauty did not touch him, for it was cold and sharp as a scythe. She turned away from him. She walked toward the entrance to the cave.

Galdar managed with great effort to move his shaking limbs. He dared not look into that face, dared not meet those eyes that held in them eternity. He had no weapon that could fight her. No such weapon existed in this world. He had only his love for Mina, and perhaps that was what gave him courage to place his own body between Queen Takhisis and the cave.

"You will not pass," he said, the words squeezed out of him. "Leave her alone! Let go of her! She did what you wanted and without your help. You abandoned her. Leave it that way."

"She deserves to be punished," Takhisis returned, cold, disdainful. "She should have known the wizard Palin was treacherous, secretly plotting to destroy me. He nearly succeeded. He destroyed the totem. He destroyed the mortal body that I had chosen for my residence while in the world. Because of Mina's negligence, I came close to losing everything I have worked for. She deserves to punished! She deserves death and worse than death! Still—" Takhisis's voice softened— "I will be merciful. I will be generous."

Galdar's heart almost stopped with fear. He was panting and shaking, yet he did not move.

"You need her," said Galdar harshly. "That's the only reason you're saving her." He shook his horned head. "She's at peace now, or soon will be. I won't let you have her."

Takhisis moved closer.

"I keep you alive, minotaur, for only one reason. Mina asks me to do so. Even now, as her spirit is wrenched from its shell of flesh, she begs me to be merciful toward you. I indulge her whim, for now. The day will come, however, when she will see that she no longer has need of you. Then, what lies between you and me will be settled."

Her hand lifted him up by the scruff of his neck and tossed him carelessly aside. He landed heavily among the sharp rocks and lay there, sobbing in anger and frustration. He pounded his left hand into the rocks, pounded it again and again so that it was bruised and bloody.

Queen Takhisis entered the cavern, and he could hear her crooning softly, sweetly, "My child . . . My beloved child . . . I do forgive you. . . ."

22

Lost in the Maze

Gerard was determined to reach the Knights' Council with the urgent news of the return of Queen Takhisis as quickly as possible. He guessed that once she had built her totem and secured Sanction, the Dark Queen would move swiftly to secure the world. Gerard had no time to waste.

Gerard had found the elf, Samar, without difficulty. As Silvanoshei had predicted, the two men, though of different races, were experienced warriors and, after a few tense moments, suspicion and mistrust were both allayed. Gerard had delivered the ring and the message from Silvanoshei, though the Knight had not been exactly honest in relating the young king's words. Gerard had not told Samar that Silvanoshei was captive of his own heart. Gerard had made Silvanoshei a hero who had defied Mina and been punished for it. Gerard's plan was for the elves to join the Solamnics in the attempt to seize Sanction and halt the rise of Takhisis.

Gerard trusted that the elves would want to free their young king, and although Gerard had received the distinct impression that Samar did not much like Silvanoshei, Gerard had managed to impress the dour warrior with the true story of Silvanoshei's courage in the fight with Clorant and his fellow Knights. Samar had promised that he would carry the matter to Alhana Starbreeze. He had little doubt that she would agree to the plan. The two had parted, vowing to meet each other again as allies on the field of battle.

After bidding farewell to Samar, Gerard rode to the sea coast. Standing on a cliff that overlooked the crashing waves, he stripped off the black armor that marked him as a Knight of Takhisis, and one by one he hurled the pieces into the ocean. He had the distinct satisfaction of seeing, in the pre-dawn light, the waves lift the black armor and slam it against the jutting rocks.

"Take that and be damned to you," Gerard said. Mounting his horse, clad only in leather breeches and a well-worn woolen shirt, he set off west.

He hoped that with fair weather and good roads he might reach Lord Ulrich's manor in ten days. Gerard soon glumly revised his plan, hoped to reach the manor house in ten years, for at that point everything began to go strangely wrong. His horse threw a shoe in a region where no one had ever heard of a blacksmith. Gerard had to travel miles out of his way, leading his lame horse, to find one. When he did come across a blacksmith, the man worked so slowly that Gerard wondered if he was mining the iron and then forging it.

Days passed before his horse was shod and he was back in the saddle, only to discover that he was lost. The sky was cloudy and overcast. He could see neither sun nor stars, had no idea which direction he was heading. The land was sparsely populated. He rode for hours without seeing a soul. When he did come upon someone to ask directions, everyone in the land appeared to have suddenly gone stupid, for no matter what route he was told to take, the road always landed him in the middle of some impenetrable forest or stranded him on the banks of some impassable river.

Gerard began to feel as if he were in one of those terrible dreams, where you know the destination you are trying to reach, but you can never quite seem to reach it. At first he was annoyed and frustrated, but after days and days of wandering he began to feel uneasy.

Galdar's poisoned sword lodged in Gerard's gut.

"Am I making the decisions or is Takhisis?" he asked himself. "Is she determining my every move? Am I dancing to her piping?"

Constant rain soaked him. Cold winds chilled him. He had been forced to sleep outdoors for the past few nights, and he was just asking himself drearily what was the use of going on, when he saw the lights of a small town shining in the distance. Gerard came upon a road house. Not much to look at, it would provide a roof over his head, hot food and cold drink and, hopefully, information.

He led his horse to the stable, rubbed the animal down and saw to it that the beast was fed and resting comfortably. This done, he entered the road house. The hour was late, the innkeeper had gone to bed and was in a foul mood at being wakened. He showed Gerard to the common room, indicated a place on the floor. As the Knight spread out his blanket, he asked the innkeeper for the name of the town.

The man yawned, scratched himself, muttered irritably, "The town is Tyburn. On the road to Palanthas."

Gerard slept fitfully. In his dreams, he wandered about inside a house, searching for the door and never finding it. Waking long before morning, he stared at the ceiling and realized that he was now completely and thoroughly lost. He had the feeling the innkeeper was lying about the town's name and location, although why he should lie was a mystery to Gerard, except that he now suspected everyone he met of lying.

He went down to breakfast. Sitting in a rickety chair, he poked at a nameless mass that a scullery maid termed porridge. Gerard had lost his appetite. His head ached with a dull, throbbing pain. He had no energy, although he'd done nothing but ride about aimlessly the day before. He had the choice of doing that again today or going back to his blanket. Shoving aside the porridge, he walked over to the dirty window, rubbed off a portion of soot with his hand, and peered out. The drizzling rain continued to fall.

"The sun has to shine again sometime," Gerard muttered.

"Don't count on it," said a voice.

Gerard glanced around. The only other person in the inn was a mage, or at least that's what Gerard presumed, for the man was clad in reddish brown robes—the color of dried blood—and a black, hooded cloak. The mage sat in a small alcove as near the fire burning in the large stone hearth as he could manage. He was ill, or so Gerard assumed, for the mage coughed frequently, a bad-sounding cough that seemed to come from his gut. Gerard had noticed him when he first entered, but because he was a mage, Gerard had left his fellow traveler to himself.

Gerard hadn't thought he'd spoken loudly enough to be heard on the other side of the room, but apparently what this inn lacked in amenities it made up for in acoustics.

He could make some polite rejoinder or he could pretend he hadn't heard. He decided on the latter. He was in no mood for companionship, especially companionship that appeared to be in the last stages of consumption. He turned back to continue staring out the window.

"She rules the sun," the mage said. His voice was weak, with a whispering quality to it that Gerard found eerily compelling. "Although she no longer rules the moon." He gave what might have been a laugh, but it was interrupted by a fit of coughing. "She will soon rule the stars if she is not stopped."

Finding this conversation disturbing, Gerard turned around. "Are you speaking to me, sir?"

The mage opened his mouth, but was halted by another fit of coughing. He pressed a handkerchief to his lips, drew in a shuddering breath. "No," he rasped, irritated, "I am speaking for the joy of spitting up blood. Talking is not so easy for me that I waste my breath on it."

The shadow of the hood concealed the mage's face. Gerard glanced about. The maid had vanished back into a smoke-filled kitchen. Gerard and the mage were the only two in the room. Gerard moved closer, determined to see the man's face.

"I refer, of course, to Takhisis," the mage continued. He fumbled in the pocket of his robes. Drawing out a small, cloth pouch, he placed it on the hob. A pungent smell filled the room.

"Takhisis!" Gerard was astounded. "How did you know?" he asked in a low voice, coming to stand beside the mage.

"I have known her long," said the mage in his whispering voice, soft as velvet. "Very long, indeed." He coughed again briefly and motioned with his hand. "Fetch the kettle and pour some hot water into that mug."

Gerard didn't move. He stared at the hand. The skin had a gold tint to it, so that it glistened in the firelight like sunlit fish scales.

"Are you deaf as well as doltish, Sir Knight?" the mage demanded.

Gerard frowned, not liking to be insulted and not liking to be ordered about, especially by a total stranger. He was tempted to bid this mage a cold good morning and walk out. The mage's conversation interested him, however. He could always walk out later.

Lifting the kettle with a pair of tongs, Gerard poured out the hot water. The mage dumped the contents of the pouch into the mug. The smell of the mixture was noxious, caused Gerard to wrinkle his nose in disgust. The mage allowed the tea to steep and the water to cool before he drank it.

Gerard found a chair, dragged it over.

"Do you know where I am, sir? I've been riding for days without benefit of sun or stars or compass to guide me. Everyone I ask tells me something different. This innkeeper tells me that this road leads to Palanthas. Is that right?"

The mage sipped at his drink before he answered. He kept his hood pulled low over his head, so that his face was in shadow. Gerard had the impression of keen, bright eyes, with something a bit wrong with them. He couldn't make out what.

"He is telling the truth as far as it goes," said the mage. "The road leads to Palanthas—eventually. One might say that all roads that run east and west lead to Palanthas—eventually. What you should be more concerned with now is that the road leads to Jelek."

"Jelek!" Gerard exclaimed. Jelek—the headquarters of the Dark Knights. Realizing that his alarm might give him away, he tried to pass it off with a shrug. "So it leads to Jelek. Why should that concern me?"

"Because at this moment twenty Dark Knights and a few hundred foot soldiers are bivouacked outside of Tyburn. They march to Sanction, answering Mina's call."

"Let them camp out where they will," said Gerard coolly. "I have nothing to fear from them."

"When they find you here, they will arrest you," said the mage, continuing to sip at his tea.

"Arrest me? Why?"

The mage lifted his head, glanced at him. Again, Gerard had the impression there was something wrong with the man's eyes.

"Why? Because you might as well have 'Solamnic Knight' stamped in gold letters on your forehead."

"Nonsense," said Gerard with a laugh, "I am but a traveling merchant—"

"A merchant without goods to sell. A merchant who has a military bearing and close-cropped hair. A merchant who wears a sword in the military manner, counts cadence when he walks, and rides a trained war-horse." The mage snorted. "You couldn't fool a six-year-old girlchild."

He went back to drinking his tea.

"Still, why should they come here?" Gerard asked lightly, though his nervousness was increasing.

"The innkeeper knew you for a Solamnic Knight the moment he saw you." The mage finished his tea, placed the empty mug upon the hob. His cough had noticeably improved. "Note the silence from the kitchen? The Dark Knights frequent this place. The innkeeper is in their pay. He left to tell them you were here. He will gain a rich reward for turning you in."

Gerard looked uneasily toward the kitchen that had grown strangely quiet. He shouted out loudly for the innkeeper.

There was no response.

Gerard crossed the room and flung open the wooden door that led to the cooking area. He startled the scullery maid, who confirmed his fears by giving a shriek and fleeing out the back door.

Gerard returned to the common room.

"You are right," said Gerard. "The bastard has run off, and the maid screamed as though I was likely to slit her throat. I had best be going." He held out his hand. "I want to thank you, sir. I'm sorry, but I never asked your name or gave you mine. . . ."

The mage ignored the outstretched hand. He took hold of a wooden staff that had been resting against the chimney and used it to support himself as he regained his feet.

"Come with me," the mage ordered.

"I thank you for your warning, sir," said Gerard firmly, "but I must depart and swiftly—"

"You will not escape," said the mage. "They are too close. They rode out with the dawn, and they will be here in minutes. You have only one chance. Come with me."

Leaning on the staff, which was decorated with a gold dragon claw holding a crystal, the mage led the way to stairs that went to the upper floor. His motions were quick and fluid, belying his frail appearance. His nondescript robes rustled around his ankles. Gerard hesitated another moment, his gaze going to the window. The road was empty. He could hear no sounds of an army, no drums, no stamp of marching feet.

Who is this mage that I should trust him? Just because he seems to know what I am thinking, just because he spoke of Takhisis . . .

The mage paused at the foot of the staircase. He turned to face Gerard. The strange eyes glittered from the shadows.

"You spoke once of following your heart. What is in your heart now, Sir Knight?"

Gerard stared, his tongue stuck to the roof of his mouth.

"Well?" said the mage impatiently. "What is in your heart?"

"Despair and doubt," said Gerard at last, his voice faltering, "suspicion, fear . . ."

"Her doing," said the mage. "So long as these shadows remain, you will never see the sun." He turned, continued walking up the stairs.

Gerard heard sounds now, sounds of men shouting orders, sounds of jingling harness and the clash of steel. He ran for the stairs.

The lower level contained the kitchen, an eating room, and a large common room where Gerard had passed the night. The upper level contained separate rooms for the convenience of better-paying guests, as well as the innkeeper's private quarters, protected by a door that was locked and bolted.

The mage walked straight up to this door. He tried the handle, which wouldn't budge, then touched the lock with the crystal of his staff. Light flared, half blinding Gerard, who stood blinking and staring at blue stars for long moments. When he could see, the mage had pushed open the door. Tendrils of smoke curled out from the lock.

"Hey, you can't go in there—" Gerard began.

The mage cast him a cold glance. "You are starting to remind me of my brother, Sir Knight. While I loved my brother, I can truthfully say of him that there were times he irritated me to death. Speaking of death, yours is not far off." The mage pointed with his staff into the room. "Open that wooden chest. No, not that one. The one in the corner. It is not locked."

Gerard gave up. In for a copper, in for a steel as the saying went. Entering the innkeeper's room, he knelt beside the large wooden chest the mage had indicated. He lifted the lid, stared down at an assortment of knives and daggers, the odd boot, a pair of gloves, and pieces of armor: bracers, grieves, epaulets, a cuirass, helms. All of the armor was black, some stamped with the emblem of the Dark Knights.

"Our landlord is not above stealing from his guests," said the mage. "Take what you need."

Gerard dropped the lid of the chest with a bang. He stood up, backed off. "No," he said.

"Disguising yourself as one of them is your only chance.

There is not much there, to be sure, but you can cobble something together, enough to pass."

"I just rid myself of an entire suit of that accursed stuff—'

"Only a sentimental fool would be that stupid," the mage retorted, "and thus I am not surprised to hear that you did it. Put on what armor you can. I'll loan you my black cloak. It covers a multitude of sins, as I have come to know."

"Even if I am disguised, it won't matter anyway," Gerard said. He was tired of running, tired of disguises, tired of lying. "You said the innkeeper told them about me."

"He is an idiot. You have a quick wit and a glib tongue." The mage shrugged. "The ruse may not work. You may still hang. But it seems to me to be worth the risk."

Gerard hesitated a moment longer. He may have been tired of running, but he wasn't yet tired of living. The mage's plan seemed a good one. Gerard's sword, a gift from Marshal Medan, would be recognized. His horse still bore the trappings of a Dark Knight, and his boots were like those worn by the Dark Knights.

Feeling more and more as if he were caught in a terrible trap in which he was continually running out the back only to find himself walking in the front, he grabbed up what parts of the armor he thought might fit him, began hastily buckling them onto various parts of his body. Some were too big and others painfully small. He looked, when he finished, like an armored harlequin. Still, with the black cloak to cover him, he might just pull it off.

"There," he said, turning around. "How do I—"

The mage was gone. The black cloak he had promised lay on the floor.

Gerard stared about the room. He hadn't heard the mage depart, but then he recalled that the man moved quietly. Suspicion crept into Gerard's mind, but he shrugged it off. Whether the strange mage was for him or against him didn't much matter now. He was committed.

Gerard picked up the black cloak, tossed it over his shoulder, and hastened from the landlord's room. Reaching the stairs, he looked out a window, saw a troop of soldiers drawn up outside. He resisted the urge to run and hide. Clattering down the stairs, he walked out door to the road house. Two soldiers, bearing halberds, shoved him rudely in their haste to enter.

"Hey!" Gerard called out angrily. "You damn near knocked me down. What is the meaning of this?"

Abashed, the two halted. One touched his hand to his forehead. "I beg pardon, Sir Knight, but we're in a hurry. We've been sent to arrest a Solamnic who is hiding in this inn. Perhaps you have seen him. He is wearing a shirt and leather breeches, tries to pass himself off as a merchant."

"Is that all you know of him?" Gerard demanded. "What does he look like? How tall is he? What color hair does he have?"

The soldiers shrugged, impatient. "What does that matter, sir. He's inside. The innkeeper told us we would find him here."

"He *was* in there," said Gerard. "You just missed him." He nodded his head. "He rode off that way not fifteen minutes ago."

"Rode off!" The soldier gaped. "Why didn't you stop him?"

"I had no orders to stop him," said Gerard coldly. "The bastard is none of my concern. If you make haste, you can catch him. Oh, and by the way, he's a tall, handsome man, about twenty-five years old, with jet-black hair and a long black mustache. What are you standing there staring at me for like a pair of oafs? Be off with you."

Muttering to themselves, the soldiers dashed out the door and down the street, not even bothering to salute. Gerard sighed, gnawed his lip in frustration. He supposed he should be grateful to the mage who had saved his life, but he wasn't. At the thought of yet more lying, dissembling, deceiving, of being always on his guard, always fearful of discovery, his spirits sank. He honestly wondered if he could do it. Hanging might be easier, after all.

Removing his helm, he ran his fingers through his yellow hair. The black cloak was heavy. He was sweating profusely, but dared not discard it. In addition, the cloak had a peculiar smell—reminding him of rose petals combined with something else not nearly as sweet or as pleasant. Gerard stood in the doorway, wondering what to do next.

The soldiers were escorting a group of prisoners. Gerard paid little attention to the poor wretches, beyond thinking he might have been one of them.

The best course of action, he decided, would be to ride away during the confusion. If anyone stops me, I can always claim to be a messenger heading somewhere with something important.

He stepped out into the street. Glancing up in the sky, he noted with pleasurable astonishment that the rain had ceased, the clouds departed. The sun shone brightly.

A very strange sound, like the bleat of a pleased goat, caused him to turn around.

Two pairs of gleaming eyes stared at him over the top of a gag. The eyes were the eyes of Tasslehoff Burrfoot, and the bleat was the glad and cheerful bleat of Tasslehoff Burrfoot.

The Tasslehoff Burrfoot.

23

In Which It Is Proven That Not All Kender Look Alike

The sight of Tasslehoff there, right in front of him, affected Gerard like a lightning blast from a blue dragon, left him dazed, paralyzed, incapable of thought or action. He was so amazed he simply stared. Everyone in the world was searching for Tasslehoff Burrfoot—including a goddess—and Gerard had found him.

Or rather, more precisely, this troop of Dark Knights had found the kender. Tasslehoff was among several dozen kender who were being herded to Sanction. Every single one of them probably claimed to be Tasslehoff Burrfoot. Unfortunately, one of them really was.

Tasslehoff continued to bleat through the gag, and now he was trying his best to wave. One of the guards, hearing the unusual sound, turned around. Gerard quickly clapped his helm over his head, nearly slicing off his nose in the process, for the helm was too small.

"Whoever's making that noise, stop it!" the guard shouted. He bore down on Tasslehoff, who—not watching where he was going—stumbled over his manacles and tumbled to the street. His fall jerked two of the kender who were chained to him off their feet. Finding this a welcome interlude in an otherwise dull and boring march, the other kender jerked themselves off their feet, with the result that the entire line of some forty kender was cast into immediate confusion.

Two guards, wielding flails, waded in to sort things out. Gerard strode swiftly away, almost running in his eagerness to leave the vicinity before something worse happened. His brain hummed with a confusion of thoughts, so that he moved in a kind of daze without any real idea of where he was going. He blundered into people, muttered excuses. Stepping into a hole, he wrenched his ankle and almost fell into a water trough. At last, spotting a shadowy alley, he ducked into it. He drew in several deep breaths. The cool air soothed his sweat-covered brow, and he was at last able to catch his breath and sort out the tangle.

Takhisis wanted Tasslehoff, she wanted the kender in Sanction. Gerard had a chance to thwart her, and in this, Gerard knew he followed the dictates of his own heart. The shadow lifted. The seeds of a plan were already sprouting in his mind.

Giving a mental salute to the wizard and wishing him well, Gerard headed off to put his plan, which involved finding a knight Gerard's own height and weight and, hopefully, head size, into action.

The Dark Knights and their foot soldiers set up camp in and around the town of Tyburn, bedded down for the night. The commander and his officers took over the road house, not much of a triumph, for its food was inedible and its accommodations squalid. The only good thing that could be said of the ale was that it made a man pleasantly light-headed and helped him forget his problems.

The commander of the Dark Knights drank deeply of the ale. He had a great many problems he was glad to drown, first and foremost of which was Mina, his new superior.

The commander had never liked nor trusted Lord Targonne, a small-minded man who cared more for a bent copper than he did for any of the troops under his command. Targonne did nothing to advance the cause of the Dark Knights but concentrated instead on filling his own coffers. No one in Jelek had mourned Targonne's death, but neither did they rejoice at Mina's ascension.

True, she was advancing the cause of the Dark Knights, but she was advancing at such a rapid pace that she had left most of them behind to eat her dust. The commander had been shocked to hear that she had conquered Solanthus. He wasn't sure that he approved. How were the Dark Knights to hold both that city and Solanthus and the Solamnic lord city of Palanthas?

This blasted Mina never gave a thought to guarding what she'd taken. She never gave a thought to supply lines stretched too thin, men overworked, the dangers of the populace rising in revolt.

The commander sent letters explaining all this to Mina, urging her to slow down, build up her forces, consolidate her winnings. Mina had forgotten someone else, too—the dragon overlord Malys. The commander had been sending conciliatory messages to the dragon, maintaining that the Dark Knights had no designs on her rulership. All this new territory they were conquering was being taken in her name, and so forth. He'd heard nothing in response.

Then, a few days ago, he had received orders from Mina to pull out of Jelek and march his forces south to help reinforce Sanction against a probable attack by a combined army of elves and Solamnics. He was to set forth immediately, and while he was at it, he was to round up and bring along any kender he happened to come across.

Oh, and Mina thought it quite likely that Malys was also going to attack Sanction. So he was to be prepared for that eventuality, as well.

Even now, rereading the orders, the commander felt the same shock and outrage he'd experienced reading them the first two dozen times. He had been tempted to disobey, but the messenger who had delivered the message made it quite clear to the commander that Mina and this One God of hers had a long reach. The messenger provided several examples of what had happened to commanders who thought they knew better than Mina what course of action to take, starting with the late Lord Targonne himself. Thus the commander now found himself on the road to Sanction, sitting in this wretched inn, drinking tepid ale, of which to say it tasted like horse piss was to give it a compliment it didn't deserve.

This day had gone from bad to worse. Not only had the kender slowed up their progress by tangling themselves in their chains—a tangle that had taken hours to sort out—the commander had lost a Solamnic spy, who'd been tipped off to their coming. Fortunately, they now had a good description of him. With his long black hair and black mustache, he should be easy to apprehend.

The commander was drowning his problems in ale when he looked up to see yet another messenger from Mina come walking through the door. The commander would have given all of his wealth to hurl the mug of ale at the man's head.

The messenger came to stand before him. The commander glowered balefully and did not invite him to be seated.

Like most messengers, who needed to travel light, this one was clad in black leather armor covered by a thick black cloak. He removed his helm, placed it under his arm, and saluted.

"I come in the name of the One God."

The commander snorted in his ale. "What does the One God want with me now? Has Mina captured Ice Wall? Am I supposed to march there next?"

The messenger was an ugly fellow with yellow hair, a pockmarked face, and startling, blue eyes. The blue eyes stared at the commander, obviously baffled.

"Never mind." The commander sighed. "Deliver your message and be done with it."

"Mina has received word that you have captured several kender prisoners. As you may know, she is searching for one kender in particular."

"Burrfoot. I know," said the commander. "I have forty or so Burrfoots out there. Take your pick."

"I will do that, with your permission, sir," said the messenger respectfully. "I know this Burrfoot by sight. Because the matter of his capture is so very urgent, Mina has sent me to look over your prisoners to see if I can find him among them. If he is, I'm to carry him to Sanction immediately."

The commander looked up in hope. "You wouldn't like to take all forty, would you?"

The messenger shook his head.

"No, I didn't think so. Very well. Go look for the blasted thief." A thought occurred to him. "If you do find him, what am I supposed to do with the rest?"

"I have no orders regarding that, sir," said the messenger, "but I would think you might as well release them."

"Release them . . ." The commander stared more closely at the messenger. "Is that blood on your sleeve? Are you wounded?"

"No, sir," said the messenger. "I was attacked by bandits on the road."

"Where? I'll send out a patrol," said the commander.

"No need to bother, sir," said the messenger. "I resolved the matter."

"I see," said the commander, who thought he noted blood on the leather armor, too. He shrugged. None of his concern. "Go search for this Burrfoot, then. You, there. Escort this man immediately to the pen where we keep the kender. Give him any assistance he requires." Raising his mug, he added, "I drink to your success, sir."

The messenger thanked the commander and departed.

The commander ordered another ale. He mulled over what to do with the kender. He was considering lining them all up and using them for target practice, when he heard a commotion at the door, saw yet another messenger.

Groaning inwardly, the commander was about to tell this latest nuisance to go roast himself in the Abyss, when the man shoved back his hat, and the commander recognized one of his most trusted spies. He motioned him forward.

"What news?" he asked. "Keep your voice down."

"Sir, I've just come from Sanction!"

"I said keep your voice down. No need to let everyone know our business," the commander growled.

"It won't matter, sir. Rumor follows fast on my heels. By morning, everyone will know. Malys is dead. Mina killed the dragon."

The crowd in the alehouse fell silent, everyone too stunned to speak, each trying to digest this news and think what it might mean to him.

"There's more," said the spy, filling the vacuum with his voice. "It is reported that Mina is dead, too."

"Then who is in charge?" the commander demanded, rising to his feet, his ale forgotten.

"No one, sir," said the spy. "The city is in chaos."

"Well, well." The commander chuckled. "Perhaps Mina was right, and prayers are answered after all. Gentlemen," he said, looking around at his officers and staff, "no sleep for us tonight. We ride to Sanction."

One down, thought Gerard to himself, tramping off behind the commander's aide. One to go.

Not the easiest, either, he thought gloomily. Hoodwinking a half-drunken commander of the Dark Knights had been goblin-play compared to what lay ahead—extricating one kender from the herd. Gerard could only hope that the Dark Knights, in their infinite wisdom, had seen fit to keep the kender gagged.

"Here they are," said the aide, holding up a lantern. "We have them penned up. Makes it easier."

The kender, huddled together like puppies for warmth, were asleep. The night air was cold, and few had cloaks or other protection from the chill. Those who did shared with their fellows. In repose, their faces looked pinched and wan. Obviously the commander wasn't wasting food on them, and he certainly wasn't concerned about their comfort.

The kenders' manacles were still attached, as were their leg irons and—Gerard breathed a hefty sigh of relief—their gags were still in place. Several soldiers stood guard. Gerard counted five, and he suspected there might be more he couldn't see.

At the bright light, the kender lifted their heads and blinked sleepily, yawning around the gags.

"On your feet, vermin," order the Knight. Two of the soldiers waded into the pen to kick the kender into wakefulness. "Stand up and look smart. Turn toward the light. This gentleman wants to see your dirty faces."

Gerard spotted Tasslehoff right away. He was about three-quarters of the way down the line, gaping and peering about and scratching his head with a manacled hand. Gerard had to make a show of inspecting every single kender, however, and this he did, all the while keeping one eye on Tas.

He looks old, Gerard realized suddenly. I never noticed that before.

Tas's jaunty topknot was still thick and long. Gray streaks were noticeable here and there, however, and the wrinkles on his face were starkly etched in the strong light. Still, his eyes were bright, his bearing bouncy, and he was watching the proceedings with his usual interest and intense curiosity.

Gerard walked down the line of kender, forcing himself to take his time. He wore a leather helm to conceal his face, afraid that Tas would recognize him again and make a glad outcry. His scheme did not work, however, for Tasslehoff shot one inquisitive look through the eyeslits of the helm, saw Gerard's bright blue eyes, and beamed all over. He couldn't speak, due to the gag, but he gave a wriggle expressive of his pleasure.

Coming to a halt, Gerard stared hard at Tas, who—to Gerard's dismay—gave a broad wink and grinned as wide as the gag would permit. Gerard grabbed hold of the kender's topknot and gave it a good yank.

"You don't know me," he hissed out from behind the helm.

"OfcourseIdont," mumbled the gagged Tas, adding excitedly, "Iwassosurprisedtoseeyouwherehaveyoubeen—"

Gerard straightened. "This is the kender," he said loudly, giving the topknot another yank.

"This one?" The aide was surprised. "Are you sure?"

"Positive," said Gerard. "Your commander has done an outstanding job. You may be certain that Mina will be most pleased. Release the kender immediately into my custody. I'll take full responsibility for him."

"I don't know . . ." The aide hesitated.

"Your commander said I was to have him if I found him," Gerard reminded the man. "I've found him. Now release him."

"I'm going to go bring back the commander," said the aide.

"Very well, if you want to disturb him. He looked pretty relaxed to me," Gerard said with a shrug.

His ploy didn't work. The aide was one of those loyal, dedicated types who would not take a crap without asking for permission. The aide marched off. Gerard stood in the pen with the kender, wondering what to do.

"I overplayed my hand," Gerard muttered. "The commander could decide that the kender is so valuable he'll want to take him himself to claim the reward! Blast! Why didn't I think of that?"

Tasslehoff had, meanwhile, managed to work the gag loose, dislodging it with such ease that Gerard could only conclude he'd kept it on for the novelty.

"*I don't know you,*" said Tasslehoff loudly and gave another conspiratorial wink that was guaranteed to get them both hung. "What's your name?"

"Shut up," Gerard shot out of the corner of his mouth.

"I had a cousin by that name," observed Tas reflectively.

Gerard tied the gag firmly in place.

He eyed the two guards, who were eyeing him back. He'd have to act quickly, couldn't give them a chance to cry out or start a racket. The old ruse of pretending to find scattered steel coins on the ground might work. He was just about to gasp and stare and point in astonishment, readying himself to whack the two in the head when they came over to look, when a commotion broke out behind him.

Torchlight flared up and down the road. People began shouting and rushing about. Doors slammed and banged. Gerard's first panicked thought was that he'd been discovered and that the entire army was turning out to seize him. He drew his sword, then realized that the soldiers weren't running toward him. They were running away from him, heading for the road house. The two guards had lost interest in him entirely, were staring and muttering, trying to figure out what was going on.

Gerard heaved a sigh. This alarm had nothing to do with him. He forced himself to stand still and wait.

The aide did not return. Gerard muttered in impatience.

"Go find out what's going on," he ordered.

One guard ran off immediately. He stopped the first person he came to, then turned and pounded back their direction.

"Malys is dead!" he shouted. "And so is that Mina girl! Sanction is in turmoil. We're marching there straight away."

"Malys dead?" Gerard gaped. "*And* Mina?"

"That's the word."

Gerard stood dazed, then came to his senses. He'd served in the army a good many years, and he knew that rumors were a copper a dozen. This might be true—he hoped it was—but it might not be. He had to act under the assumption that it wasn't.

"That's all very well, but I still need the kender," he said stubbornly. "Where's the commander's aide?"

"It was him I talked to." The guard fumbled at his belt. Producing a ring of keys, he tossed them to Gerard. "You want the kender? Here, take 'em all."

"I don't want them all!" Gerard cried, aghast, but by that time, the two guards had dashed off to join the throng of troops massing in the road.

Gerard looked back to find every single kender grinning at him.

Freeing the kender did not prove easy. When they saw that Gerard had the keys, the kender set up a yell that must have been heard in Flotsam and surged around him, raising their manacled hands, each kender demanding that Gerard unlock him or her first. Such was the tumult that Gerard was nearly knocked over backward and lost sight of Tasslehoff in the mix.

Bleating and waving his hand, Tasslehoff battled his way to the front of the pack. Gerard got a good grip on Tas's shirt and began to work at the locks on the chains on his hands and feet. The other kender milled about, trying to see what was going on, and more than once jerked the chains out of Gerard's grip. He cursed and shouted and threatened and was even forced to shove a few, who took it all in good humor. Eventually—he was never to know how—he managed to set Tasslehoff free. This done, he tossed the keys into the midst of the remaining kender, who pounced on them gleefully.

Gerard grabbed the bedraggled, disheveled, straw-covered Tasslehoff and hurried him off, keeping one eye on Tas and the other on the turmoil among the troops.

Tas ripped off his gag. "You forgot to remove it," he pointed out.

"No, I didn't," said Gerard.

"I am so glad to see you!" Tas said, squeezing Gerard's hand and stealing his knife. "What have you been doing? Where have you been? You'll have to tell me everything, but not now. We don't have time."

He came to a halt, began fumbling about for something in his pouch. "We have to leave."

"You're right, we don't have time for talk." Gerard retrieved his knife, grabbed Tas by the arm and hustled him along. "My horse is in the stable—"

"Oh, we don't have time for the horse either," said Tasslehoff, wriggling out of Gerard's grasp with the ease of an eel. "Not if we're going to reach the Knights' Council in time. The elves are marching, you see, and they're about to get into terrible trouble and—well, things are happening that would take too long to explain. You'll have to leave your horse behind. I'm sure he'll be all right, though."

Tas pulled out an object, held it to the moonlight. Jewels sparkled on its surface, and Gerard recognized the Device of Time Journeying.

"What are you doing with that?" he asked uneasily.

"We're going to use it to travel to the Knights' Council. At least, I *think* that's where it's going to take us. It's been acting funny these past few days. You wouldn't believe the places I've been—"

"Not me," said Gerard, retreating.

"Oh, yes, you," said Tasslehoff, nodding his head so vigorously that his topknot flipped over and struck him in the nose. "You have to come with me because they won't believe *me*. I'm just a kender. Raistlin says they'll believe you, though. When you tell them about Takhisis and the elves and all—"

"Raistlin?" Gerard repeated, trying desperately to keep up. "Raistlin who?"

"Raistlin Majere. Caramon's brother. You met him in the road house this morning. He was probably mean and sarcastic to you, wasn't he? I knew it." Tas sighed and shook his head. "Don't pay any attention. Raistlin always talks like that to people. It's just his way. You'll get used to it. We all have."

The hair on Gerard's arms prickled. A chill crept up his back. He remembered hearing Caramon's stories about his brother—the red robes, the tea, the staff with the crystal, the mage's barbed tongue . . .

"Stop talking nonsense," said Gerard in a decided tone. "Raistlin Majere is dead!"

"So am I," said Tasslehoff Burrfoot. He smiled up at Gerard. "You can't let a little thing like that stop you."

Reaching out, Tas took hold of the Knight's hand. Jewels flashed, and the world dropped out from under Gerard's feet.

24

The Decision

When Gerard was young, a friend of his had concocted a swing for their entertainment. His friend suspended a wooden board, planed smooth, between two ropes and tied the ropes to a high tree branch. The lad then persuaded Gerard to sit in the swing while he turned him round and round, causing the ropes to twist together. At that point, his friend gave the swing a powerful shove and let loose. Gerard went spinning in a wildly gyrating circle that ended only when he pitched out of the swing and landed facedown on the grass.

Gerard experienced exactly the same sensation with the Device of Time Journeying, with the notable exception that it didn't dump him facedown. It might as well have, though, for when his feet touched the blessed grass, he didn't know if he was up or down, on his head or his heels. He staggered about like a drunken gnome, blinking, gasping, and trying to get his bearings. Wobbling about beside him, the kender also looked rattled.

"As many times as I've done that," said Tasslehoff, mopping

his forehead with a grimy sleeve, "I never seem to get used to it."

"Where are we?" Gerard demanded, when the world had ceased to spin.

"We *should* be attending a Knights' Council," said Tasslehoff, dubious. "That's where we wanted to go, and that's the thought I thought in my head. But whether we're at the *right* Knights' Council is another question. We might be at Huma's Knights' Council, for all I know. The device has been acting very oddly." He shook his head, glanced about. "Does anything look familiar?"

The two had been deposited in a heavily forested tract of land on the edge of a stubbly wheat field that had long since been harvested. The thought came to Gerard that he was lost yet again, and this time a kender had lost him. He had no hope that he would ever be found and was just about to say so when he caught a glimpse of a large stone building reminiscent of a fortress or a manor. Gerard squinted, trying to bring the flag fluttering from the battlements into focus.

"It looks like the flag of Lord Ulrich," said Gerard, astonished. He looked all around him more closely now and thought that he recognized the landscape. "This *could* be Ulrich manor," he said cautiously.

"Is that where we're supposed to be?" Tas asked.

"It's where they were holding the Knights' Council the last time I was here," said Gerard.

"Well done," said Tasslehoff, giving the device a pat. He dropped it back carelessly into his pouch and stared expectantly at Gerard.

"We should hurry," he said. "Things are happening."

"Yes, I know," said Gerard, "but we can't just say we dropped out of the sky." He cast an uneasy glance upward.

"Why not?" Tas was disappointed. "It makes a great story."

"Because no one will believe us," Gerard stated. "I'm not sure I believe us." He gave the matter some thought. "We'll say that we rode from Sanction and my horse went lame and we had to walk. Got that?"

"It's not nearly as exciting as dropping out of the sky," Tas said. "But if you say so," he added hurriedly, seeing Gerard's eyebrows meet together in the middle of his forehead.

"What is the horse's name?" he asked, as they started off across the field, the stubble crunching beneath their feet.

"What horse?" Gerard muttered, absorbed in his thoughts that continued to whirl, even though he was, thankfully, on solid ground.

"Your horse," said Tas. "The one that went lame."

"I don't have a horse that went lame . . . Oh, that horse. It doesn't have a name."

"It *has* to have a name," said Tas severely. "All horses have names. I'll name it, may I?"

"Yes," said Gerard in a rash moment, thinking only to shut the kender up so he could try to sort out the puzzle of the strange mage and the extremely fortuitous and highly coincidental discovery of the kender in exactly the right place, in exactly the right time.

A walk of about a mile brought them to the manor house. The Knights had transformed it into an armed camp. Sunlight glinted off the steel heads of pikes. The smoke of cook fires and forge fires smudged the sky. The green grass was trampled with hundreds of feet and dotted with the colorful striped tents of the Knights. Flags representing holdings from Palanthas to Estwilde flapped in the brisk autumn wind. The sounds of hammering, metal on metal, rang through the air. The Knights were preparing to go to war.

After the fall of Solanthus, the Knights had sent out the call to defend their homeland. The call was answered. Knights and their retainers marched from as far as Southern Ergoth. Some impoverished Knights arrived on foot, bringing with them nothing but their honor and their desire to serve their country. Wealthy Knights brought their own troops, and treasure boxes filled with steel to hire more.

"We're going to see Lord Tasgall, Knight of the Rose and head of the Knights' Council," said Gerard. "Be on your best behavior, Burrfoot. Lord Tasgall doesn't tolerate any nonsense."

"So few people do," said Tas sadly. "I really think it might be a better world all the way around if more people did. Oh, I've thought of your horse's name."

"Have you?" Gerard asked absently, not paying attention.

"Buttercup," said Tasslehoff.

"That is my report," said Gerard. "The One God has a name and a face. Five faces. Queen Takhisis. How she managed to achieve this miracle, I cannot say."

"I can," Tasslehoff interrupted, leaping to his feet.

Gerard shoved the kender back into his chair.

"Not now," he said, for the fortieth time. He continued speaking. "Our ancient enemy has returned. In the heavens, she stands alone and unchallenged. In this world, though, there are those who are willing to give their lives to defeat her."

Gerard went on to tell of his meeting with Samar, spoke of the promise of that warrior that the elves would ally themselves with the Knights to attack Sanction.

The three lords glanced at each other. There had been much heated debate among the leadership as to whether the Knights should try to recapture Solanthus before marching to Sanction. Now, with Gerard's news, the decision was almost certainly going to be made to launch a major assault on Sanction.

"We received a communiqué stating that the elves have already begun their march," said Lord Tasgall. "The road from Silvanesti is long and fraught with peril—"

"The elves are going to be attacked!" Tasslehoff sprang out of his chair again.

"Remember what I said about the nonsense!" Gerard said sternly, shoving the kender back down.

"Does your friend have something to say, Gerard?" asked Lord Ulrich.

"Yes," said Tasslehoff, standing up.

"No," said Gerard. "That is, he always has something to say, but not anything we need to listen to."

"We have no guarantee that the elves will even arrive in Sanction," Lord Tasgall continued, "nor can we say *when* they will arrive. Meanwhile, according to reports we have been receiving from Sanction, all is in confusion there. Our spies confirm the rumor that Mina has vanished and that the Dark Knights are engaged in a leadership struggle. If we judge by events of the past, someone will rise to take her place, if that has not happened already. They will not be leaderless for long."

"At least," said Lord Ulrich, "We don't have to worry about Malys. This Mina managed to do what none of us had the guts to do. She fought Malys and killed her." He raised a silver goblet. "I drink to her. To Mina! To courage."

He gulped down the wine noisily. No one else raised a glass. The others appeared embarrassed. The Lord of the Rose fixed a stern gaze upon Lord Ulrich, who—by his flushed features and slurred words—had taken too much wine already.

"Mina had help, my lord," said Gerard gravely.

"You might as well call the goddess by name," said Lord Siegfried in dire tones. "Takhisis."

Lord Tasgall looked troubled. "It is not that I doubt the veracity of Sir Gerard, but I cannot believe—"

"Believe it, my lord," called Odila, entering the hall.

She was thin and pale, her white robes covered in mud and stained with blood. By her appearance, she had traveled far and slept and eaten little.

Gerard's gaze went to her breast, where the medallion of her faith had once hung. Its place was empty.

Gerard smiled at her, relieved. She smiled back. Her smile was her own, he was thankful to see. A bit tremulous, perhaps, and not quite as self-assured or self-confident as when he had first met her, but her own.

"My lords," she said, "I bring someone who can verify the information presented to you by Sir Gerard. His name is Mirror, and he helped rescue me from Sanction."

The lords looked in considerable astonishment at the man Odila brought forward. His eyes were wrapped in bandages that only partially concealed a terrible wound that had left him blind. He walked with a staff, to help him feel his way. Despite his handicap, he had an air of quiet confidence about him. Gerard had the feeling he'd seen this man somewhere before.

The Lord of the Rose made a stiff bow to the blind man, who, of course, could not see it. Odila whispered something to Mirror, who bowed his head. Lord Tasgall turned his complete attention to Odila. He regarded her sternly, his face impassive.

"You come to us a deserter, Sir Knight," he said. "It has been reported you joined with this Mina and served her, did her bidding. You worshiped the One God and performed miracles in the name of the One God, a god we now learn is our ancient foe, Queen Takhisis. Are you here because you have recanted? Do you claim to have discarded your faith in the god you once served? Why should we believe you? Why should we think that you are anything more than a spy?"

Gerard started to speak up in her defense. Odila rested her hand on his arm, and he fell silent. Nothing he could say would do any good, he realized, and it might do much harm.

Odila bent down on one knee before the lords. Although she knelt before them, she did not bow her head. She looked at all of them directly.

"If you expect shame or contrition from me, my lords, you will be disappointed. I am a deserter. That I do not deny. Death is the punishment for desertion, and I accept that punishment as my due. I offer only in my defense that I went in search of what we all are seeking. I went in search of a power greater than my own, a power to guide me and comfort me and give me the knowledge that I was not alone in this vast universe. I found such a power, my lords. Queen Takhisis, our god, has returned to us. I say 'our' god, because she is that. We cannot deny it.

"Yet I say to you that you must go forth and fight her, my lords. You must fight to halt the spread of darkness that is fast overtaking our world. But in order to fight her, you must arm yourselves with your faith. Reverence her, even as you oppose her. Those who follow the light must also acknowledge the darkness, or else there is no light."

Lord Tasgall gazed at her, his expression troubled. Lord Siegfried and Lord Ulrich spoke softly together, their eyes on Odila.

"Had you made a show of contrition, Lady, I would not have believed you," said Lord Tasgall at last. "As it is, I must consider what you say and think about it. Rise, Odila. As to your punishment, that will be determined by the council. In the meantime, I am afraid that you must be confined—"

"Do not lock her away, my lord," urged Gerard. "If we are going to attack Sanction, we are going to need all the experienced warriors we can muster. Release her into my care. I guarantee that I will bring her safely to trial, as she did me when I was on trial before you in Solanthus."

"Will this suit you, Odila?" asked the Lord of the Rose.

"Yes, my lord." She smiled at Gerard, whispered to him in an undertone. "It seems our destiny to be shackled together."

"My lords, if you're going to attack Sanction, you could probably use the help of some gold and silver dragons," Tasslehoff stated, jumping to his feet. "Now that Malys is dead, all the red dragons and the blue dragons and the black and the green will come to Sanction's defense—"

"I think you had better remove the kender, Sir Gerard," said the Lord of the Rose.

"Because the gold and silver dragons *would* come," Tasslehoff shouted over his shoulder, squirming in Gerard's grasp. "Now that the totem is destroyed, you see. I'd be glad to go fetch them myself. I have this magical device—"

"Tas, be quiet!" said Gerard, his face flushed with the exertion of trying to retain a grip on the slippery kender.

"Wait!" the blind man called out, the first words he'd spoken. He had been standing so quietly that everyone in the hall had forgotten his presence.

Mirror walked toward the sound of the kender's voice, his staff impatiently striking and knocking aside anything that got in his way. "Don't remove him. Let me talk to him."

The Lord of the Rose frowned at this interruption, but the man was blind, and the Measure was strict in its admonition that the blind, the lame, the deaf, and the dumb were to be treated with the utmost respect and courtesy.

"You may speak to this person, of course, sir. Seeing that you are sadly afflicted and lack sight, I think it only right to tell you, however, that he is naught but a kender."

"I am well aware that he is a kender, my lord," said Mirror, smiling. "That makes me all the more eager to speak to him. In my opinion, kender are the wisest people on Krynn."

Lord Ulrich laughed heartily at this odd statement, to receive another reproving glance from Lord Tasgall. The blind man reached out a groping hand.

"I'm here, sir," said Tas, catching hold of Mirror's hand and shaking it. "I'm Tasslehoff Burrfoot. *The* Tasslehoff Burrfoot. I tell you that because there's a lot of me going around these days, but I'm the only real one. That is, the others are real, they're just not really me. They're themselves, if you take my meaning, and I'm myself."

"I understand," said blind man solemnly. "I am called Mirror and *I* am, in reality, a silver dragon."

Lord Tasgall's eyebrows shot up to his receding hairline. Lord Ulrich sputtered in his wine. Lord Siegfried snorted. Odila smiled reassuringly at Gerard and nodded complacently.

"You say that you know where the silver and gold dragons are being held prisoner?" Mirror asked, ignoring the Knights.

"Yes, I know," Tasslehoff began, then he halted. Having been termed one of "the wisest people on Krynn," he felt called upon to tell the truth. "That is, the device knows." He patted his pouch where the Device of Time Journeying was secreted. "I could take you there, if you wanted," he offered, without much hope.

"I would like to go with you very much," said Mirror.

"You would?" Tasslehoff was astonished, then excited. "You would! That's wonderful. Let's go! Right now!" He fumbled about in his pouch. "Could I ride on your back? I love flying on dragons. I knew this dragon once. His name was Khirsah, I think, or something like that. He took Flint and I riding, and we fought a battle, and it was glorious."

Tas halted his fumbling, lost in reminiscences. "I'll tell you the whole story. It was during the War of the Lance—"

"Some other time," Mirror interrupted politely. "Speed is imperative. As you say, the elves are in danger."

"Oh, yes." Tas brightened. "I'd forgotten about that." He began once again to fumble in his pouch. Retrieving the device, Tas took hold of Mirror by the hand. The kender held the device up over his head and began to recite the spell.

Waving to the astonished Knights, Tas cried, "See you in Sanction!"

He and Mirror began to shimmer, as if they were oil portraits that someone had left out in the rain. At the last moment, before he had disappeared completely, Mirror reached out, seized hold of Odila, who reached out to take hold of Gerard.

In an eyeblink, all four of them vanished.

"Good grief!" exclaimed the Lord of the Rose.

"Good riddance," sniffed Lord Siegfried.

25

Into the Valley

The elven army marched north, made good time. The warriors rose early and slept late, speeding their march with songs and tales of the old days that lightened their burdens and gladdened their hearts.

Many of the Silvanesti songs and stories were new to Gilthas, and he delighted in them. In turn, the stories and songs of the Qualinesti were new to their cousins, who did not take so much delight in them, since most were concerned with the Qualinesti's dealing with lesser races such as humans and dwarves. The Silvanesti listened politely and praised the singer if they could not praise the song. The one song the Silvanesti did not sing was the song of Lorac and the dream.

When the Lioness traveled among them, she sang the songs of the Wilder elves, and these, with their stories of floating the dead down rivers and living wild and half-naked in the treetops, succeeded in shocking the sensibilities of both Qualinesti and Silvanesti, much to the amusement of the Wilder elves. The Lioness and her people were rarely among them, however. She and her Wilder elves acted as outriders, guarding the army's flanks from surprise attacks, and riding in advance of the main body to scout out the best routes.

Alhana seemed to have shed years. Gilthas had thought her beautiful when he'd first met her, but her beauty had a frost upon it, as a late-blooming rose. Now, she walked in autumn's bright sunshine. She was riding to save her son, and she could ride with honor, for she believed that Silvanoshei had redeemed himself. He was being held prisoner, and if he had landed himself in this predicament by his near fatal obsession with this human girl, her mother's heart could conveniently forget that part of the tale.

Samar could not forget it, but he kept silent. If what Sir Gerard had told him about Silvanoshei proved true, then perhaps this hard experience would help the young fool grow into a wise man, worthy of being king. For Alhana's sake, Samar hoped so.

Gilthas marched with his own misgivings. He had hoped that once they were on the road, he could cast off his dark fears and forebodings. During the day he was able to do so. The singing helped. Songs of valor and courage reminded him that there had been heroes of old, who had overcome terrible odds to drive back the darkness, that the elven people had undergone greater trials than this and had not only survived, but thrived. In the night, however, trying to sleep while missing the comfort of his wife's arms around him, dark wings hovered over him, blotted out the stars.

One matter worried him. They heard no news from Silvanesti. Admittedly, their route would be difficult for a runner to follow, for Alhana had not been able to tell the runners exactly where to find them. She had sent back runners of her own to act as guides, however, while every chipmunk would be able to give news of their passing. Time passed without word. No new runners came, and their own runners did not return.

Gilthas mentioned this to Alhana. She said sharply that the runners would come when they came and not before and it was not worth losing sleep and wasting one's energy worrying about it.

The elves traveled north at a prodigious pace, eating up the miles, and soon they had entered the southern portion of the Khalkist Mountains. They had long ago crossed the border into ogre lands, but they saw no signs of the ancient enemy, and it seemed that their strategy—to march along the backbone of the mountains, hiding themselves in the valleys—was working. The weather was fine, with cool days that were cloudless and sunny. Winter held back her heavy snow and frost. There were no mishaps on the trail, none fell seriously ill.

If there had been gods, it might have been said that they smiled upon the elves, so easy was this portion of their march. Gilthas began to relax, let the warm sun melt his worries as it melted the light dusting of snowflakes that sometimes fell in the night. Exhaustion from the long day's march and the crisp mountain air forced sleep upon him. He slept long and deeply and woke refreshed. He could even remind himself of the old human adage, "No news is good news," and find some comfort in that.

Then came the day that Gilthas would remember for the rest of his life, remember every small detail, for on that day life changed forever for the elves of Ansalon.

It began as any other. The elves woke with the first gray light of dawn. Packing up their bedrolls with practiced haste, they were on the march before the sun had yet lifted up over the mountaintops. They ate as they walked. Food was harder to come by in the mountains where vegetation was sparse, but the elves had foreseen this and filled their packs with dried berries and nutmeats.

They were still many hundred miles from Sanction, but all spoke confidently of their journey's end, which seemed no more than a few weeks away. The dawn was glorious. The Qualinesti elves sang their ritual song to welcome the sun, and this morning the Silvanesti joined in. The sun and the marching burned away night's chill. Gilthas marveled at the beauty of the day and of the mountains. He could never feel at home among mountains, no elf could, but he could be moved and awed by their stark grandeur.

Then, behind him came the pounding of horse's hooves. Ever after, when he heard that sound, he was swept back in time to this fateful day. A rider was pushing the horse to the limit, something unusual on the narrow, rocky trails. The elves continued to march, but many cast wondering glances over their shoulders.

The Lioness rode into view, the sun lighting her golden hair so that it seemed she was bathed in fire. Gilthas would remember that, too.

He reined in his horse, his heart filled suddenly with dread. He knew her, knew the grim expression on her face. She rode past him, heading for the front of the column. She said nothing to him, but cast him a single glance as she galloped by, a glance that sent him spurring after her. He saw now that there were two people on the horse. A woman sat behind the Lioness, a woman clad in the green, mottled clothing of a Silvanesti runner. That was all Gilthas noticed about her before the Lioness's mad charge carried her around a bend in the narrow trail and out of his sight.

He rode after her. Elves were forced to scatter in all directions or be ridden down. Gilthas had a brief glimpse of staring eyes and concerned faces. Voices cried out, asking what was going on, but the words whipped past him and he did not respond. He rode recklessly, fear driving him.

He arrived in time to see Alhana turn her horse's head, stare back in astonishment at the Lioness, who was shouting in her crude Silvanesti for the queen to halt. The runner dismounted, sliding off the back of the horse before the Lioness could stop the plunging animal. The runner took a step, then collapsed onto the ground. The Lioness slid off her horse, knelt beside the fallen runner. Alhana hastened to her, accompanied by Samar. Gilthas joined them, gesturing to Planchet, who marched at the head of the column with the Silvanesti commanders.

"Water," Alhana commanded. "Bring water."

The runner tried to speak, but the Lioness wouldn't permit her, not until she had drunk something. Gilthas was close enough now to see that the runner was not wounded, as he had feared, but weak from exhaustion and dehydration. Samar offered his own waterskin, and the Lioness gave the runner small sips, encouraging her with soothing words. After a draught or two, the runner shook her head.

"Let me speak!" she gasped. "Hear me, Queen Alhana! My news is . . . dire. . . ."

Among humans, a crowd would have gathered around the fallen, ears stretched, anxious to see and hear what they could. The elves were more respectful. They guessed by the commotion and the hurry that the news this runner bore was probably bad news, but they kept their distance, patiently waiting to be told whatever they needed to know.

"Silvanesti has been invaded," said the runner. She spoke weakly, dazedly. "Their numbers are countless. They came down the river in boats, burning and looting the fishing villages. So many boats. None could stop them. They entered Silvanesti, and even the Dark Knights feared them, and some fled. But they are allies now. . . ."

"Ogres?" Alhana asked in disbelief.

"Minotaurs, Your Majesty," said the runner. "Minotaurs have allied with the Dark Knights. The numbers of our enemies are vast as the dead leaves in autumn."

Alhana cast Gilthas one burning-eyed glance, a glance that seared through flesh and bone and struck him in the heart.

You were right, the glance said to him. *And I was wrong.*

She turned her back on him, on them all, and walked away. She repulsed even Samar, who would have gone to her.

"Leave me," she commanded.

The Lioness bent over the runner, giving her more water. Gilthas was numb. He felt nothing. The news was too enormous to comprehend. Standing there, trying to make sense of this, he noticed that the runner's feet were bruised and bloody.

She had worn out her boots, run the last miles barefoot. He could feel nothing for his people, but her pain and heroism moved him to tears. Angrily, he blinked them away. He could not give in to grief, not now. He strode forward, determined to talk to Alhana.

Samar saw Gilthas coming and made a move as if to intercept him. Gilthas gave Samar a look that plainly said the man could try, but he might have a tough time doing it. After a moment's hesitation, Samar backed off.

"Queen Alhana," said Gilthas.

She lifted her face, that was streaked with tears. "Spare me your gloating," she said, her voice low and wretched.

"This is no time to speak of who was right and who was wrong," Gilthas said quietly. "If we had stayed to lay siege to Silvanesti, as I counseled, we would all probably be dead right now or slaves in the belly of a minotaur galley." He rested his hand gently on her arm, was shocked to feel her cold and shivering. "As it is, our army is strong and intact. It will take some time for the armies of our enemies to entrench themselves. We can return and attack, take them by surprise—"

"No," said Alhana. She clasped her arms around her body, set her teeth and, through sheer effort of will, forced herself to stop shaking. "No, we will continue on to Sanction. Don't you see? If we help the human armies conquer Sanction, they will be honor-bound to help us free our homeland, drive out the invaders."

"Why should they?" he asked sharply. "What reason would humans have to die for us?"

"Because we will help them fight for Sanction!" Alhana stated.

"Would we be doing that if your son were not being held prisoner inside Sanction's walls?" Gilthas demanded.

Alhana's skin, cheeks, lips were all one, all ashen. Her dark eyes seemed the only living part of her, and they were smudged with shadow.

"We Silvanesti will march to Sanction," she said. She did not look at him. She stared southward, as if she could see through the mountains and into her lost homeland. "You Qualinesti may do what you like."

Turning from him, she said to Samar. "Summon our people. I must speak to them."

She walked away, tall, straight-backed, shoulders squared.

"Do you agree with this?" Gilthas demanded of Samar as he started to follow her.

Samar cast Gilthas a look that might have been a backhanded blow across the face, and Gilthas realized he had been wrong to ask. Alhana was Samar's queen and his commander. He would die before he questioned any decision she made. Gilthas had never before felt so utterly frustrated, so helpless. He was filled with raging anger that had no outlet.

"We have no homeland," he said, turning to Planchet. "No homeland at all. We are exiles, people without a country. Why can't she see that? Why can't she understand?"

"I think she does," said Planchet. "For her, attacking Sanction is the answer."

"The wrong answer," said Gilthas.

Elven healers came to tend to the runner, treating her wounds with herbs and potions, and they shooed the Wilder elf away. The Lioness walked over to join him.

"What are we doing?"

"Marching to Sanction," Gilthas said grimly. "Did the runner have any news of our people?"

"She said that there were rumors they had managed to escape Silvanesti, flee back into the Plains of Dust."

"Where they will most certainly *not* be welcome." Gilthas sighed deeply. "The Plainspeople warned us of that."

He stood, troubled. He wanted desperately to return to his people, and he realized now that the anger he was feeling was aimed at himself. He should have followed his instincts, remained with his people, not marched off on this ill-fated campaign.

"I was wrong, as well. I opposed you. I am sorry, my husband," said the Lioness remorsefully. "But don't punish yourself. You could not have stopped the invasion."

"At least I could be with our people now," he said bitterly. "Sharing their trouble, if nothing else."

He wondered what he should do. He longed to go back, but the way would be hard and dangerous, and the odds were he would never make it alone. If he took away Qualinesti warrriors, he would leave Alhana's force sadly depleted. He might cause dissension in the ranks, for some Silvanesti would certainly want to return to their homes. At this time, more than any other, the elves needed to be united.

A shout rang from the rear, then another and another, all up and down the line. Alhana stopped in the midst of her speech, turned to look. The cries were coming from every direction now, thundering down on them like the rocks of an avalanche.

"Ogres!"

"What direction?" the Lioness called out to one of her scouts.

"All directions!" he cried and pointed.

Their line of march had carried the elves into a small, narrow valley, surrounded by high cliffs. Now, as they looked, the cliffs came alive. Thousands of huge, hulking figures appeared along the heights, stared down at the elves, and waited in silence for the order to start the killing.

26

The Judgment

The gods of Krynn met once again in council. The gods of light stood opposite the gods of darkness, as day stands opposite night, with the gods of neutrality divided evenly in between. The gods of magic stood together, and in their midst was Raistlin Majere.

Paladine nodded, and the mage stepped forward.

Bowing, he said simply, "I have been successful."

The gods stared in wordless astonishment, all except the gods of magic, who exchanged smiles, their thoughts in perfect accord.

"How was this accomplished?" Paladine asked at last.

"My task was not easy," Raistlin said. "The currents of chaos swirl about the universe. The magic is wayward and unwieldy. I no more set my hand upon it than it slides through my fingers. When the kender used the device, I managed to seize hold of him and wrench him back into the past, where the winds of chaos blow less fiercely. I was able to keep Tas there long enough for him to have a sense of where he was before the magic whipped away from me and I lost him. I knew where to look for him, however, and thus, when next he used the device, I was ready. I took him to a time we both recognized, and he began to know me. Finally, I carried him to the present. Past and present are now linked. You have only to follow the one, and it will lead you to the other."

"What do you see?" Paladine asked Zivilyn.

"I see the world," said Zivilyn softly, tears misting his eyes. "I see the past, and I see the present, and I see the future."

"Which future?" asked Mishakal.

"The path the world walks now," Zivilyn replied.

"Then it is not possible to alter it?" Mishakal asked.

"Of course, it is possible," said Raistlin caustically. "We may all yet cease to exist."

"You mean that the blasted kender is not yet dead?" Sargonnas growled.

"He is not. The power of Queen Takhisis has grown immense. If you are to have any hope of defeating her, Tasslehoff has yet one important task to accomplish with the Device of Time Journeying. If he accomplishes this task—"

"—he must be sent back to die," said Sargonnas.

"He will be given the choice," Paladine corrected. "He will not be forced back or sent against his wishes. He has freedom of will, as do all living beings upon Krynn. We cannot deny that to him, just because it suits our convenience."

"Suits our convenience!" Sargonnas roared. "He could destroy us all!"

"If that is the risk we run for our beliefs," said Paladine, "then so be it. Your queen, Sargonnas, disdained free will. She found it easier to rule slaves. You opposed her in that. Would your minotaurs worship a god who made them slaves? A god who denied them their right to determine their own fate, a right to find honor and glory?"

"No, but then my minotaurs have sense. They are not brainless kender," muttered Sargonnas, but he muttered it into his fur. "That brings us to the next question, however. Providing this kender does not yet get us all killed"—he cast a baleful glance at Paladine—"what punishment do we mete out to the goddess whose name I will never more speak? The goddess who betrayed us?"

"There can be only one punishment," said Gilean, resting his hand upon the book.

Paladine looked around. "Are we all agreed?"

"So long as the balance is maintained," said Hiddukel, the keeper of the scales.

Paladine looked at each of the gods. Each, in turn, nodded. Last, he looked at his mate, his beloved Mishakal. She did not nod. She stood with her head bowed.

"It must be," said Paladine gently.

Mishakal lifted up her eyes, looked long and lovingly into his. Then, through her tears, she nodded.

Paladine rested his hand upon the book. "So be it," he said.

27

Tasslehoff Burrfoot

asslehoff's life had been made up of glorious moments. Admittedly, there had been some bad moments, too, but the glorious moments shone so very brightly that their radiance overwhelmed the unhappy moments, causing them to fade back into the inner recesses of his memory. He would never forget the bad times, but they no longer had the power to hurt him. They only made him a little sad.

This moment was one of the glorious moments, more glorious than any moment that had come before, and it kept improving, with each coming moment shining more gloriously than the next.

Tas was now growing accustomed to traveling through space and time, and while he continued to feel giddy and disoriented every time the device dumped him out at a destination, he decided that such a sensation, while not suited to everyday use, made for an exhilarating change. This time, after landing and stumbling about a bit and wondering for an exciting instant if he was going to throw up, the wooziness receded, and he was able to look around and take note of his surroundings.

The first thing he saw was an immense silver dragon, standing right beside him. The dragon's eyes were horribly wounded by a jagged scar that slashed across them, and Tas recognized the blind man who had spoken to him in the Knights' Council. The dragon, like Tas, appeared to have taken the journey through time in stride, for he was fanning his wings gently and turning his head this way and that, sniffing the air and listening. Either traveling through time did not bother dragons, or being blind kept one from getting dizzy. Tas wondered which it was and made a mental note to ask during a lull in the proceedings.

His other two companions were not faring quite as well. Gerard had not liked the journey the first time, so he could be excused for really not liking it the second time. He swayed on his feet and breathed heavily.

Odila was wide-eyed and gasping and reminded Tas of a poor fish he'd once found in his pocket. He had no idea how the fish had come to be there, although he did have a dim sort of memory that someone had lost it. He'd managed to restore the fish to water, where, after a dazed moment, it had swum off. The fish had the same look that Odila had now.

"Where are we?" she gasped, clinging to Gerard with a white-knuckled grip.

He looked grimly at the kender. One and all, they looked grimly at the kender.

"Right were we're supposed to be," Tas said confidently. "Where the Dark Queen has kept the gold and silver dragons prisoners." Gripping the device tightly in his hand, he added a soft, "I hope!" that didn't come out all that softly and rather spoiled matters.

Tas had never been anywhere like this before. All around him was gray rock and nothing except gray rock as far as the eye could see. Sharp gray rocks, smooth gray rocks, enormous gray rocks, and small gray rocks. Mountains of gray rock, and valleys of the same gray rock. The sky above him was black as the blackest thing he'd ever seen, without a single star, and yet he was bathed in a cold white light. Beyond the gray rock, on the horizon, shimmered a wall of ice.

"I feel stone beneath my feet," said Mirror, "and I do not smell vegetation, so I assume the land in which we have arrived is bleak and barren. I hear no sounds of any kind: not the waves breaking on the shore, not the wind rushing through the trees, no sound of bird or animal. I sense that this place is desolate, forbidding."

"That about sums it up," said Gerard, wiping sweat from his forehead with the back of his hand. "Add to that description the fact that the sky above us is pitch black, there is no sun, yet there is light; the air is colder than a troll's backside, and this place appears to be surrounded by what looks like a wall made of icicles, and you have said all there is to say about it."

"What he didn't say," Tas felt called upon to point out, "is that the light makes the wall of ice shimmer with all sorts of different colors—"

"Rather like the scales of a many-colored dragon?" Mirror asked.

"That's it!" Tas cried, enthused. "Now that you come to mention it, it does look like that. It's lovely in a sort of cold and unlovely way. Especially how the colors shift whenever you look at them, dancing all along the icy surface . . ."

"Oh, shut up!" ordered Gerard.

Tas sighed inwardly. As much he liked humans, traveling with them certainly took a lot of joy out of the journey.

The cold was biting. Odila shivered, wrapped her robes around her more closely. Gerard stalked over to the ice wall. He did not touch it. He looked it up and down. Drawing his dagger, he jabbed the weapon's point into the wall.

The blade shattered. Gerard dropped the knife with an oath, wrung his hand in pain, then slid his hand beneath his armpit.

"It's so damn cold it broke the blade! I could feel the chill travel through the metal and strike deep into my bone. My hand is still numb."

"We can't survive long in this," Odila said. "We humans will perish of the cold, as will the kender. I can't speak for the dragon."

Tas smiled at her to thank her for including him.

"As for me," said Mirror, "my species is cold-blooded. My blood will thicken and grow sluggish. I will soon lose my ability to fly or even to think clearly."

"And except for you," said Gerard grumpily, looking around the barren wasteland on which they stood, "I don't see a single dragon."

Tasslehoff was forced to admit that he was feeling the chill himself and that it was causing very unpleasant sensations in his toes and the tips of his fingers. He thought with regret back to a fur-lined vest he'd once owned, and he wondered whatever became of it. He wondered also what had become of the dragons, for he was absolutely positive—well, relatively certain—that this was the place where he'd been told he would find them. He peered under a few gray rocks with no luck.

"You better take us back, Tas," said Odila, as best she could for her teeth clicking together.

"He can't take us back," said Mirror, and the dragon was oddly complacent. "This place was constructed as a prison for dragons. It has frozen the magic in my blood. I doubt if the magic of the device will work either."

"We're trapped here!" Gerard said grimly. "To freeze to death!"

Tasslehoff drew himself up. This was a glorious moment, and while admittedly it didn't look or feel very glorious (he'd lost all feeling in his toes), he knew what he was doing.

"Now, see here," he said sternly, eyeing Gerard. "We've been through a lot together, you and I. If it wasn't for me, you wouldn't be where you are today. That being the case," he added hurriedly, before Gerard could reply, "follow me."

He turned around, bravely confident, ready to proceed forward, without having the least idea where he was going.

A voice said softly, distinctly, in his ear, "Over the ridge."

"Over the ridge," said Tasslehoff. Pointing at the first ridge of gray rock that he saw, he marched off that direction.

"Should we go after him?" Odila asked.

"We don't dare lose him," said Gerard.

Tas clamored among the gray stones, dislodging small rocks that slid and slithered out from under him and went clattering and bounding down behind him, seriously impeding Odila and Gerard, who were attempting to climb up after him. Glancing back, Tas saw that Mirror had not moved. The silver dragon continued to stand where he had landed, fanning his wings and twitching his tail, probably to try to keep his blood stirring.

"He can't see," said Tasslehoff, stung by guilt. "And we've left him behind, all alone. Don't worry, Mirror!" he called out. "We'll come back for you."

Mirror said something in response, something that Tas couldn't quite hear clearly, what with all the noise that Odila and Gerard were making dodging rocks, but it seemed to him that he heard, "The glory of this moment is yours, kender. I will be waiting."

"That's the great thing about dragons," Tas said to himself, feeling warm all over. "They always understand."

Topping the ridge, he looked down, and his breath caught in his throat.

As far as the eye could see were dragons. Tasslehoff had never seen so many dragons in one place at one time. He had never imagined that there were so many gold and silver dragons in the world.

The dragons slumbered in a cold-induced torpor. They pressed together for warmth, heads and necks entwined, bodies lying side by side, wings folded, tails wrapped around themselves or their brother dragons. The strange light that caused rainbows to dance mockingly in the ice wall stole the colors from the dragons, left them gray as the rocky peaks that surrounded them.

"Are they dead?" Tas asked, his heart in his throat.

"No," said the voice in his ear, "they are deeply asleep. Their slumber keeps them from dying."

"How do I wake them?"

"You must bring down the ice wall."

"How do I do that? Gerard's knife broke when he tried it."

"A weapon is not what is needed."

Tas thought this over, then said doubtfully, "Can I do it?"

"I don't know," the voice said. "Can you?"

"By all that is wonderful!" Gerard exclaimed. Pulling himself up to the top of the ridge, he now stood beside Tasslehoff. "Would you look at that!"

Odila said nothing. She stood long moments, gazing down at the dragons, then she turned and ran back down the ridge. "I will go tell Mirror."

"I think he knows," said Tasslehoff, then he added, politely, "Excuse me. I have something to do."

"Oh, no. You're not going anywhere!" Gerard cried and made a snatch at Tasslehoff's collar.

He missed.

Tasslehoff began running full tilt, as fast as he could run. The climb had warmed his feet. He could feel his toes—essential for running—and he ran as he had never run before. His feet skimmed over the ground. If he stepped on a loose rock that might have sent him tumbling, he didn't touch it long enough to matter. He fairly flew down the side of the ridge.

He gave himself to the running. The wind buffeted his face and stung his eyes. His mouth opened wide. He sucked in great mouthfuls of cold air that sparkled in his blood. He heard shouts, but their words meant nothing in the wind of his running. He ran without thought of stopping, without the means of stopping. He ran straight at the ice wall.

Wildly excited, Tas threw back his head. He opened his mouth and cried out a loud "Yaaaa" that had absolutely no meaning but just felt good. Arms spread wide, mouth open wide, he crashed headlong into the wall of shimmering ice.

Rainbow droplets fell all around him. Sparkling in a radiant silver light, the droplets plopped down on his upturned face. He raced through the curtain of water that had once been a wall of ice, and he continued to run, out of control, running, madly running, and then he saw that just ahead of him, almost at his feet, the gray rock ended abruptly and there was nothing below it except black.

Tas flailed his arms, trying to stop. He struggled with his feet, but they seemed to have minds of their own, and he knew with certainty that he was going to sail right off the edge.

My last moment, but a glorious one, he thought.

He was falling, and silver wings flew above him. He felt a claw seize hold of his collar (not a new sensation, for it seemed that someone was always seizing hold of his collar), except that this was different. This was a most welcome seize.

Tas hung suspended over eternity.

He gasped for breath that he couldn't seem to find. He was dizzy and light-headed. Tilting back his head, he saw that he dangled from the claw of a silver dragon, a silver dragon who turned his sightless eyes in the general direction of the kender.

"Thank goodness you kept yelling," said Mirror, "and thank goodness Gerard saw your peril in time to warn me."

"Are they free?" Tasslehoff asked anxiously. "The other dragons?"

"They are free," said Mirror, veering slowly about, returning to what Tas could see now was nothing more than an enormous island of gray rock adrift in the darkness.

"What are you and the other dragons going to do?" Tas asked, starting to feel better now that he was over solid ground.

"Talk," said Mirror.

"Talk!" Tasslehoff groaned.

"Don't worry," said Mirror. "We are keenly aware of the passing of time. But there are questions to be asked and answered before we can make any decision." His voice softened. "Too many have sacrificed too much for us to ruin it all by acting rashly."

Tas didn't like the sound of that. It made him feel extremely sad, and he was about to ask Mirror what he meant, but the dragon was now lowering the kender to the ground. Gerard caught hold of Tasslehoff in his arms. Giving him a hug, he set him on his feet. Tas concentrated on trying to breathe. The air was warmer, now that the ice wall was gone. He could hear wings beating and the dragons' voices, deep and resonant, calling out to each other in their ancient language.

Tas sat on the gray rocks and waited for his breathing to catch up with him and for his heart to realize that he'd quit running and that it didn't need to beat so frantically. Odila went off with Mirror to serve as his guide, and he soon heard the silver dragon's voice rising in joy at finding his fellows. Gerard remained behind. He didn't tromp about, as usual, peering into this and investigating that. He stood looking down at Tas with a most peculiar expression on his face.

Maybe he has a stomach ache, Tas thought.

As for Tasslehoff, since he didn't have breath enough to talk, he spent some time thinking.

"I never quite looked at it that way," he thought to himself.

"What did you say?" Gerard asked, squatting down to be level with the kender.

Tas made up his mind. He could talk now and he knew what he had to say. "I'm going back."

"We're all going back," Gerard stated, adding, with an exasperated glance in the direction of the dragons, "eventually."

"No, I don't mean that," said Tas, having trouble with a lump in his throat. "I mean I'm going back to die." He managed a smile and a shrug. "I'm already dead, you know, so it won't be such a huge change."

"Are you sure about this, Tas?" Gerard asked, regarding the kender with quiet gravity.

Tas nodded. "'Too many have sacrificed too much . . .' that's what Mirror said. I thought about that when I ran off the edge of the world. If I die here, I said to myself, where I'm not supposed to, everything dies with me. And then, do you know what happened, Gerard? I felt scared! I've never been scared before." He shook his head. "Not like that."

"The fall would be enough to scare anyone," said Gerard.

"It wasn't the fall," Tas said. "I was scared because I knew if everything died, it would all be my fault. All the sacrifices that everybody has made down through history: Huma, Magius, Sturm Brightblade, Laurana, Raistlin . . ." He paused, then said softly, "Even Lord Soth. And countless others I'll never know. All their suffering would be wasted. Their joys and triumphs would be forgotten."

Tasslehoff pointed. "Do you see that red star? The one there?"

"Yes," said Gerard. "I see it."

"The kender tell me that people in the Fifth Age believe Flint Fireforge lives in that star. He keeps his forge blazing so that people will remember the glory of the old days and that they will have hope. Do you think that's true?"

Gerard started to say that he thought the star was just a star and that a dwarf could never possibly live in a star, but then, seeing Tas's face, the Knight changed his mind.

"Yes, I think it's true."

Tas smiled. Rising to his feet, he dusted himself off, looked himself over, twitched his clothes and his pouches into place. After all, if he was going to be stepped on by Chaos, he had to look presentable.

"That red star is the very first star I'm going to visit. Flint will be glad to see me. I expect he's been lonely."

"Are you going now?" Gerard asked.

"'No time like the present,'" Tas said cheerfully. "That's a time-travel joke," he added, eyeing Gerard. "All us time travelers make time-travel jokes. You're supposed to laugh."

"I guess I don't feel much like laughing," Gerard said. He rested his hand on Tas's shoulder. "Mirror was right. You are wise, perhaps the very wisest person I know, and certainly the most courageous. I honor you, Tasslehoff Burrfoot."

Drawing his sword, Gerard saluted the kender, the salute one true Knight gives to another.

A glorious moment.

"Goodbye," Tasslehoff said. "May your pouches never be empty."

Reaching into his pouch, he found the Device of Time Journeying. He looked at it, admired it, ran his fingers over the jewels that sparkled more brightly than he ever remembered seeing them sparkle before. He caressed it lovingly, then, looking out at the red star, he said, "I'm ready."

"The dragons have finally reached a decision. They're about ready to return to Krynn," said Odila. "And they want us to go with them." She glanced about. "Where's the kender? Have you lost him again?"

Gerard wiped his nose and his eyes and thought, smiling, of all the times he'd wished he could have lost Tasslehoff Burrfoot.

"He's not lost," Gerard said, reaching out to take hold of Odila's hand. "Not anymore."

At that moment, a shrill voice spoke from the darkness.

"Hey, Gerard, I almost forgot! When you get back to Solace, be sure to fix the lock on my tomb. It's broken."

28

The Valley of Fire and Ice

The ogres did not attack immediately. They had laid their ambush well. The elves were trapped in the valley, their advance blocked, their retreat cut off. They weren't going anywhere. The ogres could start the assault at a time of their own choosing, and they chose to wait.

The elves were prepared to do battle now, the ogres reasoned. Courage pumped in their veins. Their enemy had come upon them so suddenly and unexpectedly that the elves had no time for fear. But let the day linger on, let the night come. Let them lie sleepless on their blankets and stare at the bonfires ringed around them. Let them count the numbers of their enemies, and let fear multiply those numbers, and by next day's dawning, elf stomachs would shrivel and elf hands shake, and they would puke up their courage on the ground.

The elves moved immediately to repel the enemy attack, moved with discipline, without panic, taking cover in stands of pine trees and brush, behind boulders. Elven archers sought higher ground, picked out their targets, took careful aim and waited for the order to fire. Each archer had an adequate store of arrows, but those would soon be spent, and there would be no more. They had to make every shot count, although the archers could see for themselves that they might spend every arrow they possessed and still not make a dent in the numbers of the enemy.

The elves were ready. The ogres did not attack. Understanding their strategy, Samar ordered the elves to stand down. The elves tried to eat and sleep, but without much success. The stench of the ogres, that was like rotting meat, tainted their food. The light of their fires crept beneath closed eyelids. Alhana walked among them, speaking to them, telling them stories of old to banish their fears and lift their hearts. Gilthas did the same thing, talking to his people, bolstering their spirits, speaking words of hope that he did not himself believe, that no rational person could believe. Yet, it seemed to bring comfort to the people and, oddly, to Gilthas himself. He couldn't understand it, for he had only to look all around to see the fires of his enemies outnumbering the stars. He supposed, cynically, that hope was always the last man standing.

The person Gilthas most sought to comfort refused to be comforted. The Lioness disappeared shortly after bringing the elven runner into camp. She galloped away on her horse, ignoring Gilthas's shout. He searched the camp for her, but no one who had seen her, not even among her own people. He found her at last, long after darkness. She sat on a boulder, far from the main camp. She stared out into the night, and although Gilthas knew that she must have heard him approach, for she could hear a sparrow moving in the woods twenty feet away, she did not turn to look at him.

No need to tell her that she was placing herself in danger of being picked off by some ogre raider. She knew that better than he.

"How many of your scouts are missing?" he asked.

"My fault!" she said bitterly. "My failure! I should have seen something, heard something to keep us from this peril!" She gestured toward the mountain peaks. "Look at that. Thousands of them! Ogres, who shake the ground with their feet and splinter trees and stink like warm cow dung. And I did not see them or hear them! I might as well be blind, deaf, and dumb with my nose cut off for all the good I am!"

After a pause, she added harshly. "Twenty are missing. All of them friends, loyal and dear to me."

"No one blames you," said Gilthas.

"I blame myself!" the Lioness said, her voice choked.

"Samar says that the some of the ogres have grown powerful in magic. Whatever force blocks our magic and causes it to go awry works in the ogres' favor. Their movements were cloaked by sorcery. You could not possibly be faulted for failing to detect that."

The Lioness turned to face him. Her hair was wild and disheveled, hung ragged about her face. The tracks of her tears left streaks of dirt on her cheeks. Her eyes burned.

"I thank you for trying to comfort me, my husband, but my only comfort is the knowledge that my failure will die with me."

His heart broke. He had no words to say. He held out his arms to her, and she lunged into them, kissed him fiercely.

"I love you!" she whispered brokenly. "I love you so much!"

"And I love you," he said. "You are my life, and if that life ends this moment, I count it blessed for having you in it."

He stayed with her, far from camp, all through the night, waiting for those who would never return.

The ogres attacked before dawn, when the sky was pale with the coming of morning. The elves were ready. None had been able to sleep. Each knew in his heart that he would not survive to see the noontide.

The hulking ogres began the assault by rolling boulders down the sides of the cliffs. The boulders were enormous, the size of houses, and here was proof of a goddess's magic, for although ogres are huge, averaging over nine feet in height, and massively built, not even the most powerful ogre was strong enough to wrench those gigantic rocks out of the ground and fling them down the mountainside. The voices of the ogre mages could be heard chanting the magic that was a gift from Queen Takhisis. .

The boulders careened into the valley, forcing the elves who had taken refuge among the rocks to flee and sending elven archers leaping for the lives. The dying screams of those crushed by the rocks echoed among the mountains, to be answered with gleeful hoots by the ogres.

A few angry or panicked elven archers wasted arrows, shooting before the enemy was in range. Samar angrily rebuked those who did, reiterated the command to wait for his orders. Gilthas was no archer. He gripped his sword and waited grimly for the charge. He wasn't very good with his weapon, but he'd been improving—so Planchet told him—and he hoped he would be good enough to at least take a few of the enemy with him and make the spirit of his father and mother proud.

Gilthas was strangely conscious of his mother this morning. He had the feeling that she was beside him, and once he thought he heard her voice and felt her touch. The feeling was so intense that he actually turned to look to see if she stood near him. What he saw was the Lioness, who smiled at him. They would fight together, here at the end, and lie together in death as they had lain together in life.

The ogres were black upon the mountain tops. They raised their spears and shook them, giving the elves a clear view of their fate, and then the ogres gave a cheer that rebounded down the mountain.

The elves gripped their weapons and waited for the onslaught. Gilthas and the Lioness stood among the command group, gathered around Queen Alhana and the elven standards of both the Qualinesti and the Silvanesti.

Finally we are united, only when we face annihilation and it is too late. Gilthas quickly put the bitter thought out of his mind. What was done was done.

Having cleared their way, the ogres began to move inexorably down the mountain, their numbers so great that they blackened the mountain side. The entire ogre nation must be here, Gilthas realized.

He reached out, clasped hold of the Lioness's hand. He would fill his soul with love and let that love carry him to wherever it was souls went.

Samar gave the order to prepare to fire. The elven archers nocked their arrows and took aim. Samar raised his hand, but he did not drop it.

"Wait!" he cried. His eyes squinted as he tried to see more clearly. "What is that, my queen? Am I seeing things?"

Alhana stood on a knoll, from which she could have a view of the battlefield and direct the battle, such as it would be. She was calm, beautiful as ever. More beautiful, if that were possible, fell and deadly. She shaded her eyes with her hands, stared into the east and the sun that had just now lifted above the mountaintops. "The forces near the mountaintop have slowed," she reported coolly, no emotion in her voice, neither elation nor despair. "Some are actually turning around."

"Something has them frightened," cried the Lioness. Lifting her gaze skyward, she pointed. "There! Blessed *E'li!* There!"

Light flared above them, light so brilliant that it seemed to catch the sun and drag its bright rays into the valley, banishing the shadows. At first, Gilthas thought that some miracle had brought the sun to the elves, but then he realized that the light was reflected light—the sun's rays shining off the scales of the belly of a golden dragon.

The Gold dived low, aiming for the side of the mountain that was thick with ogres. At the sight of the resplendent dragon, the marching ranks of the enemy dissolved into a jumbled mess. Mad with terror, the ogres ran up the mountainside and down and even sideways in their panicked effort to escape.

The dragon blasted the hillside with a fiery breath. Jammed together in knots of fear, the ogres died by the hundreds. Their agonized screams echoed among the rocks, screams so horrible that some of the elves covered their ears to blot out the sound.

The Gold sailed up and over the mountain. Smaller silver dragons flew in behind, breathing killing hoarfrost that froze the fleeing ogres, froze their blood, froze their hearts and their flesh. Hard and cold as rock, the bodies toppled over, rolled down into the valley. More golden dragons flew to the attack, so that the sky was aflame with the glitter of their scales. The ogre army that had been racing down gleefully upon their trapped enemy was now in full retreat. The dragons followed them, hunted them down wherever they tried to hide.

The ogres had sent thousands of their people into this fight that was supposed to lop off the head of the elven army and rip out its heart. United under the command of the ogre titans, trained into a disciplined fighting force, the ogres had tracked the elven march with cunning patience, waited for them to enter this valley.

The ogres lost a great many in the battle that day, but their nation was not destroyed, as some elves and humans would later claim. The ogres knew the land, they knew where to find caves in which to hide until the dragons departed. Skulking in the darkness, they licked their wounds and cursed the elves and vowed revenge. The ogres were now firmly allied with the minotaur nation. Penned up on northern islands, its burgeoning population spilling out into the ocean, the minotaurs had long eyed the continent of Ansalon as an area ripe for expansion. Although the ogres had been defeated this day, they would remain firm in their alliance with the minotaurs. A day of reckoning was yet to come.

Those ogres who dashed into the valley and accosted the elves were mad with fury, forgot their training, sought only to kill. The elves dispatched these with ease, and soon the battle was over. The ogres named the battlefield the Valley of Fire and Ice and proclaimed it accursed. No ogre would set foot there ever after.

The tide of battle had turned so swiftly that Gilthas could not comprehend they were safe, could not adjust to the fact that death was not advancing on him with club and spear. The elves were cheering now and singing anthems of joy to welcome the dragons, who wheeled overhead, the sun blazing off their glistening scales.

Two silver dragons broke free of the pack. They circled low, searching for a smooth and level patch of ground on which to land. Alhana and Samar advanced to meet them, as did Gilthas. He marveled at Alhana. He was shaking with the reaction of the sudden release of fear, the sudden return of life and of hope. She faced this reversal in fortune with the same cool aplomb that she had faced certain destruction.

The silver dragons settled to the ground—one of them with swooping, graceful movements, and the other landing as awkwardly as a young dragon fresh from the egg. Gilthas wondered at that, until he saw that this second dragon was maimed, his eyes disfigured and destroyed.

The dragon flew blind, under the guidance of his rider, a Solamnic Knight. Long black braids streamed down from beneath her shining helm. She saluted the queen, but did not dismount. She remained seated on the dragon, her sword drawn, keeping watch as other dragons hunted down and destroyed the remnants of the ogre army. The rider of the second dragon waved his hand.

"Samar!" he shouted.

"It is the Knight, Gerard!" exclaimed Samar, shocked out of his usual stoic complacency. "I would know him anywhere," he added, as Gerard ran toward them. "He is the ugliest human you are ever likely to see, Your Majesty."

"He looks very beautiful to me," said Alhana.

Gilthas heard tears in her voice, if he did not see them on her face, and he began to understand her better. She was frost without, fire within.

Gerard's face brightened when he saw Gilthas, and he came hastening forward to greet the Qualinesti king. Gilthas gestured obliquely with his head. Gerard took the hint and looked to Alhana. He halted dead in his tracks, stared at her, rapt. Too awestruck by beauty to remember his manners, he gaped, his mouth wide open.

"Sir Gerard," she said. "You are a most welcome sight."

Only then, at the sound of her voice, did he recall that he was in the presence of royalty. He sank down on one knee, his head bowed.

"Your servant, Madam."

Alhana extended her hand. "Rise, please, Sir Gerard. I am the one who should kneel to you, for you have saved my people from certain destruction."

"No, Madam, not me," said Gerard, flushing red, looking about as ugly as it was possible for a human to look. "The dragons came to your aid. I just went along for the ride and . . ." He seemed about to add something, but changed his mind.

Turning to Gilthas, Gerard bowed deeply. "I am overjoyed to see that you are alive and well, Your Majesty." His voice softened. "I was deeply grieved to hear of the death of your honored mother."

"Thank you, Sir Gerard," said Gilthas, clasping the Knight by the hand. "I find it strange that the paths of our lives cross once again—strange, yet fortuitous."

Gerard stood awkwardly, his keen blue eyes going from one to the other, searching, seeking.

"Sir Gerard," said Alhana, "you have something else to say. Please, speak without fear. We are deeply in your debt."

"No, you're not, Your Majesty," he said. His speech and manner were clumsy and awkward, as humans must always look to elves, but his voice was earnest and sincere. "I don't want you to think that. It's for this very reason I hesitate to speak, yet"—he glanced toward the sun—"time advances and we stand still. I have dire news to impart, and I dread to speak it."

"If you refer to the minotaur seizure of our homeland, we have been made aware of that," said Alhana.

Gerard stared at her. His mouth opened, shut again.

"Perhaps I can help," she said. "You want us to fulfill the promise Samar made and ride with you to attack Sanction. You fear that we will feel pressured into doing this by the fact that you came to our rescue."

"Lord Tasgall wants me to assure you that the Knights will understand if you feel the need to return to fight for your homeland, Madam," said Gerard. "I can say only that our need is very great. Sanction is guarded by armies of both the dead and the living. We fear that Queen Takhisis plans to try to rule both the mortal world and the immortal. If that happens, if she succeeds, darkness will encompass all of us. We need your help, Madam, and that of your brave warriors if we are to stop her. The dragons have offered to carry you there, for they will also join the battle."

"Have you had news? Is my son Silvanoshei still alive?" Alhana asked, her facing paling.

"I do not know, Madam," Gerard replied evasively. "I hope and trust so, but I have no way of knowing."

Alhana nodded, and then she did something unexpected. She turned to Gilthas. "You know what my answer must be, Nephew. My son is a prisoner. I would do all in my power to free him." Her cheeks stained with a faint flush. "But, as king of your people, you have the right to speak your thoughts."

Gilthas might have felt pleased. He might have felt vindicated. But he had been awake all night. He felt only bone tired.

"Sir Gerard, if we aid the Knights in the capture of Sanction, can we expect the Knights to aid us in the retaking of our homeland?"

"That is up to the Knights' Council, Your Majesty," Gerard replied, uncomfortable. As if aware that his answer was a poor one, he added with conviction, "I do not know what the other Knights would do, Your Majesty, but I willingly pledge myself to your cause."

"I thank you for that, sir," said Gilthas. He turned to Alhana. "I was opposed to this march at the beginning. I made no secret of that. The doom I foresaw has fallen. We are exiles now, without a homeland. Yet as this gallant Knight states, if we foreswear the promise Samar made to aid the Knights in their fight,

Queen Takhisis will triumph. Her first act would be to destroy us utterly, to annihilate us as a people. I agree. We must march on Sanction."

"You have our answer, Sir Gerard," Alhana declared. "We are one—the Qualinesti and the Silvanesti—and we will join with the other free people of Ansalon to fight and destroy the Queen of Darkness and her armies."

Gerard said what was proper. He was obviously relieved and now eager to be gone. The dragons circled above them, the shadows of their wings sliding gracefully over the ground. The elves greeted the dragons with glad cries and tears and blessings, and the dragons dipped their proud heads in response to the salutes.

The silver dragons and the gold began to swoop down into the valley, one or two at a time. The elven warriors mounted on the backs of the dragons, crowding as many on as possible. Thus had the elves ridden into battle during the days of Huma. Thus had they ridden to battle during the War of the Lance. The air was charged with a sense of history. The elves began to sing again, songs of glory, songs of victory.

Alhana, mounted on a golden dragon, took the lead. Raising her sword into the air, she shouted an elven battle cry. Samar lifted his sword, joined in. The Gold carried the queen of the Silvanesti into the air and flew off over the mountains toward the west, toward Sanction. The blind silver dragon departed, guided by his human rider.

Gilthas volunteered to remain to the last, to make certain that the dead were given proper rites, their bodies cremated in dragonfire, since there was no time to bury them and no way they could be returned to their homeland. His wife stayed with him.

"The Knights will not come to our aid, will they?" said the Lioness abruptly, as the last dragon stood ready to bear them away.

"The Knights will not come," Gilthas said. "We will die for them, and they will sing our praises, but when the battle is won, they will return to their homes. They will not come to die for us."

Together, he and the Lioness and the last of the Qualinesti warriors took to the skies. The songs of the elves were loud and joyful and filled the valley with music.

Then all that was left was the echoes.

Then those faded away, leaving only silence and smoke.

29

The Temple of Duerghast

Galdar had not seen Mina since her triumphant return to Sanction. His heart was sore as his body, and he used his wounds as an excuse to remain in his tent, refusing to see or speak to anyone. He was considerably surprised that he was still alive, for Takhisis had good reason to hate him, and she was not merciful to those who had turned on her. He guessed that Mina had much to do with the fact that he was not lying in a charred lump alongside Malys's carcass.

Galdar had not stayed to listen to the conversation between Takhisis and Mina. His fury was such that he could have torn down the mountain, stone by stone, with his bare hands, and fearing that his fury would hurt Mina, not help her, he stalked away to rage in solitude. He returned to the cave only when he heard Mina call for him.

He found her well, whole. He was not surprised. He expected nothing less. Nursing his bruised and bloodied hand—he had taken out his anger on the rocks—he regarded her in silence, waited for her to speak.

Her amber eyes were cold and hard. He could still see himself frozen inside them, a tiny figure, trapped.

"You would have let me die," she said, accusing.

"Yes," he replied steadily. "Better that you should have died with your glory fresh upon you than live a slave."

"She is our god, Galdar. If you serve me, you serve her."

"I serve you, Mina," Galdar said, and that was the end of the conversation.

Mina might have dismissed him. She might have slain him. Instead, she started off on the long trek down the Lords of Doom. He went with her. She spoke to him only once more, and that was an offer to heal his injuries. He declined. They walked to Sanction in silence and they had not talked since.

The joy at Mina's return was tumultuous. There had been those who were sure she was dead and those who were sure she lived, and so high was the level of anxiety and fear that these two factions came to blows. Mina's Knights argued among themselves, her commanders bickered and quarreled. Rumors flew about the streets, lies became truth, and truth degenerated into lies. Mina returned to find a city of anarchy and chaos. The sound of her name was all that it took to restore order.

"Mina!" was the jubilant cry at the gate as she appeared. "Mina!"

The name rang wildly throughout the city like the joyous sound of wedding bells, and she was very nearly overrun and smothered by those who cried out how thankful they were to see her alive. If Galdar had not wordlessly swept her up in his arms and mounted her on his strong shoulders for everyone to see, she might well have been killed by love.

Galdar could have pointed out that it was Mina they cheered, Mina they followed, Mina they obeyed. He said nothing, however, and she said nothing either. Galdar heard the tales of the destruction of the totem, of the appearance of a silver dragon who had attacked the totem and who had, in turn, been attacked and blinded by Mina's valiant troops. He heard of the perfidy and treachery of the Solamnic priestess who had joined forces with the silver dragon and how they had flown off together.

Lying on his cot, nursing his injuries, Galdar recalled the first time he'd seen the lame beggar, who had turned out to be a blue dragon. He had been in company with a blind man with silver hair. Galdar pondered this and wondered.

He went to view the wreckage. The pile of ash that had been the skulls of hundreds of dragons remained untouched, undisturbed. Mina would not go near it. She did not return to the altar room. She did not return to her room in the temple, but moved her things to some unknown location.

In the altar room, the candles had all melted into a large pool of wax colored dirty gray by the swirling ashes. Benches were overturned, some blackened from the fire. The odor of smoke and magic was all pervasive. The floor was covered with shards of amber, sharp enough to puncture the sole of a boot. No one dared enter the temple, which was said to be imbued with the spirit of the woman whose body had been imprisoned in the amber sarcophagus and was now a pile of ashes.

"At least one of us managed to escape," Galdar told the ashes, and he gave a soldier's salute.

The body of one of the wizards was gone, as well. No one could tell Galdar what had happened to Palin Majere. Some claimed to have seen a figure cloaked all in black carry it off, while others swore that they had seen the wizard Dalamar tear it apart with his bare hands. At Mina's command, a search was made for Palin, but the body could not be found, and finally Mina ordered the search ended.

The body of the wizard Dalamar remained in the abandoned temple, staring into the darkness, apparently forgotten, his hands stained with blood.

There was one other piece of news. The jailer was forced to admit that during the confusion of Malys's attack, the elf lord Silvanoshei had escaped his prison cell and had not been recaptured. The elf was thought to be still in the city, for they had posted look-outs for him at the exits, and no one had seen him.

"He is in Sanction," Mina said. "Of that, you may be certain."

"I will find him," said the jailer with an oath. "And when I do, I will bring him straight to you, Mina."

"I am too busy to deal with him," said Mina sharply. "If you find him, kill him. He has served his purpose."

Days passed. Order was restored. The elf was not found, nor did anyone really bother to look for him. Rumors were now whispered that Mina was having the ancient Temple of Duerghast, that had long been left to lie in ruins, reconstructed and refurbished. In a month's time, she would be holding a grand ceremony in the temple, the nature of which was secret. It would be the greatest moment in the history of Krynn, one that would be long celebrated and remembered. Soon, everyone in Sanction was saying that Mina was going to be rewarded with godhood.

The day Galdar first heard this, he sighed deeply. On that day, Mina came to see him.

"Galdar," she called outside his tent post. "May I come in?"

He gave a growl of acquiescence, and she entered.

Mina had lost weight—with Galdar not around, no one was there to persuade her to eat. Nor was anyone urging her to sleep, apparently, for she looked worn, exhausted. Her eyes blinked too often, her fingers plucked aimlessly at the buckles of her leather armor. Her skin was pale, except for a hectic, fevered stain on her cheeks. Her red hair was longer than he had ever known her to wear it, curled fretfully about her ears and straggled down her forehead. He did not rise to greet her, but remained sitting on his bed.

"They say you keep to your quarters because you are unwell," Mina said, regarding him intently.

"I am doing better," he said, refusing to meet her amber eyes.

"Are you able to return to your duties?"

"If *you* want me." He laid emphasis on the word.

"I do." Mina began to pace the tent, and he was startled to see her nervous, uneasy. "You've heard the talk that is going around. About my becoming a god."

"I've heard it. Let me guess, Her Dark Majesty isn't pleased."

"When she enters the world in triumph, Galdar, then there will be no question of whom the people will worship. It's just that . . ." Mina paused, helpless to explain, or perhaps loath to admit to the explanation.

"You are not to blame, Mina," said Galdar, relenting and taking pity on her. "You are here in the world. You are something the people can see and hear and touch. You perform the miracles."

"Always in her name," Mina insisted.

"Yet you never stopped them from calling out *your* name," Galdar observed. "You never told them to shout for the One God. It is always 'Mina, Mina.' "

She was silent a moment, then said quietly, "I do not stop it because I enjoy it, Galdar. I cannot help it. I hear the love in their voices. I see the love in their eyes. Their love makes me feel that I can accomplish anything, that I can work miracles . . ."

Her voice died away. She seemed to suddenly realize what she had said.

That I can work miracles.

"I understand," Mina said softly. "I see now why I was punished. I am amazed the One God forgave me. Yet, I will make it up to her."

She abandoned you, Mina! Galdar wanted to shout at her. If you had died, she would have found someone else to do her bidding. But you didn't die, and so she came running back with her lying tale of "testing" and "punishing."

The words burned on his tongue, but he kept his mouth shut on them, for if he spoke them, Mina would be furious. She would turn from him, perhaps forever, and he was the only friend she had now, the only one who could see clearly the path that lay ahead of her. He swallowed the words, though they came nigh to choking him.

469

"What is this I hear of you restoring the old Temple of Duerghast?" Galdar asked, changing the subject.

Mina's face cleared. Her amber eyes glimmered with a glint of her former spirit. "That is where the ceremony will be held, Galdar. That is where the One God will make manifest her power. The ceremony will be held in the arena, and it will be magnificent, Galdar! Everyone will be there to worship the One God—her foes included."

Galdar's choked-down words were giving him a belly-ache. He felt sick again, and he remained sitting on the bed, saying nothing. He couldn't look at her, couldn't return her gaze, couldn't bear to see himself, that tiny being, held fast in the amber. Mina came to him, touched his hand. He kept his face averted.

"Galdar, I know that I hurt you. I know that your anger was really fear—fear for me." Her fingers closed fast over his hand. "You are the only one who ever cared about me, Galdar. About *me*, about Mina. The others care only for what I can do for them. They depend on me like children, and like children I must lead them and guide them.

"I cannot depend on them. But I can depend on you, Galdar. You flew into certain death with me, and you were not afraid. I need you now. I need your strength and your courage. Don't be angry with me anymore." She paused, then said, "Don't be angry with *her.*"

His thoughts went back to the night he'd seen Mina emerge from the storm, heralded by thunder, born of fire. He remembered the thrill when she touched his hand, this hand, the hand that was her gift. He had so many memories of her, each one linked with another to form a golden chain that bound them together. He lifted his head and looked at her, saw her human, small and fragile, and he was suddenly very much afraid for her.

He was so afraid that he could even lie for her.

"I am sorry, Mina," he said gruffly. "I was angry at—"

He paused. He had been going to say "Takhisis," but he was

loath to speak her name. He temporized. "I was angry at the One God. I understand now, Mina. Accept my apology."

She smiled, released his hand. "Thank you, Galdar. You must come with me to see the temple. There is still much work to be done to make ready for the ceremony, but I have lighted the altar and—"

Horns blared. Rumbling drumbeats rolled over her words.

"What is this?" Mina asked, walking to the tent flap and peering out, irritated. "What do they think they are doing?"

"That is the call to arms, Mina," said Galdar, alarmed. He hastily grabbed up his sword. "We must be under attack."

"That cannot be," she returned. "The One God sees all and hears all and knows all. I would have been warned. . . ."

"Nevertheless," Galdar pointed out, exasperated, "that *is* the call to arms."

"I don't have time for this," she said, annoyed. "There is too much work to be done in the temple."

The drumbeat grew louder, more insistent.

"I suppose I will have to deal with it." She stalked out of the tent, walking with haste, her irritation plain to be seen.

Galdar strapped on his sword, snatched up the padded leather vest that served him for armor, and hastened after her, fastening buckles as he ran.

The streets were awash in confusion, with some people staring stupidly in the direction of the walls, as if they could divine what was going on by just looking, while others were loudly demanding answers from people who were just as confused as they were. The levelheaded raced to their quarters to grab their weapons, reasoning that they'd arm themselves first and find out who they were fighting later.

Galdar opened up a path through the panic-clogged streets. His voice bellowed for people to make way. His strong arms picked up and tossed aside those who didn't heed his command. Mina followed closely behind him, and at the sight of her, the people cheered and called her name.

"Mina! Mina!"

Glancing back, Galdar saw her still annoyed by the interruption, still determined that this was nothing. They reached the West Gate. Just as the huge doors were thundering shut, Galdar caught a glimpse of one of their scouts—a blue dragon, who had landed outside the walls. The dragon's rider was talking to the Knight commanding the gate.

"What is going on? What is happening?" Mina demanded, shoving her way through the crowd to reach the officer. "Why did you sound the alarm? Who gave the order?"

Knight and rider both swung toward Mina. Both began talking at once. Soldiers and Knights crowded around her, adding to the chaos by trying to make their own voices heard.

"An army led by Solamnic Knights is on its way to Sanction, Mina," said the dragonrider, gasping for breath. "Accompanying the Knights is an army of elves, flying the standards of both Qualinesti and Silvanesti."

Mina cast an irate glance at the Knight in charge of the gate. "And for this you sound the alarm and start a panic? You are relieved of your command. Galdar, see that this man is flogged." Mina turned back to the dragonrider. Her lip curled. "How far away is this army? How many weeks' march?"

"Mina," the rider said, swallowing. "They are not marching. They ride dragons. Gold and silver dragons. Hundreds of them—"

"Gold dragons!" a man cried out, and before Galdar could stop him, the fool had dashed off, shouting out the news in a panicked voice. It would be all over the city in minutes.

Mina stared at the rider. Blood drained from her face, seemed to drain from her body. She had looked more alive when she was dying. Fearing she might collapse, Galdar put his hand out to steady her. She pushed him away.

"Impossible," she said through pale lips. "The gold and silver dragons have departed this world, never to return."

"I am sorry to contradict you, Mina," the rider said hesitantly, "but I saw them myself. We"—he gestured outside the walls, where his Blue stood, her flanks heaving, her wings and head drooping with exhaustion—"we were caught off-guard, nearly killed. We barely made it here alive."

Mina's Knights gathered tensely around her.

"Mina, what are your orders?"

"What is your command, Mina?"

Her pale lips moved, but she spoke to herself. "I must act now. The ceremony cannot wait."

"How far away are the dragons?" Galdar asked the rider.

The man glanced up fearfully at the sky. "They were right behind me. I am surprised you cannot see them yet—"

"Mina," said Galdar, "send out an order. Summon the red dragons and the blue. Many of Malys's old minions still remain close by. Summon them to fight!"

"They won't come," said the dragonrider.

Mina shifted her gaze to him. "Why not?"

He gestured with a jerk of his thumb over his shoulder to his own blue dragon. "They won't fight their own kind. Maybe later, the old animosities will return, but not now. We're on our own."

"What do we do, Mina?" her Knights demanded, their voices harsh and filled with fear. "What are your orders?"

Mina did not reply. She stood silent, her gaze abstracted. She did not hear them. She listened to another voice.

Galdar knew well whose voice she heard, and he meant that this time she should hear his. Grabbing her arm, Galdar gave her a shake.

"I know what you're thinking, and we can't do it, Mina," Galdar said. "We can't hold out against this assault! Dragonfear alone will unman most of our troops, make them unfit for battle. The walls, the moat of fire—these won't stop dragons."

"We have the army of the dead—"

"Bah!" Galdar snorted. "Golden dragons have no fear of the souls of dead humans or dead goblins or any of these other poor wretches whose spirits the One God has imprisoned. As for the Solamnics, they have fought the dead before, and this time they will be prepared to face the terror."

"Then what do you advise, Galdar?" Mina asked, her voice cold. "Since you are so certain we cannot win."

"I advise we get the hell out of here," Galdar said bluntly, and her Knights loudly echoed his opinion. "If we leave now, we can evacuate the city, escape into the mountains. This place is honeycombed with tunnels. The Lords of Doom have protected us before, they'll protect us again. We can retreat back to Jelek or Neraka."

"Retreat?" Mina glared at him, tried to wrench her arm from his grasp. "You are a traitor to even speak those words!"

He held onto her with grim determination. "Let the Solamnics have Sanction, Mina. We took it away from them once. We can take it away from them again. We still own Solamnia. Solanthus is ours, as is Palanthas."

"No, we don't," Mina said, struggling to free herself. "I ordered most of our forces to march here, to come to Sanction to be witness to the glory of the One God."

Galdar opened his mouth, snapped it shut.

"I did not think there would be dragons!" Mina cried out.

He saw the image of himself in her eyes growing smaller and smaller. He loosed his hold on her.

"We will not retreat," she stated.

"Mina—"

"Listen to me, every one of you." She gathered them together with a glance, all the tiny figures frozen in the amber eyes. "We must hold this city at all costs. When the ceremony is complete and the One God enters this world, no force on Krynn will be able to stand against her. She will destroy them all."

The officers stared at her, not moving. Some flinched and cast glances skyward. Galdar felt a twinge of fear twist his gut—the dragonfear, distant yet, but fast approaching.

"Well, what do wait for?" Mina demanded. "Return to your posts."

No one moved. No one cheered. No one spoke her name.

"You have your orders!" Mina shouted, her voice ragged. "Galdar, come with me."

She turned to leave. Her Knights did not move. They blocked her path with their bodies. She bore no weapon. She had not thought to bring one.

"Galdar," said Mina. "Kill any man who tries to stop me."

Galdar laid his hand on the hilt of his sword.

One by one, the Knights stepped aside, cleared a path.

Mina walked among them, her face cold as death.

"Where are you going?" Galdar demanded, following after her.

"To the temple. We have much to do and little time to do it."

"Mina," he said, his voice low and urgent in her ear, "you can't leave them to face this alone. For love of you, they will find the courage to stand and fight even golden dragons, but if you are not here—"

Mina halted.

"They do not fight for love of me!" Her voice trembled. "They fight for the One God!" She turned around to face her Knights. "Hear my words. You fight this battle for the One God. You must hold this city in the name of the One God. Any man who flees before the enemy will know the wrath of the One God."

Her Knights lowered their heads, turned away. They did not march proudly back to their posts, as they might once have done. They slunk back sullenly.

"What is the matter with them?" Mina asked, dismayed, confused.

"Once they followed you for love, Mina. Now they obey you as the whipped dog obeys—in fear of the lash," said Galdar. "Is this what you want?"

Mina bit her lip, seemed to waver in her decision, and Galdar hoped that she might refuse to heed the voice. That she would do what she knew to be honorable, knew to be right. She would remain loyal to her men, who had remained loyal to her through so much.

Mina's jaw set. The amber eyes hardened. "Let the curs run. I don't need them. I have the One God. I am going to the temple to prepare for the ceremony. Are you coming?" she demanded of

Galdar. "Or are you going to run away, too?"

He looked into the amber eyes and could no longer see himself. He could no longer see anyone. Her eyes were empty.

She did not wait for his answer. She stalked off. She did not look to see if he was following. She didn't care, one way or the other.

Galdar hesitated. Looking back at the West Gate, he saw the Knights gathered in knots, talking in low voices. He doubted very much if they were determining a strategy for battle. A babble of screams and cries rose from the streets as word spread that hundreds of golden and silver dragons were bearing down on Sanction. No one was acting to quell the terror. Each man thought only of himself now, and he had only one thought in his mind—to survive. Soon there would be rioting, as men and women devolved into wild beasts, bit and clawed and fought to save their own hides. In their miserable panic, they might well destroy themselves before the armies of their enemies ever arrived.

If I stay here on the walls, I might rally a few, Galdar thought. I might find some who would brave the horror and fight alongside me. I would die well. I would die with honor.

He watched Mina walking away, walking alone, except for that shadowy five-headed figure that hovered over her, surrounded her, cut her off from everyone who had ever loved her or admired her or cared about her.

"You great bitch!" Galdar muttered. "You won't get rid of me that easily."

Gripping his sword, he hastened after Mina.

Mina was wrong when she told Galdar that he was the only one who had ever cared for her. Another cared, cared deeply. Silvanoshei hurried after her, shoving and pushing his way through the crowds that now milled about in panic in the streets, trying to keep her in sight.

He had stayed in Sanction to hear some word of Mina. Silvanoshei's joy when he heard she was alive was heartfelt, even as her return plunged him once more into danger. People suddenly remembered having seen an elf walking about Sanction.

He was forced to go into hiding. A kender obligingly introduced Silvanoshei to the system of tunnels that criss-crossed beneath Sanction. Elves abhor living beneath the ground, and Silvanoshei could remain in the tunnels for only short periods of time before he was driven to the surface by a desperate need for air. He stole food to keep himself alive, stole a cloak with a hood and a scarf to wrap around his face, hide his elven features.

He lurked about the ruins of the totem, hoping to find a chance to talk to Mina, but he never saw her there. He grew fearful, wondered if she'd left the city or if she had fallen ill. Then he overheard a chance bit of gossip to the effect that she had moved out of the Temple of the Heart and had taken up residence in another temple, the ruined Temple of Duerghast that stood on the outskirts of Sanction.

Built to honor some false god dreamed up by a demented cult, the temple was notorious for having an arena where human sacrifices were sent to die for the entertainment of a cheering crowd. During the War of the Lance, Lord Ariakas had appropriated the temple, using its dungeons to torture and torment his prisoners.

The temple had an evil reputation, and there had been talk in recent days, during the reign of Hogan Bight, of razing it. Tremors had caused gigantic cracks to open in the walls, weakening the structure to the point where no one felt safe even going near it. The citizens of Sanction had decided to let the Lords of Doom complete the destruction.

Then came the news that Mina was planning to rebuild the temple, transform it into a place of worship of the One God.

The Temple of Duerghast lay on the other side of the moat of lava that surrounded Sanction. The temple could not be reached overland, not without bridging the moat. Therefore, Silvanoshei reasoned, Mina would be forced to enter the temple via one of the tunnels. He traipsed about the tunnel system, losing himself more than once, and at last found what he was searching for—a tunnel that ran beneath the curtain wall on the southern side of the city.

Silvanoshei had been planning to explore this tunnel when the alarm was raised. He saw the dragonrider fly overhead and land outside the West Gate. Guessing that Mina would come to take charge of the situation, Silvanoshei concealed himself in the crowds of people who were eager to see Mina. He pressed as close as he dared, hoping against hope just to catch a glimpse of her.

Then he saw her, surrounded by her Knights, speaking to the dragonrider. Suddenly one man broke from the group and raced into the crowd, shouting out that silver and gold dragons were coming, dragons ridden by Solamnic Knights. People swore and cursed and started to push and shove. Silvanoshei was jostled and nearly knocked down. Through it all, he fought to keep his eyes on her.

The news of dragons and Knights meant little to Silvanoshei. He thought of it only in terms of how this would affect Mina. He was certain she would lead the battle, and he feared that he would have no opportunity to talk to her. He was astonished beyond measure to see her turn around and walk off, abandoning her troops.

Their loss was his blessing.

Her voice carried to him clearly. "I am going to the temple to prepare for the ceremony."

At last, maybe he could find a way to speak to her.

Silvanoshei entered the tunnel he had found, hoping that his calculations were correct and that it led beneath the moat of fire to the Temple of Duerghast. Hope almost died when he found that the tunnel roof had partially collapsed. He made his way past the chunks of rock and soil, continued on, and eventually found a ladder that led to the surface.

He climbed swiftly, had sense enough to slow as he neared the top. A wooden trapdoor kept the tunnel opening concealed from those above. As he pushed against the door, his hand broke through the rotting wood. A cascade of dirt and splinters fell down around him. Cautiously, he peered out of the hole in the trapdoor. Bright sunshine half-blinded him. He blinked his eyes, waited for them to become accustomed to the light.

The Temple of Duerghast stood only a short distance away.

To reach the temple, he would have to cross a space of open ground. He would be visible from the walls of Sanction. Silvanoshei doubted if anyone would see him or pay attention to him. All eyes would be turned skyward.

Silvanoshei wormed his way out of the hole and ran across the open patch of ground, hid himself in a shadow cast by the temple's outer wall. Constructed of black granite blocks, the temple's curtain wall was built in the shape of a square. Two towers guarded the front entrance. Circling around the wall, hugging the building, he searched for some way inside. He came to one of the towers, and here he found two doors, one at either end of the wall.

Heavy slabs of iron controlled by winches served for gates. Although they were covered with rust, the iron gates remained in place and would probably still be standing when the rest of the temple fell down around them. He could not enter there, but he could enter through a part of the outer wall that had collapsed into a pile of rubble. The climb would be difficult, but he was nimble. He was certain he could manage.

He started toward the wall, then halted, frozen in the shadows. He had caught movement out of the corner of his eye.

Someone else had come to the Temple of Duerghast. A man stood before it, gazing at it. The man stood in the open, the sunshine pouring down on him. Silvanoshei must have been blind to have missed seeing him. Yet, he could have sworn that there had been no one there when he came around the corner.

Judging by his looks, the man was not a warrior. He was quite tall, above average height. He wore no sword, carried no bow slung across his shoulder. He was clad in brown woolen hose, a green and brown tunic, and tall leather boots. A cowl, brown in color, covered his head and shoulders. Silvanoshei could not see the man's face.

Silvanoshei fumed. What was this simpleton doing here? Nothing, by the looks of it, except gawking at the temple like a kender on holiday. He had no weapon, he wasn't a threat, yet Silvanoshei was reluctant to have the man see him. Silvanoshei was determined to talk to Mina, and for all he knew this man might be some sort of guard. Or perhaps this stranger was also waiting to speak to her. He had the look of someone waiting.

Silvanoshei wished the man away. Time was passing. He had to get inside. He had to talk to Mina. Still the man did not move.

At last, Silvanoshei decided he could wait no longer. He was a swift runner. He could outdistance the man, if the stranger gave chase, lose himself in the temple confines before the man figured out what had happened. Silvanoshei drew in a breath, ready to run.

The man turned his head. Drawing back his cowl, he looked straight at Silvanoshei.

The man was an elf.

Silvanoshei stared, riveted, unmoving. For a petrifying moment, he feared that Samar had tracked him down, but he recognized immediately that this was not Samar.

At first glance, the elf appeared young, as young as Silvanoshei. His body had the strength, the lithesome grace of youth. A second glance caused Silvanoshei to rethink his first. The elf's face was unmarred by time, yet in his expression held a gravity that was not youthful, had nothing to do with youth's hope and high spirits and joyful expectations. The eyes were bright as the eyes of youth, but their brilliance was shadowed, tempered by sorrow. Silvanoshei had the odd impression that this man knew him, but he could not place the strange elf at all.

The elf looked at Silvanoshei, then he looked away, turned his gaze back to the temple.

Silvanoshei took advantage of the elf's shift in attention to sprint to the opening in the wall. He climbed swiftly, one eye on the strange elf, who never moved. Silvanoshei dropped down over the side of the wall. He peered back through the rubble to see the elf still standing there, waiting.

Putting the stranger from his mind, Silvanoshei entered the ruined temple and set off in search of Mina.

30

For Love of Mina

ina fought her way through the crowded streets of Sanction. Her movement was hampered by the people who, at the sight of her, surged forward to touch her. They cried out to her in fear of the coming dragons. They begged her to save them.

"Mina, Mina!" they shouted, and the din was hateful to her.

She tried to block it out, tried to ignore them, tried to free herself from their clutching, clinging hands, but with every step she took, they gathered around her more thickly, calling out her name, repeating it over and over as a frantic litany against fear.

Another called her name. The voice of Takhisis, loud and insistent, urging her to make haste. Once the ceremony was complete, once Takhisis had entered the world and united the spiritual realm with the physical, the Dark Queen could take any form she chose, and in that form she would fight her enemies.

Let the foul Golds and the craven Silvers go up against the five-headed monster that she could become. Let the puny armies of the Knights and the elves battle the hordes of the dead that would rise up at her command.

Takhisis was glad that the wretched mage and his tool, the blind Silver, had freed the metallic dragons. She had been furious at the time, but now, in her calmer moments, she remembered that she was the only god on Krynn. Everything worked to her own ends, even the plots of her enemies.

Do what they might, they could never harm her. Every arrow they fired would turn to their own destruction, target their own hearts. Let them attack. This time she would destroy them all— knights, elves, dragons—destroy them utterly, wipe them out, crush them so that they would never rise up against her again. Then she would seize their souls, enslave them. Those who had fought her in life would serve her in death, serve her forever.

To accomplish this, Takhisis needed to be in the world. She controlled the door on the spiritual realm, but she could not open the door on the physical. She needed Mina for that. She had chosen Mina and prepared her for this one task. Takhisis had smoothed Mina's way, had removed Mina's enemies. Takhisis was so close to achieving her overweening ambition. She had no fear that the world might be snatched from her at the last moment. She was in control. No other challenged her. She was impatient, however. Impatient to begin the battle that would end in her final triumph.

She urged Mina to make haste. Kill these wretches, she commanded, if they will not get out of your way.

Mina grabbed a sword and raised it in the air. She no longer saw people. She saw open mouths, felt clutching hands. The living surrounded her, plucking at her, shrieking and gibbering, pressing their lips against her skin.

"Mina, Mina!" they cried, and their cries changed to screams and the hands fell away.

The street emptied, and it was only when she heard Galdar's horrified roar and saw the blood on her sword and on her hands and the bleeding bodies lying in the street that she realized what she had done.

"She commands me to hurry," Mina said, "and they wouldn't get out of my way."

"They are out of your way now," Galdar said.

Mina looked down at the bodies. Some she knew. Here was a soldier who had been with her since the siege of Sanction. He lay in a pool of blood. Her sword had run him through. She had some dim memory of him pleading with her to spare him.

Stepping over the dead, she continued on. She kept hold of the sword, though she had no skill in the use of such a weapon and she grasped it awkwardly, her hand gummed with blood.

"Walk ahead of me, Galdar," she ordered. "Clear the way."

"I don't know where we're going, Mina. The temple ruins lie outside the wall on the other side of the moat of fire. How do you get there from here?"

Mina pointed with the sword. "Stay on this street, follow the curtain wall. Directly across from the Temple of Duerghast is a tower. Inside the tower, a tunnel leads beneath the wall and underneath the moat to the temple."

They proceeded on, moving at a dead run.

"Make haste," Takhisis commanded.

Mina obeyed.

The first enemy dragons came into view, flying high over the mountains. The first waves of dragonfear began to affect Sanction's defenders. Sunlight glittered on gold and silver scales, glinted off the armor of the dragonriders. Only in the great wars of the past had this many dragons of light come together to aid humans and elves in their cause. The dragons flew in long lines—the swift-flying Silvers in the lead, the more ponderous Golds in the rear.

A strange sort of mist began to flow up over the walls, seep into the streets and alleyways. Galdar thought it odd that fog should arise suddenly on a sunny day, and then he saw suddenly that the mist had eyes and mouths and hands. The souls of the dead had been summoned to do battle. Galdar looked up through the chill mist, looked up into the blue sky. Sunlight flashed off the belly of a silver dragon, argent light so bright that it burned through the mists like sunshine on a hot summer day.

The souls fled the light, sought the shadows, slunk down alleyways or sought shelter in the shade cast by the towering walls.

Dragons do not fear the souls of dead humans, dead goblins, dead elves.

Galdar envisioned the blasts of fire breathed by the gold dragons incinerating all those who manned the walls, melting armor, fusing it to the living flesh as the men inside screamed out their lives in agony. The image was vivid and filled his mind, so that he could almost smell the stench of burning flesh and hear the death cries. His hands began to shake, his mouth grew dry.

"Dragonfear," he told himself over and over. "Dragonfear. It will pass. Let it pass."

He looked back at Mina to see how she was faring. She was pale, but composed. The empty amber eyes stared straight ahead, did not look up to the skies or to the walls from which men were starting to jump out of sheer panic.

The Silvers flew overhead, flying rapidly, flying low. These were the first wave and they did not attack. They were spreading fear, evoking panic, doing reconnaissance. The shadows of the gleaming wings sliced through the streets, sending people running mad with terror. Here and there, some mastered their fear, overcame it. A lone ballista fired. A couple of archers sent arrows arcing upward in a vain attempt at a lucky shot. For the most part, men huddled in the shadows of the walls and drew in shivering breaths and waited for it all to go away, just please go away.

The fear that descended on the population worked in Mina's favor. Those who had been clogging the streets ran terrified into their homes or shops, seeking shelter where no shelter existed, for the fire of the Golds could melt stone. But at least they left the streets. Mina and Galdar made swift progress.

Arriving at one of the guard towers that stood along Sanction's curtain wall, Mina yanked open a door at the tower's base.

The tower was sparsely inhabited, most of its defenders had fled. Those who were left, hearing the door bang open, peered fearfully down the spiral stairs. One called out in a cracked voice, "Who goes there?"

Mina did not deign to answer, and the soldiers did not dare come down to find out. Galdar heard their footsteps retreat farther down the battlements.

He grabbed a torch, fumbled to light it from a slowmatch burning in a tub. Mina took the torch from him and led the way down a series of dank stone stairs to what appeared to be a blank wall, through which she walked without hesitation. Either the wall was illusion, or the Dark Queen had caused the solid stone to dissolve. Galdar didn't know, and he had no intention of asking. He gritted his teeth and barged in after her, fully expecting to dash his brains out against the rock.

He entered a dark tunnel that smelled strongly of brimstone. The walls were warm to the touch. Mina had ranged far ahead of him, and he had to hurry to catch up. The tunnel was built for humans, not minotaurs. He was forced to run with his shoulders hunched and his horns lowered. The heat increased. He guessed that they were passing directly under the moat of fire. The tunnel looked to be ancient. He wondered who had built it and why, more questions he was never going to have answered.

The tunnel ended at yet another wall. Galdar was relieved to see that Mina did not walk through this wall. She entered a small door. He squeezed in after her, a tight fit, to find himself in a prison cell.

Rats screeched and chittered at the light, scrambled to escape. The floor was alive with some sort of crawling insects that swarmed into the nooks and crevices of the crumbing stone walls. The cell door hung on a single rusted hinge.

Mina left the cell, that opened up into a corridor. Galdar caught a glimpse of other rooms extending off the main hall and he knew where he was—the Temple of Duerghast.

Thinking back to what he had heard about this temple, he guessed that these were the torture chambers where once the prisoners of the dragonarmy were "questioned." The light of his torch did not penetrate far into the shadows, for which he was grateful.

He hated this place, wished himself away from it, wished himself anywhere but here, even in the city above, though that city might be crawling with gold dragons. The screams of the dying echoed in these dark corridors, the walls were wet with tears and blood.

Mina looked neither to the right nor the left. The light of her torch illuminated a flight of stairs, leading upward. Climbing those stairs, Galdar had the feeling he was clawing his way back from death. They reached ground level, the main part of the temple.

Cracks had opened in the walls, and Galdar was able to catch a whiff of fresh air. Though it smelled strongly of sulfur from the moat of fire, the smell up here was better than what he'd smelled below. He drew in a deep breath.

Rays of dust-clouded sunlight filtered through the cracks. Galdar started to douse the torch, but Mina stopped him.

"Keep it lit," she told him. "We will need it where we are going."

"Where are we going?" he asked, fearing she would say the altar room.

"To the arena."

She led the way through the ruins, moving swiftly and without hesitation. He noted that piles of rubble had been cleared aside, opening up previously clogged corridors.

"Did you do this work yourself, Mina?" Galdar asked, marveling.

"I had help," she replied.

He guessed the nature of that help and was sorry he'd asked.

Unlike humans, Galdar was not disgusted to hear a temple had an open-air arena where people would come to witness blood sports. Such contests are a part of a minotaur's heritage, used to settle everything from family feuds to marital disputes to the choosing of a new emperor. He had been surprised to find that humans considered such contests barbaric. To him, the malicious, backstabbing political intrigue in which humans indulged was barbaric.

The arena was open to the air and was visible from the highest walls of Sanction. Galdar had noted it before with some interest as being the only arena he'd ever seen in human lands. The arena was built into the side of the mountain. The floor was below ground level and filled with sand. Rows of benches, carved into the mountain's slope, formed a semicircle around the floor. The arena was small by minotaur standards, and was in a state of ruin and decay. Wide cracks had opened up among the benches, holes gaped in the floor.

Galdar followed Mina through dusty corridors until they came to a large entryway that opened out onto the arena. Mina walked through the entryway. Galdar followed and went from dusty daylight to darkest night.

He stopped dead, blinking his eyes, suddenly afraid that he'd been struck blind. He could smell the familiar odors of the outdoors, including the sulfur of the moat of fire. He could feel the wind upon his face. He should be feeling the warmth of the sun on his face, as well, for only seconds before he had been able to see sunshine and blue sky through the cracks in the ceiling. Looking up, he saw a black sky, starless, cloudless. He shuddered all over, took an involuntary step backward.

Mina grabbed hold of his hand. "Don't be afraid," she said softly. "You stand in the presence of the One God."

Considering their last meeting together, Galdar did not find reassuring the knowledge that he was in Takhisis's presence. He was more determined than ever to leave. He had made a mistake in coming here. He had come out of love for Mina, not love for Takhisis. He did not belong here, he was not welcome.

Stairs led from the ground floor into the arena.

Mina let go of his hand. She was in haste, already hurrying down the stairs, certain he would follow. The words to say goodbye to her clogged in his throat. Not that there were any words that would make a difference. She would hate him for what he was going to do, detest him. Nothing he could say would change that. He turned to leave, turned to go back into the sunlight, even though that meant the dragons and death, when he heard Mina give a startled cry.

Acting instinctively, fearing for her life, Galdar drew his sword and clattered down the stairs.

"What are you doing here, Silvanoshei? Skulking about in the shadows like an assassin?" Mina demanded.

Her tone was cold, but her voice trembled. The light of the torch she held wavered in her shaking hand. She'd been caught off-guard, taken unawares.

Galdar recognized Mina's besotted lover, the elf king. The elf's face was deadly pale. He was thin and wan, his fine clothes tattered, ragged. He no longer had that wasted, desperate look about him, however. He was calm and composed, more composed than Mina.

The word "assassin" and the young man's strange composure caused Galdar to lift his sword. He would have brought it down upon the young elf's head, splitting him in two, but Mina stopped him.

"No, Galdar," she said, and her voice was filled with contempt. "He is no threat to me. He can do nothing to harm me. His foul blood would only defile the sacred soil on which we stand."

"Be gone then, scum," said Galdar, reluctantly lowering his weapon. "Mina gives you your wretched life. Take it and leave."

"Not before I say something," said Silvanoshei with quiet dignity. "I am sorry, Mina. Sorry for what has happened to you."

"Sorry for me?" Mina regarded him with scorn. "Be sorry for yourself. You fell into the One God's trap. The elves will be annihilated, utterly, finally, completely. Thousands have already fallen to my might, and thousands more will follow until all who oppose me have perished. Because of you, because of your weakness, your people will be wiped out. And *you* feel sorry for *me?*"

"Yes," Silvanoshei said. "I was not the only one to fall into the trap. If I had been stronger, I might have been able to save you, but I was not. For that, I am sorry."

Mina stared at him, the amber of her eyes hardening around him, as if she would squeeze the life out of him.

He stood steadfast, his eyes filled with sorrow.

Mina turned away in contempt. "Bring him," she ordered Galdar. "He will be witness to the end of all that he holds dear."

"Mina, let me slay him—" Galdar began.

"Must you always oppose me?" Mina demanded, rounding on him angrily. "I said bring him. Have no fear. He will not be the only witness. All the enemies of the One God will be here to see her triumph. Including you, Galdar."

Turning, she entered the door that led into the arena.

The hackles rose on the back of Galdar's neck. His hands were wet with sweat.

"Run," he said abruptly to the elf. "I will not stop you. Go on, get out of here."

Silvanoshei shook his head. "I stay as do you. We both stay for the same reason."

Galdar grunted. He stood in the doorway, debating, though he already knew what he would do. The elf was right. They both stayed for the same reason.

Gritting his teeth, Galdar stalked through the door and entered the arena. Glancing back to see if the elf king was following, Galdar was astonished to see another elf standing behind Silvanoshei.

Ye gods, the place is crawling with them! Galdar thought.

The elf looked fixedly at Galdar, who had the sudden uneasy feeling that this elf with the young face and the old eyes could read the thoughts of his head and of his heart.

Galdar didn't like this. He didn't trust this new elf, and he hesitated, wondering if he should go back to deal with him.

The elf stood calmly, waiting.

All the enemies of the One God will be here to witness her triumph.

Assuming that this was just one more, Galdar shrugged and entered the arena. He was forced to follow the light of Mina's torch, for he could not see her in the darkness.

31

The Battle of Sanction

The silver dragons flew low over Sanction, not bothering to use their lethal breath weapons, relying on fear alone to drive away the enemy. Gerard had flown on dragonback before, but he'd never flown into battle, and he had often wondered why any person would risk his neck fighting in the air when he could be standing on solid ground. Now, experiencing the exhilaration of a diving rush upon Sanction's defenses, Gerard realized that he could never again go back to the heave and crush and heat of battle on land.

He yelled a Solamnic war cry as he and his Silver dived down upon the hapless defenders, not because he thought they would hear him, but for the sheer joy of the flight and the sight of his enemy fleeing before him in screaming panic. All around him, the other Knights yelled and shouted. Elven archers seated on the backs of golden dragons loosed their arrows into the throngs of soldiers trying desperately to escape the glittering death that circled above them.

The river of souls swirled around Gerard, seeking to stop him, seeking to wrap their chill arms around him, submerge him, blind him. But the army of the dead was leaderless now. They had no one to give them orders, no one to direct them. The wings of the golden and silver dragons sliced through the river of souls, shredding them like the rays of the sun shred the morning mists that drift along the riverbank. Gerard saw the clutching hands and pleading mouths of the souls whirl about him. They no longer inspired terror. Only pity.

He looked away, looked back to the task at hand, and the dead vanished.

When most of the defenders had been swept from the walls, the dragons landed in the valleys that surrounded Sanction. The elven and human warriors who had been riding on their backs dismounted. They formed into ranks, began to march upon the city, while Gerard and the other dragonriders continued to patrol the skies.

The Silvanesti and Qualinesti placed their flags on a small knoll in the center of the valley. Alhana would have liked to lead the assault on Sanction, but she was the titular ruler of the Silvanesti nation and reluctantly agreed with Samar that her place was in the rear, there to give orders and guide the attack.

"I will be the one to rescue my son," she said to Samar. "I will be the one to free him from his prison."

"My Queen—" he began, his expression grave.

"Do not say it, Samar," Alhana commanded. "We will find Silvanoshei alive and well. We will."

"Yes, Your Majesty."

He left her, standing on the hill, the colors of their tattered flag forming a faded rainbow above her head.

Gilthas stood beside her. Like Alhana, he would have liked to be among the warriors, but he knew that an inept and unpracticed swordsman is a danger to himself and everyone unfortunate enough to be near him. Gilthas watched his wife race to battle. He could pick her out of a crowd of thousands by her wild, curling mass of hair and by the fact that she would always be in the vanguard along with her Kagonesti warriors, shouting their ancient war cries and brandishing their weapons, challenging the enemy to quit skulking behind the walls and come out and fight.

He feared for her. He always feared for her, but he knew better than to express that fear to her or to try to keep her safe by his side. She would take that as an insult and rightly so. She was a warrior with a warrior's heart and a warrior's instincts and a warrior's courage. She would not be easy to kill. His heart reached out to her, and as if she felt his love touch her, she turned her head, lifted her sword, and saluted him.

He waved back, but she did not see him. She had turned her face toward battle. Gilthas could do nothing now but await the outcome.

Lord Tasgall led the Knights of Solamnia from the back of a silver dragon. He still smarted from the defeat of Solanthus. Remembering Mina's taunts from the walls as she stood victorious in the city, he was looking forward to seeing her once again upon a wall—her head on a pike on that wall.

A few of the enemy had managed to overcome the dragonfear and were mounting a defense. Archers regained the battlements, launched a volley of arrows at the silver dragon carrying Lord Tasgall. A golden dragon spotted the volley, breathed on it, and the arrows burst into flame. Lord Tasgall guided his silver dragon into the heart of Sanction.

The armies in the valley marched up to the moat of fire that guarded the city. The silver dragons breathed their frost-breath on the moat, cooling the lava and causing it to harden into black rock. Steam rose into the air, providing cover for the advancing armies as a few staunch defenders began to fire at them from the towers.

Elven archers halted to fire, sending wave after wave of arrows at the enemy. Under cover of the fire, Lord Ulrich led his men-at-arms in a rush upon the walls. A few catapults were still in operation, sent a boulder or two crashing down, but they were fired in panicked haste. Their aim was off. The boulders bounded harmlessly away. The soldiers flung grappling hooks up over the walls, began to scale them.

A few daring bands of elven archers dropped down off the backs of the low-circling dragons, landing on the roofs of the houses inside Sanction. From this vantage point, they fired their arrows into the backs of the defenders, wreaking further havoc.

They had not been able to bring with them a battering ram to smash open the gates, but as it turned out, they had no need. A golden dragon settled in front of the West Gate and, paying small heed to the arrows being fired at her from the battlements, breathed a jet of flame on the gates. The gates disintegrated into flaming cinders. With a triumphant cry, the humans and elves stormed into Sanction.

Once inside the city, the battle became more intense, for the defenders, faced now with certain death, lost their fear of the dragons and fought grimly. The dragons could do little to assist, afraid of harming their own forces.

Still, Gerard guessed that it would not be long before the day was theirs. He was about to order his dragon to set him down, so that he could join the fighting when he heard Odila shout his name.

As the blind silver dragon, Mirror, could not join in the assault, he and Odila had volunteered to act as scouts, directing the attackers to places they were needed. Calling out to Gerard, she pointed northward. A large force of black-armored Knights of Neraka and foot soldiers had managed to escape the city and were retreating toward the Lords of Doom. They were not in panicked flight but marched in ragged ranks.

Loath to let them escape, knowing that once they were in the mountains, they would be impossible to ferret out, Gerard urged his own dragon to fly to intercept them. A flash of metal from one of the mountain passes caught his eye.

Another army was marching out of the mountains to the east. These soldiers marched in rigid order, moving swiftly down the mountainside like some enormous, deadly, shining-scaled snake.

Even from this distance, Gerard recognized the force for what it was—an army of draconians. He could see the wings on their backs, wings that lifted them up and carried them easily over any obstacle in their way. Sunlight shone on their heavy armor, gleamed off their helms and their scaled skin.

Draconians were coming to Sanction's rescue. A thousand or more. The army of escaping Dark Knights saw the draconians heading in their direction and broke into cheers so loud that Gerard could hear them from the air. The retreating army of Dark Knights shifted about, intending to regroup and return to the attack with their new allies.

The draconians moved rapidly, racing down the sides of the mountains. They would soon be over Sanction's walls, and once they were in the city, the dragons could do nothing to stop them for fear of harming the Knights and elves fighting in the streets.

Gerard's Silver was preparing to dive to the attack, when, staring in astonishment, Gerard bellowed an order for his dragon to halt.

Wheeling smartly, the draconians smashed into the astonished ranks of Dark Knights that had, only moments before, been hailing the draconians as friends.

The draconians made short work of the beleagured Knights. The force crumbled under the attack, and as Gerard watched, it disintegrated. The job done, the draconians reformed again into orderly ranks and marched on toward Sanction.

Gerard had no idea what was going on. How was it possible that draconians should be allies of Solamnics and elves? He wondered if he should try to halt their march, or if he should allow the draconians to enter the city. Common sense voted for one, his heart held out for the other.

The decision was taken out of his hands, for the next instant, the city of Sanction, the snaking lines of marching draconians, the silver wings, head, and mane of the dragon on which he rode dissolved before his eyes.

Once again, he experienced the dizzying, stomach-turning motion of a journey through the corridors of magic.

Gerard found himself seated on a hard stone bench under a night-black sky, staring down into an arena that was illuminated by a chill, white light. The light had no source that he could see at first, but then he realized with a shudder that it emanated from the souls of the countless dead who overflowed the arena, so that it seemed to him that he and the arena and everyone in it floated upon a vast, unquiet ocean of death.

Gerard looked around to see Odila, staring, open-mouthed. He saw Lord Tasgall and Lord Ulrich seated together, with Lord Siegfried some distance off. Alhana Starbreeze occupied a seat, as did Samar, both staring about in anger and bewilderment. Gilthas was present, with his wife, the Lioness, and Planchet.

Friend and foe alike were here. Captain Samuval sat in the stands, looking dismayed and baffled. Two draconians sat there, one a large bozak wearing a golden chain around his neck, the other a sivak in full battle regalia. The bozak looked stern, the sivak uneasy. More than one person in that crowd had been snatched bodily from the fray. Their faces flushed and hot, spattered with blood, they stared about in amazed confusion. The body of the wizard Dalamar was here, sitting on a bench, staring at nothing.

The dead made no sound, and neither did the living. Gerard opened his mouth and tried to call out to Odila, only to discover that he had no voice. An unseen hand stopped his tongue, pressed him down into his seat so that he could not move except as the hand guided him. He could see only what he was meant to see and nothing more.

The thought came to him that he was dead, that he'd been struck down by an arrow in the back, perhaps, and that he'd been taken to this place where the dead congregated. His fear subsided. He could feel his heart beating, hear the blood pounding in his ears. He could clench his hands into fists, dig his nails into his flesh and feel pain. He could shuffle his feet. He could feel terror, and he knew then that he wasn't dead. He was a prisoner, brought here against his will for some purpose that he could only assume was a horrible one.

Silent and unmoving as the dead, the living were constrained to stare down into the eerily lit arena.

The figure of a dragon appeared. Ephemeral, insubstantial, five heads thrust hideously from a single neck. Immense wings formed a canopy that covered the arena, blotting out hope. The huge tail coiled around all who sat in the dread shadow of the wings. Ten eyes stared in all directions, looking forward and behind, seeing into every heart, searching for the darkness within. Five mouths gnawed hungrily, finding the darkness and feeding upon it.

The five mouths opened and gave forth a silent call that split the eardrums of all listening, so that they gritted their teeth against the pain and fought back tears.

At the call, Mina entered the arena.

She wore the black armor of the Knights of Neraka. The armor did not shine in the eerie light but was one with the darkness of the dragon's wings. She wore no helm, and her face glimmered ghostly white. She carried in her hand a dragonlance. Behind her, almost lost in the shadows, stood the minotaur, faithful guard at her back.

Mina faced the silent crowd in the stands. Her gaze encompassed both the dead and the living.

"I am Mina," she called out. "The chosen of the One God."

She paused, as if waiting for the cheers to which she'd become accustomed. None spoke, not the living, not the dead. Their voices stolen, they watched in silence.

"Know this," Mina resumed, and her voice was cold and commanding. "The One God is the One God for now and forever. No others will come after. You will worship the One God now and forever. You will serve the One God now and forever, in death as in life. Those who serve faithfully will be rewarded. Those who rebel will be punished. This day, the One God makes manifest her power. This day, the One God enters the world in physical form and thus joins together the immortal with the mortal. Free to move between both of them at will, the One God will rule both."

Mina lifted up the dragonlance. Once lovely to look upon, the shining silver lance glimmered cold and bleak, its point stained black with blood.

"I give this as proof of the One God's power. I hold in my hand the fabled dragonlance. Once a weapon of the enemies of the One God, the dragonlance has become her weapon. The dragon Malystryx died on the point of the dragonlance, died by the will of the One God. The One God fears nothing. In token of this, I shatter the dragonlance."

Grasping the lance in both hands, Mina brought it down upon her bent knee. The lance snapped as if it were a long-dead and dried-up stick, broken in twain. Mina tossed the pieces contemptuously over her shoulder. The pieces landed on the sandy floor of the arena. Their silver light flickered briefly, valiantly. The dragon's five heads spat upon them, the dragon's breath smothered them. Their light diminished and died.

The living and the dead watched in silence.

Galdar watched in silence.

He stood behind Mina, guarding her back, for somewhere in the darkness lurked that strange elf, not to mention the wretch, Silvanoshei. Galdar had not much fear of the latter, but he was determined that no one should get past him. No one would accost Mina in this, her hour of triumph.

This will be her hour, Galdar told himself. She will be honored. Takhisis can do no less for her. He told himself that repeatedly, yet fear gnawed at him.

For the first time, Galdar witnessed the true power of Queen Takhisis. He watched in awe to see the stadium fill with people, taken prisoner in the midst of their lives and brought here to watch her victorious entry into the mortal realm. He looked in awe at her dragon form, her vast wingspan blotting out the light of hope, bringing eternal night to the world.

He realized then that he had discounted her, and his soul sank to its knees before her. He was a rebellious slave, one who had tried foolishly to rise above his place. He had learned his lesson. He would be a slave always, even after death. He could accept his fate because here, in the presence of the Dark Queen's full might and majesty, he understood that he deserved nothing else.

But not Mina. Mina was not born to be a slave. Mina was born to rule. She had proven herself, proven her loyalty. She had walked through blood and fire and never blanched, never swerved in her unwavering belief. Let Takhisis do with him what she would, let her devour his very soul. So long as Mina was honored and rewarded, Galdar would be content.

"The foes of the One God are vanquished," Mina cried. "Their weapons are destroyed. None can stop her triumphant entry into the world."

Mina raised up her hands, her amber eyes lifted to the dragon. "Your Majesty, I have always adored you, worshiped you. I pledged my life to your service, and I stand ready to honor that pledge. Through my fault, you lost the body of Goldmoon, the body you would have inhabited. I offer my own. Take my life. Use me as your vessel. Thus, I prove my faith!"

Galdar gasped, appalled. He wanted to stop this madness, wanted to stop Mina, but though he roared his protest, his words came out a silent scream that no one heard.

The five heads gazed down on Mina.

"I accept your sacrifice," said Queen Takhisis.

Galdar lunged forward and stood still. He raised his arm and it didn't move. Bound by darkness, he could do nothing but watch to see all he had ever loved and honored destroyed.

Clouds, black and ghastly and shot with lightning, rolled down from the Lords of Doom. The clouds boiled around the Dragon Queen, obscuring her from view. The clouds swirled and churned, raised a whipping wind that buffeted Galdar with bruising force, drove him to his knees.

Mina's prayer, Mina's faith unlocked the prison door.

The storm clouds transformed into a chariot, drawn by five dragons. Standing in the chariot, her hand on the reins, was Queen Takhisis, in woman's form.

She was beautiful, her beauty fell and terrible to look upon. Her face was cold as the vast, frozen wastelands to the south, where a man perishes in an instant, his breath turning to ice in his lungs. Her eyes were the flames of the funeral pyre. Her nails were talons, her hair the long and ragged hair of the corpse. Her armor was black fire. At her side, she wore a sword perpetually stained with blood, a sword used to sever the souls from their bodies.

Her chariot hung in the air, the wings of the five dragons fanning, keeping it aloft. Takhisis left the chariot, descended to the arena floor. She trod on the lightning bolts, the storm clouds were her cloak, trailing behind her.

Takhisis walked toward Mina. The five dragons lifted their heads, cried out a paean of triumph.

Galdar could not move, he could not save her. The wind beat at him with such force that he could not even lift his head. He cried out to Mina, but his voice was whipped away by the raging wind, and his cry went unheard.

Mina smiled a tremulous smile. "My Queen," she whispered.

Takhisis stretched out her taloned hand.

Mina stood, unflinching.

Takhisis reached for Mina's heart, to make that heart her own. Takhisis reached for Mina's soul, to snatch it from her body and cast it into oblivion. Takhisis reached out to fill Mina's body with her own immortal essence.

Takhisis reached out, but her hand could not touch Mina.

Mina looked startled, confused. Her body began to tremble. She reached out her hand to her Queen, but could not touch her.

Takhisis glared. The eyes of flame filled the arena with the hideous light of her anger.

"Disobedient child!" she cried. "How dare you oppose me?"

"I do not!" Mina gasped, shivering. "I swear to you—"

"She does not oppose you. I do," said a voice.

The strange elf walked past Galdar.

The wind of the Dark Queen's fury howled around the elf and struck at him. Her lightning flared over him and sought to burn him. Her thunder boomed and tried to crush him. The elf was bowed by the winds, but he kept walking. He was knocked down by the lightning, but he rose again and kept walking. Undaunted, unafraid, he came to stand before the Queen of Darkness.

"Paladine! My dear brother!" Takhisis spat the words. "So you have found your misplaced world." She shrugged. "You are too late. You cannot stop me."

Amused, she waved her hand toward the gallery. "Find a seat. Be my guest. I am glad you came. Now you can witness my triumph."

"You are wrong, Sister," the elf said, his voice silver, ringing. "We can stop you. You know how we can stop you. It is written in the book. We all agreed."

The flame of the Dark Queen's eyes wavered. The taloned fingers twitched. For an instant, her crystalline beauty was marred with doubt, anxiety. Only for an instant. Her doubts vanished. Her beauty was restored.

She smiled.

"You would not do that to me, Brother," Takhisis said, regarding him with scorn. "The great and puissant Paladine would never make the sacrifice. "

"You misjudge me, Sister. I already have."

The elf thrust his hand into a pouch he wore at his side and drew out a small knife, a knife that had once belonged to a kender of his acquaintance.

Paladine drew the knife across the palm of his hand.

Blood oozed from the wound, dripped onto the floor of the arena.

"The balance must be maintained," he said. "I am mortal. As are you."

Storm clouds, dragons, lightning, chariot, all disappeared. The sun shone bright in the blue sky. The seats in the gallery were suddenly empty, except for the gods.

They sat in judgment, five on the side of light: Mishakal, gentle goddess of healing; Kiri-Jolith, beloved of the Solamnic Knights; Majere, friend of Paladine, who came from Beyond; Habakkuk, god of the sea; Branchala, whose music soothes the heart.

Five took the side of darkness: Sargonnas, god of vengeance, who looked unmoved on the fall of his consort; Morgion, god of disease; Chemosh, lord of the undead, angered at her intrusion in what had once been his province; Zeboim, who blamed Takhisis for the death of her loved son, Ariakan; Hiddukel, who cared only that the balance be maintained.

Six stood between: Gilean, who held the book; Sirrion, god of nature; Shinare, his mate, god of commerce; Reorx, the forger of the world; Chislev, goddess of the woodland; Zivilyn, who once more saw past, present and future.

The three children, Solinari, Nuitari, Lunitari, stood together, as always.

One place, on the side of light, was empty.

One place, on the side of darkness, was empty.

Takhisis cursed them. She screamed in rage, crying out with one voice now, not five, and her voice was the voice of a mortal. The fire of her eyes that had once scorched the sun dwindled to the flicker of the candle flame that may be blown out with a breath. The weight of her flesh and bone dragged her down from the ethers. The thudding of her heart sounded loud in her ears, every beat telling her that some day that beating would stop and death would come. She had to breathe or suffocate. She had to work to draw one breath after the other. She felt the pangs of hunger that she had never known and all the other pains of this weak and fragile body. She, who had traversed the heavens and roamed among the stars, stared down with loathing at the two feet on which she now must plod.

Lifting her eyes, that were gritty with sand and burning with fury, Takhisis saw Mina, standing before her, young, strong, beautiful.

"You did this," Takhisis raved. "You connived with them to

bring about my downfall. You wanted them to sing your name, not my own!"

Takhisis drew her sword and lunged at Mina. "I may be mortal, but I can still deal death!"

Galdar gave a bellowing roar. He leaped to stop the blow, jumped in front of Mina to shield her with his body, raised his sword to defend her.

The Dark Queen's blade swept down in a slashing arc. The blade severed Galdar's sword arm, hacked it off below the shoulder.

Arm, hand, sword fell at his feet, lay there in a widening pool of his own blood. He fell to his knees, fought the pain and shock that were trying to rob him of his senses.

The Dark Queen lifted her sword and held it poised above Mina's head.

Mina said softly, "Forgive me," and stood braced for the blow.

His own life ebbing away, Galdar was about to make a desperate lunge, when something smote him from behind. Galdar looked up with dimming eyes to see Silvanoshei standing over him.

The elf king held in his hand the broken fragment of the dragonlance. He threw the lance, threw it with the strength of his anguish and his guilt, threw it with the strength of his fear and his love.

The lance struck Takhisis, lodged in her breast.

She stared down in shock to see the lance protruding from her flesh. Her fingers moved to touch the bright, dark blood welling from the terrible wound. She staggered, started to fall.

Mina sprang forward with a wild cry of grief and love. She clasped the dying queen in her arms.

"Don't leave me, Mother," Mina cried. "Don't leave me here alone!"

Takhisis ignored her. Her eyes fixed upon Paladine, and in them her hatred burned, endless, eternal.

"If I have lost everything, so have you. The world in which you took such delight can never go back to the way it was. I have done that much, at least."

Blood frothed upon the queen's lips. She coughed, struggled to draw a final breath. "Someday you will know the pain of death. Worse than that, Brother"—Takhisis smiled, grimly, derisively, as the shadows clouded her eyes—"you will know the pain of life."

Her breath bubbled with blood. Her body shuddered, and her hands fell limp. Her head lolled back on Mina's cradling arm. The eyes fixed, stared into the night she had ruled so long and that she would rule no more.

Mina clasped the dead queen to her breast, rocked her, weeping. The rest, Galdar, the strange elf, the gods, were silent, stunned. The only sound was Mina's harsh sobs. Silvanoshei, white-lipped and ashen-faced, laid a hand upon her shoulder.

"Mina, she was going to kill you. I couldn't let her. . . ."

Mina lifted her tear-ravaged face. Her amber eyes were hot, liquid, burned when they touched his flesh.

"I wanted to die. I would have died happily, gratefully, for I would have died serving her. Now, I live and she is gone and I have no one. No one!"

Her hand, wet with the blood of her queen, grasped Takhisis's sword.

Paladine sought to intercede, to stop her. An unseen hand shoved him off balance, sent him tumbling into the sand. A voice thundered from the heavens.

"We will have our revenge, Mortal," said Sargonnas.

Mina plunged the sword into Silvanoshei's stomach.

The young elf gasped, stared at her in astonishment.

"Mina . . ." His pallid lips formed the word. He had no voice to speak it. His face contorted in pain.

Furious, grim-faced, Mina thrust harder, drove the sword deeper. She let him hang, impaled on the blade, for a long moment, while she looked at him, let the amber eyes harden over him. Satisfied that he was dying, she yanked the sword free.

Silvanoshei slid down the blade that was smeared with his blood and crumpled into the sand.

Clutching the bloody sword, Mina walked over to Paladine, who was slowly picking himself up off the floor of the arena.

Mina gazed at him, absorbed him into the amber. She tossed the sword of Takhisis at his feet.

"You *will* feel the pain of death. But not yet. Not now. So my Queen wished it, and I obey her last wishes. But know this, wretch. In the face of every elf I meet, I will see your face. The life of every elf I take will be your life. And I will take many . . . to pay for the one."

She spat at him, spat into his face. She turned to the gods, regarded them in defiance. Then Mina knelt beside the body of her queen. She kissed the cold forehead. Lifting the body in her arms, Mina carried her dead from the Temple of Duerghast.

All was silent in the arena, silent except for Mina's departing footfalls. Galdar laid down his head in the sand that was warm from the sunshine. He was very tired. He could rest now, though, for Mina was safe. She was safe at last.

Galdar closed his eyes and began the long journey into darkness. He had not gone far, when he found his path blocked.

Galdar looked up to see an enormous minotaur. The minotaur stood tall as the mountain on which the red dragon had perished. His horns brushed the stars, his fur was jet black. He wore a leather harness, trimmed in pure, cold silver.

"Sargas!" Galdar whispered. Clutching his bleeding stump, he stumbled to his knees and bowed his head. His horns touched the ground.

"Rise, Galdar," said the god, his voice booming across the heavens. "I am pleased with you. In your need, you turned to me."

"Thank you, great Sargas," said Galdar, not daring to rise, tentatively lifting his head.

"In return for your faith, I restore your life," said Sargas. "I give you your life and your sword arm."

"Not my arm, great Sargas," Galdar pleaded, the pain burning hot in his breast. "I accept my life, and I will live it to honor you, but the arm is gone and I do not want it back."

Sargas was displeased. "The minotaur nation has at last thrown off the fetters that have bound us for so many centuries. We are breaking out of the islands where we have long been imprisoned and moving to take our rightful place upon this continent. I need gallant warriors such as yourself, Galdar. I need them whole, not maimed."

"I thank you, great Sargas," said Galdar humbly, "but, if it is all the same to you, I will learn to fight with my left hand."

Galdar tensed, waited in fear of the god's wrath. Hearing nothing, Galdar risked a peep.

Sargas smiled. His smile was grudging, but it was a smile. "Have it your way, Galdar. You are free to determine your own fate."

Galdar gave a long, deep sigh. "For that, great Sargas," he said, "I do truly thank you."

Galdar blinked his eyes, lifted his muzzle from the wet sand. He couldn't remember where he was, couldn't imagine what he was doing lying here, taking a nap, in the middle of the day. Mina would need him. She would be angry to find him lazing about. He jumped to his feet and reached instinctively for the sword that hung at his waist.

He had no sword. No hand to grasp it. His severed arm lay in the sand at his feet. He looked at where the arm had been, looked at the blood in the sand, and memory returned.

Galdar was healthy, except for his missing right arm. The stump was healed. He turned to thank the god, but the god was gone. All the gods were gone. No one remained in the arena except the body of the elf king and the strange elf with the young face and the ancient eyes.

Slowly, clumsily, fumbling with his left hand, Galdar picked up his sword. He shifted the sword belt so that he wore it now on his right hip, and, after many clumsy tries, he finally managed to return the sword to its sheath. The weapon didn't feel natural there, wasn't comfortable. He'd get used to it, though. This time, he'd get used to it.

The air was not as warm as he had remembered it. The sun dipped down behind the mountain, casting shadows of coming night. He would have to hurry, if he was going to find her. He would have to leave now, while there was still daylight left.

"You are a loyal friend, Galdar," said Paladine, as the minotaur stalked past him.

Galdar grunted and trudged on, following the trail of her footprints, the trail of her queen's blood.

For love of Mina.

32

The Age of Mortals

he fight for the city of Sanction did not last long. By night-fall, the city had surrendered. It would have probably surrendered much sooner, but there was no one willing to make the decision.

In vain, the Dark Knights and their soldiers called out Mina's name. She did not answer, she did not come, and they realized at last that she was not going to come. Some were bitter, some were angry. All felt betrayed. Knowing that they if they survived the battle they would be executed or imprisoned, a few Knights fought on. Most fought because they were trapped or cornered by the advancing enemy.

Some had decided to act on Galdar's advice and tried to find refuge in the caves of the Lords of Doom. These formed the force that had run into the army of draconians. Thinking that they had found an ally, the Dark Knights had been prepared to halt their retreat, turn around to try to retake the city. Their shock when the draconians smashed into them had been immense but short-lived.

Who these strange draconians were and why they came to the aid of elves and Solamnics would never be known. The draconian army did not enter Sanction. They held their position outside the city until they saw the flag of the Dark Knights torn down and the banners of the Qualinesti, the Silvanesti, and the Solamnic nation raised in its stead.

A large bozak draconian, wearing armor and a golden chain around his neck, marched forward, together with a sivak, wearing the trappings of a draconian high commander. The sivak called the draconian troops to attention. He and the bozak saluted the banners. The draconian troops clashed their swords against their shields in salute. The sivak gave the order to march, and the draconians wheeled and departed, heading back into the mountains.

Someone recalled hearing of a group of draconians who had taken control of the city of Teyr. It was said that these draconians had no love for the Dark Knights. Even if this was true, Teyr was a long march from Sanction, and no one could say how the draconians had managed to arrive at the critical time. Since no one ever saw the draconians again, this mystery was never solved.

When the victory in Sanction had been achieved, many of the golden and silver dragons departed, heading for the Dragon Isles or wherever they made their homes. Before they left, each dragon lifted up and carried away a portion of the ashes from the totem, taking them for a proper burial on the Dragon Isles. The Golds and Silver took all the remains, even though mingled among them were the ashes of Reds and Blues, Whites, Greens, and Blacks. For they were all dragons of Krynn.

"And what about you, sir?" Gerard asked Mirror. "Will you go back to the Citadel of Light?"

Gerard, Odila, and Mirror stood outside the West Gate of Sanction, watching the sunrise on the day after the battle. The sunrise was glorious, with bands of vibrant reds and oranges darkening to purple and deeper into black as day touched the departing night. The silver dragon faced the sun as if he could see it—and perhaps, in his soul, he could. He turned his blind head toward the sound of Gerard's voice.

"The Citadel will have no more need of my protection. Mishakal will make the temple her own. As for me, my guide and I have decided to join forces."

Gerard stared blankly at Odila, who nodded.

"I am leaving the Knighthood," she said. "Lord Tasgall has accepted my resignation. It is best this way, Gerard. The Knights would not have felt comfortable having me among their ranks."

"What will you do?" Gerard asked. They had been through so much, he had not expected to part with her so soon.

"Queen Takhisis may be gone," Odila said somberly, "but darkness remains. The minotaurs have seized Silvanesti. They will not be content with that land and may threaten others. Mirror and I have decided to join forces." She patted the silver dragon's neck. "A dragon who is blind and a human who was once blind—quite a team, don't you think?"

Gerard smiled. "If you're headed for Silvanesti, we may run into each other. I'm going to try to establish an alliance between the Knighthood and the elves."

"Do you truly believe the Knights' Council will agree to help the elves recover their land?" Odila asked skeptically.

"I don't know," Gerard said, shrugging, "but I'm damn sure going to make them think about it. First, though, I have a duty to perform. There's a broken lock on a tomb in Solace. I promised to go fix it."

An uncomfortable silence fell between them. Too much was left to say to be said now. Mirror fanned his wings, clearly eager to be gone. Odila took the hint.

"Goodbye, Cornbread," she said, grinning.

"Good riddance," said Gerard, grinning back.

Odila leaned close, kissed him on the cheek. "If you ever again take a bath naked in a creek, be sure and let me know."

She mounted the silver dragon. He dipped his sightless head

in salute, spread his wings, and lifted gracefully into the air. Odila waved.

Gerard waved back. He watched them as they dwindled in size, remained watching until long after they had vanished from his sight.

Another goodbye was said that day. A farewell that would last for all eternity.

In the arena, Paladine knelt over the body of Silvanoshei. Paladine closed the staring eyes. He cleansed the blood from the young elf's face, composed the limbs. Paladine was tired. He was not accustomed to this mortal body, to its pains and aches and needs, to the range and intensity of emotions: of pity and sorrow, anger and fear. Looking into the face of the dead elven king, Paladine saw youth and promise, all lost, all wasted. He paused in his labor, wiped the sweat from his forehead, and wondered how, with such sorrow and heaviness in his heart, he could go on. He wondered how he could go on alone.

Feeling a gentle touch upon his shoulder, he looked to see a goddess, beautiful, radiant. She smiled down upon him, but there was sadness in her smile and the rainbows of unshed tears in her eyes.

"I will carry the young man's body to his mother," Mishakal offered.

"She was not witness to his death, was she?" Paladine asked.

"She was spared that much, at least. We freed all those who had been brought here forcibly by Takhisis to view her triumph. Alhana did not see her son die.

"Tell her," said Paladine quietly, "that he died a hero."

"I will do that, my beloved."

A kiss as soft as a white feather brushed the elf's lips.

"You are not alone," Mishakal said to him. "I will be with you always, my husband, my own."

He wanted very much for this to be so, willed that it should be so. But there was a gulf between them, and he saw that gulf grow wider with every passing moment. She stood upon the shore, and he floundered among the waves, and every wave washed him farther and farther away.

"What has become of the souls of the dead?" he asked.

"They are free," she said and her voice was distant. He could barely hear her. "Free to continue their journey."

"Someday, I will join them, my love."

"On that day, I will be waiting," she promised.

The body of Silvanoshei vanished, born away on a cloud of silvery light.

Paladine stood for a long time alone, stood in the darkness. Then he made his solitary way out of the arena, walked alone into the world.

The children of the gods, Nuitari, Lunitari, Solinari, entered the former Temple of the Heart. The body of the wizard Dalamar sat upon a bench, staring at nothing.

The gods of magic took their places before the dark and abandoned altar.

"Let the wizard, Raistlin Majere, come forth."

Raistlin emerged from the darkness and ruins of the temple. The hem of his black velvet robe scattered the amber shards that still lay upon the floor of this temple, for no one could be found who dared touch the accursed remnants of the sarcophogus that had imprisoned the body of Goldmoon. He trod upon them, crushed the amber beneath his feet.

In his arms, Raistlin held a body, shrouded in white.

"Your spirit is freed," said Solinari sternly. "Your twin brother awaits you. You promised to leave the world. You must keep that promise."

"I have no intention of remaining here," Raistlin returned. "My brother awaits, as do my former companions."

"They have forgiven you?"

"Or I have forgiven them," Raistlin returned smoothly. "The matter is between friends and none of your concern." He looked down at the body he held in his arms. "But this is."

Raistlin laid the body of his nephew at the feet of the gods. Then, drawing back his hood, he faced the three siblings.

"I ask one last boon of you, of all of you," said Raistlin. "Restore Palin to life. Restore him to his family."

"And why should we do this?" Lunitari demanded.

"His steps strayed onto the path that I once walked," said Raistlin. "He saw his mistake at the end, but he could not live to redeem it. If you give him back his life, he will be able to retrace his wandering footsteps and find the way home."

"As you could not," said Lunitari gently.

"As I could not," said Raistlin.

"Brothers?" Lunitari turned to Solinari and Nuitari. "What do you say to this?"

"I say that there is another matter to be decided, as well," said Nuitari. "Let the wizard Dalamar come forth.

The elf's body sat unmoving on the bench. The spirit of the wizard stood behind the body. Wary, tense, Dalamar approached the gods.

"You betrayed us," said Nuitari, accusing.

"You sided with Takhisis," said Lunitari, "and we nearly lost the one chance we had to return to the world."

"You betrayed our worshiper Palin," said Solinari sternly. "By her command, you murdered him."

Dalamar looked from one shining god to the next and when he spoke, his soul's voice was soft and bitter. "How could you possibly understand? How would you know what it feels like to lose everything?"

"Perhaps," said Lunitari, "we understand better than you think."

Dalamar kept silent, made no response.

"What is to be done with him?" Lunitari asked. "Is he to be given back his life?"

"Unless you give me back the magic," Dalamar interposed, "don't bother."

"I say we do not," said Solinari. "He used the dead to work his black arts. He does not deserve our mercy."

"I say we do," said Nuitari coolly. "If you restore Palin to life and offer him the magic, you must do the same for Dalamar. The balance must be maintained."

"What do you say, Cousin?" Solinari asked Lunitari.

"Will you accept my judgment?" she asked.

Solinari and Nuitari eyed each other, then both nodded.

"This is my decree. Dalamar shall be restored to life and the magic, but he must leave the Tower of High Sorcery he once occupied. He will henceforth be barred from entry there. He must return to the world of the living and be forced to make his way among them. Palin Majere will also be restored to life. We will grant him the magic, if he wants it. Are these terms satisfactory to you both, Cousins?"

"They are to me," said Nuitari.

"And to me," said Solinari.

"And are they satisfactory to you, Dalamar?" Lunitari asked.

Dalamar had what he wanted, and that was all he cared about. As for the rest, he would return to the world. Someday, perhaps, he would rule the world.

"They are, Lady," he said.

"Are these satisfactory to you, Raistlin Majere?" Lunitari asked.

Raistlin bowed his hooded head.

"Then both requests are granted. We grant life, and we gift you with the magic."

"I thank you, lords and lady," Dalamar said, bowing again. His gaze lingered for a moment on Nuitari, who understood perfectly.

Raistlin knelt beside the body of his nephew. He drew back the white shroud. Palin's eyes opened. He gazed around in shocked bewilderment, then his gaze fixed on his uncle. Palin's shock deepened.

"Uncle!" he gasped. Sitting up, he tried to reach out to take his uncle's hand. His fingers, flesh and bone and blood, slid through Raistlin's hand that was the ephemeral hand of the dead.

Palin stared at his hand, and the realization came to him that he was alive. He looked at his hands, so like the hands of his uncle, with their long, delicate fingers, and he could move those fingers, and they would obey his commands.

"I thank you," Palin said, lifting his head to see the gods in their radiance around him. "I thank you, Uncle." He paused, then said, "Once you foretold that I would be the greatest mage ever to live upon Krynn. I do not think that will come to pass."

"We had much to learn, Nephew," Raistlin replied. "Much to learn about what was truly important. Farewell. My brother and our friends await." He smiled. "Tanis, as usual, is impatient to be gone."

Palin saw before him a river of souls, a river that flowed placidly, slowly among the banks of the living. Sunlight shone upon the river, starlight sparkled in its fathomless depths. The souls of the dead looked ahead of them into a sea whose waves lapped upon the shores of eternity, a sea that would carry each on new journeys. Standing on the shore, waiting for his twin, was Caramon Majere.

Raistlin joined his twin. The brothers raised their hands in farewell, then both stepped into the river and rode upon its silvery waters that flow into the endless sea.

Dalamar's spirit flowed into his body. The magic flowed into his spirit. The blood burned in his veins, the magic burned in his blood, and his joy was deep and profound. Lifting his head, he looked up into the sky.

The one pale moon had vanished. Two moons lit the sky, one with silver fire, the other with red. As he watched in awe and thankfulness, the two converged into a radiant eye. The black moon stared out from the center.

"So they gave you back your life, as well," said Palin, emerging from the shadows.

"*And* the magic," Dalamar returned.

Palin smiled. "Where will you go?"

"I do not know," said Dalamar carelessly. "The wide world is open to me. I intend to move out of the Tower of High Sorcery. I was prisoner there long enough. Where do you go?" His lip curled slightly. "Back to your loving wife?"

"If Usha will have me," said Palin, his tone and look somber. "I have much to make up to her."

"Do not be too long about it. We must meet soon to discuss the reconvening of the Orders," said Dalamar briskly. "There is work to be done."

"And there will be other hands to do it," said Palin.

Dalamar stared at him, now suddenly aware of the truth. "Solinari offered you the magic. And you refused it!"

"I threw away too much of value because of it," said Palin. "My marriage. My life. I came to realize it wasn't worth it."

You fool! The words were on Dalamar's lips, but he did not say them aloud, kept them to himself. He had no idea where he was going, and there would be no one to welcome him when he got there.

Dalamar looked up at the three moons. "Perhaps I will come to visit you and Usha sometime," he said, knowing he never would.

"We would be honored to have you," Palin replied, knowing he would never see the dark elf again.

"I had best be going," Dalamar said.

"I should be going, too," said Palin. "It is a long walk back to Solace."

"I could speed you through the corridors of magic," Dalamar offered.

"No, thank you," said Palin with a wry smile. "I had best get used to walking. Farewell, Dalamar the Dark."

"Farewell, Palin Majere."

Dalamar spoke the words of magic, felt them bubble and sparkle on his lips like fine wine, drank deeply of them. In an instant, he was gone.

Palin stood alone, thoughtful, silent. Then he looked up at the moons, which were for him now nothing but moons, one silver and one red.

Smiling, his thoughts turning to home, he matched his feet to the same direction.

The Solamnic Knights deployed their forces on Sanction's battlements, started hasty work repairing the West Gate and shoring up the holes that had been made in Sanction's walls. Scouts from the ranks of the Knights and those of the elves were sent to search for Mina. Silver dragons flying the skies kept watch for her, but no one found her. Dragons brought word of enemy forces marching toward Sanction, coming from Jelek and from Palanthas. Sooner or later, they would hear word that Sanction had fallen, but how would they react? Would they turn and flee for home, or would they march on to try to retake it? And would Mina, bereft of her god-given power, return to lead them, or would she remain in hiding somewhere, licking her wounds?

None would ever know where the body of Queen Takhisis lay buried—if she had been buried at all. Down through the years, those who walked on the side of darkness would search for the tomb, for the legend sprang up that her unquiet spirit would grant gifts to those who found her final resting place.

The most enduring mystery was what became known as the Miracle of the Temple of Duerghast. People from all parts of Sanction, all parts of Ansalon, all parts of the world, had been snatched abruptly from their lives by the Dark Queen and brought to the arena in the Temple of Duerghast to witness her triumphant entry into the world. Instead, they witnessed an epoch.

Those who saw firsthand the death of Queen Takhisis retained the images of what they saw and heard forever, feeling it branded into their souls as the brand burns the flesh. The shock and pain were searing, at first, but eventually the pain faded away, as the body and mind worked to heal themselves.

At first, some missed the pain, for without it, what proof was there that this had all been real? To make it real, to insure that it had been real, some talked of what they had seen, talked volubly.

Others kept their thoughts locked away inside and would never speak of the event.

As with those on Krynn who had witnessed other epochs—the chaotic travels of the Gray Gem, the fall of Istar, the Cataclysm—they passed their stories of the Miracle from one generation to the next. To future generations living on Krynn, the Fifth Age would begin with the theft of the world at the moment of Chaos's defeat. But the Fifth Age would only come to be widely called the Age of Mortals on the day when the Judgment of the Book took away the godhood of one god and accepted the sacrifice of the other.

Silvanoshei was to be laid to rest in the Tomb of the Heroes in Solace. This was not to be his final burial place. His grieving mother, Alhana Starbreeze, hoped to one day take him home to Silvanesti, but that day would be long in coming. The minotaur nation poured in troops and supplies and were firmly entrenched in that formerly fair land.

Captain Samuval and his mercenaries continued to raid throughout the elven lands of Qualinesti. The Dark Knights drove out or killed the few elves who remained and claimed the land of Qualinesti as their own. The elves were exiles now. The remnants of the two nations argued over where to go, what to do.

The elven exiles camped in the valley outside of Sanction, but they were not at home there, and the Solamnic Knights, now the rulers of Sanction, urged them politely to consider moving somewhere else. The Knights' Council discussed allying with the elves to drive the minotaurs out of Silvanesti, but there was some question in regard to the Measure, and the matter was referred to scholars to settle, which they might confidently be expected to do in ten or twenty years.

Alhana Starbreeze had been offered the rulership of the Silvanesti, but, her heart broken, she had refused. She suggested that Gilthas rule in her stead. The Qualinesti wanted this, most of them. The Silvanesti did not, though they had no one else to recommend. The two quarreling nations came together once more, their representatives traveling together to the funeral of Silvanoshei.

A golden dragon bore the body of Silvanoshei to the Tomb of the Heroes. Solamnic Knights, riding silver dragons, formed a guard of honor, led by Gerard uth Mondar. Alhana accompanied the body of her son, as did his cousin Gilthas.

He was not sorry to leave the quarrels and intrigues behind. He wondered if he had the strength to go back. He did not want the kingship of the elven nations. He did not feel he was the right person. He did not want the responsibility of leading a people in exile, a people without a home.

Standing outside the tomb, Gilthas watched as a procession of elves carried the body of Silvanoshei, covered in a shroud of golden cloth, to its temporary resting place. His body was laid in a marble coffin, covered over with flowers. The shards of the broken dragonlance were placed in his hands.

The tomb would be the final resting place of Goldmoon. Her ashes were mingled with the ashes of Riverwind. The two of them together at last.

An elf dressed in travel-stained clothes of brown and green came to stand beside Gilthas. He said nothing but watched in solemn reverence as the ashes of Goldmoon and Riverwind were carried inside.

"Farewell, dear and faithful friends," he said softly.

Gilthas turned to him.

"I am glad to have this chance to speak to you, E'li—" he began.

The elf halted him. "That is my name no longer."

"What, then, should we call you, sir?" Gilthas asked.

"So many names I have had," said the elf. "E'li among the elves, Paladine among the humans. Even Fizban. That one, I must admit, was my favorite. None of them serve me now. I have chosen a new name."

"And that is—" Gilthas paused.

"Valthonis," said the elf.

"'The exile?'" Gilthas translated, puzzled. Sudden understanding rushed upon him. He tried to speak but could not manage beyond saying brokenly, "So you will share our fate."

Valthonis laid his hand upon Gilthas's shoulder. "Go back to your people, Gilthas. They are both your people, the Silvanesti and the Qualinesti. Make them one people again, and though they are a people in exile, though you have no land to call your own, you will be a nation."

Gilthas shook his head.

"The task before you is not an easy one," Valthonis said. "You will work hard and painstakingly to join together what others will endeavor to tear apart. You will be beset with failure, but never give up hope. If that happens, you will know defeat."

"Will you be with me?" Gilthas asked.

Valthonis shook his head. "I have my own road to walk, as do you, as does each of us. Yet, at times, our paths may cross."

"Thank you, sir," said Gilthas, clasping the elf's hand. "I will do as you say. I will return to my people. All my people." He sighed deeply, smiled ruefully. "Even Senator Palthainon."

Gerard stood at the entrance to the tomb, waiting for the last of the mourners to leave. The ceremony was over. Night had fallen. The crowds who had gathered to watch began to drift away, some going to the Inn of the Last Home, where Palin and Usha joined with his sisters, Laura and Dezra, to comfort all who mourned, giving them smiles and good food and the best ale in Ansalon.

As Gerard stood there, he thought back to all that had happened since that day, so long ago, when he had first heard Tasslehoff's voice shouting from inside the tomb. The world had changed, and yet it had not.

There were now three moons in the sky instead of one. Yet the sun that rose every morning was the same sun that had ushered in the Fifth Age. The people could look up into the sky again and find the constellations of the gods and point them out to their children. But the constellations were not the same as they had once been. They were made up of different stars, held different places in the heavens. Two could not be found, would never be found, would never be seen above Krynn again.

"The Age of Mortals," Gerard said to himself. The term had a new significance, a new meaning.

He looked inside the tomb to see one last person still within— the strange elf he had first seen in the arena. Gerard waited respectfully, patiently, fully prepared to give this mourner all the time he needed.

The elf said his prayers in silence, then, with a final loving farewell, he walked over to Gerard.

"Did you fix the lock?" he asked, smiling.

"I did, sir," said Gerard. He shut the door to the tomb behind him. He heard the lock click. He did not immediately leave. He was also loath to say goodbye.

"Sir, I was wondering." Gerard paused, then plunged ahead. "I don't know how to say this, but did Tasslehoff— Did he . . . did he do what he meant to do?"

"Did he die when and where he was meant to die?" the elf asked. "Did he defeat Chaos? Is that what you mean?"

"Yes, sir," said Gerard. "That's what I mean."

In answer, the elf lifted his head, looked into the night sky. "There once used to be a red star in the heavens. Do you remember it?"

"Yes, sir."

"Look for it now. Do you see it?"

"No, sir," said Gerard, searching the heavens. "What happened to it?"

"The forge fire has gone out. Flint doused the flame, for he knew he was no longer needed."

"So Tasslehoff found him," said Gerard.

"Tasslehoff found him. He and Flint and their companions are all together again," said the elf. "Flint and Tanis and Tasslehoff, Tika, Sturm, Goldmoon and Riverwind. They wait only for Raistlin, and he will join them soon, for Caramon, his twin, would not think of leaving without him."

"Where are they bound, sir?" Gerard asked.

"On the next stage of their souls' journey," said the elf.

"I wish them well," said Gerard.

He left the Tomb of the Last Heroes, bade the elf farewell, and, pocketing the key, turned his steps toward the Inn of the Last Home. The warm glow that streamed from its windows lit his way.

Report on the Order of Creation and the Progression of Souls

by Valthonis

as told to Tracy Hickman and Matthew L. Martin

Introduction

My name? Ah, I have so many. Paladine, El'i, Fizban, Bah'Mut, Draco Paladin—that last was a special favorite. Forgive the digression; I sometimes find these academic discourses a little disconcerting, even with old friends. In a way, though, all my friends are old friends, since I knew you before you were born, not that you'd know that. In any case, I understand that you desire a record of my observations on the War of Souls. I'm glad to help, especially since this series of events spans times and concepts only the gods and High Gods fully understand. Of course, because of that, I'll have to be careful how I put things. The gods don't experience time in the same way mortals do; it sometimes frustrates us when you can't grasp the totality of simultaneous existence and the stream of probability. You see what I mean? In any case, I'll try to keep this simple.

Foundation of the World

The origin of the War of Souls traces its origins to a time just after the creation of the gods by the High God, before the world was completed and the Order of Creation and the Destiny of Souls fully established.

The Beginning

There is, forever has been, and forever will be the High God, who chose to bring forth spirits out of love so that they might share in the glory, joy, and love He possessed. To this purpose, he conceived the Order of Creation and the Progression of Souls.

As a vital part of this plan, souls are born into the mortal world. From whence these souls come and what their condition was before their birth is not given to mortals to know. Nor is it given to us to know to where these souls eventually depart and to what state they may exist in the life beyond mortality. The progression of souls stretches into eternity—of which mortality is but a single moment. Nevertheless, that part of the progression of souls we designate as mortality consists of souls brought into the world to live, to learn faith in the gods and in each other. Thus mortals learn to love the purposes of the High God, to draw closer to him as they follow the ways of goodness and virtue, and to share in his glory and reflect it in their behavior. Yet some come to reject the goodness of the High God, even stand against him.

The High God conceived the Order of Creation and outlined his plan for the world's development in the Tobril. He created the gods, powerful beings who would help carry out the plan of Creation and shepherd mortals in their evolution. Greatest among the gods was Ionthas, chief among the shapers of the material world, who possessed more might than any of his brethren.

Gilean, Keeper of the Book, held the Tobril and guided Ionthas in the forging of the world, while Reorx, Sirrion, and other gods aided the many tasks. Paladine and Takhisis arose to counsel the mortals who were born to this world during the first ages. Majere served as advisor to Paladine and Takhisis, and lesser gods helped with the spiritual guidance.

After speaking the world into existence, the High God commanded Ionthas and the other gods to shape it, bringing it to fullness. As the gods molded the world in conformity with the Plan, Ionthas grew proud and haughty. Deviating from the Tobril, he declared himself the true deity and supplanter of the High God. Paladine, Gilean, and most of the other gods challenged him in this, although some remained silent. Ionthas sent his might forth across Krynn, undoing the work of the other gods and doing his best to remake the world in his own image. As he fought against the High God and the others, however, Ionthas found that his attempt to dominate Krynn did little more than drain him, and that while he could damage and distort what had been, he could not truly make anything new.

Ionthas's anger at his impotence, his failure to create a world in his own image, coupled with his overweening pride, caused him to turn against the High God, his fellow gods, and everything that was not himself. Ionthas even repudiated his old name and identity, from that moment on known to all as Chaos. Many of the other gods, led by Paladine, took up the struggle against their renegade brother. Though Chaos might have stood against them all, even in his now-weakened state, the High God granted Paladine, whose love for and obedience to the High God was second to none, the power necessary to vanquish and chain Chaos. Defeated by the Platinum Dragon, Chaos was cast beyond creation, to drift there, alone, his pride shattered. Thereafter, Chaos descended into an abyss of twisted thought, rather than face reason. He convinced himself that *he* was the creator of All and of Nothing, that the other gods were his children, that he was simply letting them play in his world. He denied the very existence of the High God, although deep within himself he dreaded

and hated the High God and all that had sprung from his brow—
everything, including to some degree, Chaos himself.

Though he was gone from the universe, Chaos's wrath had
undone much. Had they united their natural gifts, perhaps the
gods could have healed this marring of Krynn, but such good-
will was not to be. For Chaos had not only harmed Krynn, his
malice and rebellion had spread adversely among the gods
themselves.

The High God had appointed as co-regent of the young world
Takhisis, who was expected to rule jointly with Paladine. However, Chaos' evil had influenced Takhisis, for she was closely
associated with Ionthas and admired his many skills. Like Chaos,
she began to desire sole dominion of Krynn. Where Chaos had
lusted after the physical universe, Takhisis was more concerned
with the spiritual. She wished to be worshiped by the other gods,
and she sought to possess the very souls of the mortals who came
to inhabit Krynn. Subtly, she began to steer others among the
gods to her side; the names of these apostates were Morgion, Sargonnas, Chemosh, Hiddukel, Zeboim, and Nuitari. These renegade gods began to draw their strength and might not from the
High God and the unfolding of His will, but like vampires from
negative energies, drawing power from decay and wickedness
and mastering those elements of creation that sold themselves to
the darkness. This rising of the dark came to fruition as the creation of Krynn drew to an end and the next phase of the Celestial
Plan began.

The first creatures to populate Krynn were the dragons, who
were tightly bound to Paladine and Takhisis, as well as to Krynn.
Paladine and Takhisis, assisted by Reorx and Mishakal, crafted
the Five Dragons, and the High God provided their souls. Seeing
these creatures of might, the first free-willed beings to inhabit
Krynn, Takhisis and Morgion seduced them to follow her dictates. In this alliance, Takhisis and the gods who stood with her
declared themselves dedicated to usurping mastery of Krynn and
thwarting the execution of the plan. They opposed the Order of
Creation and the progression of souls.

Takhisis and her cohorts thus became the gods of Evil, falling from their lofty state into the Abyss, consumed by their own envy and malice. Their rebellion convinced several gods that the further development of Krynn would lead only to decay and disorder. These gods nurtured specific aspects of the Creation, while acting neither to thwart the will of the High God nor serve him as they were intended. Even Gilean took this point of view. These became known as the gods of Neutrality, because they saw themselves as aloof from the struggle between Good and Evil.

This struggle reached a frenzy with the birth of mortals. Takhisis, Sargonnas, and the other gods of Evil declared their intention to enslave the mortals, for, as Takhisis said, "We forged this world. Why should we now surrender it to lesser beings?"

The gods of Good stood against the evil ones, faithful to the High God. Paladine declared, "These coming mortals are children of the High God, just as we are. This world was made for them, as much as for us, and in the end, the mortals shall be greater and brighter than any of us."

The gods of Good pledged to guide the mortals, to protect them from the Evil ones and the remnants of Chaos. They would not betray the High God.

Thus began the All-Saints War, as Good strove against Evil. The gods of Neutrality originally intended to ignore the conflict, tending to their own gardens. In the end, Paladine and Majere persuaded Gilean and the other Neutrals to side with the gods of Good, for Takhisis sought dominion over the *entire* world, which would leave those elements cherished by the Neutral gods enslaved to her ends or destroyed.

The alliance of Good and Neutrality pushed the forces of Evil back, but without a decisive resolution. The High God was obliged to intervene directly.

"Know ye that I am the High God, and thou art my children, just as are these mortals whom I shall soon create.

"Paladine, thou and thine allies hath done well in remaining faithful to thy calling and desiring to aid the mortals. Though they shall be free to choose for Good or against it, thou shalt be free as well to aid and protect them so that this freedom may be maintained. And as it shall be with the mortals who choose Good, so shall it be with thee. Thy labors shall in the end bring about Good, though Evil may surround thee. For Goodness, sought truly and for its own sake, shall redeem its own.

"Takhisis, thou hast followed Ionthas in foolishness, and those who follow thee shall likewise know their folly, should they not repent. Thou and thine shalt be free to mar, wound, and tempt the mortals, yet in the end, thou shalt regret this most grievously. For I am farther above thee than thou canst conceive, even more above thee than thou perceivest thyself to be above the mortals. All that thou shalt do to thwart my designs shall in the end fulfill them and be used to bring about Good. But, Evil, thy work remains, and thou shalt suffer for this, even more than the mortals who serve thee suffer for their misdeeds. For Evil, even pursued in the guise of Good, shall turn in upon itself.

"Gilean, though thou hast not acted directly against mine designs, still thou and those who declare themselves Neutral hath failed to fullfill the Plan. Thou shalt fulfill it despite thyself, and I shall permit thy declared Neutrality, for even in thy silence, thou all shalt bring Goodness. As thou art free, so are the mortals. Yet thou shalt not remain betwixt forever; in the end, thou must stand either with us in the Light or with Takhisis and her compatriots in the Darkness. For all are free to choose for Good or against it, but all will make a choice between sides in the end.

"Know ye all that there shall be a Balance. I will permit Good, Evil, and Neutrality all to work upon this world, and the mortals shall be free to choose between the three and garner the consequences of their choosing. They may alter the Balance, but the decision must come from within, and not be forced upon them from without. Know thee, Paladine, that if those mortals in thy service seek to force Goodness upon the others, they shall fall into Evil and bring about great suffering. Know thee, Gilean, that if thy servants try to forbid the mortals from choosing between the two, they shall likewise fail and bring about devastation. Know thee, Takhisis, that when thou dost attempt to enslave the world to thine service, thou shalt be thwarted in the end, and yet in thy folly, thou shalt continue to seek such dominion until the end of thy presence upon this world."

Thus ended the All-Saints War, named because it affected the destiny of all who could become saints on Krynn.

Of the Gods

Though the gods numbered twenty-two in the beginning, Chaos was cast from their number in the first days of the Age of Starbirth. By the end of the All-Saints War, there were twenty-one gods on Krynn, divided into three orders of seven, the Gods of Light, the Gods of Neutrality or Twilight, and the Gods of Darkness.

The Gods of Light

Greatest among the righteous gods is Paladine, the Celestial Paladin and Platinum Dragon. Mightiest of all gods, save Chaos, Paladine is the exemplar of virtue and holiness, patron of the great virtue of Charity. Leader of the Order of Light, he protects Krynn against the schemes of Takhisis and leads both mortals and his fellow gods in the path of righteousness. Thus, he guides all who protect the innocent and seek to lead others in truth and goodness. His role as leader and keeper of Krynn, though, is tempered by a deep and sincere humility, which he strives to inculcate in his followers as well.

Majere is only slightly less in might than Paladine. Paladine loves the High God most fiercely and deeply of all the Powers. Majere is said to have the greatest understanding of the High God's wisdom and the Celestial Plan, surpassing even Gilean. Thus, Majere serves an advisor to Paladine and fosters the virtue of Faith, as well as the diligence that encourages mortals to pursue values of the spirit despite effort and trial. Monks are the most conspicuous among Majere's followers, but he is also revered by many mystics and theologians, as well as the intellectual and spiritual gold dragons.

Mishakal, third among the gods of Good, is nearly as beloved as Paladine among the people of Krynn. Healer and Consoler, Mishakal strives to bring aid and comfort to those suffering in body and mind. Of the virtues, Hope is Mishakal's special concern, as she inspires mortals to trust in the promises and plans of the High God and the inevitable triumph of Good. She is also the patron of natural love, be it between parents and children, brother and sister, or man and wife. The silver dragons, who share Mishakal's concern and empathy for mortals, revere her deeply.

Of all the gods of Light, Kiri-Jolith, Sword of Justice, is the most martial. Tireless in his pursuit of Justice, Kiri-Jolith inspires his followers, among them the copper dragons, to protect the innocent and punish the forces of Evil. He is not merciless in this crusade, though, and directs his servants and those who look to him for guidance to temper justice with mercy and not to be carried away by bloodlust and wrath.

Habbakuk, close ally to Kiri-Jolith, is Prince of Beasts and Lord of the Seas. He promotes respect for the natural glories of Krynn and teaches mortals to see in them a reflection of the glory and virtue of the eternal. At the same time, he inspires Temperance, which keeps the passions of mortals' animal qualities in harmony and balance. With the metallic dragons, he shares a fondness for the sea.

While Habbakuk teaches devotion to natural beauty, Branchala inspires art, courage, and generosity. He encourages the people of Krynn to use artistic talents to lift the eyes of others heavenward and to muster courage, face fear, and strive for goodness despite danger and opposition.

Last among the gods of Light is counted Solinari, Keeper of the Silver Moon and the White Archmage. All White Magic falls under his dominion, and all wizards in service to good pay him honor and accord. In return, Solinari teaches them Wisdom, helping guide them in knowing when to use their great gifts to best further the goals of Good and keeping them from being consumed by their hunger for magical power, as happens to so many mages of the Black Order.

The Gods of Neutrality

Brass and bronze dragons often consort with the neutral gods. Gilean, the Observer and Keeper of the Tobril, is the most impressive of the neutral gods in terms of power, but he has very few followers on Krynn. Cold in heart and passionless in spirit, Gilean merely watches, intervening only when it appears one side in the great conflict may end the 'experiment' prematurely. Though he does not seek followers, he accepts the allegiance of historians, scientists, and others who strive for pure and objective knowledge.

Reorx, Lord of Earth, is also patron of craftsmen. His concern is with the attention of the maker to his craft and the quality of the results. He is the special patron of the dwarves, who are descended from humans he took into his service and taught secrets.

While Reorx takes an interest in craftsmanship, Shinare is patroness of trade, taking a delight in the cycles of exchange, commerce, and economic development. Though admired by honest merchants, she is only revered by those who, while trustworthy, see nothing in life beyond their business. Many such tradesmen eventually fall prey to avarice and slip, knowingly or unknowingly, into Hiddukel's grasp.

Sirrion, Master of Flame, is primarily concerned with his chosen element, but also maintains an interest in inspiration and creativity. Alchemy is a favored subject, as well as other pursuits that seek transformation, or singular moments of beauty or intensity. Most chaotic among the Neutral powers, his tendency to focus on the moment without a thought for consequences has made him often a pawn of the gods of Evil.

Chislev, Lady of the Woods, concerns herself with the natural world of Krynn, as it is and for its own sake rather than as a reflection of Good, as is true of Habbakuk; nor does she attempt to dominate nature and use it as a weapon, in the manner of Zeboim. She concerns herself above all with the plants and trees of Krynn, more so than the beasts of the world. Of all the Neutral powers, she is perhaps the most likely to intervene in the affairs of the world, trying to protect nature from the ravages of Evil or the unintended damage caused as a side effect when Good defends itself and the world against the assaults of darkness.

Zivilyn, Seeker of Wisdom, is aide to Gilean and companion to Chislev. Unlike Gilean, who pursues knowledge of what is outside mortals, Zivilyn encourages mortals to look within, finding wisdom in their own hearts. His approach sometimes brings tranquility, sometimes madness. Zivilyn sees both as viable paths to self-knowledge and enlightenment.

Last and seventh among the gods of Neutrality is Lunitari, Lady of the Crimson Moon and Red Sorceress. As the Mistress of Red Magic, wizards of the Red Robes pay her homage. Lunitari has a fondness for illusion and trickery, which makes her favored by confidence men, but her primary concern is magic for magic's sake, rather than as a part of the order of creation or a tool for her own domination.

The Gods of Darkness

With Chaos banished, Takhisis, Queen of Darkness, became the foremost opponent of Truth and Light upon Krynn. It is said by some that she betrayed Chaos and stole much of his power. What is generally accepted is that she inherited his megalomaniacal pride. She sees herself as the center and rightful master of all creation. Though she finds this, the queen of vices, distasteful in others, it is useful in tempting mortals away from the High God and into her clutches. The Dragon Queen also retains an interest in lust. She seeks disordered pleasures of the spirit—adoration and submission—for herself, and she stirs up disordered desires for pleasures of the flesh in mortals, so as to more easily entice them down the path of darkness.

Sargonnas the Vengeful stands next to Takhisis in the courts of the gods of night, and resents this deeply. Indeed, Sargonnas resents every slight and insult, and thus he is dominated by the vice of wrath which he champions, encouraging rampant blood-shed and harsh punishment for the slightest offense. Blue drag-ons, who evince fiery tempers, are his special favorites.

Chemosh, the Lord of the Undead, stands as counterpart to Majere and a master of wicked counsel. He specializes in sloth, that chill of the spirit that quenches the flames of love and faith and, while promising comfort and ease, turns life into a cold, joy-less, loveless mockery. In many cases, this culminates in the shad-owed life of the undead that Chemosh nurtures and cherishes. The white dragons, prone to this same coldness and long slum-bers, are often associated with the Prince of Bone.

Morgion the Seething dwells alone. He lost the glory and majesty that he so prized in the early days, when he chose to stand with Takhisis in her rebellion. He was wounded in the All-Saints War, reduced to wrack and ruin. Like his fellow gods of Evil, he both suffers from and encourages his particular vice. In his case, it is the sin of envy, which resents the good of others and seeks to reduce all to common misery. Morgion especially enjoys the spread of disease, which causes suffering of the flesh, and deceit, which often brings about torture of mind and soul. Any who feel themselves injured by the good of others or seek to bring someone low find the Spreader of Disease a ready ally. Because of this, he is favored by the spiteful green dragons, who resent and hate virtue and desire to cause pain and anguish in body and spirit.

Hiddukel, Prince of Tarnished Gold, is perhaps the most often invoked of all the Evil Powers, being the patron of avarice. Thus he is honored by thieves, corrupt merchants, and all seduced by the lure of gold. Hiddukel does much to foster this devotion, being himself dominated by the greed for souls. Red dragons, the most avaricious of all their kind, often pay tribute to Hiddukel and seek his aid in their acquisitions.

Zeboim, Lady of Tempests, pays scant attention to the intrigues of the gods or the affairs of mortals. As representative of gluttony, she spends much of her time trying to consume as much as she can beneath the seas of Krynn, ranging from individual sailors to entire ships, cities, or islands. Black dragons are her pets, due to their love for water and their own insatiable hungers.

Nuitari, Master of the Dark Moon and Black Wizard, stands last among the gods of Evil. Desiring recognition and prone to vanity, he fosters the growth of black magic and attempts to choke out the work of Solinari and Lunitari so that he alone will be recognized as the source of magic in the world. His followers are often obsessed with increasing their magical abilities, becoming the greatest wizards in history, and being feared or revered as such.

The Creation of Mortals

When the All-Saints War was brought to an end, the Firstborn mortals were created on Krynn, male and female.

All mortals spring from the thought of the High God and have their souls created by him. The gods of Good and Neutrality, as well as the High God himself, bestowed gifts upon the first parents to help them function in the world and achieve their destinies. The gods of Evil, though, were at work from the beginning of these new mortals' lives, and though they also promised gifts, they in truth lured the Firstborn to fall from their original state, be weakened in body and soul, and be cast under the shadow of the Dragon Queen.

Whether the three oldest races were created distinct from each other, or diverged from one father and mother into three races at some point in history, is a matter best left to your scholarship and dispute. Suffice it for now that within the earliest generations, elves, ogres, and humans were all present on Krynn.

Of the three races, the elves proved most faithful to the High God and least seduced or deceived by the wiles of Takhisis. Thus, they have retained many of the original gifts, such as a long life-span, physical health, and a clearer, more focused will. Their greater control of their passions makes them less likely to succumb completely to the temptations of Evil, although they still must guard against that weakness. Pride, selfishness, and sloth are the most dangerous characteristics of elvenkind.

The Irda, being strongest and physically most beautiful of the races, were coveted by the Dark Queen, who expended much effort to seduce them, and largely succeeded. The Irda did not lose their physical or mental gifts immediately, yet their will and intellect were darkened, and a seed of decay was planted within them, which would bear bitter fruit in the Age of Dreams. Thus did they become ogres.

Regardless, ogres retain a crude moral sense and a capacity to choose Good. However, while there are differences in ogrish cultures, especially those before and after the collapse of the last ogre empire and the historical decline of their race, all ogres exhibit anger, vanity, avarice, lust, and gluttony. Most ogres shrug off concerns about "Good" and "Evil" and willingly enslave themselves to their desires. Despite this, ogres still must be dealt with in a compassionate fashion, for they are not wholly Evil nor irredeemable.

Humans occupy something of a middle ground, neither as committed to Good as the elves nor as enslaved by Evil as the ogres. Despite this, humans have the greatest potential for either Good or Evil and are often the key movers in the historic events of Krynn, as they have achieved the greatest glory and goodness, yet also fallen into the most appalling depravity.

And so the Age of Starbirth ended and the Age of Dreams began, with the gods of Good determined to do their best to realize a wondrous future for Krynn.

The Progression of Souls

Mortals are born into the world of Krynn for two purposes—each ordained by the High God. The first is internal: for the growth and enhancement of their own souls and those of others as they develop faith and exercise their agency of choice between Evil, Neutrality and Good. Some souls, when challenged by Evil, choose to darken or lose themselves in the fires; others pass through such tests without failing but without attaining higher virtue; still others are purified and shine brighter than the stars, reflecting and radiating the High God's Light.

The second purpose is external: that mortals should take up their role in shaping the world of Krynn, bringing it to perfection, and, in the wake of the deeds of Chaos and the fall of Takhisis and her cohorts, repairing the wounds of Evil. The freedom of will given to mortals by the High God means that mortals may turn to dark ends. Yet the High God weaves Neutrality and Evil into the unfolding of the Tobril, inevitably bringing forth Good out of Evil. What mortals have called Fate is the expression of the High God's subtle but prevalent will upon Krynn.

Death, feared by so many mortals, is both an end and a beginning. For souls who have chosen by their faith and actions to stand with the High God, death is an end to the trials of this life and a gateway to sharing in the love and glory of the High God. Those who chose to turn their backs on the High God, though, cast themselves into the Abyss, tormented by the wickedness they embraced in life. More than that I cannot say, for some things must be left to faith.

Some mortals fear the passage to the world beyond, either out of fear of the unknown or, if they are wicked mortals, a suspicion of what awaits them. In some cases, the Evil god Chemosh responds to this fear and offers mortals a chance at a fake and perverted form of immortality. This attempt to "cheat death" and circumvent the progression of souls is but a sad joke that Chemosh delights in perpetrating. Those who accept his temptation find themselves trapped within their dead bodies or otherwise bound to the world of Krynn, doomed to a horrid existence until destroyed or freed from Chemosh's bonds. Even dragons are not immune to Chemosh's seductions, as the recent case of Cyan Bloodbane indicates. Some wizards have pursued a similar fate through dark magic. I have heard it said that Chemosh and Nuitari conspired to release the secrets of lichdom into the world for their own gain.

Glory of the Gods: The Four Powers

The life and death of mortals upon Krynn gives strength to the gods. This was ordained by the High God, both for the sake of the gods (that they might benefit and learn from the unfolding of the Tobril's Plan) and for the sake of mortals (that the gods of Evil would not destroy the balance). As mortals act on Krynn, their beliefs and deeds lend power to the gods aligned to their actions. This is especially true when they die and make their final commitments of the spirit. The gods not only benefit from this power but return it to their followers. **(Fig. 1)**

Spirits Progress to
Next World/Reality

Increased
Glory
(Faith)

Increased
Power
(Creation)

Clerical
Powers
(Focused
Faith)

High
Sorcery
(Focused
Creation)

Ambient Spirit Force

Ambient Creation Force

Spirit-Children from
Previous World/Reality
Progress to Krynn Mortality

Fig. 1

Two kinds of power can be said to exist on Krynn: the spiritual energy of faith, fueled by the heart and spirit of mortals, and the elemental energies driven by creation. These powers exist in two states, the ambient power of Krynn and the directed energies of the Cycles of Faith and Creation, which connect gods and mortals. From these sources comes the magic of Krynn.

The ambient power of the world is the source for the magic of the Fifth Age, both mystical (ambient spiritual energy) and sorcerous, or "wild magic" (ambient elemental and creative energy). These arts were also practiced in the Age of Dreams but largely forgotten after that era. This magic is fueled by mortals and their relationship with Krynn and thus survived even during the gods' absence. Wild magic is "wild" precisely because of the damage done to Krynn by the forces of Chaos and Evil. As it reflects the state of creation, it also shares in the disordering of the world.

It is from the harmony between gods and mortals that the powers of High Sorcery and clerical magic derive. As mortals revere the gods and pursue the acts of living faith, they channel power to the gods. The gods complete the circuit by returning that power, whether Good, Neutral, or Evil. The cycle thus rewards both gods and mortals, providing magic to the mortals and energy for the gods in their cosmic struggle. However, the gods are not equal, nor are all mortal beings, and there is constant flux and volatility.

The Fifth Age—Another Perspective

Despite the turmoil of Krynn and occasional disruptions of the Cycles of Faith and Creation, the Progression of Souls remained unthreatened until the Chaos War. **(Fig. 2)**

Krynn normal motion in space, time & reality

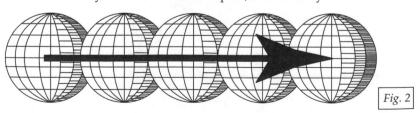

Fig. 2

Chaos, released from the Greygem that had trapped him, resumed his challenge to the High God for mastery over Krynn. Some say that Takhisis enticed him into this mad scheme, but it certainly seems likely that she was the one who coaxed the Irda to crack the Greygem. It must be understood that the Chaos War was not fought merely over the world of Krynn, but over the souls of mortals.

The Theft of the World

The ultimate defeat of Chaos at the end of the Chaos War was the last cog in her own master plan, which Takhisis apparently had been developing for centuries. In the last instant of Chaos's fall, the Dragon Queen stole the world of Krynn, removing it to a place, time, and reality unknown and unnoticed by the other gods. She adopted many guises as she endeavored to achieve this and other ends . . . including that of a Shadow Sorcerer. **(Fig. 3)**

However, Takhisis, badly weakened from the terrible theft of the world and deception of the gods, needed time to rest and regather her strength. She felt comfortable in doing this, for

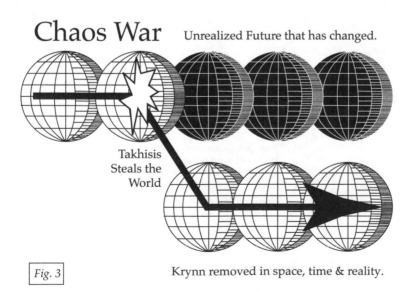

Chaos War — Unrealized Future that has changed.

Takhisis Steals the World

Fig. 3 — Krynn removed in space, time & reality.

Spirit Krynn
After Takhisis Steals the World

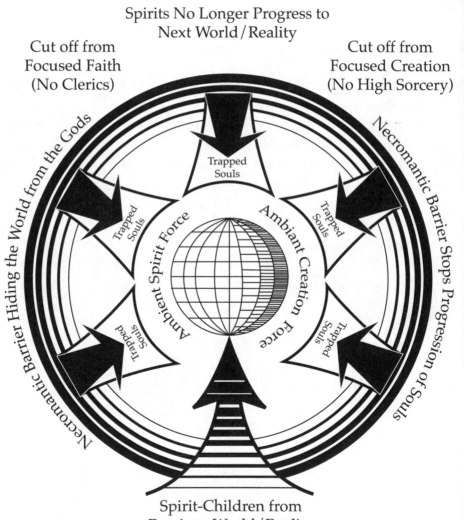

Spirits No Longer Progress to
Next World/Reality

Cut off from
Focused Faith
(No Clerics)

Cut off from
Focused Creation
(No High Sorcery)

Trapped
Souls

Trapped
Souls

Trapped
Souls

Necromantic Barrier Hiding the World from the Gods

Necromantic Barrier Stops Progression of Souls

Ambient Spirit Force

Ambient Creation Force

Trapped
Souls

Trapped
Souls

Spirit-Children from
Previous World/Reality
Progress to Krynn Mortality

Fig. 4

while new souls continued to be born into the world, the progression of souls had been stopped. Instead of moving on to a higher plane after death, the souls of mortals were stopped, doomed to remain on Krynn. Takhisis drew power from their spirits as they were trapped in this hideous fate, in a fashion similar to that of her favored children, the Evil dragons, during the early days of this age. As the power of the Dark Queen waxed, these souls became more enslaved. She even began to send them forth to drain magic from the spells of mortals, and spellcasters even began to detect her foul taint corrupting wild magic and mysticism. **(Fig. 4)**

The world became a closed source of power for the Queen of Darkness. While other gods were deprived of the energies of mortal souls, the Dragon Queen drew power not only from those who served her but from the energy put forth by all mortals. In time, she believed that she would have enough power not only to retain supremacy over Krynn but to challenge the High God for mastery over all creation. Thus did she follow in Chaos' path, and bring about great misery in the world in doing so.

The Curious Case of the Kender: Then and Again

Time is key to understanding the unfolding of this history of Krynn. As creation would be meaningless without a past, present, or future, long ago the High God forbade the powers to tamper with the River of Time. Takhisis, typically, believed that this commandment had no real meaning for her, even though her theft of Krynn displaced the world both in space *and* time . . . with unforeseen consequences.

The Future That Never Would Be

Prior to the Chaos War, Tasslehoff Burrfoot—a kender of some renown—was able to travel forward in time . . . to a future that would never take place, because of Takhisis's subsequent sin against the High God.

Chaos War

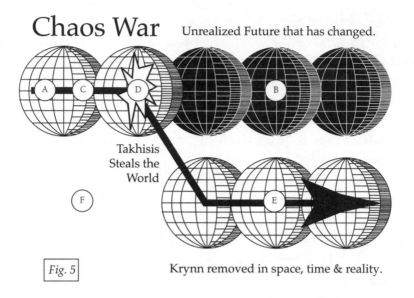

Unrealized Future that has changed.

Takhisis
Steals the
World

Krynn removed in space, time & reality.

Fig. 5

Perhaps this illustration will best serve to clarify the matter **(Fig. 5)**. The kender went forward in time (A) prior to his deadly conflict with Chaos. He visited a future (B) where the elves were at peace and Palin had attended Caramon's funeral. He then returned to the past (C) where he was caught up in the Chaos War. At the moment Chaos might have destroyed him (D), he gratefully recalled my admonition to trigger the device once more. In that very moment, Tahkisis stole the world, establishing it along a new and different timeline. Tasslehoff leaped forward once more to the same time—Caramon's funeral—but an entirely different future. (E) Another way of looking at it is that Tasslehoff jumped "down" the River of Time a ways, then returned and continued on his regular path through life. At the end of the Chaos War, Tas tried to jump forward again, but at the same moment, Takhisis dammed the river and forced it into a new course, sweeping Tasslehoff along with it.

Time travel, it is true, is a highly speculative subject. Inarguable is the fact that Tasslehoff had memories of two distinct futures because of the simple fact that he had indeed visited two separate futures.

The Past That Never Was

I have spoken with Palin Majere at length since the end of the War of Souls. He was most curious as to why, when he tried to travel back in time, he found no past beyond the Chaos War. As you can see from the diagram, when Palin used the device inside the War of Souls timeline, he attempted to travel back beyond the point in time when Takhisis absconded with the world. Thus, while everyone on Krynn from that time had lived in the original timeline and could thus remember it, from the point of view of the River of Time itself, there was no past at all (F).

Palin also expressed some confusion as to the relationship between the High God and Chaos, drawing from what he overheard in the Abyss and while working with Reorx to try and stop Chaos. When he was in the Abyss, the domain of Takhisis, observing the gods, his perceptions were influenced by Takhisis. While much of what he overheard was accurate in substance, his perspective was colored by the Dark Queen. Confusing Chaos with the High God, in Palin's mind, must have seemed to Takhisis an excellent way to advance her plans for dominion.

As to Reorx referring to Chaos as "Himself" and "the Father of All and Nothing". . . . Chaos remained the mightiest of the gods until the end, and the magnitude of his presence could be overwhelming even for Reorx. When Reorx came face to face with Chaos, it shook him to the core and left him fleetingly believing Chaos's deluded claims. After the Chaos War, the Forger recovered, but by then the world had been stolen and the mistaken impression lingered.

The Future of the Fifth Age

With the return of the gods, the progression of souls has been restored, and mortals can now move on to their just rewards or punishments. High sorcery once again functions, and the gods have been reunited with the lost world with tremendous joy. However, Mysticism and wild magic have also blossomed in the Fifth Age and no doubt are here to stay.

As for me and my future, who can say? The justice of the High God has been satisfied. We know there are struggles ahead. There is still evil that threatens the balance, and there are still dragon overlords who oppress vast portions of Krynn. The minotaurs now threaten the continent of Ansalon more than ever before in history.

The best that may be said is that there will be a future . . . though what future will be up to each of us. We look forward, if not to a new age, to clearer understanding of this Age of Mortals in which we live. We may not know the future, but as for me . . . I look forward with wonder to see it unfold.

P9-DHN-567

Area I

Area II

Area III

Area IV

Area V

Area VI

palacios

The Rockwells'
COMPLETE GUIDE
TO SUCCESSFUL
GARDENING

BY F. F. ROCKWELL and ESTHER C. GRAYSON

THE COMPLETE BOOK OF ANNUALS

THE COMPLETE BOOK OF BULBS

THE COMPLETE BOOK OF LAWNS

THE COMPLETE BOOK OF LILIES
(with Jan de Graaff)

THE COMPLETE BOOK OF FLOWER ARRANGEMENT

THE ROCKWELLS' NEW COMPLETE BOOK OF
FLOWER ARRANGEMENT

THE ROCKWELLS' COMPLETE BOOK OF ROSES

10,000 GARDEN QUESTIONS (Editors)

GARDENING INDOORS

BY F. F. ROCKWELL

Senior Editor, *Flower Grower Magazine,*
formerly Garden Editor, New York Sunday *Times,*
The Home Garden, and *McCalls' Magazine.*

THE TREASURY OF AMERICAN GARDENS
(with James Fitch)

AROUND THE YEAR IN THE GARDEN

THE BOOK OF BULBS

THE HOME GARDEN HANDBOOKS

HOME VEGETABLE GARDENING

GARDENING UNDER GLASS

PAUL E. GENEREUX

The Rockwells'
COMPLETE GUIDE
TO SUCCESSFUL
GARDENING

The homeowners' step-by-step counselor in planning, laying out, planting, and caring for his place; and monthly reminders of what to do in his particular region, *including direct page references on* how *to do it; lists of plant material for specific purposes and regions.*

With more than a hundred photographs by the authors (except as otherwise noted); and more than a hundred line drawings by Virginia Howie, to supplement the text.

FREDERICK F. ROCKWELL
and ESTHER C. GRAYSON

AN AMERICAN GARDEN GUILD BOOK
1965
DOUBLEDAY & COMPANY, INC.
GARDEN CITY, NEW YORK

ACKNOWLEDGMENTS

Grateful acknowledgment is made to the following for the use of copyrighted material:

JONATHAN CAPE LIMITED
"The Villain" from *The Complete Poems of W. H. Davies*. Reprinted by permission.

NORMA MILLAY ELLIS
"Northern April" and "The Hardy Garden" from *Collected Poems*, Harper & Row, Publishers. Copyright 1928, 1955 by Edna St. Vincent Millay and Norma Millay Ellis. Reprinted by permission.

ESTHER GRAYSON
"October Ale." Reprinted by permission.

THE MACMILLAN COMPANY
"The Buds," "The Petal of a Rose," "In Green Ways," "The Wind." Copyright 1915 by The Macmillan Company, renewed 1943 by James Stephens. "Spring 1916," copyright 1916 by The Macmillan Company, renewed 1944 by James Stephens. All from *Collected Poems* by James Stephens. Reprinted by permission of The Macmillan Company, Macmillan & Co. Ltd., The Macmillan Company of Canada Limited, Mrs. James Stephens and St. Martin's Press, Inc.

THE NEW YORK TIMES
"Across the Plains of April" by F. F. Rockwell. Reprinted by permission.

CARL ROSE
"It's Broccoli, dear." "I say it's Spinach, 'and I say the Hell with it' "! Copyright © 1928, 1956 by *The New Yorker Magazine, Inc*. Reprinted by permission.

CHARLES SCRIBNER'S SONS
"The Heavenly Hills of Holland" from *The Poems of Henry Van Dyke* by Henry Van Dyke. Copyright 1911 by Charles Scribner's Sons; renewal copyright 1939 by Tertius Van Dyke. Reprinted by permission.

DEDICATION

To our good friend Arno Nehrling, who, as long-time executive secretary of the Massachusetts Horticultural Society, director of its publication *Horticulture,* and manager of the Annual New England Spring Flower Show, has contributed so much to the advancement of distinguished gardening in America.

Contents

Foreword   *xv*

PART I. YOUR HOME GROUNDS: HOW TO PLAN, PLANT, AND MAINTAIN THEM

1. Planning the New Place   *3*

The importance of having a long-range plan. How to set about making a plan. The preliminary work: existing features, divisions, elevations. The important areas: utility, play and rest. Screening and protection: hedges, fences, walls, shrubbery. Special gardens: flower beds, borders, rock and wall gardens, vegetables and fruits.

2. The Soil and How to Manage It   *15*

Over-all importance. Possibility of altering. Types of soil and their origins: clay, sand, loam, humus. Subsoil and its importance. Drainage. Special area soil types: peat, gumbo, muck, adobe. Remaking and maintaining soils.

3. The Plant and How It Grows   *37*

Plant anatomy: roots, stems, leaves. Reproduction: how plants grow: air, water, food, light, temperature. Deterrents to growth: light, air, cold, heat, drought, pests, old age.

4. New Plants from Old: Methods of Propagation   *49*

Growing from seed: timing, control of conditions, the mechanics of sowing, equipment for seed sowing, sterilizers, watering, temperature, transplanting, repotting. Asexual propagation: layering, divisions, cuttings, grafting, budding.

5. Keeping Plants Vigorous and Healthy   *76*

The gardener's job: temperature, micro-climates, light, moisture, mulches, watering, watering equipment, wind barriers. Feeding plants: fertilizers, manures, green manures. Soil preparation: organic gardening, fertilizers and fertilizer formulas. Plant pests, diseases. Weeds and their controls.

6. Pruning and Training Plants   *94*

Definitions. Pruning objectives: renewing old plants, increasing yields of flowers, fruits, repairing injured or diseased plants. Training objectives: controlling size, habit of growth, shape. Pruning equipment, pruning techniques.

7. Coldframes and Hotbeds   *107*

Definitions: types of frames, types of sash; location, drainage, building the frame, soil for frames. Frame management, temperature control, planting, watering, ventilation, feeding, shading. The hotbed: construction, methods of heating, management.

8. Tools and Equipment   *120*

Tools for many purposes: the question of quality. Hand tools for many tasks. Power tools. Tools for transplanting, cultivating, pruning. Equipment for training and supporting plants: fences, trellises, arbors; for dusting, spraying, lawn care.

PART II. SPECIAL GARDENS, AREAS, AND PLANT MATERIALS

9. Trees, Shrubs, and Vines   *137*

Dominant and permanent features of the landscape plan: advantages of establishing them early, possibilities of a home nursery and its advantages, problems of selection. Suggestions for deciduous, evergreen, and ornamental subjects. Shrubs for various purposes. Vines and other climbers. Supports.

10. Lawns and Turf Areas   *156*

The lawn, an important feature: what type of lawn to use. Preliminary preparations: grading, drainage, preparation of seedbed, sowing. After care, sodding, stripping, plugging, sprigging, and other methods of lawn making. Lawn renovation. Lawn maintenance: mowing, feeding, rolling, pests, diseases, weed control. Lawns and grasses for hot climates, for cool climates, for dry land areas. Ground-cover substitutes for grasses.

11. Flower Beds and Borders   *178*

Placement. Backgrounds. A definite plan. Annuals from seed: setting out plants, culture, support for, fall clean-up. Biennials. Perennials. Planning the border. Buying plants. Dividing and replanting. Bulbs: selecting, planting, storing.

12. Rock, Bank, and Wall Gardens   *204*

Specialized gardens have many advantages. Rock garden location, preliminary work, background trees and shrubbery, a definite plan, construction, rock plants, culture. The bank garden. The wall garden.

13. Pools, Streams, and Water Gardens   *218*

The fascination of water. Importance of good design, location, construction, water supply, water control, winter care. The question of fish.

14. The Patio Garden, Mobile Gardening, Window Boxes   *227*

Definitions. Location. Suitable plants. Added protection. Plants for walls. Lilies and other bulbs for succession of bloom in pots. Patio pools. Modern mobile gardening. Window boxes.

15. Roses and Rose Gardens   *237*

The Queen still reigns! The all-purpose flower. Various types of roses. Their selection for different purposes. Preparation of soil. Supports. Fall *vs.* spring planting. Planting techniques. Culture: feeding, pruning, pruning climbers. Spring care. Pest control. Winter protection.

16. Vegetables for Better Eating   *257*

Why "grow your own"? Location. Size. What to grow. A definite plan. Soil preparation. Planting. Cultivation. Thinning. Fertilizing. Mulching. Harvesting. Winter storage. Detailed culture for popular vegetables.

17. Tree Fruits, Small Fruits, and Berries   *280*

Definitions; and again, why "grow your own"? Locations. Planting. Pruning. Spraying. Harvesting. Storing. Tree fruits: apples, pears, plums, peaches, figs, grapes. Bush and cane fruits: blueberries, raspberries, strawberries.

18. The Home Greenhouse   *299*

Year-round gardening. Uses and types of construction: even span or lean-to. Work space. Heating. Ventilation. Shading. Watering. Greenhouse operations: timing, sowing dates, soil mixes, seed sowing, transplanting, watering. Pots, potting, and repotting. Pest control. Propagation.

PART III. SELECTIVE, COUNTRY-WIDE MONTHLY CALENDAR

How to Use the Calendar   317
Alphabetical List of States Showing Areas   320
The Calendar   325
Notes on Country-wide Gardening Problems: 394
     West Coast, Southwest, Mountain, Intermountain, Great Northern Plains, Central Plains and Heartland, North Central, Northeast, East Central, Mid-Atlantic, South Central, Upper South, Lower South and Gulf Coast, Seashore.

PART IV. APPENDIX

Hardy trees and shrubs   412
Trees, shrubs, and other plants for very cold climates   425
Trees, shrubs, and other plants for the South and for reclaimed
  desert lands   434
Trees, shrubs, and other plants for the Atlantic seashore   448
Garden flowers: annuals, biennials, perennials. Bulbous plants.
  Plants for rock, wall, water, and bog gardens. Fragrant plants
  and herbs   451
Garden troubles: Pests, diseases, weeds, and their controls   461
Botanical gardens and Arboretums   472
Parks and display gardens   477
Agricultural colleges and Agricultural Experiment Stations   491
Special plant societies   495
Other national organizations   497
Books for further reference   498
Bibliography   501

Index   *503*

Photographic Illustrations

BY THE AUTHORS, EXCEPT AS NOTED

Frontispiece

Buttrick garden, Concord, Mass.	10
Garden with rocks (*Paul E. Genereux*)	11
Perennial garden with yew hedge (*Paul E. Genereux*)	12
Horizontal landscape design in harmony with house (*Paul E. Genereux*)	13
"Green manuring"	26
Compost heap	28
Frame for sowing	51
Seed sowing in frame	52
Equipment for seed sowing	53
Small plastic seed flat	54
Seeds in bulb pan covered with plastic	54
Seedlings in small composition box	58
Seedlings showing root masses	58
Tomato seedlings	59

ASEXUAL REPRODUCTION:

Root division	60
Leaf cuttings (2)	61
Hardwood cuttings (2)	62
Softwood cutting	63
Increase in tulip bulbs	65
Daffodils increase by offsets	66
Candidum-lily splitting	67
Summer mulch	79
Watering equipment (2)	82, 83
Wind barrier	84
Pruning a vigorous climbing rose	97
Pruning tools	101
Tulip tree damaged by hurricane	103
Horizontal rose cane showing vertical growth	104
How to remove a tree limb	105

Coldframes and their uses (4)   108, 109
Building a coldframe   112
Shading for the coldframe   116
Ventilation for the coldframe   117
Forcing hardy bulbs in a coldframe   118
Melon boxes   126
Climbing rose on post-and-rail fence   127
Wisteria over gate   128

STEPS IN TRANSPLANTING: (4)   138, 139, 140, 141
Guy wire for bracing tree or shrub   140
Star Magnolia   143
Flowering Dogwood   144
Spirea vanhouttei   145
Pieris japonica   145
Wisteria   151
Materials and equipment for lawn making   158

FOUR STEPS IN LAWN MAKING: (4)   159, 160
The remade lawn   161
Watering equipment for the lawn   165
"Plugging" a new lawn   166
Grass substitute: *Arctostaphylos uva-ursi*   175

PLANNING AND PREPARING THE BORDER: (4)   180, 181
Annual border with shrub background   183
Hillside garden of annuals   184
Perennial borders (2)   188, 189
Tulips along a driveway   196
Daffodil planting (*Laurie Wiener*)   197
Tuberous begonias   198
Knot garden—Courtesy of Brooklyn Botanic   201
Rock garden (*Paul E. Genereux*)   205
Spring rock-garden bloom in shade (*Paul E. Genereux*)   207
Perennials growing in rock wall at GrayRock   213
Water garden (*Paul E. Genereux*)   220
Garden with pool (*Paul E. Genereux*)   221
Hardy water-lilies in pool   221
Tropical water-lilies   222

Artificial stream and pools that *look* natural, GrayRock 224

Small pool in authors' rock garden 226

Paved terrace for outdoor living (*Paul E. Genereux*) 228

Terrace with plants in tubs (*Paul E. Genereux*) 229

"Built-in" planter box harmonizing with house architecture 234

Tuberous begonias in semishaded window boxes 235

Moderate-sized rose garden (*Paul E. Genereux*) 238

Roses well arranged in limited space (*Paul E. Genereux*) 238

ROSE TYPES:

Hybrid Tea 240

Floribunda 240

Grandiflora 241

Single 241

Shrub 242

Miniature 243

FOUR STEPS TO FINE ROSES: 248–249

Roses hilled for winter 255

Vegetable garden, GrayRock 259

Oakleaf lettuce 268

Arrangement of salad materials (*Boutrelle*) 269

Tomatoes 271

Pole beans 273

Sweet corn 274

Melons 277

Peaches 287

Raspberries 288

Strawberries in the garden and ready to serve (2) 288, 289

Authors' curved-eave greenhouse 300

Seedling plants 306

Three hose nozzles 308

Lettuce in peat pots 310

Line Illustrations

by Virginia Howie

Garden plan 5

Measure for tree shade 8

pH scale   19
Double digging   21
How to install drainage tile   22
Compost heap   29
How to take soil samples for testing   32
Plant anatomy   38

LIFE CYCLES OF:

annuals; biennials;   40
perennials; tubers;   41
bulbs   42
Methods of asexual reproduction   44
Details of air layering   64
"Scaling" a lily bulb   67
Preparing different types of cuttings   68
Propagation box   70
Whip and tongue graft   73
Wedge and cleft graft   73
Budding   74
Measure for watering   81
Pruning objectives   95
Espaliered fruits   99
Pruning tools   102
Method of securing coldframe sash   113
Hand tools for the garden   122, 123
Trellises and arbors   129
Spraying and dusting equipment   130
Lawn tools   132
Operation planting   154
A dry well to save a tree where grade is changed   162
"Chocolate layer" preparation of lawn soil   163
Cutting garden plan   179
How to thin seedlings   185
Supports for tall plants   186
Plan for mixed herbaceous border with lilies   191
Division of perennials   192
Plan for a herb garden   202
Rock garden   208

BUILDING THE ROCK GARDEN:

Make it three dimensional   209

Placing largest stones   211

Setting large rocks in soil   211

Rock garden with steps   212

Making retaining wall   216

A wall garden   216

Small garden pool   222

Patio with "plunging" bed for potted plants   230

Patio with garden plan   232

How to construct a self-watering window box   234

Self-watering system for rose garden   245

Post-and-chain support for roses   250

Removing rose suckers   251

Pruning roses   253

Vegetable garden plan   262

Trellis for tomatoes   270

Pinching out new growth on tomatoes   271

Supports for pole beans   273

Hilling up corn   274

"Heeling in" nursery stock   282

Dwarf fruit trees   285

Pruning apple trees   286

Pruning peach trees   290

Grape supports   291

Pruning grape vines   291

Raspberry culture   295

Strawberry plants   297

Rooting strawberry runners   298

Even-span and lean-to greenhouses   301

Potting shed with storage space   303

Portable potting bench   303

"Crocking" for potted plants   311

CALENDAR HEADINGS:

January   325

February   331

March   337

April   343
May   349
June   355
July   361
August   367
September   371
October   377
November   383
December   389

Foreword

Here is a different kind of garden book.

While designed especially to guide and aid the beginner, it will also, we believe, be valuable to the experienced gardener in enabling him to make sure that all his garden operations are attended to just when they should be done. Furthermore this is accomplished without the usual time-consuming research, sometimes in other books, for those unfamiliar details about operations that to him have not yet become routine.

In order to make this book of the widest possible use, the information concerning things to be watched for and attended to from month to month has been sectionalized in PART III, SELECTIVE, COUNTRY-WIDE MONTHLY CALENDAR. Therefore in whatever part of the country the reader may live, he will find, concentrated in one place, definite suggestions that apply to his own local climate.

These suggestions are in the form of brief reminders. As he looks them over—in a matter of fifteen or twenty minutes for each month—he will decide which of them apply to *his own particular interests and conditions*.

Then, in case he needs information as to the details of just *how* to do the jobs indicated, he will find these given in the preceding chapters of the book, which cover garden planning, planting, and maintenance. Reference page numbers, inserted in the calendar section, enable him to turn immediately to the instructions he seeks, with no time wasted in hunting through other books or magazine files to find out *how* to do any task that has been suggested. In other words, in this one book, he has a whole garden library at his fingertips, with just the information he needs, *when he needs it*.

The very great advantage of such an arrangement will at once be evident to any home gardener who, with many other matters on his mind, has so often suddenly realized that the time for doing something that he wanted to do has slipped by. Frequently this may mean a delay of an entire year!

Very often, too, it means the loss of money that might have been saved, as when one has to pay a half dollar or more apiece for perennial plants that could just as well have been started from seed the previous summer at a cost of a few cents each. The same thing applies to shrubs, trees, evergreens, hedges, and other components of attractive home surround-ings. Most of these will cost dollars where they might have cost dimes had they been purchased in small sizes and then grown on to landscape-size specimens in a home nursery—*if* the homeowner had only been reminded of it at the proper time!

At least once every month in the year, and in most cases much more frequently, the average home gardener lets some garden operation slip by that costs him money because it was not done on time. It is just such expensive omissions and mistakes that this book is planned to obviate.

In addition to these omissions there are dozens of others which, while not involving actual loss of money, result in home surroundings much less attractive than they should be—a less perfect lawn, for instance, or poorer displays in the flower borders, or vegetables or fruits that are not as fine as they might be. Such misadventures and losses often are the direct re-sults of failure to feed, spray, or provide protection for plant material just when one or perhaps all of these things should have been done to assure best results.

The sum total of such errors of omission, even on the average small place, is the difference between well-cared-for grounds and gardens, of which the owner is justly proud, and the mediocre or ill-kept property that never commands a second look from the passer-by, and of which the owner is secretly ashamed.

More than a half century of practical gardening experience, under widely varying conditions, is condensed in this volume. It is the hope of the authors that it may bring to others much of the same pleasure they have enjoyed in acquiring the information that has gone into its making.

PART ONE

YOUR HOME GROUNDS: HOW TO PLAN, PLANT, AND MAINTAIN THEM

I'd leave all the hurry, the noise, and the fray
For a house full of books, and a garden of flowers.
Ballade of True Wisdom by ANDREW LANG

CHAPTER 1

Planning the New Place

At last you have a place of your own to plan! There is no thrill in the world quite like it, unless perhaps the building of your own house; and even in that case it is quite likely that the architect and the builder will not leave you as free a hand as you have in developing your grounds and gardens.

Furthermore it is not a thrill that will be finished in a few weeks or a few months. It continues for years, with each passing season bringing new projects, new changes, and new successes. It is, in more than one sense of the word, a growing entertainment and satisfaction.

Even when one is not starting from scratch but taking over a place already established, the adventure is almost as exciting. The house may be more or less permanently set in a definite pattern; but the grounds are not. Here, quite literally, the sky is the limit. There may be old trees or large shrubs which cannot readily be moved, but with few exceptions they can be worked into the planting plan.

Frequently old trees, too large to move, but occupying an undue amount of space or casting shade over too large an area, are tolerated much longer than they should be. We recall, with some amusement from this distance in time and space, a very old tulip tree that had grown up in the remains of a stone wall on land where we built a house. This tree was for several years our pride and joy. Nothing grew under it but a tangle of weeds and poorly nourished wild benzoin that had become tall and leggy. Then one night in a hurricane it blew down—falling away from the house fortunately. We heard the crash, and a flashlight revealed what had happened. We spent most of the remainder of the night lamenting our loss, but in the morning something wonderful had happened. Our study and bedroom were flooded with sunshine, where formerly they had always been filled with filtered green light. The same was true of one end of the big living room. We liked the change immensely—though we were somewhat reluctant to admit that fact even to ourselves.

After the wreckage (which incidentally revealed that our fine old tree was rotten at the heart) had been cleared away, we discovered that it had left us a perfect site for a rock garden, with stones on the spot. These, moved into proper position and supplemented by larger ones to form a ledge with water dripping in a natural manner from the crevices, formed an area that attracted more attention from visitors than anything else on the place. Best of all, most people assumed it to be not man-made but a bit of nature's handiwork with merely a few cultivated plants added.

We have told this story not to point a moral—though one might be found without digging very deeply—but to bring out two facts: one, that the homeowner should not hesitate to make radical changes about the grounds; and two, that it takes a comparatively short time to give a garden area a completely new look.

MAKE A LONG-RANGE PLAN

By far the first and most important step to be taken in developing an attractive place, and one that will provide the greatest returns in everyday satisfaction, is to make a definite long-range plan.

If the place is a fairly large one, and you feel that you are not capable of developing such a plan, by all means consult a landscape architect. By so doing you can avoid making serious mistakes that in all probability would cost you more than his fee. Not only that, but he undoubtedly can make suggestions that will give you better immediate effects than you would otherwise be likely to achieve.

Lacking the services of a landscape architect or of the more modest "garden consultant," you can do your own planning by thoroughly studying one or more of the several excellent books available on the subject. (See Books for Further Reference, Appendix.) You will find these helpful in any event, because you will undoubtedly be adding to your plantings for many years; that is part of the fascination of the game!

THE MASTER PLAN

It saves much time and trouble in the long run to make a very complete master plan at the beginning. This need not show detailed plantings, but it should cover the entire grounds, including buildings, driveways and other traffic lanes, service and recreation areas, and projected plantings. This should be drawn to scale on a large sheet of squared paper such as architects and engineers use, obtainable at any stationery store. Paper ruled ten squares to the inch is convenient to use.

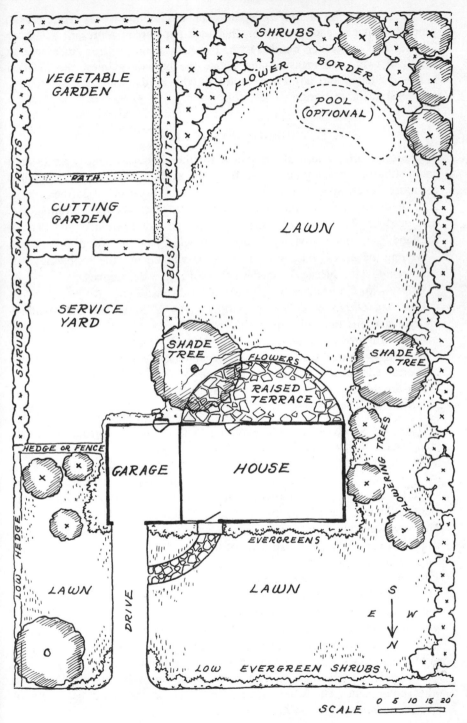

The scale to be adopted depends of course upon the size of the property. That is, each square on the ruled paper may represent 5, 10, or 20 feet (or any other number). A two-man team, with a stake and a length of twine can measure and locate the boundary lines, the location of the residence and any other buildings, the roads, walks, walls, fences, and existing large trees.

THE IMPORTANT AREAS

Regardless of the size of the place, whether it be a country estate or a small suburban development plot, there are certain areas to be designated for more or less specific uses—just as in the house itself, regardless of its size, there are specific areas for cooking, lounging, sleeping, bathing, etc. The outdoor areas will vary because of the size of the place, the "lay of the land," and the individual interests or whims of the owner.

Among the areas which are likely to be wanted are the following:

Screening (for privacy)—hedges, shrubbery, walls, fences.

Utility—for clotheslines, dog house, trash disposal, etc.

Rest and Outdoor Living—providing areas of both sun and shade, a view of gardens or a distant vista.

Play—for grownups' games and/or children's playground.

Gardens—Flower Beds, Borders, Vegetables, Fruits

Special Gardens—Cutting, Herb, Rose, Rock, Wall, Water

Locomotion

Lawn

Only the vitally interested gardener with expansive grounds should plan for all of these areas; on a small place it would not be possible. The lawn, for instance, must probably be utilized for play, and possibly (if it extends to the rear of the house) for outdoor living. There may not be space for a separate flower garden, in which event the flower borders may include flowers for cutting as well as for decoration where they grow. The vegetable and fruit areas may be combined or omitted altogether. If the owner does not wish to do this, a few vegetables may be incorporated in a wide flower border.

In one of the most interesting small places we ever saw this was done. The vegetables were not in rows, but in small groups; a few dwarf fruits and everbearing raspberries formed part of the screen planting that extended around three sides of the plot. At the rear of the house, out of sight from the road, a well-kept shaded lawn provided space for lounging, with a hammock and rocking chairs that invited complete relaxation. At one side a small, neat garden house took care of tools, mowers, and other equipment. The whole layout was one of the finest examples of *multum in parvo* that we have ever seen.

Now we are ready to begin the plan. We have to start with the given dimensions and the location of the house and other buildings, if any.

The next step is to locate on the plan any other existing features, such as big trees, rocks, banks, or other marked changes in elevation.

Next we fit into the remaining space the other special areas desired, and for which *room can be found.* One of the worst mistakes that can be made is to try to crowd in too much. If there is not sufficient space for all, then an effort should be made to *combine* some of them, as suggested previously.

Screening. If the place is a small one, and privacy is a consideration, then a fairly tall but dense-growing hedge is one solution. A strip at least three feet wide should be allowed, even if the hedge is to be kept trimmed —a task in these days of electric hedge trimmers not nearly so time consuming as it used to be. Where space is at a premium, a stout wire or wattle fence, or a barrier of louvers covered with vines, may be a better solution.

On the somewhat larger place, a mixed border planting of trees and shrubs, or shrubs alone, provides more effective screening and at the same time makes a most attractive addition to the landscape picture. It should be kept in mind however that a planting of this type cannot be kept under such complete control as to height and breadth as can a hedge or planted fence; and that it may eventually shut out prevailing breezes, a view, or sunshine that is desirable.

With the "walls" of the outdoor living area provided for, the next step is to decide on the number of "rooms" and their locations.

Utility Area. This should include the tool house, if there is to be one, a yard for drying clothes, a sunken garbage can with heavy lid and foot pedal, etc.

In many modern houses the garage serves as the tool house. In our own home in fact, it is the tools (power mowers, power cultivator, power edger) that really are the masters of space, with barely enough room left for the car and opening the door to the driver's seat. Of course about once a month we say we are going to clear out a lot of hand tools, flats, unplanted bulbs, etc., which somehow collect in what should be free floor space, but it's always *next* month. This in spite of the fact that we have a garden house for storing hand tools and materials *and* a potting shed. By all means plan for a separate tool house if you can!

Play and Rest. For both grownups and youngsters, a large part of the summer will be spent out of doors. Where enough space is available it is well to have separate areas for active play and for peaceful relaxation, but with the decreasing size of the average home plot of ground this becomes more and more difficult. It is often possible, however, to find space for at least one play area, even if for nothing more than a spot for practicing basketball, a croquet or badminton court, a putting green, or an area for pitching horseshoes. The advantage, where teen-agers or near teen-agers are involved need not be stressed here, for it will mean children staying and playing at home instead of wandering off to find entertainment elsewhere.

If there is to be an area for rest and relaxation—and occasional outdoor entertainment of a few guests—this may be placed at the rear or to one side of the house, protected as much as possible from the street. The ideal thing is to have it connected with the porch (in an old-fashioned house) or with the terrace in a modern one. Even a slight difference in elevation helps to set it off.

Shade. This subject we have touched upon, but it should be given a bit more consideration. Most of the things that are done about the new place, or one that is being renewed, show immediate results. A hedge, for instance, may be only 18 inches or 2 feet high when it is set out, but the owner can readily visualize what it will be like in two or three years when it has attained a height of 4 to 5 feet. A flower garden, when first made, is a two-dimensional flat area; but it doesn't take such imagination to behold it in full bloom with 4- to 6-foot hollyhocks, delphinium, cosmos, lilies, and hardy asters making a background for the lower-growing bedding plants in front of them.

With a shade tree it is a very different matter. When you set out a spindly whip of an elm, oak, beech, or even a dogwood or a clump of birches, the area it will eventually shade, even after a few years, is almost unbelievable. Adequate shade, even in a very moderate-sized place,

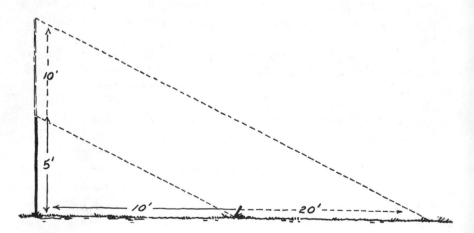

In deciding on location for tall trees, take into consideration how much dense shade they will cast as they mature. This can be estimated by measuring the shade cast by a pole of given length. If, for instance, a 5-foot pole casts a 10-foot shadow, a 25-foot tree will throw a 50-foot shadow.

is desirable. Nothing else can contribute quite so much comfort, not to mention esthetic value, to its owners during the summer and milder months of the year.

There is a present trend among nurserymen, as a result of the shrinking size of average rural and suburban homes, to develop lower-growing forms of our popular shade trees, and the small place owner will be well repaid for hunting them up.

To measure how far the shade of a tree will reach in 5 to 8 years, hold an old-fashioned bamboo fishing pole erect at the location of planting, check where the shadow falls, and use a little simple arithmetic.

The Foundation Planting is less important than it was when houses were constructed on stone or cement foundations extending several feet above the ground level. One still sees the dire results of planting tall-growing evergreens or shrubs against such houses in order to get an immediate effect. Lists of plants on pages 413 and 416 include many low-growing species suitable for planting close to house walls and under windows.

SPECIAL GARDENS

Whether or not special gardens of any sort may be desirable depends upon three factors: the size of the place; the character of the location; *and* the zeal and stick-to-itiveness of the gardener! In any event the beginner will do well not to attempt too much at first. Only after he has acquired some of the techniques of gardening, and has gained some idea of the time required to accomplish certain things, should he venture far in specializing.

On the other hand there certainly is no doubt that making a specialty of some phase of gardening or some single group of plants does bring its own particular rewards—interests and achievements which are to be had in no other way.

What the specialty will be depends primarily on the predilections of the individual gardener, who may find, for some reason known not even to himself, that roses or cacti or rock plants, azaleas or lilies or even dahlias, are more fascinating than all other flowers. However, there may be other impelling considerations; for instance, a rocky slope ideal for a rock garden; a sandy spot in a hot climate that would suit cacti to a "T"; or boggy low land that could readily be converted into a water garden. If such is the case, by all means make the most of it.

The Hardy Border. The mixed border (a long, comparatively narrow bed) containing a varied assortment of perennials, with or without annuals and biennials added, is generally the most satisfactory single garden feature. In it one may enjoy almost unlimited varieties of plant forms, flower forms, and colors. Most important of all, a continuous succession

Part of the old and very lovely Buttrick garden at Concord, Mass. From here an ancestor of the present owner led the embattled farmers who fired "the shot heard 'round the world." The house and grounds look out over gently sloping fields to the famous bridge where the Minutemen made their stand. The importance of evergreens is well illustrated here where they are used as background material and for protection.

of bloom may be achieved from the time the snow melts in spring (with such early bulbs as snowdrops and crocus and spring perennials like arabis, iberis, and creeping phlox) until the first snow in autumn, when the last hardy chrysanthemums and asters, monkshood and late-blooming annuals finally succumb.

Flower Beds, or special areas for some particular type of flower, or for cutting, serve a somewhat different purpose. Some plants, because of special requirements in culture, do best when given a space to themselves. Roses—with the possible exception of the climbers and some shrub roses —do much better in a bed of their own, as do dahlias, most lilies, chrysanthemums, and species requiring support, such as sweet peas and snapdragons.

A common mistake, especially in these days of bulldozer operations, is to fail to take advantage of the lay of the land. Here the addition and rearrangement of a few rocks have created a charmingly naturalistic setting.

The frame for each garden picture should be planned at the very start. Here a yew hedge, though but recently set out, already adds much to the effectiveness of the perennial planting.

Here is an excellent example of keeping the landscaping in harmony with the house. The horizontal design of the planting and the spreading yews and other plant materials used achieve a very happy effect.

Rock, Wall, and Water Gardens. Any of these, properly incorporated in the landscape scheme, add immensely to the charm and beauty of a place. But they are not to be stuck haphazardly into the garden picture. To be really effective they must have, at least to a passable degree, the appearance of having been placed there by nature.

Often a mound, a steep slope, or a gully which at first seems to present a serious problem may be developed into a distinctive special feature. Anything that can be done to add the third dimension of *height* to a level plot greatly adds to its attractiveness. *Where such a possibility exists, the area in question should be considered when planning the landscaping,* even though development of the area must be left until later.

Vegetable and Fruit Gardens. One of the unfortunate things about the shrinking size of ground plots for suburban homes in most sections of the country is that there is less room for home vegetable and fruit growing. Even more regrettable is the fact that this is only half the story. There are millions of places where vegetables and possibly some fruit could be grown, with both profit and pleasure to the owners, but where never a seed is planted or a tree set out.

This indifference to home food growing is on the increase even though most home-grown vegetables and fruits are infinitely more flavorful and tender than those that have been developed by the plant breeders particularly for "eye appeal" and shipping quality rather than for flavor. Shipped thousands of miles to the chain-store outlets which dispense them, most vegetables today are either withered by the time they're sold or kept plump by constant syringing or by storage in cellophane bags. Many fruits that are likely to spoil in transit are shipped so green that they reach the table still unripe, even though artificial skin coloring may make them appear appetizing. More concerning this is said in chapters 17 and 18. It is suggested that, before the complete plan the development of the home place is decided upon, a space for vegetables and or fruits be allotted to this use. It is always easier to eliminate projects on the plan than to find space for them afterward.

TAKE TIME IN PLANNING YOUR PLACE

One final word on making your planting plan:

Don't be in too great a hurry. You can move a tree, even a big one, or transplant a whole hedge *on your planting plan* in just a couple of minutes. The actual operation, once a mistake has been made, may take hours or even days.

When you have prepared the plot plan do not at once begin to fill in the different areas—lawn, play and rest areas, garden plots—directly upon it. Instead use a tissue or tracing-paper overlay and mark the areas, drives, walks, and paths on this. Then try a different arrangement, and if unsatisfied with it, still another. Only after comparing several possibilities can you be certain that you have the one which will best suit your purposes. The same is true of placement of each flower bed, border, and any other landscape feature.

Leaf after leaf drops off, flower after flower,
Some in the chill, some in the warmer hour:
Alike they flourish and alike they fall,
And earth who nourished them receives them all.
                    WALTER SAVAGE LANDOR

CHAPTER 2

The Soil and How to Manage It

No matter how much or how little gardening the owner of a small country place or a suburban home may plan to do, his basic problem—after the planning is done—is the *soil*. The soil is the home in which his plants have to live, and it is the major factor in determining whether they prosper vigorously, merely manage to exist, or fail utterly. In fact his soil—next to climate (temperature, moisture, and wind)—will determine *what* he can grow successfully.

The character of the soil depends upon two factors; its *physical* structure and its *chemical* content. Both of these, fortunately, can to a considerable extent be altered by the way the soil is handled, what is done in its mechanical treatment, and what is added to it. While this is true, the fact remains that much less work and care is involved when the owner uses plant material that is naturally adapted to the type of soil he happens to possess.

This of course is not always possible. The soil, for instance, upon which the authors have established their present garden was about as unproductive as any that could well be imagined, boasting only scrub pine, barren areas of wild tuft grasses that could establish themselves on bare sandy spots, and, where the best "soil" was, wild black locusts and an impenetrable tangle of cat brier and the Cape's famous "trippin' briers." There was also a bumper crop of poison ivy to add to our problem.

Friends, especially those who had seen our former home, thought we were bemused to select such a location. It suited our requirements, however, in every other respect and it was a challenge to our skill as gardeners, which we rather welcomed. The results we have achieved make a very good demonstration of what can be done in the way of soil alteration, even from a very unpromising beginning.

TYPES OF SOIL

Almost everyone, even the apartment-house dweller, knows that there are different types of soil, though his experience with them may be limited to having to clean mud off his shoes or shake sand out of them.

The two best known and the two extremes of texture are found in *sandy* soils and *clay* soils. Within these two types there are again marked differences. If the sand particles are sufficiently coarse we have a gravel which is really not a soil at all, as the individual particles merely fall apart if one attempts to move it. If, on the other hand, clay particles are sufficiently fine, we have a plastic, monolithic mass like modeling clay which, if dried out, forms a stonelike substance or, if sufficiently wet, may be smeared like paint.

When sand and clay (or silt, which contains clay as a rule) are mixed together they blend to form what we know as *loam*. This may be a sandy or a clay loam but differs from its component parts in that it will hold water instead of letting it all drain through as does sand. Unlike clay, it does not remain in sodden lumps and masses, which when they do dry out become as hard as bricks.

To grow good crops or good turf, or to support vigorous shrubs and trees, the soil must be in such physical condition as to absorb and hold a large amount of moisture, but at the same time be open enough to let *surplus* water drain down through it without creating a muddy mass. The ideal soil should hold approximately equal amounts of air and of water; for roots of plants, in order to function normally, must have both.

This knowledge takes us the first step on our way to understanding what type of soil is needed to grow plants successfully. Two other steps, however, remain. One of these is to know the function of organic materials in soil building; the other is to learn the part played by various chemical elements.

ORGANIC MATERIALS IN SOIL BUILDING

Let's look first at the role played by organic materials—animal and vegetable matter undergoing the process of decomposition. It is part of nature's scheme of things that every living plant or animal, when it dies, shall contribute something to the lives of the plants or animals that come after it. This holds true whether the plant or animal is returned directly to the soil, or whether, after having served as food, it is transformed into the waste materials we call manures.

Organic materials when mixed into the soil improve it in many ways. They provide small amounts of the chemicals required by plants in their growth; they add humus to the soil structure; and they provide food for the soil bacteria, which, in turn, releases those chemicals in the soil that are otherwise unavailable to the plants.

· *Humus* (decaying animal and vegetable matter) is an all-important factor in soil fertility. It makes an open, porous soil which allows both air and water to penetrate freely; and also, acting in the soil like millions of tiny sponges, absorbs and holds the water and *the chemical food elements that are in solution in it*. These chemical food elements *must* be in solution before the roots of plants can take them up.

On the other hand humus permits free drainage of *surplus* water down to lower levels. Most forms of plant life, including all the trees, shrubs, flowers, grasses, fruits, and vegetables usually found around a home, cannot long survive in a sodden soil.

One further benefit provided by humus is that, as it forms no provoking clods, it is easy to work. A humusy soil warms up quickly in the spring, making possible earlier preparation and more successful planting. It is in fact a "friable" soil—one that you love to touch!

PLANT FOODS: CHEMICAL ELEMENTS IN THE SOIL

So far we have discussed the physical aspects of soils—the materials which go to make them up, and their various characteristics. We can have all of these in favorable amounts and combinations and still have a soil that is not fertile, that will not make plants *grow*.

There are a number of elements essential to the successful growth of plants. First of all they must have oxygen, carbon, and hydrogen, all of which they obtain from the air and from water.

Next come the three chief nutrients: nitrogen, phosphorus, and potassium. One or often all of these must be supplied or supplemented in the form of fertilizers.

Calcium, magnesium, iron, and sulfur are other important elements that must be present, but most soils contain these in sufficient quantities so that they need not be added. Desert and other alkaline soils are among the few exceptions to this rule. Most of them lack sulfur, and sometimes other elements such as boron.

The so-called trace elements: manganese, boron, copper, zinc, and molybdenum contribute to plant growth, but are needed in such infinitesimal quantities that they seldom have to be added. Many complete fertilizers today, however, do contain these trace elements.

Not only must all of these elements be present in the soil, air, and water, but they must be in forms that are soluble or that will readily become so through soil acids and bacterial action.

The three elements contained in all "complete" fertilizers are nitrogen, phosphorus, and potassium. The precentage of each which commercial fertilizers contain must, by law, be marked on each bag or package. A 5–

10–10 formula for example contains 5 per cent nitrogen, 10 per cent phosphorus, and 10 per cent potassium. If boron is present, that is expressed by a fourth figure. The numerals representing the percentages of the several elements are always given in the order mentioned above.

Often, too, the material or materials used in the mixture to provide the given amounts of nitrogen, phosphorus, and potassium are stated. For instance nitrogen may come from sodium nitrate (nitrate of soda) or from tankage or blood and bone (slaughterhouse by-products); phosphorus from superphosphate (processed phosphate rock); and potassium from potassium chloride or wood ashes (potash).

CHEMICAL *vs.* ORGANIC SOURCES

It will be noted that some of these sources of plant-food elements are chemical, others organic. In theory this should make no difference; in actual practice it does.

In the first place, the rapidity with which the chemical is released and can be taken up by the plant roots is an important factor. The nitrogen from nitrate of soda, for instance, is available almost instantly, while that from bone meal is released very slowly.

As a rule the chemical elements in organic matter become available more quickly than those from mineral sources. The latter take longer to break down in the soil and release the chemical elements in forms that can go into solution and be taken up by the plant roots.

The great big plus in favor of organic sources is that they add not only essential chemical elements to the soil, but also organic matter—and how vitally important that is we have already seen in the discussion on humus earlier in this chapter.

Acid and Alkaline Soils. There is still another respect in which soils differ from one another. They may be acid, sweet, (alkaline), or neutral.

The great majority of plants thrive in soil that is neutral to slightly or moderately acid; a few demand an acid soil; and still fewer a really sweet or alkaline soil.

Soil acidity or alkalinity is measured by what is known as the pH scale, arranged like a thermometer, with 1 representing maximum acidity and 7 as the neutral point (see diagram).

The question of soil acidity, while important, does not cause as much concern as formerly. More gardeners have come to realize that *a soil in which the humus content is maintained at a high level* greatly decreases the likelihood of injury to plant growth from too great a degree of acidity. It should be noted, however, that the key word here is *maintained,* for soil humus, like an unfed fire, is quickly consumed unless kept replenished.

The Subsoil and Its Importance. The subsoil is, as the word implies,

THE pH SCALE

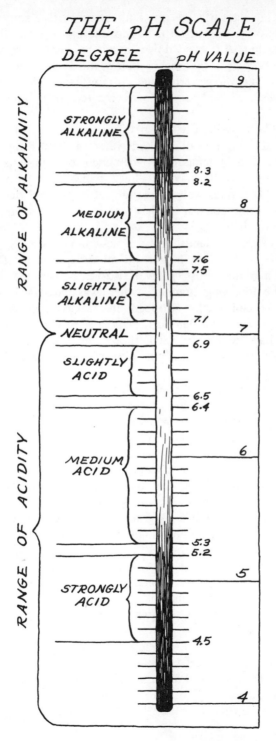

the soil beneath the surface layer. Unlike the surface soil, it has remained for hundreds of years with little or no alteration, other than gaining the nutrients and humus leached down into it by rainfall. In some places the subsoil may be only a few inches below the surface, in others a foot to 20 inches. In our Midwestern states, for instance, where for centuries the prairie grasses grew and rotted down, the topsoil is often up to two feet deep.

Subsoils, like topsoils, vary greatly in composition. They may be sandy or gravelly, allowing rain or applied water to drain away so quickly that plant roots are only temporarily benefited by nutrients in the topsoil above; or they may be clay or "hard pan," an impervious cementlike layer that holds surplus water so long that air is excluded and plants are quite literally drowned, just as they are in areas that are flooded by the construction of dams.

Some years ago, in landscaping a new home, we had two American elms, each some 25 feet in height, put in for our client. The nurseryman, for a small additional cost, gave a two-year guarantee that they would live. Late the following summer, which was excessively rainy, one tree turned yellow and finally dropped its leaves and died. Examination showed that it had been planted in a pocket of clay subsoil, and for lack of drainage had literally drowned, though no water had collected on the surface. The replacement tree, put in with proper tile drainage to a lower level, grew lustily.

Where the topsoil is very shallow, only 3 to 5 inches, it may be made deeper by turning up, whenever the garden is dug or plowed, 2 to 3 inches of subsoil to be mixed with the surface soil. Or the English system of double digging may be employed.

In extreme cases, where a tenacious clay subsoil exists not far below the surface, the only solution is to put in a drainage system that will carry off the surplus water. While this may be made a do-it-yourself job, it is usually better to have it done professionally.

The first step is to establish a grade from the high point on the area to be drained to some low point such as a roadside gutter or a drainage ditch. The drains should be sufficiently below the surface to escape accidental breakage or disturbance, usually a minimum of 8 to 12 inches. Either ceramic drain pipes (which are 24 inches long, with an open collar at one end that permits soil water freely to enter the joints), or the newer composition drain pipe (which has perforations along its entire length) may be used. The latter has the advantage that it can be laid in a continuous strip to a more even slope, thus saving much time. Also there is less chance of accidental breakage after it is laid.

If some coarse, nonpacking material such as small stones, crushed stone, very coarse gravel, or brick and mortar rubble is filled in around and over the drain tile or pipe, the effectiveness of the drainage system

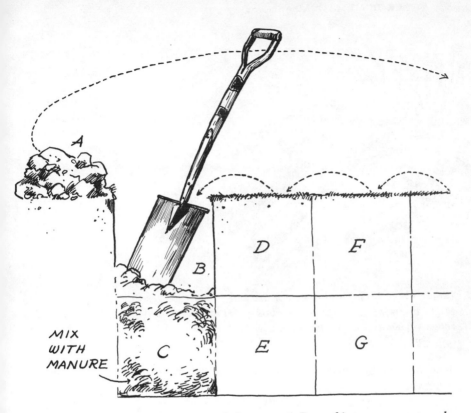

MIX WITH MANURE

DOUBLE DIGGING. A—*Soil is removed from area B, making an open trench.* C—*Subsoil in area C is forked over and mixed with manure or peatmoss and compost.*
D—*Topsoil from this area is forked over, mixed with compost and fertilizer, and placed in trench C.*
E—*This area is forked over and treated as area C.*
F—*Is treated as area D, the enriched soil being placed in area D. This operation is repeated over the entire area to be dug.*
A—*Topsoil A is enriched and carried across at the end of the digging operation to fill in the remaining open trench at the far side of the garden.*

is greatly increased. The sketch on page 22 shows the layout for a drainage system for a moderate-sized area.

A most important point in installing a drainage system is that there shall be no sags or low spots. If there are, the whole purpose is defeated, for water that has drained *into* the system from a higher elevation will, at such places, drain *out* of it, back into the soil.

Too porous subsoil, so sandy or gravelly that little or no moisture is retained, creates a very serious condition. The only remedy here is to build up the amount of humus in the surface soil by every means available

Where heavy (clay) soil does not dry out promptly after rain, it is necessary to install drainage tile, with open joints to admit water. This greatly increases the range of plants which may be grown.

—such as adding manure, peatmoss, and other forms of organic matter; using mulching materials wherever possible; and growing "green manure" crops such as rye, ryegrass, oats, clover, and vetch (see pages 26–27).

SPECIAL AREA SOIL TYPES

While our discussion so far has covered average soils such as are encountered over most of the United States, there are areas where non-typical soils present special problems. In some instances such soil types are almost state-wide, in others less than the size of a county, or even of a township.

Though we cannot go into complete details about such soils, we can guide the reader in recognizing them, and tell him how to set about making them better fitted for growing the average run of trees, shrubs, and other plants.

Clay and Sandy Soils. These, as we have seen, are the two extreme types of average soils found everywhere. The way to improve the structure of either is to add the other, *plus humus.*

Peat Soils. These are composed basically of vegetable matter that has started to decay but has been arrested in the process by being covered with water or with soil. (Under some conditions the process continued to eventually form coal.)

If the vegetable material happened to be sphagnum moss, it was converted to what we know as moss-peat: or more generally, but incorrectly, as peatmoss, for it is peat formed from moss, *not* moss formed from peat.

If the vegetable matter was made up of sedges and other bog plants, the eventual product became peat—or sedge peat—quite different in its physical make-up from moss-peat. This is true particularly of its more limited capacity to absorb and hold water.

Both types of peat are extremely valuable for horticultural uses—but to home gardeners especially so in their processed commercial forms, added to other soils.

Muck Soils, found in drained or dried-up bog and marsh areas, also contain much decayed or semidecayed vegetable matter and serve for the extensive growing of special crops such as celery, lettuce, onions, and cranberries, which are suited to the conditions they provide.

Frequently such muck soils, partially dried, are dug and sold or peddled locally to inexperienced homeowners and gardeners who are misled, by their nice crumbly structure and black-as-your-hat color, into thinking that they are necessarily "rich." They may be; but there is an equal or better chance that they may be next to worthless. The novice is well advised to consult his local county agent before buying. He is likely to have some knowledge of such materials offered for local sale.

Adobe and Gumbo Soils cover extensive areas of low rainfall in the West and Southwest. Often they are naturally well supplied with plant-food elements but these are unavailable because there is not enough moisture to release them and because of the soil's physical properties. For their treatment and improvement see page 34.

A BRIEF LOOK AT THE SOILS OF THE UNITED STATES
(See map on back endpapers.)

Roughly, the soils of this country are divided in half by an imaginary line running north and south in the vicinity of Lincoln, Nebraska.

West of this line, soils are largely unleached (except in areas of high rainfall along the Pacific coast and in a few fertile valleys and river basins). That is to say there is so little rainfall that the soluble salts of potassium and sodium and the less soluble calcium and magnesium salts remain near the soil surface, unleached and unavailable to plant roots, thus contributing in varying degrees to aridity.

East of this line, rainfall gradually increases, and as it does so, salts, mineral nutrients, and humus are increasingly leached down below the surface to varying depths, but usually not beyond the reach of plant roots. In the east and central parts of the United States, a great variety of ornamental and food plants may be grown, not because the soil is more fertile than much of that farther west, but because of the long growing season, and because the high rainfall makes readily available to plant roots the nutrients from the topsoil.

The Alkaline Soils, some of which are so saline that they cannot be made fertile until their salt content has been artificially leached away, occur in those parts of the country where rainfall is very low, for fertility is closely related to humidity, since, to be available for plant growth, nutrients must be in solution.

In the driest regions we find pale *desert soils* (*adobe*), practically without humus, where the surface salts contribute to their gray color; or very dark, fine-grained, silty *gumbo* soils which, when wet, become soapy, waxy, or sticky, and are completely unworkable in that condition. Often desert areas are so strongly alkaline that only alkaline-resistant plants can survive except where conditions have been improved through irrigation and when necessary, also by leaching of the surface salts (page 35).

East of the desert areas, *grayish-brown soils* occur which contain some humus and a considerable content of soluble salts. Instead of accumulating on the surface, as in the desert itself, calcium carbonates are here leached down by a little more rainfall (5 to 18 inches annually) to a depth of 12 to 15 inches. On these unimproved soils, low, sparse grass and wild shrubs are found. With irrigation other things may be grown, but commercially these lands are used largely for grazing.

Chestnut soils occur east of the grayish-brown, in areas where rainfall is 15 to 22 inches per annum. Here calcium salts are leached down 14 to 24 inches below the surface. There is more humus content, enough to give it a chestnut-brown color, and on it cereal grains can be grown where artificial irrigation is used. Providing adequate water makes this land highly productive.

East of this again, we find the Great Plains of the central United States, the soil containing little potassium or sodium but a heavy content of calcium salts 24 to 36 inches below the surface. In the thick humus layer, 15 inches or more in depth, formed by the prairie grasses that originally grew there, there exists ample nitrogen and mineral nutrients, released only by moisture.

The true *prairie soils,* very dark or almost black in color, are to be found still farther east, in the area of which the present Iowa corn belt is the heart. Here, where rainfall is heavy, the wild prairie grasses originally grew to the height of a man, and created a humus layer of 20 inches or more. This humus layer retains large quantities of nutrients and moisture, providing the richest soil in the country for the commercial growing of corn, oats, wheat, and fodders.

Eastward from the prairie lands, the country was originally timbered. Rainfall is high—30 to 50 inches—and humus considerable, though, except in northern forest sections, it has been carried well below the surface together with calcium salts, iron, and aluminum. Because of favorable climate and plentiful rainfall, however, these soils become highly productive when well fertilized and regularly supplied with supplementary humus.

In the far northern lands, which are both cold and wet, more of the ample humus, salts, and other nutrients remain near the surface because of the natural mulch on the forest floor, but for many plants the growing season is too short.

Along the border states from Minnesota to New York, on the Atlantic Seaboard and along the Gulf coast, areas of high rainfall and humidity have created soils largely made up of decomposed organic matter and therefore called *organic soils*. These, when drained and correctly handled, are highly fertile.

REMAKING AND MAINTAINING SOILS

So now we come to the all-important part of this chapter: how to improve unsatisfactory soils and how to maintain good ones. For even a good soil has to be *kept* good. Otherwise it will run down—and in time run out!

Every homeowner or gardener has, of course, to start with the soil he has, but unless it is a *very* exceptional soil, he can within the course of two or three years change it to the type that will support most of the plants he desires to grow. In most instances this development need not involve any very great expense.

The one thing he should *not* expect to do, if his soil is lacking in humus, is to convert it into a productive loam merely by adding large quantities of chemical fertilizers. Yet, as a result of ignorance and exaggerated and misleading claims made by some unscrupulous advertisers, this is exactly what hundreds of thousands of gullible new homeowners annually do expect to accomplish.

Here is a safe and sane program for creating productive soil in areas where there are no *acute* soil problems of alkalinity, salinity, alkalisalinity, or acidity. First, determine the character of the soil you have to start with.

One need not be a chemist to determine if he has sandy soil or a clay soil. If decidedly of either type, it may be improved by adding, if it is procurable, soil of the opposite type. A one- to two-inch layer of either type will usually work wonders, especially if supplemented by a dressing of lime (see page 33) and by humus.

A heavy application of *manure*—a layer two to three inches thick, is the quickest method of improving both the physical condition of the soil and providing immediately available plant foods. It should be partly rotted; and a mixture of horse and cow manure is better than either one alone.

Hen manure and sheep manure are very strong, and best used only after they have been mixed with compost, dead leaves, or other organic roughage and have begun to decay.

All animal manures are becoming, in most sections, more and more difficult to get. Therefore, to add sufficient amounts of humus to build up a soil in such areas, it becomes increasingly necessary to use substitutes for them.

The two most useful substitutes are *peatmoss* and *green manures*. The latter is made up of crops which are grown for the purpose of digging or plowing under before they mature, to decay in the soil, and thus add to it large amounts of humus (see also page 86).

Peatmoss has the advantage of being immediately effective, furnishing humus in an ideal form. Green manures have the advantage of being very much less expensive—just the cost of the seed and sufficient ferti-

"Green manuring," or turning under a growing crop to add humus to the soil, is the best and most economical method of improving poor soil. Here the incorporation of three successive crops of winter rye has been the chief factor in converting a thin, barren soil into a deep, rich garden loam.

lizer to give them a good start—but they require several months to a year from the time of sowing until they have been turned under and have decayed in the soil. Some of them, such as rye, ryegrass, and winter vetch, may be sown in the fall to make winter growth and be turned under the following spring. Other good, green manure crops are vetch, sweet clover, crimson clover, alsike clover, and hairy vetch. All the clovers and vetches are legumes and so have the extra advantage of adding nitrogen to the soil.

A procedure which we have used successfully in bringing much of our barren soil into a high degree of productivity is that of sowing winter rye on flower beds or vegetable plots as soon as they are cleared in late summer or fall, adding a high nitrogen fertilizer to give them a quick start, and turning them under as the ground is needed in spring. No patch of soil, at any time of year, is left long without a cover crop on it to manufacture humus.

The Compost Heap is another most valuable source of humus to the home gardener. In an efficiently run garden there is always one mature heap ready for use, plus a more recently made pile in the process of decomposition.

If one heap is built each autumn, using vegetable wastes stored for the purpose during the summer in a rough pile, plus undiseased, pest-free plants which have completed their growth cycle, and weeds which have not gone to seed, the gardener will at all times have compost available when needed.

To build an ideal compost heap, the following materials should be at hand:

1. Coarse dead stalks and stems such as those of corn, zinnia, or marigold for the bottom layer.
2. Grass cuttings, dead leaves, young weeds, and other vegetable wastes and garbage such as rotting or overmature fruits and vegetables, and peelings.
3. Garden soil.
4. Peatmoss and/or well-rotted leafmold.
5. Agricultural lime.
6. Manure, if available.
7. Complete fertilizer.

Location should be in part shade, where water is available, and in a position screened from flower gardens and the outdoor living areas.

Size can be as desired; 4 to 8 feet by 4 feet is convenient. After measuring off the area, a shallow pit one foot deep is dug; or a bin, built of cement blocks or boards, may be used as a base.

First layer. Fill the pit with coarse stems and stalks and with any large lumps of undecomposed compost left over from siftings of older, mature heap.

Maintaining a compost heap is an important factor in successful gardening. Every autumn we make up a pile such as this from materials accumulated during spring and summer. Nothing that will decay (unless diseased or pest-ridden) should ever be burned.

Second layer, 6 inches deep, is of grass cuttings, weeds, garbage, etc., from rough storage pile. Sprinkle this with complete fertilizer and lime, and wet down.

Third layer, 3 inches deep, is of garden soil.

Fourth layer, 3 to 6 inches deep, should be of manure if available, or peatmoss mixed with dry commercial manure such as Bovung or Dricanure.

Repeat sequence, beginning with the second layer, until heap is 4 to 6 feet high.

The heap should be built with the sides sloping gently inward, and the top left with a saucerlike depression to hold water. When completed, enough water is given to saturate all materials in the heap without leaching.

The entire heap may be turned "inside out" with a spading fork at the

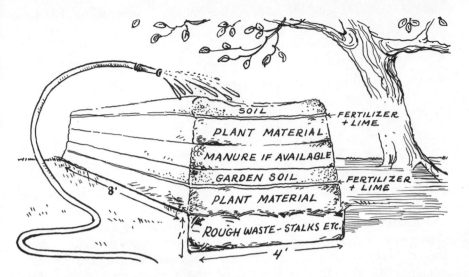

One of the greatest aids in growing plants of all kinds is the maintenance of a well-made compost heap, sprinkled occasionally to keep it moist. It may not look as neat as our artist's sketch, but if it can be placed near the garden itself, much time will be saved as the rotted, sifted compost is transported to beds and borders.

end of one and a half months to hasten decomposition; and again a month later. We seldom turn our compost but depend on the varied contents of the heaps, including manure, fertilizer, lime and peatmoss, to complete decomposition in 4 to 6 months.

In climates subject to extended dry spells the heap should be watered frequently to facilitate rapid rotting; it must be moist at all times.

In from three to six months, depending on how well it has been built and the materials it contains, the compost is ready for use. It may be sifted through an inch-mesh screen for potting up seedlings or setting out young plants; or to place in rows and beds for outdoor seed sowing; or may be used unsifted in perennial beds and borders and in the bottoms of holes when planting trees and shrubs. The product should be very dark in color, light in texture, but rich, easily sifted, and crumbly.

Martin E. Weeks, of the College of Agriculture, University of Massachusetts, in his booklet *Composts for the Home Grounds* states that well-made compost is the equivalent of the best grade of animal manures, *plus* its added content of chemical fertilizers and lime.

Many State Experiment Stations issue bulletins on compost making, stressing the use of locally available materials.

So much for the first step in building up productive soils—getting them well supplied with humus in order to keep them open, to hold moisture, provide good drainage and conditions favorable for beneficial soil bacteria.

Now we come to the second step.

PROVIDING THE ESSENTIAL CHEMICAL ELEMENTS

Having built a solid foundation—that of getting the soil into first class *mechanical* condition, or setting the table so to speak—we are now ready to bring on the food, the chemicals in the soil which plants need to make lusty growth.

We have already seen that these are chiefly nitrogen, phosphorus, and potassium (the meat and vegetables of the meal) plus the minor or trace elements usually present in sufficient amounts—the sugar, salt, pepper, and vinegar that stay on the table and seldom need to be replenished.

Nitrogen. There are many materials which provide nitrogen: organic sources such as animal manures and processed animal and vegetable materials like tankage, cottonseed meal, and a number of others, seldom in these days used by the amateur gardener. Chemical sources include ammonium nitrate and sodium nitrate (nitrate of soda) ranging from 5 to 15 or 20 per cent of nitrogen in very quickly available but not long-lasting forms. The effect of nitrate of soda, for instance, can often be seen within two or three days after it is applied. Newly developed types of nitrogen-bearing chemicals—such as urea—release the nitrogen slowly and so are much more effective as season-long fertilizers. Nitrate of soda and similar quick-acting forms are excellent for giving plants a strong, quick start, but should be used with judgment and caution. Otherwise their use may result in too luxuriant, soft growth, or may even "burn" the roots. The chief function of nitrogen in nature's plan is to assure luxuriant growth of foliage of good color and substance.

Phosphorus, second of the big-three plant-food elements, is effective in vigorous root, tuber, and seed development, and so complements or balances nitrogen.

Many soils are low in phosphorus, particularly in forms that can be taken up by plant roots. Fortunately this element, in forms readily available as plant food, is to be had in superphosphate, and in triplephosphate. The former contains 20 per cent and the latter 45 per cent phosphorus. Both are commonly used in commercial fertilizers as a source of phosphorus. Bone meal contains 20 to 25 per cent phosphorus, plus some nitrogen, and is a very safe (nonburning) fertilizer to use, *especially in transplanting.*

Potassium, third of the big three, is important because it contributes to vigorous root growth and strong, sturdy stems. It is present in ample quantity in most soils but, unfortunately for gardeners, in forms that cannot be taken up by plant roots until abundant humus in the soil and the action of soil bacteria have made it so.

In most soils that are well supplied with humus, potassium in available forms will be ample. Where a soil analysis shows that it is deficient, it may be added by applying sulfate or muriate of potash. Where wood ashes are to be had, either homemade or purchased, they provide an excellent organic source of potash.

"COMPLETE" FERTILIZERS

Few homeowners these days attempt to mix their own fertilizers, but some knowledge of their ingredients is essential to those who wish to procure the best types and use them to the best advantage. Millions of dollars are wasted annually on "special" fertilizers for this, that, and the other purpose, which can accomplish no more than standard mixtures.

Every fertilizer must carry an analysis showing how much of each of the three important plant-food elements—nitrogen, phosphorus, and potassium—it contains. The best give information as to the sources from which these are derived. If the fertilizer mixture is an honest one, and carries the ingredients your particular soil needs, it will grow roses just as well as it will grow potatoes. No special formula is needed for "special" purposes, with the exception of such special groups as azaleas, rhododendrons, and other acid-loving plants which thrive best on acid-forming plant foods or those supplemented by acids.

It is infinitely more important to find out what your soil *needs, and procure a fertilizer that will provide it, than to buy special fertilizers for the* plants *you intend to grow.*

SOIL TESTS AND ADVICE ON SOIL IMPROVEMENT

For the gardener whose land is in an area where lack of fertility, extreme alkalinity, salinity, alkali-salinity, or acidity is a general problem, the first act should be to take soil samples from various spots on his grounds and have these analyzed by the nearest Agricultural Experiment Station.

The results of these tests then determine what must be done to improve each particular soil and to maintain it in a state of fertility. Specific advice on his soil problem is what each gardener needs in such areas, and it is what he will get if he submits soil samples to his county agent or Experiment Station.

Soil tests should be taken in the following manner:

In a 10-quart pail 5 to 10 samples are taken from each area to be planted—the number of samples depending on the size of each plot. Each sample is taken to the full depth of a transplanting spade, but

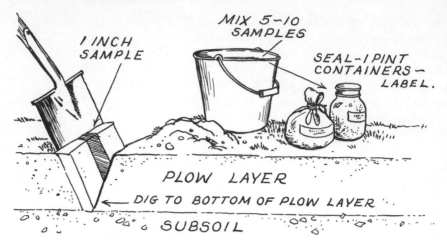

How to take soil samples for testing.

need be only an inch in width and one in thickness. The various samples for one plot are then mixed thoroughly together in a pail, and a pint of each mixture is packed in glass or in a heavy plastic bag. Seal each container to prevent contamination and label each so that it can be identified as to the part of the garden from which it came. A sample of subsoil taken at 18 to 24 inches in depth may also help, especially in muck or peat soils.

Other information that will assist the analyst in determining what should be done is:

When the plot was last limed, manured, green manured, and fertilized, with rates of application. Any other amendment that may have been used should be mentioned, giving, if possible, date and quantity applied per 100 square feet.

Drainage conditions and what, if anything, has been done to improve them if they are unsatisfactory.

When the report comes back it should include specific recommendations for improvement and how often these corrective measures are to be repeated. In dealing with problem soils, new tests should be made every 2 to 5 years.

Does this seem like too much trouble? It may take you an hour at most to prepare such samples. The result is likely to save you many hours of labor that will not yield maximum results, to say nothing of wasted expenditures for seed, plants, and fertilizers. *Think it over!*

Pretty much every county in these widespread United States—including ice-locked Alaska and sun-flooded Hawaii—has a man waiting to help you with your particular soil problems. He is your local county agent. Your taxes help to support him; do not hesitate to ask for the assistance he is glad to provide.

SPECIAL SOIL PROBLEMS AND THEIR SOLUTIONS

ACID SOILS AND THEIR IMPROVEMENT

In the eastern part of the United States, soils which have proved unsatisfactory for growing most plants are frequently too acid for all but a comparatively small group of acid-lovers.

Acid soils may be improved and their pH raised to a point where most plants readily grow by:

1. A regular program of *green manuring* (pages 26; 86) which, by adding humus, reduces acidity while improving the soil's mechanical condition.

2. The application of *raw ground limestone,* the material most commonly used to correct moderate soil acidity. This can be applied in fall or spring at the rate of 10 pounds to 150 square feet; or as directed by the county agent after soil samples have been analyzed.

3. *Wood ashes,* which contain large percentages of lime as well as potash, may be used at the rate of six pecks per 100 square feet.

A pH between 5.5 and 6.5 or 7 (neutral) is suitable for most flowers and vegetables.

TABLE

POUNDS OF RAW GROUND LIMESTONE PER 1000 SQUARE FEET TO RAISE pH TO 6

Original soil acidity	Light sandy soil	Medium sandy	Loam and Silt	Clay
pH 4.0	90 lbs.	120 lbs.	172 lbs.	217 lbs.
4.5	82	112	157	202
5.0	67	90	127	150
5.5	52	67	97	120

AMOUNTS OF SULFUR REQUIRED TO CHANGE pH OF A SILT-LOAM SOIL

from pH	to	lbs. sulfur per 100 sq. ft.
8	6.5	3.0
8	6.0	4.0
8	5.5	5.5
7.5	6.5	2.0
7.5	6.0	3.5
7.5	5.5	5.0
7.5	5.0	6.5

ACIDIFYING AND FERTILIZING NEUTRAL
OR NEAR-NEUTRAL SOILS IN ORDER
TO GROW *ACID-LOVING PLANTS*

Azaleas and rhododendrons prefer a pH of 4.5 to 5.5; hollies and camellias 5 to 5.5. Special treatment must be given neutral or near-neutral soils to attain the needed pH. For this purpose the following mixture may be used:

Equal parts by weight of aluminum sulfate
iron sulfate
ammonium sulfate

Sulfur (325 mesh) or superfine, can be worked into the soil before planting, or added to acid mulches such as hardwood leaves, pine needles, or acid peatmoss, before applying these to established plantings.

An acid fertilizer (4–6–8 formula) suitable for feeding acid-loving plants consists of a mixture of:

10 lbs. ammonium sulfate
35 lbs. 16% superphosphate
17 lbs. 50% sulfate of potash
28 lbs. cottonseed meal
10 lbs. aluminum sulfate

This is applied at the rate of *not more than* 1 to 1½ lbs. per 100 square feet, acid leafmold and/or acid peatmoss being applied at the same time.

For clay soils which need acidifying, cottonseed meal alone makes an effective acid fertilizer.

ALKALINE AND SALINE SOILS AND THEIR IMPROVEMENT

Much can be done to improve highly *alkaline* soils where excessive sodium is present; *saline* soils which contain high percentages of salts, but not sodium; and those *alkaline-saline* soils which are plagued by too much sodium and also large amounts of saline salts.

ALKALINE SOILS

Should be tested by the nearest Agricultural Experiment Station to determine just what corrective measures are needed.

Such soils exist in arid regions of very low rainfall and also in some parts of the West (as in Washington State) where a high water table and impervious soil texture cause surface accumulations of salts.

Symptoms of alkalinity are: light gray color (exceptions are gumbo soils, which are almost black but of a sticky or waxy texture that cannot be worked when wet); excessive washing (erosion); and the characteristic of forming hard, brick-like or fragile clods or crumbs when dry.

Correctly amended these soils release their calcium—a most important plant nutrient—which is unavailable in their natural state. When improved many such soils can be made highly productive. In dry regions, irrigation is necessary for reclamation.

Amendments applied commonly contain sulfur:

Gypsum (calcium sulfate) contains 19.5 to 21 per cent calcium and 16 to 18 per cent sulfur. It dissolves quickly and easily in irrigated soils and releases its calcium at once, so it is the fastest acting amendment.

Iron sulfate must be carefully handled, because when wet it is converted into sulfuric acid. It works fast in moist soil to form gypsum.

99 per cent dry sulfur, if ground very fine (40 mesh or finer), forms sulfuric acid quickly and converts to gypsum. Lower grades and coarser grinds require greater quantities—up to 3 times as much as the 99 per cent fine ground—to give comparable results.

Lime-sulfur (*calcium polysulfide*) and *Blue Chip Sulfur* are other forms often used.

The county agent or nearest Agricultural Experiment Station should be consulted as to the best material to use in any specific area, and the quantity needed per 1000 square feet.

SALINE SOILS

Where salinity occurs without excessive alkali, leaching is the only solution. It is impossible to remove or change these salts by the application of any chemical or other soil amendment. In irrigated land (as in the California desert regions) and where the water table is high (as in some parts of Washington State), excessive soluble salts are often deposited in the surface soil and must be washed away.

Sometimes a temporary pond is created on saline land until enough salt has been leached down to a lower level to make the land usable. The area is then permitted to dry out, is fertilized, and planted. Where much irrigation must be resorted to, the salts may reform in time. In this case, leaching is repeated at intervals, as needed.

Where salinity is present but less pronounced, beds may be built on a slant so that, when irrigated, the salts can drain off.

In the case of salinity, as in that of alkalinity, tests of the soil should be taken and recommendations of the State Agricultural Station followed.

ALKALINE-SALINE SOILS

When both problems discussed above occur in conjunction, leaching *and* amendments containing sulfur must be resorted to. Here the advice of a government soil expert is essential to success and no time should be wasted in seeking his help through the nearest State Agricultural Experiment Station.

Drainage. Alkaline and/or saline soils which are poorly drained, with a water table a minimum of 3 feet below the surface, must be made porous enough so that the water is lowered to at least 5 feet.

Wind erosion may also be a problem both in dry land areas and in such sections as the Columbia River Basin. Dust bowl conditions develop in windy country where unplanted soil is very finely pulverized and does not contain enough clay and humus to hold it in a wind.

Such soils should be rough-dug or tilled *when wet,* leaving the clods that form until planting time, to prevent blowing of the fine particles. As little time as possible is left between the operations of cultivating and planting. When watered, fragile clods or crumbs such as are formed by many of these soils break up or dissolve very readily.

Humus, HUMUS, HUMUS. In preparing new beds and borders in these soils, the wild growth is dug under to decay and form humus. Under no circumstances should it be removed! The more humus in the soil, the less danger of soil erosion. As soon as matured plants have been removed from beds and borders in autumn, a cover crop should be planted to hold the soil. Summer cover crops are also planted on fallow land.

Windbreaks are helpful in preventing erosion from excessive blowing.

FERTILITY AND FERTILIZERS FOR ARID SOILS

In arid soils ample *potassium, calcium,* and needed trace elements are often present and can be made available by means of irrigation, which puts them in solution.

Where *potassium* and *nitrogen* are lacking in slightly alkaline soils, potassium sulfate and ammonium sulfate are good sources, both reducing alkalinity and providing major nutrients. Phosphoric oxide is recommended to supply phosphorus where needed.

Boron is a trace element sometimes found to be lacking in arid lands, and where it is not present certain plants will not thrive (walnuts, clover, and strawberries are examples). Borax can be used to supply this deficiency, 4 to 6 pounds being applied to the soil around each mature tree; beds and borders in similar proportion.

Through the dear intercourse of sun and dew
Of thrilling root, and folding earth, anew
They come, in beauty.
The Buds by JAMES STEPHENS

CHAPTER 3

The Plant and How It Grows

This is not a book about botany—"the branch of biology dealing with plant life," according to Mr. Webster.

There are many successful gardeners—that is people who succeed in making plants grow—who know next to nothing about botany. However a certain amount of information about plant anatomy and growth helps both in selecting plants which will give the results we wish to attain and in achieving success in their culture.

THE PLANT'S ANATOMY

A plant, like an animal, is a wonderful combination of specialized parts or organs which work together in their own mysterious ways to maintain a living entity capable both of supporting itself and of creating offspring in its own image.

The most significant difference between animals and plants is that the former can move about at will to search for and find their food and drink. They can even leave their environment if it becomes too hostile and seek another. A plant is anchored to one spot and either lives upon what nature provides or perishes.

Without being technical it may be said that the plant is made up of these several distinct parts.

Roots   Flowers
Stems or trunks Fruits
Foliage   Seeds

The function of the roots is to take in water, which carries chemical elements up through the stem or trunk to the leaves and other portions of the plant. This chemical solution is the food that sustains the plants'

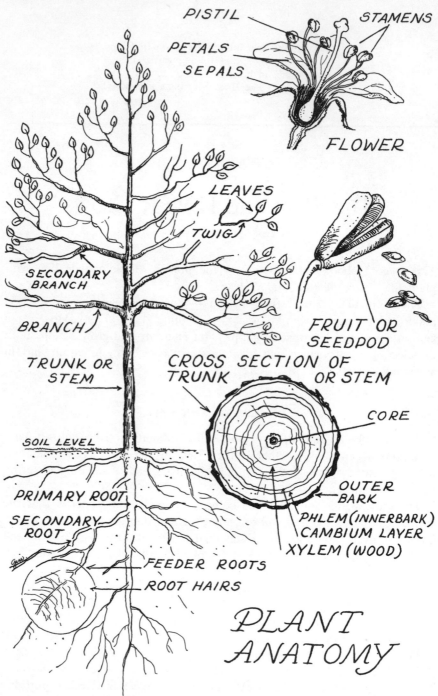

PISTIL

STAMENS

PETALS

SEPALS

FLOWER

LEAVES

TWIG

SECONDARY
BRANCH

BRANCH

TRUNK OR
STEM

FRUIT OR
SEEDPOD

CROSS SECTION OF
TRUNK   OR STEM

CORE

SOIL LEVEL

PRIMARY ROOT

SECONDARY
ROOT

OUTER
BARK

PHLEM (INNERBARK)
CAMBIUM LAYER
XYLEM (WOOD)

FEEDER ROOTS

ROOT HAIRS

PLANT
ANATOMY

structure and growth and nourishes the flowers and eventually the seeds that are to carry on the species.

While plants, unlike animals, cannot move about to search out conditions or environments that are most favorable to sustaining life, they do possess a remarkable capacity for adapting themselves to their own environments. There are, of course, limits to such capacities; but no one who has ever climbed even a moderate-sized mountain can have failed to notice how shrubs and trees accommodate themselves to the conditions of the increasing elevation. Species which on the lower levels towered far above him have gradually grown smaller and smaller until, at the wind-swept summit, the giants of the valley have become gnarled, misshapen dwarfs clinging precariously to any crack or crevice offering them a toe hold. Personally we always feel a great admiration for these tough and indomitable high-altitude characters. On several occasions we have brought home and planted such half-starved, under-privileged subjects. In each case they have suffered less from transplanting than more vigorous specimens would have, but made little growth for two or three years. Then, when the root systems seemed finally to have got over their surprise at an abundant food supply, they began to take hold and make normal, vigorous growth. One of these specimens is a little moosewood (*Acer pennsylvanicum*) which came from the hill country of Vermont. Last summer, after having taken two years to decide that it liked its new home, it finally took hold and nearly doubled its height in one season.

The Roots. The growth patterns of the roots of many trees and shrubs in a way duplicate those of the plants above ground. The main roots send out others which become branch roots, and these still others; but instead of developing foliage as the branches above ground do, the root branches develop root hairs or feeding roots which absorb from the soil the water and the chemical nutrients which feed the plant.

Comparatively recently it was discovered that many plants can also absorb plant foods through their leaves. This has led to the theory and practice of *foliar feeding* in which liquid fertilizer is sprayed on the foliage.

Often the main roots of very old trees, where they join the trunk, gradually become more like branches than like roots, as in the case of ancient elms, oaks, and some evergreens.

Stems and Trunks. As a seed sprouts and begins to grow, that portion above ground pushes up into the air "reaching for the sun." It develops leaves and eventually a central stem or group of stems. In the case of trees and of many shrubs and vines, this central, permanent growth becomes the trunk (or trunks) which, like the main or taproot, branches and rebranches. Just as the terminal roots cover themselves with fine hair-like roots which absorb food, so the terminal branches or twigs clothe themselves with leaves through which they "breathe."

While the description above applies particularly to trees, shrubs, and

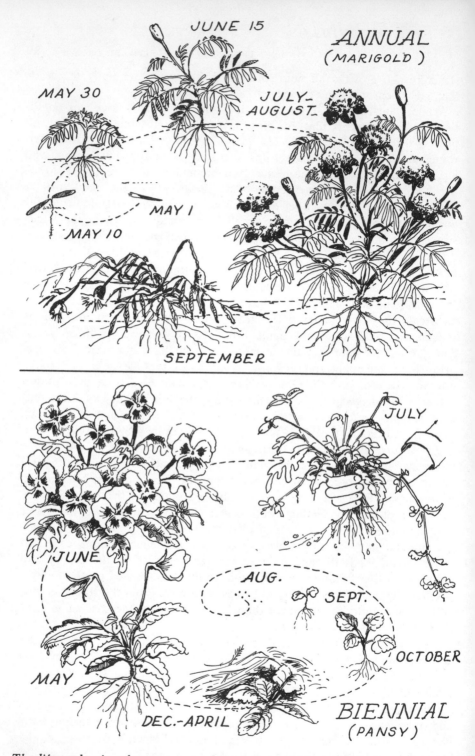

JUNE 15

ANNUAL
(MARIGOLD)

MAY 30

JULY-
AUGUST

MAY 1

MAY 10

SEPTEMBER

JULY

JUNE

AUG.

SEPT.

OCTOBER

MAY

DEC.-APRIL

BIENNIAL
(PANSY)

The life cycle of a plant may extend for a few weeks or months, or may con-
tinue for several hundred years. It is important that the gardener know the
growth habit of any plant which he attempts to grow. Annuals (above) live but
a single growing season. Biennials (below) take two growing seasons to reach
maturity, bloom, seed, and die.

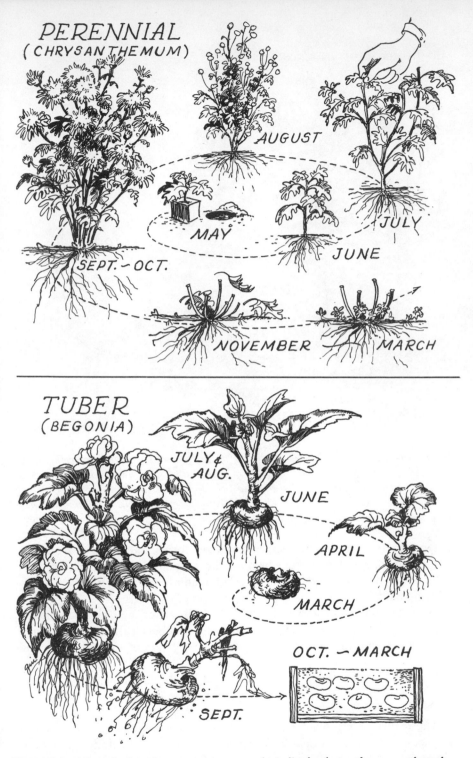

PERENNIAL
(CHRYSANTHEMUM)

AUGUST

MAY

JUNE

JULY

SEPT. – OCT.

NOVEMBER

MARCH

TUBER
(BEGONIA)

JULY & AUG.

JUNE

APRIL

MARCH

OCT. – MARCH

SEPT.

Perennials (*above*) live from year to year but die back to the ground each winter where freezing occurs. Hardy roots throw up new growth each spring. Tubers (*below*), as well as corms, are like true bulbs in that they live on from year to year. Many are frost-tender and must be given frost-free storage in winter. Started into new growth in spring, they produce summer flowers and are dug and dried off for storage each autumn.

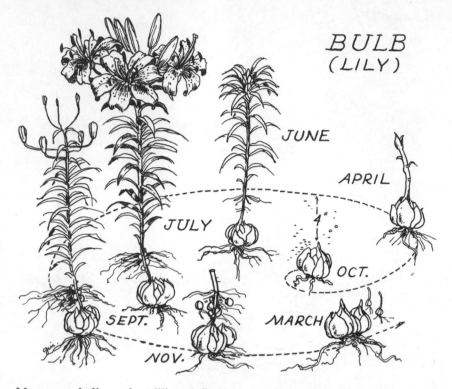

BULB
(LILY)

JUNE

APRIL

JULY

4"

OCT.

SEPT.

MARCH

NOV.

Many true bulbs such as lilies, daffodils, tulips, and other spring-flowering sorts are winter-hardy in the north. Once planted, they live and bloom for some years. Most hardy bulbs are fall-planted for bloom the following spring or summer. Tender bulbs like amaryllis or veltheimia are grown in pots in the north and wintered indoors, but remain in the garden year-round in warm climates.

perennial vines, it is true also, in modified forms, of annuals, biennials, perennials, and bulbs that die back to the ground each year. The growth cycles of a number of different types of plants are shown in the accompanying sketches.

Here the miracle of growth begins. The soil, water, and chemicals combine to be transformed into life-giving sap which is carried onward and upward, defying the law of gravity, to the very tips of every branch and leaf.

This pipeline system of trunk or stem, with its branches, continues growth until the plant is mature—which may be a matter of a few weeks or of several centuries!

The *leaves* of the plant (or in some species the scales, bracts, or skin surfaces that take the place of leaves) form the breathing apparatus through which it gets the oxygen that, like any living thing, it must have in order to exist.

This combination of roots, stem structure, and leaves continues to function in perfect balance until the plant dies.

Reproduction. Just as every animal possesses, or more accurately is possessed by, the overpowering instinct to reproduce itself and thus continue the species, so also do plants make sure that future generations will follow them.

They accomplish this in various ways but by far the most universal method is through the production of seeds, which like the creation of the embryo in animals results from the merging of male and female germ cells. One of the most interesting things in all nature is the variety of ingenious devices employed to accomplish this mating. Most usual of these is the production of nectar to lure the bee or other insect so that he will carry away on hairy legs the pollen (male) from the anthers of one flower to be dusted over the sticky stigma (female) of the next flower visited. The result of this mating of course, is the development of seed—seed which can hold life suspended for weeks, months, even decades or (reportedly) centuries until the right conditions trigger the mysterious spring that starts it ticking again when, with a force out of all proportion to its size, it bursts its imprisoning shell.

ASEXUAL REPRODUCTION

There are also other methods of reproduction, some accomplished by nature, others by the ingenuity of man. Nature, for instance, equips some plants such as strawberries or the strawberry-begonia (*Saxifraga sarmentosa*) with "runners" at the tips of which new plants are formed. Blackberries and some shrubs and vines whose canes or branches bend over and touch the ground root at the point of contact or self-layer as the gardener puts it. Then, like Antaeus, son of Terra, the earth goddess, they spring up from contact with the soil, full of renewed energy, to form new plants.

Asexual reproduction stimulated by man includes artificial layering, which occurs when a branch is partially cut through and then buried in soil or wrapped in sphagnum moss to encourage rooting, and the simpler method of rooting stem or leaf cuttings described in Chapter 4.

All plants produced by any of these methods are exact replicas of those from which they were obtained.

In contrast to this uniformity, plants produced from *seed* may "come true" or may vary widely. Seedlings from a natural species will be like their ancestors, although occasionally a "break" or "sport" occurs—one chance in a thousand or million. Plants resulting from a "cross" between two different species or forms are likely to vary greatly, and thus we get new varieties.

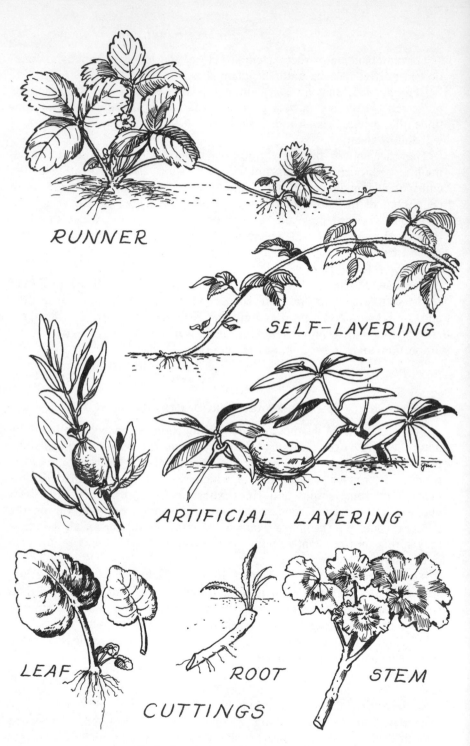

RUNNER

SELF-LAYERING

ARTIFICIAL LAYERING

LEAF

ROOT

STEM

CUTTINGS

Methods of asexual reproduction.

Books have been written on the science and the techniques of plant breeding, but that does not concern us here. We are interested in how best to keep the plant we have growing satisfactorily.

HOW PLANTS GROW

The more we know about a plant, the better we can care for it. As we have seen, the root system gathers food, in solution, from the soil. This is passed up through the trunk or stem and branches to the foliage, new growth, flowers, and, eventually, to the seed containers (fruits, nuts, pods, etc.) and into the seeds themselves. This is greatly oversimplifying an extremely complicated and mysterious process, but it may help the beginner to get an idea of the plant machine and how it works.

To keep this living mechanism, the plant, in operation, there must be available air, water, food, light, and a suitable range of temperature. To provide these is the function of the gardener—YOU. Of course you will have a very capable assistant—nature. Without a garden and without you, she would attend to all these matters in her own way—*the survival of the fittest!* But since, in having a garden at all, you have elected to take over from nature, the responsibility becomes yours. You can't lick the old gal, but you can join her, or, more accurately, coax and persuade her to join you.

Air, the first of the elements with which you are concerned, is always available. But pure, nonstagnant air is best for plants, as it is for humans. Plants can't be expected to thrive as well in the smoke-laden, dusty atmosphere of a city or in the smog of a factory district as they do in open country. If adverse air conditions exist in the gardener's locality, he can, unfortunately, do little about it unless the entire community cooperates. He can, however, keep his plants uncrowded and provide adequate air circulation.

Water, if plants are to do their best, must be available when they require it. If it is lacking, their food supply is also cut down, as all plant nutrients are taken in solution. Certain types of plants, such as those in deserts and other low-rainfall areas, go "dead" for weeks or months, and revive almost overnight when the dry season ends. Most of our garden plants suffer quickly and severely when the water supply gets much below normal. They may survive but they are stunted or otherwise injured, and during the dry spell are anything but ornamental. *The money spent on an adequate watering system* (Chapter 5) *is likely to be the most rewarding of any investment the garden-minded homeowner can make.*

Food. As with all living things, a plant must have food if it is to continue to live. The three most important items in its diet are nitrogen, phosphorus, and potash. In addition to these, there are several others, called trace elements, less important but still essential. All of these and the relative parts they play in plant nutrition are also discussed in Chapter 5. The essential point here is that these elements must *all* be present: the lack of any one may check or even completely halt normal growth and development.

Light is another essential for practically all living things. Many, to make normal or maximum growth, require direct sunshine. Even the shade-lovers do not tolerate darkness. One of the tests of skill of a gardener is that of choosing locations for the various trees, shrubs, perennials, and bulbs he wishes to grow; and vice versa, of selecting species and varieties of plants that will be happy in the locations he has available. Fortunately for beginners, catalogs of the most reliable firms provide, in their descriptions of plants, information on these important points.*

Temperature. One need not be a gardener to realize that temperatures —high, low, and averages for the year—are a major factor in determining what may be grown where. Few persons, however, realize to what extent temperatures may vary as a result of local conditions, either natural or man-made. Elevation is one very important factor. One friend of ours, for instance, has part of his garden at water level by a stream that runs through his grounds. The temperature here is occasionally ten degrees lower than it is at his home on a hilltop less than three hundred feet away. Ten degrees makes a big difference in what can and cannot be grown.

We have fig trees and camellias that have lived through several successive winters without covering except for a heavy mulch about the roots. They are in sunny locations, sheltered from wind. Moved a hundred feet in any direction they would certainly have perished during one of the winters they have gone through.

Micro-climate areas may be created on most places. A suitably placed wall or even a tight board fence screened with vines or shrubs to make it less obtrusive may move one section of your garden at least one and possibly two zones south! Leave one side open to leeward, however, so that in severe weather cold air cannot be bottled up inside the wall or

---

* *One for the book:* This note is for believe-it-or-not Ripley. As the senior partner in this co-author team was correcting the typescript of this page, dealing with *light,* the junior partner (who had just been to town for the mail) handed him a letter from Canada from which the following is a quotation: We are also gardening in our basement, under fluorescent lights, during winter months and with quite satisfactory results. . . . This morning I found in *Illuminating Engineering* an article (copy enclosed) on Experimental Gardening on a Polaris submarine. The article described plant culture in horticultural vermiculite plus water and chemical plant foods, by members of the submarine crew. A number of crops were successfully grown but lettuce proved to be the most satisfactory and the most popular.

Thank you again very much for the opportunity you gave us last summer to visit you at your very lovely place.

fence and possibly kill borderline subjects. We once saw hundreds of rare specimens killed or injured inside such a protective barrier on the eastern shore of Maryland after a very severe winter.

DETERRENTS TO GROWTH

Having looked at one side of the coin, let us for the sake of emphasis turn it over and for a moment examine the other side—conditions that may deter or interfere with normal growth.

Lack or Excess of Light and Air. Avoid placing sun-loving plants in shady spots on the north sides of buildings, or in the shade of trees or shrubs, or *where trees or shrubs now small may in a few years be casting dense shade.* Vegetables and many plants that require full sun show a difference in growth if they are in shade for even two or three hours a day. Conversely, shade-lovers soon wither and dry up if subjected to full sun.

Avoid planting shrubs or even vigorous-growing perennials too close together. They may shade and crowd each other when they attain full growth as well as shutting off the air circulation so important to their well-being. It is equally dangerous to subject doubtfully hardy species to rough, prevailing winds.

Cold. Make sure that the tree or shrub you would like to have will be hardy in your section of the country. If in doubt, consult your county agent. If he doesn't know from personal experience he can find out for you; that's part of his job. But keep in mind what has been said above about micro-climates. There is often a good deal of satisfaction in growing something that is out of the ordinary for your locality.

Heat. High temperatures, in themselves, are less likely to prove fatal or even injurious to plants than are low temperatures. High readings however, are frequently accompanied by severe drought—a devil's tandem of black funeral horses for the gardener! Under such conditions those who have made good use of mulching have much to be thankful for. Mulches keep the ground cooler and also decrease the loss of moisture by evaporation.

Dryness. Even in cool weather the ground may get excessively dry. High winds, especially dry ones, suck moisture from the soil as rapidly as do excessively high temperatures. Moisture is an absolute essential for plant growth, and once it is gone there is only one remedy: to replace it. Water is the cheapest "fertilizer" one can buy, but few gardeners fully realize its importance.

Pests and Diseases. Despite improved controls, insects and other plant pests are still a serious factor in damaging plant growth and—equally important to the home gardener—the appearance of plants. Fortunately materials for control have been tremendously improved. All-purpose sprays and dusts containing chemicals to control sucking and chewing insects as well as fungicides to keep diseases in check are particularly helpful to the home gardener. To assure normal, healthy growth of such plants as roses, for instance, regular applications of all-purpose sprays or dusts are essential. With less susceptible subjects, an application should be made *as soon as* trouble appears; or in advance as a preventive in cases where it can be anticipated, as for mildew on phlox or lilacs, or thrip on gladiolus. Remember the old adage about an ounce of prevention? It still goes—double!

Old Age, for which there is no known cure in spite of the advances science is making these days. However, old age in some types of plants may be postponed almost indefinitely. The lilac that once in the dooryard bloomed just goes on indefinitely. We have a clump on our river bank where, reportedly, a tidewater mill once stood some two hundred years ago. This specimen, the main trunk recumbent like a sleeping giant, has now spread into a colony and apparently is ready to go on till doomsday. Even the oldest portion, we suppose, is not literally the original plant. The death of most shrubs, even those which do not sucker and form colonies, is most often due to failure to cut out old wood—thus admitting more light, air, and moisture. An azalea which we have had for over twenty years (and so far as we could find out was around fifty when we bought it) has been moved three times and was once nearly lost due to mishandling in a long-distance truck ride in the wind. It has finally decided to make one more comeback, however, and presented us again last spring with a few flowers on new wood sprouting from the roots! Neglect, resulting in overcrowding and slow starvation, kills many more trees and shrubs than old age.

Let here no seed of a season that the winter
But once assails, take root and for a time endure;
But only such as harbor at the frozen centre
The germ secure.

EDNA ST. VINCENT MILLAY

CHAPTER 4

New Plants from Old: Methods of Propagation

GROWING PLANTS FROM SEEDS AND CUTTINGS, AND BY BUDDING AND GRAFTING

Everyone who gardens, no matter on how modest a scale, sooner or later becomes a plant propagator. An unscientific but perhaps sufficiently comprehensive definition of propagation might be: *The growing of new plants from parts of old plants.* These "parts" may be seeds; pieces of stems, roots, or leaves, single buds or eyes.

One usually starts gardening with plants growing in pots or other containers, which someone else (usually the nurseryman) has propagated. There is of course much pleasure to be had from nurturing such plants, but nothing to be compared to the exciting thrills that come when the gardener begins to grow his own plants from their very start in life.

The several methods of propagating plants include growing them from seed; from bulbs, corms, or tubers; from cuttings; by budding and grafting. The first two of these methods are nature's way of doing the job; the others are man's. The skillful gardener employs them all.

GROWING FROM SEED

The simplest method of propagating plants is from seed.

Seeds are among the most intricate of all the many marvels of nature. They vary in size from the fine dustlike particles of the begonias to the near football dimensions of the coconut. Yet each individual seed is a time bomb so delicately adjusted that, although many of them will withstand extreme degrees of heat, cold, and even moisture, it will, when just the right combination of conditions prevail, explode into a living organism. It is the gardener's province to provide these conditions; and to do so at a time, and under such circumstances, that the baby plantlet may prosper.

In growing plants from seed there are three things of vital importance to be considered. They are:

The quality of the seed itself

Correct timing

Control of conditions

The question of quality is not merely a matter of having fresh, live seed that will sprout. Of equal importance is having seed that are *well bred*. It's the old truism that one cannot make a silk purse out of a sow's ear.

The beginning gardener will do well, before ordering seeds, to make some inquiry among friends more experienced in gardening as to which firms have the best reputations. Usually a concern that specializes in some flower—such as pansies, primulas, delphinium, sweet peas, or even zinnias—will have first-quality seed bred from selected strains. Some firms state on each package the per cent of germination, based on recent tests.

Price is a matter of very secondary consideration. A single superior plant from a packet of seed is worth several times the difference in cost between just good seed and really superior seed.

Timing in seed sowing is important because upon it depends to a large degree the prospect of ultimate success. Some seeds, for instance, germinate better at low temperatures than at high; others just the opposite. Some germinate within a few days, others require a considerable time; some, indeed, need a period of stratification or prolonged burial in soil before they will sprout. Some make very rapid growth after they come up; others require more time to develop strong root growth and "crowns" before they send up flowering stalks. Others such as many of the lilies germinate but for a long period make growth only underground, developing root strength before sending up slender green spears into the sunlight.

The control of conditions under which seeds are sown is, within limits imposed by nature, up to the gardener. He can provide almost any type of soil by making special mixtures for the small amounts that will be required. He can control the amount of moisture they get during the germination period. With modern, inexpensive equipment such as automatically regulated heating cables, he can provide the desired temperature. Fluorescent lights take care of the requirements of timing seed sowing even where they must be started in cellar or basement.

The beginner who may not wish to bother with all, or even with any, of these contrivances, may still start all the plants he is likely to require with no other equipment than a small frame made of a few boards and covered with an old window sash or two.

THE MECHANICS OF SOWING

Each one of the several factors involved in starting plants from seed contributes its part to ultimate success. If any one of them goes far wrong, the result may be total failure. Let's briefly consider each in order.

Equipment. First item here is a *place* in which to start seed. For outdoor sowing this may be a simple frame or seed bed located where it gets full sun and all the protection possible from prevailing early spring winds. A typical frame, with glass sash to cover, is shown in Chapter 7. Temporary sash may be made of light wooden frames covered with plastic, but glass sash are more satisfactory in the long run.

Frame for Sowing. Preparation: Thorough preparation of the soil in the frame is an important factor in growing sturdy seedlings.

Drainage is very important, as a single flash flood can ruin a whole crop of seedlings. Provision should be made for shading the glass when necessary. Light, slatted shutters giving shifting shade are ideal; old burlap bags fastened together provide dense shade and also protection from severe frosts.

Soil for the frame should be both rich and porous. We use a mixture of two thirds compost, which contains plenty of humus, and one third peatmoss. Seeds are sown in a thin layer of sharp sand, vermiculite, or pulverized sphagnum moss sifted over the surface.

Some strong-growing seedlings such as calendulas, zinnias, and large marigolds may be started directly in the frame, sown in rows 3 to 6 inches apart. Most, however, are started in small flats of wood or pressed fiber, and later transplanted to the frame. These may also be potted up in

Sowing: Seeds are sown thinly in rows (each variety clearly labeled). This simplifies care in weeding, thinning, and transplanting after germination takes place.

plastic, clay, or fertile peat pots which are then plunged to their rims in the frame. If peat pots are used, seedlings root through into the rich frame soil, and carry much of it with them when transferred to the garden.

In addition to the frame, a supply of containers should be on hand. These will include flats, pots, and bulb pans (shallow flower pots). The old clay flower pots and pans have now been almost completely replaced by plastic ones (which for most purposes are decidedly superior), and by pots made of compressed peat with plant nutrients added, which are planted out "pot and all."

The standard flat is a shallow (2½- to 3½-inch-deep) wooden box with a slatted bottom that provides ready drainage—and makes possible *watering from the bottom* by placing the flat in an inch or so of water until moisture shows on the surface, a method which we swear by.

In the greenhouse—and sometimes in a coldframe or hotbed—seeds are started in pots, small flats, or composition boxes rather than directly in the soil. This makes possible care which can better meet the requirements of individual species and varieties. Equipment for doing a good job of seed sowing includes (right to left) float to press soil mixture down firmly; V-shaped marker to make furrows for large seeds; labels and pencil to mark varieties; a seed protectant and root-stimulant powder; a seed sower to assure even distribution; a bulb spray to moisten soil without disturbing seeds.

One of several modern devices to aid the inexperienced: a small plastic flat with seed already planted. All the "gardener" need do is to add water.

Seeds sown in a bulb pan may be covered with a plastic dome and watered from below by placing water in saucer. This creates a miniature greenhouse, conserving moisture and humidity. Remove cover as soon as seeds germinate.

Standard florists' flats are usually 20 or 22 inches long by 14 or 15 inches wide, but smaller ones are often more convenient for the gardener. The small wooden or fiber boxes in which seedlings are grown, and sold by retailers in the spring, are of a convenient size for small plantings.

Seed Sowing Mixtures. Success in starting plants from seed depends *very largely* upon the medium in which the seeds are started. In the old days a 50–50 mixture of garden loam and sifted leafmold or "woods soil" or "chip dirt," gathered in the forest or from the half-rotted debris around the chopping block by the wood pile, answered well. Now these are no longer available, and probably would not serve if they were, for certain diseases which cause tiny seedlings to damp-off (decay at the soil line or before they emerge) have become so prevalent that, without some defense against them, failure is more likely than success.

Certain soil mixtures have been developed which help to assure success. Best known of these are the famous John Innes mixtures in England and the University of California soil mixes developed in this country. The seed mixture recommended by John Innes is made up of 7 parts composted medium loam, 3½ parts peatmoss, and 3½ parts coarse sand, all measured by volume. To this is added 2 pounds of superphosphate and 1 pound of chalk. For use in this country the above materials might be translated as follows: 7 parts good loam, 3½ parts peatmoss, and 3½ parts sharp sand. Add 2 pounds of superphosphate and 1 pound agricultural lime.

The U. C. Soil Mix B, recommended for seed sowing, is composed of 75 per cent by volume of fine sand and 25 per cent by volume of pulverized peatmoss, to each cubic yard of which is added 6 ounces potassium nitrate, 4 ounces potassium sulfate, 2½ pounds single superphosphate, 4½ pounds dolomite lime, 1¼ pounds carbonate lime, and 1¼ pounds gypsum. The pH of this mixture with fertilizers added should be 6.8.

For years we have used in our own seed flats one third by weight of sifted compost, one third pulverized peatmoss, and one third sharp sand, well mixed and covered with a surface layer of sterile vermiculite, perlite, or milled sphagnum moss.

Even with these special mixtures, however, success is not assured, for the worst of the damping-off diseases, Rhizoctonia, (Rhizoc. for short) is so contagious and persistent and has become so widely disseminated, that unless all containers, equipment, and soil are kept sterilized, good results can by no means be assured.

Most amateurs are finding that the use of new or sterilized containers and an absolutely sterile material in which to sow the seeds gives the greatest assurance of success. *Composition planter trays, plus either milled sphagnum moss or vermiculite (an expanded mineral product) provide these conditions.*

The standard trays are about 6 by 4 inches, with holes in the bottoms to provide drainage. Even when filled with either material, and thoroughly moistened, they are light and easy to handle. Roots of seedlings develop marvelously and can be lifted out for transplanting with little or no breakage. Naturally, planted in such a sterile medium without nutrients, seedlings must be transplanted very young to a richer mixture or, if this operation must be delayed, plant nutrients must be supplied when watering.

Watering Devices. Maintaining the correct degree of moisture at all times is another most important factor in starting seedlings. Too much water, or serious lack of it for even a few hours, may cause failure.

The ordinary hose nozzle and the usual watering-can sprinkler head apply water with too much force and in too large droplets to be ideal for very small seedlings. A shallow pan or tray of galvanized sheet iron 2 inches deep (which a tinsmith can make up) will permit moistening the soil from the bottom up. A mist nozzle, to replace the ordinary hose nozzle, moistens the surface without knocking over or washing out even the tiniest seedling. See illustration, Chapter 18.

Trays, pots, or boxes in which seeds are planted may be kept moist for days without watering by covering them tightly with a pane of glass, or with a sheet of cellophane of suitable size held in place by a rubber band.

Labels are an important part of garden records. It is well to have several sizes (say 4-, 8-, and 12-inch) available. Painted labels, being weather-resistant, are well worth the slight additional cost.

Seed sowing is something of an art. Even distribution of the seed is essential because the less the tiny roots—often more extensive than the top growth at this stage of development—are tangled together, the better. Very fine seed such as that of begonias and large-flowered petunias may be mixed with fine sand to aid in securing even distribution. Never sow all the seed in a packet just to use it up. Extra seedlings that mean overcrowding *are just weeds,* often very harmful ones. Two dozen good, strong seedlings in a pot or flat often make more of an ultimate show in the garden than a hundred or more overcrowded, spindly ones.

Some gardeners like to sow seed directly from the packet, but we get better results with a 6-inch piece of plastic hose cut at an angle to a sharp point and plugged at the other end with a cork. By tapping this with the forefinger, it is possible to distribute sizable seeds almost one by one, and even very small ones with some degree of accuracy. Gadgets similar to the home-made one described above are available at seed stores.

Inoculants. Disinfectants. The seed sower also makes it easy to apply inoculants such as Legume Aid, Nod-O-Gen, and Nitricin; and disinfectants such as Spergon, Semesan, or Rootone, to the seeds being sown. These materials are advantageous (1) in introducing nitrogen-gathering bacteria into the soil where legumes (peas, beans, etc.) are being sown; and (2) in protecting seeds against harmful bacteria which cause seed-borne disease. A pinch of powder or a few drops of liquid is placed with the seed in the sower, which is then closed with the thumb and shaken thoroughly.

Correct temperature is essential in securing good seed germination. Optimum temperatures vary with different plants. Peas (including sweet peas), for instance, will germinate and grow in soil that is little above freezing; while others, such as tomato and torenia or portulaca, prefer 70 to 80 degrees. Most seeds will germinate satisfactorily at 70 to 80 degrees, but should be given 5 to 10 degrees less soon after they are up.

Moisture can be maintained to and through the germination period by the means already described above.

Light is not essential while seeds are germinating, but once they have begun to show above the surface soil they should be brought *immediately* to full light. Otherwise they grow spindly, on weak stems, straining toward whatever source of light may be available.

STARTING THE SEEDLINGS

Seeds may be sown in the open ground, where they are to grow. This is the method used with most vegetables and many flowers. The thing here is to prepare the seedbed, or at least the surface inch or two, so that the soil is finely pulverized and smooth, also making sure that it contains plenty of humus. The latter may be provided by a light layer of compost or of peatmoss, sifted or pulverized, and raked into the surface soil. There should also be provision for watering with a very fine spray, such as that from a "mist" or "fog" nozzle, (page 309).

Much more certain results, especially with difficult subjects, may be had by starting seeds in a frame, no matter how crude a one, as described in Chapter 7.

Until the seeds have germinated their first true leaves, usually quite different from the seedling leaves or cotyledons, the soil should never be allowed to dry out completely on the surface.

Thinning out the seedlings where germination has been good is vitally important. To neglect it for even a week or so may mean very serious injury to the remaining plants. This operation is just as essential where seedlings are to be transplanted later or where they have attained considerable size. Give each plant room to grow freely.

Transplanting is the next step in growing plants from seed. As a general rule, the earlier this is done the better. It consists of removing the tiny seedlings from the pot, flat, or seedbed in which they have been started, and replanting them, either in the open ground, in well-prepared and enriched soil where they will grow to maturity, or in flats or small pots in soil containing enough nutrients to bring them to a size where they can hold their own in the open garden or in the spot where they are to grow.

Seedlings growing in small, lightweight composition box.

Seedlings removed from box similar to that shown just above, with root masses formed in the rooting medium of peatmoss and perlite.

Month-old tomato seedlings ready for transplanting. Two in center grown in peat-sand mixture; others in soil.

The soil to be used in transplanting to flats or pots will depend upon the type of planting. A soil mixture suitable for the great majority of plants is made up of sifted material from the well-rotted compost heap (page 27) to which may be added peatmoss, loam, and/or sand in varying proportions, according to the character of the plants to be grown. Lime (a half cup per bushel) may be added for plants requiring an especially "sweet" soil, and a complete, organic plant food at the rate of 1 pint per bushel if loam must be substituted for sifted compost or if the compost available has no fertilizer or manure in its composition.

For transplanting into flats, we like to use a layer of old, well-decomposed manure (or if this is not available, of peatmoss plus a generous sprinkling of commercial dried manure) in the bottom of each flat before filling it with the soil mixture. This has the triple advantage of providing a sponge which holds moisture, of supplying extra plant food, and of providing a fibrous mass into which the seedling roots will pass and hold together in a dense root ball when the plants are cut out of the flat for transplanting or setting out in their permanent positions.

Repotting. As the plants in small pots, which are usually placed side by side, begin to crowd, repotting is in order. According to the type of plant, this will take place anywhere from a few weeks to several months.

When clay or plastic pots are used, a look at the root ball indicates if repotting is needed. Invert a pot, secure plant and root ball with the fingers of one hand, and with the other rap the pot against the edge of bench or table. A close network of roots around the ball means that more soil, and hence a larger pot, is needed. With the root-through type of peat or fiber pot, repotting should be done as soon as roots have thoroughly penetrated the pot's walls and before they begin to form a tangled mass.

After repotting, plants should be well watered and provided with moderate shade to prevent excessive wilting. An occasional misting or fogging may be needed, but usually this is not required.

ASEXUAL PROPAGATION

While the propagation of plants by means of seed is the method most generally employed by amateur gardeners, obtaining new plants by other means is not too difficult.

To begin with, many plants, and especially man-made varieties (*cultivars,* as the botanists call them) will not come true from seed, and can only be propagated by means of growing new plants from sections (cuttings, buds, or pieces of root or bulb) of the parent plant.

Dividing. The simplest and quickest of these methods is the use of sections of the parent plant that are provided with both tops and roots.

ASEXUAL REPRODUCTION. *The simplest way to propagate many plants is by* root division.

Some species (such as gesnerias and many begonias) are easily propagated by leaf cuttings.

CUTTINGS. Hardwood cuttings *of holly and many other woody plants may be rooted in winter in a frame out of doors or—more quickly—in the greenhouse.*

Japanese Euonymus (hardwood) cuttings in a double pot. Even moisture to stimulate rooting is maintained by adding water, as needed, to the small inner pot.

House plants such as geraniums are usually increased by softwood stem cuttings.

These we acquire when we take up and "divide" such plants as irises, chrysanthemums, and phlox; such clump-forming bulbs as daffodils; shrubs like forsythia, spirea, and Rugosa roses; or when we cut off and replant a young lilac that has come up several feet from its parent bush; or transplant the "runners" of strawberries.

The rankest amateur can scarcely fail to succeed with this method of propagation. It is desirable to damage roots as little as possible in dividing clumps or in removing offshoots of parent plants; and also to do the job while the parent is dormant, in early spring or sometime after bloom is over in the case of bulbs and such perennials as iris and Oriental poppies. Where plants form "crowns," like chrysanthemums for example, the old woody centers are discarded and root cuttings, with stems and leaves attached, are taken from around the outer edge where growth is vigorous. It may be desirable to cut back the top growth of shrub divisions, but this is more for the purpose of encouraging compact new growth than to assure the success of the operation. Naturally we take care to provide good soil, plenty of water, and a mulch, if the weather is dry, to keep the soil moist.

Layering is actually a modified form of division. All that the gardener does, actually, is to lend a helping hand to nature in order to produce new plants, still attached to their parents, until sturdy root systems have been developed. It is an easy method of obtaining new plants of azaleas and shrubs like forsythia and old-fashioned shrub roses, to name but a few. New, half-hardened growths of these plants may be induced to form roots by fastening them down in loose, friable soil and covering them with a suitable rooting medium as shown in the accompanying sketch. At a point where a branch of comparatively young, but well-hardened growth may be bent down to the ground, a slanting cut is made, on the lower side, half to two thirds of its thickness. This is held open with a small pebble or twig. A forked stick, brick, or stone serves to hold it in place. Success can be made more certain by preparing the soil at the point of contact with the ground with a pocket of peatmoss or a peatmoss-sand mixture, and treating the cut with a root stimulant such as Rootone. Some shrubs form roots naturally along branches which come in contact with the ground and in propagating these no cut need be made though otherwise the process is the same.

The rooting medium should be maintained in a moist condition by the mulch and by watering as frequently as necessary, especially during the first few weeks. After rooting—which may take anywhere from a few weeks to a year according to the subject and to conditions—the new plant is severed from its parent and transplanted to a permanent position.

Air layering differs from ordinary layering in that the job is done above ground instead of in it. It is used principally in the propagation of greenhouse plants such as rubber-plant (ficus), dieffenbachia, philodendron, and gardenia, but also with some hardy subjects.

CUT OR
GIRDLE
STEM

APPLY
SPHAGNUM MOSS
AND PLASTIC

SEVER
BELOW
ROOT BALL

Details of air layering. Especially prepared kits are available for doing this work. The rooting material must remain moist until rooting occurs.

In air layering, the top of a plant, or the tip of a branch the wood and bark of which have not yet become really hardened, is selected for the operation. At the point determined, a short cut is made a half to two thirds through the stem. This cut—which should be made cleanly with a sharp blade, leaving no frayed edges—is then held open with a bit of wood. Or the bark may be "ringed" or "notched" (see illustration). The cut parts are then dusted with a root stimulant such as Hormodin or Rootone, and firmly wrapped in sphagnum moss that has been thoroughly moistened by dipping it in water and squeezing it to remove the surplus.

The ball of moss is then wrapped in a sheet of polyethylene of suitable size, and tied securely at top and bottom to make it as nearly airtight as possible. A special propagating kit, by the name of Airwrap, may be purchased, which makes the operation a very simple one.

The ball of moss is left on, in its wrapping, until roots have begun to penetrate it—a period which varies with the subject and conditions from several weeks to several months. The rooted tip, with root-filled moss intact, is then severed just below the root mass, and potted up. It should be kept in a moist, sheltered place or in a glass-covered frame until new

Increase in tulip bulbs. The small ones require a year's growth before flowering.

growth indicates its recovery from the operation. The number of plants with which this method is successful is limited. Before trying it, the amateur would do well to consult his State Experiment Station or a book on propagation as to which plants, in his area, are likely to root under these conditions.

Bulbous, Cormous, and Tuberous-rooted plants are propagated largely by natural or artificial division, though some species such as tuberous-rooted begonias come readily from seed.

Daffodils and many other bulbous plants produce bulbs which become double and finally split and separate, forming dense clumps with interlaced feeding roots. When these clumps become so dense that they stop blooming, they are dug, the bulbs in each clump are separated, and replanted to grow on.

Tender bulbs like amaryllis, veltheimia, and ismene also increase naturally by producing small side bulbs or offsets above or below ground. When these are ready to split off, they may be removed and planted separately. This is increase by natural division.

Daffodils increase by small offsets *which form on the outer surfaces of mature* bulbs.

Candidum-lily bulbs "splitting" to produce more bulbs.

"Scaling" a lily bulb to promote the growth of bulblets. A rapid method of increase where it can be used.

Lilies increase naturally by bulbils formed at the stem nodes above ground in some varieties, or by bulblets which develop underground in others. Gladiolus cormlets form around the parent corm underground in much the same way.

To increase lilies asexually by artificial methods, individual scales are removed from a parent bulb and each of these is rooted like a cutting to form a separate plant.

Many tubers can be cut into several pieces, each containing one or more "eyes," and each of these pieces, planted and grown on, will produce a separate plant. Examples are dahlias, potatoes, and tuberous begonias.

CUTTINGS

A cutting, as the name implies, is a severed portion of a plant. *Stem cuttings* are made from portions of the stem of a plant. As these are by far the most widely used for propagation, we will have more to say about them.

Root cuttings, used to propagate plants with tuberous roots—like Oriental poppies and butterfly weed (*Asclepias tuberosa*)—are portions of the root itself, cut during dormancy. Each is planted, with threadlike feeding roots adhering, to grow on and produce a separate plant.

Leaf cuttings of certain species will also produce new plants. *Gesneriads* like African violets and *episcias* are propagated by taking mature leaves with one-inch stems, treating the base of the stems with a rooting stimulant and sinking the stems in a rooting medium until new plants form at the soil line.

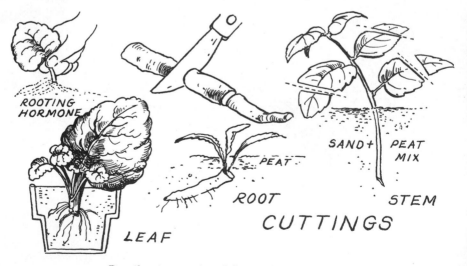

Details of preparing different types of cuttings.

The leaves of Rex and other large-leaved begonias, cut at the veins, and laid flat on a bed of moist sand, will produce roots at the cuts which may be developed into new plants.

Some greenhouse subjects such as piggyback plant (*Tolmiea*), twelve apostles (*Marica*), and Bryophyllum (*Kalanchoe verticillata*), and some other succulents, produce plantlets on the leaves which may be detached and potted up. Others, like the *Echeverias* and other sedums propagate new plants readily from individual leaves. The bases of these are sunk in the rooting medium which, in this case, may be pure sand.

Softwood stem cuttings of a great many annuals, biennials, and perennials, many shrubs (including roses, azaleas and camellias), and not a few trees, may be rooted by the amateur. They provide a quick, easy, and fairly sure way of increasing one's supply of a great many favorite plants, both to extend one's own garden material and to supply extras to give to friends or to "swap," a good old-fashioned custom that adds much to the pleasure of gardening.

Such cuttings are made of terminal new growth which has hardened sufficiently to be "firm" but which is still pliable or crisp like a fresh snap-bean, and capable of reviving quickly after being cut. They may vary in length from 3 to 6 inches, and usually at least two eyes or leaf joints are left above the surface when they are inserted in the rooting medium. Large leaves should be trimmed back a third to a half.

If cuttings must be transported or held for any length of time, they may be kept from wilting by rolling them in a damp cloth or newspaper. For instance, geraniums (which root easily from soft-wood cuttings) are left lying on the bench for 24 hours after they are cut before being placed in the rooting medium. This gives time for the stems to dry or callus at the cuts and, as they are grown and even propagated with less moisture than most other plants, they root more quickly after this treatment.

ROOTING MEDIA

A very important factor of success is the selection of the material in which the cuttings are to be rooted. In former days the standard rooting medium was clean, sharp (gritty), medium-coarse sand. For many plants (including geraniums, *Impatiens holsti,* and *Daphne cneorum*) this is still a perfectly satisfactory material. Other materials have come into use, however, and whether by themselves or in combinations are now more generally employed.

Among these are vermiculite (expanded mica); perlite, a volcanic mineral; milled sphagnum moss, and pulverized peatmoss. All of these are sterile when used fresh from the package or bag. A mixture of one half sterilized sand and one half pulverized peatmoss is perhaps the safest and most foolproof medium for the beginner.

After the base of each cutting is cleanly recut just where the stem is firm and crisp, it is dipped in a root stimulant such as Rootone or Hormodin and set *firmly* in the moist rooting medium. Do not try to root cuttings in water. This method is slower and less efficient.

If many cuttings of one variety or one species are to be rooted, an ordinary flat may be used as the container. For outdoor propagation, one section of a frame may be filled with the selected rooting medium, and the cuttings set in in rows.

Where only a few each of different plants are to be propagated, bulb pans or flower pots serve well because they can be given individual treatment if required, as concerns temperature, moisture, and light. Moreover, some cuttings root vigorously in a few weeks, while others may require months. With practically all, however, rooting is hastened by maintaining moist air around the *tops* as well as keeping the rooting medium moist.

The nurseryman accomplishes this by using a propagating frame or box, which can be kept closed to hold the moisture. In greenhouses an automatic "misting" system is often employed to keep the air saturated with moisture. The amateur can make a small propagating box by taking a wooden box of any convenient size, 5 or 6 inches deep, and constructing sides and ends of double-thick window glass, held together at the corners with waterproof tape. (Your hardware dealer will cut the glass to your specifications.) Glass should extend 6 to 10 inches above sides of box,

Simple propagation box, with glass sides and top. Plastic bag or a plastic plant-dome, fastened over a bulb pan, is a useful device for rooting a few cuttings of one kind.

according to the size of cuttings to be rooted. A pane of glass 1 to 2 inches longer and wider than the box forms the cover.

The method we have most frequently employed for rooting a few cuttings at a time is very simple. We merely take a bulb pan of suitable size —usually 6 or 8 inches—and cover the bottom with drainage material (broken pieces of clay pots), add a half-inch layer of coarse peatmoss or sphagnum, and then fill to within a half inch of the rim with the rooting medium. After the cuttings have been inserted, the bulb pan is covered with a cellophane bag or a plastic dome which gives an almost airtight seal, and allows the condensation to run back into the edge of the pot. The pot is placed in a saucer which serves as a sub-irrigating device whenever lack of moisture on the inside of the cover indicates that the rooting medium is getting dry.

Whatever method of rooting is used, the cuttings, as soon as well rooted, should be transferred to individual pots in a soil mixture well supplied with nutrients. If roots get more than an inch or so long, many of them are likely to be injured in the operation.

Hardwood cuttings are made from firm, stout stems of woody plants, usually taken in autumn from the oldest of the current year's growth. Generally 4 to 12 inches are the best lengths to root, though with easy subjects such as willow and mulberry, they may be as long as 3 or 4 feet. Often they are taken with a "heel" or piece of the main stem of older wood attached at the base. Autumn-cut hardwood cuttings are tied in bundles and buried, laid horizontally in moist soil in a frame so that the cut ends may callus. In early spring they are separated and planted in rows in a moist rooting medium in an outdoor propagation bed to develop roots and grow. Many shrubs, trees, and small fruits may be increased in this way, as may also some broad-leaved and coniferous evergreens.

GRAFTING AND BUDDING

Grafting and budding are methods of propagation in which a piece of one plant is transferred to another and eventually becomes a part of it. They may be used to provide a stronger growing root system; to obtain several varieties of fruits or flowers on one plant, as is often done with apples; or to create a special type or form of plant, as when a bush or trailing rose is grown on a stout cane of another type to produce a small tree or a trailing effect.

In *grafting,* a section of stem or branch is used which has several "eyes" or leaf joints. *Budding* is really a type of grafting in which a single bud or eye is employed instead of a cutting containing several eyes.

In both operations the essential thing to keep in mind is that the union must first be effected by bringing together sections of the cambium layer or *bark* of both plants. In the bark alone can this new growth be initiated, just as all new growth of any plant develops.

In *simple or whip grafting,* a section of year-old growth, usually—in the case of fruits or flowering trees—about the thickness of a pencil, is cut into sections each of which contain three to five eyes. These are known as scions. A long, sloping cut is then made at the lower end with a razor-sharp blade, so as to leave the bark uninjured and the cambium layer firmly attached to the wood itself. A branch or trunk of a young tree of the same thickness (the understock) is similarly cut at its top with a long slope. Then the scion is closely bound to the understock, the cadmium layer of bark of the two pieces meeting at all possible points (see sketch). The graft may then be covered with grafting wax until it "takes."

In *whip and tongue grafting,* after the sloping cuts are made, the grafting knife is driven straight down, first into the scion and then into the understock near the points of the cuts, to form a "tongue" in each (see sketch). Scion and understock are fitted closely, the two tongues interlocking, and the cambium layers of bark of each neatly meeting the other. The graft is then wrapped with cotton cord and covered with grafting wax.

In *wedge or cleft grafting,* a large branch of understock may be used. This is cut straight off (see sketch) and a cleft made down its center with a grafting chisel or heavy knife driven to the desired depth with a wooden mallet. One or two scions are then trimmed at the lower ends to tapering wedges and fitted snugly down into the cleft at the outer edges so that the cadmium bark of the scions meets that of the understock on the outside. The graft is then bound and covered with wax.

There are many other more complicated types of grafting, such as bark, rind, saddle and veneer, but for readers who wish to try these, we recommend one of the books on propagation listed in the Appendix.

While grafting is usually done early in spring—February to April, according to climate and the species to be grafted—the scions may be prepared any time during the winter if they are afterward buried in moist soil or kept in damp peatmoss wrapped in plastic, at a temperature close to freezing.

In *budding,* a T-shaped cut is made in the bark of a young branch of a tree or shrub of another variety of the same species as the bud. The vertical portion of the T may vary from half an inch to an inch, or according to the size of the bud. The buds are taken from young stems of the current year's growth, each bud being sliced off the stem with about half an inch of rind above and below it (see sketch). The wood inside is best removed, leaving only the bud and bark on each side of it—including of course the precious cambium layer. Great care must be exercised, however, not to remove the base of the bud with the inner wood. The upper corners of the T-cut on the understock are now carefully turned back

WHIP & TONGUE GRAFT-

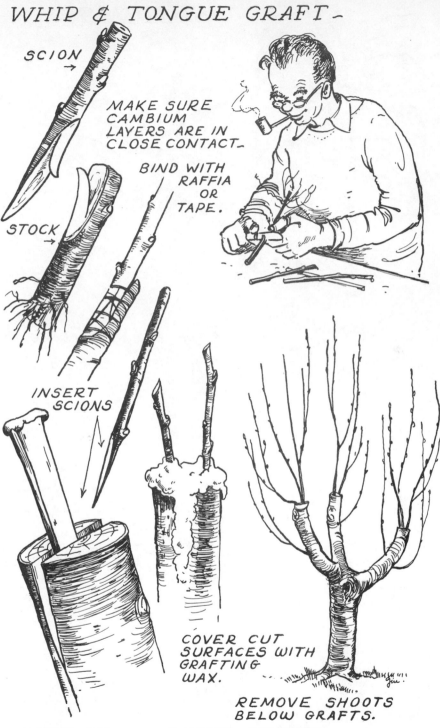

SCION

MAKE SURE
CAMBIUM
LAYERS ARE IN
CLOSE CONTACT-

BIND WITH
RAFFIA
OR
TAPE.

STOCK

INSERT
SCIONS

COVER CUT
SURFACES WITH
GRAFTING
WAX.

REMOVE SHOOTS
BELOW GRAFTS.

WEDGE or CLEFT GRAFT

BUDDING

BUD STICK — REMOVE LEAVES EXCEPT FOR ½ INCH OF LEAFSTALK.

BUD

CUT BUD FROM BUD STICK.

a. CUT MADE IN BARK.

b. BUD INSERTED.

c. BIND WITH RUBBER BAND.

REMOVE LOWER LEAVES FROM ROOT STALK.

FOLLOWING SPRING—CUT JUST ABOVE BUD.

with the end of the budding knife (designed for this purpose) and the bud is slipped into place so that the bark of bud and understock are in close contact. If the operation is carefully done, there will be no rough or torn edges. The bud is then securely held in place by bandaging the wound with a rubber band under slight tension, the end slipped under the last two or three turns (see illustration).

If conditions are right, the inserted bud will begin to grow normally and in a surprisingly short time the wood will have callused over. After the wound has completely healed and the bud has developed into a vigorous shoot or branch, the top of the original or root-stock plant is severed. Usually this is done early in the spring following the operation.

The best time to attempt budding is when sap is beginning to flow and when the bark is soft, plastic, and least likely to tear during the operation. For most plants these conditions exist early in spring, just as growth is being renewed.

In either budding or grafting the amateur will do well, if it is at all possible, to watch the operation actually performed before attempting it himself. If he belongs to a garden club, some member may in all likelihood be able to demonstrate it for him; or he may suggest that it be made the subject for discussion at a meeting. In our experience, few subjects for programs "draw" better than this one. If one does not happen to be a club member, the local county agricultural agent will in all probability be glad to assist. There is no reason why, with a little patience, any serious amateur should not succeed by himself, especially if he invests in a book on the subject, preferably one with plenty of "how-to-do-it" illustrations.

CHAPTER 5

Keeping Plants Vigorous and Healthy

Gardening is the technique and the science of keeping plants growing vigorously. Landscaping is the art of employing plant material to produce effects which are esthetically pleasing. The two are often confused. In this chapter we are concerned only with what makes plants tick—and how to keep them ticking happily.

The beginning gardener must learn to realize that plants are living organisms which, if they are to prosper, must breathe, eat, drink, sleep, and have periods of rest, all in a congenial environment. The old proverb that one man's meat is another man's poison applies equally to plants. One grows lustily where another would perish.

It is the gardener's job, first of all, to select plants which prosper in the environment which he can provide. This includes temperature; light, sun, and shade; moisture; the physical character of the soil; and the chemical elements it contains, as discussed in Chapter 3.

Next he must make sure that his plants receive adequate amounts of such foods as they demand. In many instances nature provides all that is needed in this department. Giant trees, some of them centuries old, survive to remind humanity that plants can get along without man better than he can without them!

However, the gardener is not content to let plants exist where *they* choose to grow, and so in many cases—and in fact in more and more as man continues to alter and ravish the face of the earth—he must provide plants with foods that will enable them to live, let alone to thrive and multiply. Water, of course, as well as food, is essential.

In the third place, the gardener must protect his plants from their enemies, both insects and diseases. Here again the gardener has provided himself with an ever-increasing amount of work since he has destroyed the natural enemies of plant enemies—birds for instance, who live largely on insects. Furthermore, many of the fruits, flowers, and ornamentals which he himself has developed are much more susceptible than were their original forms in nature. Fortunately, science is constantly producing materials which simplify the process of protecting plants from their enemies.

With this over-all glance at the picture, let us now take a closer look at some of the details.

TEMPERATURE

One need not be a gardener to realize that not all plants grow in all climates. The chief factor determining what will grow where is temperature. That is why planting zones—such as those indicated on the end-paper map—are based on average temperatures, and especially on "first frost" and "last frost" dates.

Altitude is another factor to be considered. Hence many gardens in any particular zone are either much warmer or much colder than the average for most gardens in that zone. The gardener must ascertain where his property fits into the picture. This he can do by consulting his local county agent and experienced gardeners in his local garden club, which, incidentally, he should join if he would like to have friendly assistance in meeting many of his garden problems.

Micro-climates, as the word implies, are variations, within limited areas, from the normal conditions surrounding them. Protection against prevailing winter winds, too strong sunshine, and heavy storms can make a big difference in the kind of plants that can be grown successfully. A hill, a house, or even a hedge can provide the necessary protection.

A wall may dam up the flow of cold air down a slope, resulting, on cold nights, in a difference in temperature of a few degrees. If those few degrees have been just above or just below freezing, they may mean the end of a display of flowers that could have gone on blooming for weeks longer. Results may often be more serious. We have seen the loss of several beds of rare plants, including many fine shrubs, due to just such a condition. Our house is near the edge of a steep bank running down to a salt-water river; there frost often strikes, or ice forms, at times when we escape it. The difference in the growth of plants, in areas only a few hundred feet apart, is often very perceptible.

A coldframe is the outstanding example of a micro-climate reduced to the *n*th degree. Within its boundaries of a few boards and a frail cover of glass, a tiny bit of your garden is moved one to two hundred miles to the south!

Water features, either natural or artificial, can be used to create micro-climates—most desirable in climates where summer heat is a problem. A wide, shallow pool which throws off moisture just as a pan of water does on an old-fashioned steam radiator, creates a cool little oasis in a hot, dry landscape. Running streams and fountains are even more helpful in reducing dry heat, for the water is constantly in motion and so is more readily absorbed into the air.

The forming of micro-climates, by utilizing natural variations in topography, building walls, planting windbreaks or hedges, is of practical help to any gardener who wishes to extend the range of the plants he can grow. On larger places, a planting of evergreens or a wide border of mixed shrubs provides shelter from prevailing winter and spring winds that will advance the flowering of early perennials and bulbs by as much as two weeks, and in addition lessens the danger of injury from summer storms.

Shade. While the majority of our cultivated ornamentals like full sun, there are many that are happier in partial shade, and some that demand it (see list, Appendix). Shade may readily be provided for these plants by a few quick-growing, leafy trees such as birches, Chinese elms, and pin oaks. For this purpose, greedy and shallow-rooting trees such as maples, poplars, and magnolias are to be avoided.

MOISTURE

The country over, season after season and year after year, more plants are injured or lost for lack of sufficient moisture than from any other one cause. Yet the average gardener spends many times as much per annum on plant foods and gadgets as he does on providing an adequate watering system.

The reason? It's simple: No one makes any money selling *water*. No company puts on a multithousand-dollar advertising campaign to convince the home gardener that he needs it to make his plants grow successfully.

The homeowner who can have his own water supply is fortunate; for if it is adequate he will not be faced with an ordinance forbidding him to use it just when his plants and his garden most need it. Unfortunately the privately owned water supply is a vanishing luxury. What then?

Well, there are many ways of making such water as is available count to the last drop.

First: keep the soil in which your plants grow well supplied with *humus*. This holds water like a sponge and keeps it from leaching down into the lower layers of soil out of reach of thirsty roots—and incidentally carrying with it essential plant foods.

Second: keep bare surfaces *mulched*. This not only greatly decreases the amount of moisture lost through evaporation from the soil surface (which in dry windy weather can be tremendous) but it also keeps the soil surface many degrees cooler than when it is fully exposed to the sun. Mulching also saves a great deal of labor in controlling weeds. Under a mulch many weeds fail to germinate; or if they do, and succeed in push-

Next in importance to applying water to the soil when needed is the prevention or decrease of its loss through evaporation from the surface. This is accomplished by the use of mulching, the application of any material that curtails evaporation. Frequent cultivation, which creates a "dust mulch," is helpful. More effective is covering the soil around and between plants with any material that makes a moisture-holding blanket. Among such are peatmoss, chopped sugar cane, buckwheat hulls, and others.

ing up through it, they are weak, leggy, and easy to remove, roots and all. Mulching does not actually provide moisture, but it does work wonders in conserving it once it has been provided.

A mulch is any material spread around and between plants to cover the soil and thus prevent, or at least curtail, the loss of soil moisture through surface evaporation. Nature's own mulch is the matrix of decayed and decaying vegetable matter—leaves, twigs, needles of coniferous evergreens, surface roots, and plants to be found in any forest, or even under a group of shrubs or trees, unmolested by the hand of man.

As man, at an ever-accelerating pace, takes over the surface of the earth from nature and strips it of its natural mulch mantle, it becomes increasingly important that he should replace it wherever he can.

For this purpose almost any material that will decay may be used, but some are better than others. Half-decomposed material from the compost heap is excellent. Grass clippings, if not applied so thickly as to ferment or pack and keep out air circulation, are good. Dry hardwood leaves, pine needles, or other materials locally available, such as cranberry vines, seaweed from the shore, sawdust, wood chips, and the chopped stalks of sugar cane or corn, redwood or fir bark can be utilized. Among the numerous commercial products available are peatmoss, buckwheat hulls, chicken litter made from ground peanut shells, bagasse, shavings, and well-rotted strawy manure, where it may be obtained. Even flat stones, pebbles, or coarse pebbly sand will serve in a pinch, conserving moisture in the soil beneath, though of course they add no humus.

Mulches are applied in a layer from 2 to 4 inches thick, according to the material and the purpose for which they are used. Some types, notably sawdust and wood chips, may, in the process of decomposition, temporarily reduce the available nitrogen in the soil, due to its use by the bacteria affecting the decay. This is the reason that sawdust is often condemned as a mulch. Although this "loan" of nitrogen is later repaid to the soil bank, it is well, in using mulches of this type, to supplement them with an application of nitrogen, raked in before applying the mulch at the rate of 1 pound of sulfate of ammonia or 1½ pounds of nitrate of soda per 100 square feet.

Third: if, for any reason, a mulch cannot be used, *cultivate frequently,* even if no weeds are in evidence. The best tool for this purpose is a scuffle hoe, which has a thin, double-edged blade on a long handle and is worked by "scuffling" it back and forth. With it one can clean ground of small weeds almost as fast as walking, and the soil surface is left in a nice, loose mulch. Our two scuffle hoes—one 6, the other 8 inches wide —get more constant use than any other hand tools we have.

Watering. If despite everything that can be done to conserve moisture —by the use of humus, windbreaks, mulches—the soil still dries out to a degree that interferes with normal growth, then plants must be watered.

The average home gardener wastes a large percentage of the water he uses for his plants by "sprinkling." The first thing to learn about watering is that a sufficient amount should be given at each application to penetrate the soil well down into the root zone of the plant, crop, or bed being watered. If the surface only is made moist, to a depth of a fraction of an inch (or a few inches in the case of trees or large shrubs) it never reaches the *feeding* roots.

The depth to which water penetrates depends upon the character of the soil. In sandy or gravelly soils deficient in humus, it goes down immediately—and keeps going! (Much of the soil in our grounds on Cape Cod is the type of which natives say, "Rain goes faster after it hits the ground than it does coming down; fog's a lot better!") On a heavy clay soil, water

Use a coffee-can measure when watering. After watering, measure depth accumulated in can. Then dig nearby to see how deep moisture has penetrated soil. You now know, when water is X inches deep in can, just how deep it will have moistened the soil.

penetrates very slowly, and if applied too rapidly accumulates on the surface and is lost by running off or by evaporation.

On a loamy soil (which is a mixture of sand and clay) it will penetrate readily, and if enough humus is also present is then absorbed and held.

Each gardener must determine for himself the method of watering best suited to his needs. If he has more than one type of soil, or grows a wide variety of plants, he will get best results by employing several methods.

Until he becomes familiar with the moisture requirements of his soil and his crops, he should do a little experimenting. A simple method of determining how much water is required to moisten any particular soil to a depth of 4 inches (the minimum for any but very shallow-rooting crops) is as follows: Take a fairly wide-mouthed, straight-sided can and mark the inside to indicate inches and half inches. Place the tin—being careful to have it level—where it will get the average "rainfall" from a sprinkler or other watering device. When it indicates that ½ inch of "rain" has fallen, shut off the water. Then take a trowel and dig down into the soil, making a straight-sided hole that will clearly show just how deep the moisture has penetrated.

A few trials will indicate how much water you should apply to moisten the soil to the depth desired, and the coffee-can measure, left in place, will show when it has been applied. This, of course, is a rule of thumb rather than a scientific way of estimating your soil's moisture requirements, but serves all practical purposes.

Watering Equipment. There are all kinds of devices for applying water, from the time-honored one of holding the thumb over the end of a hose to get a fanlike spread, to automatic oscillating devices that throw very

WATERING EQUIPMENT. *The oscillating rain machine, of which there are many types available, is the best substitute for natural rain. In most gardens water is the critical factor in determining how well plants will prosper. Without it no amount of plant foods or care in culture can assure success. The more closely the application of water approaches natural rainfall, the better the results. The machine shown above covers areas up to 2500 square feet from one position and applies rainlike drops in "waves," allowing the water to penetrate the soil without forming surface puddles or knocking down plants. (Self-propelled types are available, but we have found them satisfactory only under ideal conditions for operation.)*

realistic raindrops in alternating waves from side to side, so that they have a chance to soak in without forming puddles on the surface. In our experience such rain machines are far superior to the various revolving sprinkers which apply water much too rapidly and much less uniformly.

For watering freshly sown seeds and small transplants, a mistlike spray is the most desirable. Similar to this in effect are the perforated plastic

This cast-aluminum "sprinkler" throws a very fine mist covering 100 square feet or more, depending on water pressure.

In planning any garden, the possible effect of winds *should be considered. It is one of the chief factors determining the successful development of many plants, including trees. A substantial wind barrier which creates a micro-climate substantially lessens wind hazard.*

hoses which may be attached to the regular hose. Laid along the length of a bed or border, one of these will deliver fine mistlike sprays from a number of small openings. Where only small areas are to be watered, these are more practical than the oscillators, which cover quite large areas.

For vegetable or other large gardens, a permanent irrigation system, controlled from a central valve, is the most convenient—and also the most expensive. These are usually installed by professional concerns and are a bit too complicated for the average do-it-yourself gardener.

Wind Barriers. The rate of evaporation of moisture from the soil is controlled to a large degree by its exposure to wind passing over it. Anything that protects an area from strong air currents materially helps to conserve moisture. In the case of new plantings in beds or borders, or of individual plants, a temporary screen of any sort is of assistance. Small plants may be covered with newspapers or strips of plastic held in place by stones, berry baskets, plastic domes, or Hotkaps.

THE FEEDING OF PLANTS

We have already discussed (in Chapter 2) the fact that plant growth is dependent upon the presence of certain chemicals in the soil; and that those chemicals must be in available form, i.e. readily soluble, because plants can take up their foods only when it is in solution.

Of the three principal plant foods—nitrogen, phosphorus, and potassium—the first is the one likely to be soonest exhausted; and the third, potassium, the least likely. A superabundance of one type of food does not make up for the shortage of another. The gardener therefore should so arrange his plant-feeding program that *all three* are available in adequate supply.

Nitrogen may be obtained in a number of materials. Quickest acting of these are nitrate of soda and sulfate of ammonia. The former, applied in small pellets or crystals, followed by rain or a thorough watering, may noticeably stimulate new growth of foliage in a few days. By the same token, its beneficial effect is soonest exhausted. Recently, forms of nitrogen that are much slower acting have been developed. Such synthetic organic nitrogen carriers as calcium cyanamide and urea take a little longer than nitrate of soda but are still quick-acting. The new combination nitrogenous fertilizers, using several nitrogen-bearing materials, continue to provide this vital nutrient throughout the season. These have proved particularly valuable in fertilizing lawns, but are equally important for other long-season crops.

The *fertilizers* most commonly used about the home grounds—and for commercial crops, too—are termed "complete" fertilizers. That is, they contain all three of the principal elements, nitrogen, phosphorus, and potassium, and minor trace elements as well.

It is mistaken economy to purchase fertilizers on the basis of the price per bag. The lower the percentage of nutrients present, the more you pay for useless "fillers" that are combined with these to make up the total weight. As a rule the total percentage of the complete plant foods should be at least 20, as in a 5–10–5 or 10–6–4 mixture. (See also Chapter 2.)

It is seldom necessary to apply any one of the three main nutrients separately, except in the case of nitrogen for lawns. With the other two elements, phosphorus and potassium, a complete fertilizer can be used, with a formula high in the elements most needed and low in the others.

The beginning gardener should learn to distinguish between organic and inorganic (chemical) fertilizers.

The former are made up of processed animal and vegetable materials: bone, dried blood, slaughter-house wastes (tankage), cottonseed meal, and the like. The chemical fertilizers are derived from inanimate substances such as nitrate and potash salts, phosphate rock, and various manufacturing by-products.

The *organic fertilizers* are safer to use, that is there is less danger of "burning" or otherwise injuring plants in case of an accidental overdose. In *transplanting* especially it is better to avoid the use of chemicals; in fact many instructions for transplanting or setting out even sizable trees or shrubs advise using no fertilizer in the planting holes. We have never observed any injury from this practice, however, but have had good results from the reasonable use of *organic* fertilizers in such operations.

In using fertilizers, best results are usually obtained by making two or more moderate applications rather than one large one.

A satisfactory system is to make the first application just before sowing seeds or setting out plants, and a second one considerably later; with vegetables and annuals, when they are half grown. Most perennials and shrubs may be fertilized just as growth starts in the spring, and again just before or after the flowering period. Usual amounts to be used are suggested in connection with different types of plants, throughout this volume.

Humus (discussed in Chapter 2), in addition to its other advantages, acts as a sponge to absorb and hold plant nutrients that have gone into solution, thus preventing their loss through leaching from excessive rain or watering.

Manures and composts have the double advantage of adding both plant foods and humus to the soil. In fact the most effective—as well as the pleasantest—way to utilize animal manures is to incorporate them with organic materials in the compost heap. This is like starting a bank account, and requires some planning ahead—but it pays excellent dividends. We keep a series of heaps going. (See Chapter 2 for details of constructing the compost heap.)

Green manures are crops sown to be plowed or dug under, usually in an immature state, where they are grown. The growing roots penetrate the soil and improve its friability, and also gather food elements which are brought nearer the surface.

Crops used for this purpose include several of the legumes, such as cowpeas, vetch, and clover, that add to the nitrogen in the soil. Others, such as winter rye and oats, produce a mass of green material, while the soil is not otherwise occupied, to provide humus when it is turned under. (See also Chapter 2.)

PREPARATION FOR PLANTING

The information given so far in this chapter will be of no use in providing a green lawn, bigger roses, or more vigorous trees and shrubs—*unless it is put to use*. In most instances nine tenths of the successful growth of a plant depends upon what is done to the soil *before* it is planted.

England is famous for its beautiful gardens. The climate, with its abundant moisture and the absence of the extremes of winter cold and scorching summer heat which we experience, may be credited with a great deal of this horticultural success, but much is due to the extreme thoroughness practiced in preparing the soil for planting. No one who reads English books on gardening can fail to be impressed by this. In connection with our editorial work we read many of these volumes, and the constant emphasis on what should be done *before* planting stands out like a bandaged thumb at a bridge party.

Too often American gardeners sow their seeds or set out their plants in soil that is completely *un*prepared. This is especially true of beginning gardeners, but by no means limited to them. Misled by blatantly extravagant, if not patently false claims in advertising—which go unchallenged in most editorial columns—they plant with little or no real preparation of the soil, depending upon wonder-working "miracle" chemicals to give them Jack-and-the-beanstalk results. Recently we saw a full-page ad in one of the country's leading—and in many ways most reliable—newspapers, devoted to a new method of lawn making purporting to provide a perfect, weed-free turf. Supposedly this could be achieved in a few weeks merely by spreading over the ground a combination of three layers of especially prepared fabric, carrying seed, and fertilizer contents. This might be possible, but how long would such a lawn last? Its remains, of course, might be rooted up to make a good, but rather expensive, addition to the compost heap.

As we have seen, the soil factors involved in obtaining and maintaining good plant growth are:

> its physical condition,
> its capacity for retaining moisture,
> its nutrient content.

Our problem, therefore, is to provide, as far as is practical, the maximum in each of these factors for the plant or crop to be grown.

Physical condition. The soil should be "worked up"—by hand digging, plowing, or rototilling—to a depth adequate for the plants or crops to be grown. Where there is a hard subsoil this may be broken up with a pickax or a crowbar to improve drainage. Usually it is left in place, but if too close to the surface it may be advantageous to remove some of it entirely to make possible a larger prepared planting hole or a deeper bed.

If the subsoil is sandy or gravelly, usually the best course is to leave it undisturbed, or to mix with it clay soil and peatmoss or other humusy material to increase its water-holding capacity.

Either of these treatments is more readily employed in preparing planting holes for trees or shrubs than in the case of a lawn, a large flower garden, or a vegetable plot. For such extensive areas, poor drainage may be improved by extra-deep digging or by subsoil plowing. Too rapid draining may be slowed up by the incorporation of humusy materials such as manure, green manures, sod turned under (either broken up in small pieces or grass side down), peatmoss, or compost.

The *depth* to which ground should be prepared varies with different types of plants. But as we stress throughout this book *the deeper the better*. The following figures should be taken as minimum:

Flower borders:

annuals	5 to 6 inches	
perennials	6 to 8 inches	
Lawn	4 to 6 inches	
Roses	18 to 24 inches	
Shrubs (holes)	18 to 24 inches; 24 inches in diameter	
Trees (holes)	24 to 36 inches; 36 inches in diameter	

In the preparation of planting holes it is advisable to remove soil from holes completely (placing it on burlap or in a wheelbarrow) and then refill with prepared compost.

The *nutrient content* of any soil is determined by the amounts of the several elements in *available form* which it contains, as discussed earlier in this chapter. Different plants, in growing, use up these elements in different amounts, foliage plants like lawn grass demanding more nitrogen than others, some more potash, etc.

In commercial farming and vegetable growing, special formulas, designed to provide these plant food elements in just the right proportions for the crop being grown, are employed. Special formulas are also put out, in fancy packages and at fancy prices, for the home gardener's use. He can get them for lawns, for roses, for this and that special purpose, but they are by no means essential. We have grown just as good roses with potato fertilizer as with any other, though of course if we were growing roses by the acre we would try to get a formula especially suited to the crop *and* the soil in which they were grown.

For the amateur's garden, the most important distinction is between plants that demand or prefer an acid soil—such as rhododendrons, azaleas, kalmias, and camellias—and plants which particularly demand neutral or alkaline soil. In the former case, a fertilizer with an acid reaction should be used, and in the latter, lime may be applied if needed. See the table at the close of this chapter.

Final preparation for planting then includes these three steps:

First: digging or plowing the area and, if necessary, improving the drainage and removing large stones or roots.

Second: applying and *digging in* peatmoss, compost, and/or other humus-forming material, and lime if required.

Third: applying and raking in fertilizers, either inorganic (chemical) or processed (pulverized) organic materials.

Just before planting, it is advantageous to go over, with an iron rake, the area where seeds are to be sown.

ORGANIC GARDENING

We are often asked what stand we take on organic gardening—as though it were a challenge to our religion or our politics!

We make a practice of using all of the organic material, of whatever sort, that we can get. In addition to this, every fall and spring we plant cover crops of winter rye, vetch, clover, or some other fast-growing ground cover for turning under as "green manure" (pages 26; 86).

We do not, however, eschew the use of all chemical fertilizers, insecticides, and fungicides as do the dedicated organic gardeners. As a matter of fact, we would have had great difficulty in growing green manure crops (to provide the humus so badly needed on our sandy, porous soil) without the assistance of chemical fertilizers to give them a start.

We have never seen convincing evidence that organically grown vegetables and flowers can be made immune to insect and disease attacks, and we have encountered numerous instances of evidence to the contrary. When possible, we use natural organic materials such as rotenone or pyrethrum for spraying and dusting, but in an emergency we resort to chemical materials. We do agree that vegetables and fruits—practically "manufactured" on vast areas with chemicals and irrigation and harvested prematurely—are lacking in flavor and probably in nutritional value.

In short, we use all the organic material we can obtain, but do not hesitate to employ chemicals where they are likely to beneficially supplement the organics, or save a diseased or insect-ridden crop from ruin.

SYMPTOMS OF NUTRIENT DEFICIENCY

Nitrogen: Light green to yellow leaves starting at bottom of plant, turning first pale green, then yellow.
    Cucumber: pointed blossom end.
    Fruit: poor set; early leaf fall.
    Corn: leaves with yellow midrib, edges green. Most likely to occur in sandy or water-logged soils.
Phosphorus: "Leaf scorch," often mistaken for drought or fire blight.
    Corn: yellows at leaf tips and along margins.
    Cucumber: small stem end.
    Potato: marginal scorch of lower leaves.
Boron: Celery: cracked stems.
    Beets: heart rot and canker (cracking of outer skin near soil surface, followed by breaking down of root tissue).

FERTILIZERS, THEIR NUTRIENT CONTENTS,
REACTION AND APPLICATION

Reaction	Fertilizer	Source	Application per 100 sq. ft.
alkaline	bone meal	organic	3 to 6 pounds
acid	cottonseed meal	"	3 to 6 "
alkaline	cyanamid	inorganic	combined with others
acid	dried blood	organic	2 to 4 pounds
	manure		
	dried cow		
	or sheep	"	1 to 2 pecks
	dried poultry	"	½ peck
none	muriate of potash	inorganic	1 to 3 pounds
alkaline	nitrate of soda	"	1 to 3 "
acid	sulfate of ammonia	"	
none	superphosphate	"	3 to 6 "
acid	tankage	organic	4 "
slightly acid	urea	inorganic	combined with others
alkaline	wood ashes	organic	6 pecks

GENERAL FERTILIZER FORMULAS AND THEIR RECOMMENDED USES

Applications as noted or as directed on the packages

Plant	Formula			Pounds per 100 sq. ft.
annuals	5–10–5 or 4–12–4			3 to 4
azaleas and rhododendrons	4–12–4		plus 25% organic nitrogen—	3 to 4
			or 2 parts cottonseed meal and 1 part ammonium sulfate	1 to 2
lawns	10–6–4 or 11–4–8			3 to 4
perennials	4–12–4 or 2–10–10			3 to 4
roses	4–12–4			3 to 4
shrubs	4–12–4 or 10–6–4			3 to 4
trees	4–12–4 or 10–6–4			3 to 4
vegetables, leafy,	4–12–4		and side dress with	3 to 4
root	2–10–10		nitrogenous fertilizer	3 to 4

UPKEEP

The general appearance of the home and grounds depends not only upon how much thought and good care have been employed in planning it, and expense and labor in planting it; there is a third factor which too often is neglected. It may be expressed in the word "upkeep"—but that is perhaps a little too all-inclusive. What is specifically referred to here is vigorous growth and good health.

To cover the former, little need be added to the information and suggestions given in preceding chapters. Pests and diseases, however, are another matter; and the novice at gardening will not have gone far before he begins to encounter them. If he takes the trouble to learn what he can about them *in advance,* he will save himself much trouble, disappointment, and heartbreak.

In the first place he will learn to be *constantly on the watch* for the first sign of injury to his plants caused by pests or diseases. In fighting many of them, promptness is almost as important as it is in fighting a fire. And so the wise gardener keeps on hand, ready for instant use, one or more of the all-purpose controls, and equipment with which to apply them. (See Appendix and page 129.)

As a rule the more vigorous and healthy a plant, the less likely it is to be attacked. But exceptions to this rule are so frequent that one cannot rely upon it.

In guarding against many plant pests and diseases, sanitation is quite as essential in the garden as in the house. Plants that are kept well fed and uncrowded are less likely to be attacked by either pests or disease, and are more likely to make a recovery if they are attacked. With feeding, as with most things, it is possible to overdo. Plants forced into abnormally lush growth—as for instance by the use of an excess of nitrogen—may be unduly susceptible to trouble.

Weeds, too, are pests when growing where they are a menace to cultivated plants. A weed has been described as a plant growing where it is not wanted. (One of the worst "weeds" we had in our vegetable garden last year was a vigorous, self-sown crop of that excellent "greens" *Tetragonia expansa,* more commonly known as New Zealand spinach.)

Of recent years various chemicals have been more and more frequently employed in the control of weeds in large-scale vegetable growing and farming operations, as well as for destroying unwanted growth along highways and roadsides. In the home garden and about the home grounds these materials should be used with great caution (as in the eradication of poison-ivy) or applied by a professional operator. The control of weeds in lawns by the use of chemicals is an exception to the above statement; but in our experience and observation, these "patent medicines"—with monosyllabic names dreamed up by high-salaried advertising experts who would not know a weed from a watering can—are in general not nearly so effective as the extravagant claims made for them would imply. We suggest a small-scale test treatment under one's own conditions before making any considerable investment in any such panacea. For weeds and their control see Appendix.

INSECTICIDES, FUNGICIDES, AND HERBICIDES

New or improved insecticides, fungicides, and herbicides are constantly coming on the market in these days of rapid scientific discovery. By the time this volume reaches the reader, a number of materials may be available which were unknown at the time this was written. We can only list the best materials for home garden use known to us at this writing.

Products are offered in garden centers, seed and hardware stores, usually under trade names. The label of each package, however, bears a list of ingredients, with percentages of active and inactive content. Our recommendations in the Appendix (pages 467 and 469) for insecticides and fungicides, with but few exceptions, do not use trade names, but those of the chemicals themselves. In the table of herbicides (page 470, Appendix) trade names are used without any intention on our part of recommending a single product over all others. Commercial products manufactured by reputable companies are as represented. By consulting the list of ingredients on each package displayed in the store, the buyer can select the one best suited for his purpose.

Many products are available as dusts, concentrated liquid sprays to be diluted in water, or powders to be dissolved in water and used in spray guns. Dusts are easiest to apply. In general, sprays do a more thorough job. Directions on each package tell exactly how each material should be prepared for use, how much water is to be added to a given amount of material to make a spray, and, in cases where the material or spray mixture is to be applied to the soil or lawn surface, how much is needed to cover 100 or 1000 square feet.

Since the publication of Rachel Carson's controversial book, *Silent Spring,* and the articles, lectures, government research, and legislation resulting from the furor it caused, all gardeners are aware of the potential dangers to man, animals, birds, and even fish from the indiscriminate or careless use of many insecticides and other related materials.

The label on every product bears explicit directions and precautions if the material is toxic to man or to animals. These must be *followed to the letter* for ensurance against injury to any living thing.

Sometimes beginners increase the given dosage of an insecticide, or even of a fertilizer, on the theory that if a little is good, more is better. Nothing could be further from the proven facts. Following such a course may well result in injury to plants, materials, birds, or wild creatures, or worst of all, to the operator.

The following precautions should be observed in all cases. (From Home & Garden Bulletin No. 46, U. S. Dept. of Agriculture.)

Most insecticides and fungicides are poisonous. Those that are recommended . . . can be used with safety provided these precautions are carefully followed.

Handle insecticides and fungicides with care. Follow all directions and heed all precautions on the labels.

In handling, mixing, or applying insecticides and fungicides, avoid inhaling them; keep them out of eyes, nose and mouth. Work on the windward side of the areas treated.

For detailed lists of insecticides, fungicides, and herbicides, see Appendix.

For information of dusters and sprayers, see page 129.

Good cultural practices will do much to prevent and control pests, diseases, and weeds in the home garden. The following measures should be taken:

1. Good drainage is essential.
2. Fertile soil containing a constant supply of humus.
3. Good-quality, appropriate fertilizers applied as needed.
4. Plants suited to the soil and climate should be grown.
5. Weeds should be kept under control and never permitted to go to seed.
6. Best-quality grass seed contains few weed seeds. Buy only certified seed.
7. Before sowing seeds, treat with seed protectant. See page 56.
8. Check purchased plants to be sure they are pest and disease free.
9. Disease-resistant varieties of many plants are available. These reduce danger of trouble.
10. When pests or diseases have been present during growing season, burn all garden trash which might harbor them through the winter, to appear again next season. A thorough garden clean-up each fall makes for a clean garden in spring.

The lopped tree in time may grow again,
Most naked plants renew both fruit and flower.
                                    ROBERT SOUTHWELL

Just as the twig is bent, the tree's inclin'd.
                                    ALEXANDER POPE

CHAPTER 6

Pruning and Training Plants

Almost all trees, shrubs, and perennial vines grown about the modern home place require, at one time or another, some attention involving pruning or training.

While both these operations necessitate the removal of parts of the plants, let us at the outset make clear the distinction between the two.

Pruning is done primarily to ensure better growth, more bloom, or greater health for the specimen. *Training* may also involve such removal, but it is done for the benefit of the pruner rather than of the plant: to make the plant grow, or assume a form that, for esthetic reasons, he prefers. Often the two objectives overlap, but it should always be kept in mind that they are distinct.

Few people realize the fact that nature herself does a great deal of pruning. Forest trees, as they struggle upward in the competition for light, lose their lower branches. The same thing happens with ornamental trees if planted too close together, and with shrubs about the home grounds that are allowed to crowd each other. Storms, too, often remove branches or even tear out the tops of trees and shrubs. The results of this type of pruning are likely to be anything but desirable. In fact much of the pruning done by the gardener is designed particularly to prevent what would happen were the job left to nature!

PRUNING OBJECTIVES

The gardener should never take a pruning tool in hand without having some definite objective as to what and why he is going to prune. Among the several things he can set out to accomplish are:

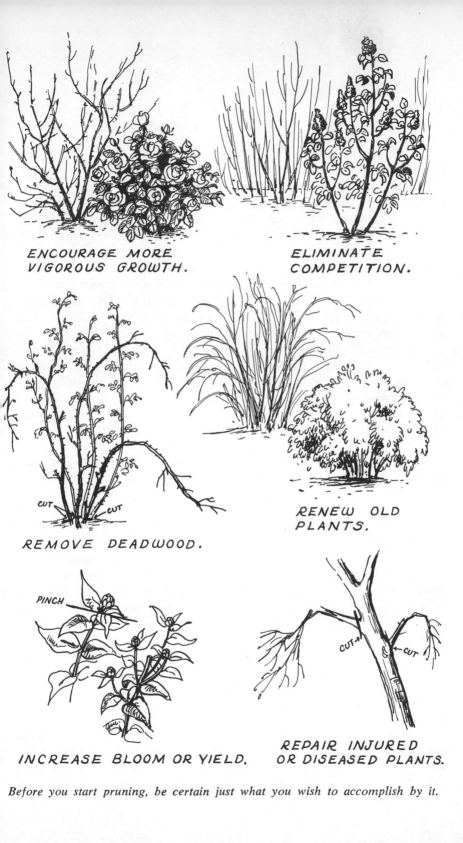

ENCOURAGE MORE
VIGOROUS GROWTH.

ELIMINATE
COMPETITION.

REMOVE DEADWOOD.

CUT   CUT

RENEW OLD
PLANTS.

PINCH

INCREASE BLOOM OR YIELD.

CUT   CUT

REPAIR INJURED
OR DISEASED PLANTS.

Before you start pruning, be certain just what you wish to accomplish by it.

To encourage more vigorous growth. Plants that are cut back grow with renewed vigor—as when, for instance, roses that have barely pulled through a tough winter are pruned severely to encourage the development of new, healthy shoots nearer the base of the plant; or when an injured branch of a tree or shrub is severed in order to induce the development of vigorous new growth below the cut.

To eliminate competition. Some trees and many shrubs develop so many branches or new growths from the ground, and the fight for survival is so intense, that none can fully develop. Most fruit trees, and especially peaches, are examples of the former; lilacs that have been allowed to send up suckers or sprouts around the original plant until they have formed a thicket typify the latter.

To remove dead wood is another essential form of pruning and one which is always safe for the gardener to undertake. Many shrubs can be kept vigorous and full of bloom indefinitely if all dead and dying wood is cut away *at ground level* once each year.

To renew old plants. Frequently a tree, shrub, or vine that still has a vigorous root system becomes so overgrown as to outlive its purpose as far as its decorative value is concerned. Usually such plants can, by severe pruning—or even cutting back practically to the ground—be remade into new, attractive plants. The rambler type of climbing rose, which flowers only on new wood, and should have all old canes cut out immediately after flowering, is one example of this. Peach trees that have borne many crops, and occasionally apples, when "dehorned" (cut back to leave only stubs of the original branches), typify this kind of severe pruning. Other plants like mountain-laurel and lilacs are, in time, completely rejuvenated by being cut back to mere stubs. If plants become too tall, leggy, and sprawling for repair, try this severe pruning before rooting them out altogether.

To increase bloom or yield. Many fruits, if left to grow naturally, are almost sure to set more flowers or fruit than can be properly matured or ripened. Nature is not interested in the size or perfection of blossoms or fruit set. And so, even though she removes part of the crop by letting it fall off while immature, if the pruning is left to nature alone, it is not likely to be well done.

The pruning away of dead flower stalks or branches, as with roses, lilacs, and other flowering shrubs, with perennials like delphinium and lupine, and even with most annuals, is calculated to produce more or higher quality bloom later on. Disbudding of dahlias and chrysanthemums is really a form of this type of pruning.

To repair injured and diseased plants. Pruning often plays an important part in the restoration of injured plants, as after storm or ice-breakage, and also in the cure of diseased specimens. Here on Cape Cod, where we have so many hurricanes and northeast storms, we often find

Most shrubs and vines tend to smother themselves with an accumulated tangle of old wood, which chokes and shades new growths trying to establish themselves. To maintain vigorous growth, much of the old wood, even if still alive, should be severely pruned out, or even cut back to the ground, as with this vigorous climbing rose.

it necessary to perform such repair operations. A fine young tulip tree, brought with us from New York, lost 15 feet of its top two years ago, and the unsightly stub seemed hardly worth rehabilitating. However, we cut the main trunk neatly just above a strong branch, and fastened the branch in an upright position by attaching it to a long bamboo stake bound to it and to the tree trunk. After a few months it had formed a vigorous new leader and the support was removed. Today the tree is handsomer than ever, more dense, but not so tall as it would have been if uninjured.

Where disease has begun to attack a plant, as in the case of rose cancer for instance, cutting back to clean, live wood before the trouble has gone too far may save the plant.

Equally important is the use of pruning to *forestall* injury, by eliminating weak crotches, poorly placed limbs, entangled boughs or roots and the like.

TRAINING OBJECTIVES

When pruning is to be undertaken to change or modify the shape or habit of a plant in order to make it more beautiful, or to induce it to fit better into a certain space or garden picture, the gardener should be perfectly clear in his mind just what he is going to do before starting to use the pruning shears.

To control size and habit of growth. It often happens that a tree or shrub is planted where it fits in all right for a few years, but later completely outgrows its surroundings. Who, for instance, has not seen, under low windows, foundation plantings of evergreens that have been allowed to grow until they nearly obliterate the front of the house? Often a maple or other shade tree or evergreen almost completely occupies a front yard until no space is left for a lawn or for any other use.

There is a limit to the control of size by pruning, but if taken in time, and faithfully continued, the results which can be accomplished are almost unbelievable.

The same holds true for the control of *habit of growth*. Many years ago when the famous Seabrook Farms in New Jersey undertook an extensive orchard operation, I complimented—in the column of a Seabrook house organ which I edited at the time—the little German who had charge of the pruning, stating that he could do anything with an apple tree except make it jump through a hoop. Instead of being flattered, he burst into my office in a very irate mood, with the statement that his skill had been greatly underestimated. A year later he stopped in again and asked me to take a ride in his jeep. We ended up in the yard of his neat little home, where, with pride, he showed me a young apple, growing lustily, topped by three perfect hoops formed by the willowy branches. "Ja," he exclaimed triumphantly. "You see, I *can* make heem jump through a hoop!"

The extreme example of controlling growth habit is to be found in topiary work in which dense-growing shrubs, especially box, are trained, trimmed, and tortured into the forms of urns, roosters, animals, or what-have-you. Fortunately this garden "art" is now seldom encountered in this country, although still to be seen in famous old gardens in Great Britain and Europe.

Espaliered fruits or vinelike shrubs such as *Pyracantha coccinea* or *Hydrangea petiolaris* (climbing hydrangea) represent another extreme example of training plants to desired forms by means of pruning away unneeded branches or tops and guiding the remainder by tying the young, pliable branches to a frame or fastening them to a wall in exactly the positions in which the gardener wishes them to grow.

ESPALIER FORMS

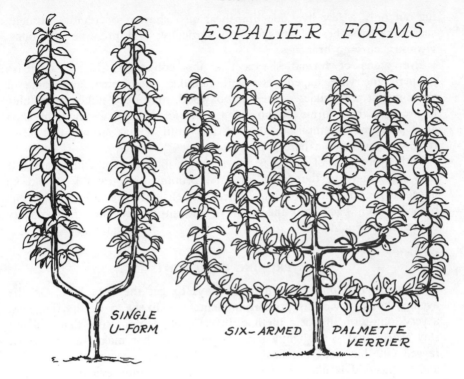

SINGLE
U-FORM

SIX-ARMED

PALMETTE
VERRIER

In formal gardens, or against a sunny wall, espaliered fruits or certain types of flowering shrubs may be used effectively.

Hedge pruning, when sheared to shape, is simply a less difficult and less tortuous form of topiary work. To be successful this must be begun when the plants are small—whether they are privet, barberry, or trees such as hemlock or arborvitae. Shaping, topping, and shortening of side branches must be done frequently to assure dense growth over each entire plant. A season of neglect may result in bare spots which fail to fill in after the too large, neglected branches have finally been removed.

Informal hedges, where plants are permitted to retain their natural habit of growth, must still be shaped frequently by pruning, to keep "wild" branches in check and to remove all dead or dying wood back to the main stems.

Shrubs. The training or shaping of shrubs need not be confined to chopping graceful flowering specimens like spirea and forsythia into ball or club-shaped atrocities, though one too often sees these on places where untrained help is brought in by the day to mow and "prune."

The correct way to prune and train all flowering shrubs of fountainlike growth is to preserve and assure the continuance of their natural, graceful forms. Remove wood too old to bloom or any that is dying, throwing out only a few live side branches; also shorten or remove straight, suckerlike branches which shoot up vertically; and preserve all young, vigorous, curving branches.

Evergreens of formal shapes like the columnar Chinese or Irish junipers; the vase-shaped yews and globular mugo pine, and some of the compact arborvitaes as well as boxwood, may need judicious pruning to preserve their forms. Removing a maverick branch or shoot as soon as it appears accomplishes this. If left until it has grown too large, removal may leave a bare gap.

With evergreens of informal growth habit like the Spreading Japanese Yew and many of the dwarf junipers, pruning and training should be aimed at preserving their *natural* forms. Often cutting a few too vigorous branches well back into the heart of the shrub prevents the necessity of frequent pruning.

PRUNING EQUIPMENT

When buying tools for pruning it pays to get the very best. On the average home place any pruning implement is likely to be, barring loss, a very long-term, if not a lifetime, investment. A poor tool that will not stay sharp, that gets slightly out of alignment, that makes a bruised or ragged cut that does not heal properly, becomes a constant annoyance, and in the end is likely to have to be replaced, thus eventually costing more than would have been required to get a first-class tool in the first place.

Hand pruning shears are of two basic types: the anvil, in which the cutting blade comes down upon a flat bed; and the two-bladed, or scissor type, in which the two cutting edges shear past each other. The anvil type has the advantage that even in the toughest use, the tool remains in alignment; while in the scissor type the blades may be forced apart, resulting in a ragged cut and in injury to the tool. The anvil type of shears, however, is more likely to crush the bark if it is soft than is the scissor type with its two cutting blades that pass each other as they shear a twig or branch. Even the scissor type, unless of excellent quality, and kept very sharp, is likely to spread apart slightly as the blades are pressed together, resulting in a badly bruised cut. Where much pruning is to be done, it is advisable to have both types.

Pole pruning shears are similar to hand shears except that they are operated at the end of a pole, making it possible to reach very high branches. The better types, equipped with levers, easily cut off quite large branches.

Pruning knife, made with an extra-strong blade, terminates in a curved point. It can be used in many places difficult to get at with shears, and is in general very useful about the garden.

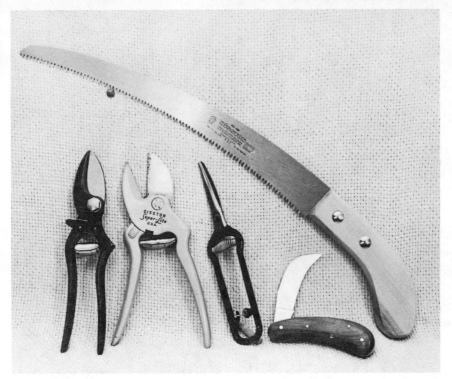

Our most frequently used pruning tools: curved-blade pruning saw and (left to right) small-sized, top-grade pruners; featherweight pruner that may conveniently be carried in pocket or garden basket; slim-bladed shears good for cutting back small rose canes or for cutting flowers; and curved-blade pruning knife (German design) especially useful for pruning close without leaving stubs or injured bark.

Lopping shears, with two long handles, are designed to cut larger branches than hand shears. They are especially useful in caring for shrubs and hedges, and quite an essential tool on a large place or one that is wooded.

Pruning saw. The blade may be straight or crescent-shaped, and used either in the hand or at the end of a pole. A *pole saw* is effective for making neat, clean cuts of branches too heavy or too high to be handled with shears. The straight-bladed type with teeth on both sides is likely, in the amateur's hands, to do more harm than good!

No pruning tool is better than its edge. The use of a dull pair of shears or saw may, by bruising or tearing bark and wood, initiate decay or disease, and so do much harm. Kept on hand, for frequent use along with one's pruning tools, should be a good sharpening stone. We find the small type (illustrated) to be most useful. Occasionally—once every

POLE
SAW

POLE
PRUNER

COMBINATION
TREE TRIMMER
AND SAW.

LOPPING
SHEARS

*Select your pruning tool to do the job required; and keep all cutting edges
razor-sharp to avoid leaving bruised bark and thus inviting disease.*

year or two according to the amount of use—it pays well to have all pruning tools professionally sharpened. This is an early winter job, so that they will be ready for late winter, spring, and summer use.

THE TECHNIQUES OF PRUNING

To employ the art of pruning effectively it is essential to know something of the growth habits of plants in general; and then—from observation or study—of the plant being pruned, in particular.

If you observe the growth of a tree, shrub, or vine in your garden, you cannot fail to note that the *terminal* bud of a main stem, or of any

Hurricane damage to a vigorous young tulip tree. Main trunk was cut back as indicated, treated with tree-wound paint, and branch at left tied to stake to encourage more upright growth. Three seasons later this branch had established itself as a new leader, making a normal-looking tree.

In controlling the growth of a plant, one should consider training along with pruning. New growth in most plants tends upward—as that from the horizontally trained rose cane illustrated.

lateral, usually makes the most vigorous growth. If this bud is injured or removed, then the one next below it takes its place as the leader. In the case of a tree such as a pine or spruce, if the terminal growth—the "leader"—is broken or removed, then *one* of the cluster of branches just beneath it will outgrow the others, turn upright, and take its place just as in the illustration of the tulip tree which had its top torn out in a hurricane.

What is not so commonly known—although examples of it may be observed in almost any garden—is that if a branch or cane of any plant is bent down, then the buds that remain highest up will tend to take the lead in new growth.

Furthermore, if part of a plant (the cane of a vigorous climbing rose, for instance) is trained horizontally or in an arch, then the buds in the *upper* surface are those to grow most vigorously (see photograph).

It is essential to keep these three points in mind in pruning to control or direct plant growth.

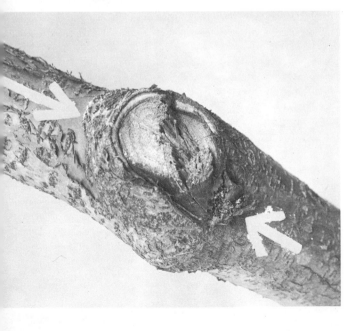

In pruning limbs or branches, it is essential to avoid having the bark stripped from the trunk below the cut. To prevent this, first make an undercut (A) six inches or so from the main trunk; then saw off the branch at (B); and finally remove the stub close to the main trunk (C). Failure to do this may result in a torn, ragged wound (as in the photograph below) that will invite disease and eventual decay.

Another most important fact for the beginning pruner to realize is that any pruning cut should be made close to a growing part of the plant, or to an "eye" that will make new growth. Any "stub" that is left beyond growing wood is very likely to die back and eventually may decay and result in serious injury. This is the reason for removing entire branches of trees or shrubs as close as possible to the main trunk of the plant.

Nature tends to cover up wounds left by pruning with new bark. It is often surprising how quickly and how thoroughly she can do this. But pruning wounds of more than an inch or two in diameter are best treated with tree-wound paint immediately after they have been made. If this special paint is not available, any ordinary outside paint will serve.

It is best, wherever possible, to *anticipate* in pruning. A forefinger and thumbnail pinch in spring may save fifteen minutes' work in autumn or next spring. Much light pruning can be done with a pruning knife (see illustration, page 122), which takes up less pocket space than a penknife. I always carry one about the garden and grounds. It is kept— along with folding rule, garden gloves, hand weeder, pruning shears, and other frequently used and easily mislaid small items—on the "snatch" shelf by our garage door, where it can be picked up or put down on the way to or from the garden.

CHAPTER 7

Coldframes and Hotbeds

Perhaps the most exciting day that can come to the novice at gardening is the one when he finally resolves no longer calmly to accept the verdict of gray-bearded Old Man Winter when he snarls, *"This is where we stop!"*

Oddly enough the gardener's most helpful assistant at rebelling against this age-old command is glass. Glass, one of the frailest of all materials; glass made of sand!

The simplest of structures employed in growing things out of season is the coldframe—a small rectangular pit covered with removable glass sash. When temperatures in the frame get too high the sash may be taken off entirely or partly raised to admit only the desired amount of cooler air.

A hotbed is similar to a coldframe, but there is the essential difference that some means of *artificial* heating is provided. Thus the operator ceases to be entirely dependent upon the vagaries of the weather. If, in addition to artificial heat within the frame, the glass sash is also covered with some form of insulation, then frost may be kept out even in sections where long periods of very cold weather are experienced. Hotbeds originally were heated by fermenting manure—hence the name. Nowadays electric heating cable provides the heat.

The greenhouse differs basically from a coldframe or hotbed in that it is designed to be not merely an accessory to outdoor growing, but to serve as an indoor garden with a succession of flowering and foliage plants from one end of the year to the other. For this reason the greenhouse, in this book, is discussed separately (see Chapter 18).

What type of frame? The amateur gardener will do well to start moderately for a season or two when he decides to tackle the adventure of gardening under glass. Success in this field depends very largely upon the gardener's being able—as well as willing—to give regular attention to

A substantial coldframe can add four to six weeks at each end of the season to the gardener's outdoor activities. The cost of maintenance, if it is well made in the beginning, is next to nothing. A portable short plank (like that with the hand weeder on it) is a convenience in thinning and transplanting.

A frame is useful not only for starting new plants but also for providing out-of-season vegetables and flowers in early spring and fall. Except in very cold regions many hardy plants may be carried right through the winter if glass is covered during very cold spells.

The frame, like the garden, must be kept well enriched if good growth is to be maintained. Here the annual fall preparation for winter and spring use is being made—lime, compost, bone meal (and soil if needed) are applied in successive layers and dug in.

Plants set out or seeds sown in such soil make vigorous growth. A spotting stick saves time in transplanting. The movable frame-divider, supported by attached legs, makes possible the maintenance of different temperatures.

it. The flower garden or the vegetable garden may be left to itself for a week or even longer; but a hotbed or even a coldframe, for most of the season for which it is in use, requires daily attention, particularly in the matter of ventilation. A few hours of bright sunshine, even if the temperature is down to freezing or below, may run the temperature in the frame up to 80 or 90 degrees or even more, and quickly dry out and severely injure any plants in it, especially any that are in flats or pots. Opening the sash to provide ventilation is easily done, but there must be someone available who will attend to it.

Frames may be bought, ready-made, complete with sash. These can be set in place quickly and with very little work. The do-it-yourself-er, however, may get more space for his money by purchasing only the sash, and then constructing his own frame.

Sash is available in three sizes: the standard 3×6 feet; half-sash 3×3 feet; and the zephyr or home garden type 2×4 feet. Standard-size sash are too heavy for a woman—or for many white-collar men these days—to handle. Of the two smaller sizes, we much prefer the 2×4 foot as it provides more direct sunshine in proportion to the area covered inside of the frame. This is important during late fall, winter, and early spring, when sunshine strikes the frame at a very low angle—just the period when it is of most use.

The 2×4 sash, weighing but 14 to 20 pounds, is easily handled. In case of breakage it is readily repaired, as the glass, instead of being held in place by putty, is merely slipped into grooves. For general-purpose gardening, two frames of small or moderate size are much more useful than one larger one. The only additional material required will be that needed to make two more ends.

Where two frames are used, one may well be placed in semishade or where it will be shaded at least during midsummer. We have one long frame under an old cherry tree trimmed up to form a huge umbrella. This frame gets filtered sunshine during late autumn and early spring, but just the right amount of "high" shade during late spring, summer, and early fall. It makes an excellent spot for growing on tuberous begonias and other plants, after they have been taken out of the greenhouse, to develop until they are set out in beds, flower boxes, or planters for the summer.

Another method of providing conditions for plants that do not like full, direct sunshine, is to make a board 12 or 15 inches wide and the exact length of the frame, and to nail to this two or more pairs of 1×2-inch cleats 3 or 4 feet apart. These are placed so that they extend 4 inches or so below one edge of the board. When the board is placed on top of the lower side of the frame, the cleats hold it in place, thus converting what was the lower side into the high side. Consequently when sash are put on they slant in just the opposite direction from which they formerly did, and the sun's rays are deflected, thus keeping the frame cooler.

A removable divider for the frame often proves useful. This is a piece of ¼- or ½-inch plywood cut at an angle to match the slant of the sash, and sufficiently wide to penetrate a couple of inches into the soil. Two pointed pieces of 1×2 extending 6 inches below the lower (straight) edge and nailed to it are pushed down into the soil in the frame to hold the divider firmly in place. In use it is, of course, so located as to match the edge of a sash. This makes it possible to maintain two different temperatures within the frame.

LOCATION

The location of the frame will have much to do with its contribution to the success of the garden. Its two chief requirements are full exposure to direct sunshine and protection from prevailing cold winds. If you have a pet cat or a dog, turn it out of doors on a sunny winter day and it will pick out the spot for you! If there is no location against the sunny side of a wall, there may be a hedge that will serve the purpose. In warmer climates, one of the fast-growing evergreen privets or any other evergreen shrub may be used. In the north, hemlock, pine, yew, or red-cedar, all of which may be kept sheared or pruned to any desired height, will answer. A tight board or picket fence—which later can be "planted out" with vines or evergreens—may be utilized.

Drainage. Equally important in selecting a location for the frame is the matter of drainage. There must be provision for any surplus water within the frame to be absorbed or to drain away quickly. In locations where natural drainage is poor, the quickest way to improve this condition may be to dig out the soil to a depth of 2 to 3 feet and fill in gravel or cinders to provide drainage for any surplus water within the frame. Allowance should be made for at least 6 to 8 inches of soil over the drainage material.

BUILDING THE FRAME

The frame itself may be built with 2×4-inch stakes and 1-inch rough boards, preferably 12 inches wide. As a result of many, many years of experience with frames, we would recommend the use of 2-inch planks. These will last not only twice, but many times as long as 1-inch material. Top board for each end of frame may be cut (see sketch) on an angle, 9 inches at one end and 3 at the other. End posts to hold the sides and ends in place may be made of 2×4s. A 3×3, sawed diagonally, is stronger and will prove more convenient when flats are being placed in the frame. As the dimensions of hotbed sash of different makes vary somewhat, the sash should be on hand before the frame is constructed so that all measurements can be carefully checked. After the top sides and the ends of

Building a "super frame." This coldframe-hotbed combination, heated by electric cable, served as a sort of miniature greenhouse until we got our real greenhouse.

the frame are in place, the additional boards or planks can be fitted beneath them to extend the frame any desired depth into the ground. It is advisable to batten the cracks where the top boards and those placed beneath them come together as there will be some expansion and contraction according to the season and the weather. Also a piece of 3×1, nailed along the back of the frame and projecting an inch or so above it, helps to hold the sash steadily in position and also to check any leakage of warm air.

In many years of experience we have found that it pays well to treat very thoroughly, with creosote or some similar preservative such as Conservo, all wood to be used in building a frame. Also we have learned to take the precaution of placing on the outside (near the top of each end of the frame) two stout screw eyes. To one of these is secured a piece of plastic clothesline, which is then run the length of the frame *over* the sash, passed through the screw eyes at the other end of the frame, and then back over the sash again to the fourth screw eye at the end from which the line started. Here it is securely tied. This makes the

FRAME CONSTRUCTION
FOR FIVE 2×4' SASH

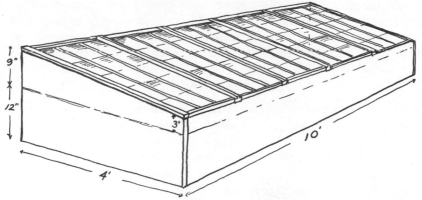

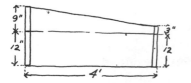

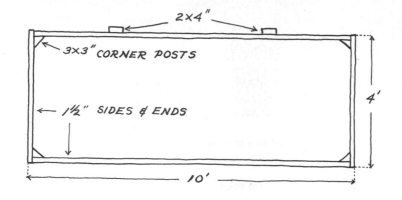

2×4"

3×3" CORNER POSTS

1½" SIDES & ENDS

Method of holding sash (also burlap or other covering used over glass to keep out extreme cold) securely in place with plastic clothesline.

quickest and most permanent method we have ever found of protecting the sash from being blown off during gale winds or freak storms. When not in use the plastic cord is laid along the outside of the frame or coiled up at one end. A further use for this cord is to hold securely in place any burlap or mat covering that may be put on over the glass (to keep out frost, or to prevent deep freezing inside the frame) in winter.

SOIL FOR FRAMES

Under some conditions the soil where the frame is built is suitable for use as is, but in the great majority of cases it is much better to remove it and replace it with a mixture prepared for the purpose. This is especially true if existing soil is either heavy clay or very sandy. Usually some of the original soil removed from the frame can be used in making up the mix to be put back into it.

Soil for a general-purpose frame should be such as will drain rapidly, but at the same time should contain sufficient humus to retain moisture, when the surplus has drained through, so that too frequent watering is not required.

The mix we use is made up of sifted compost to which peatmoss is added if necessary. In any event, about one third coarse peatmoss is mixed into the bottom layer of 3 inches or so. This provides an additional reservoir for moisture, beneficial not only to plants grown directly in the frame but also to pots plunged to their rims; and even to flats or trays placed on the surface. If the only available soil for the frame is of clay, sand and peatmoss should be added to the mix. If very sandy, add more peatmoss.

FRAME MANAGEMENT

No matter how well the frame may be constructed, the attempt to grow plants in it is likely to result in failure unless the gardener understands at the outset that *it is not a garden area,* and that it cannot be treated as such. Even when, during frost-free periods, the sash is left off entirely, the frame needs careful attention in regard to watering; and flats and even pots plunged into the soil should be moved frequently to prevent overcrowding and rooting through into the soil.

Temperature. The greatest problem in handling plants in frames is the control of temperature. Even on a very cold winter day a few hours of bright sunshine may skyrocket the temperature up to a dangerous point. If for any reason a frame must be left untended for a considerable period, it is much better to leave the sash partly open. The risk that the temperature may drop lower than is desired is less serious than that it may go too high if it remains closed. Plants are much more likely to recover from a severe chill than from dehydration.

In moderate sections plants in large pots, tubs, or planters are sometimes wintered over in extra-deep frames or pits. They are best placed on a layer of pebbles or turkey gravel to assure good drainage. If there is danger of frost penetrating the frame, most large plants may be left for days on end with the sash covered with mats made for the purpose or with heavy burlap bags.

Plants in peat pots that are scheduled to be transplanted later to the open are sunk part way into a layer of sifted compost or a sand-peat mixture so that roots that have penetrated the pot walls will suffer minimum injury when they are moved out.

Plants in clay or plastic pots are best sunk half their depth and should be moved often enough to prevent their rooting through into the soil below, which they are prone to do very quickly.

Cuttings in peat pots should be sunk to the rims as they are much more likely to be injured by having their roots disturbed than are seedling plants. Roots growing out through the sides of the pots form wonderful root balls for transplanting as they do not have to undergo a recovery period before renewing growth in their new environment.

Spacing. Plants in frames require elbow room and air just as much as they do if growing in the open. This is especially true of young plants in flats, pots, and multiple peat pots or "strips." As soon as plants begin to crowd they should be moved further apart or every other row of strip pots may be removed and placed elsewhere. Hardy vegetables—such as cabbage, broccoli, and lettuce—and hardy annuals and perennials may be removed from the frame as soon as danger of hard freezing is past and placed in a sheltered location until they can be planted out, thus leaving more space for the really tender things.

Watering. The inexperienced gardener very soon will learn that he cannot trust to nature to do this job for him. Plantings in flats and in pots and even those planted directly in the soil of the frame, and particularly in a hotbed, dry out in an astonishingly short time. This is especially true in bright, sunny, or windy weather. A spigot near the frame, or a length of hose extending to it and left permanently in place during the growing season, is a great time and labor saver. A good nozzle for this purpose is a type with an adjustable spray and an automatic shut off (see page 305).

Feeding. Plants placed temporarily in frames usually require no additional feeding before they are moved out to their permanent locations. Plants being *grown* in a frame, even if the soil has been well enriched, benefit from an occasional feeding with a general-purpose fertilizer. Materials with an extra-high nitrogen content are best avoided however. "Little and often" is the rule to follow.

Keep frames clean! Litter such as dead and possibly diseased leaves or plants, weeds, empty flats, and pots all encourage pests and diseases. An

Slatted shades, same size as sash, are used with or without the glass sash. If Visqueen or other sturdy plastic material is placed over slat shades and firmly fastened down with two-by-fours or other weights, a dead air space, which provides a very effective frost barrier, is created over the glass.

occasional spraying with an all-purpose pesticide and fungicide, even when no trouble shows itself, is good practice.

Shading. Plants in a frame, cut off from ordinary air circulation, are much more likely to suffer in hot weather than those in the open. One way of compensating for this is to provide some method of shading. The good gardener, instead of depending on sheets of last Sunday's newspaper, will have on hand substantial slatted sash. These are of the same size or very slightly larger than the glass sash and are made up of two pieces of 2×2 the length of the sash, with cross slats of ¼-inch wood ¾ of an inch wide spaced at intervals of 1 inch. Either redwood, white pine, or cypress, all light and decay resistant, are excellent for this purpose. While providing shifting shade, the slat sash do not interfere with full ventilation.

THE HOTBED

Hotbeds, as has already been explained, are merely coldframes provided with some artificial means of heating. The most satisfactory and most easily regulated kind of heating is an electric cable. Heating kits including thermostatic controls are available in a wide range of sizes.

To give good results without exorbitant expense for heating, the hotbed must be of substantial construction and very thoroughly insulated. It may very well be sunk deeper into the ground than a coldframe—provided of

Ventilation is a vital part of frame management. Two-by-four blocks of wood, six or eight inches long, provide moderate ventilation without having to raise ends of sash. This method also lessens danger of wind damage.

course that adequate drainage is maintained. Or it may have soil mounded up against the outside. Also, if a choice is available, it is well to have it so located that it will get full, direct morning sun from November on, as midwinter afternoon sunshine has no more strength than a twice watered-down highball.

Further protection during the winter in the form of mats, Fiberglas bats, burlap, old quilts, or what-have-you, will not only cut down the cost of heating but provide assurance against possible loss of plants from too low temperatures.

Another method of providing additional insulation is to erect a temporary frame of rough boards or of chicken wire outside the hotbed, leaving a space of 4 to 6 inches between it and the walls of the frame. This is stuffed with marsh hay, straw, dry leaves, or peatmoss. The latter material is much the best and really costs nothing as it can be used in the garden after it has served to protect the frame. Lining the walls with heavy building paper held in place by lath strips affords still further insulation.

BULBS FOR INDOORS

One of the most rewarding of all uses for the coldframe is in connection with "forcing" bulbs for bloom indoors in the winter, or in the greenhouse. In our opinion, and based on long experience, there is no

The frame makes an ideal place in which to prepare hardy bulbs for winter bloom indoors. Here they are safe from rodents and readily got at to bring in. After bloom they may be returned to frame, pots plunged to the rims, until they can be planted out of doors.

gardening operation that brings more certain and satisfactory returns in proportion to the effort involved.

Although the term used for this particular method of growing hardy bulbs is "forcing," it is a misleading one. To get the best results the plant must be grown *cool*—just as when Mother Nature takes charge of the job in the garden.

The bulbs best adapted to this method of growing are the so-called Dutch bulbs—tulips, daffodils, hyacinths, crocuses, and the like. To get the best results it is important to use first-quality or top-size bulbs. While they may be grown in pots, it is much better to get bulb pans—which are merely more squatty flower pots—as these are both more sightly and less tippy. Soil from the compost heap—or garden soil with about one fourth each of sand and peatmoss added to it—gives good results.

Bulbs are placed in the pots or pans, and these are sunk to the rims in the frame and covered with leaves or straw. No attempt is made to prevent freezing; in fact sash is best left off until soil begins to freeze and then opened or removed during any prolonged mild or sunny spell during October to mid-December. (We once had a number of pans of bulbs buried in a trench which filled with water during a midwinter thaw and then froze into a solid cake of ice, locking them tight until late February. But when we finally were able to extricate them and bring them indoors, they bloomed perfectly.

Any time after mid-December the pots may be brought in, a few at a time, and placed where they will receive light but only moderate temperatures (40 to 50 degrees if possible) until they have made a few inches of growth, after which they will be happy in a sunny window sill. Once the flowers have opened, they should be kept as cool as possible—*especially at night*—until they fade. After that the pots are returned to the frame, or covered with soil or mulch out of doors to complete growth. They may be planted, deep, in a permanent location in the garden as soon as the ground can be worked. Many bulbs, after possibly skipping one year of flowering, re-establish themselves satisfactorily after forcing and become permanent occupants of the garden. (For discussion of spring-flowering bulbs, see Chapter 11.)

CHAPTER 8

Tools and Equipment

No owner of a new home can go far before realizing that he will need adequate equipment—in addition to big ideas and willing hands—to create the little paradise he envisions in his mind's eye.

Unless he has someone to guide him, he is quite likely to make costly mistakes in the tools he buys. The amount and the type of equipment he should eventually possess depends upon both the size of the place and how he expects to develop it. The sign above his tool-house door should read GO SLOW.

To begin with, the tools required to maintain home grounds in good condition are of two types: those used for many different tasks, such as digging, cultivating, raking; and the more specialized ones, employed for mowing, hedge trimming, pruning, and the like.

With tools that are to be kept in more or less constant use—such as hoes, rakes, pruning shears, spades, trowels, and lawn mower—it is good policy, and in the end least expensive, to get the very best, which does not necessarily mean the highest in price. With those used less constantly—such as shovels, a crowbar, a wheelbarrow—it may be advisable, if funds are limited, to settle for a less expensive grade; but even here, in the long run, this is doubtful economy.

HAND TOOLS FOR MANY TASKS

One of the first operations in gardening is preparation of the soil. With the ever-increasing use of power tools, real digging has become almost a lost art, but even so the modern gardener must occasionally dabble a bit in the dirt and get his fingers soiled.

Spades. The one tool most useful for preparing soil for planting, and for general use around the place, is a round-pointed, long-handled shovel. It may well be supplemented by a square-pointed, short-handled digging spade.

If much transplanting is to be done, a transplanting spade with a narrower blade, rounded at the tip, will prove extremely useful, as it does a neater, more efficient job, with less effort. In fact we find the transplanting spade our favorite for many jobs other than actual transplanting.

Spading fork. In ground that is already in good tilth, and for turning under cover crops or other humus such as peatmoss or manure, our preference is the spading fork, with its broad, flat tines. This is an ideal tool for breaking up clods of soil, leaving a fairly smooth surface ready for raking. It is also our preferred digging tool in preparing beds or borders for planting and transplanting.

Power tools. The investment of a considerable sum of money in a tractor, or other power-driven equipment, does not make good sense unless one is certain that there will be sufficient work to be done to make it pay off. Many inexperienced homeowners find out too late that they might better have hired the tractor work done, and expended the money saved on hand tools and plants. Many garden centers, seed stores, and hardware stores rent small power equipment for the do-it-yourself gardener.

For transplanting. Back through the ages the trowel has been the symbol of gardening, yet only recently have there been any changes to improve it. Modern trowels are made from one piece of metal so the head no longer keeps separating from the handle. The blade has been curved so that a rounded, firm ball of roots is taken up with the plant, and in some types the handle has been curved to fit the operator's hand. We find most generally useful a long-shanked type with a wooden handle that fits into the metal ferrule. These are heavy-duty hand tools which never bend or break under pressure. For taking up seedlings or separating young plants grown in a flat, we like a small-sized mason's trowel with a flat, diamond-shaped blade, which makes it possible to cut out plants with minimum injury to the roots. It is also convenient for many other garden operations on young plants and is indispensable in the greenhouse.

Two other hand tools useful in setting out plants in the garden are the dibble and the holemaker. The former is merely a development of the pointed stick, used to make holes to receive the roots of small plants—such as those from a seed flat, or strawberry runners—for transplanting. The holemaker is a device for *removing* the soil to leave a hole to receive larger plants, especially those from pots or from seed or nursery rows or bulbs. Both tools are used quite frequently on a place of any size but can scarcely be classed as essential, since the trowel and the spade will accomplish the same jobs, even if not quite so neatly and rapidly.

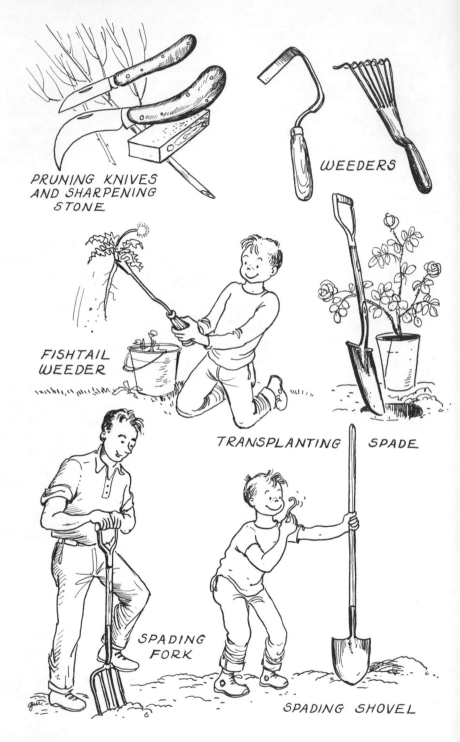

PRUNING KNIVES
AND SHARPENING
STONE

WEEDERS

FISHTAIL
WEEDER

TRANSPLANTING SPADE

SPADING
FORK

SPADING SHOVEL

It is poor economy and time-wasting to skimp on essential hand tools. Keeping them clean and sharp saves time, temper, and money.

MODERN—
ONE PIECE
TROWEL

STRAIGHT
SHANK

MASON'S TROWEL

STEEL
BOW
RAKE

LAWN
RAKE

DIBBLE

TULIP

ONION HOE

ALL-PURPOSE
HOE

SCUFFLE HOE

For cultivating. Cultivating, as has been explained, is necessary not only to control weeds but also to conserve moisture in the soil. Usually both operations are accomplished at the same time. The ideal method is to stir the soil around plants or between rows of plants so frequently that weeds never get beyond the seedling stage. This keeps the surface soil in a condition known as a dust mulch, so dried out that few, if any, weeds will start in it. This surface soil, although completely dry, oddly enough forms a blanket that helps to keep the soil beneath it moist, just as it is to be found under a flat stone or a piece of plank.

The oldest and simplest tool for cultivating is a hoe, and to this day it remains the most useful for home garden areas. The beginning gardener often makes the mistake of purchasing the largest hoe he can find, the type known as a field hoe. Much more useful for the average home garden is the small-bladed or "onion" hoe. In fact the one hoe that we use more than any other is an old field hoe so worn down that it is even smaller than an onion hoe. It was half gone when we acquired it, out of sentiment, at an auction some forty years ago. The original hickory handle, long since worn satin smooth, is still tight in its ferrule. It serves excellently for taking out weeds close to a row or between plants, although no longer of use for cutting out big plants or hilling up potatoes or roses. Equally useful is the modern, "all-purpose" hoe, which has a small, sharp triangular blade attached to a curved steel shank. This tool is favored by the distaff side of the family. See sketch.

The scuffle or push-hoe has a very narrow blade sharpened at both the front and the rear edge. Pushed along the ground just beneath the surface, it cuts off all weed seedlings and leaves a good soil mulch. The blade cuts on both the push and the backward pull and so can be used as the operator walks backward. This has the decided advantage that the newly cut weeds and the soil are not trampled and pushed back into the soil after the ground is worked over. Some weeds, purslane and chickweed, two of the worst garden pests, for instance, reroot quickly if trodden into the soil. In rainy weather they may be even worse in a few days than they were before being hoed.

Rakes. Both in handling the soil and in caring for the lawn, the rake is an essential tool. For the former job an iron rake is best. For all-round general use, a "bow" rake with slightly curved teeth proves most useful. Where there is much lawn raking to be done, a rake with straight teeth, either metal or wood, proves a worthwhile addition. For raking up cut grass or leaves or any extensive area, a fan-shaped, larger capacity but lightweight rake with spring teeth is a great time and labor saver. Originally this type of rake was made of bamboo and these are still available, but the modern metal ones do a better job and are much more durable.

Hand weeders. Where vegetables or annual flowers are grown in beds or garden rows, a hand weeder is one of the most useful of all tools. These are of various types and sizes. The one we like best has a flat blade turned at right angles to the shaft. This may be held in different positions to cut off weeds, to destroy sprouting weed seedlings, or, turned vertically, to root out larger ones. Another has seven stiff wire fingers and is especially good for cultivating crusted clay soil. The "fish tail" weeder with a V-shaped blade like an asparagus knife is the kind to use for going well below the surface for deep-rooted weeds like dandelions, dock, or poke seedlings. It is available with either a short or a long handle. We find rather inefficient the cuplike hand weeder of cast aluminum with three broad teeth at the edge of the cup; and even more exasperating, the claw weeder made of soft metal with broad teeth, which often bends or comes out of its wooden handle before it gets the weed out. Long-handled spring types for dandelions and similar garden weeds are fine as long as they work, but the springs are often short-lived.

Knives. Anyone who does much gardening has use for at least two knives: a small one for light pruning and cutting flowers and a much heavier one for real pruning jobs and for heavy cutting. For the former, we use a flat-handled, one-bladed knife which is very light; and for the latter, a heavy, hook-bladed pruning knife. To make work easy, and what is more important to leave smooth, clean cuts that heal evenly, any knife used about the garden should be kept *very* sharp. For this purpose it is well to have on hand a sharpening stone *kept with the edged tools,* in addition to the usual whetstone for grass clippers, scythes, sickles, and other equipment.

For protecting plants. Throughout the year there is almost no season when some plant or crop is not in danger of injury from one source or another, in addition to those caused by pests and diseases. Protecting plants from such potential threats is possible *if* one acts quickly.

MECHANICAL PROTECTORS

Hotkaps made of treated paper or domes made of plastic, placed over plants threatened by frost or by too hot sun or drying winds, lessen the danger of injury or total loss. The plastic domes cost more but are less expensive in the end since they can be used repeatedly, season after season. Some of ours have been in constant use for more than fifteen years and are still doing duty. These miniature, transparent tents not only keep off light frosts but also protect plants from pest injury.

Box protectors. A homemade plant protector that we have found most useful in our gardening (especially for covering young vine crops) consists of a box 12×16 inches and 6 inches deep, covered with fine mesh copper wire. The boxes are made of 6-inch wide ship lap, or ¼-inch white pine, cedar, or cypress nailed to pointed corner posts that extend

Wire-covered, bottomless boxes for covering hills of vine crops or blocks of seedlings likely to be severely injured by pests during early stages of growth. These are placed over plants as Hotkaps (front-center) are removed.

3 inches below the bottoms of the boxes and are pushed down into the soil to hold them in place. They are set over newly planted or set-out hills or groups of flowers or vegetables particularly subject to attack by insects, birds, or small animals. They also afford some protection against low temperatures and wind. We often place them over plants or hills which have been covered with Hotkaps when the plants have grown so large that the Hotkaps must be removed. Some of these boxes are still in use after fifteen years, though careful storage is essential if the screening is to be kept intact.

Treewrap is a weatherproof, stretchable paper 3 to 6 inches in width, that comes in 50-yard rolls. It is used to wrap up the trunks and branches of newly or recently set trees as a protection against sun scald, rabbits, field mice, and other pests. It is wrapped from the top down. In areas where deep snow may be expected, the wrap should be started high enough to ensure protection above the snow level.

A post-and-rail fence makes a sturdy support for climbing roses.

Wilt-Pruf is a liquid to be sprayed on shrubs, trees, and other woody plants to provide a thin coating that prevents excessive evaporation, which may cause dehydration of plants just after transplanting or during transportation.

PLANT SUPPORTS

Supporting plants and training them often go hand in hand. Let us consider available supports on which the training can be done, for if inadequate equipment is chosen for this purpose, it will be both expensive and time consuming to correct later on.

Fences, gates, trellises, and arbors sold at garden centers and chain stores, although neat-looking, are constructed of lightweight material and often do not remain erect or plumb for longer than the second or third year. Often they are too small to support a vigorous climbing rose or a trumpet creeper through more than a couple of seasons' growth.

A gate or arbor designed to support a perennial vine such as wisteria must be of substantial construction.

The do-it-yourself gardener can find no more rewarding garden feature to construct than a well-designed and *substantial* trellis or arbor. If this is beyond his skill or takes more time than he has to spare, he may have it made to order *to his own specifications.* If of good material and well constructed, such equipment will last for many years. If the cost is too great, he may use a post-and-chain support (page 247) or a substantial aluminum chain-link trellis that may be secured to a wall or to a vertical post.

Whatever type is employed, if it is to be held in place at the ground level, it should have its foot posts or anchor blocks *set in concrete.* If only a small job is to be done, a ready-mixed concrete will answer. This material need have only water added to it to be ready for use.

There are a number of strong, decorative fences and gates on the market which look well, are sturdy and long-lasting—but not cheap! If a fence is to support climbing roses or perennial vines, the cheapest and sturdiest permanent type is post-and-rail. Frail fencing of lightweight wood, like the arbors and trellises, are hardly worth erecting. If time is

Trellises and arbors are both useful and ornamental, but most of those put up have to be replaced in a few years. They should always be of substantial construction. It requires little more work to place the bases in concrete, and at least trebles their life expectancy.

not important, it may be less expensive to plant a young hedge instead of a fence, using sheared evergreens, barberry, Korean box, box-leaved holly, or one of the hedge materials listed in the Appendix. Time and reasonable care will create a beautiful, impenetrable barrier.

DUSTING AND SPRAYING EQUIPMENT

Dusters. Though spraying has largely replaced dusting in the control of insects and diseases in the home garden, there are many occasions when "spot" dusting saves time and is effective. In the last few years several small hand dusters of the ball-bearing type have come on the market, sold frequently by rose companies and others that offer rose dusts for sale.

Those illustrated in the sketch are effective and not likely to get out of order. The old-fashioned puff-gun type, formerly sold, is almost useless as it is practically impossible to deliver from it a fine, even distribution of

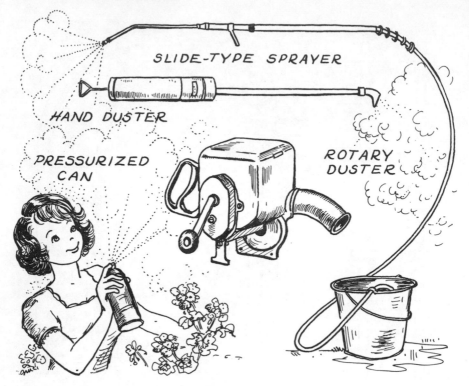

The effectiveness of any spray or dust depends upon getting thorough, even coverage. Inadequate equipment means constant waste of money. The type that automatically mixes spray material with water as it comes from the hose is easy to use and effective, as is the slide-type sprayer. Pressure cans are expensive for use on large areas. The hand duster (second from top) is short-lived and not very efficient while the rotary duster (center) does a really good job. Keep equipment clean!

dust. The best obtainable is none too good, for dusting is hard work at best.

Sprayers. The application of insecticides and fungicides has been revolutionized by the development of devices which screw onto the end of a garden hose and automatically mix spray materials with water as it is applied. While dusts tend to lodge on the upper surfaces of leaves—and, with any hand duster, more or less unevenly—a fine mistlike spray covers all parts of the plant uniformly, and where necessary, the soil mulch beneath it. The material to be sprayed on is placed in a small container in the specified quantity, and then sucked up into and mixed with the water from the hose. This equipment may also be used for applying fertilizers in liquid form as in lawn or other foliar feeding.

Pressure-tank sprayers of various types are used extensively in commercial growing, and smaller models are available for the home gardener. Tank sprayers have two advantages: they give more accurate control of the exact spray formula to be used; and they can be carried about wherever needed, without having any hose to be bothered with. However, they must frequently be pumped up to maintain pressure and must be thoroughly cleaned after each use. Sometimes it is difficult to get parts when needed, such as new leather washers which must be renewed occasionally, especially if oily materials are used.

Our own choice is a so-called "trombone" sprayer, a development from the crude bucket sprayer, which came into use in the First World War. The spray material is placed in a pail and mixed with water according to directions. The "trombone," attached to a long rubber hose, sucks up the spray at each stroke and then expels it forcibly, either in a mistlike spray or in coarse droplets through the adjustable nozzle. We find it much easier to clean than a tank sprayer and have little trouble in getting sufficient pressure as long as the leather washers remain soft and pliable. Here again the best available type should be purchased if efficiency is wanted, and *extra washers* should be bought or ordered at the same time.

For house plants, and for spot spraying in the greenhouse or cold-frame, one of the all-purpose pressurized can sprays is invaluable, though expensive. Read the directions carefully before buying, to make sure the spray material is suitable for your purposes.

LAWN EQUIPMENT

On many modern suburban grounds, the lawn receives more attention than any other feature. In fact it becomes a sort of status symbol, not quite in the class with a swimming pool, but a lawn that is better than that of the Smiths' or the Jones' is something worth striving for!

Unless one's lawn is fairly extensive, an old-fashioned hand mower may be a much better investment than a power mower. The term "old-fashioned" does not apply to the efficiency of the machine, for modern, manpower-propelled mowers are very great improvements over the much heavier out-dated ones of the past. And they leave less hand trimming to be done than does a power mower.

A riding power mower will, of course, make you feel like a king—or at least a major general on horseback. A walking-type power mower, however, costs only a fraction of the price of a riding type and requires less storage space and less expense for upkeep. In fact many small power mowers cost little more than hand mowers, though they need repairs and tuning up more often, as well as the expensive "white gas" on which they run.

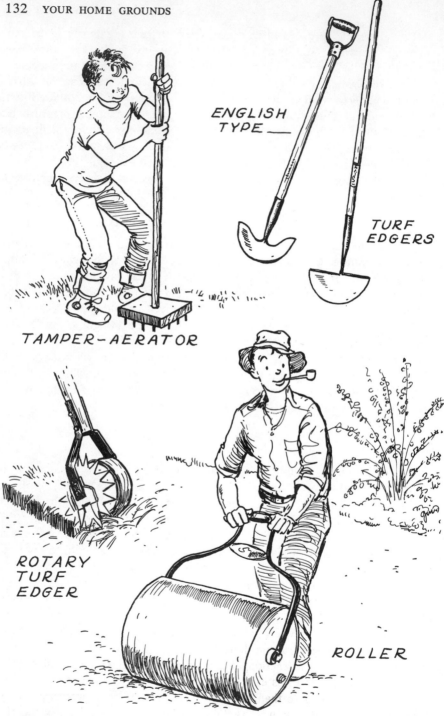

ENGLISH TYPE

TURF EDGERS

TAMPER-AERATOR

ROTARY TURF EDGER

ROLLER

Very important tools for making and maintaining an attractive lawn are the turf edger, the tamper-aerator, and the water-ballast roller.

When purchasing a power mower it is always a good idea to get an extra blade *at the same time.* It is just as important to keep the blade sharp on a power type as on a hand mower. With an extra blade on hand, the machine will never be laid up just when it is most needed. The size and type to be purchased depends largely on the area and type of turf to be cared for. Some rotaries are heavy enough to cut light brush, such as berry vines and heavy weeds, while small, light machines are just right for well-kept, smooth lawns.

Next to an adequate mower, or perhaps even ahead of it, the most essential tool for lawnmaking and maintenance is a good *fertilizer and seed distributor* (see page 160). It is a costly mistake to get a too cheap, inadequate machine which will never do the job properly and which, after a season or two, will have to be consigned to the dump. The good machines both sow seed and distribute fertilizers or herbicides with speed and accuracy, and with proper care last a decade or more. Ours is twelve years old and works as well as ever. It is absolutely essential, however, as with any equipment that comes in contact with fertilizers, *that it be kept scrupulously clean.* The best method is to *wash* it out and then dry it thoroughly after each use.

A *roller* of small or medium size is essential for good lawn maintenance. The best are made of heavy steel, and must be partly filled with water to provide the needed weight. The smaller water-weight rollers weigh 40 to 60 pounds empty, 160 to 220 filled; but the wise gardener only partially fills his roller, usually one third to one half.

A *tamper-aerator* (see sketch) is needed for the aerator feature if the lawn is on heavy soil. The tamper is of special value when sods are being laid, or just after the frost comes out in spring.

Edgers. It might be said that a lawn, especially a small one, is only as good as its edges, for any roughness or unevenness shows up not only along a drive or path but along the edge of every flower bed and border. There are edgers of several types. The one we like best has a semicircular or moon-shaped blade. The English pattern has a fork-handle-grip which makes it somewhat easier to use. Where long grass or trailing flowers such as petunias or sweet alyssum create a problem, a rotary turf edger does a much faster and neater job than the old-fashioned grass clipping shears, though the latter will serve where there is little of this work to do. A long-handled type with a squeeze-handle control saves stooping but lacks accuracy of aim. We also have an electric edger which runs like a house afire until the blades become clogged with grass cuttings—which is about once every five minutes. To use this gadget, a hundred feet or more of heavy-duty electric cord is needed—and a handy outlet. We use it frequently to "edge up" the small lawn near the front door, which is completely surrounded by beds, a holly border on one side and a bank rock garden on the other.

PART TWO

SPECIAL GARDENS, AREAS, AND PLANT MATERIALS

Go then, and plant a tree, lovely in sun and shadow.

CHAPTER 9

Trees, Shrubs, and Vines

Let us begin by emphasizing again that the owner of a new home should give first consideration to the location and planting of trees, shrubs, and perennial vines.

This is contrary to the usual procedure. Naturally the new owner of a piece of property is anxious to beautify it as quickly as possible. By the time the house is finished and the last throes of moving in are over, the bank balance is likely to be at a very low ebb. Small wonder then that the prospect of colorful flowers and a green lawn seems much more appealing than plantings like trees and shrubs that make so little show the first year and, with many trees, not for several years. Nevertheless there are cogent reasons for planting *trees, shrubs, and vines first:*

Relating them to other features of the landscape is of primary importance.

They will form the most striking and the most permanent part of the plantings around the home, and give it more character than any others.

Since they require more time to mature and to form an effective part of the landscape, the sooner they are started, the sooner the grounds will have a finished look.

They will add greatly to the value and salability of the property, especially after the first few years—and this added value increases year after year.

Finally, if one wishes to plant a few fairly large trees to obtain immediate effects, they should be put in before anything else. Moving and planting operations, if delayed until after other parts of the landscaping have been done, are likely to cause damage to lawns and gardens, and possibly even to walks or driveways.

Second Choice. If you are the owner of an established home and grounds but want to change or add to the existing plantings, you have another choice. By purchasing trees, shrubs, and even vines in small

STEPS IN TRANSPLANTING. *Dig a generous-sized, extra-deep hole.*

sizes one can start a little home nursery, which will save considerable money—possibly even make some!—and assure excellent results. The inexperienced home gardener should not be afraid to attempt this even though it sounds overambitious for a beginner.

As a matter of fact, young trees and shrubs can be planted and "grown on" for a few years, till ready for transplanting to their permanent locations, with greater assurance of success than the beginner can expect with most flowers. Set out a foot or two apart, in rows two to three feet apart to permit easy cultivation, shrubs and most trees will, in two to four years, have made husky small specimens that may be transplanted in late autumn or early spring to their permanent positions.

This system has the further advantage that transplanting may be done under the most favorable conditions. When we moved to our present home we nursery-planted many small trees and shrubs, most of them young seedlings from our former place. In six years, many of these have become tall, vigorous young trees. An elm (brought here in the back seat of our car, the roots wrapped in damp sphagnum) now has a typical vase-shaped top 22 feet tall. A similar "baby" tulip tree now measures 18 feet in spite of having lost nearly half its top in a hurricane. If they do

Mix in peatmoss and compost for the refill.

not suffer for want of food and water, the growth made by many small trees is almost incredible.

One of our favorite trees is the White Pine (*Pinus strobus*), but only the Pitch Pine that is common on the Cape today grew on our acreage. We procured several hundred 2-year seedlings and planted them about one foot apart in nursery rows. For the first year they had to shift for themselves as we had not yet moved in. We had some losses but most of them grew vigorously to transplanting size and we now have several groups of fine specimens 9 to 12 feet tall, in addition to an extensive White Pine hedge planting—all at an initial cost of pennies per tree!

What Trees for You? Before purchasing trees, the homeowner should have two kinds of information:

First, what species thrive in his locality.

Careful observation of the surrounding countryside is a pretty safe guide, but don't be entirely limited by this. Consultation with a local nurseryman or with the county agricultural agent will help further and perhaps give you added ideas. Marked distinction and beauty in the home landscape are often achieved by obtaining species and varieties of trees and shrubs that succeed in the local climate and soil, but which are

Handle plants carefully to keep root ball intact.

In bracing a tree or a limb, pass wire through short piece of hose to prevent chafing or bruising of bark. Wires may be drawn taut by twisting with a spike or short piece of wood.

Plant a few inches deeper than surrounding ground level, leaving a soil dish to hold water; tamp soil thoroughly around root ball or bare roots. Trees of any size should be braced.

seldom or never used in the area. Most homeowners are content to "follow the leader" when it comes to selecting plant materials, and automatically plant the same things they see on other places around them. In certain parts of Pennsylvania and Connecticut for instance, magnificent specimens of Copper or Purple Beech are to be seen on many old estates and even in modest gardens. At the time these were planted, they were probably a novelty in these sections, but today their dignity and beauty characterize the countryside.

Don't be afraid to venture a bit! Here on Cape Cod and on the Islands, one frequently finds fine old specimens of unusual trees that have survived the years, because the sea captains who brought them home from the Orient did not realize they were not supposed to be hardy here! Micro-climates very often make a great difference in what may be grown.

Second, how the species chosen will fit into his particular landscape scheme, *when they approach their full size.*

One constantly sees examples of what happens when cute little evergreens of the wrong varieties are set out in foundation plantings under windows. If left there, as frequently happens, the windows are blocked and the flower borders beneath them rendered useless.

Even more serious is the result of planting a potentially large tree such as a maple, oak, horse-chestnut, fir, or spruce in a space that will be much too small long before the tree reaches maturity. The owner cannot bring himself to cut it down; the lawn beneath it gradually goes to pot; and if the place is a small one, all chance of achieving an attractive, comprehensive planting is lost.

HOW TO SELECT TREES

The great importance of our former warning must now be apparent: an over-all plan for the planting of grounds should be prepared before *any* purchasing or planting is done. It is so easy to shift trees and shrubs around on paper, and so difficult and expensive to do it with the actual living materials!

Before a decision can be made as to the types and varieties to be planted, it is essential to know just where each is to be placed. It is important to visualize, as nearly as possible, how the plantings will appear ten years or so hence, and this is not easy. On occasion we have tried to help an inexperienced client to "get the picture" by placing trimmed branches or wood strips of various heights where trees were to be planted. The result shows roughly how much sunshine will be shut out, or how much of a distant view may be obliterated when trees in such locations begin to approach maturity. Results are sometimes startling. The proper time to move big trees, very definitely, is before planting them!

What Trees for Me? That is a puzzling question. You can get a fairly good idea of the various sizes, shapes, and characters by borrowing a book on trees from your library. It will be more rewarding, however, to visit a park or a botanical garden, where mature specimens may be seen and studied.

The most noticeable difference is that between evergreens, which are green throughout the years, and deciduous trees, which drop their foliage during the winter. There are even a few needled, cone-bearing trees that drop their foliage during the winter. The larches are typical of this group.

Especially on small places it often makes a big difference whether or not a tree retains its foliage throughout the year. Shade that is welcome in summer may be exactly what is *not* wanted during the winter. On the other hand, an evergreen hedge which shuts out street noises and provides a degree of privacy may be just as desirable in December as in July.

The following list includes a number of the most desirable trees for

The Star Magnolia (M. stellata), *one of the loveliest of all early, spring-flowering small trees, is hardy to southern New England but occasionally the flower buds are nipped by a late, hard frost. Ideal for milder climates.*

Flowering Dogwood (Cornus florida) *is a hardy, fast-growing, and trouble-free native of the eastern seaboard. Thrives in the open or in semishade. Indispensable for informal planting. There are pink-flowered forms as well as the usual creamy white.*

home landscaping in Areas II, III, and IV. Trees especially adapted to the South, Southwest, and other special areas or conditions will be found listed in the Appendix.

Although trees may be bought by mail, it is usually much better (except in the case of seedlings or very young specimens) to purchase at a nursery where they may be personally selected. Even at a young age they have begun to show some individuality in size, shape, and, in the case of certain evergreens, in color. The nurseryman tries to grow his stock to be as uniform as possible, but often an irregular specimen gives the homeowner a much more interesting and artistic effect if good judgment is used in placing it. At almost any big flower show one may find displays that illustrate this point. Such offbeat plants can usually be obtained at considerably reduced prices.

Spirea vanhouttei *provides fountains of foamy white bloom; old-fashioned but still a lovely subject for the mixed shrub border or as an informal hedge. Single specimens may also be used as accents. Requires annual pruning.*

Andromeda (Pieris japonica) *has glossy, handsome evergreen foliage. Graceful, drooping panicles of greenish-white blossoms are freely produced in very early spring (ultimate height 10 feet).*

SHADE TREES

Deciduous	Evergreen	Ornamental
** Beech, American	Arborvitaes	Cherries, Flowering
** Purple	in variety	Crabs, Flowering
Birch, Canoe or Paper	** Fir, Balsam	Dogwood, Flowering
** Elm, American	** Hemlock, American	Dogwood, Kousa
Chinese	** Canadian	Hawthorns
Siberian	Carolina	** Horse-chestnut
** Larch, American	Junipers,	Laburnum
** European	in variety	Magnolias,
** Linden, American	Pine, Japanese	in variety
European	Scotch	Maple, Japanese
** Locust, Honey	** White	Mountain-ash
Maple, Amur	** Spruce, Blue	(Sorbus)
** Norway	** Norway	Oxydendron
Red	** Red.	** Paulownia
Scarlet	** White	Silver Bell
** Sugar	** Umbrella-pine	(Halesia)
** Oak, Pin	(Sciadopitys	Witch-hazel
Red	verticillata)	(Hamamelis
Black		japonica;
Scarlet	Yews,	virginiana)
** White	in variety	
Sassafras		
Sweet Gum		
** Tulip		
Willows		

** Very tall—over 60 ft.

SHRUBS

While the use of trees, except in very small numbers, is limited to the fairly extensive property, shrubs may be employed freely on all but the smallest of places. Judiciously placed, they help to make an area appear considerably larger than it actually is. Many of the taller shrubs give much the effect of trees, and to that extent increase the *apparent* size of their surroundings.

Types of Shrubs. As with trees, the shrubs, once established, are usually lifetime fixtures and therefore should be selected with consideration for the size they are likely to attain at maturity.

Catalog illustrations are often misleading. First of all, they are usually close-ups of small specimens in full bloom. The inexperienced gardener is quite likely to visualize them as pictured, in strategic locations around his grounds. He may forget that many of them will be in flower for only two or three weeks out of the entire season and may be quite lacking in decorative effect when not in flower. Then, too, in the course of three or four years, they may become entirely too large for the locations in which they have been placed.

Again, as was true in choosing trees, the best way for the inexperienced homeowner to procure a really satisfactory selection of shrubs is to make a few visits to a neighboring botanic garden, arboretum, or genuine nursery (not merely a sales center). Even though such a trip may take the best part of a day, it will pay off handsomely in the long run.

Shrubs for Color. On either the large or the small place, shrubs are more effective than any other plants in providing masses of color above the ground or flower bed level. For really striking mass color effects, the two may be combined, as they often are in public or private show gardens. For the average home grounds, however, where a pleasing prospect is desirable week after week through the season, something less spectacular but more continuous is to be preferred.

In most cases, therefore, it is important to plan for a long succession of bloom in selecting flowering shrubs. Especially in northern latitudes, the great majority of shrubs flower in the spring, but one should try to plan for color during the summer and autumn also. There are several not-too-large trees that flower in summer or autumn and where space permits these may well be included in planning the shrub planting. Following is a list of some of the most satisfactory flowering shrubs. Fragrance and fall coloring in foliage or fruit is also noted.

DECIDUOUS FLOWERING SHRUBS

Early spring	Late spring and early summer	Late summer	Autumn and winter
Azaleas F	Callicarpa B AC	Albizzia	*Baccheris halimifolia*
Almond, Flowering F	Calycanthus F	Buddlei F	Gordonia AC
Cydonias	Carnelian-cherry B	Buckeye	(*Franklinia alatamaha*)
Forsythia F	Deutzias	Clethra F	*Tamarix hispida*
Jasmine F	Dogwood shrubs B	Hibiscus	Witch-hazels F
nudiflorum	Eleagnus F	Hydrangea	
Kerria japonica	*Euonymus alatus* AC	Hypericum	
Lilacs F	Kolkwitzia	Sorbaria	
Mockorange F	Lilacs F	Stewartia	
(Philadelphus)	Potentilla	June to Aug.	
Peony, Tree	Roses, Shrub F	*Vitex macrophylla*	
Spireas	Stephanandra AC		
Snowberry B	Viburnums B AC F		
Symplocos B			
Tamarix tetrandrus			AC—autumn color
Wintersweet			B—autumn fruit
			F—fragrant

HARDY SHRUBS AND EVERGREENS SUITABLE FOR SCREENS AND HEDGES

Deciduous	Height with some pruning	Evergreen * Must be kept well-pruned
Azaleas, in variety	2–6	Arborvitae Tom Thumb
Barberries, in variety	3–4	Little Gem
Bayberry	2–9	Chinese
		Rosedale
Cornus (Dogwood)		Compacta
Gray	6–15	Golden
Mas	6–15	
Tatarian	6–10	
		Boxwood, English*
Cotoneaster lucida	3–10	Korean
Cydonias	3–10	Hemlock, Japanese*
Deutzias	6	Hollies, American*
		Chinese
Euonymus	6	English*
Dwarf Burningbush	6	Japanese
Winged	6–8	
		Juniper Andorra
Hawthorn, Cockspur	6–25	Hill Japanese
English	6–15	Hillbush
Washington	6–25	Meyer
		Needle
Hibiscus, Chinese	6–20	Savin
Shrub Althea	6–12	
Lilacs	6–20	
		Pine, Mugo
Maple, Hedge	6	Waterer
Mockorange	6–10	
		Yew, Brown's*
		Intermedia*
Ninebark, Yellow	6	Hicks'*
		Hatfield*
Osage-orange	6–20	Dwarf Japanese*
Privets, improved varieties	4–12	Spreading "
Rosa multiflora		
rugosa & hybrids		Evergreen–Flowering
Red Robin	4–6	
setigera		Abelia grandiflora
Russian-olive	6	Firethorns (Pyracanthas)*
Sea-buckthorn	6	Hollygrape, Oregon
		Laurel, Mountain (Shade)*
		Leucothoe
		catesbaei
		racemosa
Spireas	3–10	Pieris floribunda
		japonica*
Viburnums	6–12	Rhododendrons*

For a list of hardy evergreen and flowering shrubs, with the zones in which they are at home, see Appendix.

Shrubs for Screens. One of the most practical uses for shrubs, especially in suburban development areas, is to secure some degree of privacy or to shut out undesirable views.

Here the ultimate height required for the screen should be carefully calculated. Left to itself, such a screen often grows taller than is necessary and consequently shuts out much wanted sunshine or light. Of course, it may be kept within bounds by pruning and trimming, but this takes time and labor—more each season as the hedge grows older.

Privet, widely used as a tall screen as well as for trimmed hedges, will attain a height of from 10 to 15 feet. Most deciduous types hardy in northern climates are not too attractive in winter—especially when littered up with bits of newspaper and other wind-blown debris.

In selecting plants for a screen, it is best to procure something that will provide the desired height *with a minimum of pruning.* A low-growing evergreen such as Hicks' Yew or Mugo Pine is more decorative and requires less constant care than hedge material such as barberry. These are, however, more expensive to start with.

Lists of hedge and screen material for the South, California, and the cold areas of the northern United States appear in the Appendix.

Shrubs for Hedges. Many of the considerations which apply to the selection of plants for screens apply also to hedges. It might be said that the screen begins where the hedge leaves off. There is a difference, however, for the *bottom* of the hedge is as important as the upper growth, and many plants cannot be kept green and dense down to ground level.

The various privets and barberries are the plants most widely used for hedges. Of the privets, the fastest growing is the ubiquitous California Privet (*Ligustrum lucidum*), which under favorable conditions attains a height of 3 to 4 feet the first season. This, however, is not reliably hardy in northern sections and at best it lends no distinction to a planting. The hardier Amur River Privet (*L. amurense*), more upright and compact, is well worth the extra cost.

Many improved forms of barberry are now available, including *Berberis mentoriensis,* one of the best, which requires very little pruning and holds its foliage well into midwinter as far north as southern New England and Chicago. *Crimson Pygmy* is a new dwarf barberry only a foot or so in height, suitable for a very low hedge or border.

In considering the cost of a hedge or a border planting one should remember that one is dealing not only with a long-term investment, but with probably the most conspicuous feature of the landscaping. Summer and winter it is there for every passer-by to see and to appraise—even without any conscious effort on his part to do so. It seems only common sense then to give extra thought—and if necessary an extra generous allowance—to this item in the landscaping budget.

VINES AND OTHER CLIMBERS

The third general group of plants used in making the home grounds more interesting and attractive includes those that climb, either of their own accord or if provided with suitable support. Virginia creeper (*Parthenocissus quinquefolia*) and wisteria are examples of the former, though one clings by tendrils, and the other by twisting stems. Climbing roses on the other hand, do not really climb but can be tied to supports such as a trellis or post. There are also many shrubs with long, arching or trailing branches that, with suitable encouragement, give a vinelike effect. *Forsythia suspensa, Cotoneaster horizontalis,* and *Pyracantha c. lalandi* are examples.

Correctly placed, vines and climbers, by the very habit of their growth, form highlights in the general picture, and take up little ground space. Many of them, however, grow vigorously and may take over if not kept well pruned. Therefore it is necessary to give some of them an occasional, severe cutting back in order to keep them within the allotted spaces. Wisteria, trumpet creeper, akebia, and honeysuckle are examples of this type.

Some of the annual vines are so vigorous as to make an almost unbelievable amount of growth during their single season. Typical of these are moonflower (*Ipomaea bona-nox*), balloon-vine (*Cardiospermum halicacabum*), and cup-and-saucer vine (*Cobaea scandens*)—semitropicals that, in northern climates, are treated as annuals. They are started in greenhouse or frame and set out after all danger of late frost. We have had Cobaeas so handled, grow thirty-five feet up a house wall of rough stucco, with no other support, reaching the peak of the second-story roof by August. We always plant moonflowers (started under glass) where we can enjoy the great, white, morning-glory-like blooms as they open, very slowly at first, and then with an almost explosive burst. A favorite game when guests are present, is to bet which unfolding bud will be next to open—something not easy to predict.

As the methods by which vines climb vary, it is important to know what type of support should be provided for each. Some, such as wisteria and passion vine, are twiners, often hugging their supports so tightly that only with great difficulty can they be torn off. They coil around twigs or branches, while the tip of the growing plant actually waves slowly about in a circle, seeking to find the next support to be

Wisteria, so rampant in the South that it becomes a pest, is a popular, hardy-flowering vine in colder climates. Even in the north it requires "heading back" each year after bloom to keep it within bounds.

encircled. They move clockwise or counterclockwise, but *always* in the same direction for any one species. And they just cannot be made to turn the other way!

Another type sends out tendrils that grasp and cling tightly to twigs or branches, other plants, or similar supports. Typical of this group are springlike tendrils issuing—like those of smilax—from the leaf stems or from the main stem of the plant, as with Virginia creeper. Still others are wall climbers such as ampelopsis, and have tendrils ending in tiny suction discs that cling tightly to a flat (but not to a polished) surface. A few, of which English ivy (*Hedera helix*) and creeping fig (*Ficus pumila*) are examples, have aerial roots that penetrate the slightest crack, fissure, or unevenness, thus holding the main stems securely.

Types of Supports. The differences to be found among climbing plants are not merely of botanical interest. They are definitely to be considered when it comes to selecting a vine or a climber for some specific location.

A disregard for the manner in which a species supports itself may result in its failure to give the desired effect, no matter how much care may be lavished upon it in the way of feeding, watering, and spraying.

The mistake most commonly made in providing supports for vines is that of not having them substantial enough or ready soon enough. This is especially true in the case of climbing roses, and of such heavy vines as wisteria, trumpet-vine, and bougainvillea. Most of the neat-looking but all too flimsy arches and arbors sold by garden centers and hardware stores will scarcely stand up by themselves for more than four or five seasons, especially if the wooden posts supporting them are buried directly in soil instead of with concrete footings as they should be. How can they be expected to stand up under the weight of heavily foliaged growth in heavy winds? Little wonder one so frequently sees sagging or half-fallen specimens that completely destroy the attractiveness of an otherwise well-cared-for garden!

In planning supports for vines or climbers of any sort, it is essential that they be of types that will fulfill their purpose. A rough wall, well suited to provide support for ivy, climbing hydrangea (*H. petiolaris*) or creeping fig would be useless for wisteria, moonflower, or passion-flower. A trellis, suitable for the latter, would be shunned by the ivy or climbing hydrangea (see page 128).

Cultural pointers. As a class, vines require less care than most other types of plants. Nevertheless one cannot expect satisfactory results from a plant that has merely been stuck into the ground, watered a couple of times until it "takes hold," and then left to shift for itself. Yet this happens frequently. Of all groups of plants, vines are the most likely to be neglected. The wonder is that as many succeed as well as they do.

The majority of vines are not particular as to soil. The clematis group are happiest in a "sweet" soil (see page 33). Ordinary garden loam in good tilth suits most of the others. Planting holes should be large, deep, and well prepared, as most vines are likely to be pretty much "on their own" after the first year's growth.

As the majority of established vines are more likely to be too vigorous than too weak and spindling, often little or no annual feeding is required unless the soil is very poor. Pruning, however, is needed, though often neglected or altogether omitted. Most vigorous-growing vines should be pruned annually, especially during the first few years of growth. This is especially true of such rampant growers as wisteria and trumpet creeper.

Along with the pruning should go training of the main stems, securing them in position if need be until they have taken the permanent form which is planned for them. (Lists of vines will be found in the Appendix.)

Espaliered plants are particularly attractive in formal surroundings. These are fruits, shrubs, or even suitable vines that are trained into more or less geometrical designs by the nurseryman or the gardener. They are especially effective against a house or a sunny wall surrounding a patio. Consistent pruning is required to maintain these attractive designs, and unless one is prepared to provide this, they are best not attempted.

POINTERS ON PLANTING

Trees, shrubs, and vines, the most expensive landscape features, are often planted with less care than are perennials and even annuals. To do a really good job of planting, it is important to have all preparations made before receiving the stock. Once received, the earlier they are put into the ground, the better start they will get.

The first step is to mark, with fairly substantial stakes, the exact locations where they are to go. In placing the stakes, careful thought should be given to their ultimate height and diameter. It is easy to shift stakes around until one is satisfied that the best locations have been selected, but very difficult and sometimes fatal to trees or shrubs once they have been planted.

All planting holes should be made *large* and *deep*. Eighteen inches in depth and at least that much in diameter is none too much for bare-root stock. For "B and B" (balled and burlapped) stock the holes should be a least 6 inches deeper and 12 inches larger in diameter than the root balls themselves.

Unless the holes are being made in excellent soil, all earth removed from them should be discarded. (It is well to shovel it into a wheelbarrow and remove it at once if the holes are being dug in turf areas.) Holes made where a clay subsoil is encountered should be pierced at the bottom with a crowbar to improve the drainage.

Into the bottom of each hole put 6 inches or so of the best soil available, or of good compost mixed with a peck or two of peatmoss. Instructions for planting trees and shrubs usually advise against using any fertilizers in the planting holes. We go along with this so far as *chemical* fertilizers are concerned; but personally we always use a mixture of one part bonemeal to two or three parts of an all-organic fertilizer, at the rate of a quart or so for a small (15-inch) hole, to double or triple that for larger ones. Any fertilizers should be thoroughly mixed with the soil in the bottom of the planting hole.

Care of plant material. If nursery stock cannot be set out the same day it is received, it should be kept in shade and out of the wind. Remember that these are *living* plants, even when they are dormant. If for any reason there must be a delay of more than a day or two, roots should be buried in a trench and kept thoroughly moist. Shrubs, trees, or vines tied in bundles should be separated sufficiently to assure that all roots are in contact with the soil.

Often in packing or during shipment, portions of roots or branches may

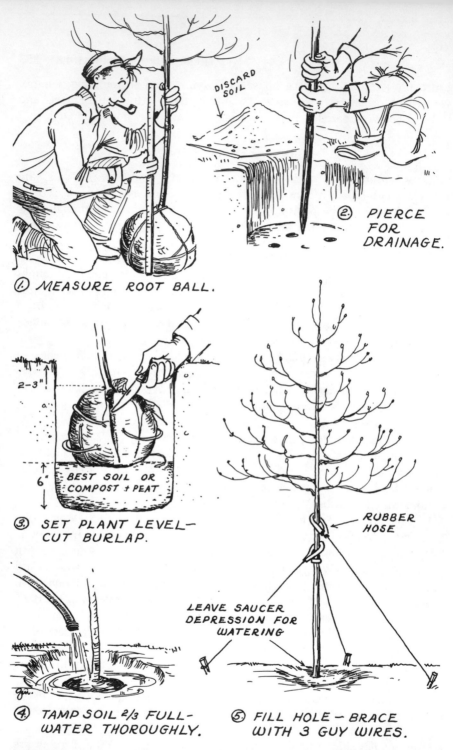

DISCARD SOIL

② PIERCE FOR DRAINAGE.

① MEASURE ROOT BALL.

2-3"

6"

BEST SOIL OR COMPOST + PEAT

③ SET PLANT LEVEL — CUT BURLAP.

RUBBER HOSE

LEAVE SAUCER DEPRESSION FOR WATERING

④ TAMP SOIL ⅔ FULL — WATER THOROUGHLY.

⑤ FILL HOLE — BRACE WITH 3 GUY WIRES.

OPERATION PLANTING. *Measure root ball and dig hole 6 to 10 inches wider and deeper. Loosen or punch holes in subsoil if it is clay or hardpan. Put prepared soil or compost in bottom of hole. Cut slits in burlap around root ball, but do not remove it if soil is loose around roots. Partly fill hole, after setting tree; firm soil around roots and water. Then fill hole, leaving saucerlike depression, and water again. If tree or shrub is large, brace in three directions—especially important with evergreens.*

be broken or injured, or may have begun to dry out. All such should be pruned back to clean, live wood with sharp shears that leave no broken or bruised ends.

Planting. During the operation of planting, especially in windy, sunny weather, it is advisable to keep roots covered with wet peatmoss to prevent excessive drying out. Root balls wrapped in burlap can be kept intact merely by cutting long slits in the covering instead of attempting to remove it, as this sometimes results in breaking the root ball.

Trees and shrubs are set in the planting holes at a depth that will bring the top of the root ball (or, if bare-rooted, the soil mark on the stem or trunk indicating the depth at which it previously grew) 2 to 3 inches below the surface of the surrounding turf or soil. This will leave a shallow basin that tends to catch and hold water, and which will keep neatly in place any temporary mulching that may be used around them.

In planting fairly large specimens—which is usually best done by two persons—the soil level at the bottom of the hole should be adjusted until it will support the tree or shrub at just the desired level. Then soil is filled in around it to about half to two thirds the depth of the hole and, with the feet or a blunt-ended tamping stick made moderately firm. (The youngsters' baseball bat is ideal for the purpose!)

Before completing the filling, run water in the hole and let it soak in, repeating this operation two or three times if necessary, until no more water is readily absorbed. Then complete the filling, treading the soil until it is well firmed.

For the next few weeks, until new growth indicates that the tree, shrub, or vine has actually begun to grow in its new quarters, water frequently enough to make certain that the soil about the roots never dries out. Mulching helps greatly in keeping the soil moist. If weather is dry and windy it is well to sprinkle the tops occasionally.

In the case of tall trees, especially of evergreens in windy areas, bracing in three directions with well-secured guy wires (see sketch) is essential. Where any wire touches the tree, it is passed through a piece of old hose to prevent its cutting into the bark (see illustration). Rope is of no use for bracing as it will sketch too much to provide lasting support.

Valuable specimens are often given still further protection by wrapping the trunks in Treewrap, by mist spraying the tops, if in foliage, frequently for a few weeks after transplanting, or by spraying the foliage with Wilt-Pruf.

Grass is the forgiveness of nature . . .
Forests decay, harvests perish, flowers vanish,
but grass is immortal.

JOHN JAMES INGALLS

CHAPTER 10

Lawns and Turf Areas

There is an old saying that "the lawn makes the place." Like most old sayings, this is an overstatement. The fact remains, however, that poor turf will ruin the general effect and attractiveness of any home grounds, no matter how good the rest of the landscaping may be.

The lawn is usually the first work to be undertaken when a place is being improved. This is not always the most desirable method of procedure, for new turf can easily be damaged in the process of bringing in and planting trees and shrubs, laying out permanent walks, making a pool, or getting other outdoor operations under way.

The owner has to decide when the lawn is to be made—or remade. In reaching a decision he should keep in mind not only the considerations suggested above, but also *when* it is best to undertake lawnmaking or remaking in his particular region. In general, in short-season sections of the country (Areas I, II, III, and IV) first choice would be autumn and second choice the earliest possible moment in spring. In long-season sections (Areas V and VI) the recommended time varies with the *type* of lawn, the grasses (or other plants) to be used, and the rainy season. In some very warm climates both a summer lawn and a winter lawn are employed, one overplanted on the other, to keep a green turf the year around.

What type of lawn? Before any work on lawnmaking is undertaken, the homeowner should consider the uses to which the turf will be put—whether principally as an important part of the all-over landscape plan, "for to admire and for to see," a play area, or just ordinary lawn requiring no special care and expensive upkeep, but both usable and attractive (page 4).

It must be admitted that the show (or perhaps we would be justified in saying the "show-off") lawn, if adequately maintained, contributes greatly to the over-all appearance of a place—but the IF is a very big one. We have made such lawns for ourselves and for others. Our present "lawn," which attracts much favorable comment here on Cape Cod, where fine turf is difficult to maintain, is the result of merely cooperating with nature. After clearing from about an acre of wild land a tangle of poison ivy, catbriers, and woodbine, we began to mow regularly with a rotary mower and to root out clumps of coarse tuft-forming grasses such as witch, crab, and orchardgrass, filling in the resulting holes with compost, and encouraging natural turf-type grasses to spread. A top-quality lawn grass mixture containing Merion Bluegrass was sown where the fill-ins were extensive.

This lawn was made under the light, partial shade of a grove of native black locust trees, well thinned out and trimmed high up. Although rather light and sandy, the soil is well supplied with humus, and also with nitrogen (provided by the nodules on the roots of the locust trees). Such a lawn could not be made so readily just anywhere. But it frequently happens that areas around new homes are torn up and remade at great expense, when a very good turf could have been developed at a fraction of the expense merely by surface dressing, oversowing, and regular mowing.

By an odd freak of circumstance, our smaller lawn, along the front of the house, illustrates the other extreme of lawnmaking. Here we started with an excavation over 5 feet deep, resulting from the fact that, when building our home, we removed a pocket of coarse, gritty sand ideal for mixing our concrete and mortar. The gaping hole that was left—some 20 feet long by 6 wide—was filled with a mixture of poor soil, plus the "chocolate icing" layer described on page 163. On this was sown a top-quality, general-purpose lawn seed—plus white Dutch clover as a "seek-no-further" device to keep young rabbits from investigating the flower beds on the bank and the terraces above the lawn.

This strip of lawn, made six years ago, and maintained by our standard lawn treatment (as explained in the following pages) has remained in excellent condition with no remaking or reseeding, although the traffic over it is heavier than normal.

PRELIMINARY PREPARATIONS

Most beginners fail to realize that using good seed is only half, and much the smaller half, of making a good lawn. The preliminary preparation of the soil is what really counts, but except in very rare instances, this is not to be accomplished merely by using a large dose of a high-power, quick-action fertilizer.

On most moderate-sized places the lawn is both the most conspicuous and the most permanent feature of the landscape. Why then does it not merit the best that can be put into it?

Materials and equipment required to make a new lawn or remake an old one: lime (in pail); peatmoss or humus (in wood basket); fertilizer; and—if required—excellent topsoil for surface layer. Tools needed are: a spading fork, a rake, and a roller. In dry weather, especially on light soil, adequate facilities for watering are essential.

What use? A quick glance at the over-all landscape plan for a small place (Chapter 1) will show that there are likely to be several lawn areas. In the average place these may all be treated in the same way, but sometimes it is worthwhile to consider them separately, at least to the extent of having a "show" or front lawn, and a play and work area. For these, different types of grasses are desirable. But in both cases, thorough preliminary preparation of the soil is the same.

Grading is the first step if the house is new. After building is completed, grading of the entire area should be undertaken. This must not be neglected. Before any soil is moved, all refuse left from building—empty cans, scraps of metal, bits of paper, pieces of wood, and bottles—should be cleared away. Frequently the builder uses these as part of the back-fill against the house foundations, with the result that they cause future trouble, starving and stunting struggling plant material.

The soil, or any section of an established lawn needing repair, is dug up; fertilizers and compost are spread and worked in to make a deep, rich, root run.

The next step is to have topsoil—for future lawn and prospective flower beds—pushed to one side, in one or more heaps. Otherwise, when grading is being done, good soil in certain areas is almost certain to be buried. When this happens, the lawn is more than likely to have poor spots, or areas that quickly turn brown at the first touch of hot, dry weather, no matter how much water or fertilizer is applied. (The removed topsoil is used in preparing the "chocolate icing" layer later described.)

In establishing the over-all grading for the property, it is advisable to have the surface slope away from the house at an angle sufficient to carry off heavy rains. Where the property lies considerably above street or road level, the creation of a steep bank should by all means be avoided —even if it is necessary to build a wall of suitable height instead of carrying the turf down to the sidewalk level. Banks or steep slopes are not only very difficult to mow, but also difficult to maintain in good turf.

Surface is leveled and raked smooth to make a perfect seedbed.

Seed is sown, preferably with a spreader, to get even distribution. One may be rented where seed is purchased. It will save seed and time and do a better job. Eventually you will want to own one (it also spreads fertilizer, etc.).

Seed is raked in lightly and the area is rolled.

This remade lawn is not quite as perfect as a completely new one, but serves for all practical purposes. Topsoil and seed were spread over the entire area.

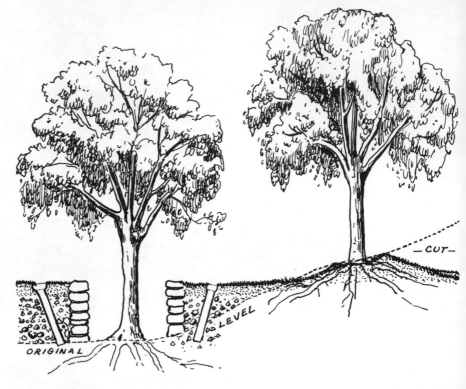

Where soil level must be raised around trees, making a dry well may save it.

If existing trees present a problem in establishing a grade this difficulty may be overcome either by building "wells" of suitable size around the trunks, or by sloping the surface up to them.

The next step is to *mark off* definitely the area or areas that are to be put into turf. This should be done even if the lawns are not to be finished until after other planting (trees, shrubs, etc.) has been done. In laying out lawn areas we find it convenient to use ¾-inch rope or a flexible hose that may readily be adjusted to curves until both the size and the shape of the areas desired for grass can be definitely determined. Such lines may then be marked permanently by driving in short stakes at intervals.

Drainage. To produce and maintain good turf, uniform even in appearance, and permanent, the lawn area must be well drained. Low areas where water may collect and stand after rain or during winter and early spring result in poor or even dead turf. If drainage is needed, installing it is the very first step toward satisfactory results. (For a general discussion of drainage see page 20). Unless the lawn area is fairly level to start with, it should be worked over, first to establish gradual, even slopes, and then to eliminate any minor high spots or ridges. The latter, if left, will not only appear unsightly, but also will result in "scalping" or cutting the grass too short in spots. A smooth, even surface is particularly important when cutting is done with a power mower.

After the surface has been rough-graded, turn your attention to improving the soil. If it is heavy clay or very sandy, add a layer 2 to 4 inches deep of soil of the opposite type or good loam. This supplementary material is then thoroughly dug, or cultivated in, to a depth of 4 to 6 inches. At the same time, animal manures or unsifted compost from a well-rotted heap may be applied by spreading a layer 2 to 4 inches in depth over the entire surface and digging it in together with the soil supplement.

In the case of newly cleared land, on which roots of trees or brush, rocks, and newly exposed subsoil areas and the like are excavated, often it actually *saves* time in the long run to delay making the lawn for a season or even for a year.

Rather than attempt to establish a finished lawn under such conditions, one may sow a cover crop of winter rye, (for cold weather) or annual ryegrass, clover, or other green manure crop for summer. This is dug under to add valuable humus and to help break up a stiff soil before the area is prepared for seeding lawn grass.

SURFACE SOIL—THE "CHOCOLATE ICING" LAYER

Having made lawns in many localities and on many types of soil, we are convinced that the surest and quickest results are to be attained by applying, *after* the ground has been prepared as described above, a 2- to 3-inch top dressing of especially prepared compost—a chocolate icing layer to the lawn cake.

Such a specially prepared seedbed offers the most favorable conditions

Thorough preparation in making a lawn means better turf, minimum upkeep.

for quick and even germination, and a vigorous start for the tiny grass seedlings, particularly the finer grasses where a mixture is used.

The making of this compost does not involve a great deal of additional labor. Any extra time spent in preparing it is more than made up for in getting the turf well established. The compost is made up of two parts (by bulk) compost-heap soil (or clean, rich loam) and one part peat-moss (preferably sphagnum peat). To this add, for each bushel, 2 to 3 quarts of dried organic manure (such as Bovung, Driconure, or Milorganite) and 1 quart of bonemeal. The ingredients are thoroughly mixed by being sifted in alternate shovelfuls through a ½-inch mesh screen. The fertilizer may be added either during the process of sifting the soil and peat or after it has been spread. The former method is preferable as it helps start immediate bacterial action in the heap. If it is applied after spreading, rake in thoroughly.

A pre-emergence weed killer or a combination weed killer and fertilizer may be applied at this time. This precaution is well worthwhile unless one is sure he has weed-seed-free compost. If any weed killer is used, be sure to *follow directions to the letter,* allowing the full time stipulated between its application and seed sowing.

Seed. In order to decide wisely what grass or grass mixture is best suited to *your* climate and soil, see the discussion on *What Grass for You?* in this chapter, or consult your county agent or nearest State Agricultural Experiment Station.

Sowing. While small, hand-operated gadgets are available for sowing grass seed, it is much better, except for very small areas, to use a combination fertilizer and seed sower. One of these may be rented from most garden supply centers or hardware stores that sell grass seed. For the owner of an extensive lawn it is better to purchase a spreader. This will prove useful at all seasons in fertilizing flower beds and borders as well as the lawn itself.

If soil is very dry, water *thoroughly* and let the surface dry off before sowing. To assure an even stand, divide the seed into two equal parts and sow the second part at right angles to the first. Use for each operation, only *half* the amount of seed recommended per 100 or 1000 square feet.

Sowing should be followed immediately by a light raking. We like best for this job a generous-size bamboo rake, but an ordinary garden rake, wooden or iron, will serve. This raking must be done with a light hand, merely to cover the seed, or most of it, from sight. Any ridges or furrows formed will result in an uneven stand of grass.

Follow the raking with rolling, using a roller with just enough water in it to compact the soil so that it is firm but not hard. For small areas it is easier to use an iron tamper, or one made of a 12- to 18-inch piece of 2×8-inch plank, with a vertical handle.

Keep surface moist! After rolling, water the soil again, slowly but

In establishing a new lawn of any type, adequate watering, in a form that will neither compact nor wash away the surface soil, is a prime factor in achieving success.

thoroughly enough so that no puddles stand on the surface. A "mist" nozzle (page 308) on the hose is ideal for this purpose as it is for many others. A perforated hose or an oscillating sprinkler may be used instead. Do *not* apply water so rapidly that it cannot be immediately absorbed. Many a lawn has been badly damaged even before seed germinates by such careless watering that seed has been washed out or dried out in spots.

Surface must be *kept* moist, constantly, until the grass is well up, if an even stand is to be obtained. In very dry or windy weather this may mean watering twice or even three times daily for the first week or two. Some of the best lawn grasses—such as bluegrass, especially Merion and other selected strains—appear in 14 to 28 days, while fescues require 5 to 10 days to germinate. In exposed, windy, or extremely sunny places, a temporary light surface covering of straw, light brush, or something similar, if coarse in texture, may be placed on the surface. (One bale of straw will cover up to 1000 square feet.) Any such covering, however, must be removed *immediately* after germination has taken place.

Banks and Slopes. If, after grading, it is still necessary to establish grass on a sharp slope, two courses are open. The first, and best, is to cover with sods; the second is to use sods in strips or panels to hold the soil in place, and sow seed on the soil between these, keeping the seed in place with Erosionet or some similar porous ground covering.

SODDING, STRIPPING, PLUGGING, SPRIGGING

Sometimes, for one reason or another, methods other than seed sowing are used for making or renewing lawns. Some of these methods are quicker, others slower, than using seed. In all cases, however, the soil must be thoroughly prepared in advance—as outlined previously—if success is to be attained.

Sodding, as the term implies, involves the use of growing turf to establish the new lawn. It is the surest, quickest, and most expensive method.

In warm climates, Zoysia, Bermudagrass, Centipedegrass and other hot climate grasses are used. Some are established by setting in strips of sod; by the use of "plugs"—small pieces of turf; or by "sprigs"—single plants with roots. It is well to get the advice of a local county agent.

Sods, usually 12 inches wide and 12 to 18 inches long and about 2 to 4 inches thick, are cut from an old lawn, a pasture, or from new turf grown for the purpose. The latter cost more, but are by far the most satisfactory as they are uniform in quality and in the grasses they contain. They should be laid close together, breaking joints in alternate strips, rolled or tamped down evenly, and given light but very frequent watering —at least daily in hot, sunny weather until new roots have been established.

Stripping is similar to sodding except that narrow sods, usually 4 or 6 inches wide, are handled in rolls and set in strips about 3 to 6 inches apart. These are left to spread until the intervening soil strips are covered. The strips are rather conspicuous at first, but usually disappear by the middle of the first season if a good job of planting has been done.

Plugging. This is simply a modification of sodding, used chiefly in the case of warm climate grasses, seed of which is not available. Instead of sods, the turf to be used is cut up into small pieces, 2 to 4 inches square. In cutting, as much soil as possible is left on the roots, which should be kept moist. In planting, the plugs are set firmly, 12 to 18 inches apart each way, in holes or in furrows. On slopes, furrows should follow contours, to prevent washing in heavy rains. If soil is poor, use compost in holes or furrows. Soil must be kept moist until new growth starts. With plugging, it usually takes a season, or even a full year, before lawn develops a uniform appearance. During this time of course the surface between plugs must be kept clear of weeds.

Sprigging is a modification of plugging in which individual root clusters (stolons) are used. These are readily shipped by mail or express. They are set a foot or so apart each way except in the case of Zoysia grasses (see photo). Care must be taken not to cover the growing tips, to have the soil moist, and to keep it so until new growth starts.

LAWN RENOVATION

It often happens that the lawn problem is not that of making a new lawn, but what to do with a lawn that, either through neglect or having been improperly made in the first place—as in many subdivisions and developments—has become hopelessly run down. Possibly attempts have been made to renovate it with special seed mixtures, certain-death weed eradicators, and magic fertilizers. But unless the *soil* conditions are corrected, all of these efforts are likely to produce only temporary improvement.

This does not necessarily involve digging or plowing up the entire area. The following procedure will usually put the area back into good condition provided proper care is maintained afterward. However, if there is not proper drainage, or if the soil is so porous (sandy or gravelly) that water passes through it as through a sieve, then complete remaking is required.

Assuming fairly good soil, the following method should provide a good turf that, with continued maintenance, will *stay* good.

First, mow the old lawn, setting the blades as low as possible. Next dig up bare spots and weedy or poor areas and dig and work in a heavy application of compost. Use a weed eradicator (following directions carefully) where these are prevalent in turf otherwise fairly good. Top-dress and rake these areas over evenly with compost. Water *thoroughly*. When dry on the surface, sow seed, using full amount recommended for a new lawn on bare spots, less where some turf remains. Rake seed in and roll. Keep surface *constantly* moist by light watering for at least two weeks.

The best time to carry out this operation is *very* early spring or early fall for cool-climate grasses and according to local practice and State Agricultural Experiment Station advice for warm sections.

LAWN MAINTENANCE

Even the best of lawns is not an investment that is made and then forgotten, to go on paying rich dividends without further attention. In fact, the more perfect the lawn is, the more constant will be the attention required to keep it in A-1 condition.

Mowing, of course, is the first consideration. Mowing should begin when the new grass, if of a cool-climate type, is 2 to 3 inches tall. The mower blades—or blade, if a rotary mower is used—should be set at least 2 inches high. Mowing is best done on a cloudy day, to avoid possible injury from hot sun, and should be followed by watering if the soil is dry. Do not attempt mowing when grass is wet.

Subsequent mowings may be somewhat closer, but it should be remembered that this will mean mowing more frequently, and also that the closer grass is cut, the more likely it is that crabgrass—which loves full, direct sunshine and does not grow in even moderately heavy shade—will get a start. Never let the grass get so long between mowings that it is necessary to rake up and remove the clippings. Left where they fall they form a beneficial mulch and eventually work back into the soil, *thus returning most of the plant food elements that they have removed.*

Feeding is best done in early spring and again in late summer for cool-climate grasses; for hot-climate grasses, at the *beginning* of most active growth, and then at two-month intervals. This can be continued through the year if an overplanting is made to give a green winter carpet.

While the market is flooded with all sorts of special lawn fertilizers, the most important point in getting good turf is taking care that the *soil* is well supplied with the plant nutrients it requires—plus lime if needed, as in most cases it is—*before* the seed is sown. If that is done, a general-purpose fertilizer with a generous nitrogen content such as 10–6–4, will give satisfactory results, especially if the nitrogen is in a form in which it is released slowly, over a long period.

Some of the modern lawn fertilizers are designed both to provide nourishment for the grass and to kill weeds at the same time. While these are constantly being improved, they should be applied strictly in accordance with directions; and without depending too much on the claims made for them. Practically all advertising these days is given over to more and more extravagant claims, and lawn advertising is no exception to the rule.

For *Pest, Disease, and Weed Control,* see Appendix.

WHAT GRASS FOR YOU?

When it comes to the point of deciding just what grass to sow, there are two main points to consider:

What grasses grow best in your particular area?

What *type* of lawn will best suit your needs?

In the majority of cases—especially in the northern or cool-climate Areas (I, II, and III)—a good mixture with Merion Bluegrass, the chief ingredient, is likely to give the most satisfactory results. In the South, each general area has its most suitable warm-climate grass, Bermudagrass being used over the largest area, with one or more of the Zoysias rapidly increasing in popularity. In many parts of the Midwest and on the Great Plains, the question is one of moisture. Where irrigation or ample water is available, the cool-climate grasses are successfully grown; but without water, one of the native dryland grasses must be used. Many State Experiment Stations carry on extensive tests with various species and mixtures of grass. Anyone putting in a large lawn will do well to consult his Agricultural Experiment Station, or better still visit it and see for himself the results of its tests.

When buying grass seed do not be influenced by price. The cost of seed, compared with other construction costs *and upkeep,* is such a minor figure that, in the long run, the best *is* the cheapest. Bargain mixtures contain large quantities of short-lived "nurse" grasses, which soon disappear. If there is an insufficient quantity of the more expensive, permanent grass seed, an open turf is left which encourages the germination of unwanted weeds.

Here are some of the most widely used and most satisfactory grasses:

FOR COOL CLIMATES

BENTS include such special strains as Astoria, Colonial, Highland, and Rhode Island, and comprise the finest and most beautiful turf grasses. When correctly handled they produce fine, dense, handsome carpets such as are generally seen only on large estates and well-kept golf courses. A pH of 5.5 to 6.5 is required on extra-well-prepared soil. Full sun, close cutting, brushing, ample watering, regular fertilization and top dressing, and a rigid program of pest and disease control are essential to success. Northeast; North Central; East Coast; Northwest Coast.

Creeping Bents include many strains—Arlington, Pennlu, Penncross, Old Orchard, Seaside, and Toronto being some of the best known. These fine bentgrasses are used almost exclusively for putting greens and estate lawns near the seashore, for they resist salt spray. Like the other bents these produce an extremely fine turf when meticulously cared for. Northeast; East Coast; Northwest Coast.

Redtop, also a bentgrass, is a quick germinating, short-lived "nurse" grass often used in mixtures to give a temporary turf until the permanent grasses become established; or for overplanting Bermudagrass or other summer lawns for winter color in the South. Northeast; North Central; East Coast; Northwest Coast.

Velvet Bent produces the densest and most finely textured turf of all. It is used for show lawns and putting greens in areas that suit its growing requirements. It is heat, cold, shade, drought, and disease-resistant and is suited to the same climatic conditions as the other bentgrasses. It would be wise, however, to get local advice from an authority as to the advisability of using it in a locality where one lacks previous experience.

BLUEGRASSES are generally considered the best of the cool-climate lawn grasses. Kentucky or Merion Blue dominate most mixtures of high quality for the northern and central parts of the country and for other areas as well. Northeast; North Central; East Coast; Midwest; South Central; parts of the Southeast; Northwest Coast; all cool and cold areas north (including Alaska) and west where irrigation or ample water is available; 2–3 pounds per 1000 square feet.

Kentucky Bluegrass is a fine-bladed, blue-green perennial grass, long-lived and producing—when grown in full sun—a rather open turf of good, deep texture. Preferred pH 6–7. Cut at 2 inches.

Merion Bluegrass is deeper rooted, more dense, darker in color, more vigorous, and resistant to heat, drought, and fungus disease, but not to rust. As rust is less likely to attack it when it is planted with Kentucky Bluegrass, a mixture is often used of 30 to 50 per cent Merion, the balance or most of it Kentucky Blue. Merion can be cut closer than Kentucky Blue—½ to 1½ inches.

Canada Bluegrass is coarse, deep-rooted, tolerates poor soil and shade, if it has plenty of moisture, is used for athletic fields and playgrounds where it can be cut high (3–4 inches) and infrequently.

Rough Bluegrass (*Poa trivialis*) or *Meadowgrass,* prefers damp, cool weather, moisture, and partial shade but must have a fertile soil. It produces a low-growing, light green carpet not unlike Kentucky Blue except in color. This grass is almost sure to be included in any shady seed mixture for cool climates. Sometimes as much as 80 per cent is used in such mixtures. Northeast and North Central only.

FESCUES take rough treatment, endure sun or shade, moist or dry soil, and low fertility, but cannot stand the broiling summer heat of the South. They are slow-growing, producing a wiry but fine-textured turf of deep green; are mowed high, 2–3 inches; 2–3 pounds per 1000 square feet.

Red Fescue, or one of its improved strains—such as Chewings, Illahue, Pennlawn, and Ranier—are included in most cool-climate mixtures in the proportion of from 15 to 40 per cent, depending on the area where it is to be used and the use to be made of the finished lawn. Northeast; North Central; Northwest Coast.

Tall Fescue (and its strains Alta and Kentucky 31) are best suited for use on play areas, athletic fields, and airports. They are tall-growing, perennial pasture grasses producing dense leaf systems and heavy roots. Northeast; North Central; Midwest; Northwest Coast.

RYEGRASSES

Domestic or *Italian Ryegrass* is an annual used as a "nurse" grass in cool-climate mixtures to make a show of green before the permanent grasses establish themselves. By then the short-lived annual ryegrass has disappeared. It is also much used for overplanting Bermuda and Centipedegrass lawns in the South to give a green winter color; 2 pounds per 1000 square feet. Northeast; North Central; East Coast; Midwest; South Central; Southeast; Southwest; West Coast.

Perennial Ryegrass makes a permanent, coarse, tough turf though generally it is supposed to be a short-lived grass. It is often planted temporarily to form a quick green ground cover around a new house, to be turned under as green manure when the owner is ready to prepare the area thoroughly and seed a permanent lawn. Northeast; North Central; East Coast; Southeast; South Central; West Coast.

CLOVER, (White Dutch variety) though not a grass at all, is used in many grass seed mixtures. Where a homeowner wishes to include it as part of his own lawn, however, it is really better if he sows it *separately* from the grass seed, placing it in areas where he wants it. It grows almost anywhere in the United States, given enough moisture. Though it prefers a slightly alkaline soil, it endures slight acidity and grows well in full sun or part shade. It has the added advantages of adding nitrogen to the soil through the leguminous nodules on its roots, and of being so attractive to rabbits that they eat it in preference to most flowers. It may also be planted alone as a ground cover or a grass substitute.

GRASS MIXTURES

In cool climates, lawn seed is usually sold in mixture, the content depending on the use to which the lawn is to be put, and local weather conditions.

For Full Sun

Kentucky Bluegrass	50%		Merion or Kentucky Blue	40%
Merion Bluegrass	40%	OR	Red Fescue Strain	50%
Redtop	10%		Bent, Astoria, or Colonial	10%

For Moist Shade

Rough Bluegrass	40%		Ryegrass, perennial	25%
Fescue, Chewings	50%		Redtop	15%
Bent, Colonial	5%	OR	Rough Bluegrass	30%
Redtop	5%		Fescue, Chewings	25%
			Bent, Colonial	5%

2 lbs. per 1000 sq. ft.

2 lbs. per 1000 sq. ft.

For Dry Shade

Red Fescue, any variety	50%
Merion or Kentucky Bluegrass	30%
Redtop	5%
Perennial Ryegrass	15%

Grass mixtures vary considerably in different climates. If possible consult your county agent or State Agricultural Experiment Station about what mixture best suits your locality and soil.

HOT-CLIMATE GRASSES

BERMUDAGRASS and its hybrids, such as Everglades ⅟1, Gene Tift, Ormond, Sunturf, Tift 57, 127, or 328 are the most generally satisfactory grasses for the South. Bermudagrasses need full sun, slightly acid soil; 4 to 6 fertilizations per year; frequent mowings at ¾ of an inch; and deep watering in dry weather. In general, however, these grasses are the most drought-resistant of all. They are pale- to dark-green, upright-growing, wear-resistant, the hybrids of finer texture than the species. Seed is planted from March to April at the rate of 1 pound per 1000 square feet; or it may be sprigged or sodded at any time during the growing season. Except in frost-free areas it must be overplanted for winter green with domestic ryegrass or a lawn mixture. Southeast; South Central; Gulf·Coast; Southwest Coast.

CARPETGRASS is tall, coarse, broad-leaved species which spreads by creeping rootstocks. Light green in color and disease-resistant, it stands moderate wear and needs but one fertilization a year. It is adapted, however, only to low, moist, acid situations in sun or part shade. Growing 8 to 10 inches in height, it creates a mowing problem. Seed fall, winter, or early spring at the rate of 2½ pounds per 1000 square feet; or sprig or plug. Like Bermudagrass, Carpetgrass must be overplanted in winter to get year-round color. Southeast; South Central; Gulf Coast.

CENTIPEDEGRASS makes a low-growing dense sod of light green. It prefers slightly acid soil; needs little mowing as it grows to only 3 or 4 inches; is disease-resistant; endures some shade but also, if kept watered, does well in dry, sandy soils and on steep banks. Seed at the rate of 3 to 5 ounces per 1000 square feet, mixing the fine seed with a gallon of dry sand to assure even distribution; or sod, plug, or sprig. Overplant in winter with ryegrass. Southeast, especially coastal regions; Gulf Coast; South Central; Southwest Coast.

ST. AUGUSTINEGRASS, and its improved varieties such as Bitter Blue, makes coarse, deep green turf which grows in sun or shade; endures salt spray but is subject to chinch-bug injury. It prefers a pH of 6–6.5; needs 4 fertilizations a year and watering in dry periods. As it is very tender, St. Augustine should be planted only in frost-free areas where it remains green the year-round. Sod or sprig: seed is not available. Southeast coastal areas and Gulf Coast.

ZOYSIAS are rapidly becoming the most popular grasses for the South and some species are being widely planted in the North. They are low-growing, making dark green, ruglike turf which stays green over a longer period than Bermudagrass. Their slow growth at first and the fact that they must be sprigged or plugged because of lack of seed are their two major drawbacks. Two years are needed to establish a Zoysia lawn, and during that time it requires plenty of fertilizer and water. Once established, the dense growth crowds out all weeds and care is then minimal. Regular fertilization (4 per year) and watering and frequent mowings at 1½ inches maintain a dark green, handsome sod. All Zoysia grasses brown off in cold weather and the density of the turf makes it difficult to overplant as is the practice with Bermuda and other southern grasses. (Some authorities suggest *painting* the lawn green for the winter!) By sprigging end to end in rows 4 to 6 inches apart, instead of at the usual intervals, a Zoysia lawn can be established in less than the two years generally needed. If the sprigs are in good condition when planted and the area is carefully tended, a fairly good cover should be attained in 6 to 9 months. Sods should be carefully revived on delivery by "heeling in" in damp peatmoss before they are separated into sprigs. After separating, sprigs are planted at once.

Zoysia matrella or Manillagrass is a fine-leaved, medium-dark species growing 3 to 4 inches in height. It forms a dense, ruglike turf; grows in sun or shade on a wide variety of soils; is pest-, disease-, and weed-resistant. It is green from early spring to late fall, unless temperatures drop below 40 degrees. Southeast; South Central; Southwest Coast.

Emerald Zoysia is similar to *Z. matrella* but grows faster, is a richer green in color, and is more frost-resistant.

Zoysia japonica (Korean Lawngrass) and its improved Korean variety, *Meyer Zoysia,* are those recommended for northern lawns. They are coarser than *Z. matrella* and slower-growing, but form similar, dense, dark green turfs. They prefer full sun and are drought-resistant, though they turn brown in winter. As far as hardiness goes, the Japanese *Zoysias* can be grown from Florida to Massachusetts, Ohio, and even Michigan, though *Z. matrella* is better suited to southern conditions. Northeast; North Central; East Coast; South Central; West Coast; also Southeast and Gulf Coast if desired.

DRY LAND GRASSES

BUFFALOGRASS is a native prairie species of the West which needs full sun but stands cold, heat, and drought. It spreads by runners, is low-growing so needs little mowing, and forms a dense, gray-green turf. Midwest; Great Plains; Southwest; Intermountain.

CRESTED WHEATGRASS and its variety, Fairway, are pasture grasses which grow like Buffalograss. Though it browns badly in hot weather it grows vigorously in cool temperatures. Midwest; Great Plains; Intermountain below 5000 feet.

LEMMONS ALKALIGRASS is a tufted native adapted to moist alkaline soils. It can be used where soil is too alkaline for other grasses, if water and plant food can be supplied. West Coast.

GRAMAGRASSES are pasture grasses of the western United States which can be treated like Buffalograss.

Blue Grama is recommended for dry areas in Montana, Wyoming, and the Southwest where no irrigation is available.

Black Grama, another species, grows best in the Southwest.

GROUND COVERS AS GRASS SUBSTITUTES

In areas and climates where it is difficult to establish and maintain lawns, ground-cover substitutes are often tried. Unfortunately many of

In deep shade, and under other unfavorable conditions, grass substitutes may be used. For shade Vinca minor *or* Pachysandra terminalis *are commonly planted. In sandy, poor soil near the seashore Bearberry* (Arctostaphylos uva-ursi), *shown above, makes a handsome, evergreen ground cover in full sun or part shade. A number of early spring bulbs such as chionodoxa, scilla, and muscari may be interplanted under such conditions to give a welcome touch of early color.*

these are very limited in their adaptability. It is well therefore to experiment before investing heavily in seed or plants in this category.

Arctostaphylos uva-ursi (Hog-cranberry or Bearberry) is a creeping, broad-leaved evergreen of the Heath Family, a native of northern coastal areas, where it completely covers moors and sandy slopes not far from the ocean front. It is prostrate, with small, glossy oval leaves, pink flowers, and red berries in fall. Prefers full sun, sandy and quite acid soil. It is drought-resistant but difficult to transplant.

Ajuga reptans (Bugle-weed) is a hardy perennial with rosettes of glossy, dark green or bronze leaves, and 4- to 6-inch spikes of deep blue flowers in spring. (There are also white and pink varieties.) It spreads rapidly by stolons from which new-rooted leaf rosettes develop; sun or shade; needs moisture.

Clover, White Dutch (see page 171 for description).

Cotula squalida (Camomile) is a ground cover with light-green, fernlike leaves. Good sandy loam, full sun, and water in dry weather are essential. It is especially suited to California and the Southeast.

Dichondra carolinensis is a native of our own Southeast. Small, fernlike, kidney-shaped, dark green leaves form dense mats only 1½ inches in height, spreading by runners. It requires a deep, well-drained soil but needs plenty of moisture and grows in sun or shade. Sow 1–2 pounds per 1000 square feet, in June. Tender. Southeast; South Central; Southwest Coast.

Hedera helix or English Ivy is an excellent ground cover in shade, especially under trees. One of the small-leaved varieties makes a good choice. Most of these, though sold as house ivies, are hardy as far north as New York City.

Lippia canescens is used as a substitute for lawn grass in warm climates. It is of creeping habit, with gray-green foliage and small lavender flowers; grows in sun or shade; in dry and rather poor soil; and is drought-resistant. Southeast; South Central; Southwest; Southwest Coast.

Liriope muscari, a member of the lily family, has narrow, grasslike, dark green foliage which forms a dense turf 12 inches tall. Lavender-blue flower spikes in late summer. There is an attractive variegated form. It is tolerant of many soil types and grows well in sun or quite heavy shade. Hardy. Northeast; North Central; Southeast; Northwest.

Matricaria tchihatchewi or Turfing-daisy is a mat-forming perennial with finely cut leaves and small, white daisylike flowers; 12 inches, moisture and full sun are required. Hardy. Northeast; North Central; Southeast; South Central; Northwest.

Pachysandra terminalis, or Japanese-spurge, is a fine, dense, evergreen plant for shade which grows by underground stems and throws up umbrellalike stems topped by whorls of glossy, dark leaves. Flowers white. It prefers shade, moisture, and good, humusy loam. Northeast; North Central; Northwest.

Thymus serpyllum, and others: Creeping thymes are among the best of the small-leaved, completely prostrate ground covers. A variety of these gives many shades of green and gray and red, and flowers from white through pink to deep rose. They stand traffic well and are aromatic when the leaves and stems are crushed under foot.

Vinca minor, or periwinkle, is second only to *Pachysandra* as a shade-loving, evergreen ground cover. The dark, glossy leaves are produced on vinelike, creeping stems which root at the nodes. Showy blue or white flowers cover the plants in early spring. Good drainage and moisture are a must; it responds well to rich, woodsy soil. Northeast; North Central; Southeast.

LAWN SCHEDULE

COOL-WEATHER GRASSES

December to *March*. Prepare seedbed for new lawn whenever ground can be worked. Apply pre-emergence weed killer or weed killer-fertilizer.

March to *May*. Seed spring lawn as early as possible. Apply fertilizer-insecticide to old and new lawns. Treat old lawns with pre-emergence crabgrass eradicator. Use weed-control sprays and insecticide sprays before new growth appears on garden plants.

June. Cut new grass as soon as it is 3 to 4 inches high, setting mower blades at 3-inch height. Mow weekly thereafter at 2 inches.

July. Begin regular deep watering of lawns in dry periods. Fertilize lightly. Mow weekly.

August. Prepare seedbed for fall-planted lawns. Apply weed killers well in advance.

September. Sow seed as early as possible and keep moist until established. Renovate and fertilize established lawns.

October. Mow new lawn when grass is 4 inches high, setting mower at 3 inches. Mow weekly thereafter at 2 to 3 inches. Fertilize in mild climates.

November. If weather is dry, water deeply before freeze. Stop mowing.

WARM-WEATHER GRASSES

April. Prepare seedbed and finish grade for new lawns. Treat with pre-emergence weed killer. Remove thatch from established lawn. Order seed or sod for new lawn.

May. Sow grass seed as early as possible after fertilizing and watering. Keep moist until established. Begin to mow as soon as grass is 3 to 4 inches tall. Apply weed control-fertilizer to established lawns. Sod, sprig, or plug summer grasses. Keep moist and well fertilized.

June. Apply 1 pound nitrogenous fertilizer per 1000 square feet. Mow weekly at 1 to 2 inches. Apply post-emergent crabgrass weed killers as needed.

July. Continue fertilizer, mowing, and watering weekly. Treat for pests, diseases, and weeds as needed.

August. Continue same schedule as in July.

September. Raise mower ½ inch and continue mowing until frost. Aerate area and overplant with domestic ryegrass before the middle of the month.

October. Apply 2–4–D sprays (see Appendix, page 470) for chickweed and other winter weeds. Water thoroughly before ground freezes.

November. If area has not been overplanted, try applying a winter "lawn paint" to the dead, brown grass tops.

Where the copsewood is the greenest,
Where the fountains glisten sheenest,
Where the lady-fern grows strongest,
Where the morning dew lies longest;
SIR WALTER SCOTT

CHAPTER 11

Flower Beds and Borders

Flower beds and borders for annuals, perennials, and bulbs should be the last part of the planting to be done in landscaping a new place. If planted too early, you may find that they are not only poorly located, but are often damaged when soil and equipment has to be brought in for planting trees, making walks, grading, etc.

It is natural of course that the new homeowner should want a show of color out of doors and flowers for decoration indoors at the earliest possible moment. But certainly the more permanent and important parts of the landscaping can be laid out on a permanent, over-all landscape plan (page 5) before flower beds and borders are put in.

Placement. In deciding where flower beds or borders are to go there are several essential things to consider.

Does one want them to be seen and enjoyed from the public road or street? Are there *view windows* which make it possible to have the flower beds, or at least part of them, supplement the *interior* decoration? Does the family devote much time to *outdoor living?* If so can flower beds be employed specifically to add charm and distinction to the outdoor living area? Or maybe the lady of the house is interested in flower arranging, in which case she will want a *cutting garden* for her purpose where she may grow the flowers and foliage she especially likes to use; and where she can cut material at will without robbing flower beds designed and located to add to the beauty of the home grounds.

With the exception of the cutting garden, which may well be placed by itself, or actually concealed from view, (as are coldframes, compost heaps, and the vegetable garden) flower beds or borders should be a definite part of the landscape design.

Backgrounds. In deciding where any flower bed is to go, one of the most important things to be considered is what sort of background it will have.

The day of the raised circular bed in the center of the front lawn, we are happy to say, is long since gone. Too often, however, one still sees free-standing beds, rectangular, or in long, narrow strips, cut into closely clipped turf. These look almost as contrived and artificial as the old-fashioned, round, canna bed.

To show to best advantage, a bed of flowers should have a background of some sort. Often this may be the wall of a building, a fence, a terraced slope, a hedge. Lacking something of this sort, evergreens or a mixed planting of shrubs add tremendously to its effectiveness.

Be sure to check the growth habits of your plants so that tall-growing flowers are placed well in the rear, those of medium height in the center, and dwarf or very low-growing sorts along the front. Care must be exercised to avoid a blocked, geometric effect. This is done by placing

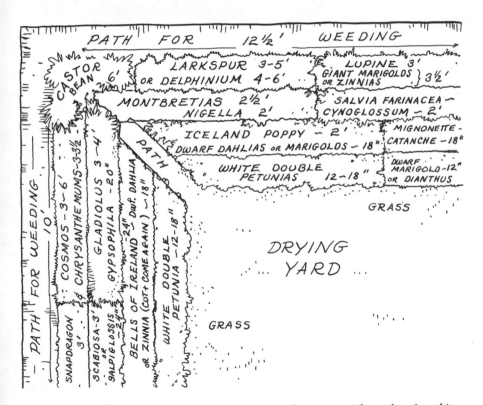

Where many flowers are wanted for cutting, plan a special garden for this purpose.

Unless the general landscape plan is a stiffly formal one— which is seldom the case these days—the flower border is best placed against a hedge or, better, against a shrubby background planting.

Usually the effect is more pleasing if the front of the border follows a curved line. This may be established by using a piece of hose or rope, adjusting it until a satisfactory curve is determined, and then cutting the turf along it with a lawn edger or a spade to leave a clean, unbroken edge. Next the turf is skimmed off and removed to the compost heap. A permanent edging of metal, wood, or brick may be put in if desired.

The remaining soil is then dug to a depth of eight inches (*or if in very poor ground, removed entirely and replaced with good soil*) and well enriched with compost and fertilizer. If the bed is not to be planted at once, a weed seed eradicant may be applied at this time.

the groups in irregular designs that tend to run together and so make a unified whole.

Long flowering season should be assured by using varieties that will flower at different times, or for exceptionally long periods (see lists, Appendix).

While flower borders may be made of either annuals or perennials, the best results for a permanent planting are to be had by using both— with some biennials and bulbs thrown in for good measure. In such a border it is possible to have some plants in bloom from early April until mid-October in the northern states, and in milder climates much longer.

Make a Plan. Even if the flower border is not to be an extensive one, it is best to prepare a planting plan *to scale,* before seeds or plants are ordered. Not only will this save time and expense, but give much more satisfactory results (page 4).

Except on a very small property, where space is at a premium, it is advisable to have at least two beds or borders; one for flowers which prefer full sun, and another for those which demand or tolerate some shade (see list in Appendix).

Soil Preparation. As most flower beds or borders are permanent landscape features, it is well worthwhile to take *extra* care in preparing the soil for them. In very poor or very light, sandy soil, it is highly desirable to excavate the beds entirely to a depth of 8 to 12 inches, and refill with good loam, plus manure or compost. It is especially important to provide plenty of humus, in the form of peatmoss, to maintain a constant supply of moisture for the roots. (For basic treatments of special types of soil, see Chapter 2.)

ANNUALS

Although most of the annuals are quite tender, and a number of them are best not sown from seed or set out as plants until after the soil has really warmed up, it is advisable to prepare the beds as early in the spring as possible. In addition to this we like to use, when setting out plants, our regular "starting" mixture of bonemeal and organic manure.

There are a few annuals which germinate quickly and spring into rapid growth, producing flowers in a few weeks. These are valuable for *quick effects* needed to give color the first year in a rock garden or border where perennials will make a show the following year. For lists of such quick growers—many of which must be sown in succession to give an all-season display—see list, Appendix.

Many other annuals require quite a *long growing season* before beginning to flower and for these it is advisable, especially in northern climates, to start seedlings in advance of planting dates, indoors or in a frame; or else to purchase plants ready for setting out. Growing one's own plants has several advantages. By so doing the gardener can secure the exact varieties he wishes to have. He can have plants that have not been forced to maintain a production timetable; he can have them properly and gradually "hardened off" before setting out; and he can plant them a few at a time as they and conditions are ready, instead of having to do a rush job as may be the case when a large number are purchased at one time.

Annuals are usually planted in beds or borders where several species and different types of the same species are used together—marigolds and zinnias for instance are available in a wide variety of colors and in plants that range from a few inches to several feet in height—but striking landscape effects may be obtained with groups of a single variety. Even a single plant such as castor-oil bean (*Ricinus*), sunflower, or angel's-trumpet (*Datura*) can be featured as a specimen.

Some of the annual vines grow with almost incredible rapidity, reaching heights of 20 to 30 feet in time to provide weeks of bloom. Examples are morning-glory, moonflower, cup-and-saucer vine (*Cobaea scandens*),

This modest border of annuals (with a few perennials) illustrates the fact that a curved design is more attractive than a straight edge. Shrubs and evergreens planted at the rear will soon blot out houses and wires and will provide privacy.

and tall climbing nasturtiums, which, though they reach only 4 or 5 feet, make up in vigor and bloom for what they lack in height.

These fast-growing annual vines are especially important for inexpensive landscape effects in first-season plantings on a new place (see list, Appendix).

In buying annuals it is advisable to procure named varieties rather than mixtures. The seed may cost a bit more, but this cost is only a small fraction of the cost of making a garden, fertilizers, sprays, watering, etc. And in buying plants, select young, vigorous ones, in bud rather than in full bloom. This applies especially to plants in flats or other multiple containers, but holds with pot plants also.

Sowing and Planting. Success with annuals depends to a great extent upon giving them the correct *start*. Both earlier and more certain results are to be had with the majority of species by starting the plants in a greenhouse, a hotbed, or a coldframe, and then setting them out—the

A unique garden of annuals, summer bulbs, and one or two perennials transforms a terraced Cape Cod hillside into a summer-long blaze of color. A dramatic illustration of what can be accomplished under adverse conditions.

hardy plants after danger of hard frosts is past and the tender ones when the ground has really warmed up.

As it takes seed a week to two weeks, or even longer, to germinate in cold soil, the hardy and half-hardy sorts, if sown outdoors, may be planted a bit in advance of these dates; but tender varieties, if sown too early, are likely to rot in the soil.

With seeds sown where they are to grow, germination will be more certain if the rows or the beds in which they are to be planted are given some extra care in the way of preparation. Where they are to be sown in rows we open up a shallow trench—2 to 3 inches in depth—and fill it with a sand and peatmoss mixture. If soil is dry, the trench is flooded with water, which is allowed to soak away before the sand-peat compost is put in, after which the soaking is again repeated. Circular or rectangular beds where seed is to be broadcast are treated in the same way.

Such preparation requires a little extra work, but is well worth it. Surplus seedlings, when the "thinning out" stage is reached, come out easily, with little disturbance to those that are left, and in ideal condition to transplant elsewhere if they are wanted. Such is not the case when seedlings have to force their way up through the usual hard-packed surface soil.

Very small seeds, sown in the open, are often washed out, or badly damaged, before or after germination. Covering the surface with a light mulch, or even with newspapers, will prevent this, but such plantings must be carefully watched and any covering *immediately removed* when germination occurs. Delay for even a day may result in losing them.

Thinning out. Probably the greatest cause of poor results, or even failure, with annuals sown where they are to grow is delay in thinning them out. *Every surplus plant is a weed!* And moreover it is a weed growing in closest proximity to the plant that is wanted, and competing with it for food, moisture, and light, from the very start. Thinning should be done as soon as possible after the first true leaves develop. Very often

Thin out seedlings while plants are still small; the earlier the better.

a second thinning, and sometimes even a third, is required to provide ample space for the remaining plants to produce maximum results.

Fertilizer. Even though the soil may have been well prepared, under most conditions an application of plant food, as the plants are coming into bud, proves beneficial. A general-purpose fertilizer, rather than one with an extra-high nitrogen content, is best for this, as forced plants usually have a shortened period of flowering. Growing plants should be watched carefully, and if they seem to lack healthy, dark green foliage, an application of a high-nitrogen fertilizer is indicated. A moderate application of nitrate of soda, well watered in, often shows results in a few days, as will foliar feeding. Such stimulation should not be overdone, however, or the plants, while making remarkable growth, may produce fewer than the normal number of flowers.

Mulching. When watering is a problem—for instance in suburban areas where its use is restricted during dry periods when it is most needed—mulching should by all means be employed. To be most effective it must be put on *before* the surface gets powder-dry or caked.

Supports. Many tall growing plants require supports. These include, of course, all of those which form vines—such as sweet peas, morning-glories, and *Cobaea scandens,* or cup-and-saucer vine; and also many that are not of climbing habit but—because of their height—are injured by strong winds. This includes such popular kinds as cosmos, larkspur, snap-dragons, sunflowers, and tall marigolds.

Supports for the real climbers are of many types—trellises of wood, metal (of which we like best the aluminum link-chain type with screw

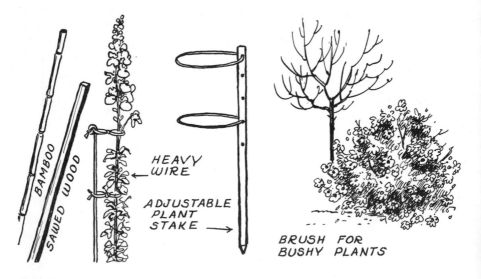

BAMBOO

SAWED WOOD

HEAVY ← WIRE

ADJUSTABLE PLANT STAKE →

BRUSH FOR BUSHY PLANTS

Tall plants need adequate support to prevent storm damage.

hooks to hold it at top and bottom), coarse twine, chains, and what-have-you. It is, however, plants of the second group, left unsupported, which are most likely to be injured.

For these, either of two types of support may be used. Typical of the first is the plant stake (made of bamboo, round or sawed wood or metal) to which the stem of the plant is securely tied. The effect is likely to be stiff and ungraceful but the plant is held securely.

For the other type of support, brush, wire, or netting may be employed. For garden use, brush provides the most natural-looking support, but it is becoming more and more difficult to procure, even in rural areas.

In using either type of support it should be *put in place early,* the plant being tied or trained on it as it grows. Plants that are left until nearly grown before being given support not only require much more work, but seldom can be made to look at all natural.

Pinching back. Many flowering plants that tend to send up a single, tall spike, such as dahlias and tall varieties of larkspur, snapdragon, and cosmos, may be made more branching and self-supporting by pinching out the top when they are well established. This induces the development of side growths and a more bushy, self-supporting plant. It may result also in more, though somewhat smaller, flowers.

End-of-season care. The first hard frost puts an end to most of the annuals. Too often they are left where they grew, to become an eyesore for the balance of the season—and to provide a nice winter mulch for seedlings of hardy weeds and undesirable grasses.

If, instead of this, they are removed at once, they make good material for the compost heap. Moreover, where annuals only have been used, the space they occupied may, if sown at once to winter rye or oats, look attractive throughout the winter and be benefited by the green manure, which is dug under the following spring.

BIENNIALS

Plants in this group normally require more than one season to complete their life cycle, making part of their growth the first summer and fall, going dormant through the winter, and flowering and maturing seed the following spring and summer. Some of them, if started inside early enough in the year will flower, even in cold regions, the same season they are sown. Among these are pansies, English daisies (*Bellis perennis*), forget-me-not (*Myosotis*), sweet William (*Dianthus barbatus*), and Siberian wallflower. In warmer regions they may be sown in autumn and brought through the colder months with suitable mulching to protect them from unusually heavy frosts (see list, Appendix).

In the well-planned perennial border great care must be exercised to keep all tall-growing plants such as delphiniums, foxgloves, and garden phlox well to the rear; those of medium height (Oriental poppies, hemerocallis, iris, veronica, and lythrum) in the center; and the low growers (heuchera, iberis, Alyssum saxatile, dianthus, and Plumbago larpentiae) (more correctly, Ceratostigma) along the front.

PERENNIALS

Perennials are plants which, after having produced flowers and seed, live on to repeat the process from year to year. Some of them are extremely long-lived; the gas-plant (*Dictamnus*) for instance, often out-lives the gardener who plants it, as do peonies. The majority of perennials, however, if left to themselves, soon form clumps of numerous offspring, becoming so overcrowded that they produce only inferior flowers, and fewer and fewer of these. So one may well realize at the start that a perennial garden is going to require more or less perennial care. Few plants in it can be left for more than two or three seasons without being taken up, divided, and replanted. And the more generously they are fed, to produce

In designing a perennial border, long strips or blocks of any one species or variety of plant are to be avoided. Groups should vary in size and shape and be placed with the time of bloom of each in mind (see plan) so that the succession of color is as nearly continuous as possible. The larger the border, the easier it is to maintain constant bloom.

vigorous growth and extra-fine bloom, the more frequently will they require replanting (see list, Appendix).

Exceptions to this general statement are the group of ground cover plants. These are used chiefly in areas where annuals and taller perennials do not thrive. They are also excellent in rock gardens and wall gardens (see lists, Appendix).

PLANNING THE BORDER

While annuals are still used extensively in the planting of beds and borders where a formal or architectural design is followed, perennials are seldom employed for this purpose. On the contrary, they lend themselves perfectly to the permanent hardy border, their astonishing variation in habit of growth, in size, in flower, in color and season of bloom, all helping to make them ideal subjects for this purpose.

As in using annuals, so with perennials, the most pleasing result is achieved when the design for planting does not follow a set pattern but produces a natural effect. Often a group of very few plants, or occasionally even a single specimen plant of some sturdy-growing variety, used as an accent creates the most pleasing picture.

As mentioned previously, low-growing species or varieties are used at the front, tall ones at the rear, and those of intermediate height in between. Care should be exercised to avoid planting in "bands." Occasionally spreading plants of medium height should run well back into the border or be brought forward near the edge. Groups of one species, planted in uneven patterns similar to those in which a group of bulbs is placed, planted informally produce unstudied, natural effects.

Much has been written about the distribution of color in the perennial garden. Many ideas advanced are alluring in theory but seldom work out in practice. Naturally one would wish to avoid putting clashing colors such as pink and yellow, or magenta and scarlet, adjacent to each other, but very pleasing borders can be achieved without too careful color planning. Such color harmonies as are commonly used by flower arrangers in their compositions may be too complicated for the average amateur gardener. For those who are keenly color conscious, however, such color planning may prove a joy. A large perennial garden that we did some years ago for a client featured the sky blue of delphiniums, the delicate salmons of Oriental poppies, sweet William, and the feathery rose of heuchera, all tied together with plenty of white blossoms and gray foliage. It was supremely satisfying to its owner, who preferred delicate colors, softly blended. A friend who prefers pure hues uses strong reds, deep oranges, heavy purples, but blends them with foliage plants of various greens and grays.

The design for a perennial border of moderate size, in sketch shown here, gives an idea of how a plan may be worked out to suit the owner.

Obtaining the plants for the perennial border may be done either by purchasing them from a nursery or growing them from seed. The new homemaker, who does not wish to wait too long for results, will find a combination of the two plans advisable.

In buying plants there is a big advantage in purchasing locally: one sees in advance what one is getting. On the other hand, unless one is within reach of a fairly large nursery where plants are actually propagated and grown as well as sold, the choice of varieties is likely to be very limited. The use of a few varieties that do not appear in every garden in the neighborhood is desirable to give the planting more individuality,

ROSA HUGONIS

DELPHINIUM DARK BLUE

HEMEROCALLIS 'AUTUMN KING'

ASTER 'BLUE LAGOON'

LILY GOLDEN SUNBURST HYB'DS

LILY 'BLACK DRAGON'

GYPSOPHILA 'BRISTOL FAIRY'

LILY 'ENCHANTMENT'

DWARF MARIGOLDS

DELPHINIUM PACIFIC GIANTS

LILY GOLDEN SPLENDOR HYB'DS

PLATYCODON GRANDIFLORUM

DAFFODILS

LILY GOLDEN WEDDING HYB'DS

PHLOX DIVARICATA

DORONICUM

VERONICA BLUE

ANTHEMIS

IBERIS SNOWFLAKE

THALICTRUM 'LAVENDER MIST'

PHLOX DECUSSATA WHITE

LILY 'SUNSTAR'

LINUM PERENNE

ANTHEMIS

IBERIS SNOWFLAKE

DAFFODILS FOLLOWED BY BACHELORS BUTTONS

LILY 'SUNSTAR'

IBERIS

LILY 'THUNDERBOLT'

DELPHINIUM CHINENSE

DOUBLE SHASTA DAISY

DWARF MARIGOLDS

PLAN FOR A PERENNIAL GARDEN FEATURING

LILY 'PAPRIKA'

ANCHUSA DROPMORE BLUE

WHITE PEACHBELLS

DORONICUM

HELENIUM

DAFFODILS FOLLOWED BY BLUE SALVIA

PHLOX DIVARICATA

LILIES

LILY 'DESTINY'

ASTER

CORAL BELLS

Lilies, being upright growers, may be interplanted with perennials of moderate height in a mixed herbaceous border.

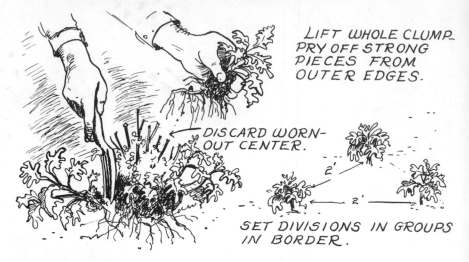

LIFT WHOLE CLUMP.
PRY OFF STRONG
PIECES FROM
OUTER EDGES.

DISCARD WORN-
OUT CENTER.

SET DIVISIONS IN GROUPS
IN BORDER.

Do not let perennials "run out" through overcrowding.

and so a combination of buying some materials locally and other items by mail is often the best solution.

By whatever method the plants are obtained, unless they can be planted immediately, they should be "heeled in"—temporarily planted —sufficiently deep to cover the roots, in a shady place where they can be kept well watered. Any plants that are tied in bundles should be separated, and the roots, if long, trimmed back a bit. It is well to have in any such temporary bed a generous amount of peatmoss.

Growing from seed is entirely practical with many species of hardy perennials. No special equipment is required. In sections where winters are severe, especially where there is likely to be alternate thawing and hard freezing, a coldframe will be helpful; but some of the most desirable perennials, such as day-lilies, heuchera, arabis, and rudbeckia, may be grown even without a frame.

The spacing for perennials in the border varies considerably. Some at maturity are quite large, with a spread of 2 feet or more; others require only a few inches. Some reach a height of 4, 5, or even 6 feet; others scarcely that many inches. Under favorable conditions of soil and climate, they attain much greater size than where soil, and exposure, are less favorable. The beginner is likely to make some mistakes in spacing—but these will be fewer if he takes the trouble to prepare a good-sized planting plan on a piece of heavy paper, and then marks this off, roughly to scale, on the prepared surface of the bed *before he begins planting.*

OFF TO A GOOD START

As is the case in attaining success with trees and shrubs, so in growing annuals, biennials, and bulbs, final results depend quite as much upon what is done *before* planting as upon good culture afterward. No amount of dosing the soil with high-pressure fertilizers during the summer will make up for lack of really thorough preparation of beds and borders before a seed is sown or a plant set out.

Preparation. As early in the spring as the frost is out, and soil can be dug without a tendency to stick together in lumps that do not easily break apart, operations are begun. If coarse manure, rough compost, seaweed, or any similar bulky material is being used it is better to spread this on the surface and dig it under. Personally we much prefer a wide digging fork to a spade or a shovel for this job, but some gardeners do not.

Soils containing a considerable amount of clay should not be dug while wet, otherwise they may form bricklike clods that do not break up and disintegrate for weeks. Such soils are much benefited by the addition of any material that helps to make them more porous (see Chapter 2).

The depth to which the soil should be dug depends upon its character. If it is a shallow soil, the gardener should aim to go an inch or two deeper each time it is dug, turning some of the raw subsoil up to the surface.

After this initial digging it may be well, if a rainy spell ensues, to wait and let the area dry for a few days before proceeding with the final preparations.

In sowing flower or vegetable seeds where plants are to grow, resist the temptation to sow the entire contents of a packet in the area available. Every surplus plant is a *weed,* and must later be removed. Otherwise the result will be a tangle of weak, struggling seedlings, none of which can properly mature. The gardener can save himself a lot of tedious, back-breaking work by having the will power to throw some seed away!

Even with carefully controlled sowing there is the need to remove many seedlings, and the earlier this is done (after the second true leaf develops) the better.

After thinning, it is helpful—unless the soil is very rich—to give a light application of an organic-base fertilizer (page 90) supplemented, if soil is at all dry, by a thorough watering with a mist nozzle spray (page 308) that will not beat down the remaining seedlings.

Setting out plants. Many gardeners these days procure seedling plants from local garden centers instead of attempting to grow their own. The plant breeders have achieved remarkable success in developing varieties of favorite annuals that come into flower at an early age on dwarf plants.

When these are grown in individual peat pots, all the purchaser need do is to set them out pot-and-all, spaced at the recommended distances apart.

If plants are growing in flats or "trays" they should be carefully separated by cutting between them with a knife so that, in removing them, they may be lifted out with the least possible injury to the roots. Transplanting or setting out—especially in very sunny or windy weather—is best done late in the afternoon. They should, however, be set out as soon as possible, for they have been growing under ideal conditions, and will quickly show the effect of the slightest neglect. After setting each in a generous hole, the soil is filled in around the roots and made very firm, leaving a slight saucer-shaped indentation to hold water. After setting, the plants are watered carefully so that the crowns are not inundated or covered with wet soil. Protection from hot sun or wind for a few days is most helpful. Berry boxes, Hotkaps, or even folds of newspaper may be used for this purpose.

Dividing and replanting. After two or three years' growth, many perennials will have formed sodlike mats; others will have developed runners with offsets; new plants will have grown up, each with its own roots, but still attached to the parent plant; and still others will form straying, fleshy roots (rhizomes) that send up new growths similar to the original one.

Examples of the first, or mat-forming type are the common, wild white daisy and the hardy garden chrysanthemum. Strawberries and ajuga are typical runner-forming types; while bearded iris and day-lilies are rhizomatous in character.

The division of plants, and their subsequent replanting, is best done when they are dormant; in northern, cold climates, the earlier in spring, the better. Some, such as irises, Oriental poppies, and day-lilies, which go into summer dormancy, are divided when the foliage ceases growth or matures. In warmer sections, replanting may be undertaken at any time when plants are dormant, or at rest.

In taking apart plants to be divided, only strong, healthy new growths should be used. The old centers or crowns (and any diseased parts) are discarded and should be consigned to the bonfire. *Sections to be replanted are kept well separated* in order to prevent their becoming overcrowded. It is better to throw away—or still better to give away—any surplus than to replant too closely.

Peonies, since they present some peculiar problems, may be mentioned specifically here. The herbaceous peony should be planted in open ground in full sun and where there can be no competition from the roots of trees or shrubs. A wind screen at some distance is an advantage if the garden is in a windy area. Light shade thrown by such a screen or by very large trees at a safe distance is not detrimental. Plant roots 3 feet apart in a bed of well-prepared, humusy soil enriched with a complete plant food and with bonemeal. *Well-rotted* manure may be used where it is available. As ample room must be allowed for future root development, the bed should be worked to at least a foot in depth.

Set the crowns 2 inches below the soil surface and fill in around the roots with good garden loam which has *not* been enriched by the addition of fertilizer or manure. Roots will quickly seek the enriched soil below. Firm in with the feet after filling the hole, and water thoroughly. In cold climates a winter mulch is advisable on a newly planted bed, though established peonies are remarkably hardy.

BULBS

A very important feature of flower beds and borders, and one all too often given little attention or even entirely overlooked, is the adequate and imaginative use of hardy bulbs.

When bulbs are mentioned the inexperienced gardener immediately thinks of daffodils, tulips, hyacinths, and crocuses. It is true that these are the ones most extensively used. However, there are many, many others; and some of these, once suitably planted, take care of themselves and gradually establish naturalized colonies.

Moreover, the flowering season of the hardy bulbs is by no means limited to spring. In milder sections where many kinds not hardy in the north may be used, their flowering periods extend pretty much around the year.

Formal beds planted with elaborate color designs of spring-flowering bulbs, once so popular, are now pretty much limited to public parks and gardens, and even there are gradually disappearing. Home gardeners have discovered that a thoughtful selection of several species and varieties, even in very limited quantities, adds immeasurably to both the beauty and interest of the mixed border.

In northern sections the season starts in February or March with snowdrops and winter-aconite and progresses to crocuses, chionodoxas, puschkinias, species tulips, early, medium, and late daffodils, hyacinths, Single Early, Cottage, and Darwin tulips.

In summer there are garden lilies; the hardy amaryllis, *Lycoris squamigera;* fall-blooming crocuses and colchicums; and, last of all, the bright yellow *Sternbergia lutea,* which blooms about the time the dogwood and Virginia creeper leaves are turning red.

For those who do not object to digging and storing in autumn, and replanting in spring, there are as well a whole galaxy of tender, summer-flowering bulbs, corms, and tubers (described at the end of this chapter) to brighten the border from early summer to autumn.

Culture. With plants as varied as those included under the general designation of hardy "bulbs" it is not possible in a general-purpose book

Flower borders along paths or roads are best kept as simple as possible. Here a planting of tulips lends spring color until the roses behind them take over, when the bulbs are overplanted with low annuals. Tulip blossoms and stems are removed after bloom but foliage, hidden by the annuals, is left to mature.

such as this to give specific cultural directions. The gardener may keep in mind, however, that most of the true bulbs (and there are many more commonly called "bulbs" (that are really corms or tubers) send down very deep roots. In some species the roots are permanent, in others they die off (as does the foliage) and the bulb goes completely dormant. Typical of these last are the so-called Dutch bulbs—tulips, hyacinths, daffodils, and others (none of which, incidentally, originated in Holland).

Because of the deep roots, and the rapidity with which these develop once growth starts, it is important for best results that bulbs have a very deep, friable, and well-drained soil. Such a soil is important too in getting them down to the full depth they should go when they are planted. If they are to be planted 4, 6, or 8 inches deep, the measurement should be *from the top of the bulb to the surface.* A Slim Jim bulb-planting trowel makes the job easier.

*Daffodils, requiring little care and remaining indefinitely, are ideal for a wood-
land setting. Flowering tree in background is Magnolia stellata.*

For summer-long color in a shaded location nothing surpasses tuberous begonias. The range of color is remarkable, and the blooms large and elegantly formed. Available in trailing forms as well as in the usual type, shown here.

Any garden border prepared according to the directions given on page 87 will be suitable. Our own experience, however, is that most bulbs seem to respond especially well to a generous application of bonemeal (the coarse ground, if obtainable) and so we add that when getting any area ready for bulbs. Most hardy species will benefit by an application of complete fertilizer cultivated in at the first sign of renewed growth in the spring.

The mistake most commonly made in the culture of bulbs, especially where they are grown in a mixed border, is to cut off the foliage before it has thoroughly "ripened," as indicated by its losing color and beginning to shrivel. The foliage of daffodils and similar species can be twisted or plaited and turned under, or may be fastened together with Twistems or other plant ties to get it out of the way and make it less conspicuous. The surest and easiest method, however, is to plant them just back of perennials that make spreading, early foliage growth, such as mertensia, myosotis, *Phlox divaricata,* stokesia, Oriental poppies, Shasta daisies, and lupines, or to set pot-grown annuals among and in front of them.

Replanting hardy bulbs. As previously mentioned there comes a time in the growth of most hardy bulbs when they begin to overcrowd and require digging and replanting. When this stage is reached the job should be attended to without delay. Otherwise the result will be not merely fewer and inferior flowers, but inferior bulbs to be replanted.

Most of the spring-flowering bulbs should be taken up as soon as the foliage dies down completely, *but while it is still attached.* Otherwise bulbs are difficult to locate and some may be lost. Also, if left in the ground too long, new roots (especially of daffodils) may have started and will be injured or destroyed.

After being dug, the bulbs are dried off, preferably in a cool place under cover, spread out in flats so that air can reach them freely. After drying, store in bags or boxes, away from direct sunshine, and safe from rodents, until time for replanting in autumn. Daffodils, being poisonous, are safe from the attacks of rodents. As they start new root growth early it is quite all right to replant these as soon as they have been pulled apart, if this is more convenient than to dry and store them.

TENDER BULBS

Overwintering. Tender bulbs, corms, and tubers such as dahlias, ismenes, gladiolus, tigridias, tuberous begonias, and such half-hardy subjects as montbretias, callas, etc., are taken up in fall as soon as the foliage has been touched by frost, or even before in sections where the first frost may be a "black" or hard, killing one. They are spread out in an airy, frost-free place to allow the tops to dry up somewhat before being cut off. After a week or two tops are removed and bulbs or corms cleaned of loose soil and packed, *carefully labeled,* in mesh bags, crates, or boxes.

They should be kept in a cool, frost-free atmosphere, away from too much heat. Where this is not possible, it is best to pack them in *slightly* moist peatmoss. They should be examined every month or so to make sure they are not drying out or rotting.

Most tender bulbs, corms, and tubers—such as ismenes, dahlias, cannas, and gladiolus—may be kept at comparatively low temperatures —35 to 50 degrees; but the very tender or tropical ones such as tuberous begonias and gloxinias are safer at 60 degrees, and some of the really tropical subjects, like caladiums, are safer at around 70 degrees. None should ever be allowed to get dry enough to shrivel.

Spring planting of most tender bulbs can be done directly in the border, after the soil has warmed up in late spring.

The very tender tropicals, like tuberous begonias, gloxinias, and caladiums, are started indoors in flats of peatmoss or in pots of rich, fibrous soil, and set outdoors in the beds where they are to grow in early summer after warm weather is established.

SOME TULIPS AND DAFFODILS

In a general-purpose book such as this, it is not possible to go into much detail concerning individual varieties of the various plants mentioned. With some of them, however, there are such marked differences as to time of flowering, size, and form, that these factors should be emphasized in order to guide the gardener who is really trying to get the most effective results from his time and effort.

Tulips are a case in point. By judicious selection they may be enjoyed for some six to eight weeks instead of for the usual two or three when the large-flowering late tulips, displayed in huge color cuts in sensational advertising, are the only type planted. Few gardeners, even some with considerable experience, realize that many of the species and species hybrid tulips bloom with, or even before such early shrubs as forsythia. These little fellows *remain* in flower two or three times as long as the May-flowering types.

To get a long succession of early spring color from tulips, start with some of the species and species hybrids such as Gaiety, Vivaldi, and the other Kaufmanniana hybrids, all very early, Dasystemon, Clusiana, Scarlet Elegance, and Praestans.

Following these come such varieties as Red Emperor (a very early hybrid which in a comparatively few years has become the most popular tulip in the world) and its companion, White Emperor; the Single Earlies like De Wet, Pink Beauty, and Rising Sun, many of which are delightfully fragrant; and the Double Earlies—Peach Blossom, Mareschal Niel, Murillo Maximus, and others.

In May-flowering, the first to bloom are the graceful Cottage and Lily-flowered forms such as Rosy Wings, Golden Duchess, Queen of Sheba, and White Triumph.

To wind up the tulip season come the Darwins and Breeders, typified by Clara Butt, Garden Magic, and Dom Pedro.

Daffodils. As is the case with tulips, so with daffodils; the period of bloom in most gardens is only half as long as it well might be. The gardener should take the trouble to procure a few bulbs of such tough and early-flowering varieties as February Gold and March Sunshine; such small-flowered gems as W. P. Milner, Moonshine, and Thalia; and a few not-too-double doubles like Cheerfulness and Golden Cheerfulness or Snowball. In addition he will have some of the usual "giant" varieties pushed in the catalogs, those seen in every bulb garden. More unusual varieties are of far greater interest, however. During the last few years a great many "breaks" have occurred in the daffodil family—bunch-flowered types, multicolored blooms, jonquil hybrids, and the like. The most startling are the many pink, rose, or apricot trumpets with white or cream perianths. These make real conversation pieces.

(For a discussion of forcing spring-flowering bulbs in pots for winter bloom indoors, see the closing pages of Chapter 7.)

HERBS AND FRAGRANT FLOWERS

Herbs are easy to grow, useful in the cuisine and for potpourris and sachets, and are always of special interest to visitors as well as to the feminine gardener.

Knot gardens or geometrically designed beds with paths running through them are the traditional way to plant and grow herbs. Full sun is a *must* and a moderately rich, rather sandy soil with a pH which is neutral or a little above suits most herbs.

In the old-fashioned knot garden, first popular in the Middle Ages, "ropes" of carefully planted and pruned herbs weave intricate patterns or knots. Low-growing plants such as dwarf lavender, germander, and santolina are used in this way, as are those culinary herbs that are not harmed by severe clipping.

The kitchen or culinary herb garden contains such perennials as sage, thyme, pot marjoram, chives, rosemary, mints, and tarragon; with annuals and biennials such as sweet marjoram, summer savory, borage, and parsley (see list, Appendix). An attractive evergreen edging plant for the

HERB GARDEN

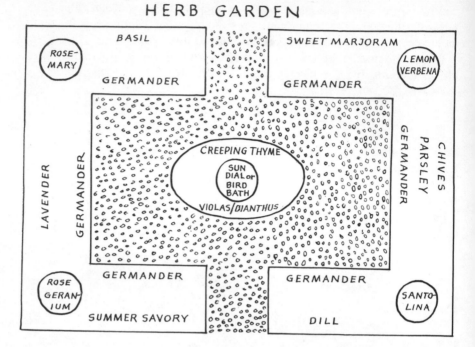

One plan for an herb garden, with suggested plantings.

beds is teucrium or germander, with small glossy leaves. It can be trimmed or sheared to the desired height.

The fragrant herb garden may feature true lavender, *Nepeta mussini,* scented geraniums, violas, and even lilies (see lists of Fragrant Plants in Appendix).

FRAGRANT GARDENS

Many gardeners not particularly interested in herbs enjoy specializing in fragrant flowers.

In addition to roses and lilies such perennials may be featured as dianthus, wallflowers, *Daphne cneorum, Datura arborea,* hostas, monarda, and buddleia (see list, Appendix).

Among the shrubs, clethra, English hawthorn, witch-hazel, the jasmines and magnolias are but a few (see list, Appendix).

Fragrant bulbs include many of the Single Early tulips, jonquil hybrid daffodils, hyacinths, and lily-of-the-valley.

Some summer bulbs such as ismenes (*Hymenocallis*), tuberoses, galtonia, and freesias are delightfully scented (see Appendix).

Fragrant annuals are numerous, but among the best known are sweet alyssum, candytuft, nasturtiums, petunias, nicotianas, stocks, and mignonette.

A garden or border with night fragrance, planted near the terrace, is a delight. Here nicotianas, petunias, moonflowers, lilies, and garden phlox give off delightful evening scents. Such a garden may be designed entirely in white and green for eye appeal after dusk as well as for fragrance.

... from the rock as if by magic grown ...
JOHN WILLIAM BURGON

Flower in the crannied wall—
ALFRED, LORD TENNYSON

CHAPTER 12

Rock, Bank, and Wall Gardens

The general types of gardens discussed in the preceding chapter are those most commonly used. There are, however, several other specialized types which are often employed, either because a location lends itself to the cultivation of certain kinds of plants or because the owner is particularly interested in some one group of plants.

Such gardens have three distinct advantages. In the first place they make it possible to feature plants that do not succeed under ordinary conditions, and in the second, these can be used to convert areas that would otherwise be problem locations, if not actual eyesores, into unique beauty spots. Not infrequently such special gardens become the highlights of the entire landscape planting, commanding more attention and admiration than any other feature. In the third place, such gardens make it possible to display, in a way that allows their full beauty to be enjoyed, many plants which in any ordinary garden would be almost completely lost.

Typical of such specialized plantings are rock, bank, and wall gardens, and water, pool, and stream gardens. This chapter deals only with the first three of these.

THE ROCK GARDEN

First of all, the prospective builder of a rock garden should be forewarned that it must be so placed and constructed as to appear to blend in *naturally* with its surroundings. Otherwise it is almost certain to be unpleasantly conspicuous. A heap of stones and soil piled up in an open space is about as distressing a sight both esthetically and horticulturally as can well be imagined, no matter how fine a collection of plants may

Often money can be saved and more pleasing and original results achieved by tailoring the house to fit the building site instead of doing it the other way around. Here the use of imagination saved a mint of money.

be wedged in the cracks. Such monstrosities are occasionally to be seen, but they are becoming rare as gardeners learn more of good design.

The immediate surroundings of the rock garden contribute quite as much to its success, as a pleasing feature of the landscape, as the plant material grown in it. A rock garden is essentially a *natural* garden; and the more its location, and the plants and trees adjacent to it, can create the effect of its having always been there the more it will add to the over-all beauty of the scene of which it is a part.

A few—even two or three—informal and picturesque evergreens such as a gnarled pine, a hemlock, juniper, or larch; a white birch, a willow, weeping cherry, a dogwood or two will accomplish wonders in blending the rock garden into the general landscape.

Location. While a rock garden may be built almost anywhere (we have seen a very successful one on the roof of a New York skyscraper) it is certain to be easier to construct it and to maintain its plants in vigorous health if certain conditions can be assured to start with.

The first of these is good drainage. While many plants commonly designated as rock plants like plenty of moisture about their roots during their periods of early growth and flowering, they do not tolerate constantly wet soil such as is favored by bog or even wet woodland plants. In fact, during most of the year many of them exist in almost desert dry conditions. Therefore, in locating the rock garden, a slight elevation or a mound or steep slope, makes a better site than a low, poorly drained area.

It is also desirable to place the rock garden in a somewhat sheltered location. While many creeping and low-growing rock plants—such as saxifrages, thymes, and sempervivums—withstand even heavy gales without injury, there are equally desirable plants—such as anemones, aquilegias, primulas, and species narcissi—which, while the foliage itself may be low-growing, thrust their flower stems or spikes proudly aloft. These, without some protection, may be twisted and broken in wind and rain.

Shelter may be provided by a background of low evergreens and shrubs, care being taken to select those that are of natural, informal habits of growth and bearing small, inconspicuous flowers, if any. Some appropriate evergreens are:

False cypress (*Chamaecyparis*): Dwarf Hinoki; Thread Sawara; Fernspray Hinoki; Plume Sawara.
Red-cedar (*Juniperus*): Koster; Silver; Goldtip; Oldfield; Common.
Juniper: Andorra; Tamarix Savin; Sargent; Hill Japanese; Waukegan; Meyer; Coffin; Blue Coast.
Pine (*Pinus*): Swiss Stone; Waterer.
Spruce (*Picea*): Pygmy; Dwarf Alberta; Weeping Blue.
Hemlock (*Tsuga*): Japanese; Sargent's Weeping.

Rocky or stony areas in shaded locations often present a special problem. In heavy shade it is advisable to concentrate on plants that bloom early, before tree foliage matures, and they should be distributed in groups or colonies which appear natural and unstudied.

Yew (*Taxus*): Spreading Japanese; Dwarf Japanese; Intermedia; Brown's; Hicks'; Upright Japanese.

Good background shrubs include: *Abelia grandiflora; Buxus* (Box), in variety.

Broad-leaved evergreens: *Cotoneaster,* in variety; *Ilex* (Holly); *crenata, opaca,* and others; *Kalmia latifolia* (Laurel); *Leucothoë catesbaei; Mahonia aquifolium* (Holly-grape); *Pyracantha coccinea* (Firethorn).

Deciduous shrubs and small trees: *Callicarpa dichotoma; Calycanthus floridus; Clethra alnifolia* (Sweet Pepperbush); *Cornus florida,* (Dogwood) *kousa; Hamamelis virginiana* (Witch-hazel); *Jasminum nudiflorum; Malus,* in variety (Flowering Crab); *Prunus,* in variety (Flowering Cherry); *Stewartia ovata; Viburnums,* in variety.

Equally important protection can be afforded by so planning the rock garden area that it slopes to the south or southeast. To look at all natural it should never be built in the form of a mound, with its highest point at the center. It should occupy an irregular slope, natural in appearance; or it may include a natural outcropping of shelf rock. Either of these, backed by the shrub planting suggested, makes it possible to grow a much greater variety of plants, and also to keep them all healthier and happier than would otherwise be possible.

While most plants ordinarily used in the rock garden are sun-loving, others enjoy partial shade; so it is desirable to have part of the area receive high shade to accommodate subjects such as terrestrial orchids,

Even on a moderate-sized place a rock garden makes possible the growing of many intriguing plants; but to be attractive, it must have a really natural appearance.

hardy cyclamens, ferns, ginger, galax, and other plants of the open woods
—trailing arbutus, pipsissewa, hepaticas, bloodroot, twin-flower, trout-
lilies, trilliums, European ginger. Many of these require more year-round
moisture than sun-loving rock plants but have a shy charm which makes
it well worthwhile to cater to their needs.

First a Plan. The location for the rock garden having been selected,
the next step is construction. It is advisable to have this begin on paper,
for changes are sure to be made as the plan is developed. Several of
the principles to be followed are illustrated in the accompanying sketches.

First of all it must be kept in mind that a rock garden is *three dimensional.* Irregularly alternating and nicely balanced elevations and depres-
sions are vital elements in its design.

This same principle of planned irregularity applies also to the ground
plan of the rock garden if it is to blend into its background and surroundings without any distinctly definite boundaries. Where ground space is
limited, greater height—and therefore more room for planting—may be
attained by digging out part of the area to form paths and steps, the soil
removed being used to build up the slopes, as indicated by the accompanying sketch.

To attain these ends it may be necessary to sketch and re-sketch the
plan several times—not a difficult task on paper, but a truly herculean
one if attempted in actual construction.

Construction. Once the location of the rock garden and the area to be

*In building the rock garden one must keep in mind that it is three dimensional.
It must have height as well as length and depth.*

occupied by it have been decided upon the next step is to assemble the materials to be used in building it.

Such a garden implies the use of rocks, but the fact that it is to be a *garden* must never be lost sight of. Hence the first consideration must be the soil to be used.

Most alpines and other plants suited to the sunny rock garden require excellent drainage, but also a soil that retains moisture well after surplus water has drained off. Both heavy clay soils and light sandy soils are unsuited for this purpose. Alpine plants growing in the wild are usually found in what might be termed a shaly soil—one in which rock debris, in various degrees of decomposition, is present together with a considerable amount of organic matter. A satisfactory mixture for the purpose consists of:

> 1 part gritty, coarse sand
> 1 part stone chips, or very coarse gravel
> 1 part peatmoss (or screened leafmold)
> 2 parts sifted compost or
> 1 part garden loam and 1 part old, spent manure

To this should be added, for lime-loving plants such as cyclamen, edelweiss, gentians, dianthus, alpine primulas, and wallflowers, a generous sprinkling of ground raw limestone. If you are planting peat or acid-lovers such as our native woodland wildlings, acid peatmoss and well-rotted acid leafmold should be used in the mixture. It is well to have a separate area for the lime-lovers.

Loam or compost should be free of weed seeds. The best way to assure this is to treat it with one of the pre-emergence weed seed destroyers before adding it to the mixture. This should be done well in advance.

The Rocks. Both the appearance of the rock garden and the way plants grow in it depend much upon the type of stone used. If native rocks must be employed, there may be little choice in the matter, except to select, as far as possible, flat stones of irregular shapes and rough surfaces rather than rounded, smooth ones. The more absorbent the character of the rock, the better. Limestone and tuffa are the best in this respect, and granite the worst. Porous sandstone and natural outcroppings of ledge rock, cracked and split by erosion to admit pockets of soil and space for root-runs for the plants are also satisfactory. Round fieldstone boulders and cut granite should never be used, as they are unsuited both in appearance and texture.

If a natural ledge is not present, long, rather flat but irregular pieces may be laid and partially buried to create the effect of a natural ledge, especially if some with mosses or lichens growing upon them can be obtained. Wide variation in size of the individual pieces is desirable.

Building. With the materials assembled, the actual construction is begun. First step, under average conditions, is to mark out the area, and

When beginning construction, place a number of the largest stones first, to determine the general design. Avoid setting in regular rows, as at left above.

excavate it to a depth of a foot or so. Some of the larger stones can be used around the perimeter, but many should be saved for placement higher up or even near the top; otherwise the result will look like a poor attempt at masonry.

After the ground layer or foundation stones are in place—buried deep enough so that they do not *look* like foundation stones but assume as natural an appearance as possible—"fill" soil is placed in back of them. Then

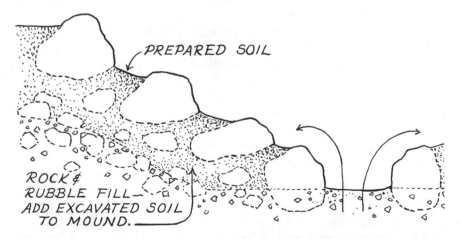

In placing the larger stones in a rock garden, a third to a half of each is covered with soil, and upper surfaces are sloped back to carry water into the soil.

If the garden is built on a slight slope, the effect of height may be considerably increased by using steps. If each is sloped slightly down *at the back, the effect of height is increased.*

the next tier of rocks is added, with the special soil mixture placed under and around these in deep pockets which run back to the fill. Most of the stones should be placed so that their surfaces slope slightly *down* into the soil behind them. Then any water striking their surfaces will drain back into the soil and be conserved for future use by the deep-penetrating roots of the plants, some of which are many, many times as long as the plants are high.

As the work proceeds, the greatest care must be taken to keep the architectural effect *irregular*. This applies not only to the stones themselves but to the contours which are being built up around them. If there can be a series of miniature ridges and valleys, with a general exposure to the south, and here and there a small level area, the desired informality will be achieved; and *also* the ideal exposure and protection for the plants that are to occupy them.

The top of the rock garden should not run up to a peak, but terminate in a series of fairly flat areas or ledges at different levels.

SELECTING THE PLANTS

In deciding what is to be grown in the rock garden, the all important matter of *scale* is most vital. A few plants which are too large, or which in a few years may grow too large, can spoil the whole effect. *The smaller the rock garden is, the more meticulously must this matter of scale be worked out and adhered to.*

Lists of plants especially suited to various types of rock gardens are to be found in Appendix. Some of these are available wherever plants are sold; others are obtainable only from firms which specialize in plants of this type (see Appendix for suggested firms). Anyone who seriously considers attempting a fair-sized rock garden should by all means visit such an establishment, or a botanical garden where rock plants are featured. The visits should preferably be made quite early in the spring as that is when most rock plants flower. Such an inspection will give the prospective rock gardener a much more definite idea of what he can grow successfully on his terrain, and of the appearance and merits of the different species and varieties than he can possibly glean from catalogs.

A great many alpine and other rock plants may easily be grown from seed. This means some delay. However it not only cuts down the expense

Many plants ordinarily grown in level beds readily adapt themselves to wall conditions. Heuchera, iberis, and aquilegia are examples. It is interesting to experiment.

involved, but provides plants that can be transferred to their permanent locations with minimum shock and under the most favorable conditions.

Culture. The rock garden differs from most other gardens in one important way. It is, in general, desirable to keep the plants within it *small* rather than to encourage them to reach maximum size. This begins with the selection of species and varieties to be planted. It is continued by doing more than the ordinary amount of pruning and cutting back; and by withholding nitrogenous and other plant foods that encourage extra-strong vegetative growth. This does not mean neglecting them.

Keep dead and old wood cut out of all plants which make woody, permanent stems or branches. Recover roots whenever soil is washed away from them or they are bared by frost action or extra-heavy rains. A top dressing made up of one part each of coarse sand, compost, and peatmoss answers for most plants. Where an acid soil is required, add acid leafmold (from beneath evergreens or oaks). For lime-lovers, add ground limestone—enough to thoroughly powder the surface of the soil. Rake in lightly. Wood ashes, scattered and raked in like limestone, may also be used for lime-loving plants. Do not apply too heavy a dose at one time as it may cake and form a crust fatal to the small plants.

Mulching conserves moisture, especially near the surface, and it also helps to keep down the temperature of the surface soil—a result greatly appreciated by the true alpines. For this type of plant material, a mulch of stone chips keeps down weeds, conserves moisture, keeps the soil cool, and adds to the permanent stone-chip content of the soil.

For partly shaded areas where small woodland wildlings are grown, a mulch of peatmoss, acid leafmold, or a mixture of the two is beneficial.

Watering. The rock garden, even when constructed with soil that is high in its capacity to absorb and hold water, is so exposed to wind and sun that it has a tendency to dry out quickly. While many rock plants are toughies that withstand drought, they do better if not subjected to extreme conditions in this direction. An occasional very thorough soaking in dry periods will be much appreciated by the plants. They well repay the extra work when their flowering season recurs.

Winter care of the rock garden involves not so much protecting the plants from cold—most of them are extra hardy—as it does preventing repeated freezing and thawing, and toward spring, the too early renewal of growth. Where the garden is well sheltered and exposed to full sun from mid-winter on, use a cover of evergreen boughs, marsh hay, or pine needles to keep the plants from getting their pretty little pink noses nipped prematurely.

THE BANK GARDEN

The "bank" garden may be merely a variation of the rock garden in which advantage is taken of an existing steep slope or bank or a "problem area" too rough or too steep to be converted into lawn or flower border. A planting of shrubs or low evergreens or of trailing roses or vines would take the curse off it; but the use of a little imagination and ingenuity and a modest collection of rock plants adapted to dry, sunny conditions, may convert it into one of the show spots of the home grounds.

Here a few large rocks, if available, may be used as the setting for a planting of azaleas and other flowering shrubs, with a background of suitable evergreens. Smaller stones and low-growing, spreading rock plants form the foreground.

THE WALL GARDEN

A great many of the rock plants may be enjoyed without building a real rock garden by growing them in a wall.

If it is a retaining wall—that is one built against a bank—the problem is a very simple one, provided the proper type of rocks are available.

In the construction of such a wall, the best effect is achieved when the stones are of the type recommended for the rock garden; rough, varying in size, and porous; preferably with some large ones that may be run well back into the soil behind the wall to give it increased stability (see sketch). Faced, cut stone, cobble stones, and large, rounded boulders are *not* suited to this type of wall as they are completely out of character with the plants to be grown.

The wall, anchored on a solid foundation, should slope back into the bank at a considerable angle, both for stability and the better to display the plants growing in it. The more robust species should be given places near the bottom, with trailing, tufted, and rosette-foliaged types above. Many flowers show off to surprising advantage in a wall garden. For instance, we discovered quite by accident how stunning coral bells (heuchera) are in such a location, the rather tall stems turning sharply upright from the rosettes of glossy leaves and giving somewhat the effect of miniature Roman candles exploding. These and short-spurred columbines, including our native eastern species, also provide irresistible targets for humming birds. Mosses, ferns, sempervivums, creeping phloxes, arabis, iberis, rock garden dianthus, *Campanula muralis,* and many more flourish in such a situation (see list in Appendix).

The free-standing, double-faced wall is another possibility. This can be used to wall in a patio, rose or herb garden, or other area where greater protection or privacy is desired within.

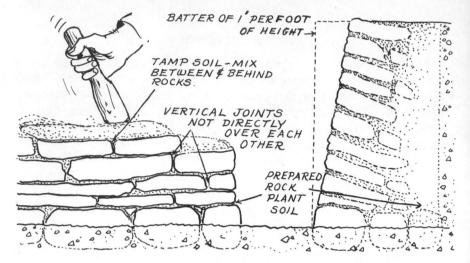

On small places where a steep slope presents a problem, often a rock-garden effect may be achieved by employing a retaining wall for planting. The more it can be sloped back the better.

Such a wall is best built 18 to 24 inches wide—or even wider where large stones are available—with a trench along the top 8 to 12 inches in depth. Plants set in deep soil pockets in the sides of the wall should not be planted too close together. The trench on top, if desired, may be filled with fibrous soil and used for a succession of flowers such as low-

The wall garden should never be overplanted. The most pleasing effect results when most of the stonework is visible.

growing, spring-flowering bulbs, followed by dwarf dahlias or fuchsias. Dwarf chrysanthemums may be set in for fall; or, if in semishade, tuberous begonias will continue to bloom from early summer to frost.

The intelligent homeowner is quick to take advantage of any unusual terrain on his property and to find some exciting and interesting solution for such a problem spot instead of letting the contractor bulldoze a bank down to the usual dead level, cover or remove natural outcroppings of rock, or otherwise destroy areas which may, with a little imagination, study, and labor, be converted into unique, colorful gardens of lasting beauty.

Some of the conditions which provide natural settings for rock, wall, or bank gardens which we have seen are: a large outcropping of ledge rock, split and checked by erosion; an old, abandoned quarry; the ruined cellar hole of a house; the foundation of a bank barn with the rock work partially intact.

Fringed pool,
Ferned grot—
The veriest school
of Peace; . . .
My Garden by
THOMAS EDWARD BROWN

CHAPTER 13

Pools, Streams, and Water Gardens

Without question there is no single feature in the home landscape that is quite so effective, in proportion to the space which it occupies, as a pool, a stream, or a water garden. Yet the number of places where any of these is to be found is very small.*

At our former home we had a steep, rocky slope that lent itself perfectly to the making of a miniature waterfall, fed by a little stream that trickled down, over, and through rough rocks to an ivy-bordered pool. The result was so natural in appearance that most visitors had to be "shown" before being convinced that it was not natural. After seeing rose gardens, bulb plantings, flower borders, vegetable garden, and whatever else they happened to find most interesting, it would be at this spot that visitors always congregated to rest in the shade and enjoy the sound and sight of water in motion.

At our present home, where we are perched above a tidewater river and overlook a fair-sized salt pond (it would be called a lake anywhere but on Cape Cod) our more intimate, man-made stream and pool, though planned, has been left until other projects have been completed.

To return, however, from our own problems to those of our readers, we would strongly urge that, before attempting to install any water feature of his own, the gardener first visit a public park, botanical garden, or the garden of a friend who has developed water features, where he can get

---

* The swimming pool will not be included in this discussion. A little imagination in planning the location of the pool, and the judicious use of shrubbery and other plant material as screening around the pool, can do much to make it fit into the over-all design. On a swimming pool project it is usually best to consult an expert.

ideas and study the mechanics involved in the construction of a pool or stream. The building of a *formal* pool or a damlike waterfall is comparatively simple. To get a really natural effect, however, though far more charming if successful, requires much more planning and skill.

Design is all-important in building a pool, a stream, or a bog or water garden. Where cement must be used—and in most instances it has to be —you can't make changes once it has begun to set. Usually it saves time in the end, as well as assuring much more satisfactory results, if one constructs in advance a small scale model of the project that is contemplated. Plasticine and small stones and stone chips of various sizes are the chief materials required. These, insofar as is feasible, should resemble in shape and character the rocks that will actually be used. Clippings from evergreens such as junipers, box, or box-leaved ilex may be used to give the effect of plantings. Bare twigs give the effect of deciduous trees in winter.

When it comes to the real construction, the result will by no means be an actual replica of the model; but the model will have served its purpose by saving many mistakes and much more time than was required to make it.

Location. The pool must be planned as an integral part of the general landscape scheme. Careful consideration should be given to the best location for the projected pool and the best *type* of pool for that location.

A lily pool, which requires full sun, is the best choice for grounds with few trees. A natural woodland pool, its outlet forming a wet area for bog plants is indicated on a property well shaded by large trees. On the small property it may be placed close to one of the boundary lines, with suitable evergreens or shrubs behind it. Here it may be the focal point of a private family retreat with the benefit of shifting shade.

One of the most attractive features of a pool may be its service as a mirror for the sky and for nearby plant material. This should always be taken into consideration in planning its location—another decided advantage, on a small property, in placing it as suggested above.

Often a pool and a stream may be combined without a great deal more expense and work than would be required for either alone. Each enhances the effect of the other, and the combination adds greatly to the illusion of naturalness.

Construction. Fortunately for those who like to do their own construction jobs about the place, the making of a small stream or pool has been very much simplified by the advent of heavy plastic sheeting such as Visqueen, obtainable at any dealer in building supplies. If a layer of this tough but pliant material is placed over the foundation layer of cement— troweled smooth of course—before the surface or finish layer is put on, the result is a sort of sandwich, leakproof even though cracks may develop in the concrete.

Every homeowner who likes to be his own jack-of-all-trades should

A little ingenuity can help work wonders. Here it converted a weed-choked drainage ditch, long used as a dumping spot for tin cans and similar refuse, into a traffic-stopping beauty spot.

A pool of water, no matter how large or how small, always becomes the mirrorlike center of interest in any garden scene. Its design and construction, however, should be in keeping with its surroundings. Skillfully placed, as in this garden, it adds greatly to the apparent length and depth of its surroundings.

The smaller-flowered hardy water-lilies are best with naturalistic surroundings. Two thirds of the water surface should be unencumbered by foliage of any sort.

The dramatic, gorgeously colored, tender species make wonderful conversation pieces.

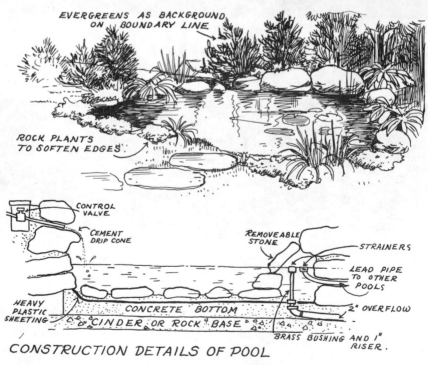

EVERGREENS AS BACKGROUND ON BOUNDARY LINE

ROCK PLANTS TO SOFTEN EDGES

CONTROL VALVE

CEMENT DRIP CONE

REMOVEABLE STONE

STRAINERS

LEAD PIPE TO OTHER POOLS

HEAVY PLASTIC SHEETING

CONCRETE BOTTOM

CINDER OR ROCK BASE

2" OVERFLOW

BRASS BUSHING AND 1" RISER.

CONSTRUCTION DETAILS OF POOL

A pool, even a very small one, may make one of the most attractive features of the home landscape.

learn to use concrete. Good handbooks on the subject are available. Some of the best are put out by cement companies, and are available where cement is sold, so we do not go into the subject in our limited space here. For small jobs, ready-mixed, concrete—containing the correct proportions of cement, sand, and gravel, and requiring only the addition of water— may be purchased. For any extensive work it is much less expensive to purchase the cement only and get the sand and gravel separately. Any surplus of either of these will be good for many other uses about the place.

Where there is a natural supply of water, and heavy clay soil, it may be possible to do without cement work in making a stream or a pool; but such conditions are seldom to be found. Without them, the best that can be done is to make all construction as inconspicuous as possible, and then to use creeping plants that will camouflage what cannot be concealed. Here are some of the most useful plants for this purpose:

Sun	*Shade*

ANNUALS

Sun	Shade
Mesembryanthemums	*Bellis perennis*
Sedums	Lobelia, dwarf
Sempervivums	Myosotis
Sweet alyssum	Virginia stock
Thunbergia	
Verbena	
Vinca rosea	

PERENNIALS

Sun	Shade
Alyssum saxatile citrinum	*Ajuga reptans*
Ajuga reptans	Arbutus, Trailing
Arabis caucasia	Campanula
Campanula carpatica	Eupatoriums
Cerastium	Ferns, dwarf
Heather	*Hedera helix*
Iberis sempervirens	Heuchera
Iris, dwarf	Hosta
Lamium maculatum	Mertensia
	Mitchella repens
	Phlox divaricata
	Primulas
	Pulmonaria saccharata
	Pulmonaria augustifolia
	Veronicas, Creeping
	Vinca minor
	Violets
	Wild ginger

An artificial stream that looks *artificial is usually a detriment to the landscape. Here the remains of an old stone wall at GrayRock was converted, with a minimum of labor, into a series of small ponds and waterfalls. The volume (controlled by a hidden valve) could be varied from a musical trickle to a rushing freshet. Visitors, to be convinced that the little stream was* not *natural, often had to be shown the pipes and valve.*

Water supply. The commonly held assumption that any water feature in the garden, with the possible exception of a static pool, requires an extraordinary supply of water is quite erroneous. Little more than a trickle is needed to keep a moderate-sized pool replenished and fresh. This same trickle, dripping down the "steps" of a miniature water course, can provide an effect of naturalness and coolness out of all proportion to its size and cost.

The line supplying the water should of course be equipped with a gate valve which permits control of the amount coming through. Then, with a turn of the wrist, the trickle may be converted into a cascading freshet whenever that is desired. A ¾-inch pipe is ample for a fairly vigorous stream.

In cold climates, provision should be made for draining the system during the winter. This means the installation of drain cocks at all low points in the supply line.

THE WATER GARDEN

It is rather difficult to make plain just what the difference is between a pool which contains plants and a water garden. Perhaps it may be helpful to say that in the former it is the pool itself which is the more important while in the latter it is the *plants*—the water being merely an adjunct to their proper culture.

The ideal water garden should have areas of both sun and shade. A small stream supplying it with water may be planted with moisture-loving shrubs like our beautiful native *Clethra alnifolia* or sweet pepperbush; the swamp azalea (*Rhododendron viscosum*); *Ilex verticillata* or winterberry, with its red berries; and *I. glabra* or inkberry, which is evergreen. Nearer the stream such moisture-loving plants as cardinal-flower, foamflower, and gentians may be grown, with a ground cover of myosotis, wild ginger, or cranberry.

In the sunny portion of the pool, pickerel-weed, water arum, pond-lilies, and other water plants are at home (see list, Appendix).

The bog or marsh garden is naturally placed at the pool's outlet, where peaty soil may be provided to hold plenty of moisture. Here water irises, including our native blue flag; Japanese iris; mallows, pitcher plants, adder's tongues; the wild turk's cap lily, *L. superbum;* Jack-in-the-pulpit; marsh-marigolds and violets may be grown in wild profusion (see list, Appendix).

Water gardening is of such a specialized type that anyone planning to go into it at all extensively should procure detailed information either from one of the specialists who supply aquatic plants, or from a book devoted to this subject (see list, Appendix).

Winter care. Except in southern sections of the United States, where low temperatures are not severe enough to form thick ice, it is best to drain pools for the winter months. An alternate ensurance against ice damage to the concrete often used with small bowl-like pools with gently sloping sides is to place a small bundle of corn or sunflower stalks upright in the center. The ice, as it forms and expands, pushes up the sides of the pool, and in at the center. A log or two thrown into the water serves the same purpose. Draining, however, is much safer and more sightly.

Fish. In pools of any size it is customary to have some fish. Naturally they go with water plants. Not only do they lend interest with their color and flashing movements, but they act as scavengers. In an outdoor pool that must be drained for winter, they present the problem of being kept

The tiniest of pools provides a center of interest in any garden; and even a very small trickle of water into it adds to the charm of the pool. Here, in the rock garden at GrayRock, the flow is so small as to be quickly absorbed by the soil around the edge, where moisture-loving plants thrive.

over until spring. They may be kept in an aquarium, but replacement with new stock each spring is not expensive, unless rare species are preferred. In a deep, natural pool where water is not drained, all but tropical varieties live comfortably in the deep water under the ice. Only a bitter winter which freezes the water in the pool to the bottom may destroy them.

I've often wished that I had clear
For life, six hundred pounds a year,
A handsome house to lodge a friend,
A river at my garden's end,
A terrace . . .

ALEXANDER POPE

CHAPTER 14

The Patio Garden, Mobile Gardening, Window Boxes

The dictionary definition of a patio is: "A court or courtyard of a house . . . especially an inner court . . . open to the sky."

The patio garden of today, in the United States at least, may be considerably less formal. Its purpose is as often to form a connecting link between the house and the grounds as it is to shut out the world beyond. In either case the patio becomes a sort of outdoor living room, with the sky for a ceiling and the walls as nearly solid, or as completely open, as the owner desires.

The patio garden most properly goes with a Spanish or other tropical or semitropical type of dwelling. It may of course be adapted to other forms of architecture, but the design and the materials used in building a patio should harmonize with the dwelling to which it is attached—or more accurately (if the design is well thought out) *of which it forms a part.*

Often an L of the house provides two walls of the patio. A free-standing wall, vine-covered fence, or louvered barrier is used as another side and the fourth is left open. Where the patio is used chiefly in summer, its open side should face east or south, never west, unless it is well protected from late sun by large shade trees. Otherwise the broiling rays of late afternoon sun in midsummer would make it too hot and uncomfortable to use during the hours when it is most needed.

In any case, it is desirable to have trees to provide some overhead shade during the warm months. These of course can be planted (or already growing) outside the boundaries of the patio garden itself. Deciduous trees, which do not completely shut out winter sunshine, are preferable to

Here a paved terrace of random slate provides an inviting and comfortable outdoor living area. Noticeable, too, is the very effective but well-masked screening-out of a neighboring property provided by the picket fence (barely visible) and the shrub and evergreen planting in front of it.

evergreens. Fast-growing species such as Chinese or Siberian elm, tulip tree, sycamore, *Paulownia tomentosa* (or Princess tree), *Magnolia soulangeana* (our early-blooming pink or white magnolia), willow, or (in Area IV) mimosa (*Albizzia julibrissin*), or *Zelkova carpinifolia,* which is hardy as far north as New England, will soon grow large enough to begin to provide shade. Maples, though fast-growing, are undesirable because of surface roots which often force up paving, even at some distance from the tree trunk.

Year-round beauty. Even though the patio—except in very warm climates—may be used as an outdoor living room only during the summer months, it should remain attractive through the winter as well, particularly if it forms a part of the vista from a view window. To achieve this end,

A paved porch and a flagstone terrace make a natural transition to the rock outcropping in the foreground. Plants in tubs and containers used against the house may be changed as desired, while terrace and natural rock are skillfully planted with alpines, sempervivums, pinks, and creeping thyme.

dwarf or semidwarf evergreens, of varied winter foliage, broad-leaved evergreen shrubs and vines, and plants like *Pyracantha coccinea lalandi* (Firethorn) and *Cotoneaster microphylla,* which can form effective silhouettes against a wall, are indispensable. Berried shrubs attract birds, an added winter dividend.

Remember that the protection afforded by the house and by the patio walls in effect moves the area at least one zone south of its actual location. As a result, many plants may be grown within the patio walls which might not survive about the grounds in the open. Among these are the less hardy types of box, evergreen azaleas; such semihardy shrubs as *Abelia grandiflora,* nandina, crape-myrtle (Lagerstroemia), and even the hardier camellias. On one of our own well-sheltered terraces we enjoy a collection of half a dozen camellias, including named varieties of both the hardier *C. sasanqua* and the more tender *C. japonica.* These get no protection except a temporary cover of a double sheet of heavy-duty pliofilm when temperatures threaten to go below 10 above zero, which seldom happens on this part of Cape Cod.

What has been said concerning evergreens and shrubs applies also to vines. The wall-clinging sorts such as the various evergreen euonymuses and the deciduous climbing hydrangea, *H. petiolaris,* appreciate the extra protection they get. Many climbers may be kept pruned to form charming traceries against a wall instead of making solid masses of greenery. Fruit trees, especially peaches, apricots, pears, and (in warmer sections) figs are suitable for espaliering. The fun of training and pruning these to the desired patterns is almost as satisfying as the lovely effects they create, silhouetted against a light-colored wall.

All hardy, permanent plants used in the patio are merely the state setting for the many ornamentals that many be grown in pots and tubs or plant boxes, to be enjoyed while they are in flower and then removed to make way for others.

If one has a greenhouse, the display may be practically continuous from the time danger of frost is over until hard freeze in the fall. Even with a coldframe it may commence long before there is any show of color in beds and borders in the open garden.

Many flowers lend themselves particularly to display in this way. Grown in pots in a greenhouse, frame, or the open-garden cutting bed, they may readily be transferred to the patio just before they come into full bloom. If plunged into prepared holes or narrow beds filled with crushed stone or sand and peatmoss, the pots are readily kept moist through the flowering period.

A *"plunging"* border around the edges of a patio makes it possible to maintain a more or less constant succession of blooming plants in pots. Sink these to the rims in gravel, marble chips, or peatmoss, depending on the subjects, exposure, etc.

The large number of flowers well suited to such use include many of the new hybrid lilies, grown in large pots holding several bulbs each. A moderate assortment of varieties provides a succession of bloom over a period of two to three months and the bulbs may be used over again in succeeding years.

Other plants for the patio are forced spring-flowering bulbs and tender summer-flowering species like callas, agapanthus, amarcrinums, nerines, *Lycoris radiata,* and amaryllis. Tuberous begonias and gloxinias are ideal for shady spots, the former giving continuous bloom from May to first frosts.

Hydrangeas, roses, and tender foliage plants in tubs are a great addition if there is man-power to move them. Large nasturtium plants (grown under glass in the north) in handmade pottery containers are colorful and appropriate, and of course for the last blaze of color, chrysanthemums, even after their buds are showing color, can be moved in pots or tubs, or set directly in prepared beds.

WATER FEATURES IN THE PATIO

The ideal place for a small wall or free-standing fountain, a tiny waterfall, or a small pool, is in the patio. Its effectiveness will depend to a very great extent, on the owner's artistic sense in designing and placing it. Resist that temptation to plunk it down in the center of the area, like an old-fashioned fountain in a public square!

Much of the charm of any water feature depends upon sound as well as on motion. The exception of course is the mirror pool, but this properly belongs in a fairly large and formal setting rather than in the outdoor living-room atmosphere of the average patio.

Consider the birds. One of the reasons for having water in the patio garden is that it attracts birds. The small pool on our terrace is used constantly by our feathered tenants from earliest spring until it freezes solid in midwinter. One reason for its great popularity is the shelter afforded on two sides by a large tree and tall-growing, moisture-loving wild shrubs that thrive in the damp soil created by the overflow before it is absorbed by our thirsty, sandy subsoil.

This little pool was not included in our original landscape plan. It just happened. A quantity of mixed concrete, left over from a masonry wall had to be disposed of—but fast! We scooped out a shallow, oval depression with slanting sides, and troweled on a three-inch layer of concrete. Later, this was covered with heavy black plastic, and a second layer finished off the edge and covered the plastic from view. Of course the area was kept covered with wet bags, permitting the concrete to dry out gradually. Around it we planted sedums, small-leaved ivies, and myrtle,

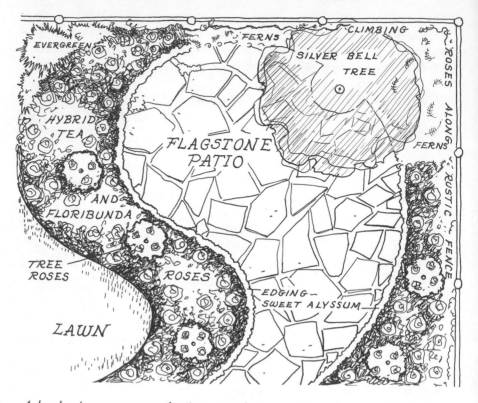

A border for permanent planting around or near the patio may add greatly to its privacy and its attractiveness when viewed from indoors.

which soon crept over the concrete edge toward the water, making it look completely natural.

From the very first this miniature pool (which is within 10 feet of the nearest view window and also visible when we are at table) has been a favorite spot for song birds of all sorts. The robins use it not only for bathing, splashing, and drinking, but also as headquarters for cherry washing and tenderizing. As soon as the wild black cherries begin to turn color, they are harvested by the hundreds from the tall, old trees on our river shore some distance away and carried to the pool. At the end of the cherry season each year we have to empty the pool and sweep out the accumulated pits. (For a further discussion of water features in the garden, see Chapter 13.)

In planning the patio, one of the most important things to consider—and one very frequently overlooked—is the view from inside the house. This applies especially in cool climates, where for more than half the year it can be enjoyed only from within doors.

Especially in a modern house with glass walls, ceiling-to-floor doors of glass, or large view windows, the patio can be an integral part of the indoor living area in summer when doors are open. In winter, the patio provides an interesting near view complete with birds, if berried shrubs and evergreens form a part of its permanent planting. Therefore it should, if possible, be placed so that it can be seen from the living or dining room. Not only is it a focal center in itself, but also forms an intimate foreground to enhance more distant garden views.

A very important supplement to the patio garden is a coldframe or, still better, a greenhouse—even a *very* small one—where plants may be brought into bud or bloom before being transferred to the patio for temporary effects. Spring-flowering bulbs, such as tulips and daffodils; small flowering shrubs like azaleas or gardenias; spring- and summer-flowering perennials and annuals in variety can provide a long succession of bloom culminating in the glorious display of chrysanthemums in autumn. The smaller the space devoted to gardening *outside* the patio, the more important it is to provide a fine succession of bloom within it. This is what is known as "mobile" gardening.

WINDOW BOXES

With or without a patio, window boxes provide a neglected opportunity for effectively displaying plants. Once very popular, they gradually went out of style and only recently they have returned as decorative features in modern homes. People have discovered that they do not *have* to be planted with geraniums, vincas, and old-fashioned, scraggly "balcony" petunias. In Europe window boxes have long played an important part in gardening and their revival in this country, especially for suburban community homes where ground areas are limited, is an encouraging sign. The modern view window provides another opportunity for the effective use of window boxes. If the window goes to the floor level, a suitable box-like bed or bed-like box with adequate drainage may be made level with it. Even more effective, however, is the eye-level, or more accurately, chair-level box, attached to the house wall just below the window sill.

Window boxes also give us another opportunity for displaying plants while in flower, or at their best. When the bloom is over they are replaced by others. Plants grown in pots are of course especially well suited for such treatment. A "succession" display of early tulips (including the new species hybrids) can be followed by geraniums, begonias, or any of the compact long-flowering annuals such as petunias, marigolds, and ageratum. Trailers like coleus, thunbergia, nasturtiums, German or Kenilworth-ivy will carry through until danger of frost. These may be followed by dwarf chrysanthemums to give color until hard freeze, especially if they are given a temporary protective covering on cold nights.

A ground-level bed or a raised planter box are more satisfactory than shrubs in front of large, view windows. Here the two are skillfully combined to provide color and protection in harmony with the horizontal lines of the window.

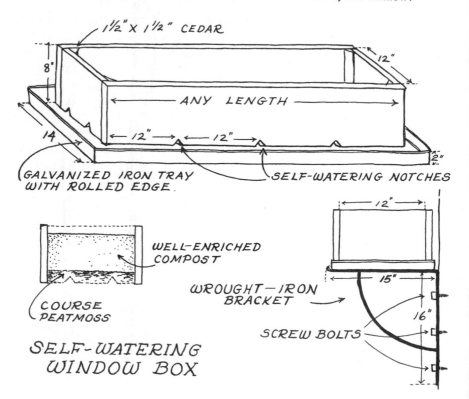

1½" X 1½" CEDAR

8"

12"

ANY LENGTH

14

12" 12"

2"

GALVANIZED IRON TRAY WITH ROLLED EDGE.

SELF-WATERING NOTCHES

WELL-ENRICHED COMPOST

COURSE PEATMOSS

12"

WROUGHT—IRON BRACKET

15"

16"

SCREW BOLTS

SELF-WATERING WINDOW BOX

For window boxes in semishaded locations, tuberous begonias in both upright and trailing types give a season-long display of color. (This self-watering, durable window box is described below.)

Our own window boxes are all on the north and northeast sides of the house, where they get plenty of light but only very early morning sunshine. The only flowers we grow in these are tuberous begonias, supplemented by trailing fuchsias and a variety of vines from the greenhouse. In our moderate autumn climate the begonias continue to flower—unless it is a hurricane year!—until late in October. In winter these boxes are either removed or filled with dwarf juniper branches and black alder berries. In summer they draw more admiration and are more photographed by visitors than any other plants on the place.

In warm climates, cacti and succulents make ideal window-box subjects the year-round, as do such showy foliage plants such as aucubas, dracaenas, and philodendrons. All these are suitable for modern homes. In the north they may be used during the growing season if there is a suitable place to over-winter them indoors.

We believe that poor construction is one of the reasons that window boxes are not more widely used. If a box rots out in a year or two it is a poor investment. Years ago we developed a simple "lifetime" window box. It isn't patented, so any reader can have one made. The accompanying line cut shows its construction. The box should be made of cypress, redwood, or Philippine mahogany. As there is no bottom, rot does not occur there, always its first point of attack. The box fits into a watertight pan of galvanized iron, 2 inches deep and about 3 inches wider and 3 inches longer than the outside dimension of the box. Water is run into the pan and rises up through the soil, which remains friable and open. A mulch of rough compost, added after plants have been set, helps to keep it that way. In case of heavy rains or overwatering, surplus water in the pans is siphoned off in a few minutes with a short piece of ¼-inch rubber hose. Supports for the boxes should be *very* rugged. We use 2×¼-inch iron brackets (see cut) fastened to the wall by ¼-inch lag bolts.

Where the petal of a rose
Blushes in the solitude!
The Petal of a Rose
by JAMES STEPHENS

CHAPTER 15

Roses and Rose Gardens

THE ROSE GARDEN

Since gardening began, the most popular of all flowers has been the rose. The appeal of other flowers may wax and wane, but the Queen of Flowers remains unrivaled in our own and many other lands.

The beginning gardener who thinks that this popularity stems from the fact that roses are easy to grow will find himself mistaken. Although certain original species of shrub roses and their direct descendants are among the most persistent of flowering shrubs, success with modern garden roses requires some knowledge of the plant's requirements and a willingness to give it the attention it needs. Hundreds of thousands of gardeners the world over, however, are convinced that roses are worth it.

Variety is one reason for the universal appeal of the rose—variety not only in flower form, color, and size of the individual blossoms, but also in the almost unbelievable range in type of plant and habit of growth. If one requires a pot plant 6 inches tall for a window sill or miniature garden; a 20-foot climber; a flowering hedge; a cover for a bank with gravelly, poor soil; a group of weatherproof and self-sufficient flowering shrubs; or exquisite, long-stemmed, fragrant blooms for indoor decoration —and winning prizes at flower shows!—one need not venture beyond the family of "la belle rosa."

Members of this grand genus flourish from Florida to Alaska and from Mexico to Nova Scotia. Not all species and varieties range over the entire area, of course, for there are tender as well as extra-hardy types. With some winter protection, however, most of the modern, strong-growing, large-flowered hybrids can be grown satisfactorily through most of North America.

This moderate-sized rose garden of semiformal design is ideal in several ways. The over-all plan makes an attractive landscape feature. The evergreens, trees, and hedge provide both privacy and effective protection against storms; the beds are so arranged as to facilitate culture and to display bloom to the best advantage; and the looking-glass pool adds charm.

A pleasing arrangement for roses in limited space. Prize-winning blooms may be grown even in a very small garden.

WHAT TYPE OF ROSE GARDEN?

Before ordering *any* plants, the wise beginner will learn the various types of roses available, what their requirements are, and how they may be used in the landscape. Then he should draw a plan, though it may be a rough one, and figure out how many plants, and *of what types,* he can accommodate. Only after this has been done should he allow himself to pore over the lavishly illustrated catalogs and make out an order for the roses that seem to suit his particular needs. A run-down on the types of roses follows:

I. *Garden Roses.* For a real rose garden of many varieties, planted in beds, for display and for cutting. Included are Hybrid Teas, Floribundas, Grandifloras, and—for southern gardens—Teas. EXAMPLES: Hybrid Teas: Peace, New Yorker, Hawaii. Floribundas: Fashion, Spartan, Betsy McCall, Betty Prior. Grandifloras: Queen Elizabeth, War Dance, Pink Parfait. Teas: Lady Hillington, Maman Cochet.

II. *Climbers.* While no roses actually climb, in the strict sense of the word, there are many which may readily be trained to supports such as trellises, posts, walls, and arbors. The more vigorous of these attain heights of 15 to 20 feet or more, especially in the south. EXAMPLES: Large-flowered Climbers: Blaze, New Dawn, and Climbing Hybrid Teas, which, as a class, are less hardy. Lower-growing Climbers are known as Pillars, attaining a height of 8 to 12 feet. EXAMPLES: Golden Showers, Inspiration, Coral Dawn. The old-fashioned, small-flowered Rambler type of Climber has been improved and reblooms throughout the season in varieties such as Chevy Chase and Crimson Shower.

III. *Trailers* are Climbers which make long canes that trail and spread horizontally over a bank, rock, wall, or even on level ground. This type used to be seen frequently on railroad embankments. EXAMPLES: Max Graf, Nearly Wild, Little Compton Creeper, Magic Carpet, Yellow Creeping Everbloom; also the Rambler group like Dorothy Perkins.

IV. *Hedge Roses* are quite tall-growing, thick, and bushy, and valuable not only for their profuse bloom, but primarily to serve as hedges. For this purpose, due to their thick growth and thorns, they are particularly effective. EXAMPLES: Red Robin, Hybrid 311, Robin Hood, Frensham. (Multiflora, much advertised for this purpose, is not recommended except for use on large farms or country places where extensive acreage is to be hedged in.)

V. *Edging Roses* are dwarf, or low, compact-growing roses, suitable for edging borders, rose gardens, or walks. They are chiefly in the small-flowered polyantha (many flowers in clusters) group. EXAMPLES: Pygmy—Yellow, Lavender, or Red; Margo Koster, Carroll Ann.

The rose, one of the first of all flowers to be brought under cultivation, is still the most popular pretty much the world over. There are several distinct types of roses, and the beginning gardener, in order to be able to select those which best suit his purposes, should learn to distinguish them.

(1) The Hybrid Teas provide the largest and loveliest individual blooms. To this type belongs Peace, the world's most popular rose. Hybrid Teas bloom intermittently throughout the season.

(2) Floribundas, as the name implies, provide more flowers, more continuously, and make the finest summer-long display in beds or borders. This is Vogue.

(3) *The new grandiflora type combines the characteristics of the two named above, but is not, as yet, quite definitely established. Queen Elizabeth, growing to shoulder height and bearing masses of handsome, well-formed blooms, is a well-known variety in this class.*

(4) *The Single roses, more or less neglected in modern, high-pressure rose advertising, possess a charm all their own, and at least one or two should be included in even a moderate-sized rose garden. Innocence, illustrated, is one of the loveliest. Dainty Bess is most in demand.*

(5) *Climbing roses should be given a place, whether or not one has a rose garden. Distinction should be made between the old-fashioned Rambler type and the wonderful, large-flowered Climbers and Pillars (see photo page 127) such as Climbing Peace and Golden Showers.*

(6) *Shrub roses such as the Rugosas and varieties like Frencham and The Fairy are excellent for landscape effects without a rose garden. Tough, pure pink, The Fairy, almost constantly in bloom until hard frost, is the one variety we would have if we could have but one.*

VI. *Miniature Roses* are quite distinct from all the above in that, although normal roses in plant habit, growth, and flowering, they are diminutive in size. The plants average 8 to 18 inches in height, and the flowers about an inch in diameter. In spite of their frail appearance, however, we have found them extremely resistant to general plant troubles and to cold. Most of them are really very small Hybrid Teas, in habit and form, though they are somewhat of a mystery in Rosedom. Their reappearance dates back to the early 1900s with the introduction of *Rosa rouletti,* which was found on a cottage window sill in the Swiss Alps; but there are records indicating importation, about 1815, to Europe from the Orient. Later they disappeared, to turn up again in Switzerland. For some years these little gems attracted attention principally as a curiosity. Recently, however, many new colors and named varieties have been introduced. Their sale has been pushed, and they have become tremendously popular, especially for indoors and for

(7) *The thimble-size Miniature roses, growing on compact bushes only a foot or so tall under average conditions, are surprisingly hardy and trouble-free; excellent too as pot plants.*

home greenhouses, where their dwarf stature and long, continued flowering period have proven great assets. EXAMPLES: Pixie, Baby Gold Star, Bo Peep.

VII. *Shrub Roses,* as the term implies, are those which in form, habit, and culture look and are treated like average ornamental shrubs. As a rule they more closely resemble the original species from which modern garden roses have been developed. While as a group they are hardier and less subject to pests and diseases than the garden roses, they are coarser in growth and much less floriferous than the modern hybrids. Many have brilliantly colored flowers and later very large or showy seed pods or "hips," which are quite as decorative as the flowers and much longer lasting. A few may well be used in any sizable planting of mixed shrubs. EXAMPLES: Harison's Yellow, an old farmyard and cemetery favorite; The Fairy; Mabelle Stearns; the Rugosas and their many hybrids; the Briers and their hybrids.

PREPARING THE ROSE GARDEN

A rose garden is one of the most rewarding horticultural projects that a homeowner can undertake—but it is not one of the simplest. You must plan and prepare it carefully, and give it care throughout the season— and this means from the time the frost leaves the ground in the spring until it freezes solid again in autumn. Otherwise, results are likely to be only mediocre.

Site. Ideal exposure for the rose garden is one to the east or south, with air drainage to a lower level, and preferably with some protection to the north and west from strong winds or storms. Soil drainage also should be excellent. In heavy, poorly drained soil, tile should be used (see page 20).

Soil. Clay soil used to be considered essential for the growing of good roses. We have seen—*and have grown*—as good roses on light sandy soil, properly handled and supplemented, as on clay. (All that is needed for success is to follow the suggestions for soil improvement given in Chapter 2.)

Soil *preparation,* however, is of the utmost importance. Roses are a long-time crop and the bed should be prepared to be adequate for many years to come. By the end of the second or third year, the roots of strong growing plants will extend down into the bed for several feet. Therefore, some of the old authorities advocated preparing the soil to a depth of 4 feet. Such an extreme is not necessary, but 18 inches, *by the ruler,* is the minimum. Most successful rose growers prepare the soil to 24 inches, and the general rule is: "the deeper the better."

Cow manure used to be considered another "must" for the rose garden, but in most localities today it can be had, if at all, only in the processed dry form. Good roses, indeed excellent roses, can be grown without it if the rose beds are well supplied with *humus,* in the form of peatmoss or other organic material, plus a goodly proportion of organic fertilizers. Roses are not overparticular about soil acidity; a pH of from 6 to nearly 7 (neutral) is agreeable to them.

Drainage, however, is another matter. Roses must have abundant moisture to provide continuous good bloom throughout the season, but water-soaked soil, even well below the surface, will prove injurious at any season of the year.

To make the best display, on the other hand, roses require a constant supply of moisture in the soil during the entire growing season. For this reason the homeowner who wishes to make a feature of his rose garden will do well to provide an adequate watering system. For a rose garden of any size, a mere sprinkling with a hose is not only time-consuming but inadequate. Watering devices of many kinds are available (see Chapter 5), but to get uniform distribution with least work in a garden of 50 or more plants, for example, a permanent system of some sort is desirable.

Overhead watering of garden roses is to be avoided because moist foliage, particularly during hot, muggy weather, encourages the develop-

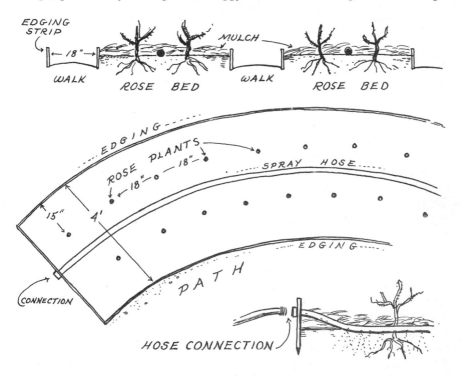

Self-watering system for rose garden. Merely connect hose and turn on spigot. No water gets on foliage to invite black spot.

ment of diseases, especially black spot and mildew—the *bêtes noire* of the rose gardener in most parts of the country. Overhead watering also is likely to deceive the novice into thinking he has given his rose beds a thorough watering when in reality moisture may have penetrated the soil but little below the surface.

Having tried many different watering systems, we have worked out one which uses a perforated hose, *inverted,* left permanently in place for the season and covered with a fairly deep (2- to 3-inch) mulch. A line of hose is stretched along the center of each bed containing two rows of plants. The open end of the sprinkler hose is passed through a short, stout stake a few inches above the ground level, at the end of the bed. A regular hose, coupled to this and allowed to run for a half hour or more, gives the soil of the rose beds a slow, deep soak, with no wetting of foliage or even of the upper surface of the mulch.

At the end of the season the lengths of sprinkler hose are rolled up and stored for the winter, so that they do not interfere with any hilling or mulching that may be required for winter protection in cold climates.

PLANTING ROSES

Preparation. Before planting a rose garden, the entire area, including the paths, should be deep dug and thoroughly prepared. Roots will extend into the soil under the paths. Beds are best laid out to accommodate two or three rows only. We prefer two, since a middle row is difficult to reach for pruning, spraying, weeding, or even gathering flowers.

Plants should be set 18 to 30 inches apart according to type, variety, and culture to be given. A satisfactory average is 20 to 24, though such extra-vigorous plants as Peace or Queen Elizabeth should have all of 30. Pruning usually helps to keep the more vigorous specimens from pre-empting too much space. In a large garden, extra-vigorous varieties may be grouped by themselves and given somewhat more room than the others.

Even when the total bed area has been thoroughly prepared and fertilized, we like to make individual planting holes, marked by stakes bearing names of varieties to be planted. These are prepared by digging to a depth of 15 to 18 inches, and mixing in the bottom of each hole a quart or two of peatmoss, and about a pint mixture of ⅔ dehydrated manure and ⅓ bonemeal.

For climbing roses and shrub and bush roses which are planted individually, it is also important to prepare planting holes very thoroughly. Once established, their roots will spread far and deep, but unless they can get off to a strong start, they may never make the display expected of them. We make planting holes at least 18 inches wide and deep and set the plants 3 inches or so below the ground level (covering the "knob" or "graft" by at least an inch) to assure their getting all available moisture.

Supports for climbing roses should be substantial and permanent. The spindle-wood trellises and arbors so widely sold are next to worthless and usually have to be replaced within a few years, at considerable expense and with some damage to the roses.

Post-and-chain supports made of sturdy cedar posts 6 to 8 feet tall with two loops of sturdy chain running from post to post are ideal for vigorous growers (see sketch page 250). The posts are sunk 3 feet in the ground and placed at 8 to 10 foot intervals. A cedar post with sturdy cleats nailed across it at intervals makes a good support for pillar roses. Rambler and other small-flowered types, the canes of which are numerous but not heavy (as old canes are removed each year), may be supported on a trellis or arbor. These should be constructed of 1×3-inch strips, with sturdy uprights to hold them. Whatever type is chosen, supports should be in place before planting.

Planting. More and more, roses are being sold as growing plants, even in bud or flower, in generous-sized composition pots. Of course, these may be planted at any time, but the earlier, the better.

Fall or spring planting? Most home gardeners, however, still buy dormant, bare-root plants which are shipped either in the late fall or very early spring. In northern sections where ground may freeze hard in late September or early October, spring planting becomes a necessity. In mild climates, fall planting gives plants an early start in spring. In either case, *the earlier the plants can be set out the better.* In fact the terms "fall" and "spring" planting are misleading. "Early-winter" and "late-winter" would be more accurate, for plants (except where they may be procured locally) cannot be purchased at the tail-end of fall. If not shipped until mid-spring, they will have started into growth, despite all attempts to keep them dormant.

Unless the plants can be set out immediately upon receipt, they should at once be buried in a coldframe or trench, with damp peatmoss about the roots and covered with moist soil.

Plants are usually pruned and ready for planting before being shipped, but even so it is well to go over them carefully with *sharp* pruning shears. Long or broken roots and bruised, broken, or spindly branches should be trimmed back by cutting just above an outward-pointing bud.

Plants are set so that, when soil has been filled in and firmed down, the level is just an inch or so above the "knuckle"—the somewhat swollen section of the stem above the roots which indicates where the plant was budded. Few garden roses are grown on their own roots. For this reason plants should always be carefully watched to see if any shoots originate *below* this point. These are removed at once, as they come from the rootstock. They may usually be identified by the fact that they have seven leaflets instead of the five which distinguish most hybrid varieties.

FOUR STEPS TO FINE ROSES
*Dig the holes both
wide and deep.
These are 18 inches
apart and about
the same depth,
with topsoil replaced
in bottoms of holes.*

*Into this topsoil,
peatmoss and a mixture
of bonemeal and
dried cow manure are
thoroughly mixed.*

*After roses are set—
so that root buds or
grafts are about level
with the soil surface—
they are very well
watered in, and balance
of soil replaced.*

*After growth starts and
any weeds have been
removed, mulch—in
this instance bagasse—
is applied to conserve
moisture, discourage
weeds, and keep soil
cool.*

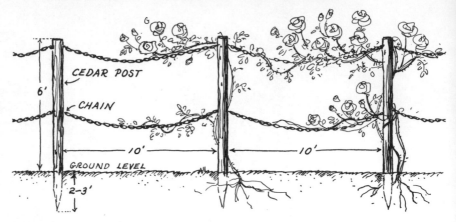

A support for climbing roses that will last a lifetime. Cedar posts (set in concrete) and galvanized chain.

Feeding. No ornamental plants in the garden are hungrier than roses. When one considers the amount of new growth that is made, much of which is removed in cutting blooms and pruning, this is not surprising.

Most display rose gardens are fed repeatedly throughout the season. The average home rose garden or border will produce satisfactorily with two or three feedings. The first should take place in spring, when any winter mulch and soil protection has been removed or worked in; the second during midsummer, after the big May–June burst of bloom; and the third in autumn, when the plants have finished their September–October show and are being readied for winter. Recently, extensive experiments have demonstrated that the autumn feeding is decidedly beneficial.

What fertilizer to use? There are many special rose foods on the market—at special prices. We have never found that the brand name made much difference in the results. We use a general-purpose fertilizer with an analysis of 6–10–4 for spring and summer, and 5–10–5 for autumn. In addition to this we apply liberal amounts of wood ashes from fireplaces and brush pile in either spring or fall—a form of potash which roses seem to particularly like. An analysis lower in nitrogen would probably serve as well for the late fall application.

The fertilizers suggested above are used at the rate of 3 to 5 pounds per 100 square feet. *Do not* apply fertilizer just in a ring around each plant but spread evenly over the entire surface of the bed, placing as little as possible within 6 or 8 inches of the main stems.

Today's tendency is toward the use of more and more concentrated fertilizers. Directions given with any of these should be followed to the letter.

PRUNING

No operation in connection with rose growing is more hotly debated than that of pruning. However, this need not cause the amateur rose-grower, who merely wishes to have a good show out of doors and some choice blooms for cutting, to get any gray hairs.

Fall and spring pruning are important for garden roses: Hybrid Teas, Floribundas, Grandifloras, and the like. Tall growths should be cut back so that the plants may not whip about in high winds and loosen the roots. If not removed, such long canes are likely to kill back during the winter. Any diseased or broken wood should also be taken out, as should spreading branches inclined to tangle with neighboring plants.

The real pruning should be left until spring. Wood that has died back or has been killed back during the winter is easily recognizable long before leaves begin to develop. This should be removed, cutting to just above an outward-pointing eye, so that the bush will tend to grow to an open center. Thin, weak growths and those that are dying (with dead cores at the center) should also be removed.

How far back to cut? is an open question.

As a general rule, very severe pruning produces fewer but better flowers. Other factors involved, however, include the type and variety of rose, the individual plant, and climatic conditions. In the average garden a colorful over-all display is more desirable than a limited number of extra-fine blooms for cutting.

In the north, where winter damage is usually severe, cutting back to healthy, new wood may involve removing most of the previous year's

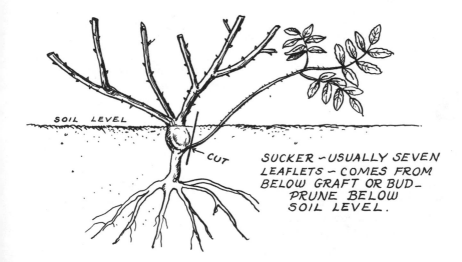

SOIL LEVEL

CUT

SUCKER — USUALLY SEVEN LEAFLETS — COMES FROM BELOW GRAFT OR BUD — PRUNE BELOW SOIL LEVEL.

growth. Farther south, more healthy new wood survives the winter, and may be kept, if tall, bushy plants with many medium-sized blooms are desired.

Light, moderate, or hard? Generally speaking, we may say that there are three types or degrees of pruning.

Light. These bushes are gone over and shaped up. Extra-tall or wayward branches and those that cross and rub against others are trimmed back. Weak, inward-growing branches are removed. Up to about a third of the total healthy wood may be cut away.

Moderate. The main stems and the more vigorous side shoots are cut back more severely, taking care always to cut above an outward-facing bud or one that will have room to develop into a sturdy branch without crossing or crowding another vigorous cane. One aims at developing a plant with an open center. The result of such pruning is a reduction in the number of blooms, especially early in the season, but the individual flowers will be larger and of better quality. On an average, a half to two thirds of the plant is removed.

Hard. This means just what the term implies. Two thirds or even more of the body of the plant is discarded. The main canes and laterals are cut back to only two to four eyes each, which will probably mean stubs less than a foot high. The result will be fewer but larger blooms, with longer and more perfect flower stems—the kind that win blue ribbons at flower shows.

Cuts resulting from correct pruning usually self-heal very promptly, but where large canes—a half inch or more in diameter—are removed, it is advisable to apply a tree paint.

Under no circumstances should a short stub be left between a cut and a branch below it, as such stubs tend to die back. Where winter injury is common, it is safer to prune to the first outward-facing bud *below* branched growth, rather than above it, as die-back may occur at the branching point.

Pruning Climbers. The newer, large-flowered remontant or ever-blooming types of climbing roses demand much less attention in the matter of pruning than do bush roses, but they do give a much finer display if pruning is not neglected. After they have attained full size—which will require two or three seasons under favorable conditions—the annual removal of one or more of the oldest canes encourages vigorous new growth. In taking out the old growths, it is best to cut into fairly short sections so that newer canes are not injured in the process of removal. The best time to do this pruning is just after the first big burst of bloom is over. A pair of lopping shears (page 102) is convenient for this work, as it is a bit heavy for ordinary pruning shears.

In the case of small-flowered, old-fashioned rambler roses, *all old*

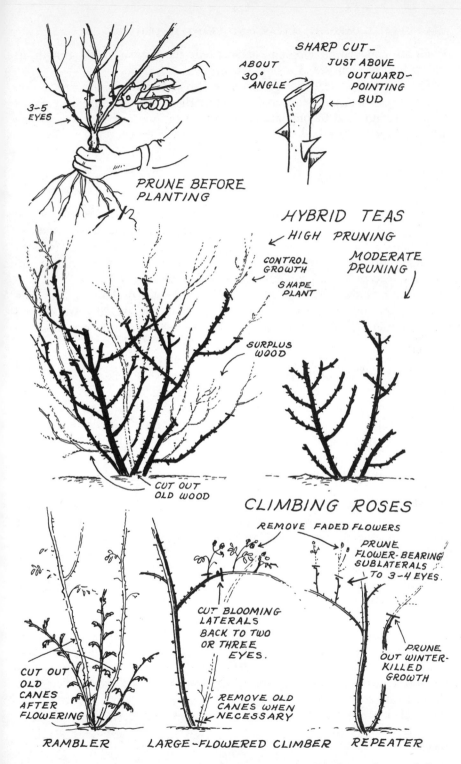

Pruning is a very important factor in growing roses. Study results carefully as a guide to future pruning.

canes are removed after bloom, leaving only the current year's growth, as bloom occurs each year on new wood.

The removal of dead flower heads is also important in the production of later blooms in large-flowered climbers. Blooms occur on side growths or laterals and dead blooms are snipped off with one or two buds, cutting just above a healthy bud or eye.

SPRING CARE

The first spring work in the rose garden, after all frost is out of the ground, is to remove mulching material and then rake down and incorporate in the soil of the beds the compost or loam that has been hilled up around the bases of canes. (In warm climates, of course, no hilling is necessary and this task does not present itself.)

Next comes the spring pruning—light, moderate, or hard as the gardener elects. In any event, all injured or doubtfully healthy wood, and weak, surplus, or intercrossing growths are removed. All prunings are carefully collected and burned.

The first or dormant spray follows. This may be lime-sulfur, an old but safe compound for the purpose. This spraying should be extra-thorough to give the plants a clean start. It must be applied *before* the leaves begin to unfold. If for any reason it has not been applied when this occurs, omit the dormant spray and make a thorough application of the usual all-purpose rose sprays. Spraying should be continued weekly throughout the growing season from the time the leaves begin to unfold.

The spring feeding comes next (page 250).

After this, the application of whatever summer mulch, if any, is in order. We are firm believers in mulching for roses. Of the many materials we have tried, we have found pine needles, tan bark, seaweed, and bagasse (chopped sugar cane stalks) satisfactory. Absorbent materials such as peatmoss may stay too wet. Buckwheat hulls and similar materials dry out and blow about.

Staking may be required for tall varieties, such as the new grandifloras, but we prefer to keep them self-supporting by pruning. Cutting long-stemmed blooms for indoor decoration helps accomplish this.

Cutting roses is really part of their culture. All blooms should be removed as soon as they begin to fade, not only for the sake of appearance, but also because fallen, decaying petals may help spread disease. Always cut just above an outfacing eye which has developed five leaflets, not three. Near the center of our rose garden we keep a large wicker basket into which spent blooms and other trimmings are tossed, then burned. We find this a great help, especially in hot weather when flowers fade quickly.

Regular spray program is essential if pests and diseases are to be fended off. A good all-purpose rose spray or dust should be applied every week or ten days without fail. The beginner who is not willing to tackle this chore regularly will do better to specialize in some less demanding flower.

Sprays are preferred to dusts both because they are more efficient if applied thoroughly and because they do not cover the leaves with residue as many dusts do. We use both a good quality trombone sprayer with a bucket to hold the spray mixture, and the glass-jar type which screws directly onto a garden hose.

Excellent, small-size ball-bearing dusters are now sold by several rose growers and purveyors of dusts. One of these is a "must" if dusting is to be used.

Winter protection. The most important step in winter care of roses is the "hilling up" around the roots in late fall, using garden loam, compost, or very well rotted, littery manure alone or mixed with loam or

Hilling up for winter is a "must" in severe climates. A mulch applied after hilling prevents thawing of the soil during warm spells and affords additional protection.

compost. In northern climates where temperatures go down to zero and below, hilling should be heaped as high as 12 inches. In milder areas, where below-freezing temperatures are common but less severe, 6 or even 4 inches may suffice. This work may be done well in advance of hard freeze if desired, but after the plants begin to go into dormancy.

In extremely cold locations like the Great Plains, climbers are removed from their supports, laid flat on the ground, and covered with soil for the winter. Where temperatures are not quite so low but heavy winter winds are frequent, pillars and lower-growing climbers may be protected with evergreen boughs or small Christmas trees stuck upright in the ground around the plants, bound over the canes and tied to the supports.

Near New York City, where we maintained a large rose garden for many years, we hilled moderately and then covered the beds with cut evergreen boughs which held the snow and kept the rose plants cozily cold, without alternate thawing and freezing, a condition which often results in winter injury.

In spring when danger of hard freeze is past, mulch is removed, and "hills" from around the main stems of the rose plants are lightly worked into the surface soil of the beds along with an early spring application of fertilizer.

Crown'd with the eares of corne, now come,
And, to the Pipe, sing Harvest home.
ROBERT HERRICK

"It's Broccoli, dear."
"I say it's Spinach,
'and I say the Hell with it.'"
CARL ROSE

CHAPTER 16

Vegetables for Better Eating

Why grow one's own vegetables when it is so easy to pick them up, all neatly wrapped in cellophane—cleverly colored to make them look riper or more perfect than they are!—at the nearest chain store? For those with freezers, frozen vegetables have become available in forms especially tempting to the busy housewife. Sliced carrots, chopped onions, potato balls, or even stuffed baked potatoes may be had all ready to heat up and serve.

"Why grow your own?" is a good question. And there are three good answers.

First: You can save money, a considerable amount of it during the year.

Second: You can, with a few exceptions, enjoy very much better quality and flavor.

Third: It's fun doing it!

The amount of money that may be saved depends upon two factors. First, that the home vegetable grower do all, or most, of the work involved. If he has to engage much help—assuming that he can find anyone to do it!—any possible savings will disappear. Second, that a suitable storage place is provided for vegetables to be kept for winter use. Most modern cellars with temperatures up to 60 or 70 degrees are not suitable for storing any of the root crops, though it will take care of winter squash as these require higher storage temperatures. An outdoor storage pit, however, is not difficult to construct. Those with freezers—an ever-increasing percentage of our population—may store most vegetables, frozen, with less effort than that required to winter-store root vegetables. As was mentioned above, even potatoes are frozen today.

As to *flavor,* there is no question that home-grown crops are far superior to most of the vegetables commercially available. This is especially true of leaf vegetables such as lettuce, spinach, and chard, the quality of which quickly deteriorates after being cut. It is also true of many others such as peas, beans, asparagus, and corn, which must be fresh-picked to be at their best. The saying that the pot should be boiling before sweet corn is picked is not an old wives' tale. Scientific tests have proved that after picking the sugar content in the kernels decreases rapidly with every passing hour. Green peas of course are in the same category. Items, such as tomatoes, when grown for sale must be picked while still "firm"—a euphemism for "half green"—when they are to be shipped, often thousands of miles, to reach retail markets before they begin to decay. How often for instance does one get, in a market, a melon that is really sweet and luscious, as this fruit should be? Tomatoes, melons, and most other fruit should not be harvested until dead ripe if the true flavor is to be experienced.

There is another, and an even more serious factor to consider in relation to table quality in vegetables. In former days the vegetable-plant breeders' first concern was to improve flavor and tenderness. Now all that has changed. Recently, in an article in a national magazine about the achievements of a famous plant breeder, much stress was laid upon the wonders he had achieved in developing such qualities as greater "eye appeal," crops "all ripe at once" to facilitate harvesting, uniform size and shape to speed up packing, tough skins to resist injury in long distance shipping—*but not one word about table quality!*

Fortunately there are still some seedsmen left who cater to the home-garden trade—though their number is small compared to what it was a half century, or even a couple of decades ago.

As to our third claim, that growing one's own vegetables is really fun, we must admit that this is a matter of taste (in both senses of the word) and there is no way of proving it. It is neither a status activity such as golf nor a group sport like sitting in the bleachers watching trained athletes sweating it out while the observer eats peanuts and puts on weight.

Growing some of your own vegetables and fruits is not an activity that can be "sold" by argument. All we can suggest is that the reader try it, on a modest scale at first, to see if he is one of the many who find it worthwhile for the table, the body and the soul!

Vegetable garden and test plot at the authors' former home.

PRELIMINARIES

The site. While there is a wealth of ornamental plants that either demand or tolerate a considerable amount of shade, when it comes to vegetables and fruits an abundance of sunshine is not only desirable but essential. Usually the more the better, except under some subtropical conditions.

Good drainage is also essential. Poorly drained soils are slow to warm up in the spring, and early planting is necessary for some vegetables that do not tolerate very hot weather; and for others which require a very long period of growth. (For information concerning drainage problems, see Chapter 2.)

A vegetable plot facing south, especially if on a gentle slope, usually may be made ready for planting a week or ten days earlier than a level piece. Buildings or shrubs—especially hedges—to the north or west also afford protection, thus providing an ideal location for frames (Chapter 7) as well as for the vegetable patch.

How big? What size should the vegetable plot be? The standard answer to that silly question is the somewhat more sensible answer: "No larger than your wife can take care of."

For one's first attempt at vegetable growing, it is advisable to start moderately; and to try only those vegetables which are most easily grown —such as beans (both bush and pole), peas, radishes, onion sets, sweet corn, squash, lettuce, and tomatoes.

How much of each? That depends largely upon the family's tastes; and further than that upon the yield, which varies with different varieties, and from season to season. Last year, for instance, our bean crop was double as much as usual from the same space planted. Despite all we gave away and packed into the freezer for winter (we are still enjoying them as this is written in April) a lot went to the compost heap. There is no way of planning so accurately as to guarantee neither want nor waste.

The figures in the chart at the end of this chapter, based on our own experience, may serve as a guide to the number of feet of row to supply two people. It may be multiplied by .5 for each additional member of the family; or by somewhat more for any item that is a particular favorite. Figures are for one planting, and where succession plantings are made (as in the case of bush beans, sweet corn, lettuce, and some others) they should of course be increased accordingly.

With no separate vegetable garden it is still possible to enjoy a few favorite vegetables, by making places for them in the flower borders or herb garden. A row, or several clumps of asparagus, for instance, yields stalks for the table in spring, and makes a decorative background for annuals or perennials during summer and fall. Rhubarb, after supplying succulent stems for sauce and pie, sends up tall spikes of creamy white flowers that are not only decorative in the garden, but effective and long-lasting in large flower arrangements.

The most intriguing and practical use of vegetables grown in a flower border that we have encountered was at a small place where we once stopped to get photographs of a striking display of annuals that extended around two sides of a very modest plot. We were astonished to discover among the flowers a fairly large assortment of vegetables growing not in rows, but in groups, spaced more or less casually among the flowers, but each with room enough to weed around it and harvest the crop. Tomatoes and pole beans were trained to lattice supports; beets, carrots, onions, radishes, lettuce, and others were in separate groups, carefully thinned out to give maximum yield. The owner—who did all the work herself—explained that vegetable seeds were sown thinly wherever spring bulbs, after flowering, could have their foliage tied up, and where early annuals like candytuft had passed their prime. Spaces for root vegetables were left among the perennials, as these root deep and must have rich, open soil in which to develop. It was a sort of continuous catch-as-catch-can operation, but certainly paid off, especially as the only fertilizer used was vegetable wastes and table scraps, dug under near the flowers and vegetables in the beds, without bothering to compost them in the usual way.

This method of growing vegetables is not recommended, if one has room for even a very small vegetable garden, but it does show what can be done.

A plan comes first. One of the things most difficult to get the beginning vegetable gardener to realize is the importance of making a definite plan. What he usually does is to look through the seed catalog, select the varieties he likes—or thinks he will like—and then makes a wild guess at the amount to order. No matter how crude the plan, it will save seed, time, labor, and disappointment.

First step is to measure the space to be devoted to the vegetable garden. Next, make a list of the vegetables to be grown, and the *width* of row each will require. These widths vary from 12 inches (for such items as onions, spinach, carrots, and beets) to 4 or more feet for "spreaders" like tomatoes and bush squash. Vine crops such as cucumbers, melons, pumpkins, and winter squash require 6 feet or more. We had a volunteer Hubbard Squash last year at the edge of a garden plot, which we trained in two directions in a straight line. It attained, with no special feeding, a total length of 73 feet and produced over a hundred pounds of squash.

It is as interesting as a jigsaw puzzle to fit what one wants to grow into the space available. At the close of this chapter are some figures that will help solve the problem.

And here is a planting plan that indicates what the results of all your figuring and planning may be. The preparation of such a plan will of course take considerable time—in the long evenings of January or February when there is plenty of that commodity. But such a plan will *save* time in spring when there is something to be done about the grounds every minute. And in addition it will result in much better results for your efforts.

Preparation for planting is best begun as soon as frost is out and the soil has dried sufficiently to be dug, plowed, or rototilled. As a general rule, the earlier the better, especially if there is a heavy winter cover crop to be turned under. We do not apply manure or fertilizer until after this has been done. Then a second going-over mixes the plant foods evenly through the soil, which is left in nice condition to be given a final

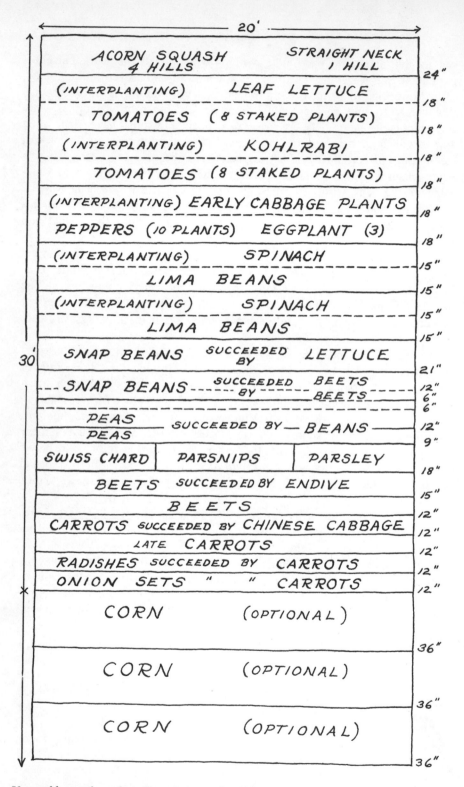

Vegetable garden plan. For those with plenty of space, an additional 15 feet has been added for sweet corn. For an ample supply, double or even triple this footage.

treatment with an iron rake to prepare a fine, smooth surface for planting.

One great advantage of preparing all the ground for planting, even if only part of it is to be used at once, is that the prompt germination of weed seeds is encouraged, and they can readily be destroyed by cultivating again before later sowings are made.

Part of the preparation for planting is to provide an ample supply of plant food. This differs little from that suggested in preparing for seeding a lawn. With many crops, however, it is beneficial to add some extra plant food in the planting holes, as described later.

If soil is extra-dry, it is advantageous to water very thoroughly before planting, preferably with a fine spray that will not make the surface muddy. One of the many oscillating or mist sprayers now available is ideal for this purpose.

PLANTING

Most vegetables are grown from seed, sown where they are to grow, but some (see page 264) do best if plants are started ahead in a greenhouse or frame. For sowing seed the surface should first be raked smooth immediately before sowing. Large-scale plantings are made with a seed drill, but in most home gardens they are sown by hand.

First step is to mark off rows the proper distance apart, with a stout garden line along which a narrow hoe or a pointed stick is drawn to make a furrow. Depth of the mark is in proportion to the size of the seed being sown. Very small seed—such as that of carrots, onions, and turnips —are covered about ⅛- to ¼-inch deep; medium sizes—beets, spinach, parsnips, etc.—½ to ¾ inches; and comparatively large seeds—peas, beans, corn—2 to 3 inches deep. In light, sandy soil or in very dry weather, planting depths may be somewhat increased.

It is important, especially in very dry weather, that the seed be firmed *in the drill* or furrow. This may be done with the back of a narrow "onion" hoe for small seeds, or an ordinary hoe for large ones. A method we have used for years, but have never seen suggested elsewhere, is to turn the wheel hoe upside down, place a light weight (such as a moderate-sized stone) on it, and run the wheel along the row. This takes very little time and nicely firms the seed into the soil. Loose soil, covered over this, serves as a mulch to hold the moisture, and delicate sprouts that would have trouble pushing up through soil firmed on the surface emerge readily.

Caution to beginners: A mistake which almost all beginners make is to sow seed—especially small seed such as that of carrots, onions, turnips, and lettuce—too thickly. *Every surplus seedling is a weed* and must be removed! Moreover, it is a weed that is growing right alongside the seedling you do want to keep, probably with roots intertangled, so that in removing it the other is sure to be loosened if not destroyed.

Much better to take an extra five or ten minutes to sow a row with seeds properly spaced (a quarter to a half inch apart for vegetables such as those mentioned above) than to have to spend half an hour or more on one's knees at the tedious job of "thinning out"—gardeners' jargon for removing surplus seedlings.

Just this past season we had a striking instance of the importance of giving individual plants in the row sufficient space to develop. Our row of parsnips germinated so poorly that we intended to replant them, but the press of other work prevented this so we finally removed all weeds, gave the plants an extra application of fertilizer, and allowed them to grow. Result: we had all of the succulent, white, sugary roots we could possibly use, and plenty to give away!

SETTING OUT

Several delicious vegetables—such as tomatoes, eggplant, peppers—require such a long season to mature that in northern sections they must be started in a greenhouse or hotbed, and later transferred to the garden as growing plants. There are others—such as cabbage and lettuce—that may be harvested much earlier in the season by starting seed early under glass and then setting out young plants. The method of doing this is described in Chapter 4. The gardener who does not possess such equipment may buy plants at any garden center. This is much easier, usually the better course for a beginner, but lacks some of the thrill of growing one's own.

Such started plants are often grown in "flats" or shallow boxes of various sizes, about 3 inches deep, but the newer method of growing them in individual pots made of peatmoss or some similar material which are planted "pot-and-all" is preferable, since by using this method there is no disturbance to the roots.

It is essential that all such started plants be "hardened off" by being exposed for several days and nights in an open frame or some other semiprotected spot before being set out in open ground. During this period they must be kept well watered as a sunny, windy day will dry them out very quickly.

In well-prepared soil, started plants may be set out with no special care in preparing the planting holes. We always feel, however, that a little extra "push" at this point is well worthwhile. Our own method is to mark out rows, and then the locations of individual plants such as tomatoes, eggplants, and peppers, and at each such point work well into the soil a shovelful of rich compost, plus half a pint of an organic fertilizer such as a mixture of Milorganite and bonemeal. This takes very little extra time and assures a fast, strong start.

CULTURE

The one great secret of success in growing vegetables is to keep ahead of the garden's greatest enemies—weeds. Unfortunately the richer the soil is made to grow fine vegetables, the more luxuriant the weeds it will produce.

In the commercial production of vegetables, chemical weed killers as well as pre-emergent treatments are now used extensively. For the small home garden we do not advocate them. Unless used with the greatest care they are likely to do more harm than good. We believe—but have no proof—that they affect the flavors of some vegetables. The methods we use to keep the weed population at a minimum are as follows:

First, *never allow a weed to go to seed.* Those that grow in corners and out-of-the-way places scatter their seeds far and wide. The first flower on any weed—and some of them, such as the chicory, wild carrot, and morning-glories, are quite lovely—should be its death warrant.

Second, *compost all fresh manure* before applying it to the garden. Very few seeds will survive the processes of decay that go on in the correctly managed compost heap (page 27).

Third, if weeds do appear, *get them out at once,* even if other more interesting and apparently more pressing jobs have to wait. Every day's delay increases the task at compound interest, and a rainy spell may easily make it hopeless.

Tools for combatting weeds are many. It will pay well to have several types, as this not only makes the job easier but will save a considerable amount of time. Some of our favorite ones are described in Chapter 8.

Thinning is the process of removing a sufficient number of plants from a row or a hill to allow those remaining to reach maximum size. As already emphasized, every surplus plant is a weed. This should be done as soon as the second or third true leaf appears. Proper space to be left between the plants in the rows varies. Averages for some of the more important vegetables are shown in the table at the end of this chapter. Crops ordinarily grown in hills—such as cucumbers, squash, and melons —are thinned out, *before they begin to crowd,* to three or four. As thinning, even when carefully done, disturbs to some extent the plants which are left, it is well to go back over the row and draw some soil up around any that may be "wobbly."

Side-dressing is a term used for the application of plant food, along the row or around individual plants. When the soil has been properly prepared this will seldom be necessary except when one has to contend with a soil that leaches badly—such as much of our Cape Cod sand— until it has been sufficiently supplied with humus. The food element most likely to become deficient is nitrogen. To correct this, a quick-acting high-nitrogen fertilizer such as Milorganite is the standard. This is not always available locally. We now use a 20–6–4 organic fertilizer sold for lawns, but equally good for vegetables. Any high-nitrogen fertilizer will be helpful.

Mulching is less frequently employed for the vegetable plot than elsewhere about the grounds. It is, however, just as effective here, and correctly used will conserve soil moisture and save a great deal of time in cultivating and weeding.

A mulch is any material, from spent manure to strips of plastic, that may be spread over the soil, around and/or between plants. Its principal purpose is to conserve moisture by checking evaporation. In addition to this it may check or even eliminate weed growth, and also affects soil temperature. Mulches which shade the soil keep it several degrees cooler in hot, sunny weather.

The mulches we use most are seaweed and "thatch" (debris from the beach such as a mixture of dead grasses and seaweed), pine needles (we have an unlimited supply of these in our pine woods), and coarse compost, sufficiently old to contain few viable weed seeds. Mulches, which may be bought commercially in bales or bags, include peatmoss, buckwheat hulls, Stay-dry (bagasse or treated sugar cane stalks), bog or meadow hay. The one thing to guard against most carefully is any material that contains weed or grass seeds.

Harvesting and storing. Most vegetables are used, as soon as ready, directly from the garden. One of the chief reasons for having a garden at all is to make possible the enjoyment of *really* fresh vegetables. As already mentioned, sweet corn and peas lose in quality by the hour as soon as they are picked.

Any of the leaf vegetables and broccoli should (unless used at once) be wrapped in a moist cloth and placed in the refrigerator. Others should be kept in the coolest, most moist spot that can be found. Any of the root vegetables placed in damp peatmoss will remain really garden fresh for days.

Winter storage of vegetables, now that the old-fashioned dirt-floor cellar and spring or pump house are things of the past, is a different problem. Potatoes, beets, carrots, and other root crops, packed as suggested above and placed in the coolest spot available, will remain fresh for a long time if the peat is not allowed to dry out. In moderate climates (where temperatures seldom drop below 10 degrees above zero) heavy mulching with straw, pine needles, or dead leaves held in place by 10- to 12-inch wide rough lumber placed on edge, will carry any of the root crops through successfully. We use this method here on Cape Cod, as it is much easier than digging and storing.

A method sometimes used is to bury a section or two of large drain tile *vertically* in the ground in a protected, shaded location, with wooden covers to fit. With extra covering in very cold weather, all root crops may thus be kept safe even in quite severe climates.

All vegetables stored, even for a short period, should be examined frequently so that any showing the least sign of decay may be removed immediately. The old saying that "one rotten apple will spoil the barrel" applies equally to vegetables.

Freezing is a method of preserving surplus vegetables which has to a large degree supplanted canning. Freezing is so quick and easy that it is really no chore. All manufacturers of freezers send out charts and instructions for blanching, freezing, and wrapping vegetables and fruits. We simply freeze surpluses that we cannot use as they mature, and even this makes a very considerable store by the time the season is over.

THE SIX LEADERS

Where space is limited it is of course impossible to grow a great variety of vegetables. One then is faced with the problem of which to attempt.

The first factor for reaching this decision is of course one's personal taste. As that differs with the individual, no rules can be laid down. Here, however, are some half dozen, which are quite universally grown.

Lettuce. This is probably the most generally liked and most constantly used vegetable, popular at all times. Unfortunately, however, few of the present generation know what really tender, tasty lettuce is. They know only the commercially grown Iceberg type, so hard and tough that it will stand shipping thousands of miles; it is fit only to be used as a garnish for so-called salads in hotels and restaurants and by individuals who do not know better varieties. Usually it is returned, uneaten, to the kitchen and goes into the garbage pail—where it belonged in the first place. The commercial-type "head" lettuces grown in most of the United States are not even listed in French or English seed catalogs.

The loose-leaf lettuces form heads of a sort, more accurately dense clusters of leaves, all of which are tender and delicious. By utilizing a deep frame, and with some protection in winter, we find we can have lettuce here on Cape Cod for nine months of the year. (For midwinter supply we grow it in peat pots in the greenhouse.) Lettuce is much hardier than is generally supposed. In moderate climates plants set out in a coldframe in late September or October come through the winter in a semidormant condition to renew growth in March. Heavy burlap over glass prevents really hard freezing in frame during midwinter.

Our favorite varieties are Bibb, Burpeeana (an improved form of Bibb), and Oakleaf. We sow a pinch of each monthly. Big Boston is an old, semihard head type with very tender leaves which is sometimes grown for local markets. Lettuce washed in cold water, shaken semidry,

The loose-heading types of lettuce are easier to grow and infinitely superior in salads to the tasteless "cabbage-head" varieties. One need not have a vegetable garden to grow lettuce; a spot in the flower garden, and a coldframe for fall and early spring supply, keeps the table supplied. Variety shown here is Oak-leaf.

wrapped in a damp cloth, and put in the refrigerator will keep crisp and fresh for more than a week.

If you want lettuce to *eat* instead of as a garnish, try two or three of the tender varieties combined and tossed in a bowl with the following dressing which we make up in quantity and keep ready in the refrigerator.

GrayRock French Dressing

1 pt. pure olive oil
2 tsp. lemon juice
   tarragon vinegar to taste
2 tsp. salt
   dash black pepper
1 clove garlic, chopped
     or pressed
½ cup chopped ripe olives

½ tsp. paprika
½ tsp. prepared mustard
½ tsp. Worcestershire sauce,
    Angostura bitters, or
    Soy sauce
1 tsp. dried salad herbs
    or fresh herbs to taste
1 tsp. celery salt

Tomatoes produce more, over a longer season, in proportion to the space they occupy than any other vegetable. They are one of the easiest to grow and most certain to yield satisfactorily; also easy to can, though in these days that is seldom done.

Seed is sown, under glass, about six weeks before the last frost date. Extra-strong, vigorous plants may be had by transplanting to 2-inch peat pots and replanting these, in their pots, to 4-inch peat pots. By spraying these with Blossom-set, when first blooms appear, it is usually possible to get them with a few small green fruits started by setting-out time. Soil used for last potting should be enriched with well-decayed rich compost, or with dehydrated commercial manure such as Bovung or Driconure. Plants are set deep—up to second or third leaf joints—as they will send out extra roots from the joints.

The essentials for mixed salads that will really win you a reputation as a gourmet cook are easily grown at home and during the summer may well save quite a bit of folding money. This "arrangement of salad materials" was all home-grown except the lemon! (We had those, too, in our greenhouse this year.)

Self-supporting trellis for tomatoes. Posts may be set 8 to 10 feet apart.

While the plants are usually tied to stakes to support them, it is better, and in the end easier, to use stout "ladders" made of uprights of 2×3 pine or cedar, with four crosspieces of 1×2-inch, about 3 feet long. If taken up and stored for the winter, these will last for many years.

As the plants grow, they send out side shoots from every leaf joint. All but three or four of these should be pinched out as they appear. Those remaining are trained, and when necessary, tied to the crosspieces with soft twine or strips of discarded sheets.

We like our tomatoes dead ripe—as they are almost never found at a supermarket. We pick them when they have turned color and then place them on a window sill in full sun, using them as they ripen. As danger of frost approaches, full-sized fruits are picked green and placed on a board in a coldframe to finish ripening under glass. Some of the green fruits are used for pickles—though our aging stomachs do not allow us to partake of these delicacies as freely as we used to. For younger gardeners, green tomato pickles, piccalilli, and India relish are all well worth the trouble of making.

Well-grown plants in peat pots are available at most garden centers for those who do not care to grow their own. Hybrid varieties may cost a bit more than others but are well worth the difference. Pot plants cost more than plants grown in and sold from flats, but again are worth the difference, as they suffer no transplanting set-back, and produce ripe fruits ten days to two weeks earlier.

Tomato troubles include the horned tomato worm, a big, green 4- to 5-inch long fellow not easily discovered until he has done considerable

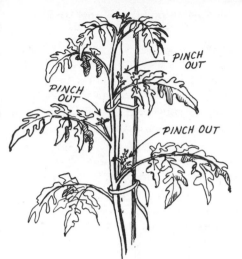

To get first-quality tomatoes, much of the new growth should be pinched out as it starts, leaving only a few main stems.

How often do you enjoy a really tender, ripe-clear-through tomato? To be shipped they must be picked half green—and they never attain full flavor. No garden is needed; merely a trellis in a flower border.

damage. Keep fruit off the ground to avoid premature rots and other soil-borne diseases.

Beans. This humble legume is one of the easiest and most rewarding of all vegetables to grow. Both its types and its uses are many and varied. Largest yields, in proportion to space occupied, are from climbing or pole beans. These also have the advantages of bearing over a long season from one planting, and of serving, if supported on chicken wire in a location getting abundant sunshine, as a most effective temporary screen.

Bush beans yield for a comparatively short time, and at least three plantings should be made, at three-week intervals, to provide tender young beans for the season. As the plants bear heavily, you may have surpluses —which are readily frozen for later use. (Leftover cooked beans used in the "snap" stage are excellent in mixed salads, or simply combined with chopped white onion, chopped, hard boiled egg, and mayonnaise. Serve on crisp leaves of Bibb-type lettuce.)

As beans are killed by the slightest frost, nothing is gained by planting them until really warm weather has arrived. This is especially true of lima beans. Largest yields are obtained by thinning out the plants as soon as the second true leaves develop, to stand 3 or 4 inches apart; 4 to 5 for bush limas.

Pole beans, which are vigorous climbers, are supported by individual poles with stubs or short branches left on; or trained up "tepees" of three poles tied together at the top. A 6-foot chicken-wire fence serves the same purpose and makes picking easier.

Varieties of beans are numerous, and favorites vary from section to section of the country. For green-pod snap beans we grow Tendergreen, Tendercrop, and Topcrop, but there are others generally popular. In wax beans we like Burpee's Brittle Wax and Eastern Brittle Wax. Golden Wax (Top Notch), Cherokee, and Chocktaw Wax are others. In pole beans Kentucky Wonder—an old, old-timer—is still the most widely grown. A comparatively new, flat-podded yellow pole bean, Burpee's Golden, is a great favorite of ours. We like to "French" or slice lengthwise all the above, unless they are picked at so immature a stage that they can be cooked whole. Lima beans may be had in either bush or climbing forms. Burpee's Fordhook is the standard type of the former. Fordhook 242 is an improved form. Burpee's Best produces a similar quality in the pole type. Ideal Pole Lima is large-podded and of good quality. Don't try limas if your growing season is very short. Pole types require 88 days; bush varieties about 74.

Sweet Corn is as typically American as baseball—and as universally liked. In proportion to its yield, however, it takes up more space than any of the preceding vegetables. In many sections it is widely grown for local markets, but unless it can be had, *really fresh picked,* it is worth-

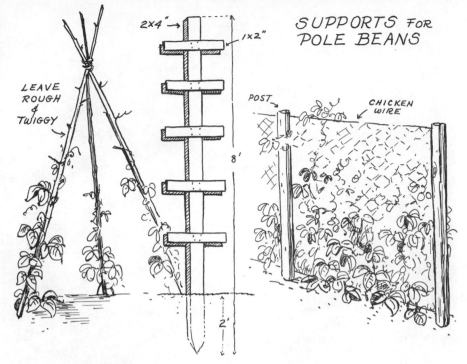

SUPPORTS FOR POLE BEANS

LEAVE ROUGH & TWIGGY

2x4"

1x2"

8'

2'

POST

CHICKEN WIRE

Pole beans require a minimum of ground space. This is Burpee's Golden—light yellow, tender, and delicious.

Sweet corn to be enjoyed at its very best must be home-grown; literally loses flavor by the hour after picking. We like the yellow varieties best. This is Wonderful.

KEEP SOIL HILLED UP TO BASE OF STALKS

Corn that is kept hilled up as it grows is less likely to be blown over in wind storms. Hilling should be started early in order to avoid damage to roots.

while to grow your own. Some local growers today make several pickings a day so that regular customers may enjoy it at its best. If there must be some delay, keep unshucked ears in a cool place, wrapped in a damp cloth.

Corn can be grown in either hills or rows. We plant kernels 4 or 5 inches apart in short blocks 3 or 4 rows wide, to assure good fertilization. (Every individual kernel, in order to develop, must have had its grain of pollen dust, reaching it through the tube-like "silk.") We thin them out to leave the strongest plants a foot or so apart. Seed is sown in a furrow about 4 inches deep, covered 2 inches, and then, as growth develops, gradually hilled up to 4 or 5 inches above ground level. This helps substantially in preventing stalks from being blown down in wind. Corn is a greedy feeder, and at least one side dressing of a high-nitrogen fertilizer should be given as stalks grow, starting when they are a foot or so high. For a continuous succession, plant both an early and a main crop variety every three to four weeks from average date of last killing frost in your locality, the last planting being calculated to mature at least ten days before average date of first fall frost.

To eat off the cob, gather when kernels are in the full "milk" stage. Drop in boiling water after shucking. We boil only 3 minutes. Others prefer to extend this to 5 or 6. Mature ears (not hard but less milky) may be used for corn fritters:

Green Corn Fritters

6 ears of corn, grated
3 eggs, beaten separately
1 large tbsp. flour
3 tbsps. cream
   salt to taste
¼ tsp. baking powder

Beat egg whites stiff and set aside. Beat egg yolks until thick. To these add cream, salt, flour, baking powder and mix. Add grated corn. Fold in beaten egg whites and bake at once on a hot griddle, preferably electric so they can be served piping hot and just baked.

When we freeze corn, we either blanch perfect young ears, cut in half, and freeze on the cob, or grate older ears, heat to boiling in a double boiler, and freeze for later use in fritters.

Many varieties of sweet corn are offered in seed catalogs. There is some variation in the way they grow in different sections, and therefore the beginner will do well, when ordering, to consult a garden-minded neighbor or the local county agent.

Asparagus is given a place in this limited list for four reasons: first, it is quite universally liked; second, it may readily be grown, even if one has no vegetable garden; third, because, with very little care, it yields for a score of years, or even more; and finally because, after being cut for the table during the spring season, the stalks—which are then allowed to grow—make a most decorative, feathery hedge, 5 feet or more in height.

Asparagus may be grown from seed, but the home gardener usually procures roots. These are set out in spring, spaced 12 to 18 inches apart in a trench a foot or so deep, well enriched with rotted manure; or, if this is not obtainable, with dried commercial manure.

For the first summer no stalks are cut, the aim being to develop strong plants as quickly as possible. Growing plants should be fertilized freely, kept clear of weeds and of any pests such as the asparagus beetle (list in Appendix). The second spring some stalks may be cut for a short period. They are best taken when 8 to 10 inches high, cutting just at the soil level, and taking care not to injure younger stalks not yet above ground. Several stalks from each plant should be left to mature.

After cutting has ceased, a heavy mulch worked in between and around the plants both keeps down weeds and conserves moisture.

Melons. The only reason for attempting to grow one's own melons is that this is the surest way to have them of really top quality. Locally grown melons have disappeared from most markets; and those grown hundreds or even thousands of miles away and packed green in order to withstand shipping are seldom worth eating no matter how attractive they may look. Unless you have tasted them home-grown and sun-ripened, you really don't know how delicious melons can be. In proportion to yield, melons take up considerable space, and they are subject to injury from animals—including impatient small boys—insect pests, and diseases. But to be of really top quality, melons (especially cantaloupes) must ripen on the vine until they part from it at the slightest touch.

Melons prefer a rich soil, rather on the light side, and—especially in the north—a protected, sunny exposure that warms up quickly. As the seedlings may be killed by the slightest frost, it is desirable, in northern sections, to plant seeds under Hotkaps or plant protectors of plastic which are removed when the plants are well up.

A still better method is to sow seeds—five or six in a 4-inch peat pot—in a coldframe or in the greenhouse, about two weeks before the last frost is likely to occur. They can then be set out in the garden, pots and all, leaving only two or three plants to a "hill." In well-enriched soil they grow vigorously and should be spaced 5 to 6 feet apart each way.

We use a combination of both methods, covering the pot-grown plants, when they are set out, with plant protectors or with wire-covered frames (page 126) for several days, taking care however to remove the former on hot, sunny days.

If kept well supplied with water, plants will cover the ground quickly. A sharp eye should be kept for the first sign of injury from such enemies as cucumber beetle, melon lice, and borers (list in Appendix).

And how about melons? To avoid the texture and tastelessness of "store-bought" cantaloupes, which often taste like a piece of rubber, find room for a few hills in a sunny spot. Delicious is a favorite variety with us.

First frost will kill the foliage but any full-grown melons may be kept and ripened in a frame or a sunny window. While the flavor will not be quite perfect, it is likely to be much better than that of supermarket specimens.

Pests and diseases of vegetables and their control are listed in the Appendix.

VEGETABLE CHART

Vegetable	Number of plants or feet of row for seeding for two persons	Distance between rows or hills (in inches)	Distance between plants after thinning (in inches)	Planting
Asparagus	25 plants	36	18	Perennial
Beans, snap, bush	50 feet	24	3–4	Succession
pole	25 feet or 4 hills	36	24	Long season
Beets	20 feet	18	3	Early and late
Broccoli	8 plants	30	30	Early and late
Brussels sprouts	8 plants	30	30	Late
Cabbage, early	12 plants	24	24	Early and late
late	12 plants	30	24	
Carrots	20 feet	24	3	Early and late
Chinese-Cabbage	10 feet	18	10	Late
Corn	100 feet	36	12	Early, midseason, and late
Cucumber	4 hills	48	8*	Late; long season; plant along one edge.
Eggplant	3 plants	30	24	Late; long season.
Lettuce plants	25 plants	18	8	Early and late
seed	15 feet	18	6	Succession
Muskmelon (Cantaloupe)	4 hills	48	8*	Late; long season; plant along one edge.
Onion seed	20 feet	12	3	Early; long season.
sets	20 feet	12	3	Early
Parsley	10 feet	12	6	Early; long season.
Pea	50 feet	30	3	Early and late
Pepper	3 plants	30	24	Late; long season.
Radish	10 plants	12	3	Succession
Rhubarb	3 plants		48	Perennial
Spinach	50	18	3	Early and late
Summer Squash	4 hills	48	8*	Late; long season; plant along edge.

* between plants in each hill

VEGETABLES

Perennial

Asparagus
Artichoke (*Cynara scolymus*) Grown on West Coast.
Rhubarb

Annual

Hardy	Half-hardy	Tender
Kale	Beet	Bean
Leek	Broccoli	Corn
Lettuce	Cauliflower	Cucumber
Onion	Cabbage	Eggplant
Parsley	Carrot	Muskmelon
Parsnip	Chard, Swiss	(Cantaloupe)
Pea	Chinese-Cabbage	Pepper
Radish		Squash
Spinach		Tomato
Turnip		

NOTE: In further reference to the last column, headed Planting (opposite page).

Perennial: Indicates a permanent planting of hardy roots.

Succession: Short season crops which must be planted in succession.

Long season: Annual vegetables which remain in the rows all season.

Late; long season: Tender vegetables, set out late, which remain in the garden all the rest of the season.

Early; long season: Hardy vegetables which can be sowed early, but which take all season to develop.

Early and Late: Cool weather vegetables which can be sown early for spring crop and late for fall crop.

Plant along edge: Suggested for vine crops for the small garden so that vines can be trained away from vegetable rows.

Thy vineyards and thy orchards are
Most beautiful and fair,
Full furnishèd with trees and fruits
Most wonderful and rare.
The New Jerusalem. ANONYMOUS

CHAPTER 17

Tree Fruits, Small Fruits, and Berries

The word "fruit" as ordinarily but not too correctly employed covers a number of quite distinct and very different plants. Consequently, their requirements and the methods employed in growing them also vary widely. Strawberries, for instance, have little in common with blueberries, peaches, or apples; yet all are commonly referred to as fruits.

As far as their culture is concerned, these several types of fruit should be considered as vines, canes, shrubs, or trees, and most of the suggestions already given in connection with those groups—as to soil preparation, planting, feeding, and general care—apply also to the fruits we are now considering.

With either fresh or frozen fruits of all kinds so generally available in the markets, why should any homeowner go to the trouble of producing his own?

The reasons are nearly the same as for growing one's own vegetables. Although the first of these is the fun of doing it, there is also the element of *quality*. Many fruits, like many vegetables, should be fully ripe before being harvested. To be handled after they have even *begun* to ripen results in bruising that develops into decay, often in an incredibly short period. Frozen fruits, *if picked and processed when fully ripe,* may be of better flavor than fresh fruits which were picked green and shipped long distances.

Here is what one of the country's leading authorities on fruit growing, commercial as well as in home gardens, has to say concerning this matter:

Home-grown fruits are as a rule much superior to market fruits. Fruits for shipment must be picked in a slightly immature condition to withstand packing and handling. They must often be harvested before the sugars and flavors are developed up to the point where the ripening process will continue. This is especially true of the more perishable fruits such as berries. . . . A fruit that is allowed to develop on the plant until it is fully ripe has quality, flavor and nutritional value that cannot be attained in fruits that must be picked for shipment. . . . Even for local handling many sorts must be picked before fully mature.

If his object is a real crop of fruit, the home gardener should attempt tree fruits, especially apples and peaches, only in localities where they are known to be successful and where spray service is available. Rainfall, frost dates, and other factors are very important in determining chances of success. Before attempting tree fruits, consult the nearest county agent and follow his advice on what *varieties* to get, as these vary with local climatic conditions.

Space is usually a determining factor in deciding what fruits, if any, are to be grown. Frequently it is *the* determining factor, since most fruits require full sun to develop and ripen properly. Overcrowded flowers will make some sort of display even if individual blooms are not up to par. Overcrowded fruits, however, will prove to be a complete waste of time and money.

The growers of tree fruits, especially of apples, have done much to make it possible for the amateur to grow his own by grafting standard varieties on dwarf-growing stocks. Fortunately, many fruits may be produced in little or no more space than is required for most shrubs or vines; and several of them, when in flower, are quite as decorative.

Location. Most of the fruits are not too particular as to soil. With the exception of blueberries, however, all prefer not to have wet feet, and even these may be grown as well on average upland ground that does not dry out excessively.

Humus in the soil, both to conserve moisture and to provide food, is as highly desirable for fruits as it is for most plants.

A rather acid soil with a pH above 5 but below 7 (the ideal is 5.5 to 6.5) best suits most fruits and is the maximum essential for blueberries, which thrive in very acid soil. In the preparation of soil for planting fruit trees and berries, the suggestions given in Chapters 2 and 9 apply.

To ripen properly and develop full flavor, fruits should be fully exposed to the sun for at least half of the day, preferably in the morning.

Planting. When to plant depends upon climatic conditions. In general, fall planting is best in sections where the ground freezes early in fall, and winter temperatures are severe. In areas where autumns are mild, fall planting gets the trees off to an earlier start. In either case, but especially when spring planting is preferable, the earlier the better. Any order for fruit trees should be placed well in advance to assure the arrival of the stock at an early date. Trees or bushes that have broken dormancy and begun to sprout even slightly get off to a bad start. Any fruit stock,

When plants from nursery cannot be set out at once, keep roots buried in moist soil to prevent drying out.

immediately upon receipt, should be unpacked and untied, the roots soaked in water, and the plants placed in wet peatmoss or sphagnum until they can be planted.

In connection with advice on ordering early, it may be well to insert a word concerning "bearing age" trees. In our experience and that of many other gardeners we know, little or nothing is to be gained and much may be lost by trying to save two or three years in this way. Bearing age trees (unless they can be bought locally and moved with generous root balls) are sure to receive such a set-back in shipping and transplanting that they seldom bear any fruit sooner than one- or two-year-old trees; and at two or three years after planting are likely to be smaller than the others, if indeed they are alive at all.

Multiple-variety trees are also likely to prove unsatisfactory, as some branches will grow much more rapidly than others, and the pruning and spraying problems involved are enough to stump even the experts. Of course they are interesting as conversation pieces.

Newly set fruit trees of all kinds should be protected from rabbits, field mice, pine mice, and other rodents during cold weather. (See Appendix, Pests and Their Control.)

Pruning. General care after planting is much the same as for other subjects. The chief difference is that trees grown for fruit require more careful pruning. Pruning fruit trees is necessary not only for the health of the tree, but also for the quality and the amount of fruit produced.

Without going into the details of pruning all the various kinds of fruit, the guiding principles will be given in connection with the several fruits discussed in the following pages.

Mulching. In general, a mulch around fruit trees saves labor and conserves moisture in the soil. Leaves, straw, old manure, grass clippings (if not too thick), spent manure, even small stones that will pack together, may be used. With the exception of apples and pears, few fruit trees (and no small fruits) do as well in sod as in soil that is kept mulched; or kept cultivated, which provides a soil mulch. This should be borne in mind when one considers using fruit trees as lawn specimens.

Under most conditions and especially in warm climates, fruit trees benefit from summer mulching.

Spraying. If satisfactory crops are to be expected, the fruit trees, more than any other group of plants, demand frequent and meticulously timed spraying. Commercial apple orchards apply from ten to thirteen sprays during the season in order to get perfect fruit. New spray materials give promise of cutting down the number of applications required. On the other hand, many pests develop immunity to sprays being used and thus create new problems.

These facts are presented not with the idea of discouraging the home-owner from growing some of his own fruit, but to make him realize what he faces in attempting the undertaking. If he succeeds it will be a bigger feather in his cap! In any event, his fruit trees, when in bloom, will be quite as beautiful as any of the ornamental trees and shrubs he grows. Indeed, among plants used specifically for decorative effects, some of the most beautiful are cherries, apples, crabapples, and quinces.

The pests most likely to be encountered in growing fruit trees are aphids, borers, codling moths, curculios, fruitworms, leaf hoppers, leaf rollers, mites of various sorts, scales, and slugs. There are also diseases like fireblight and mildew. By following the spray program recommended for your locality by your county agent or nearby Agricultural Experiment Station, all troubles can be controlled *if* the sprays are applied at exactly the times specified. An all-purpose fruit-tree spray formula and schedule appear on page 472 but consultation with one of the authorities named above is emphatically advised.

Harvesting and storing. Among the tree fruits, apples, pears, quinces, and especially peaches should be gathered before they are dead ripe, but must be handled very carefully, as any bruise quickly develops into a spot of decay. Stored in a dry, cool, dark place, best spread out on shelves, they gradually ripen to eating stage. Peaches, early pears, and plums may take just a few days. Others like winter apples and pears may not ripen for many weeks. Those fine old winter apples, the Rhode Island Greening and Winter Russet, for instance, are not at their best until well after New Year's. (A good example of the many fine fruits and vegetables that have disappeared from commercial use simply because they have no "eye appeal" on chain-store counters, and can be enjoyed only by gardeners who grow their own!)

TREE FRUITS

The culture of the various tree fruits varies in detail but follows much the same general principles. The suggestions given concerning apples apply generally to the others: pears, cherries, peaches, apricots, and plums. More detailed information may be obtained from one's local Agricultural Experiment Station.

The Apple. Unless one has a fairly large place, it is advisable to use only dwarf-growing trees. These are produced by grafting standard varieties on dwarf-growing stock, known as Malling, developed in England. The type generally used is Malling No. IX. Grown on their own roots, most orchard apples produce very large trees—with trunks a foot or more in diameter and up to 25 feet in height. A dwarf tree of the same variety would be not over 8 to 10 feet in height, with side branches in proportion. No. VII stock makes a tree somewhat larger, but still a dwarf compared to a standard. A very great advantage of the dwarf trees is that they can be pruned, sprayed, and picked with only a fraction of the effort required for standards. It should be kept in mind, however, that the *roots* as well as the tops are dwarf. It is therefore advisable, especially where high winds are likely to be encountered, to provide stakes to support the trunks until trees are well established.

In growing most fruit trees, pruning is of particular importance because *from the very start* the trees must be guided and shaped into a definite form. Left to grow normally as most ornamental trees are, they would send up strong, sky-reaching leaders with comparatively weak side branches. For this reason apples, pears, peaches, and, to a lesser degree, plums should be cut back a fourth to a third *when they are planted.* The purpose of course is to encourage as quickly as possible the development of side branches. As these increase in size, the grower must decide which ones are to be retained. The object is to keep only a few main or "scaffold" branches (four to six or eight in the case of apples) and to have these as evenly spaced as possible, but emerging from the trunk at different levels in order that the maximum amount of air and sunshine can reach all parts of the tree.

Once established, this scaffold of main branches is maintained for the life of the tree, but there should be sufficient annual pruning to keep an

Dwarf fruit trees occupy only a fraction of space required for "standard" trees. Multiple-variety dwarfs frequently end in failure.

"open head"—that is, a branch structure that freely admits fresh air and light to all parts.

The pruning of apples and of other tree fruits is best done during the winter or *very* early spring before sap starts to run (see sketch).

Pears. Pear trees, once established, require less constant care in pruning and spraying than apples. Dwarf pears are standard varieties grown on quince rootstocks. They prefer a soil on the heavy side, but with good drainage.

One-year trees are cut back about a third at the time of planting and two-year trees in about the same proportion, lowest branches being removed, and all but three or four of the rest. After that, little pruning is required except to remove lowest branches (until a suitable trunk is developed) and the weakest of any that crisscross or crowd.

Plums. Plums are of two distinct types, the Japanese and the European. The former bear much larger fruits. Where soil is light or sandy, the Japanese type is usually considered to do better. In any case, overfertilizing, especially with quickly available forms of nitrogen, is to be avoided. On sandy soils, however, a yearly feeding in spring may be required.

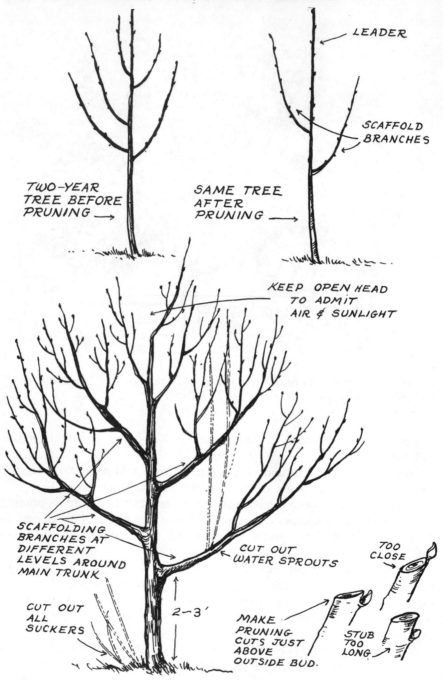

LEADER

SCAFFOLD BRANCHES

TWO-YEAR TREE BEFORE PRUNING →

SAME TREE AFTER PRUNING →

KEEP OPEN HEAD TO ADMIT AIR & SUNLIGHT

SCAFFOLDING BRANCHES AT DIFFERENT LEVELS AROUND MAIN TRUNK

CUT OUT WATER SPROUTS

TOO CLOSE

CUT OUT ALL SUCKERS

2-3'

MAKE PRUNING CUTS JUST ABOVE OUTSIDE BUD.

STUB TOO LONG

Fruit trees, in order to develop into properly proportioned producers of heavy crops, must be kept pruned from the start.

Peaches are the easiest of the tree fruits to grow—and the soonest to come into bearing. New dwarf varieties, doubling as flowering shrubs, will increase their usefulness.

With plums as with pears, only moderate pruning is needed—but enough to keep branches sufficiently thinned out to maintain an open head.

Peaches. In most sections, peaches are likely to be the most rewarding of any tree fruits to grow in the home garden. They come into bearing quickly, may readily be kept to moderate size, yield generously, and in bloom are quite as decorative as most ornamentals. With the advent of the new truly dwarf type, the owner of even the smallest place should be able to enjoy home-grown, tree-ripened peaches. The first variety of this new type grows only 4 to 5 feet tall but yields full-sized peaches.

Unlike apples and pears, peaches are not happy in sod or grass. They may be given a place along the north or west side of the vegetable garden. They often do well in soil that is rather light and sandy for other tree fruits, but under such conditions require more generous applications of fertilizer. The spraying required to control insects and diseases is much less than for apples.

To bear sizable crops of good fruit, peaches need constant attention in the matter of pruning. This starts with planting. Very young trees or "whips" up to about 4 feet high are cut back a third to a half, and any side growths are stripped off. Larger sizes, up to 6 feet or so, are cut back

Raspberries are by far the most rewarding of the cane fruits. The so-called everbearing—more correctly "repeat" (in June and September) bearing— lengthen the season at each end. This variety is September.

Strawberries are easy to grow and produce heavy crops of fruit. The secrets of success in getting lots of big berries is to set out some plants each year, and to keep soil well mulched.

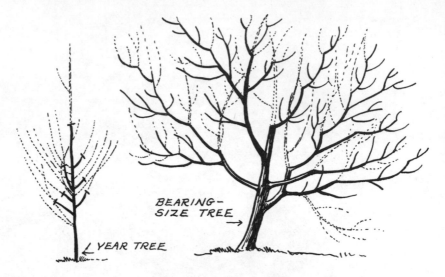

Peach trees, from the time they are planted, require annual pruning. A large part of each season's new growth becomes surplus, and if left makes a tangled, dense growth.

proportionately, but three or four of the upper side branches—evenly spaced to form a head—are left, cut back to about 5 inches each.

Peaches continue to require severe annual pruning. Branches tending to grow upright are cut back to an outside bud to encourage spreading growth; crossing or weak limbs are removed and others cut out or cut back to maintain an open head. As fruits develop, thinning may be required to keep the branches from touching each other. Heavily laden branches may require supports to prevent their breaking. In some sections the trunks need protection from rabbits, as is the case with all true fruits (see Appendix). Fruit should be gathered just before it reaches the dead-ripe stage, and handled as gently as eggs.

Apricots and nectarines require much the same culture as peaches. They are often used as espalier subjects.

Grapes, as home-grown fruit for the small place, have the great advantages that they occupy little ground area and can also serve as an important part of the landscaping. The easiest way to grow them is over an arbor, especially where shade is desired.

While grapes flourish and produce some fruit even if they are given little or no attention, really good results are to be expected only if the vines are properly supported, trained, fed and protected from possible injury from pests and diseases.

They prefer a sunny southern exposure, a slope being preferable but not essential. Even though the vines may grow vigorously, any extreme

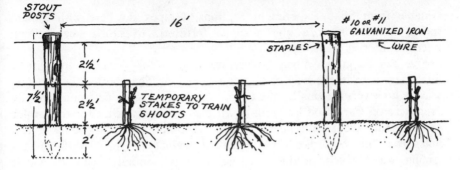

Support for grapes grown primarily for fruit.

in the way of soil, either too wet or too dry, will result in poor crops of fruit. In general, a slightly acid soil that remains fairly moist is best. Full sunshine is really essential in ripening the fruit.

If grapes are to be grown principally for eating instead of as a part of the landscape picture, it is best to support them on post and wire trellises. Stout posts, extending 5 to 6 feet above the ground and 10 to 20 feet apart, carry 2 wires or plastic ropes, the first halfway up the post and the other at the top. Vines are spaced 8 to 10 feet apart and tied to wires as they grow.

Plants when set are cut back to two or three buds, and roots to 8 or 10 inches. Plant early in spring, as soon as ground can be worked. The first year the strongest cane is tied to the wires; the second year vines are trained along wires horizontally, and so on until top wires are reached. Detailed information on pruning and other phases of grape culture is ob-

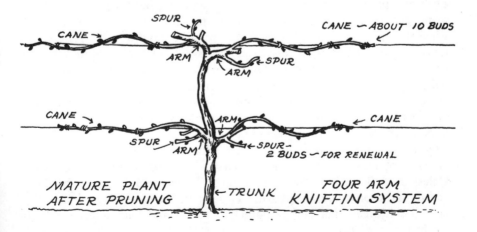

Annual pruning is required if vines are to continue to bear good crops.

tainable from State Experiment Stations. Grapes do best with annual spring application of a high-nitrogen fertilizer. Mulching keeps down weeds, conserves moisture.

Figs can be grown much farther north than they usually are with a little extra care in the way of winter protection. The shorter the growing season, however, the smaller the crop. We secure a few ripe fruits annually even here on Cape Cod by tying down the lowest branches for the winter and covering them with heavy burlap. Another enthusiast, only a few miles away, has a hardier variety planted against a high, south-facing retaining wall, which produces a good crop annually without winter protection. Roots are much hardier than growth above ground, and new branches develop quickly when severe pruning is required after winter injury. Young plants tied up, banked with leaves, dry peatmoss, or pine needles, held in place by stakes and burlap, will stand quite severe temperatures as will larger specimens if the trunks are wrapped and the tops protected by burlap, or similar material.

In the South the fig is a decorative and valuable dooryard fruit tree. It is happiest in compact clay and wet soils that are free from nematodes, which are apt to attack the roots in rich, friable, well-drained situations. A spring feeding is advisable, followed by a summer mulch. Year-round mulching is even better as figs root shallowly and so are injured by deep cultivation. Celeste, Brown Turkey, and Brunswick are standard varieties, ripening—in the order listed—from July to September.

BUSH FRUITS

Blueberries are by far the most rewarding of the several types of berries suitable for the small home garden. They yield worthwhile crops, may easily be frozen or preserved for winter, and can be fitted into the landscape plan as they form shrubs which are very decorative from spring, when the bare stems turn crimson, to late autumn, when the foliage is a rich plum-red. Their only disadvantage is the fact that birds love the ripening fruit so much that the bushes need protection during this period unless enough are planted to supply both humans and birds.

Young plants develop rapidly into good-sized specimens which assume individual characters as they mature. When specimens are to be set in a lawn or garden area for ornamental effect as well as for berries, extra large holes 4 feet or more in diameter should be prepared with a bushel or more of loose, acid peatmoss mixed with sand, if the soil is heavy. Unless the soil pH is below 6, ¼ pound of ammonium sulfate should be added, and thoroughly watered in. This treatment is repeated annually in neutral soil areas, half being applied in spring and half in early fall for the first two years.

Blueberries do best in soil that is naturally moist, or can be kept so, but that is also so perfectly drained that it never stays soggy wet. No cultivation other than the removal of weeds is needed, but a constant mulch blanket should be maintained. Sawdust is more satisfactory than peatmoss for this purpose unless the latter can be kept moist (not wet) by frequent watering. Seaweed, bog hay, cranberry vines, or ground coconut shells are satisfactory mulching materials.

Until the plants are three or four years old, little pruning is required except to clip out weak, dying, or crisscrossing growths; or to head back any inclined to become too tall. The bushes naturally assume attractive, many-branched, spreading forms.

If there is a heavy set of flower buds on newly planted bushes it is advisable to remove most of them for the first season or two in order to establish strong plants quickly. This requires will power, but pays off well in the end.

Currants and Gooseberries used to be grown more generally than they are today. Homemade currant jelly and gooseberry jam were standard treats for special occasions as well as for everyday use.

These two bush fruits are easily grown, however, and make rather neat, well-rounded shrubs 3 or 4 feet high, which are especially attractive when in fruit. A few bushes may be fitted into a planting of shrubs where they receive much, if not full, sun. Usually they are given a place in a corner of the vegetable garden. To produce well they must not be crowded. The oldest wood should be removed right down to the ground after three or four years' growth.

Gooseberries tend to grow less erect than currants, and the lowest, spreading branches should be cut out as they start. If grown as "standards" they make quite decorative conversation pieces. Ours are planted on each side of the entrance to the vegetable garden and cause much favorable comment. We have found it necessary, however, to give the tall, bare "trunks" or stems some support. We use inconspicuous, rusted iron stakes to which the stems are loosely fastened, at intervals, with raffia ties.

In pruning gooseberry bushes, all branches over four years old should be cut out, right down to the ground. One-year-old growths produce more vigorous side shoots if cut back 4 to 6 inches.

Gooseberries and currants other than the red varieties should not be planted in areas where white pine blister rust is prevalent.

Insects which attack currants or gooseberries are: aphids; sawfly; borers, including the corn borer; fruit fly. Diseases: blister rust; leaf spot; cane blight; crown gall.

THE CANE FRUITS

This group includes raspberries, blackberries, dewberries, and logan-berries. All are characterized by their vigorous, unruly, and viciously thorned canes—which bear the delectable fruits! Given half a chance, all of them increase and spread rapidly, and so they are not for the very small garden. In fact they are scarcely for the garden at all, as they are much more easily controlled in beds of their own, where they may be kept from taking over adjoining areas.

All the cane fruits prefer a loamy soil that is well drained but retains moisture. Dewberries will prosper in a somewhat sandier soil than the others. Most of them, with the exception of types recommended for the southern states, are entirely hardy and do best in the Northeast and Northwest.

Most widely grown of this group are the raspberries, which, with ever-bearing varieties now available, are well worth growing. Any surplus fruit at the height of the bearing seasons is easy to freeze or makes superb jam.

Plants received from the nursery come in the form of one-year canes with bunched roots. After tops are cut back to about 2 feet and roots trimmed, they are set out at 3-foot intervals in a row, in full sun. Planting should be done just as early as possible in spring (or in autumn in mild climates) since soil should be kept moist until they are well established.

Raspberries tend to grow erect, but should be given some support to prevent their bending over when burdened with fruit, which tends to cluster at tips of canes. A row of 2×4 posts—or better, round posts of cedar or cypress—spaced 10 to 15 feet apart can be placed along the row. To these are fastened two strands of plastic clothesline about 4 feet from the ground, one on each side of the raspberry plants. These will hold the growing canes upright and greatly facilitate both culture and picking. Old canes are removed entirely after fall fruiting, and young canes are cut back two thirds of their length.

To set out new plants, well-established suckers can be used if desired. Canes are cut back to not more than 18 inches, or to 9 inches if the grower is willing to forego any fruit the first year. In this case, the first crop will be the fall fruit of the following season, after which new canes are pruned back one third their length. Old canes are cut to the ground after fruiting. If new canes are set out every three or four years, prefer-ably in a newly prepared location, a continuous supply is assured.

Unwanted suckers between the rows, which develop rapidly during each growing season, must be hoed out or the result will be a thick tangle of canes and little fruit.

Black Raspberries, or Blackcaps, and purple and yellow raspberries, are less satisfactory than the red varieties for the home garden. By nature

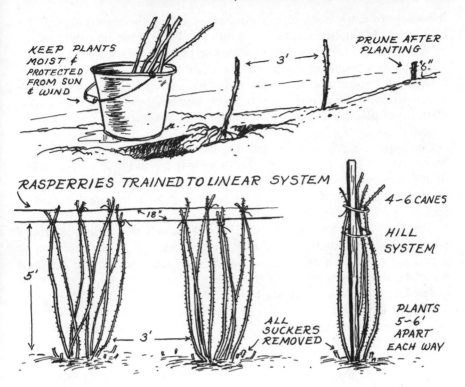

Raspberries, easily grown, are very satisfactory as a home-garden fruit crop. Old canes are cut out annually.

they are rampant, sprawling growers. To keep them under control, they must be pruned back while the tips are still soft to a height of 24 to 30 inches, according to the vigor of the variety being grown. Laterals also should be pinched back. For best flavor and easy picking, berries should be permitted to ripen on the vines, picked in the cool of the evening, and kept cool overnight.

Blackberries need room because the canes spread rapidly. Rows should be set 7 feet apart and, as with raspberries, all suckers or new canes appearing between the rows must be hoed out. Each year dead canes are cut to the ground and new canes reduced to 5 feet in length, only the strongest being left to bear. In general, culture is the same as for red raspberries. Bailey is a standard variety.

STRAWBERRIES

Strawberries, all things considered, are highly satisfactory for the home garden. They can be grown to perfection over a much wider range of territory than any of the others. The so-called everbearing varieties make it possible to enjoy home-ripe, fresh berries before the main crop in May or June, and in autumn until first frosts. To be at their very best, strawberries must be dead ripe before they are picked.

As few as a couple of dozen well-cared-for plants give much more than a token return; but for those who really like strawberries, a larger planting is desirable. With good culture most varieties provide at least a pint of fruit per plant, and yields up to twice that amount may reasonably be expected.

One important advantage in growing strawberries as compared to many other fruits is that every bit of the crop may be used. If at the height of the season there are more than enough to supply daily needs, the balance may be frozen or preserved for winter with less trouble than is required to keep most fruits and vegetables.

Varieties. There are two distinct types of strawberries: the one-crop a year June bearers, and the so-called everbearing, which produces two or occasionally three less generous crops. A more accurate term for this type would be repeat-bearing rather than everbearing.

The first everbearing varieties lacked both size and quality. These traits have been overcome in such newer varieties as Ogallala, which we consider the best of all we have tried, and Red Rich, a patented strawberry which is high-priced but worth it.

Of the numerous varieties of June-fruiting strawberries some do better in one section, some in another. One of our favorites is an old-timer, Senator Dunlop, that does well almost everywhere.

Strawberries are not fussy about either soil or climate. They thrive in many sections, from Maine to Florida and from Oregon to California. The two things they do require are good drainage and full sun. Where there is any question concerning drainage, this can readily be provided by using a slightly raised bed. Six inches or so is sufficient as strawberries do not root deeply.

Both the size and quality of the crop depend a great deal on well-enriched soil. In sandy soil, however, humus in the form of peatmoss or compost is especially helpful because strawberries, while resenting wet feet, still require ample moisture to develop large, juicy, and flavorful berries. They do especially well where irrigation or ample watering can be provided during dry weather. Abundant moisture is most important for newly set-out plants, for unless strong crowns are formed a maximum crop of berries will never be obtained.

In addition to providing plenty of humus in the soil, a general-purpose fertilizer should be applied and well worked in—preferably two weeks or so before planting. This has the advantage of destroying the first crop of weeds when the surface is again raked over in preparation for planting.

Plants may be procured either with bare roots, or established in pots. Plants locally grown in peat pots, if they can be obtained, give the quick-

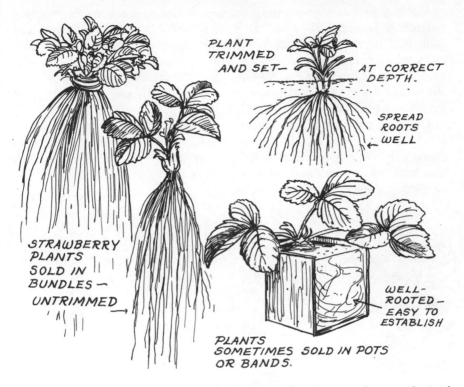

PLANT
TRIMMED
AND SET—

AT CORRECT
DEPTH.

SPREAD
ROOTS
WELL

STRAWBERRY
PLANTS
SOLD IN
BUNDLES —
UNTRIMMED

WELL-
ROOTED—
EASY TO
ESTABLISH

PLANTS
SOMETIMES SOLD IN POTS
OR BANDS.

Strawberries are readily grown in the home garden. Best results are obtained when a new bed is started each year.

est and surest results; but either pot-grown or bare-root plants, shipped by mail, are entirely satisfactory if properly cared for.

Bare-root plants are shipped in bundles of twelve or twenty-five. Upon receipt the bundle should be opened at once, even if planting must be delayed. The roots are trimmed back to 2 to 3 inches, the plants set upright on wet peatmoss, and kept in the shade. Plant as soon as possible. Fan the roots out, cover and press them in firmly, but be careful not to get soil into the centers of the crowns. If the weather is hot and dry, keep well watered for a week or so.

Mulching is always desirable on the home strawberry bed. It not only helps to retain moisture and discourage weeds but also supports the berries, keeps them clean, and encourages all-over ripening.

While strawberries are not difficult to grow, most varieties run out quickly from overcrowding. Unless one uses the hill system, in which all runners are cut off as soon as they start, one can obtain best results and the largest berries by setting out new plants every second year or, still better, by replanting half the bed every year.

The very best plants for setting out are obtained by rooting the required number of runners in 3- or 4-inch peat pots filled with rich compost and sunk into the ground up to the rims. Runners are held in place with clothespins, twigs, or small stones until roots, which develop in a surprisingly short time, are established. Tips of runners beyond the pot are cut off. Plants grown in this way can be taken up and set out in their permanent positions without the slightest check.

The most common mistake made by amateurs in strawberry growing is to assume that, once established, the plants will go on bearing good crops indefinitely. New plants formed by runners quickly become overcrowded, and bear berries so small that they are scarcely worth picking, unless carefully transplanted to new beds.

Strong new plants that receive no set-back when transplanted are grown on by rooting runners in clay or peat pots.

Plants grown by the hill system, in which runners (except for the few needed to provide new plants) are removed as described above, may be set as close as a foot apart in good soil, though a somewhat greater distance is preferable. The rows are spaced a minimum of 18 inches apart. If kept perfectly clean and well fertilized they will give good yields for three years. But here again the very best berries are obtained by setting new plants every year. In reality, this involves little more work than weeding, cleaning, and fertilizing an old bed. Runners or pot plants set each spring, or pot plants set in late summer, with no attempt to carry them on after they have finished fruiting the following summer, provide the very biggest crops and the very best berries.

CHAPTER 18

The Home Greenhouse

The day when only the wealthy could indulge in such a hobby as owning a greenhouse has long since passed. Today responsible companies all over the country sell small, home-type greenhouses, or all the materials required to assemble any size or type desired.

While inexpensive plastic ones can be bought, those made of wood, or aluminum frames glazed with heavy glass designed for greenhouse use are more reliable and substantial and in the end less expensive. Properly cared for, these will last a lifetime.

One of the most important decisions to be made when one purchases a greenhouse is whether to use it principally for growing plants, or for the enjoyment of mature plants already grown. In the latter case a conservatory rather than a greenhouse may be preferable. While a great variety of plants may be maintained and bloomed in a conservatory, it is enjoyed principally for lounging, dining, reading, possibly sun bathing.

In either case, although the construction of the house may be much the same, the floor and interior arrangement will differ greatly. In a "growing" house, a floor of dirt, gravel, or dry-laid bricks which can be freely drenched when watering, helps to maintain a moist atmosphere at all times—a great advantage in providing ideal conditions for plant growth. In the conservatory type of house such a floor would not do. Neither would the usual type of house floor. A floor of slate, tile, or terrazzo is attractive, waterproof, and can easily be kept clean. Adequate drainage should be provided.

In many situations the dual-purpose greenhouse is the answer, although such an arrangement is rare. It is entirely feasible to have a section for starting seedlings, rooting cuttings, potting and repotting plants, and other greenhouse operations along one side or end, reserving the rest of the space for decorative plants in tubs or planters, with a permanent specimen or two such as a climbing vine, palm tree, decorative orange or lemon.

The authors' curved-eave type greenhouse at West Nyack, New York. Our present one on Cape Cod is wider, with space for three benches; an attached potting shed at one end obviates the necessity of storing pots, soil mixtures, flats, etc. under the benches. This is a great advantage as it leaves space for storing bulbs to be forced, and "tapering off" those which have bloomed, as well as other plants that have flowered and are resting.

A hole may be left in the slate or tile floor where such a decorative feature may be planted.

Even-span or lean-to? Often one of the questions to be decided is whether the greenhouse should be of the even-span or the lean-to type. If it is to be entirely separate from the dwelling, the even-span type, unless some unusual conditions exist, is preferable. Even when this type of greenhouse is used, it is often more practical for it to be attached to the house. By doing this, you bring the under-glass garden within a step of the living quarters, where it can be entered without going out of doors.

EVEN-SPAN GREENHOUSE
FREE-STANDING WITH CURVED EAVES

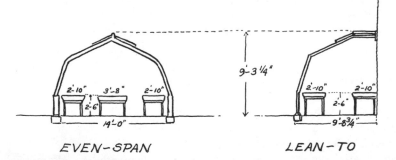

LEAN-TO GREENHOUSE
STRAIGHT EAVE – GLASS-TO-GROUND

EVEN-SPAN   LEAN-TO

*An even-span house is the most satisfactory for full-scale gardening under glass;
gives maximum light and bench space. The lean-to type requires less space,
costs less to build and heat.*

Certain conditions, however, may make it desirable to build a greenhouse of the lean-to type, directly against the house. This has the advantage of taking up less space, of being sheltered from strong winds, and of costing considerably less to heat. The curved-eave type is also better-looking—often an architectural improvement, adding to the beauty of the house design. The lean-to's disadvantages are that it gets no cross ventilation; will be much more difficult to keep cool in hot summer weather; and, in many cases, may detract from rather than enhance the architectural appearance of the house if it is not a curved-eave type. This latter difficulty often can be overcome within a short time by suitable plantings of vines, climbing roses or shrubs.

The function of a greenhouse should determine its design. A typical layout is shown in the accompanying sketch but of course the bench plan may be altered to suit the owner's wishes. No bench should be so wide that any part of it may not readily be reached.

WORK SPACE

In planning a house one should keep in mind that many operations require some elbow room. Storage space for potting soil, fertilizers, insecticides, and so on will also be needed.

Unless a potting shed is planned in connection with the greenhouse, it is desirable to leave some space at the end of a bench that can be used for this purpose. If possible, however, a potting shed should be included. Not only will it be needed for planting, transplanting, and repotting operations but also for storing compost and other soil ingredients such as peatmoss, sand, vermiculite, fertilizers.

A potting shed attached directly to the greenhouse is the most convenient, but where this is not practical, it should be placed as near by as possible. Any bins to hold soil should be made frostproof so that the contents may be available at all times.

Unlike the greenhouse, the potting shed need not receive full sun. As a considerable amount of potting, repotting, and transplanting is done during the winter and very early spring, when an unheated potting shed is not a pleasant place in which to work, a removable potting bench or board in the greenhouse will be found very useful. Cleats across the bottom to fit snugly inside the sideboards of the bench will hold it firmly in place. Upright boards are placed at the back and at one or both ends (see cut). Although our own greenhouse has an attached potting shed we find this potting board, on cold winter days, a very pleasant substitute for the sunless, chilly bench in the potting shed.

Heating. Methods of heating greenhouses vary greatly in different sections of the country. The severity and length of the winter season and the types of fuel available are factors determining the type of heating to be

Where it is possible, there is a great advantage in having a potting shed with storage space attached to the greenhouse.

The authors' portable potting bench. Can be fitted onto greenhouse bench when wanted; saves carrying plants, cuttings, seeds to the potting shed; and provides pleasanter working space on winter days.

used. In mild areas where electricity is not too highly priced, this may be the best system to employ. Hot water will prove the most satisfactory whether installed as a separate system or connected with the house heating plant. It has the great advantage of not drying out the air and the soil as rapidly as steam, hot air or electric heating. If the greenhouse is attached to or adjacent to the house, it can usually be heated conveniently and economically from any existing residence system. With modern methods of automatic control it is easy to maintain any temperature level desired, as heat in the greenhouse is required principally at night, when the needs of residence heating are at a minimum.

The following information shows the actual cost of heating home greenhouses of varying sizes in different sections of the country, based on actual records.

A recent survey found that the fuel cost of heating small houses up to 16×32 feet (in Ohio) and 15×28 feet (in Michigan) ranged from $75 to $100 per season. Smaller houses, 10×18 feet (in Illinois) and 10×21 feet (in Connecticut) ranged from $30 to $75.

In all but five of these cases, the night temperature was maintained at 60 degrees. Cost would be considerably less at 45 to 50 degrees, which is sufficient for a great many plants. Detailed information about the different types of heating systems is best obtained from the manufacturer of your greenhouse or from the county agent.

If it can be provided, a thermostat in the greenhouse helps tremendously in caring for the house and affects a considerable saving in heating costs. In most greenhouses, there are usually areas that are warmer or cooler than the average temperature of the house, but sometimes one can take advantage of this by growing cool-house subjects like snapdragons, cyclamen, and primroses in the cooler area and those which require higher temperatures where the required range is consistently maintained.

Ventilation is an important factor in the maintenance of desired temperatures in the greenhouse. Too high or too low a temperature may be equally disastrous. In fact, standard, small home greenhouses sold as "package" deals are more likely to be inadequate in providing ventilation than in the heating system.

It is possible to procure additional side ventilators and fans to blow out hot air but it is much better to make sure that there are adequate facilities for fresh air before purchasing the house. Cross ventilation provides one of the surest ways to get a flow of cool air. Doors at *both ends* of a house, for instance, are well worth the extra cost, if the model selected calls for one door only. Our own lean-to house has doors at both ends, but in addition we have installed ventilator windows above each door to carry off the trapped warm air. This is, of course, in addition to the automatic roof ventilator which runs the entire length of the house.

Shading. Almost any small greenhouse fully exposed to the sun requires some type of shading if plants are to be grown in it through the summer months. The former method of providing shade was the use of a lime whitewash, or similar material manufactured for the purpose, painted or sprayed directly on the glass. The obvious disadvantage was that, once applied, it shaded the house even during cloudy or rainy weather when all the light possible was to be desired.

Now various forms of shading that can be let down or rolled up as needed are available. We find that during certain seasons of the year—especially in spring when many young seedlings are being started—it is desirable to raise or lower the shading more than once during a day. Another great advantage of the roll-down type of shading is that one section of the bench may be shaded while the rest is left in full sun. Here on Cape Cod we also find our shading protects the glass against flying branches and other objects during heavy gales and hurricanes.

Water. The lack of adequate provision for water in most amateur greenhouses always surprises us. A single spigot can provide all the moisture the average greenhouse needs, but it requires more time to apply. We have three spigots in our moderate-sized house and another in the potting shed. We find that the time saved by not having to drag the hose around, change nozzles, and fill watering cans has repaid the cost of the extra spigots many times over.

You don't have to do much gardening under glass to realize that all types of watering cannot be done with the same nozzle. Manufacturers may claim that a nozzle can be adjusted to throw anything from a solid stream to a fine mist. In a greenhouse, however, such an all-purpose nozzle is not adequate since the tiniest seedlings and thin-stemmed transplants can easily be knocked over by a forceful spray.

We use three different nozzles and consider these the minimum for adequate greenhouse watering. The first is a "pressure breaker," which applies water freely as it flows from the hose but breaks the one solid stream into scores of tiny ones which flow out without force. The second is a "fog nozzle," which supplies water in a fine mist that settles down gently, not disturbing the soil or beating down even the most delicate seedlings. The third is an ordinary sprinkler nozzle with several adjustments which apply water evenly, either fanned out or in a heavy spray.

Another time-saver is a shut-off at the end of the hose. One type lets water flow through only while the fingers grip the shut-off tightly. The flow is stopped automatically when pressure is released. This eliminates a trip back to the spigot to turn the water off.

Other watering equipment which we find essential includes a bulb spray for moistening small trays or pots in the propagating box, and a couple of galvanized metal pans in which flats, pots, or composition planting boxes or trays may be watered from the bottom. At least one watering can should be available. We keep a second one especially for plant-food solution so that it is ready to use at a moment's notice.

GREENHOUSE OPERATIONS

The general *principles* which apply to the growing of plants under glass are much the same as those for outdoor plants. The techniques of course vary considerably. The greenhouse grower can control such factors as light, temperature, moisture, and feeding to a much greater extent than is possible in the outdoor garden. On the other hand, *unless* he controls them, troubles or even disasters are more likely to result.

Starting Seedlings. Starting plants from seed is one of the basic operations in greenhouse work. It is also one of the most fascinating and exciting. The gardener feels intimately in touch with and in control of all that goes on from the time he opens a packet of seed until the resulting plants are well on their way to maturity. Every change in the development and progress of a plant is a new thrill. Furthermore, greenhouse gardening may be indulged in all the year round.

Seedling plants (myosotis) in flats or pots, in special humusy soil mix, which keeps roots intact for transplanting.

Needless to say, it is important to procure the very best seed available —most likely those from a company specializing in varieties for under-glass culture. If the seed is not used soon after it is received, it should be kept in an airtight metal container and stored in a temperature between 40 and 50 degrees, although modern methods of packaging and storing seeds have improved the vitality to a surprising degree.

Temperature is a very important factor in starting seedlings. In the open garden or even in the coldframe or hotbed, we sow according to seasonal temperatures. In the greenhouse, however, since it is desirable, in fact essential, to be able to provide different temperatures, seeds may be started at any time the gardener wishes. Time of sowing will depend largely upon when he wants the plants.

It is best to have a miniature frame or a glass-enclosed propagation box, where temperature may be controlled independently of that in the greenhouse. Such propagating kits of various types may be purchased or made at home. An extension cord with an electric light bulb placed in or under the propagating box will provide sufficient heat to maintain a temperature five to fifteen degrees higher than that outside the box. A 25- to 75-watt bulb may be used according to the size of the box. A thermometer should be left inside to check temperature. A heating cable may be used for the same purpose. Such a difference in temperature makes a marked difference not only in the time required for flower or vegetable seed to germinate but also in the number of perfect seedlings obtained.

Sowing dates, especially for annuals, biennials, and perennials that are to be flowered in the greenhouse, are determined by the dates on which one wishes to have them in bloom and the length of time it takes them to begin to flower. A further factor, of course, is the season at which different species will flower best. One would not, for instance, attempt to have sweet peas under glass in July, or chrysanthemums in April, although both feats could be accomplished with adequate control of temperature and light.

Timing. There is considerable latitude in the time when seedlings may be started for plants to be grown under glass. But especially for the beginner, it is better to be a little bit early than late. Then if anything goes wrong with the first sowing, a second one may be made.

SEED SOWING

In recent years methods of seed starting have been greatly simplified and made much more certain. Here is the method which we now use.

Disinfecting. In order to ensure success, we first take precautions against fungus that can cause seedlings to "damp off" at the soil level, a job which must be done *before* seeds are sown. There are available today concentrated materials which, diluted in water, can be used as effective sprays or drenches. One of their great advantages is that they may be applied to soil in which seeds are to be planted and *also* in soil in which seedlings, cuttings, or young transplants are growing without causing injury. The material we use is Panodrench, but others are available.

Before sowing, we spray flats, pots, benches, watering cans, and any other equipment which may infect seedlings, as well as the soil mixture in which the seeds are to be sown.

If seedlings or young transplants are obtained from an outside source, these and the pots or trays containing them should be treated *before* being placed in the greenhouse.

Soil mixes for starting seed are a vital factor in achieving success. Many mixtures are offered for sale for this purpose; or the gardener may make up his own. A generally accepted one is half fine, gritty sand and half pulverized peatmoss, by volume. We have tried most of them but now prefer plain, sifted (milled) sphagnum moss, especially for very fine seeds.

The trick in using this mixture is to get it uniformly moist *before* placing it in the containers in which seeds are to be sown. We use composition trays about 6×8 inches, 2¼ inches in depth, with drainage holes in

Plants of varying size and under varying conditions make it desirable to have available different methods of applying water. The nozzles we find very useful are (left to right) the water-breaker, giving a gentle flow of water in tiny streams like a heavy but gentle rain; misting nozzle, which applies water in a floating mist that does not knock over or "lodge" the finest seedlings; and general-purpose spray nozzle applying water rapidly and with considerable force.

the bottom. We prefer them because of their light weight, handy size, and maneuverability.

First a ½- to ¾-inch layer of moist, medium-coarse peatmoss is placed in the bottom of the tray, to provide drainage if needed. Over this goes the moist, milled sphagnum, pressed in firmly and evenly to within half an inch of the rim.

Sowing. Seed may be broadcast over the surface, but we usually sow in rows. Shallow troughs are made with a V-shaped marker, just the length or width of the container. The depth of these varies with the size of the seed to be sown. Except for large seed, a very shallow covering is sufficient. We use an old kitchen sieve to sift the milled sphagnum over the surface after sowing. It is pressed in firmly but gently with the flat side of a light wooden tamper. To cover large seed to a greater depth, fine vermiculite or sand may be used.

Watering. We use the misting nozzle to moisten the newly sown containers. Moisture must be constant and uniform throughout the germination period. Drying out of the soil mix for even a few hours may prove fatal. On the other hand sogginess caused by poor drainage may rot the seeds before they sprout.

Fine seeds and those requiring a long time to germinate can best be kept moist by covering the container with clear plastic, such as Saran Wrap, held in place by a rubber band. This creates a miniature greenhouse so that the moisture, evaporating from the soil, is returned to it. *As soon as* germination takes place the covering must be removed. Small sheets of glass just a little larger than the containers are also effective, and in some instances easier to handle.

Nutrients. Peatmoss, sand, sphagnum, vermiculite, or perlite used as media for germinating seeds have the common disadvantage of lacking nutrients. As soon as the true leaves appear on seedlings started in any of these, plant food must be administered. Any of the complete liquid fertilizers is suitable for this purpose and a moderate feeding once a week with one of these is enough to encourage strong growth. From the time leaves begin to unfold, seedlings need all the strong sunshine they can get and fresh air, without drafts, on warm sunny days. Turn containers daily to prevent the young plants "drawing" toward the light.

Transplanting is best done as soon as the first true leaf develops. We transplant our young seedlings to peat-strip-pots, as described in Chapter 4.

Growing on. The period from the time seeds germinate until they are ready for transplanting varies greatly with different species and varieties as well as with temperature, light, and other conditions. However, as a general rule, the sooner they can be transplanted the better. It is extremely important that this shift should take place before the tops begin to crowd.

Some flowers, such as snapdragons, can be grown to maturity in peat pots. Let-
tuce, given a good start in two-inch peat pots, are repotted "pot-and-all" into
the four-inch size. By moving them apart as they begin to crowd, they can be
brought along to eating size in the four-inch peat pots.

Usually the roots become badly entangled before this happens and many
of them are broken in the operation of transplanting.

Slow-growing seedlings started in a sterile medium such as milled
sphagnum, a peatmoss-sand mixture, or vermiculite, should be given liquid
fertilizer frequently enough to prevent stunted growth from starvation.

After their first transplanting, the tiny seedlings are grown on until they
begin to crowd. Then they are again transplanted, this time into individual
pots or into peat strips or multiple pots (fiber pots joined together at the
rims so that six or eight may be handled as a unit). They remain in
these until they are ready to be shifted into larger peat or other pots, to an
outdoor frame, or to their permanent locations in beds or borders.

As plants develop, it may be necessary to move them about in the
greenhouse in order to give the young seedlings more light and air. Any
overcrowding at this period of growth quickly results in spindly, weak
plants.

A layer of coarse peatmoss over crocking, in large pots, provides a moisture reservoir that checks too rapid drying out of soil.

Potting and repotting. With plants that are to be grown on in pots, repotting at more or less frequent intervals becomes an important factor in their culture, especially during the early stages of growth. Young plants may very quickly become potbound; i.e., the rapidly forming roots become a closely woven network around the inside of the pots and consequently become hardened and more or less atrophied. *Before* this stage is reached, the roots form a good ball which can readily be removed from the pot and replanted in a pot one or two sizes larger. This is accomplished by placing the fore and middle fingers on either side of the plant stem, inverting it, and then knocking the rim of the pot sharply against the edge of the bench. The plant is then repotted in a position that will leave the surface of the old ball ¼ to ½ inch—depending on the size—below the rim of the new pot.

One great advantage in using peat or composition pots for growing on young plants is that in the operation of repotting the roots are not disturbed. Roots, pot, and all are transferred to the new and larger container.

Crocking. In using 4-inch or large-sized clay or plastic pots with hardsurfaced walls, place a few pieces of broken pot or small pebbles or turkey gravel over the drainage holes to assure unclogged drainage. Over this is put about half an inch of coarse peatmoss, which serves the double purpose of preventing any soil from clogging the drainage holes, and of acting as a moisture reservoir to prevent too-rapid drying out of the soil above it. This precaution of course is not necessary where plants are to remain in the pots for only a short period as is the case with bedding or vegetable plants that are to be set out in the open ground; or with plants in peat pots, the walls of which absorb and hold moisture.

Soil used for potting should be prepared in advance and kept for this purpose. A good basic mixture is made up of three parts sifted compost from a well-rotted heap, and one part each of gritty sand and peatmoss. If no compost is available, use in place of it two parts of good loam and two parts of peatmoss. If clay predominates in the loam, increase the proportion of sand.

Sterilizing. Soil to be used for transplanting seedlings and also for potting in most commercial operations is thoroughly sterilized by elaborate and expensive equipment. The home gardener may easily sterilize the amount of soil he requires by placing a small amount at a time in a pan, a metal tray, or any convenient container, and baking it in the oven at a temperature of 185 to 200 degrees Fahrenheit, for a half hour or more. The soil should be moist but not wet. (During this operation, any member of the household with an oversensitive nose should be warned to keep out!) This simple treatment eliminates weed seeds and practically all soil-born diseases.

Disinfecting. Sterile soil, however, does not guarantee the protection of seedlings from attack *after* they germinate and begin to grow. In fact it is after they have germinated and until they are large enough to be transplanted, that they are most likely to be attacked by the worst and most prevalent enemy of all—the dread damping-off disease, "rhizoc"— short for rhizoctonia. Many experienced gardeners as well as most beginners have had the bitter experience of having a flat of husky, healthy seedlings suddenly begin to topple over; and upon examination found them rotted through and shriveled just at the soil surface—with both root systems and tops still in perfect condition. Such a tragedy is enough to make even a Philadelphia Quaker use strong words!

Spores of rhizoctonia carried not only in soil but on plants, pots, tools, hands, and feet remain indefinitely viable. Fortunately it is now easy to guard against this menace, as described on page 307 in the introductory paragraph to seed sowing. In addition to general spraying with Panodrench we spot-spray pots and flats of newly planted seed, transplanted seedlings, and also cuttings. One of the nice things about this spray is that it does not have a disagreeable odor.

Once seedlings that have been transplanted into flats or trays begin to crowd, they should be given more space. In the case of annuals and vegetables which are to go into the open garden, the next step is to transfer them to a frame to harden off before they are set out in their permanent places. Those which are destined for pot culture are transplanted into small—usually 2- or 2¼-inch—pots.

Propagation by cuttings, as described in Chapter 4, may be carried on in the greenhouse under ideal conditions. In fact this is one of the great advantages of a greenhouse. The cutting bed we use consists of a frame that fits tightly into one end of a bench, extending about 4 inches above it. A second frame, equipped with two hinged panels covered with plastic, and which fits over the lower frame, gives additional depth. The panels forming the cover of the frame are equipped with counterbalanced weights supported by pulleys attached to the roof sash bars. These panels may be closed tight or raised to any degree wanted for ventilation; or they may be held upright and out of the way. A board divider through the center of the frame makes it possible to maintain two different temperatures within it merely by giving one section more ventilation than the other. When closed, the panels are level so that any moisture that collects drops back to the cutting bed and is evenly distributed. When not in use, this top section of the frame, with its hinged lids, is lifted off, leaving bench space available for plants in pots or trays.

WHY?

We debated a long time about whether or not to include a discussion of greenhouses in this book. But as so many of our friends and acquaintances get so much enjoyment from their gardening under glass, we finally decided to give at least enough information to guide the beginner who considers getting one.

Lack of space does not permit detailed discussion of the many intriguing plants which may be grown. We have tried, however, to point out a few things that should be considered if one is thinking of having a greenhouse, and to describe some of the basic operations in connection with operating it.

Several good books on greenhouse management for amateurs are listed in the Appendix.

PART THREE

SELECTIVE, COUNTRY-WIDE
MONTHLY CALENDAR

HOW TO USE THE CALENDAR

ALPHABETICAL LIST OF STATES SHOWING AREAS

THE CALENDAR

NOTES ON COUNTRY-WIDE GARDENING PROBLEMS

How to Use the Calendar

(Based on frost dates and length of growing seasons: *not* on state lines)

The Calendar section will be most helpful to you if you use it properly. It is simply arranged to tell:

WHAT TO DO

In any phase of gardening, from preparing the soil for planting to cutting flowers or harvesting vegetables or fruits, success depends upon doing the things that need to be done at just the right time.

This requires a great deal of *looking ahead*.

Even the experienced gardener often fails to think of all the things that should be done *just when it is time to do them*. To avoid such omissions, many garden-minded homeowners keep a running calendar, based on previous experience, to make sure that they attend to such things as ordering seeds and materials; starting seeds indoors or in a hotbed; sowing seeds and setting out plants in the open—some early and others late; transplanting; applying sprays; starting new plants from cuttings; renovating, feeding, or de-weeding the lawn—and so on through the list.

If even experienced gardeners find useful such a calendar of what-to-do and when-to-do-it, how much more valuable will one be to any beginner! With many of the things he hopes to accomplish, it may make all the difference between success and failure!

HOW

The Calendar section of this book is very simple to use. It differs from others in that, instead of giving condensed and inadequate information along with the reminder, or (as is more often the case) leaving the reader to try to track down such information as best he may, it gives wherever needed a direct reference, by number, to the *page* where this particular subject is discussed in one of the main sections of the book.

WHEN

The compilation of calendars to suit—as nearly as possible—all parts of the continental United States, has been a challenge. A calendar should be based on planting dates, frost dates and minimum winter temperatures because these factors determine when garden operations should be undertaken. Accordingly, in this calendar, the country is divided into six numbered areas based on spring planting dates, i.e., May 1, Area I; April 15, Area II; April 1, Area III; March, Area IV; February, Area V; and January, Area VI. Each of these areas has been given a Roman numeral as noted above, indicating that the states *or portions of states* included in it have similar frost dates, planting dates, and—with few exceptions—minimum winter temperatures.

Other cultural conditions in the United States, however, vary greatly and such factors as rainfall, amount of sunshine, and type of soil do make a difference in many aspects of garden operations. Since it is impossible to incorporate all of these factors in one calendar, we urge the reader who has special gardening conditions, unusual in his area, to read the calendar for the areas directly north and south of his own.

During the heart of the winter when much of the country is in the "deep freeze," operations in many areas are the same. Consequently, one January calendar applies to Areas I, II, III, and IV. Beginning in February, however, there is a change, for during that month residents of Area IV are preparing for March planting and sowing. In Area V, outdoor gardening begins in February, while in Area VI early planting dates are in January.

USE OF THE CALENDER

First: At the beginning of each monthly calendar, starting on page 326 with the month of January, the reader will find a heading of Roman numerals. One of these will correspond to his own area number—to be found on page 323 and it is *this* portion of the calendar *only* which concerns him.

For instance, the gardener living in northern Illinois finds by consulting page 321 that he is living in Area II. He then turns to the calendar for the *month* in which he is interested, and in it the section covering Area II, which includes his part of the country.

Second: The reader selects, from the list of projects or activities suggested for his area, the ones in which he is particularly interested. He may wish to jot them down, along with the accompanying page-reference numbers. This *personal* list or calendar may be made up for a month, or for several, or even for the entire year. It is well to keep it in the tool shed or in some other place where it may readily be referred to.

Don't make your personal list too all-inclusive at the start. One is quite likely to plan many more projects than there will be time, money, or energy enough to accomplish. Three projects really completed yield much more satisfaction than a dozen started but not carried through to completion, and consequently ending in a feeling of frustration.

Third: When you've decided on which projects you'll undertake, the page references included will direct you to the main portion of the book and the how-to information necessary for your project. It is well to look over one's personal calendar, once it has been made up, frequently enough to keep somewhat ahead of the game; in this way it is easy to secure and have on hand seeds, plants, bulbs, materials of various kinds that will be needed for future use. In many garden operations even a few days' delay, while not proving fatal, may mean somewhat less perfect results than might otherwise have been attained.

Many major operations—such as building a rock garden, making a pool, or constructing a new fence—can be planned in definite stages, and then the completion of each step yields its own satisfaction.

With these few words of advice—harvested from decades of experiments, experience, and a reasonable degree of success—we leave the reader to pick and choose the items that will make up *his own* tailored-to-measure calendar—and wish him Happy Hunting!

Alphabetical List of States
Showing Areas

Where you live will determine *your* AREA NUMBER for
the monthly CALENDAR REMINDERS of garden activities
and projects on pages 325 to 393

STATES LISTED ALPHABETICALLY WITH AVERAGE MINIMUM WINTER
TEMPERATURES, AVERAGE SPRING PLANTING DATES AND CALENDAR
AREAS

Area	*State*	*Average minimum winter temperature*	*Average spring planting dates*
V	Alabama, northern and		
	central	0 to 10	Feb. 1 to 15
VI	southern	20 to 30	Jan. 15
IV	Arizona, high elevations	—20 to —10	Mar. 1 to 15
V	central	—10 to 10	Feb. 15 to Mar. 1
VI	desert	20 to 30	Jan. 15
IV	Arkansas, northern	—10 to 10	Mar. 1 to Apr. 1
V	southern	10 to 20	Feb. 1 to Mar. 1
VI	California, coastal	30 to 40	Jan. 15
VI	southern and central	20 to 30	Jan. 15
V	interior valleys	10 to 20	Feb. 1 to 15
IV	mountainous	—10 to 0	Mar. 1 to 15
I	Colorado, mountainous	—40 to —30	May 1 to 15
II	eastern	—20 to —10	Apr. 15 to May 1
III	Connecticut, coastal	— 5 to 5	Apr. 1 to 15
II	central and northern	—20 to —10	Apr. 15 to May 1
IV	Delaware	0 to 10	Mar. 15 to Apr. 1
IV	District of Columbia	0 to 10	Mar. 15 to Apr. 1
VI	Florida	20 to 30	Jan. 15 to Feb. 1
VI	extreme south	30 to 40	Jan. 1 to 15
VI	Georgia, coastal and		
	southern	20 to 30	Jan. 15 to Feb. 1
V	central	10 to 20	Feb. 1 to 15
V	northern	0 to 10	Feb. 15 to Mar. 1

Area	State	Average minimum winter temperature	Average spring planting dates
I II	Idaho, mountainous intermountain	−30 to −20 −20 to −10	May 1 Apr. 15 to May 1
II III	Illinois, northern southern	−20 to −10 −10 to 0	Apr. 15 to May 1 Apr. 1 to 15
II III	Indiana, northern southern	−20 to −10 −10 to 0	Apr. 15 to May 1 Apr. 1 to 15
II III	Iowa, northern southern	−30 to −20 −20 to −10	Apr. 15 to May 1 Apr. 1 to 15
III IV	Kansas southeastern	−20 to −10 −10 to 0	Apr. 1 to 15 Mar. 15 to Apr. 1
IV	Kentucky	−10 to 10	Mar. 1 to Apr. 1
V VI	Louisiana, northern southern	10 to 20 20 to 30	Feb. 1 Jan. 15
I II	Maine, northern interior coastal and southern	−40 to −30 −20 to −10	May 1 Apr. 15 to May 1
IV	Maryland	− 5 to 10	Mar. 15 to Apr. 1
II III	Massachusetts Cape Cod	−20 to −10 − 5 to 5	Apr. 15 to May 1 Apr. 1 to 15
II	Michigan	−20 to −10	Apr. 15 to May 1
I II	Minnesota, northern southern	−40 to −30 −30 to −20	May 1 to 15 Apr. 15
V V VI	Mississippi, northern central southern	0 to 10 10 to 20 20 to 30	Feb. 15 Feb. 1 to 15 Jan. 15
III IV	Missouri, northern southern	−20 to −10 −10 to 5	Apr. 1 to 15 Mar. 15 to Apr. 1
I	Montana	−40 to −20	May 1 to 15
II III	Nebraska, northern southern	−30 to −20 −20 to −10	Apr. 15 Apr. 1 to 15
I III IV & V	Nevada, mountains western and central southwestern	−30 to −20 −20 to −10 0 to 20	May 1 Apr. 1 Feb. 15 to Mar. 1
I II	New Hampshire, northern southern	−40 to −30 −20 to −10	May 1 Apr. 15
IV	New Jersey	− 5 to 10	Mar. 15 to Apr. 1
III IV V	New Mexico, northern central southern	−20 to −10 −10 to 0 0 to 10	Apr. 1 to 15 Mar. 1 to 15 Feb. 15
I II III	New York, northern balance Long Island	−35 to −20 −20 to −10 − 5 to 5	May 1 Apr. 15 to May 1 Apr. 1 to 15

Area	State	Average minimum winter temperature	Average spring planting dates
V	North Carolina, coastal	20 to 30	Feb. 1
IV	western	0 to 10	Mar. 1 to 15
V	central	10 to 20	Feb. 15 to Mar. 1
I	North Dakota	−40 to −30	May 1
II	Ohio, northern	−20 to −10	Apr. 15
III	central and southern	−10 to 0	Apr. 1 to 15
III	Oklahoma, western	−20 to 0	Apr. 1 to 15
IV	central and eastern	−10 to 5	Mar. 1 to Apr. 1
V	Oregon, coastal	20 to 30	Feb. 1 to Mar. 1
III, IV	interior	5 to 20	Mar. 1 to Apr. 1
II	intermountain	−50 to −20	Apr. 15
II	Pennsylvania, northern	−20 to −10	Apr. 15
III	southern	−10 to 0	Apr. 1 to 15
II	Rhode Island	−10 to 0	Apr. 15
III	coastal	− 5 to 5	Apr. 1 to 15
VI	South Carolina, coastal	20 to 30	Jan. 15
V	interior	10 to 20	Feb. 1 to Mar. 1
IV	western	0 to 10	Mar. 1 to Apr. 1
II	South Dakota	−30 to −20	Apr. 15 to May 1
IV	Tennessee	0 to 10	Mar. 1 to 15
VI	Texas, gulf coast	20 to 30	Jan. 15
V	south central	10 to 20	Feb. 1
V	southwestern	10 to 20	Feb. 1 to Mar. 1
IV	northwestern	−10 to 10	Mar. 1 to Apr. 1
IV	north central	0 to 10	Mar. 1 to Apr. 1
I	Utah, mountainous	−30 to −20	May 1
II	balance	−20 to −10	Apr. 15
I	Vermont, northern	−40 to −30	May 1
II	balance	−30 to −10	Apr. 15 to May 1
IV	Virginia	0 to 20	Mar. 1 to Apr. 1
IV	Washington State, coastal	10 to 30	Mar. 1 to Apr. 1
III	interior	−10 to 10	Apr. 1 to 15
II	mountainous	−20 to −10	Apr. 15 to May 1
III	West Virginia	−10 to 0	Apr. 1 to 15
I	Wisconsin, northern	−40 to −30	May 1 to 15
II	southern	−20 to −10	Apr. 15 to May 1
I	Wyoming, mountainous	−30 to −20	May 1
II	balance	−20 to −10	Apr. 15 to May 1

AREA I

Colorado, mountainous
Idaho, mountainous
Maine, northern
Minnesota, northern
Montana
Nevada, mountainous
New Hampshire, northern
New York, northern
North Dakota
Utah, mountainous
Vermont, northern
Wisconsin, northern
Wyoming, mountainous

AREA II

Colorado, eastern
Connecticut, central
   northern
Idaho, intermountain
Illinois, northern
Indiana, northern
Iowa, northern
Maine, coastal
   southern
Massachusetts
Michigan
Minnesota, southern
Nebraska, northern
Nevada, mountainous
New Hampshire, southern
New York, central
   southern
Ohio, northern
Oregon, intermountain
Pennsylvania, northern
Rhode Island, inland
South Dakota
Utah, lower altitudes
Vermont
Washington, mountainous
Wisconsin, southern
Wyoming, lower altitudes

AREA III

Connecticut, coastal
Illinois, southern
Indiana, southern
Iowa, southern
Kansas (except southeastern)
Massachusetts, Cape Cod
Missouri, northern
Nebraska, southern
Nevada, western
   central
New Mexico, northern
New York, Long Island
Ohio, central
   southern
Oklahoma, western
Oregon, interior
Pennsylvania, southern
Rhode Island, coastal
Washington, intermountain
West Virginia

AREA IV

Arizona, high elevations
Arkansas, northern
California, mountainous
Delaware
District of Columbia
Kansas, southeastern
Kentucky
Maryland
Missouri, southern
Nevada, southern
New Jersey
New Mexico, central
North Carolina, western
Oklahoma, central
   eastern
Oregon, interior
South Carolina, western
Tennessee
Texas, northwestern
north central
Virginia
Washington, coastal

AREA V

Alabama, northern and central
Arizona, central
Arkansas, southern
California, interior valleys
Georgia, central and northern
Louisiana, northern
Mississippi, central and northern
Nevada, southwestern
New Mexico, southern
North Carolina, coastal and central
Oregon, coastal
South Carolina, interior
Texas, south central and southwestern

AREA VI

Alabama, southern
Arizona desert
California, coastal
    southern and central
Florida
Georgia, coastal and southern
Louisiana, southern
Mississippi, southern
South Carolina, coastal
Texas, gulf coast and southeastern

The Calendar

JANUARY

Every fence, and every tree
Is as white as white can be.
JAMES STEPHENS

For Areas I, II, III, IV

INDOORS

Most garden activities this month are indoors. It's a fine time to catch up on the planning you can't get done during the growing season (Chapter 1).

BOOKS: Read a few garden books on subjects of special interest to you.

CATALOGS are coming in every day. Look each one over as it arrives and then file it. Later in the month, seed, nursery stock, and roses should be ordered. If any catalogs you need have not been sent, write for them before the stock is exhausted.

PLANS made to scale are a big help in executing any garden project. If new beds, borders, or other features are to be added to the garden in spring, draw plans *now* before sending in seed and nursery orders. Plan for color combinations, periods of bloom, permanent background plantings as well as for garden design (page 5).

ORDER seeds, nursery stock, roses, tender or half-hardy, summer-flowering bulbs as soon as plans are completed. Don't order more than you have room for; but on the other hand, be sure you order everything you need. Later on, choice varieties may be sold out.

STORED BULBS, *corms, and tubers* should be examined this month. Discard rotted bulbs. Cut away withered or rotted portions of tubers and dust with sulfur. Provide ventilation to prevent further rotting. If tubers are too dry and withering, moisten peatmoss or other storage medium slightly.

Pack gladiolus corms in plastic bags, adding one ounce naphthalene flakes per 100 corms. Store at 35 to 40 degrees, to discourage thrips.

BRING AMARYLLIS BULBS, in their pots, to full light, and increase water. Feed when buds first develop.

REDUCE WATER gradually on Christmas cactus; also on poinsettias when leaves begin to drop. Keep palms on dry side this month.

GARDENIAS can bloom indoors. Give them day temperature of 60 to 70 degrees and don't let it drop below 55 degrees at night. Avoid drafts and see that they get morning sun. Water daily and soak the pot in a bucket of water once a week. Feed once a month.

HOUSEPLANTS get dusty in midwinter. Take them to the kitchen, the laundry, or the bathroom once a week. Wash glossy leaves with soapy water; rinse with clear water. Treat hairy-leaved sorts to a fine misting of the leaves and let dry completely *in the shade.* Except for hairy-leaved specimens, sprinkle or mist leaves freely during this weekly treatment. Use bath, or dish-spray head.

SOW SEEDS of *Vinca rosea* and *Nierembergia* indoors if you want them for the garden next summer. They are very slow-growing. Jerusalem-cherry berries should be dried now and sown in February. Open "cherries" and remove seeds for sowing. You'll have quite a crop for next Christmas! (Pages 49; 307.)

WOOD ASHES from the fireplace make excellent fertilizer to bring up the pH toward neutral if your garden soil is acid. *Store* in tubs or boxes and save for use around lilacs, dianthus, *Daphne cneorum,* and in rose beds.

OUTDOORS

EVERGREENS, both coniferous and broad-leaved, should have snow removed from the branches and from the centers of dense specimens soon after each storm. If it freezes on, permanent damage may result. Boxwood is especially susceptible to this sort of injury because of its dense, globular growth.

FOUNDATION SHRUBS may suffer severely if drip from the eaves or from a downspout turns to ice in a sudden temperature drop. Check eaves, gutters, and downspouts for possible leaks *before* this happens.

PRUNE GRAPES AND FRUIT TREES this month during sunny spells when a few hours outdoors are enjoyable (Chapter 17).

GRAFTING FRUIT TREES is a sport enjoyed by many amateurs. This is the time to cut the scions of trees to be used later for grafts. Mark each variety, make them into bundles, and keep them in a cool place or bury them in peatmoss in a coldframe (Chapter 4).

BAGWORMS have formed cocoons by this time and may sometimes be found on evergreens, especially arborvitae. The brown, pointed cocoons, shaped like Japanese lanterns, should be cut off and burned.

BIRDS need food now. See that they have suet as well as seeds. A bird "pudding" made of suet, seeds, oatmeal, cornmeal, and peanut butter is a real treat. If you have no evergreen cover, set up one or more discarded Christmas trees to give your feathered friends shelter.

PROTECTION FOR TREES AND SHRUBS from rabbits and other rodents should have been completed last month. If it was neglected at that time, see that something is done about it before a heavy snowfall (Appendix, page 464).

JANUARY THAWS often cause heaving of plants in perennial beds. If the ground thaws, walk around the garden and press firmly back into place any plants which have had their roots loosened.

WINDOW BOXES which hold living plants, either evergreens or bulbs, should be checked now and then for moisture. If dry, give a thorough watering when the temperature is above freezing.

TOOLS should have been checked and stored when the garden was "put to bed," but if any need sharpening or repair, January is a good time to do these odd jobs. If the handles of small hand tools like weeders and trowels are painted bright red with an enamel paint, they will be lost less easily, come spring.

COLDFRAMES which contain living plants need attention, even in midwinter. During very cold spells, additional cover over the glass is a wise precaution. Tarpaulins or heavy plastic, securely tied down, may be used. Or a covering of salt hay or of straw *under* the sash may be substituted. If a warm spell develops, give a little ventilation during the sunny hours, closing the sash again before the thermometer begins to drop sharply toward evening. If there has been a snowfall which remains on the sash, do not disturb it. The frame could not have a cozier winter blanket.

WIND BURN is a serious winter threat in some areas. Place screening, burlap, or heavy plastic on the windward side of broad-leaved evergreens. Wrap trunks of young trees and shrubs where necessary. Spray with Wilt-Pruf (page 155).

MICRO-CLIMATES: A study of midwinter conditions in your garden may reveal several micro-climates (page 77). In severe storms or after heavy snow, note sheltered areas. Doubtfully hardy trees, shrubs, and other plants should be tried out in these locations.

GRAPES may be pruned any time after they go dormant. Before sap begins to flow in February or March, remove a third of old vines and all undergrowth (page 291).

For Area V

BULBS: Check condition of stored, tender bulbs (page 199). In damp fir bark or peatmoss start tubers of tuberous begonias, gloxinias, caladiums (page 199). Pot up calla-lilies. Under glass sow seeds of gloxinias, tuberous begonias, streptocarpus. Day temperature 75°, night 55°.

SOIL PREPARATION: Prepare garden beds as soon as ground can be worked (pages 86–88). Work rich compost or well-rotted manure into beds where established perennials are about to start active growth.

PESTS: Apply dormant sprays to deciduous trees and shrubs (Appendix, page 468). Put out poison bait for mice in mole runs (Appendix, page 464).

TOP-DRESS winter-blooming primroses with all-purpose fertilizer mixed with leafmold.

VEGETABLES: Harvest winter crops as needed. These include endive, Savoy cabbage, Swiss chard, spinach, leeks, Brussels sprouts, kale, salsify, parsnips.

Sow seed of hardy vegetables in frame. Set out perennial vegetable plants (pages 262–64).

PRUNE: camellia, fuchsia, fig trees, fruit trees, grapes, hydrangeas, roses, wisteria.
Deciduous hedges: beech, hawthorn, laurel, privet, barberry, etc.
Remove dead wood: catalpa, daphne, golden-chain tree, lilacs (including suckers), locust, magnolia, paulownia (Chapter 6).

CUTTINGS: Start fuchsia and camellia cuttings from prunings (pages 62; 68).

WATER: In dry weather give deep waterings to evergreens, shrubs, and any plants soon to bloom (pages 80–84).

FRAME: Sow seeds of hardy annuals and vegetables (pages 49–60; 114).

PLANT FLOWERING TREES (pages 153–55): Among the best for the Upper South are dogwood, magnolia, mimosa (*Albizzia julibrissin rosea*), crape-myrtle, fringe tree, and redbud (see Appendix).

For Area VI

PESTS: Apply dormant spray to deciduous trees, roses, and shrubs, if not already attended to. Use general-purpose spray once a week on plants in active growth, especially roses (page 467).

WATER: In dry weather, apply deep watering to evergreens, shrubs, and plants soon to bloom (pages 80–84).

FROST: Have light covering of evergreen branches or plastic ready to protect doubtfully hardy plants if frost is predicted. After frost, water tender plants freely in early morning. In frost-free areas, Christmas gift plants do well on the patio or terrace, if brought in on cold nights.

HEDGE PLANTS which may be planted this month are listed on page 436.

BULBS: Do not disturb *Eucharis grandiflora* (Amazon-lily). Top-dress with rich fibrous soil and water well to produce winter bloom. Order new, tender, summer-flowering bulbs.

PLANT AND TRANSPLANT: azaleas, citrus fruit, deciduous trees, evergreens, evergreen shrubs, camellias, figs, fuchsias, flowering trees, fruit trees, magnolias, nut trees, rhododendron (pages 153–55), roses (Chapter 15), perennials, biennials (Chapter 11).

SOW OUTDOORS: ageratum, calendula, California poppy, candytuft, cynoglossum, dianthus, gypsophila, larkspur, lupine, petunia, salvia, snapdragon, verbena, *Vinca rosea* (Chapter 11), hardy vegetables (Chapter 16).

SOW IN FRAMES or INDOORS: wax begonia, China-aster, cinerarias, fever-few, geranium, heliotrope, lobelia, mesembryanthemum (pages 49; 114).
Tender vegetables: eggplant, peppers, tomatoes (pages 49–57).

SET OUT: onion sets; perennial vegetables; plants of cabbage, cauliflower, broccoli. *Half-hardy bulbs:* anemones, achimenes, bessera, calla, erythronium, freesia, galtonia, gladiolus, hedychium, hymenocallis, ismene, lapeirousia, leucocoryne, milla, montbretia, nerine, spreklia, tritonia, tigridia, watsonia, zephyranthes (page 199). Start sweet potato sprouts (page 264).

FROST-FREE AREAS: Plant tuberous begonias, gloxinia, caladium, amaryllis, gloxinia, etc. (page 199).

FEED: azaleas, camellias, figs, hydrangeas, irises, pansies, primulas, spring-flowering bulbs, violets, other early-blooming plants and shrubs (pages 85; 90).

PRUNE: allamanda, banana (severely if frozen back), camellia, clematis, hibiscus (past freeze), honeysuckle and other rampant vines, lantana (past freeze), mandevilla, pecans, roses, late fall-blooming shrubs (Chapter 6).

FEBRUARY

With blue and purple hollows,
With peaks of dazzling snow,
Along the far horizon
The clouds are marching slow.
The Heavenly Hills of Holland
by HENRY VAN DYKE

For Areas I, II

PRUNE, after each storm, broken and damaged branches of shrubs and trees and remove snow and ice from evergreen branches which may bear them down and cause damage.

THAW: In case of a thaw, examine perennials and other small plants to ascertain if they have "HEAVED" out of the ground. If so, press the roots in firmly, and mulch heavily.

SOWING: Do *not* be tempted to start seeds indoors too early in the far north. Ascertain from seed packets the number of days from sowing to germination. Except for those which germinate very slowly, sow about six weeks before seedlings can be hardened off in a coldframe (page 307).

STUDY your property and note areas which are wind-swept; those which lie deep in snow; are deeply or partially shaded, or in full sun. This knowledge is helpful when planting hardy specimens.

ORDER: Among the SHRUBS which may be ordered now for spring planting are the following hardy sorts: *Cotoneaster apiculata,* a low shrub with arching branches and red berries; *Cotinus coggygria* or Purple Smokebush; *Caryopteris incana* or Blue-beard, which must be treated as a perennial that is cut back in spring; Potentillas, in variety (see also lists in Appendix).

PRUNE: When weather permits, prune fruit trees, grapes, and shrubs which flower in summer or autumn (Chapter 6).

CHECK: Have all needed seeds and nursery stock, including roses, been ordered? If not this should be done at once.

POTS OF BULBS to be forced may still be brought indoors. Those which have finished blooming can be kept in a cool place, watered occasionally, and replanted in the garden when ground can be worked.

HOUSEPLANTS need all the sunshine they can get now. They do not care for cold drafts, but indirect fresh air each day is good for them.

ROOTED CUTTINGS of houseplants which have been transplanted during the winter, may be about to bloom. Feed these before buds show color.

PESTS: Keep an all-purpose houseplant insecticide on hand ready to treat any specimen which develops aphids, white fly, red spider, or other pest (Appendix, page 467).

Syringing the foliage of houseplants each week helps to keep them healthy, discouraging red spider and other troubles aggravated by dry air and dust.

For Areas III, IV

INDOORS

TUBERS: Start dahlia tubers in damp peatmoss. New shoots which have started on these may be rooted like any other cutting. Start tuberous begonia, caladium, and gloxinia tubers by placing, bud side up, in flats of damp peatmoss or fir bark. Tops should remain exposed. Pot up calla-lilies. Set out after last frost.

HOUSEPLANTS: Young flowering plants are about to bloom. Feed, until buds show color. Watch for pests and disease. Do not dry off Christmas cactus too quickly. By treating it as you did during the fall months, you may be rewarded by another burst of bloom.

FORCED HARDY BULBS which have finished bloom should be watered moderately until foliage matures, then placed in a cool dry cellar or frame until ground can be worked, when they can be replanted in the garden. (Discard bulbs of paper whites when bloom is over.) Bring in any remaining pots for forcing.

SEEDS: Sow indoors or under glass seeds of: broccoli, cauliflower, cabbage, *Cobaea scandens,* dwarf dahlias, nierembergia, verbena, stocks, Jerusalem-cherry, lobelia, *Begonia semperflorens,* etc. (page 307).

For Areas III, IV

OUTDOORS

WINTER PRUNING of fruit trees, grapes, and late-flowering shrubs can be done this month if it was not completed in January (Chapter 6).

SPRAY with dormant oil spray when temperature goes above 45 degrees—but while plants are still dormant—bittersweet, other euonymus, lilac, fruit trees, roses (Appendix, page 467).

COLDFRAMES need management from now on. When temperature rises above 40 degrees, in sun and warm rain, open to give ventilation. Close again before sundown. If soil is dry in frame 6 inches down, give slow, deep watering directly in soil (do not wet plants) on a warm day (Chapter 7).

SHRUBS AND ROSES should have been ordered by now for March planting. If not already done, see to this.

FREEZING AND THAWING may still occur. After each thaw, go over perennial beds for possible heaving and press roots back into the soil.

FLOWERING SHRUB BRANCHES force easily and quickly if brought indoors in February. Syringe the entire branches every day, and keep the stems in deep water. Hard wood absorbs water better if the ends of the branches are slit or crushed.

SOIL PREPARATION: Prepare garden beds as soon as ground can be worked (pages 86–89).

LAWN: As soon as ground is thawed, fill in bare and low spots on lawn and seed (Chapter 10). Distribute pre-emergence crabgrass killer plus plant food on lawns (Appendix, page 470).

VEGETABLES: As soon as ground can be worked in February or early March, sow peas, and sweet peas, and plant onion sets. Lettuce and radish seeds may be sown in a coldframe (Chapter 7).

PLANTING: Prepare PLANTING HOLES as early as possible for planting trees, roses. Flowering fruit trees, dogwoods, cane and bush fruits should be spring-planted (pages 153; 281).

Has your SEED ORDER arrived? Have seeds been ordered? If not, do it now! The same advice applies to perennial plants for setting out in March.

MULCH GRAPE vines with well-rotted manure if available. If not, fertilize and mulch with rough compost or peatmoss.

For Area V

PLANT: shrubs and trees (page 153), roses (page 246), half-hardy bulbs (page 199), perennial vegetable plants, potatoes, onion sets, (Chapter 16), perennial flower plants, including rock garden subjects (pages 188–92; 455).

SOW OUTDOORS: peas and sweet peas, hardy vegetables, early in month (Chapter 16), half-hardy vegetables, half-hardy annuals (page 263).

SET OUT hardy vegetable plants such as cabbage, broccoli, etc. (page 264).

SOW INDOORS or UNDER GLASS: tender annuals, tender vegetables (page 307).

PRUNE: hydrangeas (root-prune if old and not blooming well), late-blooming shrubs, geraniums, fuchsias (Chapter 6), roses, while still dormant (page 251).

FERTILIZE: newly prepared beds (page 85), lawns (page 168), roses (page 250), bulb beds as soon as bloom is over.

SPRAY PROGRAM should be started as soon as roses, shrubs, etc., start new growth. Until then, use dormant sprays where needed (Appendix, page 468).

DIVIDE and transplant mature perennials, if not done previously (page 194).

POT UP tuberous begonias, gloxinias, and caladiums started last month in damp fir bark or peatmoss (page 199).

For Area VI

LAWNS: Prepare seedbeds for new lawns which are to be sown, sprigged, or plugged. Sprigging or plugging can be done this month (Chapter 10).

All established lawns except those of Centipedegrass may be given an application of ammonium sulfate to green them up (Chapter 10).

PLANT: windbreaks and hedges (Appendix); perennials; also divide and replant established clumps (page 194); perennial vegetables; dracaena; palms; gerberias, tritomas, and tender bulbs, such as gloriosa lily, tuberose, canna (page 199); tender water-lilies in boxes to set out in March. In shade houses: begonias, gloxinias, orchids, ferns. Set out tender vegetable plants (page 264).

SOW: tender vegetable seeds (page 263), tender annual seeds (pages 51–57), decorative grasses.

SPRAY: azaleas for petal blight with dithane, camellias for scale with malathion, evergreens and shrubs for aphids with lindane, figs for mealybug with malathion, gladiolus for thrips with miticide, roses once a week with all-purpose spray (Appendix, page 467).

CUTTINGS can be taken now of: allamanda (hard or soft wood), bamboo (2 or 3 joints below ground and the same above), fig, pomegranate (hardwood), passion vine (Chapter 4).

POINSETTIAS are cut back now, leaving 12 inches of stem. When new growth starts, pinch out tips several times to assure branching growth.

PRUNE: fuchsias (Chapter 6).

FERTILIZE: azaleas (acid), camellias (acid), palms, bulbs, after bloom is over (page 90).

AZALEAS may suffer from chlorosis (yellowing). If so, spray with a mixture of 1½ ounces iron sulfate and 1½ ounces hydrated lime to a gallon of water. After bloom, prune plants severely to shape as desired (Chapter 6).

WATER deeply in dry weather (pages 80–84).

FROST may strike early this month. Cover tender subjects, if a freeze is forecast, with burlap, plastic, newspapers, or soil. Uncover as soon as possible. If shrubs freeze back, do *not* prune at once as this may encourage early, soft growth which will again freeze. Crotons, hibiscus, ixoras, etc., may be defoliated by frost but usually the wood is undamaged. Sprinkle foliage copiously early in morning after frost to prevent damage to tender subjects.

PREPARE NEW BEDS and borders for tender plants to be set out in March (pages 86–88).

MARCH

The wind at the flue, the wind strumming the shutter;
The soft, antiphonal speech of the doubled
  brook, never for a moment quiet;
The rush of the rain against the glass,
  his voice in the eaves-gutter!

EDNA ST. VINCENT MILLAY

For Areas I, II

While the rest of the country starts gardening in earnest this month, spring has not come to most parts of the far north. Some work can be done however, to save time later, when spring really arrives.

Attend spring flower shows if any are within traveling distance. Take notebook so that you can use some of the new ideas and grow some of the new varieties shown.

Those who cannot reach any of the shows can read the garden magazines and learn about what's new in plant material and gardening.

Have you a GREENHOUSE or HOTBED? If so, you are now gardening under glass and getting a head start on your neighbors. If not, read Chapters 18 and 7.

PRUNE away damaged tree and shrub branches. Paint over large wounds with tree paint, after scraping away any decay that has set in (page 106).

Prune and trim deciduous trees, late-blooming shrubs (Chapter 6) and grapes, if not already done (Chapter 17). Maples and birches should not be pruned until midsummer, as then the sap is flowing less freely than in the spring.

Do *not* prune spring-flowering shrubs until after bloom and at no time shear them so as to destroy their natural, graceful forms (Chapter 6).

ROSE BEDS which have been heavily protected should be gradually uncovered as early as possible. When snow is gone and lawns begin to green up, remove heavy mulches and gradually uncover climbers which have been laid down and buried in soil. Do not unhill until April (Chapter 15).

PLANTING: If nursery stock or roses are delivered before it is time to plant, unwrap plants, place them in a trench, and keep roots covered with moist loam or damp peatmoss until the job can be done (page 153).

As soon as frost is out of ground, prepare planting holes for evergreens, shrubs, roses (pages 153–55).

Evergreens should be planted in spring *before* new growth appears.

PESTS: Dormant oil sprays may still be applied this month (see Appendix, page 468).

FRAMES: Open coldframe or hotbed to air, sun, and rain when temperature is above freezing. Close again before evening and night temperatures drop too low (page 114).

SOW INDOORS or UNDER GLASS seeds of broccoli, cauliflower, cabbage, petunia, verbena, dwarf dahlia (page 307).

For Areas III, IV

Attend SPRING FLOWER SHOWS and make notes for use on the home place.

PRUNE away winter-damaged limbs of trees and branches of shrubs (Chapter 6). Remove dead wood and weak stems from shrubs. Do not prune spring-blooming shrubs. Never shear these in a way that will destroy their natural grace (Chapter 6).

SOIL PREPARATION: As soon as ground can be worked, prepare beds, borders, and vegetable area (pages 86–88). Prepare planting holes for the stock that is to be planted soon (pages 153–55).

Prepare soil in frames or seedbeds for sowing (pages 55–57).

LAWNS: Prepare areas to be spring-planted; treat with pre-emergence weed killer. Clean up and fertilize established lawns, repair bare spots in lawn (Chapter 10).

PLANT as soon as holes can be prepared: beech, birch, dogwood, hawthorns, lilacs, magnolias; evergreens (before new growth starts) (page 153); fruits, bush fruits, grapes, strawberries (Chapter 17); roses, (page 246).

ROSES: Remove mulch as soon as snow is gone. Unhill and work hilling into beds. Add fertilizer. Give dormant spray if plants are still dormant. Start summer spray program as soon as growth starts. Plant new roses. Prune (Chapter 15).

HEEL into trench any nursery stock, roses, or trees delivered before they can be planted. Unwrap, heel in, and water if necessary. *Keep* moist (page 153).

MULCH: Gradually remove all winter mulches.

FEED: bulb beds, fruits, perennial beds, rock gardens, shrubs and trees, roses, perennial vegetable rows (page 85).

SOW OUTDOORS: peas, sweet peas, hardy vegetables such as beets, carrots, spinach, Swiss chard, radishes, lettuce (Chapter 16), hardy annuals.

IN FRAME: half-hardy annuals (page 114).

DIVIDE AND TRANSPLANT early-flowering perennial flowers (page 194), perennial vegetables.

COLDFRAMES need much attention now. Leave open on sunny and rainy days, if above freezing. Cover only when frost threatens, or in drying winds (Chapter 7).

DORMANT SPRAYS can be applied only before plants come into growth. If scale is still present on euonymus, lilac, etc., use a combination of DDT and malathion every ten days *in late May or June* (Appendix, page 467).

When cultivating and fertilizing perennial beds where LILIES and other late-starting plants are present, be careful not to injure first shoots as they emerge or while they are still just below the soil level.

Where CRAPE-MYRTLE is root-hardy but is killed back above ground, cut back stems to 6 inches after removing mulch. Fertilize.

SUMMER TUBERS: Tuberous begonias, caladiums, and gloxinias can be started now in trays of moist peatmoss or in pots, if not already attended to in February (page 199).

For Area V

LAWNS: Feed, reseed and repair bare spots, apply crabgrass or other weed controls, begin mowing as soon as needed (Chapter 10). Use Bonus selective weed killer for dichondra lawns (Appendix, page 470).

PRUNE: albizzia, camellia after bloom, fuchsia (cuttings may be made from prunings), roses, geraniums (Chapter 6).

FEED: agapanthus (established), azaleas after bloom, camellia after bloom (page 90), bulb plantings, early-blooming perennials, trees, shrubs.

DIVIDE and transplant late-blooming perennials (page 194).

WIND SCALD: In the Southwest, guard against wind scald (page 125); provide ample water.

PREPARE all planting areas (pages 86–88); fertilize and have ready for setting out.

SOW half-hardy annual and vegetable seeds (pages 182; 263); tender annual and vegetable seeds as soon as soil warms up.

AZALEAS: Select new varieties during the blooming season when you can see them in flower.

SOW INDOORS: In cooler areas, seeds of tender annuals and perennials (page 307).

SET OUT: plants of broccoli, cabbage, cauliflower (page 264), first gladiolus corms (page 199), perennials (page 192).

PLANT: deciduous trees, shrubs (page 153), fruits (Chapter 17), roses (page 246).

SPRAY: holly and other specimens affected by scale, *before* March 15. Begin regular summer spray program as plants start into active growth (Appendix, page 467).

For Area VI

LAWNS: Mow winter grass very close. Feed established areas and apply weed killers. Sprig or plug new lawn areas, or sow seed. Repair bare spots and reseed. Treat Dichondra lawns with Bonus selective weed killer. Then apply fertilizer (Chapter 10).

SOW: seeds of tender annuals (pages 51; 182); tender vegetables (page 263); shrubs like *Cassia alata* and erythrinas.

PLANT: avocado, agapanthus, bamboo, caladiums in pots, crape jasmine, citrus fruits (pages 153–55), ground covers, subtropicals in warm areas, summer-flowering bulbs, corms, and tubers (page 199).

PRUNE: azaleas after bloom; camellias after bloom—take cuttings, fuchsia —take cuttings, geraniums—take cuttings (Chapter 4), shrubs after bloom (Chapter 6).

FEED: all established plantings; use cottonseed meal or other acid fertilizer where soil is alkaline, or for acid-loving plants such as azalea camellias, citrus fruits, evergreens, gardenias, hydrangeas (page 90) bulb beds, after bloom, summer-flowering bulbs.

SET OUT: water-lily boxes prepared last month. Leave ⅓ open water early-flowering annual plants (page 193); hardy vegetable plants tender vegetable plants in warmest sections (page 264); strawberrie (page 297).

CUTTINGS: Start chrysanthemum cuttings for fall bloom (pages 63; 69)

Select new AZALEA varieties during blooming season.

SPRAY: Start regular spring and summer spray program: azaleas an gladiolus plants for thrip; roses weekly (Appendix, page 467).

WATER: In dry areas water regularly and deeply, especially plants abou to bloom. Sprinkle foliage frequently. Protect recently planted area from drying winds (pages 78–82).

APRIL

Across the plains of April,
Fresh regiments of rain
With slanting silver bayonets
March to the front again;
And emerald green their banners fly
Against the dark, disheveled sky.
FREDERICK FRYE ROCKWELL

For Area I

In the extremely cold portions of the north and at high altitudes, winter has not loosened her grip.

On first warmer days, do not make the mistake of uncovering plants until sure that there will be no more nights of hard freeze.

As soon as weather moderates *consistently,* all operations listed for April for Area II may be undertaken in Area I.

For Area II

At last the winter should be on the run and many garden jobs can be done as the weather moderates.

UNWRAP TREE TRUNKS and branches. REMOVE MULCHES gradually from beds and shrubs.

As soon as the ground can be worked, PREPARE NEW BEDS and borders for planting (page 86); new lawn areas (page 163); planting holes for nursery stock, roses (pages 153; 246).

LAWNS can be treated with needed soil amendments (lime or sulfur) as soon as snow melts. Apply pre-emergence weed killer-fertilizer one week later. Repair bare spots. Remove snow mold. Prepare new lawn areas as soon as ground can be worked (Chapter 10).

PLANT: beech, birch, dogwoods, evergreens (until new growth appears), fruit trees, bush fruits, grapes, hawthorns, lilacs, magnolias, shrubs, roses, perennials, strawberries.

ROSES: When planting roses, hill temporarily to 6 inches until re-established. If completely dormant, apply dormant spray (page 467). Established rose beds may now be unhilled. Work hilling material into the beds. Prune roses. Start summer spray program as soon as new leaves appear (Chapter 15).

SOW INDOORS OR UNDER GLASS: seeds of annuals which germinate slowly (page 307) and tomatoes, peppers, and eggplant, late in month.

VEGETABLES: As soon as soil is prepared and enriched (page 261) sow hardy vegetable seeds (page 263). Plant onion sets, rhubarb, asparagus, horseradish.

DIVIDE and transplant perennials. Take rooted cuttings from chrysanthemum: crowns are set out in rows (pages 60–63).

FEED: bulb beds, flower beds and borders of perennials, flowering trees and shrubs (page 90), lawns (pages 90; 168), rock gardens (also add compost around roots), roses (page 250).

PESTS: Treat flower beds and lawn areas with chlordane for insects which live in soil. *Do not* use on vegetable garden (page 467).

FRAMES need careful attention now. Remove heavy mulch around plants in frames. Open sash unless mercury goes below freezing. Water if dry (page 114).

WATER: Where springs are dry, WATER as needed (pages 80–84).

CUT BACK to ground root-hardy, top-tender SHRUBS like buddleias, hydrangeas, caryopteris, etc.

BULBS: Start tuberous begonia corms and caladiums in damp peatmoss indoors. Pot up canna roots and keep indoors until May.

For Area III

As soon as it seems safe, remove all mulches; weed bulb beds and perennial borders. Do not injure emerging bulb shoots, especially lilies.

PERENNIALS: Dig all perennials that are to be divided. Cut back tops of buddleias, caryopteris, hydrangeas. Before replanting perennials, loosen soil in beds, add humus, fertilizer, compost (or well-rotted manure). Work in thoroughly. Replant divided perennials. Chrysanthemum cuttings with roots are taken from outsides of crowns and planted in rows in the garden or in peat pots in a frame, to grow on.

FERTILIZE before bloom: bulb beds, ericaceous plants, with acid fertilizer, flowering shrubs, flowering trees, early-blooming perennials, rock garden perennials, with wood ashes and bonemeal (pages 85–90).

LAWNS: If lawns were not attended to in March, see to them now (Chapter 17).

SET OUT in their beds plants of pansies, violas, English daisies, primulas, and other very early-blooming perennials supplied from your own frames or from growers (page 193).

SUMMER BULBS: As soon as danger of frost is over, plant the first gladiolus corms; follow with ismenes and other half-hardy summer-flowering bulbs, corms, tubers (pages 195–99).

START INDOORS in very early April: tender annuals; tomatoes; peppers; and eggplant later in month (page 307).

IN COLDFRAME about middle of month: half-hardy annual seeds; perennial seeds and tender annuals late in month (page 114).

PREPARE A CUTTING BED in the vegetable garden. Sow in rows now: hardy annual seeds, plants of perennials, half-hardy bulbs. When soil and air warm up: tender annual seeds, dahlia tubers, etc.

SOW now in the open garden, after ground has been thoroughly prepared: beets, carrots, Swiss chard, parsnips, spinach, turnips, and other cool-weather vegetables (page 263). Late in month try some bush beans, covering seedlings with soil on cold nights.

SET OUT plants of broccoli, cabbage, cauliflower, lettuce, and anything else not affected by slight frost (page 264). Harden young plants for a week in coldframe before setting out.

PLANT STRAWBERRIES if not already done. Place straw around established plants, after weeding and fertilizing the bed (pages 295–99).

PEST CONTROL: Use chlordane on lawns and flower beds (*not* on vegetable garden at this time) for ants, earwigs, and larvae living in soil.

USE SLUG and SNAIL BAIT once every two weeks, at night (page 467).

Spray: Begin regular fruit spray program following closely instructions of your local county agent, or State Experiment Station (page 472).

ROSES: Before growth starts take down hilling and work into beds. Last dormant spray is given at this time. If growth has started, omit dormant spray and begin regular summer spray program. Apply fertilizer, working in lightly (Chapter 15).

FEED: Before new growth starts feed azaleas, camellias, rhododendrons, *Pieris japonica,* hollies, *Leucothoe catesbei,* etc. (page 90).

PLACE NETS or strings for sweet peas, brush for garden peas, poles for beans to be planted in early May.

BULBS: Continue planting GLADIOLUS in succession, every two weeks from first planting, for six weeks. Begin spraying for thrips when plants are 6 to 8 inches tall (Appendix, page 467).

For Areas IV, V

LAWNS: Repair, fertilize and topdress with compost, aerate; on alkaline soil apply ammonium sulfate to kill weeds and feed grass; on acid soil, apply lime; plant plugs of Bermudagrass in new lawn areas; mow winter grass very close (Chapter 10).

FEED: all plants soon to bloom; azaleas and camellias *after* bloom; iris with fertilizer high in phosphorus and potash (page 90).

ROSES: Prune, feed, start regular summer spray program (Chapter 15).

SET OUT: early-blooming annuals and bedding plants, after hardening off for a week in a frame (page 193); strawberries (page 297); broccoli, cabbage, cauliflower, lettuce (page 264); tomatoes, peppers, eggplants as soon as ground warms up; American-grown lilies; gladiolus corms and other half-hardy summer-flowering bulbs (page 199); Hedges and windbreaks (page 153).

SOW SEEDS: Half-hardy annuals, half-hardy vegetables, tender annuals and vegetables as soon as ground is warm (pages 51–57).

PRUNE: shrubs after bloom, hedges, crape-myrtle, santolina, rosemary, teucrium, nierembergia (Chapter 6).

BULBS: Continue succession plantings of gladiolus corms every two weeks from first planting, for six weeks. Begin spraying for thrips when plants are 6 to 8 inches tall (Appendix, page 467).

Sow *dwarf* dahlia seeds in coldframe (page 114).

Mark clumps of daffodils so crowded they have ceased to bloom freely. Dig these next July (page 199).

Encourage foliage of spring-flowering bulbs to remain green as long as possible. Water, fertilize. Do not cut until foliage turns yellow (page 198). Set out annual plants to conceal maturing foliage.

As soon as soil warms up, plant tuberous begonias and other tender summer-flowering bulbs and corms. Caladiums should not be set out until temperature remains above 40° around the clock, as they are damaged at lower readings (page 199).

For Area VI

PLANT: tuberous begonias; caladiums when night temperature is above 40°; cannas, dahlia tubers, divide and replant; gladiolus (second or third planting); gloxinias, tuberoses (page 199); water-lilies.

SOW SEEDS of tender annuals (pages 51; 182); cool-weather vegetables (page 263).

SET OUT young annual plants, replacing old exhausted ones; perennials (page 193); crape jasmine; bamboo; chrysanthemums, rooted cuttings from old crowns.

LAWNS: Sprig or plug new lawn areas, fertilize established lawn areas, mow regularly (Chapter 10).

FEED: After bloom, spring-flowering bulb beds; azaleas, camellias, avocado, citrus fruits, grapes with superphosphate and potash, early-flowering perennials (page 90).

TAKE CUTTINGS of abutilon, geranium, fuchsia, vitex (pages 68–69). AIR-LAYER jasmine, *Magnolia soulangeana,* viburnum (page 64).

PLANT tropicals in southern or eastern exposure but where early morning sun does not strike them (in shade of building or tree); palms just before new growth starts.

DUST or SPRAY regularly for pests and diseases (Appendix, pages 467–70). Watch out for mildew. Use Mildex. For black spot on roses, use phaltan. For thrips on gladiolus, use dieldrin. Clean up all beds. Burn trash.

Begin summer mulching of all beds, borders, shrubs, trees. Use 2 to 3 inches of pine needles, coarse, rotted sawdust, peatmoss, shredded fir bark, chopped sugar cane, etc. (pages 78–80).

PICK DAILY: Pansies, violas, and other early-blooming flowers.

PRUNE any plants which were injured by freezes during winter: spring-flowering shrubs after bloom, azaleas, hedges (Chapter 6).

WATER: Give deep waterings in dry spells (pages 80–84).

BULBS: Mark clumps of spring-flowering bulbs too crowded to bloom (dig and divide in July) (page 199).

MAY

Fragrance and beauty come in with the green!
The ragged bushes put on sweet attire!

JAMES STEPHENS

For Area I

As soon as ground can be worked, add soil amendments, humus, manure, fertilizer, chlordane (except in vegetable garden where it should be applied in fall after crops are out), work over well, and prepare for planting and sowing (Chapter 2).

DIVIDE AND TRANSPLANT perennials. Set out rooted cuttings of chrysanthemums taken from outside of old crowns (pages 60–63).

SOW: As soon as ground can be prepared, sow sweet peas, peas. Plant onion sets and perennial vegetable plants (Chapter 16).

SOW INDOORS or in frame half-hardy annual seeds: tomato, eggplant, and pepper seeds (page 307); outdoors: hardy vegetable seeds (page 263).

HARDEN OFF in frame for 10 days or two weeks cool-weather vegetable and flower plants started indoors. Then set out in garden, protecting transplants from prevailing, dry winds. Keep well watered. Shade from hot sun for a week or until re-established (page 264).

LAWN: Clean up winter damage. Remove snow mold. Loosen bare spots, add compost, reseed. Fertilize and use weed killers (Chapter 10).

PLANT trees (pages 153–55; also see planting list for April, Area II).

ROSES: Uncover; unhill; prune; spray; plant new bushes (Chapter 15).

FLOWERS: After mulch is removed from beds and border, feed and water.

In WEEDING and fertilizing beds, be careful not to injure young shoots of lilies and other late-starting plants.

FRUITS: Follow spray program closely (Appendix, page 472).

SPRAY: If plants are still dormant apply dormant spray for scale to apples, crabapples, euonymus, lilacs, mountain-ash, viburnum (page 467).

FRAMES need attention this month: open for warm rain and sun; close only if temperature drops near freezing (page 114).

For Area II

SOW half-hardy annuals like marigolds, zinnias, etc., in frame (page 114) or seedbed; tender annuals late in month, cool-weather vegetable seeds outdoors (page 263).

SET OUT plants of cabbage, broccoli, cauliflower (page 264); pansies and other early-flowering, hardy plants (page 193). (Harden in frame from 10 days to 2 weeks before setting out if plants have been raised indoors or under glass.)

HARDEN OFF tomato plants in frames after May 15, ready for setting out late in month (page 264).

SET OUT peppers and eggplants when soil warms up and weather has really settled.

BULBS: If dry, WATER DAFFODILS after bloom. Keep foliage growing. Remove dead flowers. Mark clumps which are overcrowded for dividing in July (page 198).

WHEN CLEANING, CULTIVATING, AND FERTILIZING beds and borders, do not injure the young shoots of plants like lilies, which start late.

SPRAY program for fruit trees and roses should be followed (page 472).

IN WINDY AREAS, do not set houseplants outdoors without wind protection; or wait until windy period is over. Young transplants should also be protected on side of prevailing winds.

LAWN: Sow new lawns as soon as areas are ready; *the earlier the better.* Fertilize established lawns, begin mowing (Chapter 10).

PLANT gladiolus corms. Make succession plantings every two weeks, for six weeks. Other half-hardy bulbs can go in now. Tuberous begonias are set out when weather has settled and soil is frost-free; caladiums not until night temperature is above 40° (page 199).

PINCH BACK young annuals to make bushy plants; also perennials like chrysanthemums, hardy asters.

FERTILIZE all beds and borders of plants about to bloom; also spring-flowering shrubs and trees. Keep well watered in dry areas (pages 80–84).

MULCH: Begin placing summer mulch around trees and shrubs, and on beds and borders as time and opportunity offer (pages 78–80).

HOTKAPS of plastic or paper give a head start with tender vegetables. May be used over vine crops, tomatoes, eggplant, peppers (Chapter 8).

For Areas III, IV

PLANT: summer-flowering bulbs if not already attended to. Set out tuberous begonias late in month; caladiums in June (page 199).

BULBS: Keep foliage growing after bloom. Remove flower heads. Mark overcrowded clumps for transplanting in July (page 198).

THIN beets, carrots, lettuce, radishes, spinach, etc.; half-hardy and hardy annual seedlings (page 265).

SOW: After May 15 seeds of beans, corn, okra, squash, cucumber, cantaloupe—all tender vegetables; tender annuals like portulaca, torenia (page 182).

SET OUT plants of tomato, eggplant, pepper, sweet potato (page 264).

In seedbed or frame in part shade sow seeds of perennials, biennials (pages 51–55).

STRAWBERRIES: Put straw around strawberry plants.

SPRAY fruit trees according to schedule (page 472); roses regularly.

FEED: Has everything had its spring feeding? If not, do it now (pages 85; 90).

WATER if dry, then mulch, trees, shrubs, beds. Acid-lovers should have acid mulch; others any available material (pages 78–80).

PINCH BACK all too leggy young annuals and perennials.

TWIST or PLAIT BULB foliage and set out bedding plants in bulb beds.

PRUNE: All spring-flowering shrubs after bloom is over. Don't spoil their natural grace of growth (Chapter 6).

HOUSEPLANTS should be kept indoors in windy areas until wind has abated; or set out where they will have complete protection from prevailing winds. Sink to rims in well-prepared bed, with filtered sun.

STAKE tall-growing, early perennials to prevent breakage (page 186).

LAWNS: Sod new lawn areas with Zoysia or Bermuda. Plugs or sprigs of these grasses are available now (Chapter 10).

For Area V

FEED: perennials and biennials, now in strong growth, with a low-nitrogen fertilizer; roses after bloom; spring-flowering, broad-leaved evergreens, after bloom; all perennials and shrubs, after bloom; tulips, after bloom (pages 85–90).

SOW seeds of very tender annuals; perennials, biennials (pages 51–57), vine crops, corn, okra, in seedbeds or frames; second sowings of cool-weather vegetables for fall harvest (page 263); annual seeds in bulb beds (do not cut bulb foliage until mature).

SET OUT eggplant and peppers (page 264); bedding plants; summer-flowering bulbs, including tuberous begonias (page 199); water-lilies in their boxes when water temperature reaches 70°.

ROSES: Remove dead flowers; cut back blooming sprays of large-flowered climbers, removing two or three buds, after bloom; remove old canes of ramblers, after bloom; fertilize after bloom; keep well watered; spray regularly; summer mulch. Pot-grown plants can still be set out. Or keep in containers on patio (floribundas) (Chapter 15).

CLEAN UP and compost spent annual plants. Replace with young plants of summer bloomers.

SPRAY camellias after bloom; holly and lilac for leaf miner; roses weekly; elm, hackberry, honey locust, fruits for cankerworm (page 467).

CHRYSANTHEMUMS: Feed every 3 or 4 weeks; pinch back 3 times, last pinching in early July; water deeply; mulch for summer; give all-purpose spray as needed.

LAWNS: Seed or sod new areas, previously prepared; feed those already established; apply weed control; water deeply in dry spells (Chapter 10).

PINCH BACK late-flowering perennials to create bushy plants (page 187).

REMOVE DEAD FLOWERS from delphinium, foxglove, and other early-blooming perennials; also from spring-flowering bulbs. Prune all shrubs after bloom is over (page 94).

HOUSEPLANTS: Plunge pots outdoors in shady, enriched bed, after re-potting if necessary. Feature large specimens on patio.

STAKE tall-growing plants, tubers, and corms (page 186).

For Area VI

ROSES: Give plants a chance to rest a little after their first heavy bloom. Remove dead flowers. Feed lightly. Prune back very tall canes. Water as needed and do not let up on spraying. Summer mulch. Prune back old canes of ramblers to ground, after bloom (Chapter 15).

SET OUT plants of tomatoes, eggplant, and peppers, if not already done; young plants for later bloom in bulb beds (keep bulb foliage growing); all bedding plants (page 193); dahlias and other tender, summer flowering bulbs not already in (page 199).

SPRAY schedule should be rigidly adhered to. Keep ahead of pests and diseases (Appendix, page 467).

FEED chrysanthemums every 3 or 4 weeks; established lawns (Chapter 10); citrus fruit, with sulfate of ammonia; plants about to bloom (pages 85–90).

CITRUS FRUITS: Plant now; feed established trees—add iron sulfate; spray for scale, aphids (Appendix, page 467).

CLEAN UP all beds containing plants exhausted after bloom. Replace with young plants of later bloomers, or sow seed of hot-weather annuals.

BULBS: Make succession plantings of gladiolus corms every two weeks for six weeks (page 199). See list of summer-flowering bulbs for southern gardens (page 440).

WATERING should not be neglected in dry areas (pages 80–84).

DIG and STORE tulips and hyacinths when foliage matures (page 199).

VEGETABLES: Keep rows thinned as young plants develop. Give side dressing to half-grown plants. Keep after weeds. Keep watered and well mulched (Chapter 16).

SUMMER MULCH beds, borders, trees, and shrubs to retain moisture, keep down weeds (pages 78–80).

JUNE

A fragrant rose;
A tall calm lily from the waterside;
A half-blown poppy hanging at the side
Its head of dream,
Dreaming among the corn.

JAMES STEPHENS

For Area I

SOW half-hardy annual seeds in frame, or where they are to grow; late in month, tender annual and vegetable seeds, or earlier in a frame (pages 51–57).

HARDEN OFF plants started indoors or under glass by placing in frame for ten days to two weeks (page 264).

SET OUT annual, young perennial, and all but most tender vegetable plants, after hardening off; tomato plants after all danger of frost is past (page 193); peppers and eggplant somewhat later when soil warms up; summer-flowering bulbs like gladiolus, ismene; tuberous begonia, gloxinia, caladium, canna when soil warms up (page 199).

SHADE newly set out plants for a few days with berry boxes or shingles on the windward side.

IN CULTIVATING beds and borders be careful not to damage plants which are late appearing above ground.

FEED and WATER, then SUMMER MULCH all beds and garden areas.

STRAWBERRIES: Arrange straw mulch under plants in strawberry beds.

PINCH BACK late-blooming perennials like chrysanthemums, hardy asters, to make them bushy. Then feed, water, and mulch.

SPRING-FLOWERING BULBS: Keep foliage growing after bloom by giving plant food and water; remove dead blossoms; mark clumps which are overcrowded and need digging and dividing in July (page 198).

THIN seedling vegetables and annuals (page 57).

ROSES: Remove dead blooms; water, summer mulch (Chapter 15).

LAWN: Feed, water as needed, and mow once a week (Chapter 10).

FLOWER BEDS: After weeding beds and borders, add compost, fertilizer. Water well and then apply summer mulch (Chapter 5). Faded blooms should be removed from early-blooming perennials.

PRUNE spring-flowering shrubs after bloom (Chapter 6).

DIVIDE lily-of-valley, primroses, etc. after flowering (pages 192; 194).

PESTS: Watch seedling nasturtiums for black aphids. Spray with malathion or Black Leaf 40 (Appendix, page 467). Regular summer spray program should now be in full swing (Chapter 5).

CUT BACK and feed very early-blooming PERENNIALS like myosotis, pansies, violas, and others.

BEDDING PLANTS may be set out in bulb beds but *do not cut* bulb foliage (page 198).

In high altitudes of late frosts, young plants can be protected with Hotkaps until weather warms up (page 125).

For Areas II, III

LAWN: Feed, water, and mow once a week. Keep up crabgrass and other weed-control measures (Chapter 10 and Appendix, page 470).

PLANT caladiums, tuberoses, cannas, and other very tender bulbs, corms and tubers, if not done (page 199).

SET OUT very tender annual and vegetable plants, if not done previously (pages 193; 264).

SHADE and protect newly set out annuals for a few days with berry boxes or shingles on windy side (page 125). Keep watered.

STAKE tall-growing perennials that have not yet bloomed (page 186).

CUT BACK early-blooming perennials: remove dead blossoms from pansies, violas, and other early, low-growing biennials and perennials.

SOW a second lot of candytuft, nigella, cornflowers, and other annuals which bloom only a short time, to keep up succession of bloom (page 182).

PESTS: Watch nasturtium seedlings closely for black aphids. Spray with malathion or Black Leaf 40 (Appendix, page 467).

PINCH BACK tall-growing annuals, chrysanthemums, hardy asters, dahlias, and others as needed, to produce sturdy, bushy plants (page 187).

DIG and divide primroses, lily-of-the-valley. Wait until July or August f
iris and June-blooming perennials (pages 60–63; 194).

SPRAY: Continue regular summer spray program.

ROSES: Feed just before June bloom; keep dead blossoms cut, just abo
outfacing bud; spray weekly; water deeply when needed without wettir
foliage; after bloom remove old canes of ramblers; cut dead bloon
from large-flowered climbers, removing 2 or 3 eyes (Chapter 15

BULBS: Dig tulips when foliage matures, or leave in ground another yea
if still blooming well; keep daffodil and other bulb foliage growin
vigorously; water and feed if necessary (page 198); lilies, at the
height in July, should be fed and kept moist this month; mulch to kee
soil cool around roots. Set out bedding plants in bulb beds, but do *n*
remove healthy bulb foliage; simply lay it aside or tie it together.

SUMMER MULCH may now be applied to everything after beds have bee
weeded, plants fed, and watered (pages 78–80).

TROPICAL WATER-LILIES can be placed in pools when water reaches 7
degrees. Plan for one third open water, full sun.

FEED, after bloom: delphinium, lupine, Oriental poppies, aquilegia, pec
nies, iris (pages 85–90).

TOMATOES: Begin tying up plants to supports and pinching out ne
growths (page 270).

For Areas IV, V

BULBS: Remove matured yellow foliage of tulips, or dig and store bulb
for replanting in autumn. Keep foliage of other spring-flowering bulb
growing by giving deep waterings (page 198).

FEED perennials which have finished bloom, first removing dead flowe
stalks or stems. Water if dry; then summer mulch (pages 78–84; 90)

VEGETABLES: Begin tying to supports and continue pinching out ne
growths of tomatoes (page 270); side-dress half-grown plants lik
cabbage, broccoli; thin out corn, beans, planted late in May (pag
265); cut every other lettuce head, giving more room to those remair
ing; give second thinning to carrots, beets, turnips, and other hardy an
cool-weather vegetables. Beet and turnip thinnings make deliciou
greens. Make second sowing for a late crop of carrots, beets, etc. Sov
Chinese-cabbage, celery, Brussels sprouts (Chapter 16).

ET OUT all very tender plants like dwarf dahlias, caladiums, etc., if not done already (page 199).

PLANT tropical water-lilies in pool when water reaches 70 degrees. Leave one third open water.

LAWN: Mow weekly, feed, water, treat for weeds (Chapter 10).

PINCH BACK tall-growing annuals and late-blooming perennials to make bushy plants.

DIVIDE May-blooming plants such as primroses, iris, lily-of-the-valley.

SPRAY: Watch nasturtiums for black aphids. Spray with malathion. One treatment will make a 100 per cent kill (Appendix, page 467). Continue regular SPRAY program.

ROSES: Water every 7 to 10 days; apply 2- to 3-inch summer mulch; prune back lightly after June bloom; spray weekly; fertilize lightly after heavy bloom; remove all old canes to ground from ramblers; large-flowered climbers are pruned like Hybrid Teas (Chapter 15).

FEED and WATER azaleas, camellias, chrysanthemums (pages 80–84; 90).

SUMMER MULCH should be applied to all parts of the garden to conserve moisture, discourage weeds; continue deep watering in dry sections (pages 78–80).

STAKE tall-growing plants which have not yet bloomed (page 186).

FRUITS: Keep fruit trees, small fruits, and strawberries well watered while fruit is developing (Chapter 17).

SOW: For constant bloom, make monthly sowings this month and next of short-term bloomers like candytuft, nigella, and cornflower; sow seeds of torenia to take place of pansies in late garden; sow perennial and biennial seeds in frame (page 182).

PRUNE all spring-flowering shrubs which have finished blooming (Chapter 6).

AZALEAS, RHODODENDRONS: Prune and remove dead flowers (page 96); water frequently; stir and add to mulch; feed every 6 weeks with acid food (pages 81–90); make tip cuttings and layers (Chapter 6).

SET OUT young chrysanthemum plants. Feed. Water. Spray bimonthly.

FEED and water fuchsias and hydrangeas—the latter with acid fertilizer (page 90).

TUBEROUS BEGONIAS may be purchased in pots now and set out in shaded bed or patio. Mist with fine water spray on hot afternoons.

For Area VI

AZALEAS and RHODODENDRONS: Start cuttings (page 71); prune, also removing all dead blossoms (page 96); stir and add to mulch; feed with acid plant food every 6 weeks. Give iron; water frequently.

FEED and WATER established shrubs, agapanthus, bamboo, summer-flowering bulbs, citrus fruits (acid food), chrysanthemums, fuchsias, camellias (acid food), ixoras, gardenias, hydrangeas (acid food), tibouchina, palm trees, violets, ground covers (pages 81–90).

LAWNS: Mow 1½ to 2 inches high; Bermudagrass to ½ inch; apply weed controls; Bonus controls weeds in dichondra lawns; feed monthly; water weekly, twice a week when temperature is over 90 degrees; sow dichondra seed (Chapter 10).

PLANT crotons, dracaenas, large palm trees.

PRUNE bauhinia, oleander, and other tropical shrubs after bloom (use rubber gloves when handling oleander to prevent skin poisoning); keep geraniums groomed (Chapter 6).

PINCH BACK chrysanthemums, dahlias; new growths of tomatoes (pages 187; 270).

FRUITS: Keep watered. Prop up fruit-laden branches to prevent breakage.

TREES: Newly or recently planted trees and shrubs should be kept well watered and shaded to prevent sunburn (page 155).

STAKE UP gladiolus, dahlias, other tall-growing plants that have not bloomed (page 186).

DRAINAGE: If soil is poorly drained, improve by tiling or open ditches (pages 20–22).

PESTS: Regular spray program is most important; check figs for red spider, thrips, thread blight; spray roses weekly; use DDT on passion vine for caterpillars, Chlordane for ants (Appendix, page 467).

DIVIDE and replant bearded iris (page 194); leucocoryne bulbs (replant in pots).

Remove dead flower stalks from early-blooming perennials, annuals.

MULCH to protect roots from heat with well-rooted manure, compost, or straw (pages 78–80).

SOW perennial, biennial, hot-weather annual and vegetable seeds (Chapters 11 & 16).

JULY

I turned my head and saw the wind
Not far from where I stood,
Dragging the corn by her golden hair
Into a dark and lonely wood.
The Villain by WILLIAM HENRY DAVIES

For Areas I, II, III, IV

WATER deeply in drought, and regularly in areas where dry summers are the rule (pages 80–84).

MULCHING: After light cultivation of the soil, an application of fertilizer, and a deep watering, the application of a mulch is good preparation for summer heat. It conserves moisture, keeps down weeds, and maintains coolness around plant roots (pages 78–80).

LAWNS: Fertilize established lawns with high-nitrogen formula; water thoroughly as needed; mow high in hot weather; apply weed controls; spray for pests and diseases (Chapter 10).

SPRING-FLOWERING BULBS may be dug, dried off, and stored for fall planting *after* foliage turns brown; tulips may remain in ground or be dug each year and replanted in October or November; overcrowded clumps of daffodils can be dug, divided, and replanted now, or stored until September (page 198); remove dead flower stalks from all early-blooming perennials, and from lilies which have bloomed, *after* stalks die.

IRIS foliage should mature after bloom. Bearded iris can be dug, divided, and replanted, *six weeks* after bloom ceases. Cut away any rotted or pest-ridden parts, dust cuts with disinfectant, cut rhizomes into small clumps, and replant near surface. Before resetting, work over beds, adding peatmoss and superphosphate.

DIG AND DIVIDE rock garden perennials such as: arabis, *Alyssum saxatile,* heuchera, iberis, *Phlox nivalis, Phlox subulata.* Small sections, set in a row in well-prepared soil and kept watered until they root, will increase stock easily.

Do not remove foliage from peonies but keep it growing like bulb foliage. Feed peonies after bloom (page 198).

FEED: aquilegia, chrysanthemums, day-lilies, delphinium, iris, lupine, hardy asters, late-flowering annuals, roses, including climbers (lightly after heaviest bloom), peonies, potted amaryllis bulbs (pages 85–90).

REMOVE SUCKERS from roses, flowering crabs, plums, peaches, flowering almond, and any grafted plant where sucker comes from *below* graft; also from lilacs.

CHRYSANTHEMUMS: Pinch back every two weeks to July 15; feed with liquid manure.

ROSES: Remove all dead flowers, cutting above an eye or bud; ramblers *only:* cut back old canes to ground after bloom; feed lightly this month to give a little rest after heavy June bloom; keep well watered, mulched, sprayed weekly (Chapter 15).

PRUNE: wisteria runners, and other hardy perennial vines to keep growth under control; yews and sheared coniferous evergreen hedges; broadleaf evergreen hedges like box and privet; deciduous hedges. Shape up shrubs like forsythia, shrub roses, but do not destroy natural grace (Chapter 6).

CUTTINGS can now be taken and rooted of coleus, fuchsia, geraniums, lantana, heliotrope, and other tender plants for winter bloom indoors. Box, yew, euonymus, pachysandra, perennials, and deciduous shrubs are ready to be slipped for cuttings (Chapter 4).

SOW SEED of hardy perennials in partly shaded frame: delphinium as soon as seed is ripe; annuals like calendula, candytuft, sweet alyssum, to keep up succession of bloom (page 182); vegetables like beets, endive, Chinese-cabbage, lettuce, radish, spinach, turnips, for fall crop; beans and corn for a late crop (page 263).

For Areas III, IV

SET OUT late cabbage, cauliflower, and celery plants; keep well watered (page 264).

STRAWBERRIES: Keep weeded, feed with 5–10–5 formula, 2 to 3 lbs. per 100 square ft.; water and keep mulched. As soon as young plants have formed at tips or runners, pot in rich soil in peat pots and sink near parent plants without cutting runners. In August or September these can be separated from old plants, and set out in a new row (pages 295–99).

HERBS: Harvest lavender flowers before they fade; also prime leaves of culinary and fragrant herbs. Dry on trays in airy shed or attic; store in airtight containers. Pick everlastings when in early full bloom, tie in bunches, hang upside down in shed to dry (pages 227–28). Pick flowers and sprays while in perfect condition, to dry for winter bouquets in Flora-gel, or borax and cornmeal.

BULBS: Plant last gladiolus bulbs in July—by July 15 in the north; keep after thrips (page 224).

PERENNIALS: Order day-lilies, Oriental poppies, iris, madonna lilies, colchicums, fall-blooming crocus, sternbergia, and such minor bulbs as winter-aconite. All of these should be planted as soon as received.

TUBEROUS BEGONIAS, CALADIUMS: Mist spray thoroughly during hot, dry afternoons (pages 81–84); use all-purpose rose spray for mildew, leaf spot (Appendix, page 469).

SPRAY OR DUST REGULARLY and keep eyes open for midsummer pests and diseases: beetles, aphids, bag worms, berry moths, borers, ear worms in corn, clover mite (lawns), grasshoppers, mealy bugs, mites, thrips, leaf blights, mildew, lawn diseases, nematodes (Appendix, pages 467–69).

WATER IS NEEDED ESPECIALLY BY azaleas, rhododendrons, coniferous evergreens, magnolias, dogwood, flowering and other fruits (pages 80–84).

For Areas V, VI

CUT BACK exhausted annuals (replacing with young plants if necessary); remove old flower stalks of perennials.

SHEAR hedges such as box, coniferous evergreens, privet, barberry (Chapter 6).

If SPRING-FLOWERING BULBS that need division and replanting have not already been attended to, do it now; foliage has matured.

DIG AND DIVIDE bearded iris, Oriental poppies, primulas (if not done), and others; allow six weeks after end of blooming period (page 194).

CHLOROSIS (yellowing of leaves) may appear in lawns or on plants in summer. It is caused by excess alkalinity. Apply an iron chelate such as Sequestrene to soil. Also apply to foliage as a spray.

LAWN: In drought, when grass turns blue-green and wilts, sift compost over surface and work down gently around roots; if turf turns yellow, see CHLOROSIS above. Feed, on cool, cloudy days; water weekly, twice a week if temperature is above 90°; mow high in hot weather. Plug or sprig new lawn areas with St. Augustine, Centipede or Bermudagrass (this last may also be seeded) (Chapter 10).

GROUND COVERS: Shear off ground covers which are setting seeds (Chapter 10).

VEGETABLES: Cut back artichokes after bearing, to produce a crop next spring.

SOW last of warm-weather vegetables (page 263) in flats or partly shaded frame; broccoli, cabbage, cauliflower; amaryllis; perennials; winter and spring-flowering annuals (page 182).

PLANT pot-grown trees, shrubs; annuals from nurseries (page 193); *Lycoris radiata;* broad-leaved evergreens; fruits (page 281). Keep all well watered.

FEED fast-growing annuals; late-blooming perennials; chrysanthemums, with liquid manure; clivias; ixoras; hibiscus (pages 85–90). Withhold fertilizer for two months from roses to give rest; from doubtfully hardy evergreen shrubs in areas where early frosts may injure tender foliage.

BULBS: Raise amaryllis bulbs which have sunk too deep in ground.

DRAINAGE: In areas of summer rain, check drainage and install tiles or ditches if necessary; use raised beds (pages 20–22).

WATER consistently and deeply in dry areas, with special attention to all trees and shrubs, broad-leaved evergreens, fruits, and plants about to bloom (pages 80–84).

SPRAY: Keep up consistent SPRAY program. This is the peak month for pests and diseases in many areas.

PRUNE hydrangeas after bloom, poinsettias, rampant perennial vines (Chapter 6).

PINCH BACK dahlias, hardy asters, chrysanthemums, up to July 15.

SOFTWOOD CUTTINGS may now be taken of camellias (root under glass), Japanese yew, pomegranate, poinsettia (page 68).

MULCHING and GROUND COVERS protect plants from hot wind and sun (pages 78; 174).

AUGUST

For Areas I, II, III, IV

In the coldest regions, annuals from seed are at their best this month. Keep dead blooms cut off to prevent seeding. Remove weeds, give copious water, fertilize lightly between bursts of bloom, and mulch to conserve moisture and protect from heat.

Where short growing season and low winter temperatures keep roses and other plants from attaining tall, heavy growth, cut flowers with short stems to conserve stem growth and foliage.

WATER, and plenty of it, is needed this month in most sections of the country. Give deep, slow waterings and measure depth to which it permeates. It should reach to 6 or 8 inches (pages 80–84).

SUMMER MULCHES help to hold moisture, protect plants from heat by keeping root-runs cool, and help to keep down weeds (pages 78–80).

LAWN areas for fall seeding should be prepared early this month (pages 158–65); seeding can be undertaken late in August or in early September; fertilize and water established lawns; apply weed killers and spray for diseases, pests (Appendix, page 467); mow high in hot weather.

In areas subject to very early frosts, withhold plant food and water after August 15 from roses, azaleas, rhododendrons, and other woody plants, soft growth of which may be injured by early frost. Reduce water on broad-leaved evergreens in the above class.

FEED chrysanthemums, hardy asters, dahlias, tomatoes, lawns, strawberry beds for the last time (pages 85–90).

STAKE tall-growing plants before heavy blooms bend them over (page 186).

SPRAY programs should be followed closely and a sharp lookout kept for new pests. August is the time when many troubles reach their peak.

Mildew may attack delphinium, hardy asters, chrysanthemums,· lilacs, phlox, roses, zinnias (Appendix, page 469); *lawn diseases* may appear (Appendix, page 465); for *leaf hoppers, peach tree borers, spider mites, euonymus scale, Japanese and other beetles, aphids, mealy bug* (Appendix, page 467).

BULBS: Order spring-flowering bulbs; include unusual species: alliums, chionodoxas, crocus, fritillarias, scillas, winter-aconite. Minor bulbs should be planted on delivery, especially fall colchicums and *Sternbergia lutea,* and winter-aconite. Order lily bulbs. Plant madonna lilies at once; others as soon after delivery as possible.

BULB BEDS can be prepared between the time of ordering and delivery of the bulbs.

Crocus, freesia, paper-white narcissus; calla-lily, amaryllis, and other winter-flowering bulbs can now be planted in pots for winter bloom indoors (page 117).

SOW SEEDS of perennials and biennials: aquilegia, catanache, coreopsis, delphinium, gloriosa daisy, Shasta daisy, Canterbury bells, centauria, foxglove, hollyhock (page 187).

STRAWBERRY runners can now be detached from parent plants. Dig up potted runner plants and set out in a row (page 297).

DIG AND DIVIDE, if crowded, or set out new plants or bulbs of: crown-imperial, day-lilies, foxglove, bearded iris, madonna lilies, mertensia, Oriental poppy, peony, Shasta daisy (pages 60; 193).

IRIS: In Areas III and IV, where they are hardy, set out new Japanese and other tender iris plants.

CANE FRUIT: If not done previously, prune back cane fruits after bearing (page 294).

BLUEBERRIES are shallow rooted. Be sure they are well mulched and watered (pages 78–83).

ORDER: Where fall planting is safe, order azaleas and other shrubs; also perennials and roses.

VEGETABLES: Sow lettuce seed in frame for fall crop (page 263). Where autumns are long and mild, set out fall vegetable plants (page 264). When asparagus tops are faded, remove from bed. Mulch with well-rotted manure. As vegetable crops are harvested, clean up the areas, place undiseased or pest-free trash on compost heap, cultivate soil and sow winter cover crop.

FALL COLOR: Exhausted annuals can now be replaced with chrysanthemums—transplant even in bud; or with fall-blooming annuals.

For Areas V, VI

FEED: long-season annuals, between bursts of bloom; dahlias; and disbu
for show blooms azaleas, camellias, and fuchsias; chrysanthemun
with liquid plant food; roses; strawberry beds for last time; fall- an
winter-flowering shrubs; tomato plants.

STAKE as needed all tall-growing plants still in bloom or about to flowe
(page 186).

WATER: In dry areas keep watering and keep plants, beds, and border
mulched to conserve moisture, keep roots cool, and control weec
(pages 78–84).

PLANT Easter lily bulbs—varieties Croft or Creole—as soon as deliverec
also madonna lilies, Louisiana and Japanese iris, fall- and winter
flowering bulbs.

LAWNS: Last call to sow Bermudagrass now; fertilize and water estab
lished lawns, apply weed killer and spray for disease and pests (Chap
ter 10).

REFRIGERATE cool-weather perennial seeds like delphinium, pansy, an
viola before sowing (far South).

CUT BACK or remove rampant perennials in borders that threaten to crowc
out more desirable species. Continue to cut back rampant vines tha
encroach on trees, shrubs, or other plants.

SET OUT plants of cool-weather annuals, perennials, and vegetables (page
193); pot-grown shrubs, roses, broad-leaved evergreens (pages 153-
55).

PLANT calla-lily, clivia, ranunculus.

DIVIDE and TRANSPLANT day-lilies, clivia, Oriental poppies, peonies
Shasta daisy (pages 63; 193).

SOW: calendula, myosotis, stock, viola, wallflower. Transplant in si:
weeks for December bloom (page 182); beets, beans, collards, car
rots, Chinese-cabbage, radishes, for fall crop (page 263).

ROSES: Order roses for October–November planting; take cuttings and star
under glass jars; feed and water; spray weekly; remove dead bloom
and keep beds clean (Chapter 15).

WATER consistently in all dry areas or dry spells (pages 80–84). Azaleas
camellias, and fuchsias need constant moisture.

SPRAYS and DUSTS should be applied at regular intervals. This is the peak
time for pests and diseases; watch chrysanthemums and dahlias for
aphids, red spider; dahlias for stem borers (slit stems and remove
borers); watch figs for rust; pyracantha for lace-wing bug; watch
for mildew on annuals, perennials, lilacs (Appendix, page 469).

SEPTEMBER

To bronze Jove changed
Earth's golden time.
Odes by HORACE

For Areas I, II, III, IV

Though there are great variations in temperatures in the above planting areas, frost may strike even the mildest of them before the end of September. Operations suggested for this month can be executed as dictated by local weather conditions.

LAWNS: Seed new areas if not already done; the earlier the better; fertilize and repair established lawns (page 168); have soil tested and add amendments if necessary; mow high—to 2½ inches; water in dry areas (Chapter 10).

COMPOST is worth its weight in gold! Build a new heap now (page 27).

DIVIDE and REPLANT early-blooming perennials (pages 62; 193).

BULBS: Plant spring-flowering bulbs; tulips go in last; minor bulbs and lilies on delivery; lift bulbs, corms, and tubers of summer-flowering tender subjects before or just after first frost; dry off and store (page 199).

HARVEST onion and root crops and store; store winter squash at 50 to 60 degrees (Chapter 16).

CLEAN UP beds from which dead or matured plants have been removed. Cultivate and sow COVER CROPS (page 27).

WATER chrysanthemums, hardy asters, and other fall bloomers; newly set evergreens; recently planted shrubs and trees (pages 80–84).

FEED chrysanthemums, asters before they show color; use a *low*-nitrogen food to stimulate blooms, not foliage (page 90).

GATHER PODS of wildflowers and garden subjects; dry and store for winter bouquets.

EVERGREENS can be transplanted from now until ground freezes (pages 153–55).

FRAMES: If you have no coldframe, build one now (Chapter 7).

SOW completely hardy annual seeds where they are to grow: calliopsis, California-poppy, cornflower, larkspur, Shirley poppy (pages 51–57).

STOP FERTILIZING roses and shrubs: this will encourage dormancy.

SOIL PREPARATION: Where fall planting of roses is successful, prepare beds; order plants (Chapter 15).

CUTTINGS: Start cuttings of tender, flowering houseplants (page 68).

For Areas I, II, III, IV

INDOORS

Loosen pots of houseplants in their beds; in three days to a week, remove to a sheltered spot; cut back rank growth; repot where necessary, then bring indoors before first frost, which may injure tender specimens.

Place in north or west windows, ferns, ivies, tolmieas, philodendrons, tradescantias, and large-leaved begonias; place flowering plants in south or east windows; African-violets do best in east or west exposures.

Feed Christmas cactus every two weeks. Syringe frequently. Water moderately.

Watch for aphids and other pests. Treat at once. Weekly syringing of leaves discourages pests.

Houseplants which do not throw out new growth should be watered moderately, and plant food withheld until new growth starts.

If portions of houseplants die back after bringing indoors, prune back to live wood.

For Area V

LAWNS: Seed new areas; repair poor spots in established lawns, then top dress with compost and fertilize; keep up treatments for crabgrass; spray for snow mold if necessary (Chapter 10).

DIG, DIVIDE, and REPLANT peonies and other early-blooming perennia such as day-lilies, iris, Oriental poppies (pages 60; 193).

SET OUT young perennial plants in permanent locations (page 193).

MULCH young perennials after planting with light, nonmatting materi (pages 78–80).

CHRYSANTHEMUMS and HARDY ASTERS should be fed every two weeks u til buds show color; and should be kept well watered.

SOW SEEDS of hardy annuals; early-blooming perennials like primros (pages 49–57); hardy and half-hardy vegetables such as lettuce, lee mustard, spinach, Swiss chard, turnip (page 263).

BULBS: Plant spring-flowering bulbs (page 195); half-hardy bulbs; Ca didum lilies.

PRUNE roses lightly. Feed for last time. Continue spray program (Chaj ter 15).

FERTILIZER should be *withheld* after middle of month from deciduou trees, shrubs, and roses to prevent soft new growth which may be ir jured by frost. Withhold water also.

BULBS: Prepare lily beds for November planting. Feed amaryllis an other established bulb plantings with one teaspoon muriate of potash t ½ gallon of water, to harden for cold weather.

FEED camellias and winter-blooming shrubs that have not bloomed. Re move dead flowers from those which have (page 90).

CUTTINGS: Take camellia cuttings and root in frame (page 71).

TREES AND SHRUBS: Prepare planting holes for later planting (page 153–55).

SET OUT winter-blooming flower plants (page 193).

CUT BACK exhausted annuals severely, to encourage new growth.

SPRAY: Keep up regular spray program on all plants in growth (Ap pendix, page 467).

For Area VI

LAWNS: Feed; water; mow high. Overplant Bermuda or other summe grass lawns with annual ryegrass and keep constantly moist until ger mination (Chapter 10).

EED: citrus fruits for last time (early in month); avocados, camellias, with acid fertilizer (page 90); chrysanthemums; established bulb beds; sweet peas, wallflowers, and other winter bloomers (page 85).

ATER: In dry areas, keep beds, borders, trees, shrubs, and lawns well watered.

ɔW SEEDS of hardy and half-hardy annuals; perennials (page 182).

ɛT OUT plants of winter-blooming flowers. Keep moist until established (page 193).

ɪVIDE and REPLANT spring-flowering perennials: iris, peony, Oriental poppy, primula, etc. (pages 60; 193).

PRAY PROGRAM should be continued.

LANTING HOLES may now be dug for trees and shrubs to be moved later (Chapter 9).

ɪITHHOLD fertilizer and heavy watering from hibiscus, citrus fruits, figs, tibouchina, etc., in areas where soft new growth may be killed by frost.

ɪULCH tender surface roots before cool weather (pages 78–80).

EGETABLES: Sow seeds of cool-weather vegetables (page 263). Set out plants of hardy perennial vegetables now or later in fall (Chapter 16).

TAKE and TIE chrysanthemums, hardy asters, climbing roses, vines.

NNUALS: Cut back exhausted plants, feed and water.

OSES: Prune lightly to force November bloom; feed for the last time; water; spray (Chapter 15).

OIL PREPARATION: Prepare beds for pansies and other winter bloomers to be set out later (pages 86–88).

AMELLIAS: Remove dead blooms to prevent petal blight; water if needed; take cuttings and root in frame (page 71).

OCTOBER

Golden leaves in an amber pool,
And rocks all warm in the sun;
Why should we fret that summer is gone—
When autumn has just begun?

ESTHER C. GRAYSON

For Area I

PLANT spring-flowering bulbs; lilies as soon as delivered; winter rye on garden areas after they are cleaned of all trash, weeded, and cultivated (page 195).

PRUNE back tall growths of climbing roses which may whip in winter winds (page 251); cane fruits which have finished bearing (page 295).

ROSES: Hill up to 12 inches around all bush roses, with compost or top soil; have winter mulch ready to apply to rose beds over hilling just before or just after first hard freeze; prepare to lay down and cover with soil climbing and tree roses before ground freezes (Chapter 15).

GRAPES: Young vines should be laid down and covered like climbing roses, above.

GARDEN CLEAN-UP should include removal and *burning* of all trash in which pests or diseases may winter over.

VEGETABLES: Harvest before hard frost; dry off and store; follow directions (page 266).

TOOLS and POWER EQUIPMENT: Clean, check, and store after garden work is completed (Chapter 8).

For Areas II, III, IV

BULBS: Tulips can be planted as soon as the daffodils and other spring-flowering bulbs are in (page 195). Plant all lily bulbs as soon as delivered. Divide and replant lily-of-the-valley clumps (page 60). Mulch lily-of-the-valley beds with well-rotted, strawy manure, if available; otherwise with rough compost reinforced with dried manure. Pot up daffodils, tulips, muscari, hyacinths, etc., for forcing (page 117). Tender bulbs should be dug just before or just after first frost; dry off and then store (page 199).

ROSES: Have topsoil or compost dumped near rose beds ready to hill them up before hard freeze (page 255).

CHRYSANTHEMUMS: Observe and make notes on varieties which bloom well in your locality before hard freeze. Discard those which flower so late that they suffer severe frost damage before they make a show. Heel into coldframe varieties which are doubtfully hardy. Later mulch these with nonmatting mulch.

WINTER PROTECTION: Have nonmatting mulch ready to mulch beds and borders just before hard freeze (pages 78–80).

EVERGREENS and choice shrubs may be protected by placing stakes around each specimen and nailing to these a screen of burlap, canvas, or heavy plastic. Inside this screen pack dry hardwood leaves, pine needles, or locally available mulch. In milder sections, chicken wire may be used to hold the mulch in place.

GARDEN CLEAN-UP: As plant material matures or is touched by frost, clean up beds and borders, as well as vegetable garden, burning trash which may carry over pests or disease. Loosen up soil and plant winter rye as cover crop (page 27).

PESTS: Apply chlordane to soil infested by ants, earwigs, maggots, sowbugs (Appendix, page 467).

LAWNS: If grass is heavy, give last mowing. In areas where snow mold is a problem, treat with lawn fungicide to kill surviving spores (page 469). Seed new lawns; renovate old ones (Chapter 10).

WATER deeply before hard freeze all newly planted or transplanted trees and shrubs (pages 80–84).

VEGETABLES: Root crops are dug now and stored in coolest frost-free place available (page 266). Place in frame celery, lettuce, Chinesecabbage, heel in; cover on cold nights; use as needed (Chapter 7).

WINTER SQUASH and sweet potatoes should be stored in temperature 50 to 60 degrees.

SOIL PREPARATION: Prepare planting holes for nursery stock which may not be delivered until after ground freezes. Cover prepared ground with straw, leaves, or burlap, held down by boards to keep from freezing. In areas where fall planting is possible, prepare new rose beds ready for planting roses when delivered (page 244). Peonies and phlox may also be planted or divided and replanted now. Mulch beds after planting (pages 78–80).

CUT BACK long vines and rose canes which may whip in winter wind (page 251); *old* raspberry canes to the ground; and prune off a third of young canes (page 295).

HOUSEPLANTS: Bring houseplants indoors, if this has not already been attended to. Prune back rank growth and repot if needed.

Do not feed houseplants until they have recovered from shock of new environment. Watch for aphids and other pests at this time. Syringe foliage at least once a week. Keep moist but not soggy.

Feed Christmas cactus every two weeks. Water moderately, but syringe frequently.

November is the rest period for fuchsia, clivia, and crown-of-thorns. Reduce water. Do not feed until plants show signs of new growth.

While garden is in full color with berries and autumn foliage, make notes on areas which need more colorful autumn shrubs. Order these for late winter or early spring planting. If marked stakes are placed at points where new shrubbery is to be planted, this will hasten the job when it is time to dig holes and set shrubs.

FRUITS: Harvest and store tree fruits as they ripen.

For Area V

PLANT spring-flowering bulbs; half-hardy bulbs; lilies (page 195); camellias; lilacs and other shrubs and trees as soon as they become dormant; roses, fuchsias, heathers; azaleas as soon as new flower buds form (page 153). (Magnolias, dogwoods and hollies should be *spring-planted.*) Columbine, Canterbury bells, wallflower, calendula, snapdragon; ground covers such as ajuga, liriope, *Hedera helix,* and *Vinca minor* (page 218).

DIVIDE and TRANSPLANT: Peonies, iris, phlox, Oriental poppies (pages 60; 193).

PREPARE beds for pansies and other winter-blooming flowers (page 86); vegetable garden for sowing (page 261); planting holes for trees and shrubs to be planted later (pages 153–55).

SET OUT plants of cabbage, cauliflower, broccoli (page 264).

SOW late in month: carrot, beet, onion, spinach, Swiss chard, lettuce, broccoli, kale (page 263); hardy annuals (page 51); in frame: perennials and biennials (page 51); lawns with domestic ryegrass for winter color (page 171).

SPRAY broad-leaved evergreens for tea scale (Appendix, page 467).

LAWNS: Sprig new lawns with Bermudagrass. Plug St. Augustine, centipede, and Zoysia turf areas. Feed established Bermuda, carpet, St. Augustine, and Zoysia turf (Chapter 10).

REPLANT hardy water-lilies late in month.

BANK around tender shrubs and trees with soil before hard frost.

WATER deeply in dry climates so shrubs and trees will not go into cold weather with dry roots. Chrysanthemums last longer if kept well watered (pages 80–84).

HOUSEPLANTS: Bring in before hard frost; cut back and repot if necessary; watch for pests; do not feed until plants have recovered from shock of move; take cuttings of geranium, heliotrope, lantana, fuchsia (page 68).

For Area VI

PLANT and TRANSPLANT early-blooming perennials (page 193); azaleas when flower buds have set; camellias, fuchsias, heathers, lilies, bulbs. Tulip bulbs which have been in refrigerator for a few weeks may now be planted.

PLANT or TRANSPLANT tropical subjects no later than October.

FEED established bulb beds; roses; established lawns (pages 85–90).

WITHHOLD fertilizers from shrubs and tender plants which may sustain frost injury to soft growth. If dormant, or partially so, there is less danger of damage. This rule applies to citrus fruit.

SET OUT winter-blooming plants; hardy vegetables (pages 193; 264).

SOW perennial seeds in seedbed; cool-weather vegetables in garden (pages 51; 263).

LAWNS: Sprig new lawns with Bermudagrass; plug in St. Augustine, centipede, or Zoysia (page 166); feed established turf; continue mowing (Chapter 10).

WATER: See that there is ample moisture around roots of shrubs, trees, and plants to prevent cold damage (pages 80–84); after a frost, spray leaves of affected plants and protect from strong sun.

PRUNING is to be avoided in autumn, as heavy growth helps to prevent frost damage; also because pruning may encourage soft growth, which is susceptible to injury.

PROTECTION: Keep ready at hand burlap, slats, or black plastic, to protect tender specimens if frost is forecast. Remove covering as soon as danger is over. (Smaller plants may be wrapped in newspaper.)

NOVEMBER

The Wind

The wind stood up, and gave a shout;
He whistled on his fingers and

Kicked the withered leaves about,
And thumped the branches with his hand,

And said he'll kill, and kill, and kill;
And so he will! And so he will!

JAMES STEPHENS

For Area I

MULCHES: Spread well-rotted, strawy manure or compost over surface of perennial flower and vegetable beds just before or just after first hard freeze. Mulch plants in coldframes with dry hardwood leaves, pine needles, or other locally available mulching material that does not mat down. Mulch recently set or doubtfully hardy shrubs with a foot or more of nonmatting mulch (pages 78–80). Have extra insulation available to place over coldframe sash when weather becomes severe. One-inch thick Fiberglas bats covered with plastic are excellent for this purpose.

ERECT WINDBREAKS around doubtfully hardy shrubs, and those in exposed positions. Place protection on windward side to prevent sun scald. Wrap trunks of young fruit trees in heavy aluminum foil or hardware cloth to guard them from rabbits. Erect snow fence on windward side of exposed garden areas where there is no natural protection.

TREES: Place guy wires on newly set trees. Check these and metal labels to be sure they will not cut into the bark in wind or snow (page 155).

LARGE TREES may be moved by digging around them, permitting root ball to freeze, then transplanting when opportunity offers (pages 153–55).

BRING IN SOIL, sand, and peatmoss for seed sowing later. Store, damp, in plastic bags or cartons.

ROSES: Mulch hilled rose beds with nonmatting material held with evergreen boughs before they are covered by heavy snow (page 255).

BULBS: Cover newly planted bulb beds with evergreen boughs.

PERENNIALS: Pack in a pit or 3-foot-deep frame covered with sash: anemones, chrysanthemums, Canterbury bells, delphiniums, foxgloves. Heel the plants in close together.

TOOLS: When all outdoor work is completed, collect, clean, sharpen, and paint handles. Store in reasonably dry place (Chapter 8).

LAWNS: Treat for possible snow mold (Appendix, page 469).

For Areas II, III, IV

BULBS: Finish planting all spring-flowering bulbs and lilies (page 195). Where temperatures go very low in winter, cover newly planted bulb beds with evergreen boughs.

MULCH perennial and strawberry beds with strawy manure and compost, not covering crowns of plants. Where temperatures go very low, cover mulch with evergreen boughs. Use evergreen boughs *alone* to cover iberis, heuchera, madonna lily, and other plants with evergreen foliage.

ROSES: Cut rose bushes and climbers back to prevent damage from whipping. Hill up rose bushes with compost or topsoil, 6 to 12 inches, depending on severity of winter in your area. Where necessary, lay down and cover with soil climbing and/or tree roses, and young grapevines. Where winters are less severe, protect with evergreen boughs, straw or corn stalks (Chapter 15).

LAWNS: Treat lawns now for possible snow mold (Appendix, page 469).

CLEAN UP flower beds and vegetable garden after hard frost. Burn any trash which may carry over pests or disease.

SOW cleared areas to a cover crop of winter rye (page 27).

WATER evergreens deeply before hard freeze (pages 80–84).

FRAME: Dig plants of doubtfully hardy chrysanthemums and other perennials and heel in close together in a deep frame. Mulch plants with nonmatting mulch (page 78).

VEGETABLES: Bank celery in vegetable garden for blanching. Bring in roots of witloof chicory and plant in deep boxes of soil, peatmoss, and sand in cellar, for winter salads. Complete harvest of winter vegetables (page 266).

PESTS: Put out metaldehyde bait for slugs and snails; dust soil with chlordane for sowbugs and earwigs (Appendix, page 467).

DRAINAGE: Watch for poor drainage during fall rains. Few plants ca survive constantly wet feet; chrysanthemums are especially susceptibl For correcting such conditions, see pages 20; 22.

BRING IN soil, sand, peatmoss and store—preferably in plastic bags—fo use later in seed sowing or repotting (pages 307–312).

WATER PIPES in the garden and all outdoor faucets should be checke to be sure they are turned off and drained before hard freeze.

For Area V

PLANT spring-flowering bulbs (page 195); lilies; perennials (page 188) roses (page 246); evergreens, shrubs, berried shrubs, trees (page 153–55).

sow seed of hardy annuals, including sweet peas (page 57); cover crop on beds—if they are to remain unused through the winter (page 27 —after clean-up, weeding, and cultivation.

CLEAN-UP of all beds and garden areas should be undertaken as soon a plants are bloomed out or killed by frost; *burn* any trash which ma carry over winter disease or pests; place clean plant material in compos heap.

VEGETABLES: Harvest root vegetables (page 266); leave winter-hard crops such as kale, leeks, parsnips in garden and harvest as needed sow in frame or seedbed, lettuce, radishes; thin seedlings sown in Oc tober (pages 49–57).

STRAWBERRIES: Reset runners or new pot plants (page 298).

WATER where falls and winters are dry; give regular, deep waterings (page 80–84).

LAWN: If overseeded with domestic ryegrass, keep moist until seed germi nates.

BULBS: Dig summer-flowering bulbs, corms, and tubers not hardy in you locality; dry off and store (page 199); plant hardy spring-flowerin, types up to hard freeze (page 195); water established bulb beds i weather is dry.

SPRAY or dust as needed to control pests, diseases.

CUT BACK to the ground when bloom is over, chrysanthemums, hardy asters, and peonies.

UTTINGS can now be taken of tender, shrubby plants (page 69).

REES: Fertilize hardy, deciduous shade trees, 6 pounds plant food for each 100 square feet of spread; water fall-planted specimens; brace or stake recently planted trees and shrubs before winter (page 155).

ULCH doubtfully hardy garden subjects, half-hardy bulbs, or prepare mulch ready for use when needed (pages 78–80).

For Area VI

LANT refrigerated tulips, lily bulbs, bulbs listed in January calendar; evergreens, trees, shrubs, berried shrubs (pages 153–55); plants of winter-blooming annuals, biennials, perennials, including violets (page 193).

IG, dry off, and store corms, tubers, and bulbs not hardy outdoors in your locality (page 199).

RUNING, shaping, and repair of trees and shrubs can be begun this month (Chapter 6).

AWNS: Cut winter grass weekly; feed established turf each month; water as needed (Chapter 10).

EED established bulb beds, winter-blooming shrubs, shade trees, (pages 85–90).

EGETABLES: Sow seed of cool-weather sorts; thin seedlings previously sown (page 263).

OMPOST HEAP: Build a new one now (page 27).

IULCH with nonmatting material tender subjects such as amaryllis, datura, gerberia, hibiscus, plumbago; azaleas, rhododendrons, and camellias with *acid* mulch of hardwood leaves, pine needles, or acid peatmoss.

REES: Brace and stake recently set specimens before winter (page 155).

ROST DAMAGE may be prevented in many cases by covering tender plants temporarily when frost threatens. Have ready for use burlap bags, slatting, or heavy plastic. Remove as soon as possible. Sprinkling foliage copiously the morning after a frost may prevent injury. If frost damage occurs, cut back root-hardy, tender-topped plants as soon as extent of injury is ascertained. Banana, canna, and dahlias are examples.

DECEMBER

Winter! Winter! Do not fear!
You shall wear an icy crown
At the falling of the year
When the leaves are tumbled down.

JAMES STEPHENS

For Area I

INDOOR ACTIVITIES: See December calendar for Areas II, III, IV.

PRUNE and shape evergreens before Christmas; use prunings for holida
decorations; remove dead or injured branches of trees and shrubs whe
weather is pleasant (Chapter 6).

CHRISTMAS TREES may be collected after the holiday and used for extr
protection on beds and borders and for climbing or tree roses (pag
256).

Attend programs of garden clubs, special plant societies, horticultura
societies.

SNOW: After storms, remove at once from branches of trees and shrub
that might be broken by the snow's extra weight. Check that all gar
den areas and plants are adequately protected from coming storms

For Areas I, II, III, IV

INDOORS

Water Christmas cactus every other day; syringe weekly; feed with liqui
fertilizer every 10 days until buds show color.

BULBS: Start French-Roman hyacinths, Dutch hyacinths, paper
whites for bloom later.

Plant amaryllis bulbs in 6-inch pots; set in cool, dark place; wate
once a week; bring to light in eight weeks.

Bring in first spring-flowering bulbs to be forced (pages 117–18)

Go over gladiolus corms; pack in plastic bags with naphthalene
flakes.

Are other tender bulbs cleaned and stored (page 199)?

Let begonia and crassula plants dry out between waterings; this is
their rest period.

Move holiday gift plants to cool room or sunporch each night; they will last longer if not kept at too high a temperature.

Have tools been cleaned, sharpened, and stored? (Chapter 8).

For Areas II, III, IV

OUTDOORS

CUTTINGS: Take hardwood cuttings of deciduous shrubs after several hard frosts. Mark each variety, wrap in bundles, and bury in moist sand and peatmoss mixture (half and half) at a temperature between 40 and 50 degrees; do not let dry out; in spring, start in frame. Cuttings of coniferous evergreens may also be taken now (page 69).

WATER: Check outdoor water pipes and faucets before hard freeze; install one or two frostproof faucets on outer house wall for convenience in emergency winter and early spring watering.

FRAMES: Mulch plants in coldframes with nonmatting material; have extra insulation ready for placing over sash in severe weather; try one-inch thick Fiberglas bats covered with plastic; spread well-rotted strawy manure or compost over surface of perennial vegetable and flower beds just before or just after first hard freeze (page 266).

ROSES: Cut back canes on climbing roses which may whip and break in wind (page 251). In severe climates, lay down climbing and/or tree roses and cover with soil (page 256). Elsewhere, protect with evergreen boughs, straw, or corn shocks.

MULCH azaleas, shrubs, and broad-leaved evergreens with 6 inches to a foot of pine needles, hardwood dry leaves, salt hay, or other material that will not mat down when wet. Where winters are very severe, place extra mulch of nonmatting material and/or evergreen boughs over perennials and hilled rose beds (pages 78–80).

PROTECTION: Erect windbreaks around doubtfully hardy shrubs. Wrap trunks of young fruit trees in heavy aluminum foil, hardware cloth, or Tree-wrap to guard from rabbits; make it high enough for protection *when there is heavy snow on the ground* (page 464). Prevent winter traffic across lawns by erecting barriers across short cuts likely to be used by tradesmen, children, or animals. Place tree guards on windward sides of trunks of young deciduous trees to prevent sunscald.

TREES: Place guy wires on newly set trees (page 155). Larger trees may be moved by digging, permitting root ball to freeze; then transplant. Prune holly, yew, etc., before ground freezes hard, and save for Christmas decorations (Chapter 6).

Purchase or collect discarded Christmas trees after the holiday; use boughs to cover and hold mulches on top of coldframe sash, over Dutch Iris plantings. Lash several small trees in upright position around standard roses, climbers, and half-hardy shrubs to protect against wind and sun. Check labels and guy wires on shrubs and trees. Do not let these cut into bark.

TOOLS: When all outdoor activities are completed, check, clean, sharpen, and store tools; collect, check, clean, sharpen, and paint handles of hand tools; check, clean, and store power equipment (Chapter 8).

For Area V

PLANT fruit trees (page 281); deciduous shrubs and trees; broad-leaved and coniferous evergreens; heathers, avocados, pecans (pages 153–55); perennial vegetables and onion sets (page 264); plants of pansies, violas, snapdragons, dianthus, etc. (page 193); roses (page 246).

LAWN: Apply rock phosphate where lawn moss grows in winter. Agricultural lime also discourages growth of moss. Water regularly in dry areas; mow as needed (Chapter 10).

FEED winter-blooming plants like primroses, pansies, camellias; violets and pecans should be fertilized with a formula high in potash (pages 85–90). Withhold plant food from fuchsias, roses, and other plants in which dormancy should be encouraged at this time.

MULCH beds not in use with compost and strawy manure; cover perennial borders as above. Azaleas, camellias, and other acid-lovers should be mulched with an acid material as peatmoss or pine needles; have protective material ready in case a freeze threatens (pages 78–80).

SOW seeds of hardy annuals, including sweet peas; cool-weather vegetables (page 263).

PRUNE grapes as soon as dormant; remove one third to one half old wood and thin out undergrowth; roses as they become dormant (page 251); shrubs and heathers as they finish blooming.

VEGETABLES: Let parsnips, salsify, leeks, Brussels sprouts, kale, Swiss chard remain in garden; harvest as needed.

PESTS: Put out bait for slugs and snails; chlordane soil where nothing edible is to be planted before spring; use dormant sprays only while plants treated are actually dormant; before using, prune away all damaged or diseased wood (page 96).

SHIFT to sheltered positions plant boxes and tubs containing living plant material or bulbs or set in deep frame.

LAVENDER, lantana, day-lilies, dianthus, gaillardia, marguerites, and sedums grow well in soil suitable for CITRUS FRUITS.

FROST INJURY may frequently be prevented by sprinkling foliage copiously with water in *early* morning after freeze; then cover to shade from sun; if damage occurs, cut back only after extent of injury is evident; some portions of plants may recover.

For Area VI

FROST: To save plants touched by frost, water with sprinkler or hose early in the morning; keep coverings handy for tender subjects in case frost threatens.

SET OUT plants of winter bloomers like calendula, cineraria, dianthus, pansies, stock, primroses, snapdragons, violas (page 193); perennial vegetables and onion sets (page 264).

BULBS: Dig and store tuberous begonias and other tender bulbs, corms, and tubers which cannot survive winter outdoors; plant spring-flowering bulbs, if not done already (pages 195–99); plant half-hardy bulbs; see list, page 440.

SOW SEED of half-hardy annuals (pages 51–57); early vegetables (page 263).

PLANT trees, shrubs, broadleafed evergreens, evergreens; see lists (pages 434–438); for plants compatible with citrus fruits, see list in Area V.

FEED each month: lawns, camellias, roses, other winter-blooming flowers (pages 85–90).

Do not feed plants that have finished bloom and are resting.

PRUNE shrubs and heathers, as soon as they finish blooming; grapes, as soon as they go dormant; evergreens—use the prunings for holiday decorations; trees. If surgery is required, see Chapter 6.

WATER: In dry weather, give regular deep waterings to trees, shrubs, plants in active growth, especially those about to bloom; to lawns and bulb beds (pages 80–84).

PREPARE rose beds for January planting (page 244).

SPRAYS: Use summer strength oil spray on plants not fully dormant; put out bait for snails and slugs; keep after pests and diseases (pages 467–70).

Notes on Country-wide
Gardening Problems

THE WEST COAST

WASHINGTON
OREGON
CALIFORNIA

Gardening on the West Coast cannot be covered by any one set of rules because of the many micro-climates. Although some are within a few miles of each other, each has its own special conditions and limiting factors of temperature and humidity.

In the *Sunset Western Garden Book,* thirteen separate zones are specified in the coastal states alone, between the Canadian border and Southern California; and some of these are again subdivided several times for greater accuracy.

It is understandable, then, that our calendar for the West Coast must be modified to fit local conditions, especially in coordinating gardening operations with spring and fall frost dates. The selection of suitable plant material for each zone or section is also of supreme importance.

The Pacific Northwest in the *Puget Sound* area provides an average of 250 growing days near the water and about 160 a few miles inland. Winter temperatures only occasionally drop below zero, and most planting is done on the assumption that material will seldom have to weather below-zero periods.

This is a section where many borderline plants thrive, provided they do not require high summer temperatures, and if they enjoy plenty of moisture. Broadleaved evergreens of all sorts flourish in this mild but cool area, while perennials and hardy bulbs are at their best.

The northern two thirds of the Oregon coastland, in the long valley between Vancouver and Portland on the north and Rosenberg on the south, receives 80 to 120 inches of rain annually, most of it during the winter, with only 10 to 12 inches falling in the summer. Growing seasons average more than 200 days, with many nearer 300. It is small wonder that this part of the Northwest is a horticulturist's paradise: summers are cool and winter temperatures along the coast average from 20 to 30 degrees F.; 10 to 20 degrees is the average just inland from the coast, with mean temperatures in the 40s.

Winter rains taper off gradually, usually ending in May, so that spring and early summer flowers, strawberries, and hardy vegetables have ideal conditions for development.

The commercial production of spring-flowering bulbs is concentrated in this area and the best lilies in the United States are bred and grown here. Portland (known as the Rose City) commonly produces rose blooms the size of coffee cups and tea saucers! Primulas, dianthus, delphinium, and other species which thrive in a cool, moist climate are unexcelled here. These include azaleas, rhododendrons, and some of the less hardy broadleaved evergreens.

The dry summer period does not last long so that artificial watering is necessary for only a comparatively short period of time.

In fact, gardening poses few problems for the homeowner in the Pacific Northwest, unless his grounds are poorly drained. In this case, artificial drainage may be necessary (pages 20–22). Alkaline and saline soils are found in some sections of eastern Washington and this condition must be corrected (Chapter 2, page 33).

Where high rainfall constantly replenishes the humus content of the prevalent gray-brown soils characteristic of cool, humid regions, the home gardener should adhere to a consistent fertilizer program by applying home-produced compost or by adding soil amendments or complete plant foods (Chapter 2).

The intermountain areas of western Washington, Oregon, and California are covered in the Mountain and Intermountain section to be found on page 402.

In the *Siskiyous* around Medford and Grant's Pass, Oregon, and in the foothills of northern California between Redding and Bakersfield, the sharply defined climate ranges from winter lows of zero to six above, yet average 30 to 35 degrees. Crops mature quickly as the summer temperatures rise to 85 or even 90 degrees, yet the growing season lasts only about 182 days.

Because of cold winters, deciduous trees and shrubs, lilacs, flowering fruits, peonies, and hardy vegetables thrive in this area.

The *Central Valley* of California, just west of the section described above, ranges from Red Bluff on the north to Bakersfield on the south. Here the growing season averages 270 days, with some areas warm enough for the growing of citrus fruits and ornamentals like crape-myrtle, gardenias, nandinas, and oleanders. Tuberous begonias, fuchsias, and other plants which prefer cool summers can be successfully grown under shading.

Summer highs during June, July, August, and early September reach 90 to 100 degrees; but the cool, pleasant springs, lasting from February to the end of May, are ideal for gardening.

The Northern Coast of California and the San Francisco Bay runs from Eureka on the north to Carmel on the south—a narrow strip of ocean-tempered land where the growing season averages 350 days per year in and around San Francisco Bay and over 300 days in Monterey. Although the growing season is long in the foggy Bay section, summer highs average 65–68 degrees. Only plants which thrive in cool, moist air can be grown successfully here. Some, like subtropicals, are not actually injured by cold temperatures, but need more sun and many more warm days in order to flourish. Here rhododendrons, azaleas, fuchsias, ferns, geraniums, and begonias are thoroughly at home.

A few miles south, in Santa Cruz, summer temperatures average 74 to 76, with more sunshine. Here it often drops to 39 degrees in winter, as it does at the north end of the strip around Crescent City, where summer temperatures are not as high.

Gardeners along this coastal strip must select plant material by trial and error. One can experiment with all sorts of borderline plants. An area like Berkeley, where fog is less prevalent than around San Francisco, offers an opportunity to grow such tender plants as hibiscus, which cannot survive in the center of the fog belt.

Along the *Southern Coast of California* from Santa Barbara to San Diego, lies a subtropical strip where summer temperatures average in the 70s, with winter averages well up in the 40s. In this ideal climate, pleasant at all times of the year, an average of 335 growing days makes horticulture an exciting hobby. Frosts may occur, of course, sometimes years apart, sometimes several years in a row, so the tenderest of plants grown should be placed against buildings or near massed plantings that offer shelter.

The desert areas of Southeastern California are covered after the section on the Southwest on page 399.

THE SOUTHWEST

SOUTHEASTERN CALIFORNIA
ARIZONA
NEW MEXICO
NEVADA
WESTERN AND CENTRAL TEXAS

Throughout the vast areas of the Southwest, there are major problems for the home gardener which are not encountered in most other areas.

Elevation is an all-important factor here where high mountains, plateaus, and low valleys are encountered.

Maximum temperatures drop about one degree for every 225 feet of elevation. At high altitudes therefore, the number of growing days per year rapidly decreases until the period between last spring and first autumn frosts reaches less than 100 days at higher elevations. This naturally limits the kind of plant material which may be successfully grown. (See page 402 for a discussion of *Mountain and Intermountain* conditions, and the Appendix for lists of plants suitable for these regions. At the other extreme, *Desert Gardening* is discussed later on in this chapter.)

Given a similar elevation, each hundred miles of distance north or south makes a difference of from one to two weeks in seasonal changes, and therefore, in plant development. This is true everywhere in the country. (We ourselves have moved three times during the past thirty-five years, each time approximately one hundred miles farther north. We have found that the planting dates in our present home in Massachusetts are about three weeks later than in Philadelphia—and we are on Cape Cod, where the average temperatures are much milder than in the rest of the state.)

In the Southwest, where winter and summer temperatures, soils, wind, and rainfall vary so greatly, native plant life and the horticultural possibilities are equally varied.

Beginning near the Gulf, where subtropical plants are at home, each hundred miles northward marks a change in the natural vegetation, caused not only by cooler temperatures but by soil characteristics, winds, and moisture—or the lack of it.

It is impossible in a limited space to give specific gardening advice to those living in any given part of the area, but the following general directives, taken in conjunction with the rest of this chapter, should be helpful:

1. Ascertain the type of soil on which your home is built by consulting your local county agent or nearest Agricultural Experiment Station. (See also page 398 on the *soils* of the Southwest.)

2. Arrange for as generous a supply of *water* as you can afford.

3. Observe native *plants* of the area and cultivated plants successfully grown in the vicinity, and choose your plant material accordingly. (See lists in the Appendix.)

4. If drying winds present a problem in winter, summer, or both, make the planting of windbreaks a first consideration. The protection of newly or recently set trees, shrubs, and other plants is most important to success under these conditions.

5. Where winters are extremely cold, adequate winter protection for plant material should be supplied.

6. For desert conditions, see page 399.

SOILS OF THE SOUTHWEST

WESTERN NEW MEXICO
EASTERN ARIZONA

Gardeners have to work with soils composed largely of alkaline adobe sands at both high and low elevations.

EASTERN NEW MEXICO
WESTERN TEXAS
WESTERN OKLAHOMA

All have highly alkaline adobe soil—that combination of alluvial clay, silt, and sand which must be handled as clay soil (see Chapter 2). By adding humus, sand, and other needed amendments, its potential richness can be activated. Sufficient *water,* deep tilling, and an adequate drainage system are essential.

CENTRAL TEXAS

Soil is composed of black limestone on calcareous bases, reaction being alkaline to neutral to acid as the Mississippi River is approached.

These calcareous soils are extremely rich and easily managed. They are characterized by the deep cracks which develop in dry weather. Instead of forming hard clods like typical clay soil, however, they crumble easily and can be worked without difficulty. Only humus is needed to maintain their high productivity.

CENTRAL OKLAHOMA

Soil is similar in character, but less rich, being deficient in phosphorus, which must be added to make it productive. Hot summer winds and severe winter temperatures add to the problems of successful gardening in this section.

SOUTHWESTERN ARIZONA
SOUTHEASTERN CALIFORNIA

Include extensive desert regions, where special problems exist. Only where irrigation has been introduced is it possible for man to live and for plant life to flourish. Most of the soil is highly alkaline. *Salinity* may also be a problem, especially in soils irrigated by the Colorado River, which is loaded with soluble salts that sometimes build up in the surface soils to a point where many plants will not grow. In agricultural land, this is leached away by forming temporary ponds on the affected areas (see page 35).

On irrigated land, the fertility is often extremely high, especially where the Colorado River deposits its rich silts. Soils vary from heavy clay through sandy loam to pure sand. Nitrogen and phosphate are the two nutrients most needed in the growing of commercial vegetable crops, together with animal manure and other humus. Green manuring, achieved by planting a cover crop to be dug under 60 days before planting, helps keep up the humus content (see Chapter 2). If a cover crop is planted and dug under before a new home is built, or before a lawn is seeded, humus in the soil is assured for the first year at least.

DESERT LIVING

In reclaimed desert regions, where irrigation has brought fertility to vast sections formerly producing only cacti and sagebrush, temperatures reach 125 degrees in midsummer and 100 as early as March and as late as October. Frost is unusual in the short, mild winters, and the mercury occasionally climbs as high as 85 degrees.

Water. Humidity is extremely low, rainfall averaging only 2 to 3 inches per year. Because of these conditions, irrigation and wells have been introduced to make the land productive. Tremendous quantities of water are needed to produce healthy plant life, so the first need of the would-be gardener is to see that an ample supply is available.

Soil. After the soil has been analyzed and resulting recommendations carried out, it is time to consider what to grow and how to grow it.

Plantings. Once established on a home site, shade trees, shrubs, and lawns reduce wind and temper dry heat beating on roof and ground, while lawns, vines, and foliage plants cool and moisten the surrounding air by convection and evaporation. Ground surfaces ranging in temperature from 150 to 130 degrees may be cooled an average of 36 degrees when tempered by shade. Vines grown on house walls, pergolas, and verandas help to reduce the intense heat in locations where no shade is thrown by trees or shrubs.

A lawn actually reduces glare and heat radiation and so is a "must" for desert homes. Bermudagrass, lippia, or St. Augustinegrass are the three species most often used, while annual ryegrass is seeded into Bermuda-grass turf for winter color.

Trees, shrubs, and flowers which will survive and even flourish in reclaimed desert areas are found listed in the Appendix. Windbreaks for protection against blowing sand and trees to provide shade are of utmost importance.

Service areas may be screened with bougainvillea, passion-vine, climbing roses, and trumpet-vine, all husky climbers which rapidly cover a fence or lattice.

For color in the borders, tender, summer-flowering bulbs like dahlias, gladiolus, montbretias, and tigridias are showy and heat-resistant. Among the annuals, heat-loving species include marigolds, nasturtiums, and zinnias.

Completion of a home landscape may take years of planning and planting, but when the work is done it will have greatly enhanced the beauty as well as increasing the value of the property.

Important in desert areas is the tolerance of plants to alkali and saline conditions.

ALKALI TOLERANCE OF PLANTS

High	*Moderate*	*Not Tolerant*
COVER CROPS, GRASSES, AND CEREAL GRAINS		
Bromegrass	Alfalfa	Bluegrass
Millet	Barley	Giant wild rye
Orchardgrass	Field peas	
Rye	Oats	
Timothy	Ryegrass	
Tussockgrass	Sweet clover	
Western wheat	Wheat	
FRUITS AND SHRUBS		
Date palm	Desert saltbush	Creosotebush
Greasewood	Grapes	Mesquite
Salt sage		Sagebrush
White sage		
		Apples
		Figs
		Oranges
		Pears
VEGETABLES		
Sugar beets		Corn
		Potatoes

TOLERANCE OF PLANTS TO SALINITY

High	*Moderate*	*Not tolerant*
	VEGETABLES	
Asparagus	Broccoli	Beans, snap
Beets (garden)	Cabbage	Celery
Kale	Cantaloupe	Radish
Spinach	Carrots	
	Cucumber	
	Lettuce	
	Peas	
	Peppers	
	Squash	
	Sweet corn	
	Tomato	
	FRUITS	
Fig	Date	Apple
Grape		Apricot
Olive		Grapefruit
Pomegranate		Lemon
		Orange
		Peach
		Pear
		Plum
	COVER CROPS and GRASSES	
Alfalfa	Bermudagrass	Clover,
Clover, Sweet	Saltgrass	Ladino
Dallisgrass		White
Fescue, Tall		
Vetch		

ALKALINE-TOLERANT TREES AND SHRUBS

North

TREES	SHRUBS
Chinese Elm	Buckthorn
Junipers	Buffaloberry
Piñon Pine	Chokecherry
Spruce, Colorado Blue	Lilacs
	Mugo Pine
	Roses, Austrian Briar
	Russian Olive
	Silverberry
	Tamarix

South

Greasewood	Salt Sage
Date Palms	White Sage

SENSITIVE TO ALKALINE SOILS

North

Birches	Privets
Firs	Roses, Rugosa
Maples	Sandcherry
Lodgepole Pine	Spireas
Poplar, Bolleana	
Silver	
Willows	

South

Apples	Creosotebush
Figs	Mesquite
Oranges	Sagebrush
Pears	

MOUNTAIN AND INTERMOUNTAIN

WESTERN MONTANA

IDAHO

WYOMING

WESTERN AND CENTRAL COLORADO

UTAH

NEVADA (MOUNTAINOUS)

ARIZONA (MOUNTAINOUS)

NEW MEXICO (MOUNTAINOUS)

In the mountainous parts of the West most soils are lithosols—that is, they are made up of rock fragments of varied texture. Other sections are arid, most of these being alkaline and sometimes saline (pages 34–35).

Some intermountain soils like those near Salt Lake City, Utah, and Boise, Idaho, are rich in nutrients and therefore productive.

Growing conditions in high elevations vary so greatly that it is difficult to give any very specific directions to beginning gardeners. They must consult experienced neighbors and the nearest Agricultural Experiment Station. Home gardening can be attempted only if equipment for artificial watering is available during the growing season. A regular program of soil management must also be followed to maintain humus, fertilizer, and needed soil amendments at the necessary levels.

In the coldest portions of the area there are less than 100 growing days per year, temperatures dropping one degree for every 25 feet of elevation. Because of late frosts in spring, early frosts in autumn, and severe sub-zero temperatures during the winter, only very hardy trees, shrubs, and perennials can be grown. Native material is inexpensive and easy to grow if correct transplanting practices are observed (Chapter 9).

Where heavy snow covers the ground throughout the winter, a greater variety of plants can be grown than where bare ground accompanies sub-zero weather. Lists of trees and shrubs for mountain plantings will be found in the Appendix.

With a coldframe or hotbed (Chapter 7), annuals of all sorts, biennials and perennials to be treated as annuals, can be grown on for summer color. A greenhouse or conservatory attached to the home (Chapter 18) makes it possible to garden all year round instead of only during the meager number of frost-free days to be expected in many parts of this region.

In fertile *intermountain* areas, winter temperatures in mild seasons may not go below 10 degrees above, and the average number of growing days is 170 to 180. Under such conditions, successful gardening is not difficult if plenty of water is available and if good soil management is practiced (Chapter 2).

THE GREAT NORTHERN PLAINS

MINNESOTA
NORTH DAKOTA
SOUTH DAKOTA
EASTERN MONTANA
EASTERN WYOMING
NORTHERN AND CENTRAL NEBRASKA
NORTHERN IOWA

Here on the Great Plains, the climate is characterized by low winter temperatures which vary from —20 to —40 degrees. In most of the area, summer highs reach 90 degrees and rainfall is between 15 and 20 inches, 2 to 9 inches of which falls during the growing season for home gardeners.

Minnesota is favored by a higher rainfall: 25 to 30 inches annually, with 10 to 13 inches falling in summer. Here, as in the most easterly portions of the Dakotas, lies the rich "black soil" originally covered by prairie grass; year after year over the centuries this prairie grass died back and replenished the soil until it made deep, dark topsoil. Typical prairie soils are found in the southeastern portion of the state.

Soils in the west and south of the Northern Plains are mostly brown or chestnut grassland types, with some deposits of shallow, arid soils. Although most of this land is moderately rich in nutrients, home gardening is limited by the supply of available water and by the severity of the winters. With plenty of water, however, the gardener can achieve success by providing humus, needed soil amendments, fertilizers, and appropriate plant material.

The growing season varies from 150 to 120 frost-free days; fall frost occurs in September, and the last spring frosts in May in the colder regions. Only very hardy species can survive the cold and wind, but much work has been done by local State Experiment Stations in selecting and developing iron-hardy varieties of many ornamental plants, including roses and chrysanthemums (see Appendix).

Massive winter protection of many ornamentals is essential, as is wrapping or other cover to prevent sunscald and wind burn. (For windbreak material, see Appendix.)

CENTRAL PLAINS

EASTERN COLORADO
KANSAS
SOUTHERN NEBRASKA

Most of the fertile land of the Central Plains is watered by an annual rainfall of approximately 25 inches per year, though a few sections receive as little as 15 inches. Six to 9 inches falls in the growing season, when it can be helpful in the home garden.

From 140 (in the west) to 210 (in the east) frost-free days are enjoyed, but despite the comparatively long growing season, and the basic richness of the soils, which were originally covered by grasses, home gardening is difficult and in many portions impossible without plenty of supplementary water.

Given the means to irrigate as needed, it is comparatively easy to add fertilizers and humus according to local soil requirements, which can be ascertained by having samples analyzed by the county agent or nearest Agricultural Experiment Station.

An additional hazard to cultivated plants is the drying wind which sweeps across this country from the foothills of the Rocky Mountains, making it necessary for the gardener to take precautions against wind burn and winter sunscald.

HEARTLAND PRAIRIE

CENTRAL ILLINOIS
CENTRAL AND SOUTHERN IOWA
SOUTHEASTERN KANSAS
NORTHERN MISSOURI

The richest of the prairie soils of the United States lie in eastern Kansas, Iowa, and southern Minnesota, with one section east of the Mississippi in southern Wisconsin and northern Illinois. Reddish prairie soils, not quite so rich, adjoin this area on the south as do the rich "black soils" to the north.

Here in the "corn belt" lies the only soil in the country which can boast 15 to 20 inches of humus, developed by the prairie grasses over the centuries and retained in the upper soil layers because the rainfall is not excessive—30 inches annually, 10 to 13 inches falling during the growing season.

We well remember a friend who spent her childhood in northern Illinois telling us of the wonderful vegetable gardens her father raised each year, never adding a pound of fertilizer or an ounce of humus. Such practices, however, exhaust even the richest of soils in time. This is certainly true of the comparatively small areas occupied by home gardens. It is worthwhile to ask the local county agent for advice on the management of land in your vicinity.

NORTH CENTRAL, NORTHEAST, EAST CENTRAL, AND MID-ATLANTIC STATES

WISCONSIN	NEW YORK	PENNSYLVANIA
MICHIGAN	VERMONT	NEW JERSEY
NORTHERN ILLINOIS	NEW HAMPSHIRE	DELAWARE
INDIANA	MAINE	MARYLAND
OHIO	MASSACHUSETTS	WEST VIRGINIA
KENTUCKY	RHODE ISLAND	VIRGINIA
	CONNECTICUT	

Strange as it may seem to group these diverse states under one heading, the fact remains that they vary chiefly in the severity of their winter climates. The soils of the entire northeast quarter of the United States are derived from the primeval forests which covered them.

Northern Wisconsin and Michigan soils are the rich, acid forest soils also found in northern New York, Vermont, New Hampshire, and Maine. They are richer and more acid than the soils of southern Michigan, Indiana, Ohio, Kentucky, West Virginia, western Pennsylvania, and much of New York State and the Mid-Atlantic States. Soils in these areas also derive from the original forests, but much of the humus and nutrients have leached away.

Growing conditions in northern Michigan or central Maine, where winter lows may drop to —40 degrees, are the most rugged, especially as late spring and early fall frosts may reduce the growing season to little more than 120 days per year. In Maryland and Virginia, on the other hand, one can expect from 210 to 250 frost-free days and winter lows of from zero to plus 20 degrees. For directives on when garden operations should be performed, see the calendar.

Except for this disparity, however, gardening is quite similar from Michigan to Maine, and from New York to Virginia.

The entire section receives between 30 and 40 inches of rain annually, most of it nearer 40 than 30, while one section of central New York State receives an average of 50 inches. From 10 to 13 inches of this rain falls during the growing season. In short, no portion of the northeast quarter of the country suffers from prolonged dry seasons.

Soil Management. As practically all these soils are acid (alkaline soils of the West are invariably in areas of low rainfall), the addition of lime is essential (page 33). Fertilizers and humus must be applied periodically to soils in which the humus and nutrients have leached away, or been reduced by poor management in the past (Chapter 2).

Plants of a similar nature can be grown throughout the entire area, the only limitation being that of hardiness. Although Philadelphia is usually considered the northern limit for many half-hardy plants, many of these grow farther north, especially near the seashore where the cold is less severe and the climate more humid. On our home grounds on Cape Cod, for instance, we winter outdoors *Camellia sasanqua,* franklinia (*Gordonia alatamaha*), cherry-laurel (*Prunus laurocerasus*), and Virginia Boxwood. Even figs have survived for five years but we are keeping our fingers crossed.

In our north central area, where winters are extreme, only the hardiest of decorative evergreens and deciduous shrubs are safe without protection, yet a tremendous backlog of material is available. With adequate winter protection, somewhat less hardy species are successfully grown.

SOUTH CENTRAL

EASTERN OKLAHOMA
EASTERN TEXAS
SOUTHERN MISSOURI
ARKANSAS
NORTHERN LOUISIANA

Clay soils predominate in the South Central portion of the country. They are alkaline or neutral in the west and become more acid as they approach the Mississippi River. Approximately 30 per cent of Eastern Oklahoma, however, has very acid soils to which lime must be added if plants that thrive only in neutral soils are to be successfully grown (see Chapter 2).

Here the annual rainfall averages from 40 to 50 inches, of which only 10 to 13 inches fall during the summer. The growing season here has from 200 to 230 frost-free days, so that watering during the dry season and proper management of the local soils are the chief problems.

In western portions, high, drying winds make successful gardening difficult. Precautions should be taken against wind burn and sunscald.

Plants which thrive in western Louisiana are also at home in the adjoining eastern part of Texas, where soils are similar.

UPPER SOUTH

SOUTHERN KENTUCKY
TENNESSEE
NORTHERN MISSISSIPPI
NORTHERN ALABAMA
NORTHWESTERN GEORGIA

Red and yellow soils typical of warm, temperate regions prevail throughout the entire southeastern quarter of the United States. This area ranges from eastern Texas and Oklahoma (see South Central section) to North Carolina and Georgia, and from Tennessee to northern Florida, with the exception of the half-bog soils along the coast, and the alluvial deposits along the Mississippi River.

In the western portions this soil is alkaline, but gradually becomes neutral, and then acid as it nears the Mississippi, where rainfall increases.

On the eastern side of the Mississippi soils are predominantly acid, and rather low in nutrients and in humus because of the high annual rainfall of 50 inches which leaches both humus and nutrients down to a deep level.

Soil management includes the constant replacement of humus plus plentiful feedings of fertilizer. The long growing season of 200 to 250 frost-free days and the abundant rainfall make it easy to grow and turn under cover crops to keep up the humus supply. This area is ideal for the culture of a great variety of food and ornamental plants, including the acid-loving azaleas and rhododendrons which are the glory of the South.

Those who live near the southern boundary of the Upper South should read the section on the Lower South and Gulf Coast, while those residing near the northern limits will find additional information in the sections on the North Central and Mid-Atlantic States.

LOWER SOUTH AND GULF COAST

ATLANTIC COAST:
  FROM NORTH CAROLINA
  TO FLORIDA
GULF COAST OF FLORIDA
ALABAMA
MISSISSIPPI
LOUISIANA
TEXAS

Along the Coastal Plain from Charleston to Southern Florida, and along the west coast of Florida and the Gulf Coast of Florida, Alabama, Mississippi, Louisiana, and southeastern Texas, lie chiefly half-bog or waterlogged soils containing much humus, though some of it is far below the surface. Soil from the higher elevations inland is constantly being washed down by the rivers and deposited on the Coastal Plain, so that these half-bog soils are very fertile *if well drained*.

Under these conditions, open ditches running with the grades toward water courses are usually dug—especially in spots where roots of large trees would invade pipes. If the ditches are partially filled with large stones their efficiency is increased.

Tile drainage (page 20) is perfectly adequate for open lawn areas and flower beds and borders where no shrub or tree roots may clog the tile pipes.

Inland from the Coastal Plain, the soils of the Lower South are largely sandy loams with some areas of clay or clay subsoils. These soils are commonly low in nutrients and humus. Successful gardening in these areas depends upon soil management: the constant replenishment of nutrients and humus which leach away through the porous soil.

Peaty soils found in and near the Everglades, and in other portions of the Lower South, usually lack potash and phosphorus, and even nitrogen is sometimes present only in nonsoluble forms. The addition of copper sulfate at the rate of 30 to 50 pounds per acre has been found effective in improving the fertility of peat soils in Florida.

Along the Mississippi River in southern Louisiana and Mississippi, much of the soil is alluvial. This is rich in plant nutrients and high in organic matter, though in some areas it is necessary to add humus regularly by growing cover crops to be turned under. For other soil improvement methods, see Chapter 2.

Conditions along the immediate coastline, in seashore areas, are discussed on the following pages.

Although with few exceptions soils of the Lower South and Gulf Coast are acid in reaction, it is not usually necessary to add lime since many of the ornamentals and vegetables grown are acid-lovers, or at least tolerant of low pH reactions. Acidity may even have to be increased in growing azaleas and rhododendrons. This is accomplished by applying acid muck or leafmold from nearby marshes or by using one of the acidifiers described in Chapter 2.

Throughout this section of the country *air circulation* is an important consideration, because of the rapidity and luxuriance of plant growth. The objective should be to plant and maintain plantings in such a way that they permit air to circulate freely in both winter and summer and yet provide some protection from cold winter winds.

High shade is another essential feature of gardening here—shade which gives protection from too hot sun in summer and also shields shrubs, trees, and perennials that are winter bloomers.

ATLANTIC SEASHORE

There are special difficulties in establishing and maintaining gardens on the immediate seashore, either in the north or in the south.

Sand or sandy, unfertile soil, high, driving winds, and salt spray are the chief problems to be met and overcome. Each year, however, more Americans are establishing summer homes and even year-round residences in such locations. For such pioneers, a few basic principles for seashore gardening may be of considerable help in achieving success.

Wind protection is the first problem to be solved, preferably by the architect or the landscape architect. If professional help is not available, a solution must be found by the owner himself. Especially if it is to be a one-story design, a new home can be planned so that it provides considerable protection. Walls and fences extending far enough and high enough beyond the house walls to protect the foundation plantings and gardens often solve the problem. Very tough, wind-resistant native material may be used instead, or as a supplementary windbreak. The more extensive such a mixed planting may be, the better.

One objection to the wall or fence is the fact that the wind barrier obstructs the ocean view. At a recent flower show in Boston, a class for ocean-front gardens offered several practical plans. The one that we liked best was a solid fence-barrier on the ocean side with heavy gates which opened inward and fastened back against the inside of the fence. This arrangement permitted an unbroken view of the water from the garden and its lounging terrace, yet was capable of being closed and securely fastened (with iron posts fitting into metal sleeves sunk in the ground) in high winds in summer, fall, and winter. Such fences or walls also act as barriers against drifting sand, which is apt to inundate unprotected ocean-front garden areas.

Wind barriers of wind- and salt-resistant native shrubs should be a combined planting of such species as red-cedar (*Juniperus communis*), beach plum, bayberry, and scrub oak, interplanted with dwarf huckleberry and *Rosa rugosa*. Ground covers for such a planting include bearberry (*Arctostaphylos uva-ursi*), a beautiful evergreen ground cover with pink flowers and red berries, which grows all along the Atlantic in favorable areas; beach wormwood (*Artemesia stelleriana*); and the beach pea (*Lathyrus maritima*). A length of snow fence securely erected within the plant barrier helps to hold back drifting sand.

On open, shifting dunes or sand, beach grass should be plugged in (see Chapter 10). Once established, its roots will hold the slopes. Bearberry and beach wormwood, mentioned above, may also be used. Farther south, sand myrtle, with its boxlike evergreen foliage and starry pink and white flowers in May and June, may be substituted for bearberry. It is native from New Jersey to Florida.

Soil improvement is, perhaps, too polite a term for building garden soil on the ocean front. We live more than two miles back from the Atlantic, yet we have had to fill every bed, border, and planting hole with soil transported from our compost heap (Chapter 2) and from topsoil brought in for the purpose. The only exception is a locust grove where natural grass flourishes in the shallow soil. On the other hand, there are advantages to seaside gardening. One has a limitless supply of sand which can be used for everything from propagating cuttings to mixing concrete for building. And of course there is the mild climate induced by the salt water and the welcome moisture it transmits to the air.

Near the ocean front, it is advisable to remove the native sand and to build beds, borders, and lawn areas (if any) from scratch, with good loam in which plenty of humus and fertilizer are incorporated. Drainage in the sand is almost too good, so that nutrients leach away rapidly and have to be replaced frequently. When applying plant foods the rule to follow is "little and often," so that none are wasted.

Paved terraces edged by plant and flower borders are often more practical than a lawn. If a turf area is attempted, Seaside Bent in the north makes a fine lawn and is salt-resistant. Perennial ryegrass gives a coarse but adequate green cover. In the South, Bermudagrass, St. Augustinegrass, or *Zoysia matrella* resist salt spray.

All the commonly grown annuals, especially those which enjoy hot sun and sandy soil, do well at the seashore. The owner of a summer house should use them for color rather than perennials, which need winter care. Popular annuals include portulaca, petunias, ageratum, marigold, calliopsis, larkspur, sweet alyssum, and zinnia.

For shrubs, trees, and other plants especially suitable for seashore planting, north and south, see Appendix, pages 448–50.

PART FOUR

APPENDIX

HARDY TREES AND SHRUBS

TREES, SHRUBS, AND OTHER PLANTS FOR VERY COLD CLIMATES

TREES, SHRUBS, AND OTHER PLANTS FOR THE SOUTH AND FOR RECLAIMED DESERT LANDS

TREES, SHRUBS, AND OTHER PLANTS FOR THE ATLANTIC SEASHORE

GARDEN FLOWERS: ANNUALS, BIENNIALS, PERENNIALS; BULBOUS PLANTS; PLANTS FOR ROCK, WALL, WATER, AND BOG GARDENS; FRAGRANT PLANTS AND HERBS

GARDEN TROUBLES: PESTS, DISEASES, WEEDS, AND THEIR CONTROLS

BOTANICAL GARDENS AND ARBORETUMS

PARKS AND DISPLAY GARDENS

AGRICULTURAL COLLEGES AND AGRICULTURE EXPERIMENT STATIONS

SPECIAL PLANT SOCIETIES

OTHER NATIONAL ORGANIZATIONS

BOOKS FOR FURTHER REFERENCE

BIBLIOGRAPHY

I would make a list against the evil days
Of lovely things . . .

Hardy Trees and Shrubs

(See also Chapter 9.)

TALL, HARDY CONIFEROUS EVERGREENS

BOTANICAL NAME	COMMON NAME	HEIGHT (IN FEET)
Abies	Fir	
concolor	White	120'
homolepis	Nikko	120'
nordmanniana	Nordmann	60'
veitchi	Veitch	60'
others		
Chamaecyparis	False-cypress	
obtusa	Hinoki	100'
pisifera	Sawara	50–100'
Cryptomeria	Cryptomeria	
japonica	Japanese	125'
Juniperus	Juniper or Red-cedar	
chinensis	Chinese	60'
communis	Common	35'
virginiana	Eastern	100'
Picea	Spruce	
abies	Norway	150'
engelmanni	Engelmann	100–150'
glauca densata	Black Hills	40'
pungens	Colorado Blue	50'
kosteriana	Koster Blue	40'
Pinus	Pine	
bungeana	Lace-bark	70'
densiflora	Japanese Red	100'
nepalensis	Himalayan	75–100'
nigra	Austrian	50'
strobus	Eastern White	100'
Pseudotsuga		
taxifolia	Douglas-fir	100–300'
taxifolia glauca	Rocky Mountain	100'

BOTANICAL NAME	COMMON NAME	HEIGHT (IN FEET)
Taxus	Yew	
baccata	English Yew and varieties	60'
cuspidata	Japanese Yew and varieties	20–50'
Thuja	Arborvitae	
occidentalis	American	60'
orientalis	Oriental	60'
plicata	Giant	180'
Tsuga	Hemlock	
canadensis	Canadian	90'
caroliniana	Carolina	75'
heterophylla	Western	200'

LOW-GROWING, HARDY CONIFEROUS EVERGREENS

BOTANICAL NAME	COMMON NAME	HEIGHT	REMARKS
Chamaecyparis	False-cypress	6–15'	
obtusa, dwarf forms	Dwarf Hinoki		slow-growing; dense, shrub-like; after years of growth attain size of very large shrubs
compacta			
gracilis			
nana			
pisifera, dwarf forms	Dwarf Sawara		same as above, but less dense in growth; form pyramidal
filifera	Thread Sawara		
aurea	Golden Thread Sawara		
Juniperus, dwarf and spreading forms	Juniper		
chinensis varieties	Pfitzer	6'	spreading; slow-growing to large shrub
	Sargent	1½'	prostrate
communis depressa	Oldfield Common	4'	spreading
conferta	Shore	1'	procumbent, spreading
excelsa stricta	Spiny Greek	2'	spreading
horizontalis varieties		1'	prostrate
	Bar Harbor	1'	blue foliage
alpina	Alpine	2–3'	blue-gray foliage
douglasi	Waukegan	1'	blue summer, purple winter foliage; trailing

BOTANICAL NAME	COMMON NAME	HEIGHT	REMARKS
plumosa	Andorra	1½′	spreading, crested
sabina varieties	Savin	3′	spreading
squamata meyeri	Meyer	4′	prostrate stems; ascending shoots
virginiana globosa	Globe	10′	dense, rounded, slow-growing
kosteri	Koster	5′	spreading
others.			
Pinus mugo mughus	Mugo Pine	2–8′	globular
Taxus, dwarf forms	Dwarf Yews		
baccata, dwarf forms	Dwarf English	4–10′	
canadensis	Ground-hemlock	2–4′	straggling
cuspidata and dwarf varieties	Dwarf Japanese	1–8′	
media varieties	Chadwick; Hatfield; Hicks'; Stoveken	8′	hybrids of vigorous habit and fine form
others.			
Thuja	Arborvitae		
occidentalis, dwarf forms	American	2–6′	globular or dense shrubs
orientalis, dwarf forms	Oriental	4–6′	pyramidal or globular
Tsuga, low-growing forms	Hemlock		
canadensis compacta	Dwarf Canada	6–8′	conical
globosa	Globe	6–8′	globular
nana		5′	spreading
pendula	Sargent's	6′	tall
	Weeping	10′	broad

HARDY DECIDUOUS TREES

BOTANICAL NAME	COMMON NAME	HEIGHT
Acer, in variety	Maple	various
negundo	Boxelder	70′
Aesculus	Horse-chestnut, Buckeye	
carnea	Red	40′
hippocastanum	Common	100′
Ailanthus altissima	Tree-of-Heaven	60′

BOTANICAL NAME	COMMON NAME	HEIGHT
Betula, in variety	Birch	50–100'
Carpinus, in variety	Hornbeam	50–70'
Carya	Hickory	120'
laciniosa	Shellbark	120'
ovata	Shagbark	120'
Castanea	Chestnut	
mollissima	Chinese	60'
pumila	Chinquapin	45'
Catalpa bignonioides	Common Catalpa	60'
Celtis occidentalis	Hackberry	120'
Fagus	Beech	60'
grandiflora	American	
sylvatica	European	
and varieties		
Fraxinus, in variety	Ash	70–150'
Ginkgo biloba	Maidenhair Tree	120'
Gleditsia triacanthos	Honey Locust	140'
and varieties		
Gymnocladus dioica	Kentucky Coffee Tree	100'
Juglans	Walnut	60–150'
cinerea	Butternut	100'
major	Western Walnut	60'
nigra	Black Walnut	40–150'
Larix	Larch	60'
decidua	European	60'
laricina	American, Tamarack, or Hackamatack	60'
leptolepis	Japanese	60'
Liquidambar styraciflua	Sweet Gum	140'
Liriodendron tulipifera	Tulip Tree	200'
Maclura pomifera	Osage-orange	60'
Morus, in variety	Mulberries	80'
Paulownia tomentosa	Empress Tree	40'
Platanus, in variety	Plane Tree, Sycamore, or Buttonwood	100–150'
Populus, in variety	Poplars	45–90'
Prunus serotina	Wild Black Cherry	90'
Quercus, in variety	Oaks	various to 100'
Robinia pseudoacacia and varieties	Black Locust	80'
Salix, in variety	Willows	20–75'
Sassafras albidum	Sassafras	60'
Tilia	Linden, Lime, or Basswood	120'
americana	American	
europaea	European	
Ulmus	Elm	
americana	American	120'
chinensis	Chinese	40'

HARDY BROADLEAVED EVERGREENS

BOTANICAL NAME	COMMON NAME	BLOOM—FRUIT	HEIGHT
*Abelia grandiflora	Glossy Abelia	pink bloom	5'
Azaleas, hardy varieties	Snow; Torch; Kurume	various	5–10'
Berberis, hardy varieties	Barberry		
Julianae	Wintergreen	yellow bloom, blue berries	5'
mentorensis	Mentor	yellow bloom, red berries	4–6'
ilicifolia	Holly	yellow bloom, blue berries	10'
triacanthophora	Threespine	pale yellow bloom, blue berries	4'
verruculosa	Warty	yellow bloom, black berries	4'
Buxus	Boxwood		
	Littleleaf		4'
	Common		20'
	Dwarf		4'
Camellia sasanqua varieties Selected japonica varieties	Camellia	various	4–8'
*Cotoneaster	Rock-spray	red fruit	3–10'
dammeri	Bearberry	red fruit	6"
francheti	Franchet	red fruit	8–10'
horizontalis	Rock-spray	red fruit	low
microphylla	Small-leaved	red fruit	3'
salicifolia floccosa	Willow-leaved	red fruit	15'
Cytisus	Broom	various	2–10'
Daphne cneorum	Rose Daphne	pink	1'
Erica, in variety	Heaths	various	1–10'
Euonymus	Euonymus		
fortunei		pinkish fruit	1' trailing
carrierei			1' trailing
colorata		red fruit	2'
kewensis		red fruit	2'
minima		red fruit	3'
radicans		red fruit	3–4'
vegeta		orange fruit	4–5'
other			
	Corliss Emerald Hybrids	various	2–5'
Ilex	Holly	various	5–15'
crenata	Japanese	black berries	5–10'
convexa	Box-leaved	black berries	6–8'
glabra	Inkberry	black berries	5–8'
opaca	American	red berries	30–50'
pernyi	Perny	red berries	30'
rotunda	Japanese variety	red berries	15'

BOTANICAL NAME	COMMON NAME	BLOOM—FRUIT	HEIGHT
other varieties and hybrids			
Kalmia latifolia	Mountain-laurel	pink bloom	5–10'
Ledum groenlandicum	Labrador-tea	white bloom	6'
Leucothoë	Leucothoe		
catesbaei	Drooping	cream bloom	6'
keiskei	Japanese	cream bloom	3½'
*Ligustrums	Privets	white bloom	6–12'
*Lonicera pileata	Privet Honey-suckle	white bloom	4'
*Mahonia aquifolium	Oregon Holly-grape	yellow bloom	3–6'
others			
Pieris	Andromeda	white bloom	6–20'
floribunda	Mountain	white bloom	6'
japonica	Japanese	white bloom	5–10'
*Pyracantha coccinea	Firethorn	white bloom, orange berries	5–10'
Rhododendrons, in variety	Rhododendrons	various	4–20'
Viburnum rhytidophyllum	Leatherleaf	white bloom, red berries	10'

* Foliage persistent, not reliably evergreen, North.

HARDY, DECIDUOUS, FLOWERING, AND ORNAMENTAL TREES AND TREE-LIKE SHRUBS, WITH THEIR SEASONS OF BLOOM

BOTANICAL NAME	COMMON NAME	COLOR OF BLOOM	TIME OF BLOOM	FOLIAGE OR FRUIT	HEIGHT
Acer	Maple				
japonicum	Full-moon	purple	May	red foliage	30'
palmatum atropurpureum	Japanese	purple	May	red foliage	30'
multifidium		purple	May	red foliage	25'
ornatum		purple	May	red foliage	25'
rubellum		purple	all summer	red foliage	25'
Aesculus parviflora	Bottlebrush Buckeye	white	July-Aug.	spiny fruit	12'
Amelanchier canadensis	Shadbush	white	May	dark blue fruit	6-15'
Aralia chinensis	Angelica Tree	whitish	August	berry-like fruit	15-20'
Cercis canadensis	Redbud	rose-red, before leaves	spring		15-30'
alba	White Fringe Tree	white	spring	dark blue fruit	15-20'
Chionanthus virginicus		greenish-white	May	red autumn foliage	15'
Cornus	Dogwood				
florida	Flowering	white, pink	spring	red fruit	15-20'
kousa	Chinese	white	spring	red fruit	12-15'
Crataegus	Hawthorn				
arnoldiana	Arnold	white	May	red fruit	20-30'
mollis	American	white	May	scarlet fruit	20-30'
monogyna	English	pink, red, white	May	red fruit	15-20'
oxycantha	English	pink, red, white	May	red fruit	12-20'
phaenopyrum	Washington Thorn	white with pink anthers	June	red fruit	25-35'
submollis	American Thorn	white	May	orange-red fruit	20-30'
Davidia involucrata	Dove Tree	white	late May		10-30'
Eleagnus angustifolia	Russian-olive	yellowish	June	silvery foliage, yellowish fruit	15'

BOTANICAL NAME	COMMON NAME	COLOR OF BLOOM	TIME OF BLOOM	FOLIAGE OR FRUIT	HEIGHT
Franklinia alatamaha	Gordonia	white or pinkish	Aug.–Sept.	red autumn foliage	15'
Halesia	Silver-bell				
carolina		white	spring		12–20'
monticola		white	spring		20–25'
Hamamelis	Witch-hazel				
japonica	Japanese	yellow	Dec.–Jan.		20'
mollis	Chinese	reddish	Jan.–Mar.		12–20'
virginiana	American	yellow	Oct.–Nov.		12–20'
Hibiscus syriancus	Rose-of-Sharon	various	Aug.–Sept.		10'
Koelreuteria paniculata	Goldenrain Tree	yellow	July–Aug.		15–20'
Laburnum watereri	Goldenchain Tree	yellow	June		15'
Magnolia	Magnolia				
denudata		white, fragrant	spring	brown fruit	20'
liliflora nigra	Lily	purple-red	spring	brown fruit	15'
sieboldi	Siebold's	white, fragrant	June–July	crimson fruit	15'
soulangeana	Saucer	white and rose	May	brownish fruit	20'
stellata	Star	white or pink	April	red fruit	25'
virginiana glauca	Sweet Bay	white	May–Aug.	red fruit	20'
Malus, in variety	Flowering Crabs				
	Bechtel	pink	May	red fruit	30'
	Dolga	rose-red	May	red fruit	20'
	Hopa	pink	May	red fruit	10×10'
	Sargent	white	May	red fruit	10'
	Tea	rose-red	May	red fruit	20'
Oxydendron	Sourwood	white	July–Aug.	scarlet foliage	60'
Photinia villosa	Oriental Photinia	white	June	red fruit and foliage	12–15'
Prunus, in variety	Flowering Cherries				
cerasifera	Cherry Plum	white, rose-purple	May	purple fruit	15'

BOTANICAL NAME	COMMON NAME	COLOR OF BLOOM	TIME OF BLOOM	FOLIAGE OR FRUIT	HEIGHT
sargenti	Sargent's	clear pink	May	purple fruit	40'
seiboldi	Seibold's	pale pink	May	black fruit	20'
serrulata	Japanese	white, pink	May	black fruit	20'
yedoensis	Yedo	pale pink	May	black fruit	25'
Sorbus, in variety	Mountain-ash	white	fall	orange-red berries	20'
Stewartia ovata	Stewartia	white	June–Aug.	yellow autumn foliage	20'
Styrax japonica	Storax	whitish	late June		15'
Viburnum					
lentago	Nannyberry	cream	May–June	blue fruit, plum autumn foliage	12'
opulus	Cranberry-bush	cream	June	scarlet fruit, red autumn foliage	10'
prunifolium	Black-haw	cream	May	blue fruit, plum autumn foliage	15'
setigerum		cream	June	red-orange fruit	12×12'
trilobum	American Cranberry-bush	cream	June	scarlet fruit, red autumn foliage	10'

HARDY DECIDUOUS SHRUBS

BOTANICAL NAME	COMMON NAME	COLOR OF BLOOM	TIME OF BLOOM	FOLIAGE OR FRUIT	HEIGHT
Aesculus parviflora	Bottlebrush Buckeye	white	spring	red fruit	12'
Amelanchier stolonifera	Dwarf Juneberry	white	spring	red fruit	4'
Berberis, in variety	Barberries	yellow	spring		4–6'
Buddleia alternifolia	Butterfly Bush	blue, pink, white	summer		10'
Callicarpa japonica	Beautyberry	pink, white	spring	lavender fruit	5'
Calycanthus floridus	Sweet-shrub	brown	spring	yellow autumn foliage	10'
Caragana microphylla	Pea-shrub	yellow	spring		10'
Caryopteris incana	Blue-spiraea	lavender-blue	late summer		4–8'
Chaenomeles japonica (Cydonia maulei)	Flowering Quince Dwarf Japanese Flowering	red	spring	yellow fruit	3'
lagenaria (Cydonia japonica)	Japanese Flowering	various	spring	green-yellow fruit	10'
Clethra alnifolia	Pepperbush Sweet Pepper	white	late summer		10'
rosea	Pink Sweet Pepper	pink	late summer		10'
Colutea arborescens	Bladder Senna	yellow	spring	bladder-like pods	15'
Cornus, in variety	Dogwood Shrubs	white, cream	spring	red autumn foliage red or white fruit	4–10'
Corylopsis glabrescens	Winterhazel	yellow	winter		20'
Cotinus coggyria	Smoke Tree	purple	summer		15'
Cotoneaster, in variety	Rock-spray	white	spring	red fruit	3–12'
Crataegus, in variety	Hawthorns	white, pink, red	spring	red fruit	20'
Daphne mezereum	Daphne	lavender	April	scarlet fruit	4'
Deutzia, in variety	Deutzia	white, pinkish, purplish	early summer		6'

BOTANICAL NAME	COMMON NAME	COLOR OF BLOOM	TIME OF BLOOM	FOLIAGE OR FRUIT	HEIGHT
Elsholtzia stauntoni	Elsholtzia	lilac-purple	autumn		5'
Enkianthus perrulatus	Enkianthus	white	spring	red foliage	6'
Euonymus, in variety	Spindle-tree	whitish	spring	red-orange fruit	15'
Exochorda giraldi wilsoni	Pearl-bush	white	spring		15'
Forsythia, in variety	Forsythia	yellow	spring		12'
Hamamelis	Witch-hazel	yellow	spring		
vernalis	Spring	yellow	winter (Jan.–Mar.)		6'
virginiana		yellow	autumn		15'
Hibiscus syriacus	Althea; Rose-of-Sharon	various	late summer		12'
Hydrangea, in variety	Hydrangea	white, blue, pink	summer	red, blue, or white fruit	3–10'
Hypericum, in variety	St.-John's-Wort	yellow	summer		4–5'
Ilex, deciduous in variety	Holly Shrubs	whitish	spring		12'
Itea virginica	Sweet Spire	white	early spring		10'
Jasminum nudiflorum	Winter Jasmine	yellow	spring		15'
Kerria japonica	Kerria	yellow	spring		8'
pleniflora	Double	yellow, double	spring		8'
Kolkwitzia amabilis	Beautybush	pink	early summer		8'
Ligustrum, in variety	Privet	white, cream	early spring	black fruit	15'
Lindera benzoin	Spicebush	yellow	summer	yellow autumn foliage	10'
Lonicera, in variety	Honeysuckle	cream, yellow, red		red, blue, or black fruit	12'
Lycium chinense	Matrimony-vine	purple	spring	scarlet fruit	12'
Magnolia shrubs in variety	Magnolia	white, cream, pink, red, purple	spring; summer	red or brownish fruit	to 20'
Paeonia suffruticosa, in variety	Tree Peony	various	spring		6'
Philadelphus, in variety	Mock-orange	white	spring		12'

BOTANICAL NAME	COMMON NAME	COLOR OF BLOOM	TIME OF BLOOM	FOLIAGE OR FRUIT	HEIGHT
Photinia villosa	Photinia	white	spring	red fruit	15'
Potentilla fruticosa	Cinquefoil	yellow, cream	summer		4'
Prunus	Plum				
glandulosa, double	Flowering-almond	pink, white	spring	purple fruit	3–5'
maritima	Beach Plum	cream, blush, pink, white	spring	purple fruit	to 12'
triloba	Flowering-almond	cream, blush, pink, white	spring	red fruit	to 10'
Rhamnus	Buckthorn				
cathartica	Common	yellowish	spring	black fruit	6–14'
frangula	Alder	greenish	spring	red fruit	12'
Rhododendron, deciduous	Azaleas, in variety	various	spring		2–12'
Rhodotypos scandens	Jetbead	white	spring	black fruit	6'
Rhus	Sumac				
aromatica	Fragrant	yellowish	spring	red fruit	12'
copallina	Shining	white	summer	red fruit	to 20'
typhina laciniata	Staghorn	greenish	summer	red fruit	to 20'
Ribes aureum	Golden Currant	yellow, fragrant	spring	dark purple fruit	6–8'
Robinia hispida	Rose-acacia	pink	late spring	hairy pods	7'
Rosa, shrub types in variety	Rose	various	early summer	red fruit	10'
Sambucus, in variety	Elder	white, cream	spring, summer	blue, red fruit	15'
Sorbaria sorbifolia	False-spirea	white	summer		6'
Spiraea, in variety	Spirea	white, pink	spring		6'
Stephanandra incisa	Stephanandra	white	spring		8'
Symphoricarpos, in variety					
albus	Snowberry	white, pink	spring	white fruit	7'
orbiculatus	Coral-berry, Indian-currant	white	early summer	red fruit	7'

BOTANICAL NAME	COMMON NAME	COLOR OF BLOOM	TIME OF BLOOM	FOLIAGE OR FRUIT	HEIGHT
Syringa, in variety	Lilac	white, pink, lavender, purple	spring		10-20'
Tamarix	Tamarisk				
odessana		pink	summer		6'
parviflora		pink	spring		15'
pentandra		pink	late summer		15'
Viburnum, in variety	Viburnum	white, blush	spring	red, blue fruit, red or plum autumn foliage	20'
Vitex Agnus-castus	Chaste-tree	lavender, white	late summer		10'
Weigela, in variety	Weigela	pink, red	spring		10'

Trees, Shrubs, and Other Plants for Very Cold Climates

HARDY EVERGREEN GROUND COVERS

BOTANICAL NAME	COMMON NAME	BLOOM	HEIGHT	REMARKS
Arctostaphylos uva ursi	Bearberry, Hog-cranberry	white bloom, red berries	trails	seashore
Asarum europaeum	Wild Ginger	brown	5″	moist shade
Calluna, species and varieties	Heathers	white to red	4″–2′	acid, sandy soil; sun
Cotoneaster, creeping species	Rock-spray	red berries	flat	
Daphne cneorum	Rose Daphne	pink	1′	
Epigaea repens	Trailing Arbutus	pink	creeping	acid, sandy soil
Erica, species and varieties	Heaths	white to red	2″–1′	acid, sandy soil; sun
Euonymus fortunei, and varieties	Winter Creeper	white	to 1′	
Galax aphylla	Galax	white	6″	moist shade
Gaultheria procumbens	Wintergreen, Checkerberry, or Teaberry	pink, red berries	4″	moist shade
Iberis sempervivens	Evergreen Candy-tuft	white	1′	sun
Juniperus, procumbent species	Junipers		1′	procumbent shrubs
Leiophyllum buxifolium	Sand-myrtle	white, pink	2′	seashore
Liriope spicata	Lily-turf	blue	8–10″	
Mitchella repens	Partridgeberry	pink, red berries	6–10″	moist shade
Pachistima canbyi	Pachistima	reddish	1′	
Pachysandra terminalis	Japanese-spurge	white	6″	shade
Teucrium chamaedrys	Germander	rose-purple	1′	sun
Vinca minor	Periwinkle	blue or white	6″	shade

DECIDUOUS TREES FOR THE ROCKY MOUNTAINS

BOTANICAL NAME	COMMON NAME	HEIGHT
NATIVE:		
Acer negundo	Boxelder	40'
Celtis occidentalis	Hackberry	60'
Populus	Poplar	
angustifolia	Narrowleaf	60'
deltoides	Cottonwood	100'
tacamahaca	Balsam	40'
tremuloides	Quaking Aspen	50'
Salix mygdaloides	Peach-leaf Willow	80'
INTRODUCED:		
Fraxinus pennsylvanica lanceolata	Green Ash	60'
Gleditsia triacanthos	Honey Locust	60'
Populus	Poplar	
candicans	Balm of Gilead	90'
grandidentata	Largetooth Aspen	40'
Salix	Willow	
alba	White	40–60'
daphnoides	Russian	40'
Ulmus	Elm	
americana	American	80'
parvifolia	Chinese	40'
pumila	Siberian	35'

SHRUBS FOR THE ROCKY MOUNTAINS

BOTANICAL NAME	COMMON NAME	FLOWER	TIME OF BLOOM	FRUIT	HEIGHT
Amelanchier alnifolia	Serviceberry	white	spring	black	7'
Aronia arbutifolia	Chokeberry	blush	spring	red	5–10'
Caragana arborescens	Siberian Pea-shrub	yellow	spring		6–10'
Eleagnus commutata	Silverberry	white	late spring	silvery	12'
Prunus americana	Wild Plum	white	spring	red	15'
Rhamnus cathartica	Buckthorn	yellow-green	spring	black	10–14'
Rhus	Sumac				
aromatica	Fragrant	yellowish	summer	red	6'
typhina	Staghorn	greenish	summer	red	15'
Shepherdia argentea	Buffaloberry	yellowish	spring	red or yellow	6'
Tamarix odessana	Tamarisk	pink	summer		6–14'

TREES FOR THE GREAT PLAINS FOR IRRIGATED LAND

BOTANICAL NAME	COMMON NAME	HEIGHT
Acer negundo	Boxelder	50'
Celtis douglasi	Hackberry	20'
Eleagnus angustifolia	Russian-olive	15–25'
Fraxinus pennsylvanica lanceolata	Green Ash	50–60'
Gleditsia triacanthos	Honey Locust	50'
Juglans nigra	Black Walnut	40–60'
Juniperus	Juniper or Red-cedar	
*virginiana	Eastern Red-cedar	25–35'
*scopulorum	Rocky Mountain Red-cedar	20–30'
Picea pungens	Blue Spruce	30–40'
Pinus ponderosa	Ponderosa Pine	40–60'
Populus	Poplar	
alba	White	60–80'
deltoides	Cottonwood	80–100'
Prunus armeniaca siberica	Russian Apricot	20'
Salix	Willow	
amygdaloides	Peach-leaf	30'
lucida	Shiny	18'
Tilia americana	American Linden	40–60'
Ulmus	Elm	
americana	American	80'
parvifolia	Chinese	40'

* Indicates species that can be planted in unirrigated soil.

WINDBREAKS FOR THE GREAT PLAINS

BOTANICAL NAME	COMMON NAME	HEIGHT
TALL:		
Populus deltoides	Cottonwood	80–100'
Ulmus americana	American Elm	80'
MEDIUM:		
Acer negundo	Boxelder	50'
Fraxinus pennsylvanica lanceolata	Green Ash	50–60'
Ulmus parvifolia	Chinese Elm	40'
EVERGREEN:		
Juniperus	Juniper or Red-cedar	
scopulorum	Rocky Mountain	20–30'
virginiana	Eastern	25–35'
Picea pungens	Blue Spruce	30–40'
Pinus	Pine	
ponderosa	Ponderosa	40–60'
sylvestris	Scotch	40–50'
SHRUBS:		
Aronia arbutifolia	Chokeberry	5–10'
Caragana arborescens	Siberian Pea-shrub	6–10'
Prunus pumila	Sandcherry	3–5'

WINDBREAKS FOR THE CENTRAL PLAINS

BOTANICAL NAME	COMMON NAME	HEIGHT	REMARKS
EVERGREEN:			
Juniperus communis	Common Red-cedar	35'	tolerates thin, dry soils
Picea	Spruce		
excelsa	Norway	50–60'	prefers moist, well-drained, fertile soils
glauca	White	50–60'	similar to Norway Spruce but more drought-resistant
densata	Black Hills	50–60'	drought-resistant
Pinus	Pine		
resinosa	Red	60'	prefers sun; well-drained, sandy soils
strobus	White	70–80'	requires well-drained soils
Pseudotsuga texifolia	Douglas-fir	50–60'	prefers well-drained, porous soils; tolerates other soils
Thuja occidentalis	American Arborvitae	30–60'	perfers swampy, moist or thin, moist soils
DECIDUOUS:			
Eleagnus angustifolia	Russian-olive	15–25'	grows well in thin, sandy, poor soils
Populus deltoides	Cottonwood	80–100'	brittle; grows rapidly; prefers lowlands
Morus rubra	Mulberry	60'	grows well in sandy soil
Quercus palustris	Pin Oak	50–80'	prefers lowlands
Salix aurea	Golden Willow	25–40'	prefers moisture but tolerates dry soils
Ulmus	Elm		
chinensis	Chinese	35–45'	quick-growing; drought-resistant
americana	American	70–80'	subject to Dutch elm disease

HEDGE PLANTS FOR VERY COLD CLIMATES

BOTANICAL NAME	COMMON NAME	UNTRIMMED HEIGHT
Acer negundo	Boxelder	50–70'
Aronia arbutifolia	Chokeberry	10–20'
Berberis thunbergi	Japanese Barberry	4–8'
Celtis occidentalis	Hackberry	25–50'
Cornus alba	Tatarian Dogwood	6–10'
Caragana	Pea-tree	
arborescens	Siberian	10–25'
microphylla	Russian Pea-shrub	6–10'
Eleagnus angustifolia	Russian-olive	10–25'
Physocarpus	Ninebark	
bracteatus	Colorado	6–8'
monogynus	Dwarf	1½–3'
Pinus mugo mughus	Mugo Pine	3–6'
Rhamnus cathartica	Common Buckthorn	10–25'
Ribes alpinum	Mountain Currant	3–8'
Syringa	Lilac	
josikaea	Hungarian	5–10'
persica	Persian	5–10'
vulgaris	Common	5–10'
Thuja occidentalis	American Arborvitae	25–60'
Ulmus pumila	Dwarf Asiatic Elm	25–50'
Viburnum lentago	Nannyberry	10–25'

SHRUB ROSES FOR VERY COLD CLIMATES

NAME	BLOOM	TIME OF BLOOM	HEIGHT
Agnes	golden-yellow double, fragrant	May–June	4–5'
Amelie Fravereaux	bright red double	*remontant	4–5'
Belle Poitevine	large, pink double	*remontant	3½'
Betty Bland	double pink, *very hardy*	June	6'
F. J. Grootendorst	small, bright red	*remontant	3'
Hansa	reddish double, fragrant	*remontant	4–6'
Harison's Yellow	small yellow double	June	4–6'
Rosa rubrifolia	single, small pink; maroon foliage	June	4–6'
Sir Thomas Lipton	white, fragrant	*remontant	2–3'
Yellow Persian	small yellow double	June	5'

* Profuse bloom in June, repeating with fewer flowers throughout the season.

HARDY VINES FOR COLD CLIMATES

BOTANICAL NAME	COMMON NAME	COLOR OF BLOOM	HEIGHT	REMARKS
Akebia quinata	Five-leaved Akebia	purplish	15–20'	evergreen or persistent; prune severely; use as screen, climbs by twining
Ampelopsis brevipedunculata	Porcelain-berry	greenish; blue berries	10–20'	deciduous; prune severely; use as screen, wall cover; climbs by twining tendrils
Aristolochia durior	Dutchman's Pipe	yellowish	20–30'	deciduous; thin; cut back lightly; use as screen shade; climbs by twining stems
Campsis radicans	Trumpet Creeper	orange	20–30'	deciduous; thin out; blooms on new wood; use on dead trees, pergolas; climbs by aerial roots
Celastrus scandens	Bittersweet	orange fruit	10–20'	deciduous; prune frequently; spray for scale; use on rocks, banks, walls, climbs by twining stems
Clematis	Clematis			
flammula		rose	15'	deciduous; prune in fall; use on fence, trellis; climbs by twisting petioles
jackmani	Jackman	purple	12–15'	deciduous; prune in fall; use on fence, trellis; climbs by twisting petioles
paniculata	Sweet	white	30'	deciduous; prune in fall; use on fence, trellis; climbs by twisting petioles
texensis	Scarlet	red	6–10'	deciduous; prune in fall; use on fence, trellis; climbs by twisting petioles
virginiana	Virginia	white	18'	deciduous; prune in fall; use on fence, trellis, wall, or bank; climbs by twisting petioles
others				

BOTANICAL NAME	COMMON NAME	COLOR OF BLOOM	HEIGHT	REMARKS
Forsythia suspensa	Forsythia	yellow	8–10'	deciduous; train and tie; use on banks, walls
Hedera helix and varieties	English Ivy	white	50–90'	evergreen; cut back; use on walls, banks, shady areas on ground; climbs by rootlets on stems
Hydrangea petiolaris	Hydrangea	white	30–50'	deciduous; train when young; use on house walls; climbs by holdfasts on stems
Loniceras	Honeysuckles	white, yellow, red	40–80'	deciduous or evergreen; prune severely; use on banks, lattices; climbs by twining stems
Lycium halimifolium	Matrimony vine	lilac berries	5–9'	deciduous; thin; use on banks, lattices; climbs by trailing stems
Parthenocissus quinquefolia	Virginia Creeper	greenish	30–50'	deciduous, blue berries, red foliage; prune severely; use on trees and walls; climbs by rootlets with holdfasts along stems
Polygonum auberti	Fleece-vine or Silver-lace-vine	white, lacy	15–30'	deciduous, prune severely; use on trellis, walls; climbs by twisting stems
Rosa	Rose	various	4–30'	deciduous; prune after bloom; fragrant; use on trellis, fence, walls, banks; climbs by arching canes
Wisteria sinensis	Wisteria	violet, white	25–30'	deciduous; train when young; prune severely when rampant; use on pergolas, walls; climbs by twining stems

HARDY HEDGE ROSES FOR THE GREAT PLAINS

NAME	BLOOM	TIME OF BLOOM	HEIGHT
Rosa			
multiflora	small white; fragrant	June	6′
primula	small pale yellow; fragrant foliage	June	6′
rugosa and hybrids	large singles in many colors; very fragrant	June; some varieties *remontant	6′
spinossisima altaica and hybrids	various	June	6′
Therese Bugnet	pink single	*remontant	6′

* Profuse bloom in June, repeating with fewer flowers throughout season.

HARDY CHRYSANTHEMUMS FOR VERY COLD CLIMATES

HARDIEST

NAME	COLOR	TYPE	RELATIVE SEASON OF BLOOM
Aglow	orange-bronze	tall double	early-mid
Arikara	bronze	semidouble	early
Chippewa	purple	double	late-mid
Dakota	yellow-bronze	double	very early
Delight	yellow	tall double	early
Hidatsa	red	small double	late-mid
Violet	lavender	double	mid
Waku	white	large double	late

LESS HARDY

NAME	COLOR	TYPE	RELATIVE SEASON OF BLOOM
Apache	red-bronze	large double	early
Crowning Glory	wheat-bronze	tall large double	mid
Dr. Longley	lavender	double	early
Early Gold	yellow	small double	early-mid
George Luxton	bronze	double	early
Murmurs	lavender	double	early-mid
Nanook	cream	small double	early-mid
Reverence	pale yellow	large double	very early
Rouge Cushion	red	semidouble	mid
Wanda	raspberry	double	early

BEARDED IRIS FOR VERY COLD CLIMATES

White:	Gudrun, Lady Boscawen, Matterhorn
Cream:	Desert Song, Sunny Ruffles
Yellow:	Cloth of Gold, Ola Kala, Soveg
Pink:	Pink Cameo, Coralie, Twilight Sky
Light Blue:	Azure Skies, Great Lakes
Medium Blue:	Blue Frills, Blue Rhythm, Chivalry
Deep Blue:	Danube Wave
Purple:	Sable, Vatican Purple
Lavender or Violet:	Mulberry Rose, Violet Symphony
Red:	Ranger, Solid Mahogany
Bicolor:	Wabash
Plicata:	Blue Shimmer, Kansas Bouquet
Variegata:	City of Lincoln, Mexico

Trees, Shrubs, and Other Plants for the South and for Reclaimed Desert Lands

EVERGREEN TREES FOR THE SOUTH AND SOUTH CENTRAL

BOTANICAL NAME	COMMON NAME	BLOOM	FRUIT	HEIGHT
Arbutus unedo	Strawberry-tree	blush		30′
*Cedrus	Cedar			
atlantica	Atlas		cones	120′
deodora	Deodor		cones	150′
Cinnamomum camphora	Camphor Tree	yellow		40′
Cryptomeria japonica, and varieties	Cryptomeria	yellow	cones	125′
Cyrilla racemiflora	Southern Leatherwood	white		30′
*Ilex	Holly			
aquifolium	English	whitish	red berries	40′
cornuta		whitish	red berries	20′
c. burfordi	Burford	whitish	red berries	20′
crenata	Japanese	whitish	black berries	20′
opaca	American	whitish	red berries	50′
*Juniperus virginiana, and varieties	Eastern Juniper or Red-cedar		blue berries	to 100′
*Magnolia	Magnolia			
glauca	Sweet Bay	cream	red fruit	to 60′
grandiflora	Bull Bay	white	red fruit	to 100′
Myrica cerifera	Wax Myrtle		whitish fruit	35′
Osmanthus fragrans	Sweet-olive	whitish		30′
Photinia serrulata		white	red fruit	40′
*Picea, in variety	Spruces		cones	40–100′
*Pinus, in variety	Pines		cones	50–80′
Quercus virginiana	Oak, Live		acorns	to 60′
Symplocos tinctoria	Sweetleaf	yellowish	orange berries	30′
*Taxus, in variety	Yews		red fruit	various
Thuja	Arborvitaes		cones	60′

* South Central only.

ORNAMENTAL DEDICUOUS TREES FOR LOWER SOUTH AND CALIFORNIA

BOTANICAL NAME	COMMON NAME	COLOR FEATURE	HEIGHT
Acer palmatum	Japanese Maple	red foliage	25'
Aesculus	Horse-chestnut		
californica	California Buckeye	white, pink blossom	40'
carnea	Red Horse-chestnut	rose blossom	40'
Albizzia julibrissin	Silk Tree	pink blossom	40'
Catalpa bignonioides	Common Catalpa	white and lavender blossom	20–50'
Cercis	Redbud		
canadensis	Eastern	magenta blossom	25–35'
chinensis	Chinese	rose-purple blossom	25–50'
occidentalis	Western	magenta blossom	15'
siliquastrum	European	magenta blossom	25–40'
Crataegus, in variety	Hawthorn	white, pink, red blossom	to 25'
Delonix regia	Royal Poinciana	orange-scarlet blossom	40'
Firmiana simplex	Chinese Parasol Tree	green fruit	15–50'
Koelreuteria			
formosana	Chinese Flame Tree	yellow fruit; flame blossom	20–40'
paniculata	Goldenrain Tree	yellow blossom	20–30'
Lagerstroemia	Crape-myrtle		
indica	Common	various colors	20'
speciosa	Queen	purple blossom	60'
Magnolia, deciduous forms in variety	Magnolia	various colors	20–80'
Malus, flowering, in variety	Flowering Crabapples	various colors	15–25'
Melia azedarach	Chinaberry	purplish blossom	40'
Paulownia tomentosa	Empress Tree	lavender blossom	30'
Prunus, in variety	Ornamental fruits	various colors	15–20'
Zizyphus jujuba	Chinese Jujube	brown fruit	15'

FLOWERING EVERGREEN SHRUBS FOR THE SOUTH

BOTANICAL NAME	COMMON NAME	HEIGHT	BLOOM	FRUIT
Abelia grandiflora	Arbutus-shrub	6'	pink	
Aucuba japonica variegata	Gold Dust Tree	15'	purple	red
Buxus	Boxwood	various		
Camellias	Camellia	various	various	
Daphne odor	Daphne	3–4'	lavender	
Feijoa sellowiana		15'	pink	

BOTANICAL NAME	COMMON NAME	HEIGHT	BLOOM	FRUIT
Gardenia jasminoides	Gardenia	8–9′	white	
Ilex, in variety	Hollies	various	cream	red
Jasminum, in variety	Jasmines	6′	yellow or white	
Leucothoë catesbaei	Drooping Leucothoe	6′	cream	
Ligustrums	Privets	various	cream	black
Loropetalum chinense		8–9′	white	
Mahonia	Mahonia			
bealei	Chinese	12′	yellow	blue
aquifolium	Holly	6′	yellow	blue
pinnata		12′	yellow	blue
Michelia fuscata	Banana shrub	7–8′	cream, red edge	
Nandina domestica		8–9′	white	red
Neriums	Oleander	to 20′	various	
Osmanthus fortunei	Sweet-olive	6′	white	
Pieris	Andromeda			
floribunda	Mountain	6′	white	
japonica	Japanese	10′	white	
Pittosporums		10–15′	white, yellow, purple	
Pyracanthas	Firethorns	to 10′	cream	orange
Raphiolepis indica	India Hawthorn	5′	pink	
Rhododendrons	Rhododendrons	to 15′	various	
Skimmia japonica	Skimmia	5′	white	red
Viburnum tinus	Laurestinus	8–9′	blush	black
Zenobia pulverulenta	Zenobia	6′	white	

HEDGE PLANTS FOR THE SOUTH

BOTANICAL NAME	FOLIAGE	BLOOM
Abelia grandiflora	evergreen	pink
Acacia, Star	evergreen	yellow
Berberis (Barberry), in variety	evergreen	
Buxus (Box) in variety	evergreen	
Camellias, in variety	evergreen	various
Ceanothus thyrsiflorus	evergreen	blue
Cotoneaster lucida	evergreen	
Euonymus japonicus, and varieties	evergreen	pink fruit
Hibiscus rosa-chinensis	deciduous	various

BOTANICAL NAME	FOLIAGE	BLOOM
Ilex	evergreen	red fruit
aquifolium		
cornuta		
crenata		
Lantana camara	deciduous	orange and yellow
Ligustrums (Privets)	evergreen	white
Myrtis communis (True myrtle)	evergreen	white
Mahonias	evergreen	yellow
Neriums (Oleanders)	evergreen	white to rose
Osmanthus	evergreen	white
fragrans		
ilicifolius, and varieties		
Pittosporums	evergreen	
Plumbago capensis	deciduous	blue
Punica franatum (Pomegranate),	deciduous	orange-red
and varieties		red fruit
Rhamnus crocea ilicifolia	evergreen	red fruit
Red berry buckthorn		
Tamarix	heath-like	pink
aphylla		
odessana		
parviflora		
pentandra		

DECIDUOUS FLOWERING SHRUBS
FOR THE LOWER SOUTH

BOTANICAL NAME	COMMON NAME	FLOWERS	FRUIT
Aronia arbutifolia	Chokeberry	pink	
Asimina	Pawpaw	yellowish	
Azaleas		various	
Calliandra guildingi		greenish white, red stamens	
Callicarpa americana		blue	blue
Caryopteris incana		lavender-blue	
Deutzia, in variety		white	
Euphorbia pulcherrima	Poinsettia	white, pink, red	
Hibiscus, in variety		various	
Hydrangea, in variety		various	
Lagerstroemia indica	Crape-myrtle	various	
Lonicera, in variety	Honeysuckle	various	red
Philadelphus, in variety	Mock-orange	white	
Photinia		white	
Plumeria rubra	Frangipani	various	
Prunus glandulosa	Flowering Almond	pink	
Punica granatum	Pomegranate	orange-red	red
Spiraea, in variety	Spirea	white	
Thryallis glauca		yellow	
Tibouchina semidecandra	Glory Bush	purple	red
Viburnum, in variety		white	blue
Weigela		white, pink, red	

* Fragrant

BROADLEAVED EVERGREEN TREES FOR THE SOUTH

BOTANICAL NAME	COMMON NAME	FLOWERS	FRUIT	HEIGHT
*Acacias		yellow		various
Cinnamomums	Camphor Trees	yellow		to 40'
*Citrus fruits	Oranges, lemons, grapefruit	white	edible	to 40'
Eucalyptus, in variety	Gum Tree	various		tall
Ficus, in variety	Rubber-plant			various to 80'
Gordonia	Gordonia			
alatamaha	Franklinia	cream		10'
lasianthus	Loblolly Bay	white, large		60'
Grevillea robusta	Silk-oak	orange		150'
Ilex	Holly			
aquifolium	English	white	red	40'
cassine	Dahoon	white	red	25'
opaca	American	white	red	50'
Jacaranda acutifolia	Jacaranda	blue		50'
Magnolia	Magnolia			
*grandiflora	Bull Bay	cream	red	100'
*virginiana	Sweet Bay	cream	red	60'
**Palms, in variety	Palms			various
Persea americana	Avocado	white	edible	
Photinia serrulata	Chinese Photinia	white	red	40'
Quercus virginiana	Live Oak		acorns	60'

* Fragrant
** See list for Reclaimed Desert Areas for botanical names.

VINES FOR THE LOWER SOUTH AND SOUTHERN CALIFORNIA

BOTANICAL NAME	COMMON NAME	BLOOM	HEIGHT	REMARKS
Allamanda cathartica	Common Allamanda	yellow	20'	
Antigonon leptopus	Coral-vine	rose-pink	40'	prefers poor soil
Bauhinia variegata	Mountain-ebony	lavender to purple	30'	very tender
Bignonia capreolata	Trumpet-vine	yellow-red	50'	evergreen
Bougainvilleas, in variety		various	to 10'	showy
Boussingaultia baselloides	Madeira-vine	white	20–30'	fragrant
Clerodendron thomsoniae	Glory-bower	red and white	10–15'	evergreen
Clematis, in variety		various	10–20'	
Clitoria ternatea	Butterfly-pea	blue, yellow throat		very tender perennial; slender twiner

BOTANICAL NAME	COMMON NAME	BLOOM	HEIGHT	REMARKS
Clytostoma callistegioides	Trumpet Flower	lavender	10'	evergreen
Cocculus trilobus	Snail-seed	lavender	15'	evergreen; slender twiner
Doxantha unguis-cati	Rat's-claw	yellow	10'	tall
Ficus pumila	Creeping Fig		8'	wall cover
Gelsemium sempervirens	Carolina-jessamine	yellow		fragrant evergreen
Ipomoea tuberosa		yellow, showy; seed pods	15'	very tender perennial
Jasminum	Jasmine			
humile		yellow	15'	fragrant
officinale	Poet's Jasmine	white	30'	fragrant
pubiscens		white	30'	fragrant
Kadsura japonica		yellow; red fruit	6–8'	evergreen
Pandorea jasminoides	Bower-plant	white	20–30'	fragrant
Passiflora	Passion-flower		15–30'	rampant growth
alba (subpelata)		white; yellow fruit		
caerulea		white, lavender, chartreuse; yellow fruit		
coccinea		red; yellow fruit		
incarnata	Maypop	white, purple, pink; yellow edible fruit		
Plumbago capensis	Leadwort	azure blue	8'	
Senecio confusus	Mexican flame-vine	orange red	20'	rampant
Schisandra sphenanthera		green and orange	10–20'	
Smilax lanceolata	Southern smilax	red fruit	20'	slender, evergreen
Thunbergia grandiflora	Clock-vine	blue or white	30–50'	
Trachelospermum jasminiodes	Confederate-jasmine Star-jasmine	white	10'	fragrant, evergreen

BULBOUS PLANTS FOR THE SOUTH
INCLUDING BULBS, CORMS, TUBERS, TUBEROSE ROOTS, AND RHIZOMES

NAME	HEIGHT	COLOR	TIME OF BLOOM	CARE	TYPE
*Acidanthera	18"	white	S.	dig and store	C
Alpinia nutans speciosum	8'	white, pink tips	S. A.	outdoors	T
Alstroemerias	2–3'	white, pink, red	Sp. S.	outdoors	T
*Amarcrinum howardi	2–3'	pink	S.	outdoors	B
Amaryllis belladonna striata	3'	deep pink, white	S.	outdoors	B
Amaryllis—see Hippeastrum		salmon pink	W.	outdoors	B
Anemone, St. Brigid	18"	various	W. Sp.	outdoors	C
*Brunsvigia rosea	2–3'	rose	S.	outdoors (Upper South only)	B
Caladiums	1–3'	various foliage	S.	dig and store	T
Cannas	2–5'	various	S.	outdoors Lower South	root
Clivia miniata	2–4'	orange	Sp.	outdoors in pots Lower South	T
*Crinums	2–4'	white-red	Sp. S	outdoors	B
Dahlias	2–5'	various	S.	dig and store	root
Eucharis grandiflora	1–2'	white	W.	outdoors Lower South	B

NAME	HEIGHT	COLOR	TIME OF BLOOM	CARE	TYPE
Eucomis punctatum	2–3'	chartreuse-yellow	Sp. S.	outdoors	B
*Freesia	18"	various	W.	outdoors (Upper South only)	C
Gladiolus	1–3'	various	Sp. S. W.	outdoors	C
Gloriosa Lily	climbs to 8'	red and yellow	S.	outdoors	T
Habranthus	1'	pale pink	Sp. S.	outdoors	B
Haemanthus	2–3'	red, white	S.	in pots (protect from freezes)	B
Hedychium coronarium	3–5'	white, orange, yellow	S. A.	outdoors	Rhiz.
*Hymenocallis (Ismene)	2–3'	white, yellow	Sp. S.	outdoors	B
Iris	1–2'	various	Sp. W.	outdoors	B
Bulbous					
Dutch					
English					
Spanish					
Ixias	1–1½'	various	Sp.	outdoors Upper South	B
Lycoris					
alba	3'	white	A.	outdoors	B
aurea	3'	yellow	A.	outdoors	B
incarnata	2'	pale flesh	A.	outdoors	B
radiata	2'	salmon	A.	outdoors	B
sprengeri	2'	lavender	A.	outdoors	B
squamigera	3'	lavender-pink	S.	hardy	B

NAME	HEIGHT	COLOR	TIME OF BLOOM	CARE	TYPE
Montbretia	2–3'	various	S.	outdoors	C
Nerines	18"	pink, white	A.	outdoors	B
Oxalis	1'	various	S.	outdoors	B
*Polianthes (Tuberose)	18"	white	S.	outdoors	T
				Lower South	
Sparaxis	1'	various	S.	outdoors	B
Strelitzia	4–20'	blue, orange	W.	outdoors	Rhiz.
Tigridia	18"	various	S.	outdoors	C
Tritelia uniflora	8'	blue, white throat	S.	outdoors	B
Zantedeschias (Calla-lilies)	1–4'	white, pink, yellow	Sp. S.	outdoors	T

* Fragrant
Sp.–Spring
S –Summer
A –Autumn
W –Winter

BROADLEAVED EVERGREENS FOR CALIFORNIA

BOTANICAL NAME	COMMON NAME	BLOOM, FRUIT	HEIGHT	REMARKS
Acacia	Acacia or Wattle		10–20'	showy, Australian flowering trees; fragrant
baileyana		yellow bloom	10–20'	
decurrens dealbata	Silver	yellow bloom	50'	
decurrens mollis	Black	yellow bloom	50'	
longifolia	Sydney Golden	yellow bloom	20'	
melanoxylon	Blackwood	cream bloom	50'	
Arbutus menziesi	Madrone	cream bloom	50–100'	
Arctostaphylos	Manzanita	white bloom; red fruit	2–40'	
Cinnamomum camphora	Camphor Tree	yellow	40'	
Ceanothus thyrsiflorus	Ceanothus or Blue-blossom	blue bloom	8'	
Eucalyptus	Gum Tree		30–300'	
corynocalyx	Sugar	yellowish bloom	120'	tender, drought-resistant
ficifolia	Red-flowering	crimson to white bloom	30'	tender
globus	Blue	yellowish bloom	300'	coastal
maculata citriodora	Lemon-scented	white bloom	150'	tender
	Red-box	white bloom	150'	
rostrata	Red	yellowish bloom	200'	frost and drought-resistant
sideroxylon	Red Ironbark	pink bloom	60'	tender
viminalis	Manna	yellowish bloom	300'	frost-resistant
Eugenia paniculata myrtifolia	Bottle-brush-cherry	white bloom	25'	continuous bloom
Fremontia californica	Flannel bush	golden bloom	10'	drought-resistant
Grevillea robusta	Silk-oak	orange bloom	150'	for coastal areas
Melaleuca leucadendron others	Cajeput tree	white, pink, red blooms	25'	
Maytenus boaria	Mayten tree	greenish bloom	25'	coastal to Berkeley
Olea europaea	Olive	white (also olives)	25'	fragrant
Pittosporum undulatum	Orange Pittosporum	white bloom	40'	fragrant

BOTANICAL NAME	COMMON NAME	BLOOM, FRUIT	HEIGHT	REMARKS
Persea americana	Avocado	edible fruit	60'	south
Quercus	Oak		60'	Los Angeles area
ilex	Holm			
suber	Cork		60'	south
Schinus molle	California Pepper Tree	yellowish bloom; yellowish, red fruit	20'	south
Umbellularia californica	California-laurel	yellowish-green bloom; purplish fruit	80'	south

CONIFEROUS TREES FOR CALIFORNIA

BOTANICAL NAME	COMMON NAME	LOCATION	HEIGHT
Abies	Fir		60–200'
concolor	White	north	150–200'
grandis	Giant	north coastal	150–200'
magnifica	Red	north central	60–150'
nordmanniana	Nordmonn	Sacramento	60–150'
pinsapo	Spanish	San Francisco	60–100'
venusta	Bristlecone	Monterey	60–100'
Araucaria	Araucaria		
bidwilli	Bunya Bunya	south	150'
excelsa	Norfolk Island-pine	south	200'
imbricata	Monkey Puzzle	south	100'
Cedrus	Cedar		
atlantica	Mt. Atlas	entire coast	120'
deodora	Deodor	entire coast	150'
libani	Lebanon	entire coast (also in mts. to 4000')	150'
Chamaecyparis	False-cypress		
lawsoniana	Lawson	north coastal	200'
obtusa	Hinoki		120'
pisifera	Sawara		100'
Cryptomeria japonica elegans	Plume sawara	general	50–125'
Cupressus	Cypress		
arizonica	Arizona	dry land	40–70'
goveniana pygmaea	Pygmy	dry land	6'
sempervirens	Italian	general	80'
macrocarpa	Monterey	Monterey	40–70'
Libocedrus decurrens	Incense-cedar	general	100'

BOTANICAL NAME	COMMON NAME	LOCATION	HEIGHT
Picea	Spruce		
abies	Norway	general	70–80'
orientalis	Oriental	general	50–80'
pungens	Colorado Blue	general	40–100'
Pinus	Pine		80'
canariensis	Canary Island	coastal	
coulteri	Coulter	coastal	80'
halepensis	Aleppo	hot, dry	60'
pinea	Italian stone	Sacramento	80'
torreyana	Torrey	San Diego	40'
radiata	Monterey	Monterey and general	100–140'
mugo	Mugo or Swiss Mountain	general	6–40'

SHADE AND ORNAMENTAL TREES FOR RECLAIMED DESERT AREAS

BOTANICAL NAME	COMMON NAME	HEIGHT	BLOOM
DECIDUOUS:			
Brachychiton populneum	Australian Bottle-tree	60'	yellow, red
Cercidium floridum	Paloverde, Blue	25'	yellow
Chilopsis linearis	Willow, Desert	20'	lavender, white
Cydonias, (Chaenomeles)	Quinces	20'	various; edible fruit
Dalea spinosa	Smoke Tree or Thorn	25'	violet
Fraxinus velutina	Arizona Ash	50'	
Ficus carica	Fig	25–30'	
Jacaranda acutifolia	Jacaranda	50'	blue
Melia azedarah	Chinaberry	50'	purplish; fruit showy
Morus	Mulberry	60'	whitish; edible fruit
Parkinsonia aculeata	Jerusalem Thorn	30'	golden
Populus fremonti	Cottonwood	80'	
Prosopis juliflora	Mesquite	20'	yellow
Punica granatum	Pomegranate	20'	orange-red; edible fruit
Robinia pseudoacacia	Black Locust	80'	white
Tamarix aphylla	Athel Tree	30'	pink
Ulmus pumila	Siberian Elm	40'	
Zizyphus jujuba	Jujubes	40'	whitish, edible fruit
EVERGREEN:			
Acacia melanoxylon	Acacia		yellow
Casuarina stricta	Beefwood		
Citrus	Citrus fruits		white

BOTANICAL NAME	COMMON NAME	HEIGHT	BLOOM
Cupressus	Cypress	6–8'	
arizonica	Arizona	40–70'	
sempervirens	Italian	80'	
Eriobotryal japonica	Loquats	20'	white
Eucalyptus	Gum Tree		
rudis	Desert	100'	yellowish
tereticornis	Gray	150'	yellowish
ficifolia	Red Flowering	30'	red
rostrata	Red	200'	red
sideroxylon	Red Ironbark	40'	pink
Juniperus chinensis		10–15'	
pfitzeriana	Juniper, Pfitzer		
Olea europaea	Olive	25'	yellow
PALM:	Palm		
Arecastrum australe	Plume	30'	
(Cocos plumosa)			
Phoenix			
canariensis	Canary Island	60'	
dactylifera	Date	100'	
Trachycarpus fortunei	Windmill	10–40'	
Washingtonia			
filifera	Fan	80'	
robusta	Fan	100'	
Pinus halapensis	Aleppo Pine	60'	
Thuja orientalis	Oriental Arborvitae	60'	
Ulmus parviflora	Chinese Elm	40'	

SHRUBS FOR RECLAIMED DESERT LANDS

BOTANICAL NAME	COMMON NAME	HEIGHT	FOLIAGE	BLOOM
Acacia farnesiana	Sweet Acacia; Popinac	10'	evergreen	yellow fruit
Carissa grandiflora	Natal Plum	18'	evergreen	white; scarlet fruit
Cassia artemisioides	Wormwood Senna	8'	deciduous	yellow
Euonymus japonicus	Japanese Euonymus	15'	evergreen	pink fruit
Lagerstroemia indica	Crape-myrtle	20'	deciduous	white, pink, rose
Ligustrum ovalifolium	California Privet	15'	deciduous	white
Malvaviscus arboreus	Turkscap	4'	deciduous	red
Myrtus communis	Myrtle	10'	evergreen	white
Nandina domestica		8'	evergreen	white; red fruit
Nerium oleander	Oleander	20'	evergreen	various
Plumbago capensis		8'	deciduous	blue, white
Pittosporum tobira	Japanese Pitti-sporum	10'	evergreen	white bloom

BOTANICAL NAME	COMMON NAME	HEIGHT	FOLIAGE	BLOOM
Pyracantha	Firethorn	20′	evergreen	white; orange-red fruit
Spiraea vanhouttei	Spirea	6′	deciduous	white
Tamarix tetranda	Tamarisk	12′	persistent	pink
Thevetia puruviana	Yellow Oleander	30′	evergreen	yellow

Trees, Shrubs, and Other Plants for the Atlantic Seashore

NATIVE TREES AND SHRUBS FOR SEASHORE

BOTANICAL NAME	COMMON NAME	HABITAT
Amelanchier canadensis	Shadbush, Service-berry	pond edges and woodlands
Baccharis halimifolia	Groundsel bush	salt flats and swamps
Cornus	Dogwood shrubs	sandy woodlands
amomum		
racemosa		
Crataegus	Hawthorns	sandy woodlands, hedgerows
Ilex	Holly	Upper South
cassine	Dahoon	pond edges
glabra	Inkberry	swamps, moist spots
verticillata	Winterberry	Virginia and South
vomitoria	Yaupon	open fields, woods
Juniperus	Red-cedar	
communis		
virginiana		poor, sandy, dry
Myrica cerifera	Bayberry	pond edges
Nyssa sylvatica	Tupelo, Pepperidge, Black Gum	
		sandy woodlands
Pinus rigida	Pitch Pine	
Prunus		Upper South
laurocerasus	Cherry-laurel	poor, sandy, dry
maritima	Beach Plum	sandy woodlands
virginiana	Chokecherry	waste places, road-sides
Rhus copallina	Shiny Sumac	
Robinia		
pseudoacacia	Black Locust	sandy woodlands and open spaces and swamps
hispida	Rose-acacia	
Sassifras albidum	Sassifras	sandy woodlands

CULTIVATED TREES AND SHRUBS FOR THE SEASHORE

THE NORTH

BOTANICAL NAME	COMMON NAME
Berberis	Barberries, hardy varieties
Buxus microphylla koreana	Box, Korean
Cytissus and *Genista* species	Brooms, in variety
Eleagnus angustifolia	Russian-olive
Gleditsia species	Honey locusts
Hippophae rhamnoides	Sea-buckthorn
Ilex crenata convexa	Box-leaf Holly
Juniperus, spreading types	Junipers, in variety
Ligustrum	Privets, hardy varieties
Pinus	Pine
densiflora	Japanese
nigra	Austrian
resinosa	Red
sylvestris	Scotch
Pyracantha c. lalandi	Firethorn
Rosa	Rose
rugosa	
wichuraiana	
Tamarix	Tamarisk
parviflora	
pentandra	
Yucca	

THE SOUTH

BOTANICAL NAME	COMMON NAME
Agave, in variety	
Araucarias	Australian pines
Cacti	Cacti
Carissa grandiflora	Natal-plum
Coccolobia uvifera	Sea-grape
Palms	
Phoenix	
canariensis	
sylvestris	Wild date palm
Washingtonia robusta	California fan palm
Pittosporum tobira	Australian Laurel
Raphiolepis umbellata	Yeddo-hawthorn
Rosa	Roses
rugosa	
wichuraiana	
Succulents, in variety	
Yuccas, in variety	

GROUND COVERS FOR SEASHORE

BOTANICAL NAME	COMMON NAME	HABITAT	COLOR FEATURE
Arctostaphyllos uva-ursi	Bearberry		evergreen, pink flowers
Artemesia stelleriana		in sea sand	
Callunas, in variety	Heather		
Celastrus scandens	Bittersweet		red berries
Ericas, in variety	Heath		
Euonymus, creeping			evergreen
Hedera helix, varieties	English Ivy	shade	
Leiophyllum buxifolium	Sand-myrtle	New Jersey and South	
Loniceras, vines and bush forms	Honeysuckle		
Opuntia vulgaris	Prickly-pear cactus	rampant, full sun	
Vinca minor	Myrtle, Peri-winkle	shade	

Garden Flowers

ANNUALS, BIENNIALS, PERENNIALS

BULBOUS PLANTS

PLANTS FOR ROCK, WALL, WATER, AND BOG GARDENS

FRAGRANT PLANTS AND HERBS

HARDY ANNUALS

Adonis
Argemone
California-poppy
Candytuft
Centaurea cyanus
Clarkia
Collinsia
Coreopsis
Dianthus

Evening-primrose
Four O'clock
Gaillardia
Glaucium
Honesty
Larkspur
Limnanthes
Love-in-a-mist
Mexican fire plant

Pansy
Polygonum
Poppies
Rudbeckia
Snapdragon
Snow-on-the mountain
Sweet Alyssum
Sweet Pea

HALF-HARDY ANNUALS

Arctotis
Balsam
Calendula
Celosia
Centaurea americana
Cleome
Cypress vine
Datura
Dimorphotheca
Dusty Miller
Flax

Gilia
Godetia
Gypsophila
Hunnemannia
Hyacinth bean
Lavatera
Linaria
Lobelia
Lupine
Lychnis
Marigolds

Nasturtium
Nemesia
Nicotiana
Petunia
Phlox drummondi
Portulaca
Scabiosa
Statice
Sunflowers
Tahoka-daisy
Thunbergia
Zinnia

TENDER ANNUALS

Ageratum	Everlastings	Salpiglossis
Anagallis	Gourds	Salvia
Begonia	Heliotrope	Sanvitalia
Bells-of-Ireland	Immortelles	Scarlet Runner bean
Blue Lace-flower	Mesembryanthemum	Schizanthus
Browallia	Mignonette	Star of Texas
Castor-bean	Monkey Flower	Stocks
China-aster	Moonflower	Tassel Flower
Chrysanthemum	Morning-glory	Tithonia
Cobaea scandens	Nemophila	Torenia
Dahlia (bedding)	Phacelia	Verbena

LIST OF ANNUALS

FOR SUN	FOR PART SHADE	SHORT SEASON
Ageratum L	Amaranthus T	Baby's Breath M
Antirrhinum M/T	Anchusa M	Calliopsis M
Balsam M	Balsam M	Candytuft L
Bells-of-Ireland M	Calendula M	Cape-marigold M
Browallia M	Celosia T/M/L	*Centaurea cyanus* M
Calendula M	China-aster M	(Bachelor's Button)
Castor-bean T	Centaurea M	*Cobaea scandens* V
Celosia T/M/L	Clarkia M	(north)
Cleome T/M	Cleome T/M	Hunnemannia M
Cosmos T	Cosmos T	Mignonette M/L
Dahlia, bedding M	Cynoglossum M	Moonflower (north) V
Datura T	Godetia M	Nigella M
Dianthus, annual L	Larkspur T/M	Pansy (north) L
Gaillardia, annual M	Lobelia M/L	*Phlox drummondi* L
Larkspur T	*Mathiola bi-*	Poppies, annual M
Lobelia M/T	*cornis* M	Swan River-daisy L
Marigold T/M/L	*Matricaria chamo-*	Sweet Alyssum L
Mesembryanthemum L	*milla* M	Sweet Pea (north) V
Morning-glory V	Mimulus M	Thunbergia (north) V
Nasturtium V	Nemesia M	Sunflower T
Petunia M/L	Nicotiana M	
Portulaca L	Petunia M/L	
Rudbeckia M	Snapdragon T/M	
Salvia splendens M	Sweet Alyssum L	
Scabiosa M	Torenia L	
Snapdragon T/M	Virginia-stock L	
Tithonia T	Verbena L	
Vinca major M		
Zinnia T/M/L		

KEY: T–tall   M–medium   L–low   v–vine

ANNUAL VINES

NAME	HEIGHT	BLOOM	TIME	CLIMBS BY
Cardiospermum halicacabum (Balloon vine)	6–10′	white	summer	tendrils
Cobaea scandens (Cup-and-saucer vine)	10–40′	lavender-blue or white	summer	tendrils
Dolichos labab (Hyacinth bean)	15–25′	purple or white	summer	twining stems
Eccremocarpus scaber (Chilean Glory Vine)	6–12′	orange-red, showy	summer	tendrils on leaf tips
Ipomoea bona-nox (Moonflower)	10–30′	white or pink	late summer	twining stems with hold-fasts
Morning-glory	10–20′	various	summer	holdfasts
Gourds in variety	10–20′	golden	summer	vines and tendrils
Lathyrus odoratus (Sweet Pea)	6–7′	various, fragrant	all season	tendrils
Phaseolus coccineus Scarlet Runner bean	10–20′	red	summer	stems
Quomoclit pennata (Cypress vine)	1–20′	scarlet	summer	stems
Thunbergia alata Clock vine Black-eyed Susan	5–9′	white or orange-buff	summer	twining
Tropaeolum majus (Nasturtium)	3–15′	various	all season	clambering stems
Peregrinum (Canary-bird vine)	10′	yellow	summer	clambering stems

BIENNIALS

Take two years to complete growth. Planted this summer, they bloom next year, then die.

Althea rosea (Hollyhocks)
Bellis perennis (English daisies)
Campanula calycanthema (Canterbury bells)
  medium
Chieranthus allioni (Siberian wallflowers)
  cheiri (English wallflowers)
Dianthus barbatus (Sweet William)
Digitalis (Foxgloves)
Myosotis (Forget-me-nots)
Papaver nudicaule (Iceland poppies)
Pansies
Verbascum phoeniceum (Verbascum)

PERENNIALS
FULL SUN

Achilleas (Yarrow) T/M/L
Althaea (Hollyhock) T
Alyssum saxatile L
Achusas T/M
Anthemis M
Arabis L
Asclepias tuberosa
   (Butterfly-weed) M
Aster, hardy, in variety T/M/L
Aubretias L
Bellis perennis (English Daisy) L
Catanache M
Centaureas T/M
Cerastiums M/L
Chrysanthemums T/M/L
Chrysanthemum maximum (Shasta
   Daisy) M
Coreopsis M
Delphinium T
Dianthus L
Echinops (Globe Thistle) M
Gaillardia M
Geraniums (Cranesbill) M/L
Geum M
Heleniums T
Helichrysum (Everlasting) M/L
Helianthus (Sunflower) T/M
Heliopsis T/M

Hemerocallis (Day-lily) M/L
Heuchera (Coral Bells) M
Hibiscus (Mallows) T/M
Iberis sempervirens L
Kniphofia (Red Hot Poker) M
Lavender
Liatrris (Gayfeather) M
Limoniums (Statice) M/L
Linums (Flax) M
Lupines T/M
Lychnis M/L
Nepeta mussini M
Oenotheras (Evening primrose) M
Peony, herbaceous T/M
   Tree T
Penstemons T/M/L
Phlox nivalis L
   paniculata T/M
   subulata L
Physostegia T
Platycodon M
Plumbago L
Polemoniums L
Rudbeckia M
Salvias M
Thermopsis T
Veronicas M/L
Yucca T

PART SHADE

Aconitum (Monkshood) T/M
Ajuga (Bugle Weed) L
Aquilegia M
Astilbe M
Brunnera (*Anchusa myosotiflora*) M
Campanulas M/L
Cimifugas T
Corydalis lutea M
Dicentras M/L
Dictamnus (Gas Plant) M
Digitalis (Foxglove) T/M
Dodecatheons (Shooting Star) M/L
Doronicum T/M
Epimedium M
Eupatorium M
Filipendula (Meadow Sweet) T/M
Helleborus niger
   (Christmas-rose) L
   orientalis
   (Lenten-rose) L

Hemerocallis (Day-lily) T/M
Hostas M/L
Lamiums L
Lobelia, M/L
Lythrums T
Mertensia virginica M
Monardas M
Myosotis L
Phlox divaricata M
Primulas in variety M/L
Pulmonarias L
Thalictrums
   (Meadowrue) T/M
Vinca minor
Violas

KEY: T–tall M–medium L–low

BULBOUS PLANTS

HARDY AND HALF HARDY

Acidanthera hh
Alliums
Anemones, tuberous hh
Brodiaeas hh
Calochortus
Chionodoxas
Claytonia (shade)
Colchicums
Cooperias hh
Convallaria (Lily-of-the-valley)
Crocuses
Cyclamen, hardy species
Erythroniums (moist shade)
Eranthis
Fritillarias
Galanthus
Galtonia hh
Gladiolus hh
Hyacinths
Iris, bulbous hh
Ismene hh

Ixias hh
Leucojum (moist shade)
Lilies, in variety
Lycoris squamigera
Montbretias hh
Muscari
Narcissus in variety
Orchids (hardy terrestrial)
Ornithogalum
Oxalis hh
Puschkinias
Ranunculus, hardy varieties
Scillas
Sparaxis hh
Sternbergia
Tigridias hh
Tritonias hh
Tulips
Watsonias hh
Zantedeschia (Calla) hh
Zephyranthes hh

hh–half hardy

FOR ROCK AND WALL GARDEN

PLANTS FOR THE SUNNY ROCK GARDEN

Achillea
Alliums
Alyssums
Anagallis
Anchusa
Anthemis

Arabis
Arenaria
Armeria
Aubretia

Brachycome
Bulbocodium

Cacti
Calluna
Calochortus
Campanulas
Centranthus
Cerastium

Cistus
Colchicum
Crocus
Cytisus

Daffodils
Dicentra
Dianthus

Echeveria
Edelweiss
Erigeron
Erysimum
Eschscholzia
Euphorbias

Genista
Gentians
Geraniums (dwarf)
Geum
Gypsophila

Helianthemum
Heuchera

Hyacinthus *azureus*
Hypericum

Incarvillea
Iris, dwarf
Ixias
Ixiolirion

Lewisia
Linum
Lobelias
Lychnis

Mesembryanthemum
Muscari

Nepeta
Nierembergia

Oenothera

Papaver alpinum and *nudicale*
Penstemons (dwarf)
Portulaca

Puschkinia

Roses, baby

Santolina
Saxifraga
Scilla
Sedum
Sempervivum
Silene
Statice
Sternbergia

Teucrium
Thalicteum
Thymes
Tulips, species

Valerians
Veronicas

Wahlenbergia
Wallflowers

ROCK PLANTS FOR PARTIAL SHADE

Adonis
Anemones
Aquilegias
Auriculas

Campanulas
Chionodoxa
Cotyledon
Crocus
Cyclamen
Cypripedium

Daffodils
Daphnes
Dicentra

Epimedium
Eranthis

Ericas
Erythroniums

Ferns
Fritillaria
Funkias

Galanthus
Gaultheria
Gentians

Iris, dwarf

Leucojum
Linaria

Mertensia
Mimulus
Mitraria

Orchids
Ornithogalum
Oxalis

Platycodon
Primulas
Pulmonaria

Ranunculus

Sanguinaria
Saxifraga
Sedums
Shortia

Thalictrum
Tiarella cordifolia
Troillius

Violas
Vinca minor

ROCK PLANTS FOR SUMMER BLOOM

*Achillea argentea
tomentosa*
Alyssum montanum
Anchusa myosotidiflora
Arenaria
Armeria
Aubretia
Asters, dwarf

Campanulas, in variety
Cerastium tomentosum
Ceratostigma plumbaginoides
Cherianthus
Cytissus

Dianthus
Erodium
Euphorbia myrsinites

Gaultheria procumbens
Genista pilosa
Gentians, in variety
Geraniums, in variety
Geums
Globularia
Gypsophila repens

Helianthemum

Linums
Lychnis

Nepeta mussini

Oenotheras

Portulaca

Santolina
Sedums

Teucrium

Veronicas
Violas

PLANTS FOR THE SUNNY WALL

Acaenas
Achillea tomentosa
*Alyssum alpestre
montanum
saxatile*
Arabis
Arenaria
Asperula
Aubretia

Campanulas, in variety
Cerastium tomentosum
Cheiranthus

Dianthus
Draba

Erigeron

Gypsophila repens

Helianthemum
Hypericum

Iberis sempervirens

Lewisia rediviva
Linaria alpina
Linum alpinum
Lychnis alpinum

Nepeta mussini

Oenotheras
Origanum

*Phlox nivalis
subulata*

Portulaca
Primulas

Santolina incana
Saponarias
Saxifragas
Sedums
Sempervivums
Silene alpestris

Thymus, in variety
Teucrium

Verbenas
Veronicas

Wahlenbergia

PLANTS FOR MOIST WALL OR ROCK GARDEN

Aquilegias
Arenaria
Asarums (Wild Ginger)
Cornus canadensis
Eranthis
Erythroniums
Ferns
Galax

Geum reptans
Hepaticas
Heucheras
Mitchella repens
Mertensia
Myosotis
Mitraria
Oxalis

Primulas
Pyrolas
Sanguinaria
Saxifraga
Vinca minor
Violas
Violets

PLANTS FOR THE BOG GARDEN

Acorus (Sweet Flag)
Anagallis (Pimpernel)
Astilbe
Cyprepediums
Darlingtonia californica
  (California pitcher-plant)
Ferns, in variety
Hibiscus (Mallows)
Hostas
Houstonia caerulea (Bluets)
Iris aurea
  kaemferi
  monnieri
  monspur
  pseudacorus
Lilium *martagon*
  superbum
Lobelia cardinalis
  (Cardinal flower)
    syphilitica
  (Blue Cardinal flower)
Lythrums
Mitella diphylla

Mimulus, in variety
  (Monkey-flower)
Monardas
Myosotis
Orchises
Podophyllums (May-apple)
Polyogonatum multiflorum
  (Solomon's Seal)
Primulas, in variety
Ranunculus
Sarracenia drummondi
  flava
  purpurea
  (Pitcher-plants)
Spiraea aruncus (Aruncus)
  palmata (Filipendula)
Thalictrums
  (Meadowrue)
Trilliums
Trollius
Vinca minor (Myrtle)
Violas

PLANTS FOR WATER GARDENS

MARGINAL

Calla palustris (Water-arum)
Caltha palustris (Marsh-marigold)
Dracocephalums (Dragonhead)
Lobelia cardinalis
Menthas (Mint)
Menyanthes trifoliata
Mertensia virginica
Myosotis palustris semperflorens
Ranunculus aquatilis
Veronica beccabunga (Brooklime)

IN WATER

Nymphaeas (Water-lilies),
  in variety
Orontium aquaticum
  (Golden-club)
Pontederia cordata
  (Pickerel-weed)
Sagittarias, in variety
  (Arrowhead)

FRAGRANT PLANTS

Shrubs and Vines

Azalea arborescens
  canescens
  nudiflora
  poukhanensis
  rosea
  viscosa

Benzoin
Calycanthus
Clematis heracleaefolia
  paniculata
  recta
  virginiana

Clethra alnifolia
Crataegus
Cystisus
Daphne mezereum
  odora
Deutzias

Eleagunus multiflora
Forsythia
Jasmines
Leucothoë catesbaei
Lilacs

Magnolias
Philadelphus
Pieris floribunda
   Japonica
Pyrus angustifolia
   (Flowering Crabs)

Roses
Viburnums
Vitex (Chaste Tree)
Vitis (grape)
Wisteria

PERENNIALS

Achilleas
Alyssum maritimum
   saxatile
Angelica (herb)
Anthemis
Aquilegia
Artemisias
Asperula (herb)
Buddleia
Centaureas
Cheiranthus

Chrysanthemum
Cimifuga
Dianthus
Dill (herb)
Dictamnus
Iberis
Hemerocallis (Day-lily)
Lavender (herb)
Loniceras
Lupines
Melissa (Lemon Balm, herb)

Monardas
Nepeta mussini (herb)
Nymphaeas (Water-lilies)
Oenotheras
Peonies
Phlox
Primulas
Santolina (herb)
Sweet Cicely
Thymes (herb)
Teucrium (herb)
Violas
Yarrow

ANNUALS

Borage (herb)
Centaureas
Datura metel
   stramonium
Dianthus, annual
Geraniums
Heliotrope
Mignonette

Mirabilis (Four o'clock)
Moonflowers
Nicotiana
Nasturtiums
Pansy
Petunias

Scabiosa
Stocks
Summer Savory (herb)
Sweet marjoram (herb)
Sweet Pea
Sweet basil (herb)
Verbena

TENDER SHRUBS

Heliotrope
Lemon-verbena
Pelargoniums, Scented (Geraniums)
Rosemary
Sweet-olive (Osmanthus fragrans)

CULINARY HERBS

FOR SALADS

Anise A
Balm, Lemon P
Burnet P
Caraway A
Cardoon P
Chervil A
Chicory (Witloof) A
Houseleek P
Jerusalem artichoke P
Nasturtium A
Rampion P
Sorrel P

FOR FLAVORING

Angelica B/P
Basil, Sweet A
Bay, Sweet S
Borage A
Burnet P
Caraway A
Coriander A
Chives P
Dill A
Lovage P
Marjoram, Sweet A
   Pot P
Mints P
Parsley B
Pelargoniums (Geraniums) TS
Rosemary, scented TS
Sage, Garden P
   Pineapple TS
Savory, Summer A
   Winter P
Tarragon P
Thymes, in variety P

KEY: A–annual B–biennial P–perennial S–shrub TS–tender shrub

FRAGRANT BULBS

Acidanthera bicolor T
Amaryllis belladonna T
Chlidanthus fragrans T
Convallaria (Lily-of-the-valley)
Crocus
Cyclamen indicum
Eucharis T
Freesia T
Fritillaria imperialis
Galtonia candicans T
Hyacinths
Hymenocallis (Ismene)
Iris reticulata

Lilies
Muscari
Narcissus jonquilla and hybrids
   odorus
   Paperwhite T
   poetaz
   poeticus
   Soleil d'Or T
   tazetta and hybrids
Pancratium maritimum T
Tuberose
Tulip, Single Early varieties

KEY: T–tender

Garden Troubles

PESTS, DISEASES, WEEDS, AND THEIR CONTROLS

GARDEN PESTS AND THEIR CONTROLS

(See Chapter 5.)

PEST	CONTROL
Ants	Chlordane—5% dust
Aphids, various	Malathion
	or
	nicotine sulfate; trithion for citrus fruits
BEETLES	
Asiatic	Hand pick; DDT, cryolite, or methoxychlor
Asparagus	Rotenone, 5% dust in cutting season; DDT, 5% dust after season
Bean, Mexican	Rotenone after beans form; DDT before beans form; or malathion to within 3 days of harvest; or methoxychlor to within 7 days of harvest
Blister	As for Mexican Bean Beetle
Cucumber, Striped	Methoxychlor from germination until fruit forms; also hand pick
Elm bark	DDT 1 qt. 25% emulsion to 5 gal. water in mid-May; repeat at half strength in early July
Flea	Rotenone on leaf vegetables; DDT on ornamentals
Japanese	Chlordane, 5% dust for grubs; DDT on ornamentals; DOOM or JAPONEX (milky white disease) as directed; Traps, baited; hand pick
June	Chlordane for grubs; DDT for beetles
Potato, Colorado	DDT, 5% dust
White fringed	Chlordane or DDT in soil for grubs
BORERS	
Corn	Slit stalks and remove; burn all affected stalks in autumn; DDT, 10% dust 3 times, 5 days apart; or DDT, 25% emulsified, 1 tbs. per gal. water. Spray until wet when silks appear, 3 times as above; spray is most effective
Crabapple—see Peach Borer	

Dogwood—see Peach Borer

Iris — DDT and malathion mixed, 25% spray; used as directed in May and June

Lilac — As for Iris Borer, but in June and July

Peach — As for Iris Borer, but in July or August

Stalk — Slit up from entry; remove borer; bind wound and water plant

Squash — Open stem, remove borer; then mound up moist soil over wound and nearest joint to encourage root growth; also use ¾% rotenone dust

BUGS

Chinch — Chlordane spray June and early August
  gray-brown patches in lawn; small reddish bugs and larger black ones marked with white visible on grass blades

Harlequin — DDT or toxaphene; rotenone or sabadilla powder for edible plants

Lace, various — Lindane; 25% wettable powder used as directed; 2 treatments

Squash — Hand pick; remove all rubbish in fall and burn. Fertilize well; 20% sabadilla dust kills nymphs; adults hard to control

Stink
  Ornamentals — DDT
  Edible parts of food plants — 10 to 20% sabadilla dust

Tarnish Plant — As for Stink Bugs, above

Crickets, Mole — Chlordane 5% dust before planting, as directed

FRUIT PESTS AND DISEASES

(See fruit tree spray formula and schedule, pages 471–72.)

Small fruits and cane fruit — Dibrom used as directed

Grasshoppers — Chlordane or malathion

Grubs in soil, Asiatic, Japanese, and June beetles — Chlordane or dieldrin

Leaf hoppers (transmit aster yellows virus) — Malathion or methoxychlor

Leaf miners, Hawthorn, Holly, etc. — When flies are present spray with 25% lindane in 25 gals. water; repeat 10 days later

Leaf tier, Hydrangea — Arsenate of lead or DDT

Loopers, various — Arsenate of lead or DDT

Maggots, Root — 5% chlordane in soil before planting, as directed

Onion — Treat seed with heptachlor

Mealybug — Dormant oil spray
Plants in growth with malathion or all-purpose spray every 2 weeks

Millipedes — DDT, 5% dust or spray

Mites, various — Aramite, dimite, karathane, kelthane, malathion, sulfur or trithion

Moths, Berry, Codling, etc. — DDT
Nematodes — DD mixture (POISON) or Vapam
PINE PESTS
  Needle Miner
  Needle Scale
  Sawfly — DDT and malathion mixture, June 1 and June 15
  Shoot Moth, European
  Pitch Twig Moth
SCALES
  Cottony maple and vine — Dormant oil spray when temperature is *above* 60 degrees, but when plants are *dormant*
  Euonymus
  Oyster shell
    apples
    crabs — DDT and malathion mixture when plants are in bloom
    lilac
    magnolias
    mountain-ash
    Viburnum
  Pine
  Spruce
  St. Jose
Slugs — Metaldehyde bait
Snails — Metaldehyde bait
Termites — Chlordane in soil
Thrips, gladiolus, onions, etc. — Dieldrin or DDT or malathion; dust every 10 days; see limitations on food plants under insecticides

WEEVILS, ROOT — Lindane or DDT
  Taxus — Chlordane or lindane
  Vine, Black — DDT
Whitefly — Dormant oil spray
In growth, malathion or all-purpose spray every two weeks

WORMS
  Army — 5% DDT or cutworm bait
  Bag — Arsenate of lead or malathion in July; spray on; hand pick bags when they appear

  Cabbage — Rotenone dust or spray
  Canker — Arsenate of lead or malathion
    In spring on apple, elm, hackberry, honey locust, plum
    In fall on ash, box-elder, sugar maple
  Cut — DDT dust or 10% toxaphene when *preparing* soil for planting; use collars around plants set out if damage occurs
  Ear (corn) — ¼ tsp. mineral oil dropped at base of silk on each ear as silk begins to shrivel; methoxychlor or DDT if ornamentals are attacked

Eel	See nematodes
Wire	Chlordane or DDT in soil before planting
Web, Sod	Dieldrin or chlordane (moths appear in May)
Wood Ticks	10% DDT dust, dieldrin, or chlordane

ANIMAL PESTS

Dogs	Chaperone and other repellents
Gophers	Poison bait in gopher-bait dispenser (See Colo. Agr. Exp. Sta. Pamphlet 1-S)
Moles	Chlordane areas where grubs are present. Use mole bait or cyano-gas in runs
Deer	Repellent Z.I.P.; bone tar oil or electrical devices
Rabbits	Rabbit Repellent No-Nibl and others; traps; wrap trunks of young trees in heavy foil or hardware cloth to prevent winter damage. Soak soft cord or felt stripping in Conservo or other creosote mixture and place around beds that must be protected; creosote will kill grass or ornamental plants, however
RODENTS—rats, field mice	Warfarin and other rodenticides
Orchard, meadow, and pine mice, and rats	Zinc phosphide rodenticide, poison. Get from State Agr. Exp. Sta. and use as directed
Squirrels	Traps
Shrews (in coldframes)	Bait mousetraps with peanut butter
Skunks	Chlordane soil to kill grubs, which skunks eat

DISEASES

Black Spot	All-purpose rose sprays; phaltan
BLIGHTS	
Botrytis on tulips	Maneb, zineb, or ziram
Flower blight on azalea, camellia	As above
Fireblight	Agri-mycin at early and full bloom
Helminthosporium ("melting-out")	Captan
Leaf blights	Bordeaux mixture, captan, or zineb
Chlorosis	Feed with iron sulfate or chelate such as Sequestrene, applying to soil and foliage once a month or as often as needed to maintain healthy plants
Yellowing of leaves between veins; stunting; bud drop, caused by excess alkalinity	
GLADIOLUS	
Blight, Rot, and Scab	Soak corms in solution of Semesan

LAWN DISEASES

Lawn fungicides under trade names are effective, used as directed. Be sure the one purchased applies to the specific trouble

Brown patch
Circular brown spots with grayish or black edges; in hot, humid weather

Fungicide containing captan, Calo-chlor, or other calomel-corrosive-sublimate material; or captan

Copper spot
Three- to 6-inch spots, irregular margins, running together; copper colored. In warm, humid weather

A cadmium fungicide such as Cadminate or Caddy

Dollar spot
Small brown, then bluish, dollar-size spots, merging. Warm days and cool nights in late spring and early fall

As for Copper spot

Fairy ring
Bright green rings, brown on inner edge of circle

Calo-chlor or PMAS

Melting-out (Helminthosporium)

Captan

Mildew, powdery

Actidione as directed or karathane ¼ oz. to 2 gal. water; or Mildex

Pythiums
Grass dies out in spots or streaks; blackish, greasy, cottony fungus on blades. In warm, humid weather on poorly drained ground

Improve drainage; stop watering and mowing until controlled; captan or zineb applied at five-day intervals

Rust
Yellow to orange pustules on grass blades in warm weather

Zineb, 2–4 oz. to 2 gal. water; or dust with sulfur

Snow mold
Spring die-out in areas where snow is deep and long-lasting

Spray fall or/and in midwinter thaw when ground is bare with 3 oz. Calo-chlor to 2 gal. water or one of commercial lawn fungicides as directed. Give 2 fall treatments in areas where problem is serious

Leaf curl on fruits

Dormant oil spray, winter; lime-sulfur dormant spray, spring

Leaf gall (azaleas)

Bordeaux mixture, maneb, zineb

Leaf scorch (horse-chestnuts)

Ziram or zineb

Leaf spots
(attack many species)

Bordeaux mixture, ferbam, phaltan, maneb, or ziram; all-purpose sprays containing fungicides

Mildew
Downy
Powdery

Copper fungicide
See under lawn diseases
Sulfur dust

Mosaic, see virus diseases
Rhizoctonia diseases
cause damping-off in seedlings

Soil fumigants and soil drenches (see page 470)

ROTS

Blossom end (tomato)
Avoid nitrogenous fertilizer, including stable manure; use plenty of superphosphate; water *evenly*

Iris
Remove affected parts; soak unaffected rhizomes in inorganic or organic mercury

RUSTS
Bordeaux mixture, ferbam, phaltan, sulfur spray, or zineb

Scab, Potato
Do not use lime, wood ashes, or fresh stable manure if soil is already infected; preferably plant in new ground; grow scab-resistant varieties

TOMATO DISEASES
Apply maneb or zineb just before rain and every five days, beginning six weeks after setting out

VIRUS DISEASES

Mosaic, Bulb
Disinfect tools, etc.

spread by aphids
Spray or dust with malathion to destroy

Yellows, Aster
insects that spread virus

spread by leaf hoppers

WEEDS AND THEIR CONTROLS

Bermudagrass	Methyl bromide
Bindweed	Bonus; MCPA
Beggars ticks	2–4–D
Buckthorn	2–4–D
Burdock	2–4–D
Chickweeds, common and mouse-ear	2–4–5–T or silvex
	DMA or SMDC for seedlings
Cocklebur	2–4–D
Crabgrass	Pre-emergence seed killers; post-emergence: chlordane and arsenicals; Zytron
Dandelion	Bonus; MCPA; silvex
Dock, Curly	2–4–D
Field	
Ground-ivy	Silvex
Goosegrass	As for crabgrass
Knotweed	2–4–D
Heal-all	2–4–D
Henbit	Silvex
Johnsongrass	Methyl bromide
Nightshade, Black	Mow close and keep cut and cultivated
Nutgrass	Mow; hand weed
Oxalis, wild	2–4–D
Pigweed	SMDC pre-emergence
Pokeweed	Pull seedlings; dig out roots of mature plants

Plantains	2–4–D; Bonus
Poison-ivy and -oak	2–4–5–T or silvex
Purslane	2–4–D
Quackgrass	Pull by hand or cover with black plastic for a month
Ragweeds	2–4–D
Sheep laurel	2–4–D
Smartweed	Mow close and cultivate
Spurge, Leafy	Mow close and cultivate
Spotted	Silvex
Squirrel-tail grass	Mow close and cultivate
Thistle, Canada	2–4–D
Russian	Mow close and keep cultivated
Tick trefoil	2–4–D
Vetch	2–4–D
Violets	Silvex
Yarrow	Mow close and cultivate

INSECTICIDES AND PESTICIDES

NAME	USE
ALL-PURPOSE SPRAYS available under trade names marketed by many large companies	Combined insecticides and fungicides for: fruits, small perennials fruit trees roses lawns vegetables ornamentals
Aramite for ornamentals or vegetables up to fifteen days before harvest; fruits up to twenty-one days before harvest	Mites, various; 15% wettable powder emulsions, and dusts
Arsenate of lead for ornamentals only	Chewing insects—largely replaced by modern chemicals
Chlordane Long residual effects; can be absorbed through skin. Apply to food gardens *in fall* after harvest	Soil inhabiting grubs and insects; 5% and 10% dusts; 40 and 50% wettable powder
Cryolite (Do not use with Bordeaux mixture or lime, DDT, parathion, or nicotine.) If applied to food plants or fruit, must be thoroughly washed off before being eaten	Chewing insects; 2½ oz. cryolite to 1 gal. water
DD Mixture (POISON) Delay planting one to two weeks after soil treatment	Nematodes; soil fumigant
DDT Do not apply to large vegetables within seven days of harvest; to berries after fruit forms; to celery after stalk is half formed or bunching starts; to leaf vegetables after seedling stage	Chewing insects; borers; millipedes; scales; thrips; 5 or 10% dust; 25 or 50% wettable powder

Diazinon
valuable for citrus fruits, fig and olive trees

Aphids; flies; use as directed

Dibrom
on bush and cane fruits; vegetables Do not apply within four days of harvest

Aphids, caterpillars, leaf hoppers, mites; dust, low percentage; emulsion

Dieldrin (POISON)
Work into soil like chlordane; for ornamentals

Soil inhabiting insects including termites; thrips; use as directed

Dimite
ornamentals only

Mites; use as directed

Heptachlor
ornamentals only

Grasshoppers, grubs, white grubs, wireworms; soil insecticide; dusts and sprays available; use as directed

Karathane (POISON)
ornamentals only

Mites; see also under fungicides; use as directed

Kelthane
ornamentals and some vegetables and fruits, that can be washed

Mites; low percentage dust; 18½% wettable powder; use as directed

Lime-sulfur
ornamentals only

Dormant spray in spring on ornamentals, for scales; lower concentrations used during growing season for aphids, mites, and as a fungicide; see table of fungicides

Lindane
ornamentals; food crops, except roots, when plants are very young

Aphids; soil insecticide; usually combined with other materials in mixed formulations; use as directed

Malathion
ornamentals; vegetables to within seven days of harvest, except leaf vegetables, within fourteen days; okra only before pods develop

General insecticide effective against sucking and chewing insects; 5% dust, 25% wettable powder; sometimes combined with DDT

Metaldehyde

Slugs and snails; usually present in commercial baits; sold under trade names

Methoxychlor
on ornamentals; fruit and vegetables: do not use within a week of harvest; leaf vegetables within two weeks

Chewing insects, including beetle larvae; dusts; sprays and in mixed formulas, according to directions

Milky white disease
sold as Doom, Japonex, etc.

Japanese beetles; placed in soil to infect succeeding generations of beetles, thus reducing infestation over a long period

Nicotine sulfate
sold as Black Leaf 40; ornamentals; leaf vegetables to within seven days of harvest; others within three days

Aphids; lice; malathion has largely replaced this old aphicide in the home garden

OIL (Volck) SPRAYS, DORMANT
sold under trade names by all big companies

Scales; mealy bug; white fly; summer strength for use when plants are in growth, 0.24 to 2%

Pyrethrum
not harmful, as sold

General insecticide from ground flower heads; not toxic; often used with chemical insecticides

Rotenone
  not harmful; safest material for use on all food plants

An insecticide derived from ground derris and cube roots; dusts and sprays

Sabadilla
  not harmful

Chewing insects; dust or powder from ground seeds

Sevin
  for ornamentals; fruits and vegetables as directed on package

Chewing insects; 5 and 10% dusts; 50% wettable powder

Sulfur

Mites; also as fungicide, which see; dusts and sprays

Toxaphene
  ornamentals; leaf vegetables as seedlings only; others to within seven days of harvest

Chewing insects; as wettable powders and in mixed formulas

Trithion
  ornamentals, nuts, fruits, including citrus; vegetables

Mites and aphids; 5% dust; 25% wettable powder; in liquid concentrates; use as directed

Vapam (soil fumigant)
  two-week interval between treatment of soil and planting date

Nematodes; see also under fungicides and herbicides; apply when temperature is above 60 degrees

Wilt-Pruf (trade name)
  anti-transpirant

For sunburn, sunscald, salt spray and wind injury when transplanting woody subjects; also for winter protection against dehydration and sunscald; use as directed

FUNGICIDES

Available as dusts or sprays

NAME	USE
Actidione	Mildew
Agri-mycin	Fireblight, other blights, rots and bacterial wilts
Bordeaux mixture	Anthracnose, blights, downy mildew, leaf spots, etc.
Captan ornamentals	For diseases on plants and as a soil drench
Chloropicrin (POISON)	Larvacide; soil fumigant which kills weed seeds, fungi, and insects; use as directed
Copper compounds, various sold under many trade names	Use as directed
Ferbam	Rusts, scab, and as a soil drench to prevent damping-off diseases
Formaldehyde (POISON)	Soil fumigant; 1 tb. in 5 tbs. water sprinkled over a 20×14×3 flat of soil; let stand *covered* for 24 hours; then sow seed and *water well*
Karathane	Mildew; see also under insecticides
Lime-sulfur	Fungicide; see also under insecticides
Maneb (Dithane M-22; Manzate); use on food plants according to directions	Anthracnose; blights; leaf spots; 6 and 8% dusts and sprays

Nabam (Dithane D-14; Liquid Nabam Fungicide, etc.)
ornamentals and as directed on food plants
Liquid; often used with zineb, which see; soil drench

Panodrench (trade name)
Soil drench for rhizoctonia; damping-off diseases

Phaltan
ornamentals, especially roses
Blackspot, leaf spots, powdery mildew, etc.; 5 to 75% dusts

Soil Fumigants
see under chloropicrin, formaldehyde
For damping-off diseases

Seed Treatment Chemicals
available under many trade names
For seed protection before sowing

Semesan (trade name)
stunts some plants such as pansy, petunia, snapdragon when used as drench
As a seed protectant and as a drench on living plants for rhizoctonia diseases

Sulfur
Mildew, etc.; dust; see also under insecticides

Thiram (Arasan)
Fungicide; soil drench; seed treatment chemical; use as directed

Vapam
Soil fumigant; fungicide; see also under insecticides

Zineb (Dithane Z-78)
Blights; fungus leaf spots; rusts; also for russet mites on citrus; use as directed

Ziram
available under several trade names; ornamentals only except as directed; almonds; pecans
Blights; leaf spots; anthracnose; brown rot, etc.

HERBICIDES

Weed killers are available under many trade names, often sold by lawn-seed companies. Selection can be made to suit special needs.

Amiden
Brush killer; makes soil sterile for two years

Ammate
Brush and poison-ivy; sterilizes soil for two months

Ammonium sulfate
For weeds in lawns set mower low and "scalp" weeds, then apply 4 lbs. per 100 sq. ft.; poisons weeds and feeds permanent grass

Bonus (trade name)
For broad-leaved weeds in summer growth; dandelion, buckthorn, plantains, etc.; also fertilizes soil; use on dichondra lawns

Calcium cyanamid
available under trade names; allow 60 days from treatment to seeding
A high lime and nitrogen fertilizer and weed seed killer for acid soils and compost heaps; kills soil bacteria and every living seed

Chlordane
  available under trade names; apply in late winter or very early spring

Crabgrass seedlings and other weed seedlings; arrests all growth for three weeks; 5, 10, 20, and 25% granules; 40% wettable powder; see also under insecticides

Chloropicrin

Weed seed killer; see under fungicides

Dacthal
  allow 60 days from treatment to planting; use in early spring

Crabgrass and broad-leaved weeds when germinating

Dalapon

Brush killer; sterilizes soil for two months

DMA

For seedling crabgrass, common chickweed, other grasses; do not use on carpet, centipede or St. Augustine grasses; use as directed

Dybar

Brush killer; sterilizes soil for two years

MCPA

Dandelion, bindweed, ground-ivy, purslane, speedwell

Methyl bromide

For unwanted Bermuda- or Johnsongrass, annual weeds and grasses; use as directed

Pre-emergence weed killers
  available under many trade names

For seeds of crabgrass, goosegrass, etc.; use as directed

Randox

Brush killer; sterilizes soil for two years

Silvex
  see 2–4–5–T

SMDC
  allow 5 days to seeding; 21 days for food crop areas

Germinating chickweed, pigweed, ragweed, Bermuda and Johnson grasses

2–4–D

Destroys a large variety of weed seedlings and most broad-leaved weeds in growth, including many hard-to-eradicate species; use as directed

2–4–5–T (Silvex)

Chickweed, common and mouse-ear Henbit; poison-ivy and poison-oak; spotted spurge; when combined with Dalapon, kills everything and arrests growth for three weeks; grasses for six weeks

Vapam
  allow two weeks from treatment to planting

Liquid herbicide; use as directed; see also under fungicides

SPRAY AND SPRAY SCHEDULE
FOR THE HOME ORCHARD

All-purpose Spray

Captan, 50% wettable powder	1½ cups	
Methoxychlor, 50% wettable powder	1½ cups	to 10 gal. water
Malathion, 25% wettable powder	1½ cups	

The above mixture may also be used on ornamentals.

Spray Schedule for Fruit Trees

TIME			FRUIT	
	APPLE	PEAR QUINCE	PEACH PLUM APRICOT	CHERRY
Dormant				
Before buds show green tips in spring	X		X	
Prebloom				
When blossom buds show color but before they open	X	X	soil under trees only	
Petal-fall				
When most petals have fallen from apple	X	X	X	X
First Cover				
7 to 10 days after petal-fall	X	X	X	X
Second Cover				
7 to 10 days after first cover	X	X	X	X
Third Cover				
7 to 10 days after second cover	X			
Fourth Cover				
7 to 10 days after third cover	X		X	X
Fifth Cover				
10 to 12 days after fourth cover	X	X	X	X
For late apples, pears, and peaches every 10 days	X	X	X	

Eight to 10 sprays are minimal to achieve success.
(Information taken from Iowa State University Pamphlet 175.)

Botanical Gardens and Arboretums

State	Name	Address
ALASKA	Experiment Station	Palmer
	Experiment Station	College
ARIZONA	Desert Botanical Garden of Arizona	Papago Park (near Phoenix)
	Boyce Thompson Southwestern Arboretum	Superior

CALIFORNIA	Los Angeles State and County Arboretum	301 N. Baldwin Ave., Arcadia
	Regional Parks Botanic Garden	Tilden Regional Park, Berkeley
	University of California Botanical Garden	Strawberry Canyon, Berkeley
	Rancho Santa Ana Botanical Garden	1500 N. College Ave., Claremont
	University of California Arboretum	College of Agriculture, Davis (near Sacramento)
	Descanso Gardens	1418 Descanso Drive, La Canada
	Botanical Garden, University of California	405 Hilgard Ave., Los Angeles
	Joseph McInnes Memorial Botanical Gardens, Mills College	Seminary Ave. and MacArthur Blvd., Oakland
	Joseph R. Knowland State Arboretum and Park	96th Ave. at Mountain Blvd., Oakland
	Eddy Arboretum	Institute of Forest Genetics, Placerville
	Strybing Arboretum and Botanic Garden	Golden Gate Park, San Francisco
	Huntington Botanical Gardens	1151 Oxford Rd., San Marino
	Santa Barbara Botanic Garden	1212 Mission Canyon Rd., Santa Barbara
	Saratoga Horticultural Foundation	Verde Vista Lane, Saratoga
	Villa Montalvo Arboretum	Saratoga
COLORADO	The Glenmore Arboretum	Buffalo Creek
	Denver Botanical Gardens	909 York St., Denver
CONNECTICUT	Marsh Botanical Garden	Yale University, New Haven
	Connecticut Arboretum	Conn. College, New London
DELAWARE	Henry Francis du Pont Winterthur Arboretum	Wilmington
DISTRICT OF COLUMBIA	Kenilworth Aquatic Gardens	Douglas St., N.E., Washington
	United States National Arboretum	Montana Ave. and Bladensburg Rd., N.E., Washington
FLORIDA	Gifford Arboretum	University of Miami, Coral Gables
	Flamingo Groves Tropical Botanic Garden	3501 S. Federal Highway, Fort Lauderdale

	Thomas A. Edison Winter Home and Botanical Gardens	2341 McGregor Blvd., Fort Myers
	Wilmot Memorial Garden	University of Florida, Gainesville
	Fairchild Tropical Garden	10901 Old Cutler Rd., Coconut Grove, Miami
	McKee Jungle Gardens	Vero Beach
	Highlands Hammock State Park	Sebring
GEORGIA	Founders' Memorial Garden and Living Arboretum	Athens
	Ida Cason Callaway Gardens	Pine Mountain (85 miles south of Atlanta)
HAWAII	Foster Park Botanical Garden	45 North School Street, Honolulu
	Harold L. Lyon Arboretum	University of Hawaii, Honolulu
	Harold L. Lyon Botanical Garden	Koko Head, Oahu
	Wahiawa Botanical Garden	1396 California Ave., Wahiawa, Oahu
IDAHO	The Charles Houston Shattuck Arboretum	College of Forestry, University of Idaho, Moscow
ILLINOIS	Garfield Park Conservatory	300 N. Central Park Avenue, Chicago
	Lincoln Park Conservatory	2400 N. Stockton Drive, Chicago
	The Morton Arboretum	Lisle
INDIANA	James Irving Holcomb Botanical Gardens	Butler University, Indianapolis
	Christy Woods Botanical Garden	Ball State Teachers College, Muncie
IOWA	College Gardens	Iowa State Teachers College, Cedar Falls
	Lilac Arboretum, Ewing Park	McKinley Avenue and Indianola Rd., Des Moines
KANSAS	Indian Hill Arboretum	3617 West South Ave., Topeka
LOUISIANA	Jungle Gardens	Avery Island
	Gardens of the Louisiana Polytechnic Institute	Ruston
MAINE	Botanical Plantations of the University of Maine	Orono
MASSACHUSETTS	The Arnold Arboretum of Harvard University	Jamaica Plain (near Boston)
	Botanic Garden of Smith College	Northampton

	Alexandra Botanical Garden and Hunnewell Arboretum	Wellesley College Wellesley
	Walter Hunnewell Arboretum	845 Washington St., Wellesley
MICHIGAN	The Nichols Arboretum of the University of Michigan	Ann Arbor
	Anna Scripps Whitcomb Conservatory	Belle Isle, Detroit
	Beal-Garfield Botanic Garden	Michigan State University, East Lansing
	Slayton Arboretum of Hillsdale College	Hillsdale
MINNESOTA	University of Minnesota Landscape Arboretum	St. Paul (near Excelsior)
	Botanical Garden of the University of Minnesota	Minneapolis
	Hormel Foundation Arboretum	Austin
MISSOURI	Missouri Botanical Garden	2315 Tower Grove Ave., St. Louis
NEBRASKA	Arbor Lodge State Park Arboretum	Nebraska City
NEW HAMPSHIRE	Lilac Arboretum	University of New Hampshire, Durham
NEW JERSEY	Hanover Park Arboretum	Mt. Pleasant Ave., East Hanover
	New Jersey Agricultural Experiment Station Arboretum	Rutgers University, New Brunswick
NEW YORK	Cornell Plantations	Cornell University, Ithaca
	Thomas C. Desmond Arboretum	Newburgh
	Brooklyn Botanic Garden	1000 Washington Ave., Brooklyn
	The New York Botanical Gardens	Bronx Park, New York City
	Bayard Cutting Arboretum	Oakdale, Long Island, N.Y.
	Buffalo Botanic Garden	South Park Ave. and McKinley Drive, Buffalo
	Planting Fields Arboretum	Oyster Bay, L.I.
	Highland and Durand—Eastman Park Arboretum	5 Castle Park, Rochester
NORTH CAROLINA	The Coker Arboretum	University of North Carolina, Chapel Hill
	Sarah P. Duke Memorial Garden	Duke University, Durham

OHIO	Eden Park Conservatory	950 Eden Park Drive, Cincinnati
	The Dawes Arboretum	Newark
	Kingwood Center	Mansfield
	The Secrest Arboretum	Ohio Agricultural Experiment Station, Wooster
OREGON	The Peavy Arboretum	Oregon State College, Corvallis
	Hoyt Arboretum	4000 S.W. Fairview Blvd., Portland
PENNSYLVANIA	Taylor Memorial Arboretum	10· Ridley Drive, Garden City, Chester
	Botanical Garden of the Reading Public Museum and Art Gallery	500 Museum Road, Reading
	Longwood Gardens	Kennett Square
	The John J. Tyler Arboretum	Lima, Delaware County
	Masonic Homes Arboretum	Elizabethtown
	Botanical Garden of the University of Pennsylvania	38th and Spruce St., Philadelphia
	Ellis School Arboretum	Newtown Square
	The Morris Arboretum of the University of Pennsylvania	9414 Meadowbrook Ave., Philadelphia
	Elan Memorial Park	116 E. Front St., Berwick, Lime Ridge
	Phipps Conservatory	Schenley Park, Pittsburgh
	Mont Alto State Forest Arboretum	Mont Alto
	Bowman's Hill Wild Flower Preserve	Washington Crossing State Park, Washington Crossing
	Westtown School Arboretum	Westtown
	Arthur Hoyt Scott Horticultural Foundation	Swarthmore College, Swarthmore
	Arboretum of the Barnes Foundation	300 Latch's Lane, Merion
SOUTH CAROLINA	Brookgreen Gardens	near Georgetown
TENNESSEE	Southwestern Arboretum	Southwestern College, Memphis
	The W. C. Paul Arboretum	Audubon Park, Memphis
	The Tennessee Botanical Gardens and Fine Arts Center	Cheekwood Mansion, Nashville
TEXAS	Texas A. & M. Arboretum and Trial Grounds	Texas A. & M. College, College Station
	Fort Worth Botanic Garden	3220 Botanic Garden Drive, Fort Worth
UTAH	Botanical Garden	Brigham Young Univ., Provo

State	Name	Address
VIRGINIA	Virginia Polytechnic Institute Arboretum	Blacksburg
	Orland E. White Arboretum	Blandy Experimental Farm, University of Virginia, Boyce (60 miles west of Washington)
	Norfolk Botanic Garden	Granby & 35th St., Norfolk
WASHINGTON	University of Washington Arboretum	Lake Washington Blvd., Seattle
	Finch Arboretum	W. 3404 Woodland Blvd., Spokane
	Wind River Arboretum	Carson
WEST VIRGINIA	West Virginia University Arboretum	Morgantown
WISCONSIN	Alfred L. Boerner Botanical Garden	Whitnall Park, Hales Corners (near Milwaukee)
	University of Wisconsin Arboretum	Madison
	Paine Art Center and Arboretum	Oshkosh
WYOMING	Cheyenne Horticultural Field Station	Cheyenne

Parks and Display Gardens

State	Name	Address
ALABAMA	Bellingrath Gardens	Mobile
ARIZONA	Pioneer Park Rose Garden	Mesa
	Memorial Rose Garden	Prescott
	Tucson Rose Garden	Tucson
ARKANSAS	AA Gladiolus Trial Garden	Jonesboro
	Territorial Capitol Gardens	Little Rock
CALIFORNIA	Patrick's Point State Park azaleas, lilies	north of Eureka, Coast Highway
	Oakhurst Gardens bulbs, tropicals, subtropicals	345 W. Colorado, Arcadia
	Municipal Rose Garden	Berkeley
	Vetterle & Reinelt Nursery delphiniums, primroses, tuberous begonias	Capitola
	Bodger Seeds, Ltd. trial grounds	1600 S. Tyler Ave., El Monte

Roeding Park roses, trees, shrubs	Fresno
Domoto Nursery camellias, bonsai trees, gerberias, tree peonies, magnolias	Western Rd., Hayward
Howard Rose Co.	Hemet
Denholm Seed Co. trial grounds	Lompac
Exposition Park Rose Garden	Figueroa St., Los Angeles
Gardens of Sunset Magazine	Willow and Middlefield Rds., Menlo Park
Melrose Iris Gardens	Rt. 6, Modesto
Armstrong Nurseries roses	Ontario
Jackson & Perkins Co. roses	Pleasanton
White Park roses, trees	3900 Eighth St., Riverside
Capitol Park camellias	Sacramento
McKinley Park Muncipal Rose Garden	Sacramento
Ferry-Morse Seed Co. trial grounds	Salinas
Balboa Park rose garden, dahlias	San Diego
California Camellia Gardens	13531 Fenton Ave., San Fernando
Golden Gate Park	San Francisco
San Jose Municipal Rose Garden	Naglee Ave., San Jose
Palomar College cacti, succulents	San Marcos
Alameda Park	Santa Barbara
Mission Park rose garden	Santa Barbara
Memorial Rose Garden	700 E. Canon Perdido St., Santa Barbara
Redwood Highway (U.S. Rt. 101)	northern Calif.

	William McDonald Seed Co. trial grounds	Santa Maria
	Sequoia and Kings Canyon National Parks	Three Rivers
	Victory Park rose garden	Stockton
	Public Rose Garden	Visalia
COLORADO	Roosevelt Park rose garden	Longmont
	Pan-American Seeds, Inc. trial grounds, petunias	Paonia
	Washington Park (Martha Washington Gardens)	Denver
	Mineral Palace Park rose garden	Pueblo
CONNECTICUT	Bristol Nurseries chrysanthemums, perennials	Bristol
	Elizabeth Park rose garden	Hartford
DELAWARE	Josephine Gardens roses, iris	Brandywine Park, Wilmington
	Winterthur Museum and Gardens azaleas, spring flowers	Henry Francis du Pont estate (near Wilmington)
DISTRICT OF COLUMBIA	West Potomac Park Tidal Basin flowering cherries	Washington
	Dumbarton Oaks	Washington
	East Potomac Park flowering cherries	Washington
	The Bishop's Garden, Washington Cathedral	Washington
FLORIDA	Bok Tower	Lake Wales
	Simpson Park tropicals, subtropicals	Miami
	St. Petersburg Park tropicals	St. Petersburg
	Edwin A. Menninger trees	Stuart
	Killearn Gardens azaleas, gardenias	Tallahassee
	Florida Cypress Gardens	Winter Haven
	Corkscrew Swamp Sanctuary	Immokalee

GEORGIA	Hurt Park
	  magnolias,
	  shrubs,
	  flowers
		Atlanta

	Piedmont Park rare trees	Atlanta

	H. G. Hastings Co.
	  Flower Acres
	  test garden
		Lovejoy

	Dunaway Gardens
	  roses,
	  rock garden,
	  old-fashioned garden
		Newman

	Todd's Dahlia Farm	Suches
	Fulwood Park azaleas	Tifton Park
	Camellia Trail	Valdosta
HAWAII	Hawaii National Park	Kilauea-Mauna Loa Sect., Island of Hawaii
	Liliuokalani Park Japanese Garden	Hilo
IDAHO	Julia Davis Park rose garden	Boise
	Memorial Rose Garden	Lewiston
	Lakeview Park rose garden	Nampa
	Ross Park Rotary Rose Garden	Pocatello

ILLINOIS	Humboldt Park
	  roses,
	  lilies
		Chicago

	Jackson Park
	  flowering trees,
	  spring flowers,
	  chrysanthemums
		Chicago

	Marquette Park
	  roses,
	  azaleas,
	  tropicals
		Chicago

	Hill-Dundee Nursery evergreens	Dundee

	Eldorado Memorial Park
	  flowering trees,
	  bulbs,
	  roses
		Eldorado

	Merrick Park roses	Evanston
	Shakespeare Garden	Northwestern Univ. campus Evanston
	Cook Memorial Library roses	Libertyville

	Lilacia Park lilacs	Lombard
	Dr. Ernest H. Wilson Memorial Garden	Peoria

	Lincoln Memorial Garden
	   flowering trees,
	   wild flowers
		Springfield

	George K. Ball
	   trial grounds,
	   chrysanthemums
		West Chicago

	Catigny Farm; Vaughan's Seeds trial grounds	Wheaton
	David F. Hall	809 Central Ave., Wilmette

INDIANA	Foster Park
	   iris,
	   peonies,
	   lilacs,
	   tulips
		Fort Wayne

	Jaenicke Gardens
	   flowering trees,
	   azaleas,
	   bulbs
		Fort Wayne

	Lakeside Rose Gardens	Fort Wayne
	Lawton Park chrysanthemums	Fort Wayne
	Kundred Gladiolus Farms	Goshen
	Earl R. Roberts iris	Rt. 4, Indianapolis

	International Friendship Gardens
	   demonstration garden,
	   Persian roses
		Michigan City

	E. G. Hill Memorial Rose Garden	Richmond
	Leeper Park: garden of fragrance for the blind	U.S. Highway 31, South Bend
IOWA	Iowa State College test gardens	Ames
	Vander Veer Park roses	Davenport
	Grandview Park peonies	Dubuque
	Interstate Nurseries trial grounds	Hamburg
	Edmondson Park peonies	Oskaloosa
	Byrnes Park rose demonstration garden	Waterloo

KANSAS	University of Kansas campus
	   lilacs,
	   flowering crabs
		Lawrence

	Reinisch Gardens rose demonstration	Topeka

KENTUCKY	Shawnee Park perennials—old-fashioned garden	Louisville
LOUISIANA	Laurel Farms test garden	Forbing
	Southeastern Louisiana College camellia garden	Hammond
	Audubon Memorial State Park Louisiana iris	Oakley, St. Francisville
	City Park Rose Garden	New Orleans
	Cross Lake Gardens	Shreveport
	Hodges Gardens roses, camellias	Many
MAINE	Asticou Gardens	Northeast Harbor
	Bok Memorial Garden alpines	Camden
	Municipal Rose Garden	Portland
MARYLAND	Sherwood Gardens azaleas, bulbs	Stratford and Underwood Rds., Baltimore
	Dr. and Mrs. William A. Briggs' daffodil trial garden	Lutherville
	Mr. and Mrs. Jesse Hakes' daffodil trial garden	Sylvanville
MASSACHUSETTS	Harlan P. Kelsey Nurseries	East Boxford
	Bay State Nurseries	North Abington
	Worcester County Horticultural Society Orchard old apple varieties	North Grafton
	Springfield Park gardens	Pittsfield
	Mount Holyoke College greenhouses	South Hadley
	Bee Warburton iris test garden	Rt. 1, Westboro
	Berkshire Garden Center herbs	Stockbridge
	University of Massachusetts trial grounds	Waltham
	Weston Nurseries	Weston
MICHIGAN	Johnson Memorial Gardens	Detroit
	Centennial Park spring and autumn flowers	Holland
	Cooley Gardens rose demonstration	Lansing
	Grand Mere Nurseries chrysanthemum test garden	Rt. 4, Niles
	Emlong Nurseries chrysanthemum test garden, demonstration garden	Stevensville

	R. M. Kellogg Co. chrysanthemum test garden	Three Rivers
	Cranbrook Institute of Science formal gardens	Bloomfield Hills

MINNESOTA	Brand Peony Farm
	    peonies,
	    lilacs
		Faribault

	Lyndale Park rose garden	Minneapolis
	Northrup-King & Co. trial grounds	Minneapolis
	University of Minnesota chrysanthemum trial grounds	St. Paul

MISSISSIPPI	Beauvoir on the Beach
	    roses,
	    azaleas,
	    camellias,
	    woodland
		Biloxi

	Mississippi State College rose garden	Long Beach
	Mississippi State College camellia test garden	Poplarville
MISSOURI	Capaha Park rose display garden	Cape Girardeau
	University of Missouri chrysanthemum trial grounds	Columbia
	Municipal Rose Garden	Kansas City
	Forest Park Municipal Rose Garden	St. Louis
MONTANA	City Park System	Great Falls
	Roselawn Park roses	Libby
	Sunset Park municipal rose garden	Missoula
	Memorial Rose Garden	Polson
NEBRASKA	Antelope Park municipal rose garden	Lincoln
	Joslyn Art Museum conservatory	Omaha
	Omaha Hemerocallis Display Gardens	Omaha
NEVADA	Squires Park Rose Garden	Las Vegas
	Washoe Medical Center municipal rose garden	Reno

NEW
HAMPSHIRE
	Thomas Bailey Aldrich
	    Memorial
	    old-fashioned garden
		Portsmouth

NEW JERSEY	Nomahegan Park flowering cherries	Cranford
	Warinanco Park	Elizabeth
	Mattano Park Rose Garden	Elizabeth

	Cedar Brook Park varied plantings through season	Plainfield
	Julius Roehrs Co. indoor plants	Rutherford
NEW MEXICO	Baptist Assembly Gardens iris, roses, delphiniums, tuberous begonias	Glorieta
	Municipal Rose Gardens	Roswell
NEW YORK	Landscape Association, Inc. display gardens	Brookville, L.I.
	Lilac Land	Brookville, L.I.
	Louis Smirnow peonies	Brookville, L.I.
	Humboldt Park rose garden	Buffalo
	Kelly Bros. Nurseries trees, fruits, shrubs, chrysanthemums	Dansville
	Maloney Bros. Nursery	Dansville
	Beacon Hill Rock Garden Nursery	Dobbs Ferry
	Stillwell-Perine House colonial gardens	Dongan Hills, Staten Island
	Hammond House eighteenth century gardens	Grasslands Parkway, Eastview
	James I. George and Son clematis	Fairport
	Long Island Agricultural and Technical Institute trial grounds, dahlias	Farmingdale, L.I.
	Rose Garden trees, summer flowers	Great Neck
	The L. H. Bailey Hortorium	Cornell Univ., Ithaca
	Old Westbury Gardens	Westbury, L.I.
	Jackson & Perkins Co. roses, perennials, display garden	Newark
	The Cloisters: garden of the Middle Ages	Fort Tryon Park, Riverside Drive, New York City
	Van Cortlandt House formal Dutch garden	Van Cortlandt Park, The Bronx, New York City

Vassar College Campus	Poughkeepsie
flowering trees,	
shrubs	
Maplewood Park	Rochester
roses,	
flowering trees	
Chase Bros.	2405 East Ave.,
demonstration herb garden	Rochester
Joseph Harris Seed Co.	Moreton Farms,
trial grounds	Rochester
Congress Park: Italian garden	Saratoga Springs
Yaddo Estate	Saratoga Springs
rose garden,	
rock garden,	
trees	
Skyland Nursery	Sloatsburg
formerly private estate,	
great variety of material,	
large acreage,	
scenic	
Thornden Park	Syracuse
roses,	
bulbs,	
herbs,	
annuals,	
perennials	
Sterling Forest Gardens	Tuxedo Park
great variety of plant material,	
large acreage	

NORTH CAROLINA

Rhododendron Park	West Asheville
Biltmore Estate	Asheville
extensive plantings	
Sunnyside Rose Garden	Charlotte
Sarah P. Duke Memorial Garden	Duke University, Durham
Airlie Gardens	Wilmington
C. C. O'Brien	1212 Bellevue,
iris trial grounds	Greensboro
Clarendon Gardens and Nursery	Pinehurst
North Carolina State College	Raleigh
trial grounds	
Manteo Gardens	Roanoke Rapids
hemerocallis	
Municipal Iris Gardens	Runnymede Rd., Winston-Salem
Tanglewood Park	Winston-Salem
roses,	
azaleas,	
shrubs,	
wild flowers	

OHIO

Goodyear Memorial Rose Garden	East Akron
Cahoon Park Memorial Rose Garden	Bay Village
Ault Park summer flowers, dahlias	Cincinnati
Fleischman Gardens bulbs, flowers	Cincinnati
Lytle Park tulips, annuals	Cincinnati
Cleveland Cultural Gardens international	Rockefeller Park, Cleveland
Fine Arts Garden flowering trees, bulbs, formal garden, sculpture	East Blvd. at Euclid Ave., Cleveland
Wade Park herb garden	Cleveland
Municipal Rose Garden	Cleveland
Waterfront Gardens (Donald Gray Gardens) formal	Cleveland
Euclid Park Rose Garden	Cleveland
Park of Roses	4015 N. High St., Columbus
Ohio State University Rose Garden	Columbus
Bohlken Park Rose Garden	Forest City
Kingwood Center roses	Mansfield
Gerard K. Klyn, Inc. rose test garden	Mentor
Bosley Gardens roses	Mentor
Wayside Gardens nursery with many rare species and varieties, bulbs, perennials, shrubs, trees	Mentor
Library Rose Garden	Rocky River
Spring Hill Nurseries trial grounds, chrysanthemums	Tipp City

OKLAHOMA	Ardmore Rose Garden	Whittington Park, Ardmore
	Johnstone Municipal Park Rose Garden	Bartlesville
	Will Rogers Park rose garden, bulbs, hibiscus, annuals, wild plants	Oklahoma City
	Woodward Park Municipal Rose Garden	Tulsa
OREGON	Mirror Pond Park rose gardens	Bend
	Walter Marx Gardens lilies, iris, hemerocallis	Boring
	Clark's Primroses	Clackamas
	Oregon State College Experimental Gardens clematis, chrysanthemums, azaleas, hemerocallis, holly	Corvallis
	Hendricks Park rhododendrons	Eugene
	Oregon Bulb Farms lilies	Gresham
	Ambrose Brownell hollies	Milwaukie
	Rhododendron Garden	Crystal Springs Island, Portland
	Washington Park roses	Portland
	Duniway Park lilacs	S.W. Sixth and Sheridan Way, Portland
	Lewis and Clark College memorial rose garden	420 S.W. Third Ave., Portland
	Gill Bros. Seed Co. trial grounds	Portland
	Bush Park Municipal Rose Garden	Salem
PENNSYLVANIA	Independence Hall Garden	Philadelphia
	Gross Memorial Rose Garden	Allentown
	Burpee's Fordhook Farms trial grounds	Doylestown
	Rose Garden demonstration	Hershey

	Breeze Hill Gardens trial grounds	Harrisburg
	Riesenhauser Park rose arboretum	McKeesport
	Mellon Park rose garden	Pittsburgh
	City Park rose garden	Reading
	The Conard-Pyle Co. roses, demonstration garden	West Grove
	Farr Nursery Co. hemerocallis	Weiser Park, Womelsdorf
	Farquhar Park municipal rose garden	York
RHODE ISLAND	Roger Williams Park large acreage, varied plantings	Providence
SOUTH CAROLINA	Cypress Gardens azaleas	Strawberry (north of Charleston)
	Magnolia Gardens azaleas, camellias	Johns Island (west of Charleston)
	Middleton Gardens camellias, live oaks	Ashley River Rd., Charleston
	Clemson College camellias, test garden	Clemson
	Municipal Rose Garden	Florence
	Edisto Gardens camellias, azaleas, shrubs, trees, roses, hemerocallis	Orangeburg
	Memorial Park azaleas	Sumter
	Edmunds Memorial Rose Garden	Sumter
	Swan Lake Gardens iris, camellias	Sumter
	Dundale Gardens hemerocallis, camellias	Columbia Highway, Sumter
	Fortunes Spring Park roses	Winnsboro
SOUTH DAKOTA	South Dakota State College test garden for woody plants	Brookings

TENNESSEE	Warner Park Rose Garden	Chattanooga
	Happy Cabin Dahlia Garden	Signal Mt., Chattanooga
	Great Smoky Mountains National Park native trees, shrubs, flowers	Gatlinburg
	Blount Mansion (spring display)	Hill and State sts., Knoxville
	Eastern State Hospital municipal rose garden	Knoxville
	Overton Park holly, azaleas	Memphis
	Ketchum Memorial Iris Garden	Audubon Park, Memphis
TEXAS	Memorial Park rose garden	Amarillo
	W. J. Rogers test garden	Beaumont
	Spuria Iris Test Garden	2503 Wertheimer Dr., Houston
	Texas Camellia test garden	Orange
	Tyler Municipal Rose Garden	Tyler
	Arp Nursery Co. roses	Tyler
	Lindsey Lane azaleas	Tyler
UTAH	Statehouse Museum rose garden	Fillmore
	Municipal Memorial Rose Garden	Nephi
	City and County Park formal	Ogden
	Rose Garden: State Industrial School	Ogden
	Wallace Iris Gardens	Orem
	Sowiette Park memorial rose garden	Provo
	Tell's Iris Gardens	691 E. 8th St. N., Provo
	Municipal Rose Garden	Salt Lake City
VIRGINIA	Wakefield: Washington's birthplace colonial gardens	Westmoreland County
	Mount Vernon: Washington's home colonial gardens	Mount Vernon
	Memorial Rose Garden	Arlington
	Little England Daffodil Farm	Gloucester

	Lafayette Park	Norfolk
	Norfolk Municipal Gardens azaleas, camellias, woodland	Norfolk
	Colonial Williamsburg colonial gardens	Williamsburg
WASHINGTON STATE	San Benn Park roses	Aberdeen
	Cornwall Park roses	Bellingham
	Chehalis Rose Garden	Chehalis
	Lewis & Clark Park woodland	south of Chehalis
	Woodland Park Rose Gardens	Seattle
	Maneto Park varied plantings	Spokane
	Western State Hospital primroses	Stielacoom
	Point Defiance Park roses, rhododendrons, dahlias	Tacoma
	Ohme Gardens trees, alpines	Wenatchee
WEST VIRGINIA	Rose Garden, Y.M.C.A.	Charleston
	Ritter Park Rose Gardens	Huntington
	Oglebay Park gardens, peonies	Wheeling
WISCONSIN	Riverside Park flowers on the levee	La Crosse
	University of Wisconsin gardens	Madison
WYOMING	Storm Gardens	Chugwater

Agricultural Colleges
Agricultural Experiment Stations

(From U. S. D. A. Agriculture Handbook No. 116. Workers in Subjects Pertaining to Agriculture in Land-Grant Colleges and Experiment Stations, May 1962.)

State	Name	City
ALABAMA	School of Agriculture, Auburn University	Auburn
	Agricultural Experiment Station	Auburn
	Alabama Agricultural and Mechanical College	Normal
ALASKA	Department of Agriculture, University of Alaska	College
	Agricultural Experiment Station	Palmer
ARIZONA	College of Agriculture, University of Arizona	Tucson
	Agricultural Experiment Station	Tucson
ARKANSAS	College of Agriculture, University of Arkansas	Fayetteville
	Agricultural Experiment Station	Fayetteville
CALIFORNIA	College of Agriculture, University of California	Berkeley
	Agricultural Experiment Station	Berkeley
	Agricultural Experiment Station	Davis
	Agricultural Experiment Station	Los Angeles
	Agricultural Experiment Station	Riverside
COLORADO	College of Agriculture, Colorado State University	Fort Collins
	Agricultural Experiment Station	Fort Collins
CONNECTICUT	College of Agriculture, University of Connecticut	Storrs
	Storrs Agricultural Experiment Station	Storrs
	The Connecticut Agricultural Experiment Station	New Haven
DELAWARE	School of Agriculture, University of Delaware	Newark
	Agricultural Experiment Station	Newark
	Delaware State College	Dover
FLORIDA	College of Agriculture, University of Florida	Gainesville
	Agricultural Experiment Station	Gainesville
	School of Agriculture, Florida Agricultural and Mechanical University	Tallahassee
GEORGIA	College of Agriculture, University of Georgia	Athens
	Georgia Coastal Plain Experiment Station	Tifton

	Georgia Agricultural Experiment Station	Griffon
	The Fort Valley State College	Fort Valley
HAWAII	College of Tropical Agriculture, University of Hawaii	Honolulu
	Agricultural Experiment Station	Honolulu
IDAHO	College of Agriculture, University of Idaho	Moscow
	Agricultural Experiment Station	Moscow
ILLINOIS	College of Agriculture, University of Illinois	Urbana
	Agricultural Experiment Station	Urbana
INDIANA	School of Agriculture, Purdue University	Lafayette
	Agricultural Experiment Station	Lafayette
IOWA	College of Agriculture, Iowa State University of Science and Technology	Ames
	Agricultural Experiment Station	Ames
KANSAS	Kansas State University of Agriculture and Applied Science	Manhattan
	Agricultural Experiment Station	Manhattan
KENTUCKY	College of Agriculture, University of Kentucky	Lexington
	Agricultural Experiment Station	Lexington
	Kentucky State College	Frankfort
LOUISIANA	Louisiana State University and Agricultural and Mechanical College, University Station	Baton Rouge
	Agricultural Experiment Station, University Station	Baton Rouge
	Southern University and Agricultural and Mechanical College Southern Branch Post Office	Baton Rouge
MAINE	College of Agriculture, University of Maine	Orono
	Agricultural Experiment Station University of Maine	Orono
MARYLAND	College of Agriculture, University of Maryland	College Park
	Agricultural Experiment Station	College Park
	Maryland State College, University of Maryland	Princess Anne
MASSACHUSETTS	College of Agriculture, University of Massachusetts	Amherst
	Agricultural Experiment Station	Amherst
MICHIGAN	Michigan State University of Agriculture and Applied Science	East Lansing
	Agricultural Experiment Station	East Lansing
MINNESOTA	Institute of Agriculture, University of Minnesota, St. Paul Campus	St. Paul
	Agricultural Experiment Station St. Paul Campus	St. Paul

MISSISSIPPI	School of Agriculture and Forestry, Mississippi State University of Applied Arts and Sciences	State College
	Agricultural Experiment Station	State College
	School of Agriculture, Alcorn Agricultural and Mechanical College	Lorman
MISSOURI	College of Agriculture, University of Missouri	Columbia
	Agricultural Experiment Station	Columbia
	Lincoln University	Jefferson City
MONTANA	Montana State College	Bozeman
	Agricultural Experiment Station	Bozeman
NEBRASKA	College of Agriculture, University of Nebraska	Lincoln
	Agricultural Experiment Station	Lincoln
NEVADA	Max C. Fleischmann College of Agriculture, University of Nevada	Reno
	Agricultural Experiment Station	Reno
NEW HAMPSHIRE	College of Agriculture, University of New Hampshire	Durham
	Agricultural Experiment Station	Durham
NEW JERSEY	State College of Agriculture and Mechanic Arts, State University	New Brunswick
	Agricultural Experiment Station of Rutgers	New Brunswick
NEW MEXICO	College of Agriculture, New Mexico State University	University Park
	Agricultural Experiment Station	University Park
NEW YORK	New York State College of Agriculture, Cornell University	Ithaca
	Agricultural Experiment Station	Ithaca
	New York State Agricultural Experiment Station	Geneva
NORTH CAROLINA	North Carolina State College of Agriculture and Engineering, University of North Carolina	Raleigh
	Agricultural Experiment Station	Raleigh
	The Agricultural and Technical College of North Carolina	Greensboro
NORTH DAKOTA	College of Agriculture, North Dakota State University of Agriculture and Applied Science State University Station	Fargo
	Agricultural Experiment Station	Fargo
OHIO	College of Agriculture, Ohio State University	Columbus
	Ohio Agricultural Experiment Station	Wooster
OKLAHOMA	Oklahoma State University of Agriculture and Applied Science	Stillwater
	Agricultural Experiment Station	Stillwater
	Langston University	Langston

OREGON	School of Agriculture, Oregon State University	Corvallis
	Agricultural Experiment Station	Corvallis
PENNSYLVANIA	College of Agriculture, Pennsylvania State University	University Park
	Agricultural Experiment Station	University Park
PUERTO RICO	College of Agriculture, University of Puerto Rico	Rio Piedras
	Agricultural Experiment Station	Rio Piedras
RHODE ISLAND	College of Agriculture, University of Rhode Island	Kingston
	Agricultural Experiment Station	Kingston
SOUTH CAROLINA	Clemson Agricultural College of South Carolina, School of Agriculture	Clemson
	Agricultural Experiment Station	Clemson
	South Carolina State College	Orangeburg
SOUTH DAKOTA	South Dakota State College of Agriculture and Mechanic Arts	College Station
	Agricultural Experiment Station	College Station
TENNESSEE	College of Agriculture, University of Tennessee	Knoxville
	Agricultural Experiment Station	Knoxville
	Martin Branch, University of Tennessee	Martin
	Tennessee Agricultural and Industrial State University	Nashville
TEXAS	Agricultural and Mechanical College of Texas	College Station
	Prairie View A. and M. College	Prairie View
	Agricultural Experiment Station	College Station
UTAH	Utah State University of Agriculture and Applied Science	Logan
	Agricultural Experiment Station	Logan
VERMONT	College of Agriculture, University of Vermont	Burlington
	Agricultural Experiment Station	Burlington
VIRGINIA	School of Agriculture, Virginia Polytechnic Institute	Blacksburg
	Agricultural Experiment Station	Blacksburg
	Virginia Truck Experiment Station	Norfolk
WASHINGTON	College of Agriculture, Washington State University, Institute of Agricultural Sciences	Pullman
	Agricultural Experiment Station	Pullman
WEST VIRGINIA	College of Agriculture, West Virginia University	Morgantown
	Agricultural Experiment Station	Morgantown
WISCONSIN	College of Agriculture, University of Wisconsin	Madison
	Agricultural Experiment Station	Madison
WYOMING	College of Agriculture, University of Wyoming	Laramie
	Agricultural Experiment Station	Laramie

Special Plant Societies

African Violet Society of America, Inc.

Mrs. Robert Wright
P. O. Box 1326
Knoxville, Tenn.

American Begonia Society

Mrs. Margaret B. Taylor
111 Evelyn Drive
Anaheim, Calif.

American Camellia Society

Mr. Joseph H. Pyron
Box 465
Tifton, Ga.

American Daffodil Society

Mrs. Ernest J. Adams
1121 Twelfth Ave.
Huntington, W.Va.

American Dahlia Society, Inc.

Mr. Edward B. Lloyd
10 Crestmont Rd.
Montclair, N.J.

American Fuchsia Society

California Academy of Science
Golden Gate Park
San Francisco, Calif.

American Gesneria Society

Mrs. Lois B. Hammond
3917 Copeland Lane
Fremont, Calif.

American Gloxinia Society, Inc.

Miss Diantha Brown
164–20 Highland Ave.
Jamaica 32, N.Y.

American Hemerocallis Society

Miss Olive M. Hindman
404 Weigle Ave.
Sebring, Fla.

American Hibiscus Society

Mrs. C. H. Calais
Goldenrod
Orlando, Fla.

American Iris Society

Mr. Clifford W. Benson
Missouri Botanical Garden
2237 Tower Grove Blvd.
St. Louis 10, Mo.

American Orchid Society, Inc.

Mr. Gordon W. Dillon
Botanical Museum of Harvard
University
Cambridge 38, Mass.

American Penstemon Society

Mrs. Andrew Dowbridge
25 Auburn St.
Springvale, Maine

American Peony Society

Mr. George W. Peyton
Box 1
Rapidan, Va.

American Plant Life Society
(includes American Amaryllis Society)

Dr. Thomas Whitaker
Box 150
La Jolla, Calif.

American Poinsettia Society

Mrs. R. E. Gaunt
Box 94
Mission, Texas

American Primrose Society

Mrs. Alice Hills Baylor
Johnson, Vt.

American Rhododendron Society

Mrs. Ruth M. Hansen
3514 N. Russet St.
Portland 17, Ore.

American Rock Garden Society

Mr. E. L. Totten
Hendersonville, N.C.

American Rose Society

Mr. L. G. McLean
4048 Roselea Place
Columbus 14, Ohio

Bromeliad Society, Inc.

Miss Victoria Padilla
647 S. Saltair Ave.
Los Angeles 49, Calif.

Cactus and Succulent Society of America, Inc.

Mr. Scott Haselton
132 West Union St.
Pasadena, Calif.

Gourd Society of America, Inc.

Mrs. Raymond Wheeler
Elmwood, Mass.

Herb Society of America

Mrs. Edmund K. Dawes
300 Massachusetts Ave.
Boston 15, Mass.

Holly Society of America

Mr. Charles A. Young, Jr.
Bergner Mansion
Baltimore 16, Md.

International Geranium Society

Mrs. Vernon Ireland
1413 Bluff Drive
Santa Barbara, Calif.

National Chrysanthemum Society, Inc.

Miss Dorothy P. Tuthill
345 Milton Road
Rye, N.Y.

National Tulip Society

Mr. Felix R. Tyroler
55 West 42nd St.
New York 36, N.Y.

North American Gladiolus Federation

Mrs. Elna Fuller
Main Street
Boylston, Mass.

North American Lily Society

Mrs. Ervin Kulow
Waukesha, Wis.

Palm Society

Mrs. Lucita H. Wait
7229 S.W. 54th Ave.
Miami 43, Fla.

Other National Organizations

American Horticultural Society	1600 Bladensburg Rd., N.E. Washington 2, D.C.
Garden Club of America	598 Madison Ave. New York 22, N.Y.
Men's Garden Clubs of America	Mr. George A. Spader 50 Eaton St. Morrisville, N.Y.
National Council of State Garden Clubs, Inc.	Mrs. Earl H. Hath 4401 Magnolia Ave. St. Louis 10, Mo.
Woman's National Farm and Garden Association	Mrs. W. Donald Miller R.D. #2, Box 194 Havre de Grace, Md.

Books For Further Reference

LANDSCAPING AND PLANNING

The Art of Home Landscaping. Garrett Eckbo. McGraw-Hill, 1956.
Budget Landscaping. Carlton B. Lees. Holt, 1960.
Ladies' Home Journal Book of Landscaping and Outdoor Living. Richard Pratt. Lippincott, 1963.
Landscape for Living. Garrett Eckbo. McGraw-Hill, 1950.
Landscaping Your Own Home. Alice L. Dustan. Macmillan, 1955.
Color and Design for Every Garden. H. Stuart Ortloff and Henry B. Raymore. Barrows, 1951.
Garden Design Illustrated. John A. and Caroll Grant. Univ. of Washington Press, 1954.
Imaginative Small Gardens. Nancy Grasby. Hearthside Press, Inc., 1963.

GENERAL GARDENING

American Home Garden Book. Editors and staff, American Home. M. Evans, Co., 1963.
America's Garden Book. Louise and James Bush-Brown. Scribners, rev. 1958.
Better Homes & Gardens Garden Book. Meredith Press, 1954.
10,000 Garden Questions. F. F. Rockwell (ed.). Doubleday, 1959.
Taylor's Encyclopedia of Gardening. Norman Taylor. Houghton Mifflin, 1961.
How to Landscape Your Own Home. J. I. Rodale and staff. Rodale Books, Inc., 1963.

REGIONAL GARDENING

Gardening in the Lower South. Harold H. Hume. Macmillan, 1954.
Gardening in the South and West. Mrs. Gross R. and M. A. Scruggs (eds.). Doubleday, 1947.
How to Have Good Gardens in the Sunshine States. George W. Kelly. Littleton, Colo. 1957.
Modern Tropical Garden. Loraine E. Kuck and Richard C. Tongg. Tongg Publishing Co., Honolulu, 1955.
The Southern Gardener. Mary B. Stewart. Crager, 1961.
Sunset Western Garden Book. Editors of Sunset Magazine. Lane, 1961.
Your Florida Garden. J. V. Watkins and H. S. Wolfe. Univ. of Florida, 1961.

SPECIAL GARDENS

FRUITS:
Encyclopedia of Fruits, Berries and Nuts. Albert E. Wilkinson. Blakiston, 1945.
Small Fruits for Your Home Garden. J. Harold Clarke. Doubleday, 1958.

GREENHOUSE:
Greenhouse Gardening as a Hobby. James Underwood Crockett. Doubleday, 1961.
The New Greenhouse Gardening for Everyone. Ernest Chabot. Barrows, 1955.
How to Grow Rare Greenhouse Plants. Ernest Chabot. Barrows, 1952.

LAWNS:
The Complete Book of Lawns. F. F. Rockwell and Esther C. Grayson. Doubleday, 1956.
The Lawn Book. Robert W. Schery. Macmillan, 1961.

INDOORS:
Garden in Your House. Ernesta D. Ballard. Harper, 1958.
All About House Plants. Montague Free. Doubleday, 1946.
The World Book of House Plants. Elvin McDonald. World, 1963.

CONTAINERS:
Gardening in Containers. Editors of Sunset Magazine. Lane, 1959.
Outdoor Gardening in Pots and Boxes. George Taloumis. Van Nostrand, 1962.
Window-box Gardening. Henry Teuscher. Macmillan, 1956.

ROCK AND WALL:
Rock Garden Plants. Doretta Klaber. Holt, 1959.

VEGETABLES:
Burrage on Vegetables. Albert C. Burrage. Van Nostrand, 1954.

WATER:
Garden Pools, Water Lilies, and Goldfish. G. L. Thomas, Jr. Van Nostrand, 1958.
Water Gardens. Frances Perry. Penguin, 1962.

SPECIAL PLANTS AND PLANT GROUPS

AFRICAN VIOLETS:
African Violets, Gloxinias and Their Relatives. Harold E. Moore, Jr. Macmillan, 1957.
All about African Violets. Montague Free. Doubleday, 1951.

ANNUALS:
The Complete Book of Annuals. F. F. Rockwell and Esther C. Grayson. Doubleday, 1955.
How to Grow and Use Annuals. Sunset Editorial Staff. Lane, 1962.

BULBS:
The Complete Book of Bulbs. F. F. Rockwell and Esther C. Grayson. Doubleday, 1953.
How to Grow and Use Bulbs. Sunset Editorial Staff. Lane, 1963.
Hardy Garden Bulbs. Gertrude S. Wister. Dutton, 1964.

CACTI AND SUCCULENTS:
The Book of Cacti and other Succulents. Claude Chidamian. Doubleday, 1958.
Desert Plants—Cacti and Succulents. Oliver and Margaret Leese. Transatlantic. 1959.

CAMELLIAS:
Camellia Culture. E. C. Tourje (ed.). Macmillan, 1959.
Camellias in America. Harold H. Hume. McFarland, 1955.
You Can Grow Camellias. Mary Noble and Blanche Graham. Harper, 1962.
The Camellia Book. John Threlkeld. Van Nostrand, 1962.
CHRYSANTHEMUMS:
The Complete Book of Chrysanthemums. Cornelius Ackerson. Doubleday, 1957.
GERANIUMS:
Geraniums for Home and Garden. Helen K. Krauss. Macmillan, 1955.
Geraniums (Pelargoniums) for Windows and Gardens. Helen Van Pelt Wilson. Barrows, 1957.
GROUND COVERS:
Ground Covers. Daniel J. Foley. Chilton Co., 1961.
Ground Cover Plants. Donald Wyman. Macmillan, 1956.
HERBS:
Gardening for Good Eating. Helen M. Fox. Macmillan, 1943.
Magic Gardens. Rosetta E. Clarkson. Macmillan, 1939.
Herbs: Their Culture and Uses. Rosetta E. Clarkson, Macmillan, 1942.
IRIS:
Iris for Every Garden. Sydney B. Mitchell. Barrows, 1960.
Garden Irises. L. F. Randolph. American Iris Society, 1959.
LILACS:
Lilacs for America. John C. Wister (ed.). Swarthmore College, 1953.
LILIES:
The Complete Book of Lilies. F. F. Rockwell and Esther C. Grayson with Jan de Graaf. Doubleday, 1961.
ORCHIDS:
Orchids: Their Botany and Culture. Alex D. Hawkes. Harper, 1961.
Home Orchid Growing. Rebecca T. Northen. Van Nostrand, 1962.
PERENNIALS:
New Perennials Preferred. Helen Van Pelt Wilson. Barrows, 1961.
Contemporary Perennials. Roderick W. Cumming and R. E. Lee. Macmillan, 1960.
The Picture Book of Perennials. Arno and Irene Nehrling. Hearthside Press, 1964.
The Rockwells' Complete Book of Roses. F. F. Rockwell and Esther C. Grayson. Doubleday, 1958.
Anyone Can Grow Roses. Cynthia Westcott. Van Nostrand, 1960.
Climbing Roses. Helen Van Pelt Wilson. Barrows, 1955.
VINES:
Landscaping with Vines. Frances Howard. Macmillan, 1959.
All about Vines and Hanging Plants. Bernice Brilmayer. Doubleday, 1962.

TREES AND SHRUBS

Book of Broadleaf Trees. Frank H. Lamb. Norton, 1939.
The Book of Shrubs. Alfred C. Hottes. Dodd, Mead, revised, 1959.
Climbing Plants and Wall Shrubs. Douglas Bartram. Gifford, London, 1959.
The Concise Encyclopedia of Favorite Flowering Shrubs. Majorie J. Dietz. Doubleday, 1963.
Crab Apples for America. Donald Wyman. American Association of Botanical Gardens and Arboretums, 1955.
The Evergreens. James H. Beale. Doubleday, 1960.
Evergreens for Every State. Katharine M-P. Cloud. Chilton Co., 1960.
Flowering Trees. Robert B. Clark. Van Nostrand, 1963.

The Friendly Evergreens. L. L. Kumlien. Rinehart, 1954.
Handbook of Hollies. Harry William Dengler (ed.). American Horticultural Society, 1957.
Hollies. H. Harold Hume. Macmillan, 1953.
The Home Owner's Tree Book. John S. Martin. Doubleday, 1962.
Maples Cultivated in the United States and Canada. Brian O. Mulligan. American Association of Botanical Gardens & Arboretums, 1958.
Modern Shrubs. E. H. M. Cox and P. A. Cox. Nelson, 1960.
Shrubs and Trees for the Home Landscape. James Bush-Brown. Chilton, 1963.
Shrubs and Trees for the Small Place. P. J. Van Melle. Doubleday, revised, 1955.
Shrubs and Vines for American Gardens. Donald Wyman. Macmillan, 1949.
Tree Care. John M. Haller. Macmillan, 1957.
Tree Maintenance. P. P. Pirone. Oxford, 1959.
Trees for American Gardens. Donald Wyman. Macmillan, 1951.

SOILS AND THEIR MANAGEMENT

A Book about Soils. H. Stuart Ortloff and Henry B. Raymore. Barrows, 1962.
Your Garden Soil. R. Milton Carleton. Van Nostrand, 1961.

TECHNIQUES

Create New Flowers and Plants. John James. Doubleday, 1964.
Growing for Showing. Rudy J. Favretti. Doubleday, 1961.
How to Control Plant Diseases. Malcolm Shurtleff. Iowa State University Press, 1962.
How to Increase Plants. A. C. Hottes. Dodd, Mead, 1956.
Plant Breeding for Everyone. John Y. Beaty. Branford, 1954.
Plant Propagation and Garden Practice. R. C. M. Wright. Criterion, 1956.
Plant Propagation in Pictures. Montague Free. Doubleday, 1957.
Plant Pruning in Pictures. Montague Free. Doubleday, 1961.
Propagating House Plants. Arno and Irene Nehrling. Hearthside, 1962.
Pruning Guide for Trees, Shrubs, and Vines. Tom Stevenson. Robert B. Luce, Inc., 1964.
Pruning Made Easy. Edwin F. Steffek. Holt, 1958.
Simple, Practical Hybridizing for Beginners. D. G. Thomas. St. Martin's Press, 1962.

ARRANGEMENT

Contemporary Flower Arrangement. Rae L. Goldson. Hearthside, revised, 1962.
New Horizons in Flower Arrangement. Myra J. Brooks and others. Barrows, 1961.
Period Flower Arrangement. Margaret Fairbanks Marcus. Barrows, 1952.
The Rockwells' New Complete Book of Flower Arrangement. F. F. Rockwell and Esther C. Grayson. Doubleday, 1960.

Bibliography

America's Garden Book by Louise and James Bush-Brown. Scribners. New York. 1958.
Basic Horticulture by Victor R. Gardner. Macmillan. New York. 1951.

The How and Why of Better Gardening by Laurence Manning. Van Nostrand. New York. 1951.

Entoma. E. H. Fisher, editor. Entomological Society of America. 14th Edition. 1961–62.

Flower Grower, The Home Garden Magazine. New York. 1960–63.

Flower and Garden Magazine. Kansas City, Mo. 1962–63.

Gardener's Directory. J. W. Stephenson, compiler. Doubleday. New York. 1962.

Gardening in the Lower South by H. Harold Hume. Macmillan. New York. 1954.

Gardening in the South and West. Mrs. Gross R. Scruggs, editor. Doubleday. New York. 1947.

Gardening for Fun in California by Jean-Marie Consigny. George Palmer Putnam, Inc. Hollywood, Calif. 1940.

Ground Covers for Easier Gardening by Daniel J. Foley. Chilton Co. Philadelphia. 1961.

Hortus Second Compiled by L. H. Bailey and Ethel Zoe Bailey. Macmillan. New York. 1947.

Modern Gardening by P. P. Pirone. Simon and Schuster. New York. 1952.

Plant Disease Handbook by Cynthia Westcott. Van Nostrand. New York. 1960.

Plant Propagation by R. C. M. Wright. Criterion Books. New York. 1956.

Plant Propagation in Pictures by Montague Free. Doubleday. New York. 1957.

Plant Pruning in Pictures by Montague Free. Doubleday. New York. 1961.

Secret of the Green Thumb by Henry and Rebecca Northen. Ronald Press Co. New York. 1954.

Shrubs and Trees for the Small Place by P. J. Van Melle. Revised by Montague Free. Doubleday. New York. 1955.

Soil Science (Fundamentals of) by C. E. Millar and L. M. Turk. John Wiley & Sons, Inc. New York. 1961.

Standard Cyclopedia of Horticulture, 3 vol. Liberty Hyde Bailey, editor. Macmillan. New York. 1927.

Sunset Magazine. Palo Alto, Calif. 1962–63.

Sunset Western Garden Book, Staff of Sunset Magazine, and Sunset Books, 1961. Editors. Lane Publishing Co. Menlo Park, Calif.

10,000 Garden Questions. F. F. Rockwell, editor. Doubleday. New York. 1959.

The Friendly Evergreens by L. L. Kumlien. D. Hill Nursery Co. Dundee, Ill. 1946.

The Garden Encyclopedia. E. L. D. Seymour, editor. Wise & Co. New York. 1941.

The Gardener's Bug Book by Cynthia Westcott. Doubleday. New York. 1956.

The W. C. System for Producing Healthy, Container-Grown Plants. Kenneth F. Baker, editor. University of California. 1957.

What's New in Gardening by P. P. Pirone. Hanover House. Garden City, N.Y. 1956.

Brochures, bulletins, and leaflets of the agricultural colleges of all state universities, and of the U. S. Department of Agriculture, Washington, D.C.

Index

Acid-loving plants, 31, 210
Acid soils, 18; improvement, 33–34; plants for, 88
Adobe soil, 23, 34
African violets, propagation, 68
Agricultural colleges, 491–94
Agricultural Experiment Stations, 31, 33, 35, 491–94
Air, 45, 47
Air layering, 64–65, *ill*. 64
Airwrap, 65
Ajuga, 194
Akebia, 150
Alkaline-saline soils, improving, 35–36
Alabama: agricultural colleges and experiment station, 491; area, 320; gardens and parks, 477; problems, 407–8
Alaska, 472; agricultural college and experiment station, 491; gardens, 472
Alkaline soils, 18, 24; improving, 34–35
Alkali tolerance: plants, 400; trees, 401; shrubs, 401
Altitude, 77
Alyssum saxatile, 188
Amaryllis, 42, 195, 326; propagation, 66
American Horticultural Society, 497
Ampelopsis, 151
Amur River Privet, 149
Anatomy, plant, *ill*. 38
Andromeda (*Pieris japonica*), *ill*. 145
Angel's-trumpet (*Datura*), 183
Animal pests, 464
Animals—plants, difference, 37, 39
Annuals, 182–87; books on, 499; border with shrub background, *ill*. 183; buying, 184; end-of-season care, 187; fertilizer, 86, 90, 182, 186; fragrant, 203, 459; half-hardy, 451; hardy, 451; hillside garden, *ill*. 184; life cycle, *ill*. 40; list, 452; mulching, 186; pinching back, 187; for pool, 223; pruning, 96; quick growers, 182; soil preparation, 88, 185; sowing and planting, 184–85; for streams, 223; supports, 186–87, *ill*. 186; tender, 452; thinning out, 185–86, *ill*. 185; vegetables, 279; vines, 183–84, 453; water gardens, 223

Apple trees: culture, 284–85; orchards, spraying, 283; pruning, *ill*. 286
Apricot trees, 290
Aquatic plants, 225
Aquilegia, in wall garden, *ill*. 213
Arabis, 192
Arboretums, list, 472–77
Arbors, 127, 152, *ill*. 128, 129; climber roses, 239; grapes, 290; rambler roses, 247
Arborvitaes, 146
Arches, 152
Areas, states, 320–22
Area I: calendar: January, 326–28, February, 332–33, March, 338–39, April, 344, May, 350, June, 356–57, July, 362–63, August, 368–69, September, 372–73, October, 378, November, 384–85, December, 390–91; grass, 169; lawnmaking, 156; spring planting date, 318; states in, 323
Area II: calendar: January, 326–28, February, 332–33, March, 338–39, April, 344–45, May, 351, June, 357–58, July, 362–63, August, 368–69, September, 372–73, October, 378–80, November, 385–86, December, 390–92; grass, 169; lawnmaking, 156; spring planting date, 318; states in, 323; trees, 142, 144, 146
Area III: calendar: January, 326–28, February, 333–34, March, 339–40, April, 345–47, May, 352, June, 357–58, July, 362–64, August, 368–69, September, 372–73, October, 378–80, November, 385–86, December, 390–92; grass, 169; lawnmaking, 156; spring planting date, 318; states in, 323; trees, 142, 144, 146
Area IV: calendar: January, 326–28, February, 333–34, March, 339–40, April, 347, May, 352, June, 358–59, July, 362–64, August, 368–69, September, 372–73, October, 378–80, November, 385–86, December, 390–92; lawnmaking, 156; spring planting date, 318; states in, 323; trees, 142, 144, 146

Area V: calendar: January, 329, February, 335, March, 340–41, April, 347, May, 353, June, 358–59, July, 364–65, August, 370, September, 373–74, October, 380–81, November, 386–87, December, 392–93; lawnmaking, 156; spring planting date, 318; states in, 324

Area VI: calendar: January, 329–30, February, 335–36, March, 341–42, April, 348, May, 354, June, 360, July, 364–65, August, 370, September, 374–75, October, 381–82, November, 387, December, 393; lawnmaking, 156; spring planting date, 318; states in, 324

Arid soils, fertility and fertilizers, 36

Arizona: agricultural college and experiment station, 491; area, 320; gardens and parks, 472, 477; problems, 397–98, 402–3; soil, 398, 399

Arkansas: agricultural college and experiment station, 491; area, 320; gardens and parks, 477; problems, 406

Arrangement, flower, books on, 501

Asexual propagation, 60–68. See Propagation

Asparagus, 275–76; beetle, 276; in flower border, 260

Atlantic seashore, gardening problems, 409–10

Autumn: flowers, 233; rose feeding, 250; shrubs, list, 147

Azaleas, 233; acid-loving, 31; bank garden, 215; chlorosis, 336; fertilizer, 90; layering, 64; propagation, 69; soil for, 34, 88

Bagasse, 254

Bagworms, 327

Balloon-vine (*Cardiospermum halicacabum*), 150

"B and B" (balled and burlapped) stock, 153

Bank gardens, 215; advantages, 204; natural settings for, 217; trailer roses, 239

Banks: sods, 165–66; turf for, 159

Barberry, 149; for hedges, 149; pruning, 99

Bark grafting, 72

Beans, 272, *ill.* 273

Bearberry (*Arctostaphylos uva-ursi*), 175, *ill.* 175

Beech trees, 146

Beetles, 461

Begonias, 199, *ill.* 198; leaf cuttings, *ill.* 61; propagation, 69; seed sowing, 56; tuberous, propagation, 68; window box, *ill.* 235

Bents grasses, 169–70

Bermudagrass, 166, 169, 172–73; mowing, 360

Berries, picking, 295

Berry boxes, 194

Biennials, 187, 453; defined, 453; life cycle, 187, *ill.* 40

Birch trees, 146

Birds: blueberries, 292; feeding, 328; water in patio, 231, 232

Blights, 464

Blossom-set, 269

Blueberries, 292–93; acid soil, 281; location, 281; mulched and watered, 78–83, 369

Bluegrasses, 170

Bog garden, 225; design, 219; plants, 219, 458

Borders, planting, 7. See Flower beds and borders

Borers, 461–62

Boron, 36, 89

Borers, 276

Botanical gardens, list, 472–77

Bougainvillea, 152

Bovung, 28, 164, 269

Box protectors, 126–27. See Protecting plants

Boxwood, 327; pruning, 100

Bracing, 154, 155, *ill.* 140, 141, 154. See Supports

Budding, 71–72, 75, *ill.* 74; time for, 75. See Grafting and budding

Buffalograss, 174

Bugle-weed (*Ajuga reptans*), 175

Bugs, 462

Bulbils, 68

Bulblets, 68

Bulbous plants, 455; propagation, 66; for South, 440–42

Bulbs, 195–99; books on, 499; culture, 195–99; dividing, 63; early, 10; fall-planting, 42; fertilizer, 198; flowering, skipping a year, 119; foliage, care of, 198–99; "forcing," 117–19; fragrant, 202, 460; hardy, replanting, 199; life cycle, *ill.* 42; overwintering, 199; pans, 118; planting trowel, Slim Jim, 196; soil, 196; for South, 440–42; spring-flowering, 233; spring planting, 199–200; tender, 42

"Burning," 86

Bush fruits, 292–93

Bush roses, planting holes, 246

Calendar: how to use, 317–19; lawn schedule, 177

Calendulas, seed sowing, 52

California: agricultural college and experiment stations, 491; area, 320; broadleaved evergreens, 443–44; coniferous trees, 444–45; gardens and parks, 473, 477–79; ornamental deciduous trees, 435; privets, 149; problems, 394–98; soil, 399; vines, 438–39

Callas, 199

Cambium layer (bark), 71–72

Camellias: propagation, 69; soil, 34, 88

Camomile (*Cotula squalida*), 176

Canada Bluegrass, 170

Cane fruits, 294–95, 369

Carpetgrass, 173

Carson, Rachel, 92

Castor-oil bean (*Ricinus*), 183

Catalogs, 326

Centipedegrass, 166, 173

Central Plains, gardening problems, 404

Cherry trees, 146

Chestnut soils, 24

Chinese junipers, pruning, 100

Chionodoxa, 175, 195

Chlorosis, 364, 464

Chrysanthemums, 80–84, 194, 233; books on, 500; for very cold climates, 432; dividing, 63; pruning, 96; special bed, 10

Clay or plastic pots, in coldframe, 115

Clay soils, 16, 22, 193; acidifying, 34

Clematis vines, 152

Climbing roses, 150, 152, 239, *ill.* 127, 242; on greenhouse, 302; planting holes, 246; pruning, 252, *ill.* 97; supports, 128, 247, *ill.* 127, 250

Clover, 22, 27, 86, 163, 171–72; White Dutch, 112

Coal, 23

Coldframes and hotbeds, 77, 107 ff, *ill.* 108, 109, 328; attention to, 110; building frame, 111–14, *ill.* 112; bulbs for indoors, 117–19; cleaning, 115–16; combination "super frame," *ill.* 112; drainage, 111; frames, kind, 110; hotbed, 116–17; lettuce, 267; location, 111; management, 114–16; melons, 276; patio garden, 233; placement, 178; removable divider, 111; roses, 247; sash, 110; shading, 116, *ill.* 116; soil for frames, 114; spacing in, 115; temperature, 307; tomatoes, 270; vegetable plants, 263; ventilation, 334, *ill.* 117

Colleges, agricultural, 491–94

Color: evergreens, 144; in flower beds and borders, 190; shrubs, 147

Colorado: agricultural college and experiment station, 491; area, 320; gardens and parks, 473, 479; problems, 402–3, 404

Columbia River Basin, 36

Composition planter trays, 55–56

Composition box, *ill.* 58

Composition pots, 311

Compost, 86; for lawn, 163–65; storing, 302

Compost heap, 27–30, 86, *ill.* 28, 29; placement, 178; weeds and, 265

Composts for the Home Grounds, 29

Connecticut: agricultural college and experiment stations, 491; area, 320; gardens and parks, 473, 479; problems, 405–6

Conservatory, 299

Conservo, 112

Control of conditions, in seed sowing, 50–51

Copper beech trees, 141

Coral bells (*Heuchera*), in wall garden, 215, *ill.* 213

Cormous plants, propagation, 66, 68

Corms, for the South, 440–42

Corn. *See* Sweet corn

"Corn belt," 404

Cosmos, 186, 187

Cotoneaster horizontalis, 150

Cottonseed meal, 34

County agricultural agent, 77, 139, 164, 166, 275, 281, 304

Cover crops, 36; alkali tolerance, 400; salinity tolerance, 401

Cowpeas, 86

Crab trees, flowering, 146

Creeping Bents, 170

Creeping fig (*Ficus pumila*), 151

Crested wheatgrass, 174

Crimson Pygmy barberry, 149

Crocking, 311–12; *ill.* 311

Crocuses, 195; "forcing," 118

"Crowns," 63

Cucumber beetle, 276

Cultivars, 60

Cultivation, 80; necessity of, 124; rock garden, 214; tools for, 124; tree fruits, 284–92; vegetables, 265–67; of vines, 152–53

Cup-and-saucer vine (*Cobaea scandens*), 150, 183, 186

Currants, 293

Cutting garden, 178, *ill.* 179; -patio garden, 230

Cuttings, 68–69, *ill.* 62; hardwood, 71; keeping, 69; leaf, 68, *ill.* 61, 62; root, 68; rooting media, 69–71; softwood stem, 69; stem, 68

Cyclamen, 304

Daffodils, 195, 200–1, 233, *ill.* 197; dividing, 63; foliage, 198; "forcing," 118; life cycle, 42; propagation, 66, *ill.* 66; replanting, 199
Dahlias, 187, 199; propagation, 68; pruning, 96; special bed, 10
Daisy, 194; English, 187; Shasta, 199
Damp-off diseases, 55
Day-lilies, 192, 194
Dead wood, removal of, 96
Deciduous flowering shrubs, list, 147
Deciduous trees, 142; list, 146
Delaware: agricultural colleges and experiment station, 491; area, 320; gardens and parks, 473, 479; problems, 405–6
Delphinium, 188; pruning, 96
Desert living, 399–400
Desert soils, 24. *See* Adobe
Dianthus, 188
Dichondra carolinensis, 176
Dieffenbachia, air layering, 64
Disbudding, 96
Diseased plants, pruning, 96–97
Diseases, 47–48, 76, 91, 464; black spot, 246, 464; of currants and gooseberries, 293; damping-off, 55; fruit, 262–64; fruit trees, 283; lawn, 465; mildew, 246, rhizoctonia, 55, 312; rose petals, decayed, 254; tomato, 270, 272, 466; virus, 466
Disinfectants, seedlings, 56–57
Display gardens, 477–90
District of Columbia: area, 320; gardens and parks, 473, 479
Division, of plants, 194
Dogwood trees, 146; flowering, *ill.* 144
Domestic or Italian ryegrass, 171
Double digging, 20, *ill.* 21
Drainage, 20–21, *ill.* 22; alkaline-saline soils, 35; coldframes, 111; lawn, 162–63; pools in winter, 225; rock garden, 206; rose garden, 244, 245–46; for seed sowing, 52; tile, installing, *ill.* 22; vegetable garden, 259
Driconure, 28, 164, 269
Drought, mulching, 47
Dryness, 47
Dry well, *ill.* 162
Dusting: application, 92; equipment, 129–30, *ill.* 130; roses, 255
"Dust mulch," 79
Dwarf fruit trees, 284, *ill.* 285
Dwarf junipers, pruning, 100

Edging roses, 239
Elm, 146; growth rate, 138
Emerald Zoysia, 174

England: gardens, 87; John Innes mixtures, 55; Malling, 284; topiary work, 98
English daisies (*Bellis perennis*), 187
English ivy (*Hedera helix*), 151, 176
Entertainment, planning area for, 8
Erosionet, 166
Espaliered fruits, 98, *ill.* 99; apricots, 290; nectarines, 290; trees, 230
Espaliered plants, pruning, 152–53
Europe: topiary work, 98; window boxes, 233
Evaporation: mulching and, 79; *Wilt-Pruf* spray, 127
Evergreens: bank garden, 215; bracing, 154, 155; color, 144; -deciduous trees, difference, 142; importance of, *ill.* 10; patio garden, 229; planting, 339; pruning, 99; rock garden, 206, 208; for screens and hedges, list, 148; snow, 327; trees, list, 146
Experimental gardening, 46 n
"Eye," in pruning, 106

Feeding of plants, 85–86; in coldframe, 115
Fences, 7, 127, 128–29, *ill.* 127
Fertilizers, 17, 85; annuals, 86, 90, 182, 186; application, 86, 90, liquid form, 130; for arid soils, 36; bulbs, 198; "complete," 17–18, 31, 85; formulas, and recommended uses, 90; greenhouse seedlings, 309, 310; inorganic, 85–86; lawn, 90, 164, 168–69; liquid, 39, 130; nitrogenous, 85; nutrients contents, 90; organic, 85–86, -base, 90, 193; percentage in "complete," 85; in planting hole, 153; reaction, 90; roses, 90, 244–45, 250; and seed distributor, 133, 164, *ill.* 160; shrubs, 86, 90; storing, 302; strawberries, 296; trees, 90; type to use, 88; for vegetables, 86, 90, 264
Fescues, 171
Fieldstone, 210
Fig tree, 292
Fireblight, 283
Fir trees, 146
Fish, in pools, 225–26
Flats, 53, 55, 184, 264, *ill.* 54; setting out plants from, 194
Floribunda rose, *ill.* 240
Florida: agricultural colleges and experiment station, 491; area, 320; gardens and parks, 473–74, 479; problems, 407–8
Flower beds and borders, 10, 178–203; annuals, 182–87, *ill.* 183, 184; backgrounds, 179, 182; biennials, 187–88,

ill. 188; borders: edging roses, 239, placement, *ill.* 180; bulbs, 195–99, *ill.* 196, 197, 198, tender, 199–200; daffodils, 200–1; evening fragrance, 203; fragrant gardens, 202–3; herbs, 201–2; lettuce in, 268; long flowering season, 182; number, 182; perennials, 188–89, *ill.* 189; placement, 178, *ill.* 180, of flowers, 190; planning, 182, border, 189–92; "plunging border," *ill.* 230; preparation, 193–95; setting out plants, 193–94; soil preparation, 182, 193, *ill.* 181, depth of, 88; tomatoes in, *ill.* 271; tulips, 200–1; vegetables in border, 260
Flower pots, 53
Flowers: cool-house subjects, 304; overcrowded, 281. *See* Annuals, Biennials, Flower Beds and borders, Perennials *and* Plants
Foliage, roses, 245–46
Foliar feeding, 39
Food (plant), 45–46, 85–86
"Forcing" bulbs, 117–19
Forget-me-not (*Myosotis*), 187
Forsythia: *suspensa,* 150; dividing, 63; layering, 64; pruning, 99–100
Foundation planting, 9; lists of plants, 413, 416; shrubs, 327
Fountains, in patio, 231
Foxgloves, 188
Fragrant gardens, 202–3
Fragrant plants, 458–60
Frames: for seed sowing, 51, *ill.* 51; soil for, 52. *See* Coldframes and hotbeds
Freezing, vegetables, 267, 275
Fruit gardens: books, 499; pests and diseases, 462–64; planning, 13–14. *See* Fruits *and* Fruit trees
Fruits, 280; alkali tolerance, 400; blackberries, 294–95; blueberries, 292–93; bush, 292–93; cane, 294–95; culture, 280; currants, 293; dewberries, 294; frozen, 280; gooseberries, 293; grapes, 290–92, *ill.* 291; location, 281; loganberries, 294; nitrogen deficiency, 89; overcrowded, 281; pests, and diseases, 462–63; planting, 281–82; raspberries, 294, *ill.* 288, 295; salinity tolerance, 401; soil, 281; space, 281; strawberries, 295–98, *ill.* 289, 297, 298; tree, 281 (*See* Tree fruits *and* Fruit trees); why cultivate?, 280
Fruit trees: apple, 284–85; bloom, 283; diseases, 283; espaliering, 230; fig, 292; grafting, 327; harvesting, 283–84; mulching, 283; peach, 287, 290, *ill.* 287, 290; pear, 285; pests, 283; plum, 285, 287; protecting, 282; pruning, 96, 284, *ill.* 286; "scaffold," 284; spraying, 283, 472, and schedule, 472; storing, 283–84; "whips," 287
Fungicides, 92–93, 469–70; precautions, 93

Garden Club of America, 497
"Garden consultant," 4
Garden house, 7
Gardenia, 233, 327; air layering, 64
Gardening: books, 498; defined, 76; greenhouse 306 (*See* Greenhouse); "mobile," 233; organic, 89; problems, 394–410; under glass (*See* Coldframes *and* Greenhouse)
Garden roses, 239. *See* Roses *and* Rose garden
Gardens: bank, 215, 217; bog, 225; botanical, list, 472–77; clean-up, 378, 379; cutting, 178, *ill.* 179; display, 477–90; fragrant, 202–3; herb, 201–2; marsh, 225; patio, 227; pests, and control, 461–62; plan, *ill.* 5; planning area for, 6; rock, 204–14, 217; rose, 237–56; special, planning, 6; temperature for sowing, 307; vegetable, 257–79; wall, 215–17; water, 218, 219, 225–26
Gas-plant (*Dictamnus*), 188
Gates, 127, 128
Georgia: agricultural colleges and experiment stations, 491; area, 320; gardens and parks, 274, 480; problems, 407
Geraniums: dividing, *ill.* 63; propagation, 69
Germination. *See* Seed germination
Gladiolus, 199; cormlets (propagation), 68, storing, 326; diseases, 464; thrip, 48, 348
Gooseberries, 293
Grading, lawn preparation, 158–62
Grafting, 71–72, 75; and budding, 71–75; time for, 72; fruit trees, 327
Gramagrasses, 174
Grandiflora rose, *ill.* 241
Granite, 210
Grapes, 290–92, *ill.* 291; vines, mulch, 334, pruning, 328, *ill.* 291
Grass: area affinity, 169; cool climate, 169; seed, 164, 169; substitute, *ill.* 175; warm-climate, 169
Grasses: alkali tolerance, 400; for cool climates, 169–72; cool-weather schedule, 177; dry land, 174; ground cover substitutes, 174–76; hot climate, 166, 172–74; mixtures, 172; "nurse," 169; salinity tolerance, 401; types, 158; warm-weather schedule, 177
Grass seed, 164, 169

Great Northern Plains, gardening problems, 403–4
Greenhouse, 107, *ill*. 300; books on, 499; construction, 299; -conservatory difference, 299; crocking, 311–12; curved-eave, *ill*. 300; cutting bed, 313; dual-purpose, 299; equipment, 305–6; even-span or lean-to, 300–2, *ill*. 301; function determines design, 302; "growing" or construction, 299; for "growing" or "enjoyment," 299; heating, 302–4; home, 299–313; "lodge," 308; melons, 276; "misting" system, 70; operations, 306–7; patio garden, 230, 233; potting and repotting, 311; prefabs, 299; propagation box, 307; propagation by cuttings, 312–13; seed sowing, 307–13; shade, 305; spraying, 312; starting seedlings, 306–7, *ill*. 306; vegetable plants, 263, 264; ventilation, 304; water, 305–6; work space, 302–6
Green manures, 26–27, 86, 89, 163, 187, *ill*. 26; for acidity, 33; crops, 22, 26–27
Ground covers, 174–76, 189; books on, 500; for very cold climates, 425; Erosionet, 166; hardy evergreen, list, 425; for seashore, 450
Gulf Coast, gardening problems, 407–8
Gumbo soils, 23, 24, 34
Gypsum, 35

Hardwood cuttings, 71
Hardy border, 9–10
Hardy bulbs, "forcing," in coldframe, *ill*. 118
Hardy shrubs, list, 412–23
Hardy trees, list, 412–23
Harmodin, 65
Hawaii: agricultural college and experiment station, 491; gardens and parks, 474, 480
Hawthorn trees, 146
Heat, 47; greenhouse, 302, 304; water and, 77–78
Heaving, of plants, 328, 332
Hedge plants: for very cold climate, 429; for the South, 436–37. *See also* Hedges
Hedge roses, 239; for very cold climate, 432
Hedges, 7; asparagus, 276; cost, 149–50; hardy shrubs and evergreens, list, 148; hedge roses, 239; instead of fences, 128–29; pruning, 99; shrubs for, 149–50; yew, *ill*. 12
"Heeling in" nursery stock, *ill*. 282
Hemerocallis, 188

Hemlock trees, 146
Herb garden, 364; plan for, *ill*. 202; vegetables in, 260; walling in, 215
Herbicides, 92–93, 470–71; fertilizer and seed distributor, 133, *ill*. 160
Herbs, 201–2; books on, 500; fragrant, 460
Heuchera, 188, 192
Hicks' Yew, 149
Hilling: corn, 275, *ill*. 274; roses, *ill*. 255; strawberries, 297, 298
Holes, planting, 153; preparation, 88
Hollies, soil for, 34
Home greenhouse, 299–313
Honeysuckle, 150
Hormodin, 70
Horse-chestnut trees, 146
Hoses: "fog" nozzle, 56, 57, 305, 309; mist spray, 155, 165, 193, 263, 308; perforated, 165, for rose garden, 246; shut-off, 305
Hotbed, 107, 116–17; temperature, 307; vegetables in, 264. *See* Coldframes and hotbeds
Hotkaps, 84, 125, 194, 276, 351, *ill*. 126
Houseplants, 327, 333
Humus, 22, 36, 78, 86, 182; defined, 17; "friable" soil, 17; fruits, 281; lawn, 163; maintenance, 18; organic materials, 16; rose garden, 245. *See* Compost heap
Hyacinths, 195; "forcing," 118
Hybrid tea roses, *ill*. 240
Hydrangea, climbing (*H. petiolaris*), 98, 152

Iberis, 188; wall garden, *ill*. 213
Idaho: agricultural college and experiment station, 492; area, 321; gardens and parks, 474, 480; problems, 402–3
Illinois: agricultural college and experiment station, 492; area, 321; gardens and parks, 474, 480–81; problems, 404–6
Indiana: agricultural college and experiment station, 492; area, 321; gardens and parks, 474, 481; problems, 405–6
Injured plants, pruning, 96–97
Inoculants, seedlings, 56–57
Inorganic fertilizers, 85–86
Insecticides, 92–93, 467–69; precautions, 93
Insects, 76; currants, 293; gooseberries, 293
Iowa: agricultural college and experiment station, 492; area, 321; gardens and parks, 474, 481; problems, 403–5

Iris, 188, 194; bearded, 362, for very cold climates, 433; books on, 500; dividing, 63
Irish junipers, pruning, 100
Iron sulfate, 35
Irrigation, vegetable garden, 84
Ismenes, 199; propagation, 66

Japanese Euonymus (hardwood), cuttings, *ill.* 62
Japanese-spurge. *See* Pachysandra
John Innes mixtures, 55
Juniper trees, 146

Kalmias, soil, 88
Kansas: agricultural college and experiment station, 492; arboretum, 474; area, 321; gardens and parks, 481; problems, 404–5
Kentucky: agricultural colleges and experiment station, 492; area, 321; gardens and parks, 482; problems, 405–7
Kentucky Bluegrass, 170
Knot gardens, 201, *ill.* 201
Korean Lawngrass (*Zoysia japonica*), 174

Laburnum trees, 146
Landscape architect, 4
Landscaping: books on, 498; expensive features, 153; flower beds and borders, 178; trees, shrubs, vines: planting first, 137, value of, 137
Larch trees, 142, 146
Larkspur, 186, 187
Lawn, 156–77; books on, 499; "chocolate icing" layer, 157; clippings, 168; cover crop, 163; defined, 76; diseases, 369, 465; drainage, 162–63; equipment, 131–33; example, 157; feeding, 168–69; fertilizer, 90, 164, 168–69; grading, 158, 162; grass, kinds, 169–74, 177; grasses, types, 158; ground cover as grass substitutes, 174–76; humus for, 163; laying out areas, 162; lime for, 168; maintenance, 168–69; making, steps in, *ill.* 159, 160; materials and equipment, *ill.* 158; mowing, 168; nitrogen for, 85; planning area for, 6; plugging, 167, *ill.* 166; preliminary preparations, 157–63; primary work, 156; purpose, 156; remade, *ill.* 161; renovation, 167–68; "scalping," 163; seeding, 164–65; sodding, 165, 166–67; soil, 163, depth of preparation, 88; sprigging, 167; status symbol, 131; stripping, 167; summer, 156; surface soil—the "chocolate icing" layer, 163–65; type, 156–57; watering equipment, *ill.* 165; winter, 156. *See* Grasses
Layering, 64
Leaching, 24, 35
Leaf cuttings, 68, *ill.* 61, 62
"Leaf scorch," 89
Legume Aid, 56
Lemmons Alkaligrass, 174
Lettuce, 258, 267–68, *ill.* 268, 310
Life cycle, of plants, 40–42
Light, 46, 46 n, 47; seedlings, 57
Lilacs: mildew, 48; pruning, 96
Lilies, 195, *ill.* 191; germination, 50; life cycle, 42; pool, 219; propagation, 68, *ill.* 67; "scaling," *ill.* 67; special bed, 10
Lime: for lawns, 168; -loving plants, 210; sulfur, 35
Limestone, 210; raw ground for acidity, 33
Linden trees, 146
Lippia canescens, 176
Liriope muscari, 176
Loam, 16
Locomotion, planning, 6
Locust trees, 146
Long-range plan, 4
Louisiana: agricultural colleges and experiment station, 492; area, 321; gardens and parks, 474, 482; problems, 406–8
Lupines, 199; pruning, 96
Lythrum, 199

Magnolia *stellata, ill.* 197
Magnolia trees, 78, 146
Maine: agricultural college and experiment station, 492; area, 321; gardens and parks, 474–75, 482; problems, 405–6
Malling, 284
Manillagrass (*Zoysia matrella*), 174
Manures, 22, 86; commercial, 28; cow, for rose garden, 244–45; green, 22, 26–27, 33, 86, 89, 163, 187, *ill.* 26; for improving soil, 25–26; substitutes, 26
Maple trees, 78, 146; roots, 228
Marigolds, 183, 186; seed sowing, 52–53
Marsh garden, 225
Maryland: agricultural colleges and experiment station, 492; area, 321; gardens and parks, 482; problems, 405–6
Massachusetts: agricultural college and experiment station, 492; area, 321; gardens and parks, 482; problems, 405–6
Master plan, 4–6

Meadowgrass, 170–71
Melon boxes, *ill.* 126
Melon lice, 276
Melons, 276, *ill.* 277
Men's Garden Clubs of America, 497
Merion Bluegrass, 157, 165, 169, 170
Mertensia, 198
Michigan: agricultural college and experiment station, 492; area, 321; gardens and parks, 475, 482–83; problems, 405–6
Micro-climates, 141; areas, 46–47; forming, 77–78
Mildew, 283, 369
Milorganite, 164, 264, 266
Miniature roses, 243–44, *ill.* 243
Minnesota: agricultural college and experiment station, 492; arboretum, 475; area, 321; gardens and parks, 483; problems, 403–4
Mississippi: agricultural colleges and experiment station, 492; area, 321; gardens and parks, 483; problems, 407–8
Missouri: agricultural colleges and experiment station, 493; area, 321; botanical garden, 475; gardens and parks, 483; problems, 404–6
Mist spraying, 263; trees, transplants, 155
"Mobile" gardening, 233
Model, of water garden, 219
Moisture, 78–84; conservation of, 78 ff; evaporation rate, 84; mulching, 78–80; requirements, measuring, 81; seedlings, 57. *See* Water
Montana: agricultural college and experiment station, 493; area, 321; gardens and parks, 483; problems, 402–4
Moonflower (*Ipomaea bona-nox*), 150, 152, 183
Morning-glory, 183, 186
Mountain area problems, 402–3
Mountain-ash trees, 146
Muck soils, 23
Mugo pine, 149; pruning, 100
Mulberry, propagation, 71
Mulch: annuals, 185; application, 80; consistency, 80; defined, 79; "dust," 79; grass clippings, 168; rose garden, 246; for roses, 254; summer, 78–80, 368
Mulching: annuals, 186; defined, *ill.* 79; drought and, 47; fruit trees, 283; materials, 22; moisture, 78–79; rock garden, 214; roses, 254; transplants, 155; vegetable garden, 266; winter storage of vegetables, 266–67
Muscari, 175
Myosotis, 199, *ill.* 306

Nasturtiums, 184; black aphids, 357
National Council of State Garden Clubs, Inc., 497
Natural conditions, and special gardens, 9
Nature, pruning, 94, 96
Nebraska: agricultural college and experiment station, 493; arboretum, 475; area, 321; gardens and parks, 483; problems, 403–4
Nectarine trees, 290
Neutral (or alkaline) soil, 18; plants for, 88
Nevada: agricultural college and experiment station, 493; area, 321; gardens and parks, 483; problems, 402–3
New Hampshire: agricultural college and experiment station, 493; arboretum, 475; area, 321; gardens and parks, 483; problems, 405–6
New Jersey: agricultural college and experiment station, 493; arboretum, 475; area, 321; gardens and parks, 483–84; problems, 405–6
New Mexico: agricultural college and experiment station, 493; area, 321; gardens and parks, 484; problems, 397–98, 402; soil, 397
New York: agricultural college and experiment stations, 493; area, 321; gardens and parks, 475, 484–85; problems, 405–6
Nitricin, 56
Nitrogen, 30, 45, 85; deficiency, symptoms of, 89; lawn fertilizer, 169
Nod-O-Gen, 56
North Carolina: agricultural colleges and experiment station, 493; arboretum, 475; area, 322; gardens and parks, 485
North Dakota: agricultural college and experiment station, 493; area, 322; problems, 403–4
Nozzles, 305, *ill.* 308; for coldframes, 115, 305; "fog," 56, 57, 305, 309; mist spray, 155, 165, 193, 263, 308; "pressure breaker," 305; sprinkler, 305; three hose, *ill.* 308
Nursery, home, 138–39
Nursery stock: care of, 153, 155; "heeling in," *ill.* 282
Nutrient deficiency, symptoms of, 89

Oak trees, 146
Oats, 22
Ohio: agricultural college and experiment station, 493; arboretum, 476; area, 322; gardens and parks, 486; problems, 405–6

Oklahoma: agricultural colleges and experiment station, 493; area, 322; gardens and parks, 487; problems, 406; soil, 398

Old age, 48

Open ditches, 20–22

Orchard, spraying, 471–72

Oregon: agricultural college and experiment station, 493; arboretum, 476; area, 322; gardens and parks, 487; problems, 394–96

Organic fertilizers, 85–86

Organic gardening, 89

Organic materials: plus factor, 18; in soil building, 16–17

Organic soils, 25

Oriental poppies, 188, 194, 199; dividing, 63; propagation, 68

Oscillating rain machine, 84, *ill*. 82

Oscillating sprayers, 165, 263

Outdoor living: paved terrace for, *ill*. 228; planning area for, 6

Oxydendron trees, 146

Pachysandra terminalis, 176, *ill*. 175

Panodrench, 308, 312

Pansies, 187

Parks, 477–90

Passion-flower, 152

Passion vine, 150

Patio: planning, 232–33; planting border, *ill*. 232; view, importance of, 232–33; walling in, 215. *See* Patio garden

Patio garden: coldframe, 233; defined, 227; greenhouse, 233; plants for, 231; "plunging border," *ill*. 230; trees, 227–28; vines, 230; water features, 231–33

Paulownia trees, 146

Peach trees, 287, 290, *ill*. 287, 290; harvesting, 290; pruning, *ill*. 290

Pear trees, 285

Peatmoss, 22, 23, 26, 182, 282; pulverized, 69

Peat pots, 311; in coldframe, 115; snapdragons, *ill*. 310

Peat soils, 22–23

Pennsylvania: agricultural college and experiment station, 493; arboretum, 476; area, 322; gardens and parks, 476, 487–88; problems, 405–6

Peonies, 188, 194–95

Perennial ryegrass, 171

Perennials, 188–89, 198–99, 454; books on, 500; border, *ill*. 188, 189, color distribution, 190, obtaining plants, 190–92, spacing, 192; characteristics, 190; crowding, 47; dividing, 194, *ill*. 192, time for, 63; fertilizer, 86, 90; fragrant,

202, 459; growing from seed, 192; life cycle, *ill*. 41; for pool, 223; pruning, 96; replanting, 194; "run out," *ill*. 192; soil preparation, depth of, 88; for stream, 223; vegetables, 278–79; for water garden, 223; yew hedge, *ill*. 12

Periwinkle (*Vinca minor*), 176

Perlite, 69

Pesticides, 467–69

Pests, 47–48, 91; animal, 464; asparagus beetle, 276; fruit, 262–64; of fruit trees, 282, 283; garden, and control, 461–62; vegetable, 276

Petunias, seed sowing, 56

Philodendron, air layering, 64

Phlox, 188, 199; dividing, 63; mildew on, 48

Phosphorus, 30, 45, 85; deficiency, symptoms of, 89

Pillar roses, supports, 247

Pine trees, 146

Pitch pine, 139

Planning, 3–14; books on, 498; carefulness in, 14; important areas, 6–9; long-range, 4; master plan, 4–6; to scale, 326; special gardens, 9–14

Planter box, "built in," *ill*. 234

Planting: "B and B" (balled and burlapped) stock, 153; fruits, 281–82; holes, size, 152; potting shed, 302; preparation for, 86–89; shrubs, 153–55; soil preparation, 88–89; spring, dates, 320–23; trees, 153–55; vines, 153–55

Planting holes, 153, *ill*. 154; roses, 246

Plants: acid-loving, 210; adaptability of, 39; air, 45; alkali tolerance, 400; anatomy, 37–43, *ill*. 38; animals, difference, 37, 39; aquatic, 225; asexual reproduction, 43–45, methods, *ill*. 44; bog, 219; bog garden, 225; elements necessary, 17, 45–47; enemies, 76–77; environment, 76; food, 45–46; fragrant, 458–60; growth of, 45–47, deterrents to, 47–48; keeping vigorous and healthy, 76–93; leaves, 42–43; life cycle, *ill*. 40; light, 46, 46 n; lime-loving, 210; marsh garden, 225; miniature pool, 231–32; parts, 37; patio garden, 228–29, 231; pot, 184, 243, 270, 296–98; for pool, 223; reproduction, 43, asexual, 43–45; requirements, 76; rock garden, 206, 208–9, 212–13; roots, 37, 39; salinity tolerance, 401–2; seeds, 43; special and groups, books on, 499–500; stems, 39, 42; for streams, 223; submarine culture, 46 n; surplus, 193; temperature, 46–47; training, objectives of, 98–100, 194; trunks, 39,

42; wall garden, 215; water, 45; for water garden, 223, 225; window boxes, 233, 235
Plant societies, 495–96
Plant stake, 187
Play, planning area for, 6–8
Pliofilm, 229
Plugging, 167
Plumbago larpentiae, 188
Plum trees, 285, 287
Pole beans, *ill.* 273
Pools, 218, *ill.* 221, 222; annuals, 223; artificial, *ill.* 224; construction, 219, 223; design, 219; garden with, *ill.* 221; lily, 219; location, 219; looking-glass in rose garden, *ill.* 238; miniature, plants for, 231–32; mirror, 231; in patio, 231; perennials, 223; plants, 223; small, *ill.* 222; -stream combination, 219; swimming, 218 n; type, 219; -water garden difference, 225; water supply, 224–25; winter care, 225; woodland, 219
Poplar trees, 78
Post-and-chain support, 128, 247, *ill.* 250
Post-and-rail fence, 128, *ill.* 127
Potash, 31, 45; for roses, 250
Potassium, 30–31, 85
Potatoes, propagation, 68
Pot plants, 184; "crocking" for, *ill.* 311; miniature roses, 243; strawberries, 296–97, 298; tomatoes, 270
Potting, greenhouse, 311
Potting bench, 302, *ill.* 303
Potting shed, 7, 302, *ill.* 303; uses, 302
Power tools, 121
Prairie: gardening problems, 404–5; soils, 24–25
Primroses, 304
Privet(s), 149; California, 149; for hedges, 149; pruning, 99
Problems, gardening, 394–410; Atlantic Seashore, 409–10; Central Plains, 404; desert living, 399–402; East Central states, 405–6; Great Northern Plains, 403–4; Gulf Coast, 407–8; heartland prairie, 404–5; intermountain, 402–3; lower South, 407–8; mid-Atlantic states, 405–6; mountain, 402–3; North Central states, 405–6; Northeast, 405–6; South Central states, 406; Southwest, 397–99; upper South, 407; West Coast, 394–97
Propagation: asexual: air layering, 64–65, cuttings, 68–75, dividing, 60, 63, layering, 64, natural division, rooting media, 69–71; budding, 71–72, 75; by cuttings, in greenhouse, 312–13; divid-

ing, 60, 63, time for, 63; grafting, 71–72, 75; methods (*See* Propagation methods)
Propagation box, 70–71, 307; *ill.* 70
Propagation methods: asexual, 60–68; cuttings, 68–69; grafting and budding, 71–75; growing from seed, 49–57; kinds, 49; rooting media, 69–71; seedlings, starting, 57–60; sowing, 51–57
Protecting plants, 194; mechanically, 125–27; melons, 276; patio plants, 229; rock garden, 206, 208
Pruning: anticipation, 106; equipment, 100–3; espaliered plants, 152–53; to forestall injury, 97; fruit trees, 283, 284, *ill.* 286; light, 106, ill. 122; lupines, 96; objectives, 94–97; rock garden, 214; roses, 96, 246, 251–54, *ill.* 97, 253; shrubs, 96, 99–100, 153, 155; techniques, 103–6; tools, 100–3, *ill.* 101, 102; trees, 96, 153, 155; vines and other climbers, 150, 152, 153, 155; wounds, 106. *See* Training
Puerto Rico: agricultural college and experiment station, 494
Purple beech trees, 141
Puschkinias, 195
Pyracantha c. lalandi, 150
Pyrethrum, 89

Quality, of seeds, 50

Rainfall–water application ratio, *ill.* 82
Rambler roses: pruning, 252, 254; supports, 247
Raspberries, 294, *ill.* 288, 295
Recipes: GrayRock French dressing, 268; green corn fritters, 275
Reclaimed desert areas: ornamental trees, 445–46; shade trees, 445–46; shrubs, 446–47
Red fescue, 171
Redtop, 170
Regional gardening, books, 498
Renewing old plants, pruning, 96
Replanting, 194
Repotting: greenhouse, 311; potting shed, 302; seedlings, 59–60
Reproduction, 43; asexual, 43–45
Rest, planning area for, 6, 7
Retaining wall, 215, *ill.* 216
Rhizoctonia, 55, 312
Rhizomes, 194; for the South, 440–42
Rhode Island: agricultural college and experiment station, 494; area, 322; gardens and parks, 488; problems, 405–6
Rhododendrons: acid-loving, 31; fertilizers, 90; soil for, 34, 88

Rhubarb, in flower border, 260
Rind grafting, 72
Rock garden, 4, 204–14, *ill.* 11, 205, 207, 208; advantages, 204; annuals, 182; books on, 499; building, 210–12, *ill.* 211, 212; culture, 214; construction, 209–10; drainage, 206; location, 206, 208; mulching, 214; natural setting, 206, 217, *ill.* 208; plan, 13, 209, *ill.* 209; plants, 206, 455–57, selecting, 212–13; rocks, 210; soil, 210; steps, *ill.* 212; three dimensional, 209; top, 212; trailer roses, 239; watering, 214; winter care, 214
Rocky Mountains: deciduous trees, 426; shrubs, 426
Rodents, 464
Root cuttings, 68
Root division, 60, 63, *ill.* 60
Rooting media, 69–71
Rooting, stem or leaf cuttings, 43
Rootone, 56, 64, 65, 70
Roots, 37, 39
Rose garden, 237–56; drainage, 20, 244, 245–46; mulch, 246; plan, 239; planting, 246–50; preparing, 244–46; pruning, 251–54; semiformal, moderate-sized, *ill.* 238; site, 244; soil, 244, preparation, 244–45; self-watering system, *ill.* 245; spring care, 254–56; type, 239–44; walling in, 215; watering system, 245–46, *ill.* 245
Roses: bank garden, 215; black spot, 348; bush, 246; cancer, 97; climbing, 150, 152, 239, 246, 247, 252, *ill.* 127, 242, on greenhouse, 302; planting holes, 246, pruning, 252, support for, 128, 247, *ill.* 127, 250; cutting, 254; dividing, 63; edging, 239; feeding, 250; fertilizer, 90, 244–45, 250; floribundas, *ill.* 240; garden, 239; grandiflora, *ill.* 241; hedge, 239, for very cold climate, 432; hilling up, 255–56, *ill.* 255; hybrid teas, *ill.* 240; "knob" or "graft," 246–47; "knuckle," 247; miniature, 243–44, *ill.* 243; mulching, 254; pillar, supports for, 247; planting, 246–50, *ill.* 248–49; planting holes, 246; popularity, 237; potash for, 250; propagation, 69; pruning, 96, 246, 251–54, *ill.* 97, 253; rambler, 247, 252, 254; shrub, 237, 244, 246, *ill.* 242, for very cold climates, 429, layering, 64; single, *ill.* 241; soil preparation, depth of, 88; special bed, 10; spraying, 48, 254, 255; spring care, 250, 254–56; steps to, *ill.* 248–49; suckers, removing, *ill.* 251; supports, 247, *ill.* 250; trailers, 239; variety, 237; winter protection, 255–56. *See* Rose garden
Rotenone, 89
Rototilling, 87
Rots, 466
Rough Bluegrass, 170–71
Rubber-plant, air layering, 64
Rudbeckia, 192
Rusts, 466
Rye, 22, 27
Ryegrass, 22, 27, 163, 171

Saddle grafting, 72
St. Augustinegrass, 173
Salads, 269
Saline soils, improving, 35
Salinity tolerance, of plants, 401
Sandstone, porous, 210
Sandy soils, 16, 22
Sash: for coldframes, 110; slatted, 116, *ill.* 116
Sassafras trees, 146
Scale, in rock garden, 212–13, 214
Scilla, 175
Scion, 72
Screening: for patio garden, 277, *ill.* 228; planning area, 6–7; pole beans, 272; temporary, 84
Screens: hardy shrubs and evergreens, list, 148; shrubs for, 149–50
Seabrook Farms, 98
Seashore: cultivated trees and shrubs, 449; ground covers, 450; native trees and shrubs, 448
Seaweed, 266
Sedge peat, 23
Seed flat, plastic, *ill.* 54
Seed germination: light, 57; temperature, 57
Seedlings: root masses, *ill.* 58; sowing (*See* Sowing seedlings); starting, 57–60, in greenhouse, 306–7; plants, *ill.* 306; thinning out, 57; transplanting, 57
Seeds, 43; control of conditions, 50–51; grass, 164, sowing, *ill.* 160; growing from, 49 ff; protectant, 56–57; quality, 50; sowing, 193; timing, 50; watering, 82–83
Seed sowing: art of, 56; disinfectants, 56–57; equipment, *ill.* 53; in frame, *ill.* 52; greenhouse, 307–13; inoculants, 56–57; labels, 56; temperature, 307; watering devices, 56
Setting out. *See* Transplanting
Shade: coldframe, 116; creating, 78; estimating cast, 8, 9; greenhouse, 305; measure for, *ill.* 8; planning area for, 8–9; trees, 8–9, 228

Shade trees, 8–9, 228
Shaly soil, 210
Sharpening stone, 101, 125
Shasta daisies, 199
Shrub roses, 237, 244, 246, *ill.* 242; for very cold climate, 429; layering, 64; planting holes, 246
Shrubs: alkali tolerance, 400, 401; bank garden, 215; blueberries, 292; books on, 500–1; bracing, 154; for very cold climates, 426; for color, 147; crowding, 47; cultivated, for seashore, 449; currant bush, 293; dwarf peach, *ill.* 287; fertilizer, 86, 90; flowering: dwarf peach, *ill.* 287, list, 147, for the South, 435–36; foundation, 327; fragrant, 202, 458–59; gooseberry bush, 293; on greenhouse, 302; hardy, list, 412–23; for hedges, 149–50; native, for seashore, 448; patio garden, 229; planning before planting, 137, 142; planting, 137, 153–55; pruning, 96, 99–100, 153, 155; for reclaimed desert areas, 446–47; rock garden, 206, 208; Rocky Mountains, 426; roses, 237, 244, 246, *ill.* 242, for very cold climates, 429, layering, 64, planting holes, 246; for screens and hedges, list, 148–50; selecting, 147; small flowering, 233; soil preparation, depth of, 88; for the South, 437; tender, fragrant, 459; transplanting time, 138; types, 146–47; winter, list, 147
Siberian wallflower, 187
Simple or whip grafting, 72
Silent Spring, 92
Silt, 16
Silver bell trees, 146
Single rose, *ill.* 241
Slopes: plugging, 167; sods, 165–66; turf for, 159
Smilax, 151
Snapdragons, 186, 187, 304; in peat pots, *ill.* 310; special bed, 10
Snow, 390
Snowdrops, 195
Sodding, 166–67
Sods, 165–66
Soft-wood stem cuttings, 69, *ill.* 63
Soil, 15–36; acid, 18, 88, measuring, 18, improving, 33–34; adobe, 23, 34; alkaline, 18, 24, 34–35, improving, 34–35, plants sensitive to, 402; alkaline-saline, 35–36; analysis of, 31–33; arid, 36; books on, 501; character, factors in, 15; chemical elements, 17–18, providing essential, 30–31, *vs.* organic sources, 18–22; chestnut, 24; clay, 22,

193, acidifying, 34; for coldframes, 114; "complete" fertilizers, 31; compost heap, 27–30, *ill.* 28, 29; desert, 24 (*See adobe*); double digging, 20, *ill.* 21; drainage system, 20–21, *ill.* 22; erosion, 36; fertility and fertilizers, 31, 36; flower beds and borders, 182, 193, *ill.* 181; for frames, 52; "friable," 17; fruits, 281; grayish-brown, 24; gumbo, 23, 24, 34; ideal, 16; improving, 25; lawn preparation, 157–63; leaching, 24, 35; lithosols, 402; mixes for greenhouse seedlings, 308–9; moisture retention, 88; muck, 23; neutral (or alkaline), 18, 88; nitrogen, 30; nutrients, 17, 88; organic, 25, materials for building, 16–17; peat, 22–23; phosphorus, 30; physical condition, 87–88; plant foods, 17–18; potassium, 30–31; potting, 312; prairie, 24–25; preparation of, 86–89; remaking and maintaining, 25–30; rock garden, 210; rose garden, 244–45; saline, 35; samples for testing, 31–32, *ill.* 32; sandy, 22; seed sowing mixtures, 55–56; shaly, 210; Southwest, 398–99; special area types, 22–23; special problems and solutions, 33–34; sterilizing, 312; subsoil, 18–22; tests, 31–33; topsoils, 20, 159; trace elements, 17, 36; for transplanting, 59; types, 16; of United States, 23–25; vines, 152
Sound, in water feature, 231
South: broadleaved evergreen trees, 438; bulbous plants, 440–42; deciduous flowering shrubs, 437; evergreen trees, 434, 438; flowering evergreen shrubs, 435–36; grass for, 169; hedge plants, 436–37; vines, 438–39
South Carolina: agricultural colleges and experiment station, 494; area, 322; gardens and parks, 476, 488
South Dakota: agricultural college and experiment station, 494; area, 322; gardens and parks, 488; problems, 403–4
Southwest, gardening problems, 397–99
Sowing, 51–57, *ill.* 52; flower seeds, 193; grass seed, 164; vegetable seeds, 193
Sowing seedlings, *ill.* 53, 54; drainage, 52; equipment, 51; frames for, 51, *ill.* 51; seed mixtures, 55–56; soil for frames, 52
Spacing, in coldframe, 115
Special gardens: books, 499; flower beds, 10; fruit, 13–14; hardy border, 9–10; planning, 6, 9–14; rock, 13, 204–14; vegetable, 13–14, 257 ff; wall, 13, 215–17; water, 13, 218, 225–26. *See under* name of garden

Spergon, 56
Sphagnum, 282, 309
Sphagnum moss, 22, 65; milled, 69. *See* Peatmoss
Sphagnum peat, 164
Sphagnum rooting, 43
Spirea: dividing, 63; pruning, 99–100
Spirea vanhouttei, ill. 145
"Sport," 43
Spraying: all-purpose fruit tree spray formula and schedule, 472; equipment, 130–31; fruit trees, 283; in greenhouse, 308, 312; mist, of tree transplants, 155; orchard schedule, 471–72; roses, 255; tank sprayers, 131; "trombone" sprayer, 131
Sprays, 92, 340; for coldframe, 116; equipment, 130–31; for roses, 254. *See* Spraying
Spreading Japanese yew, pruning, 100
Sprigging, 167
Spring: -flowering annuals, 233; -flowering bulbs, 233; -flowering perennials, 233; planting dates, 318, 320–23; rock garden flowers, 213; rose care, 254–56; shrubs, list, 147
Spruce trees, 146
Star magnolia tree, *ill.* 143
Staking, roses, 254
Stay-dry, 266
Stem cuttings, 68
Stems and trunks, 39, 42
Steps, rock garden, *ill.* 212
Sternbergia lutea, 195
Stokesia, 199
Strawberries, 194, 295–98; *ill.* 288, 289, 298, 363; hill system, 297, 298; picking, 296; plants, *ill.* 297; reproduction, 43; rooting runners, *ill.* 298; varieties, 296
Stream(s), 218; annuals, 223; artificial, *ill.* 224; construction, 219; design, 219; perennials, 223; plants, 223; -pool combination, 219; water supply, 224–25
Stripping, 167
Submarine plant culture, 46 n
Subsoil, 18–22; composition, 20; depth, 20; "hard pan," 20; in planting hole, *ill.* 154; porous, 21–22; preparation of, 87
Suckers, 96, 100; raspberries, 294; rose, removing, *ill.* 251
Summer: bulbs, 346; -flowering annuals, 233; -flowering perennials, 233; lawn, 156; mulch, 78–80, 368; shrubs, list, 147
Sunflower, 183, 186
Sunshine, limited, providing, 110

Supports: annuals, 186–87, *ill.* 186; climbing roses, 128, 247, *ill.* 127, 250; dwarf fruit trees, 284; for gooseberries, 293; grapes, 291; plants, 127–29; post-and-chain, 247, *ill.* 250; raspberries, 294; for tomatoes, 270; for vines, 150, 151–52, 186; when to put in, 247
Sweet corn, 89, 258, 266, 272–75, *ill.* 274
Sweet gum trees, 146
Sweet peas, 186; special bed, 10
Sweet William (*Dianthus barbatus*), 187
Swimming pool, 218 n
Switzerland, miniature roses, 243
Syringing, 333

Tall fescue, 171
Temperature, 46–47, 77–78; coldframe, 114–15; greenhouse, 304; hotbed, 307; seedlings, 57, in greenhouse, 307; winter, average minimum, 320–22
Tennessee: agricultural colleges and experiment station, 494; area, 322; gardens and parks, 476, 489; problems, 407
Terrace, *ill.* 229; paved, *ill.* 228
Texas: agricultural colleges and experiment station, 494; area, 322; gardens and parks, 476, 489; problems, 397–98, 406, 407–8; soil, 398
"Thatch," 266
"Thinning out," 264; seedlings, 57; vegetables, 265; when to do, 193
Thymus serpyllum, 176
Tigridias, 199
Tile, for drainage, 20, 244; installing, *ill.* 22
Timing, in seed sowing, 50
Tomatoes, 258, 269–72, *ill.* 271; diseases, 466; seedlings, *ill.* 59; Trellis for, *ill.* 270
Tools and equipment, 120 ff; acquisition, "go slow," 120; budding knife, 106, *ill.* 122; buying, 120; care of, 133; for cultivating, 124; dibber, 121; dusting and spraying equipment, 129–31; edgers, 133; fertilizer and seed distributor, 133, *ill.* 160; field hoe, 124; greenhouse, 305–6; hand, 120–25; hand mower, 131; hand pruning shears, 100; hand weeders, 124–25; hoe, 124; holemaker, 121; knives, 125; lawn equipment, 131–33; lopping shears, 101, 102, 252; mechanical protectors, 125–27; "onion" hoe, 124, 263; plant supports, 127–29; pole pruning shears, 100; power, 121; power mower, 131, 133, 163; pruning, 100–3, *ill.* 101, 102; pruning knife, 100; pruning saw, 101; rakes, 124, 158;

roller, 133, 158; scuffle or push-hoe, 80, 124; sharpening stone, 101, 125; Slim Jim bulb-planting trowel, 196; spading fork, 121, 158; spades, 121; spike-tamper, *ill.* 132; *tamper-aerator*, 133; for transplanting, 121; trowels, 121; turf edger, *ill.* 132; types, 120; water-ballast roller, *ill.* 132; for weeding, 265

Tool shed, 318; planning, 7

Topiary work, 98

Topsoils, 20; "chocolate icing" layer, 159; shallow, 20

Trace elements, 45; "complete" fertilizers, 85

Trailers, for window boxes, 233

Trailing roses, 239

Training plants, *ill.* 104; objectives, 94, 98–100

Transplanting: greenhouse seedlings, 309–10; mulching, 155; organic fertilizers, 86; potting shed, 302; seedlings, 57, 59; time for, 194; tools for, 121; shrubs, 138–39, *ill.* 138, 139; steps in, *ill.*, 138, 139, 140, 141; trees, 138–39, *ill.* 138, 139; watering, 82

Tree fruits, 281; apples, 281; "bearing age," 282; culture, 284–92; planting, 281–82; pruning, 283; space, 281. *See* Fruit trees

Tree paint, 252

Trees: alkaline tolerance, 401; andromeda, *ill.* 145; arborvitae, 146, pruning, 99; beech, 146; birch, 78, 146; books on, 500–1; bracing, 154, 155, *ill.* 140, 141, 154; branches, pruning *ill.* 105; broadleaved evergreens for California, 443–44; cherry, 146; Chinese elms, 78; for very cold climates, 426, 426–28; coniferous, for California, 444–45; crabs, flowering, 146; cultivated, for seashore, 449; deciduous, 142, list, 146; dogwood, flowering, 146, *ill.* 144; elm, 146; evergreens, 144, -deciduous difference, 142, list, 146; fertilizer, 90; fir, 146; fruit (*See* Fruit trees); growth rate, 138–39; guy wires, 155, 384; hardy, list, 412–23; hawthorns, 146; hemlock, 146, pruning, 99; horsechestnut, 146; juniper, 146; laburnum, 146; larches, 142, 146; limb, pruning, *ill.* 105; linden, 146; locust, 146; magnolia, 78, 146; maple, 78, 146, 228; measuring shade from, 8, 9; mountain-ash, 146; native, for seashore, 448; oak, 146; ornamental: list, 146, for reclaimed desert areas, 445–46; oxydendron, 146; patio garden, 227–28; paulownia, 146; pine, 146; pin oaks, 78; planning before planting, 137, 142; planting, 137, 153–55; pruning, 96, 153, 155; purchasing, 144; Rocky Mountains, 426; sassafras, 146; selecting, 142–46; shade, 8–9, 78, 146, 228, for reclaimed desert areas, 445–46; silver bell, 146; size, 141–42; soil preparation, depth of, 88; for the South, 434–35, 438; species for locality, 139, 141–42; *spirea vanhouttei, ill.* 145; spruce, 146; star magnolia, *ill.* 143; sweet gum, 146; transplanting time, 138; tulip, 97, 138, 146, *ill.* 103; umbrella-pine, 146; "wells," 162; willow, 146; witch-hazel, 146; yews, 146

Tree-wound paint, 106

Treewrap, 126, 155

Trellises, 127, 152, *ill.* 129; climber roses, 239; grapes, 291; rambler roses, 247; for tomatoes, *ill.* 270

Trench, roses in, 247

Trumpet creeper, 150

Trumpet-vine, 152

Tuberose roots, for the South, 440–42

Tuberous begonias, *ill.* 198

Tuberous-rooted plants, propagation, 66, 68

Tubers: life cycle, *ill.* 40; for the South, 440–42; starting, 333

Tuffa, 210

Tulips, 195, 200, 233, *ill.* 196; bulb increase, *ill.* 65; "forcing," 118; life cycle, 42

Tulip trees, 146; growth rate, 138; pruning, 97, *ill.* 103

Turf: edger, *ill.* 132; effect on grounds, 156; "plugs," 166; "sprigs," 166. *See* Lawn

Turfing-daisy (*Matricaria tchihatchewi*), 176

Twiners, 150–51

U. C. Soil Mix B, 55

Umbrella-pine trees, 146

University of California, soil mixes, 55

University of Massachusetts, College of Agriculture, 29

Upkeep, 91–92

Utah: agricultural college and experiment station, 494; area, 322; gardens and parks, 476, 489; problems, 402–3

Utility area, planning, 6, 7

Vegetable garden, 257 ff, *ill.* 259; alkali tolerance, 400; annual, 279; asparagus, 260, 275–76; beans, 272; beets, 89;

books on, 499; broccoli, 266; celery, 89; chart, 278; corn, 89, 258, 266, 272–75; cucumber, 89; culture, 265–67; drainage, 259; fertilizer, 86, 90, 264; flavor, 258; in flower border, 260–61; freezing, 267; harvesting, 266, 329, 378; in herb garden, 260; leaders, 267–77; lettuce, 258, 267–68, *ill.* 310; melons, 276–78; mulching, 266; peas, 258, 266; perennial, 279; pests, 276; placement, 178; plan, 261, *ill.* 262; planning, 6, 13–14; planting, 263–64, preparation for, 261, 263; potatoes, 89; preliminaries, 259–63; reasons for growing, 257–58; rhubarb, 260; root, storing, 266; salinity tolerance, 401; setting out, 264; side-dressing, 265–66; site, 259–60; size, 260; storage, winter, 266–67; thinning, 265; tomatoes, 258, 269–72; watering, 84; weeds, 265, control of, 91, 466–67

Veltheimia, 42; propagation, 66
Velvet bent, 170
Veneer grafting, 72
Ventilation: coldframes, *ill.* 117; greenhouse, 304
Vermiculite, 69, 302, 309
Vermont: agricultural college and experiment station, 494; area, 322; problems, 405–6
Veronica, 188
Vetch, 22, 27, 86
Vinca minor, ill. 175
Vines and other climbers, 150 ff; annual, 183–84, 453; bank garden, 215; books on, 500; for very cold climates, 430–31; cultivating, 152–53; fragrant, 458–59; grape, pruning, *ill.* 291; greenhouse, 302; patio garden, 230; planting, 137, 153–55; pruning, 150, 152, 153, 155; soil, 152; for South, 438–39; supports for, 150, 151–52, 186; window boxes, 235
Virginia: agricultural college and experiment stations, 494; area, 322; gardens and parks, 477, 489–90; problems, 405–6
Virginia creeper (*Parthenocissus quinquefolia*), 150, 151
Virus diseases, 466
Visqueen, 116, 219

Walks, edging roses, 239
Wall gardens, 215–17, *ill.* 213; advantages, 204; books on, 499; natural settings for, 217; planning, 13; plants for, 215, 457; trailer roses, 239

Walls: climber roses, 239; free-standing, double faced, 215–17; temperature and, 77
Washington State: agricultural college and experiment station, 494; area, 322; gardens and parks, 477, 490; problems, 394–96
Water, 45; -ballast roller, *ill.* 132; greenhouse, 305–6; making most of, 78 ff; micro-climates, 77–78; seed sowing devices, 56
Waterfall, 218; in patio, 231
Water features: in patio garden, 231–33. *See also* Pools, Streams *and* Water Gardens
Water gardens, 218, 225–26, *ill.* 220; annuals, 223; books on, 499; design, 219; perennials, 223; planning, 13; plants, 223, 225, 458; -pool difference, 225; water supply, 224–25
Watering: amount required, 81, *ill.* 81; in coldframe, 115; equipment, 81–84, *ill.* 82, for lawn, *ill.* 165; grass seeding, 164–65, *ill.* 165; greenhouse seedlings, 309; measure for, *ill.* 81; method, 80–81; mistlike spray, 82, 84; rock garden, 214; spray, 57, 309; "sprinkler," *ill.* 83; vegetable garden before planting, 263. *See* Hoses *and* Nozzles
Watering-can, 56
Watering system, 45; rose garden, 245–46
Water-lilies, *ill.* 221; tropical, 358, *ill.* 222
Wedge and cleft grafting, 72; *ill.* 73
Weeds: chickweed, 124; control of, 91, 466–67; cultivating, 124; mulching, 78–79; purslane, 124; seeds, elimination of, 312; surplus plants, 193; tools, 265; vegetable garden, 265
Weeks, Martin E., 29
West Coast, gardening problems, 394–96
West Virginia: agricultural college and experiment station, 494; area, 322; gardens and parks, 477, 490; problems, 405–6
Whetstone, 125
Whip and tongue grafting, 72, *ill.* 73
White Dutch clover, 171–72
White pine, 139
Willow, 146; propagation, 71
Wildflowers, 372
Wilt-Pruf, 127, 155
Wind barriers, 84, *ill.* 84
Windbreaks, 36, 384, 427–28
Wind burn, 328

Wind erosion, 36
Wind scald, 125, 341
Window boxes, 233–36, *ill.* 235; self-watering, *ill.* 234; watering, 328
Winter (care of): fish in pools, 225–26; lawn, 156; pools, 225; rock garden, 214; roses, 255–56
Winter-aconite, 195
Winter rye, 163
Winter shrubs, list, 147
Wisconsin: agricultural college and experiment station, 494; area, 323; gardens and parks, 477, 490; problems, 405–6
Wisteria, 150, 152, *ill.* 151; over gate, *ill.* 128
Witch-hazel trees, 146

Woman's National Farm and Garden Association, 497
Wood ashes: for acidity, 33, 327; for roses, 250
Woodland pool, 219
Wyoming: agricultural college and experiment station, 494; area, 322; gardens and parks, 477, 490; problems, 402–4

Yew hedge, *ill.* 12
Yew trees, 146; pruning, 100

Zinnias, 183; seed sowing, 52
Zones, planting, 77
Zoysia grasses, 167, 169
Zoysias, 166, 173–74

Soil Descriptions for End-paper Soil Map

PODZOLIC AND RELATED SOILS

Pz   Strongly leached soils of cool, humid, forested regions.

AF   Acid brown soils of temperate, humid, forested regions.

GB   Grayish-brown to gray soils of temperate to cool, humid, forested regions, commonly on calcareous materials.

NB   Brown or light reddish-brown soils of warm-temperate, moist-dry regions under mixed forest-grass vegetation.

PODZOLIC-LATOSOLIC TRANSITION SOILS

RY   Leached red and yellow soils of warm-temperate humid forested regions.

CHERNOZEMIC SOILS

PC   Dark-brown to dark reddish-brown or black soils of cool to warm-temperate, humid to subhumid grassland.

CB   Brown and reddish-brown soils of cool to warm-temperate subhumid or semiarid grasslands.

Gr   Dark-brown to black self-mulching or self-swallowing clayey soils, mainly of warm subhumid regions.

DESERTIC SOILS

D   Gray soils and reddish soils of cool to warm arid regions.

HYDROMORPHIC SOILS

HGP   Gray to black soils of swamps, marshes, and flats, mainly in humid regions.

REGOSOLS

S   Deep, very sandy soils with little or no profile expression except in depressional areas among the dunes or ridges.

SOILS OF ALLUVIAL PLAINS

A   Valleys of major rivers.

SOILS OF MOUNTAINS AND STEEP SLOPES

Mp   Podzolic soils and acid brown forest soils of mountains and steep slopes in humid forested regions; commonly stony, shallow in places.

Mdc   Soils of mountains and steep slopes in arid to subhumid regions.

SOIL MAP of

CB — locations across map

Mdc — locations across map

Mp — locations across map

S — locations across map

D — locations across map

NB — locations across map

PC — location on map

A — location on map

PC, CB, Gr Dark soils in warm-temperate,
            subhumid grasslands. (Chernozemic soils)

Pz, AF Soils of cool-temperate, humid, forested regions.
GB, NB, (Podzolic and related soils)

HGP Gray to black soils of swampy, humid areas.
     (Hydromorphic soils)

RY Leached red and yellow soils of warm, temperate humid forested regions.
    (Podzolic-Latosolic Transition soils)

A Valleys of major rivers. (Soils of Alluvial Plains)

0   Miles   300

palacios